My Brother's Keeper

Jonathan Lewis

To my favorite Aunt!
Love you much!
[illegible]
Hebrews 12:1-3

AXIOM PRESS

My Brother's Keeper
by Jonathan Lewis

ISBN 1-58169-190-4
For Worldwide Distribution
Printed in the U.S.A.

Axiom Press
P.O. Box 191540 • Mobile, AL 36619
800-367-8203

Table of Contents

Dedication

To Jesus Christ,

may this story draw people to You,

and to Leffingwell Baptist Church,

my Mentors

Acknowledgments

Jesus Christ, without You, I would be only living instead of truly alive. Rachel, meine Blume, your constant support made my dream a reality.

Keith Carroll, my agent, I will never know all the work you've done, God bless you. Brian Banashak, thank you for always being there for all my questions. Axiom Press, you are truly gifted people. Reed Bernick—your maps did it Reed, thanks again!

Shawn and Melodie Walenius, you guys have been believers from the beginning, wanna go for some Nerts? Joshua Herring, my first fan, all our talks helped spur me on. Allen Simcoe, Diana Randall, Sarah Olbris, Nikki Jatindranath, Julian, and their families—you were the first to read my story, thanks for all your insights and encouragement.

Clay and Holly, what wonderful people you are. Jason Terril and Jen Ita, how in the world did such intelligent people become my friends? Rene Carey and Ruth Ford, thank you both for your honesty and direction.

Pastor Eric Thomas and John Griffin, our conversations always turned me to where I needed to be. Leffingwell Baptist Church and Salem Baptist Church—all your conditioning and nurturing shaped me more than I can explain.

First Baptist Church of Norfolk—from Martha and Jim Mason, to Julia, to George Cunningham and countless others, y'all are more than fellow believers, we're family. FBCN choir and Orchestra—Gladys Hales, Betty, John Gresham, Harvey Martin, Larry, David Polston, Irv and Rosemary Beard, Doug and Stacy Montgomery, Kathi Michael, and everyone else: each tidbit of our fellowship played into this project, thank you.

My *NIV Study Bible* (my Song of the Ages). *Roget's Thesaurus* and *American Heritage Dictionary*, my two new favorite books besides the Bible. To all of you great and small, I am humbled.

Prologue

What if this world as we know it never existed? What if the world God created were different? What if the Creator chose to shape another world instead of our own—a land where what one sees depends upon what they believe.

Imagine a place much like Earth where kingdoms align themselves according to their principles and virtues...where the lay of the land may bear clues to the inhabitants' relationship with the Creator...where a rapport of acceptance exists between all, except the scornful Keepers...where the nations speak a common tongue and yet are as distinct as what they hold to be true. Could their bonds unite them in peace, or would their realms collapse in chaos?

In this land, boundaries between the spiritual world and physical are not so clear. Would the men of this world, then, spiral into a kaleidoscope of ceaseless nightmares or would their lives taste abundantly sweeter?

Here, the spiritual is not so perceivable to some. What of them? Would they lose themselves in questioning what is real or would their hapless circumstances forward their search into the unknown?

In this place, man would be hard pressed to reconcile his fate. His precarious situation would require immense pondering unless he chose to trudge onward in time with the dull heartbeat of his everyday tasks. Dwelling somewhere among the highest servants of creation and yet lower than the heavenly beings, his life would be a passing mist in the vast order of things. Still, whom he serves and what he does would make everything hang in the balance. Or would it?

Those in Emblom had heard the rumors that such a world existed—a world where they were not the kings, but merely paupers in a great power struggle far beyond their own comprehension. They had not been privy with their own eyes, although they had not failed to listen to the whispers in the wind either. Indeed, there were numerous hints and subtleties that stretched across the Stygian Union to the far reaches of the Clonesian Empire. Tales of strange things that were peculiarly out of place and unexplainable events that were far too common to be coincidence abounded if only one scrutinized them with an unbiased attitude. All inhabitants, however, would be shocked to learn that this land of wonder described above was impossibly their own. But only the Keepers knew the truth....

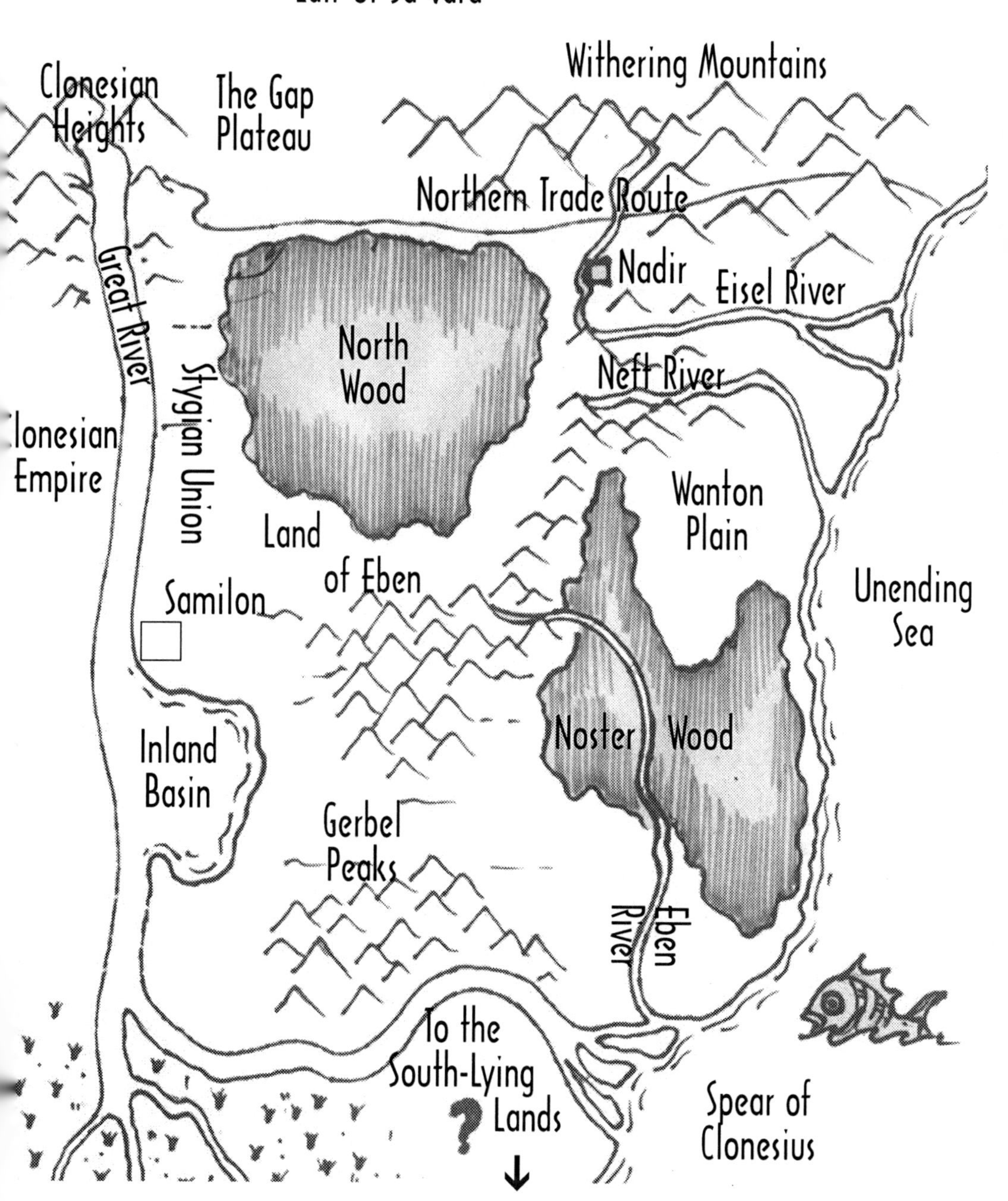
Lair of Sa´vard
Withering Mountains
Clonesian Heights
The Gap Plateau
Northern Trade Route
Great River
Nadir
Eisel River
North Wood
Neft River
Stygian Union
lonesian Empire
Wanton Plain
Land of Eben
Samilon
Unending Sea
Noster Wood
Inland Basin
Gerbel Peaks
Eben River
To the South-Lying Lands
Spear of Clonesius

THE WORLD

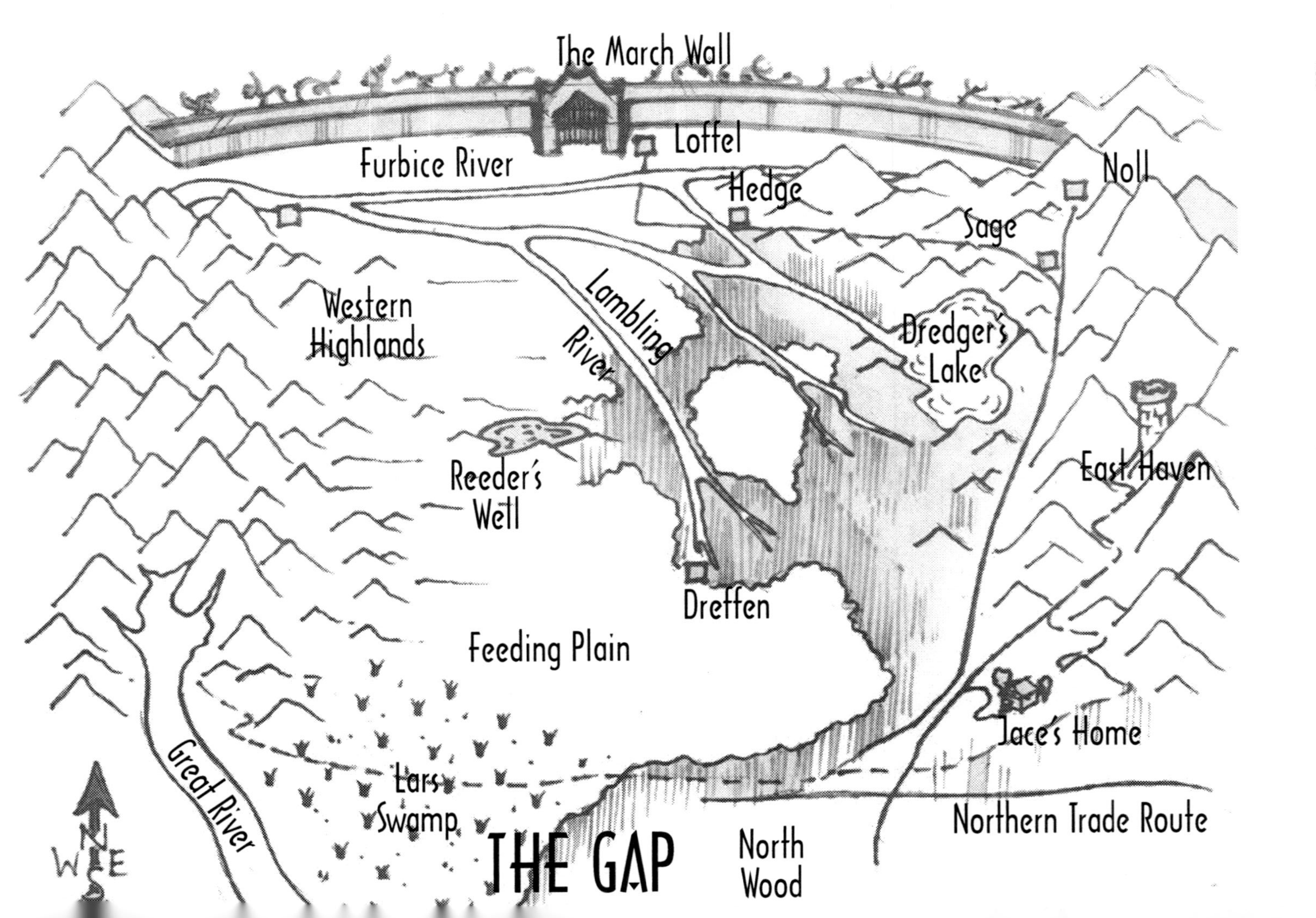

The March Wall
Loffel
Furbice River
Hedge
Noll
Sage
Western Highlands
Lambling River
Dredger's Lake
East Haven
Reeder's Well
Dreffen
Feeding Plain
Jace's Home
Great River
Lars Swamp
Northern Trade Route
THE GAP
North Wood
N
W E
S

1

A MATCH IN THE DARK

THE SMELL WAS WRETCHED. It permeated the clothes; it was in the hair, the pores of the skin, under the fingernails; it clung to the nostrils and hung in the throat. But that was only the beginning. The stench rested so heavily that it was a labor to breathe. The dank, humid air only heightened the acrid smell. It was an animal of its own accord, choking one's thoughts, quelling the appetite, and quenching one's spirit. It was the smell, some said, of hopelessness. It was the smell of the mines, hidden from human eyes deep within the earth's crust and only whispered of in lore. The outside world only spoke of such places when frightening wayward children.

The worst was the despair—knowing that he had failed, knowing that he was not good enough to be rescued. He wiped his face, but no tears came because he had already used them all. What clutched at him now was the overwhelming thought that he must resign himself to this existence. The Mines of Shorn were used for one reason only: to keep at bay the prisoners of Na'tal. The labor and the beatings were sufficient weapons to pierce the hearts of men. He had heard of this place and its treachery, but never dreamed of the despair and agony that could accompany one's existence here. Was it days or months? Maybe years had passed since he was abandoned. Time was not an inmate of this dwelling, if one could call it such. No matter, this was his home, now.

My Maker has left me, he thought. *Fine, let it be, but I will never renounce His name.* He cringed with that last thought. The responsibility to his Master was a burden he could scarcely bear. He had all but crumpled under its weight.

But that is my own burden, he argued with himself. *The one thing I cling to is that it is a welcome burden. It is lighter than the weight of shame I would have should I choose to dishonor my vows to Him and turn from His ways.*

He reached out his hand and ran it along the smooth surface of his cell. How ironic that his captors should extend the time and effort to give each prisoner a space of their own. It was void of furnishings and windows, though that mattered not. Light was rare enough that hands counted as vision. His cell was five strides by three. Long enough to lay himself down, it served for little else. Sleep was something that had to be sought, and one could hardly find it here. Many a night he merely paced back and forth, turning his thoughts to times gone by. Solitude could be the worst of enemies.

On the outside world, he had been called Jace, a name given him by his father and mother meaning "Creator's Gift," but names were the first things that were stripped from the captives. Goth was what they called all prisoners. There was no need to single out any slave since they all served the same purpose. Should they die or take ill, it mattered not; more would replace them. The name *Goth* meant "wretched"—another sign that the guards missed no opportunity to heap insults on their captors. The Goths were treated like cattle, beasts with no mind of their own, whose choices had to be made for them.

Time had turned his clothes to rags. His sandals had weathered away to nothing. His shirt was shredded and discarded long ago by the daily whippings. It did not matter; warmth was never absent this close to the earth's mantle. His leggings, though tattered, had survived thus far. They afforded him some dignity, no matter how little.

Out there, he had lived free from worries or pain. He enjoyed growing up beneath the watchful eye of his parents. He had taken their hand freely in guiding his life since they had many years of experience. There on his father's farm, he had taken hold of his everyday tasks not as a chore, but as a learning experience: a time to grow and reflect on the deeper meaning of life.

Somehow, he had always known there was more to being alive than the simple actions of breathing and working. At times, while consumed in his work on the farm, he dismissed it. Surely, the cycle of life was free of emotion, and there was no deeper meaning. He fed the cows; cows produced milk; he drank their milk and used its energy to help feed the cows once more.

Other times, it was readily apparent to him that the earth was much more profound than his simple life. He could hear it in the blowing wind, the crackling fire, a babbling brook, the birds chirping in the early morning light, or the crickets singing at dusk. He could see it in the intricacy of a spider's web, the changing leaves of autumn, or the way the sun painted the clouds each time it rose and set. The smell of the crisp winter air, a fresh baked pie, or the brush of a crow's feather across his face made it seem as though the very fabric of creation cried out that life was more than a mere cycle.

It was no coincidence when he started to ask questions to his parents: "Where does the wind come from?" "Why do the birds chirp?" "Who made the sun?" Their answers were always direct and true.

"The Creator, of course, Jace," his parents always replied, "He made it all for you. Why? Because He loves you, and He has so much more to give you, if only you will let Him."

So it was in child-like innocence that he walked in faith and met Elohim through His Son. In time He offered his life to the Almighty and Yeshua, His Son, sealing him as a Keeper. It was a small price to pay for the unbridled love of the One who sits on the everlasting throne in Par'lael. And it came to pass that Jace's family grew in their love for their Master, and the bond between them all was unbreakable. He had lived a sheltered life, but his parents had never hidden from him the Creator's love. This had shown him Elohim's saving grace.

He blinked and shook his head. What had happened to him as a child seemed like it had been just yesterday. So much had been taken from him in such a short time, but he would always have those memories, and nothing could take them away. He must sleep. Soon the guards would be back to send him to work till he collapsed, and the endless cycle would once again be set in motion. He bent his back to kneel on the floor, it seemed an odd position, but he was too tired to think. As he bent, the pain grew. First, he thought it was the aching of his muscles, then he realized he was splitting the wounds from his whippings all over again. He arched his neck in pain, but it was too late. His body gave way, and he crumpled to the floor, unconscious.

HIS HEAD STILL SWAM, so he let hang. Where was he? Certainly not in his cell.

It was too cold. And what was he doing? It felt like he was hanging. His arms were stretched out over his head. They were tied to something. If only he could open his eyes. His legs trailed out on the ground behind him. His back burned. Were those fresh whip slashes across his back?

Does it really matter? He thought. *The old ones have not yet healed.*

He listened. There were fires, no, too small—braziers, maybe: two to the left and right, and two somewhere ahead of him and overhead. His body was burning! Something dripped from the side of his mouth. It was warm and thick, blood perhaps. His head still pulsed from the fall, but no matter how he tried, he could not shake it. How long had it been since he had blacked out? Did it matter? He lay there as time passed.

There was no sound, only the soft rippling of heat from the braziers. It took an effort to breath the air. At least it was cool, if not fresh. The pain from his back made him wince whenever his chest expanded. He groaned softly.

Whippings were usually carried out in his cell. It was always the same. The Watchers would face him towards the wall and clasp his hands and feet in chains. They never said a word of approval, and never showed a sign of regret. They never uttered a word.

The guards' appearances were deceiving. They took many forms, it was said. Jace should have known their outward appearance was amiss.

They were all average height, and build, nondescript. All had shaved heads, no individual markings or blemishes. They all wore the same garb: sackcloth clothing topped by a leather vest. A baldric crossed their chest, though none wore swords. Jace never heard them talk, never saw them sneeze, itch, blink, or make any gesture that marked them as human. Their plain features and sterile habits offered no hint of their physical might or speed. Jace had learned the hard way.

The first time, there had been only two of them to carry out his punishment. He remembered them waking him from his slumber with a kick to his temple. Still dazed, they dragged him to his feet and pinned him to the wall. One had him by the throat and left arm, while the other began to bind his legs together with a leather cord. Jace remembered the guard's blank stare as his grip tightened around his throat. Stars began to form in the corner of his vision. His mind raced as he fought to breath. Jace drove his free arm up under the man's ribs. The man doubled over, releasing Jace's neck and arm. Still dazed and choking he brought both fists over the other guard's head, knocking him unconscious. As the first guard came to him, Jace fell on his back, thrusting both legs into the man's chest and catapulting him into the wall. With deft fingers, he unwound the cord, freeing his legs and sprung to his feet. He strode to the cell door.

The guards should have been unconscious. His training taught him how to immobilize a man without killing him. As he stepped over the guards, their bodies stirred. Before he could continue, they were both on their feet charging him a second time. He ducked and spun, his fist landing squarely in one of their chests, but something was different. Where he should have contacted flesh and muscle, the body was as hard as a rock. Instead of doubling over, the guard grabbed his arm, twisting it over so Jace could not move. The other guard kicked him in his knees. Jace let out a whimper between clenched teeth. The guard behind him twisted his arm further. Jace could hear the sinews of muscle and bone slowly ripping apart from each other. With that iron grip, the guard dragged him to his feet and rammed him into the wall. Before he could catch his breath, the guard took his head and pinned him up against its surface. He remembered their breath in his face—calm and steady, as if nothing had happened—and the look in their eyes that said there had been no interruption in their work. They bound one arm and then his other. There was nothing he could do. It was as if he watched himself, dazed and broken, while they beat him. Sapped of energy and strength, he was totally under the guards' control. Yet, deep in the recesses of his mind, away from the pain, he knew that it would not be the last of these meetings.

He could move his head slightly now, though it felt like fire. He never understood why they beat him, or how he had been captured. It really did not matter anymore, it seemed this was now his life. He tilted his head to the side. Were those voices? Maybe footsteps. They were coming closer. He struggled to pull himself upright, but to no avail.

Suddenly, a hand grabbed him by the scruff of the neck and whipped his head up.

"Yes, he is," said a man's voice, "I knew he would not sleep forever, that decision is in the hands of Na'tal. Bring him here."

Jace was untied and dragged forward. A hand slapped him across his face.

"Stop moaning, Goth," the voice hissed, "Do you know why you are here? Answer me!"

Jace groaned. He tried to speak, but the sound he heard coming out of his mouth was only gurgles of unintelligible utterances.

"The pig is a mute. Listen then, you fool. All Keepers have been granted the right to meet their new master before he sends them to Sheol. On your knees! The Lord of the Night's chosen draws nigh!"

He heard the sound of a legion of bodies all around him drop to bended knee with the clang of armor and swords. His carriers dropped him, leaving him sprawled on the floor. Oh, how his body ached! But he lay there listening while breathing as softly as he could. He heard the slow steady rhythm of drums signalling the processional entrance of this Na'tal. The noise echoed off the walls, making it sound as if they were in a great hall. In submissive anticipation, the chamber waited.

Jace flickered his eyes open. What he saw left him breathless. The hall he was in was one of great opulence. Indeed, he could not fathom it was part of the Mines of Shorn. Its richness was vastly different from the stark conditions he had lived in. Brilliant tapestries were hung the length of the hall—the height of ten men and twice as long! They ran for as far as the eye could see, each with its own ornate depiction of various battles and mighty deeds of history. Flanked to Jace's left and right were row after row of guards, dressed in full polished armor, their breastplates glistening in the light of a thousand torches. Their blank stares spoke only of duty and authority, though their tense, anxious muscles rippled with an urgency to fulfill their Master's bidding. Jace was laying on a carpet made of deep blood-red silk intertwined with gold, the likes of which, if sold, could have kept his family comfortable for years.

His attention turned from the carpet to the stairs and the throne beyond. There stood a man of regal stature. He was draped in a heavy robe of ruby red with cuffs of fox fur. His hair was black as night and trimmed close, though well-oiled. His beard was clipped perfectly to soften the angles of his face. There was a certain way he moved that betrayed his form. It was as if he were not all that he appeared to be or maybe much more. Whatever it was, his outward appearance was merely a formality. Though his features were soft, if not stern, his eyes glinted with authority, and his lips suggested a haughty, confident man—if he was one at all. He bore no visible adornment, crown, or ring, and his clothes bore no insignia. This man needed none for he was Na'tal, ruler of the Mines of Shorn: Sa'vard's elect. Jace suddenly remembered hearing his name whispered in the passing of his tutelage. That name was always accompanied by tales of misery and fear. It spoke of power and all too often of death.

Na'tal flowed to his throne and looked over his domain. He appeared to inspect each guard's uniform from atop his lofty height, letting his gaze linger on some, while drifting slowly by others. Nothing escaped his gaze. The drums stopped, but the silence seemed to have a noise of its own.

"Du'mas, where is the prisoner?" spoke Na'tal. His voice was rich, and his speech impeccable. Moreover it emanated confidence and demanded expediency. There was no inflection in his tone, no desire to press his influence on what was said; it seemed to be understood. The man in front of him stepped forward.

"He is here, oh lord," cried Du'mas.

This being was more a creature than human. His form was shriveled and grotesque, yet he moved with the determination of a youth. His clothing was so torn and weathered that it could only be said he dressed in rags. His right hand was hidden under his garments, close to his breast while his left clenched a jewel-studded cane, though Du'mas had no limp.

But it was his face that caught Jace's eye, if one could call it that. If his body was decrepit, his face was the embodiment of downright mutilation. Scars were slashed across it at odd angles, and the wrinkled skin beneath had a tart pinkish scar color. His hair, what was left of it, was badly singed. Where his nose should have been stood a gaping hole surrounded by loose flesh, and his eyes were glazed over by a milky white film. What horrors had this creature experienced?

It was his lips that surprised Jace. These were spotless, devoid of blemish. Why? Beyond them stood a row of brilliant gleaming white teeth, and when Du'mas spoke, his voice filled the depths of the hall. It was as clear as a blade and true as an arrow.

"He is here, oh lord," he cried, once more stepping to the side and motioning behind him. "As you commanded."

Na'tal sat as if he had not heard. The sound of soldiers shifting their restless feet filled the hall.

"Silence!" He boomed.

There was a loud hiss that followed as if someone had carelessly tossed water on white-hot coals. The very walls shook.

"Bring him hither."

At once the guards at his side pulled him up and dragged him to the foot of the steps.

"Let me see his face—his eyes."

The guards whipped his head back. Jace stood there not daring to look directly upon this man. Na'tal drew himself up, flowing down the steps. He grabbed Jace's face in his hands firmly, turning his face upward until he could gaze directly into his eyes. Na'tal's own eyes seemed to pierce Jace's soul. He struggled, but to no avail. Jace tried to speak, but his parched throat made no sound.

Na'tal curled his lips in a smile, "You wish to say something? But you already know what I want, don't you?"

Jace groaned softly. In a moment, it was clear. Na'tal did not mean to question him. He came not to give, but rather to take. He knew as he stared into those dark, empty eyes, that this man, this thing would take his life.

"So, you know," spoke Na'tal with an air of slight amusement. "But do you know why?" Na'tal breathed deeply, waiting for an answer. When he spoke, the words came slowly, like he was talking to a child, trying to help it understand.

"Your Master sent you on an errand, did He not?"

Jace groaned in reluctant agreement.

"And you failed didn't you? He promised you peace and protection, didn't He? And yet, where are your guardians? He left you alone, and why shouldn't He? What good have you done for Him? A helpless man that cannot keep his oaths—not only did He leave you unprotected, you did not know where to go, did you?"

With each passing phrase, Na'tal's voice became stronger, more forceful and deliberate. Rage seemed to cloud over his eyes as he worked himself into a frenzy.

"Where is your Master now—can He see you? Does He care?"

Tears began to form in Jace's eyes as what Na'tal was saying began to sink in. Had his Master truly discarded him? Was it possible that the Father of Goodness cared not for His children, that He watched them undergo treatment such as this for only His amusement? Could it be true? Jace shook his head—it was not possible! He had read the Song of the Ages and his Master's promises to all who chose to call on His name. Or was this man right?

"Search your heart, fool! Surely He does not need your pitiful presence. That is why you have been given to me: to meet your destiny," Na'tal hissed. "Bind him!"

The guards snatched his still, helpless body as Na'tal released his grip and walked back up the dais. They bound each hand over a brazier.

"Poor pitiful Keeper. Do you know who I am?" Na'tal sneered from his throne. "Your lord will not save you, indeed he cannot. My master holds sway over all the land, and he has given me the power to give life and to take it. Yours shall be an example. I shall offer you as a sacrifice to my master, a gift to his endless power and might, and a testimony to the impotence of the one you serve!"

With this, Na'tal flicked his hand and half a moment later, the first strike came. The whip sliced cuts anew, but this time it felt like sheer lines of fire carved into his back. With the first stroke, Jace's body went rigid.

"Behold the might and power of Na'tal!" screamed Du'mas in proclamation. At the end of his hailing, a second stroke marked Jace. His body jerked once more as the fire seemed to fill his being.

"He offers life to those who choose to follow and death to those who resist. Which shall you choose?" wailed Du'mas.

"Kra'ken! Kra'ken!" shouted the throng of soldiers. With their silence another streak of agonizing pain sliced over his back. The stars were at the edge of his vision now, and the voices around him grew distant.

"Death comes quickly, wretched, misled Keeper! Dost thou serve the mighty or the weak? The Lord of Darkness, or his powerless contender?"

A hush spilled across the mighty throng and Na'tal himself leaned forward, if ever so slightly in anticipation of the answer. It was just for a flicker of time, but Jace's spirit was alive, if only moments from his death. The question seemed to hang before his very vision. Yet, the answer was obvious. No matter the cost, he had made his choice long ago, sealed by the covenant with his Lord. He clenched his teeth to strengthen the little resolve he had left. The vast audience leaned forward, waiting for his response.

Jace gathered his strength and lifted his head to stare into the eyes of Na'tal in defiance.

"You speak lies! I will never desert Yeshua, the Almighty!"

No sooner had the words been spoken, when Jace felt the skin on his back split once again. His body went into spasms, and he shook uncontrollably. He was growing delirious. The stars were fast filling his vision, now and sounds came to him as if from afar.

"The fool, the fool!" shrieked Du'mas. "Death approaches this very threshold. My master's patience wanes, and his hunger increases. No more shall your folly be entertained, you wretch! Commit now and enter Sheol in dignity or receive your payment in full! No more shall I ask, heed it! Whom do you serve?"

The words echoed off the walls of Jace's mind. It was true, his ending lay just breaths ahead. Still, despite the anguish and utter loneliness, he would not, could not, give in. To the Lord of the Light he committed his spirit!

When he finally spoke, his words came in thick, heaving gasps. "I ... serve Him ... who over- ... comes ... all things. Him ... who ... is able ... to ... keep me ..."

Through his muffled ears, he could hear the whip being drawn back for the final blow. Yet, off in the distance arose a sound. It was small, at first, a gathering of some sort, but it grew with each passing moment. Soldiers shifted in their places and grunts of fear arose as others heard its approach. The noise grew in volume and power. It was the sound of a mighty rushing wind rapidly approaching. The soldiers stirred as a herd of horses before the breaking of a storm. Though they held their ranks, their fear was obvious.

As his vision cleared, Jace scanned the crowd. Du'mas stood listening, his milky eyes staring down the gigantic hall into nothingness. His breathing was heavy and anxious. Indeed, as he looked around, all eyes searched for the approaching wind. The sound suddenly seemed to come from everywhere at once, but no place in particular. It made the torches dance and threatened to rip the tapestries from their carved pillars. He could see Na'tal standing in front of his throne, facing him. He was clutching his robes looking beyond Jace, down the vast hall, his face etched in bewilderment.

As Jace craned his neck behind him, he saw the formless wave's effects. One by one, the torches in the great hall winked out in quick succession. A wall of blackness tumbled toward him marking the wind's advance.

Jace's skin prickled as the wind passed over him. A tingling sensation ran all over his body as blasts of air swirled around him. The immensity of the gale filled his ears like a thousand gushing rivers. Though its touch was as calm as glass, its sheer force toppled the braziers, throwing Jace among the coals. To his amazement, the shards were now as cold as ice. The masses of soldiers were pitched here and there like chaff. Chaos ensued as the gale whipped through the hall. Then all at once, it was gone.

The hall stood in darkness. He could hear the sounds of confusion all around him. Someone shouted for a torch—Du'mas, maybe. Others ran about in the blackness to repair the damage done by the enormous swell.

Jace struggled weakly to his knees. Now was his chance! He worked the bonds that tied him to the braziers. Maybe in the mounting disorder, he could find a way to escape. He bent to one knee and pulled with all his strength. His bond snapped loose and his right hand was free.

As he worked his left hand, he looked around. The Mines of Shorn were no stranger to utter darkness, and his eyes had become accustomed to such. Most soldiers worked to lower the tapestries down. The heavy woven blankets had been ripped to shreds and singed badly. Others left to find a lit torch or flint and steel. Du'mas was atop the raised platform leaning on his cane, raising his voice to calm the mass of troops, but he was barely audible above the discordant shouts and yells.

Jace continued to work the bond on his left hand. He flexed his arm and twisted his wrist, all without success. The bond held strong. He shook the brazier and worked his teeth into the leather cords, but the tie was firm.

Then, as quickly as the room was thrown into utter darkness, it was showered with blazing light. Jace sucked in a breath and threw his arm about in blind disarray. He blinked for several moments, letting his eyes adjust. A circle of pure light just below the rafters shined directly above him. The color was indescribable. It was white—no, whiter than white. Jace had never seen such a color. The light was brighter than the sun, its illumination causing the skin of each man to glow white-hot. In its presence, darkness fled. It could only be described as pure, if that were such a shade.

The circle hovered overhead, pulsing and expanding. Silence filled the hall. Many shielded their eyes, but that did little to help. Then a voice ominously spoke to the silenced throng: "If anyone of these lambs, my lambs, cries to Me out of a repentant heart in time of need, I will come to them and bring them unto Myself."

Around Jace stood four men dressed in white, their robes as spotless as mountain snow. They stood at ease, arms hanging loosely at their sides, thumbs hooked in their belts. Each bore a sword, sheathed in a plain leather scabbard. Their heads never turned to the left or right, but Jace believed these strange newcomers were somehow aware of everything.

The one in front was different. His robes were the same, and his brown hair fell to his shoulders. Unlike the others, he wore a crimson sash across his broad chest. He took a step forward. At the sight of him, Na'tal curled back his lips.

"Rendolph!" He spat. "Begone from this place, you hold no power here!"

"I come for the Keeper," spoke the red-sashed man plainly, his left hand resting on the pommel of his sword. He was tall—at least 13 hands high—taller than Jace. His build, though not heavy, was thick. Of the four white-robed intruders, he was the largest and appeared to be their leader. He carried himself with a sureness of purpose. As he spoke, he pointed skyward: "El Shaddai commands his release."

Na'tal merely laughed, "We shall see."

With that Na'tal rose. He threw back his robes revealing a wickedly curved blade. He strode down the steps to stand paces away from Rendolph. They circled each other, hands on their weapons.

"Obban, Zax, protect the Keeper," said Rendolph, his eyes never leaving Na'tal.

Two of the white-robed men came to Jace's sides. One passed his fingers over Jace's left hand and the bond dropped to the floor. They supported him under his shoulders. It was strange how tender their touch was on his ruined body as they heaved him to his feet.

"Torne, ready the gate!" barked Rendolph.

The other man raised his hands above his head with clenched fists. He was whispering something under his breath.

Jace looked around. The endless mass of soldiers that had shrunk away in fear now surrounded them. Their blank stares said little, but they crowded closer, awaiting Na'tal's order to seize their prisoner. Jace's rescuers seemed to care little. They stood perfectly still, waiting for Torne. Their faces were calm, peaceful in fact.

Jace glanced one way, then another. What had been happening was like a dream, but Jace's groggy mind was finally grasping the situation. These would-be rescuers were highly outnumbered, no matter who they were. The element of surprise had been lost, and now the mass of soldiers stood thumbing their weapons in eager anticipation of resting their captor from the doomed escape attempt. He had to do something, maybe he could talk his way out of this. He started to say something.

Rendolph heard and glanced sideways at Jace. That was all Na'tal needed. His weapon sprang from its sheath with a sickening hiss. In one fluid motion, it flashed towards Rendolph's head.

Rendolph barely had time to react. He stepped sideways at the last instant crouching down and rolling backwards out of the path of Na'tal's blade. He jumped to his feet with sword in hand.

With a cry of rage and fury, Na'tal charged him. Their swords crashed in a flurry of sparks and lightening. Rendolph was knocked off balance, crashing and sliding across the floor in front of Jace. He stood up and pointed to Jace, "Get him out of here!"

Rendolph ran to meet Na'tal. The blades met again with another supernatural shower of light. Rendolph pushed the attack. He swung his blade with the skill of an expert, his movements too quick to be seen. Yet, Na'tal's skill was equal, turning aside each thrust and then delivering his own attacks. The two's movements were quicker then the eye could follow, and soon all Jace could see was a blur of swords and bodies.

Jace looked at the man named Torne with his hands raised high. He could not make out the muttering words the man was saying, but as his chant came to an end, his words slowed.

"Ieysa!" he cried opening his fists and spreading his arms wide. With that, an incredible shower of light filled the vast hall. The circle of light winked out for a moment and then tore through the darkness again with its radiant blaze.

The crowd of soldiers that had cramped in so close now recoiled a bit, but their fear of this strange band of brightness was overcome. They came ever closer. Jace could see the hideous lust for blood behind their blank stares and hear the low buzz of their voices above the sword fight as they prepared to lunge.

He faced Rendolph now, but what he saw shook him to the core. Where once stood two skilled warriors locked in mortal combat now stood a horror. Rendolph was glorified, his robe shone like the light of all the starry skies. His face glowed. His body towered over Jace, at least twice his height. On his back, tucked closely against his body were soft, white feathers, the color of ivory. In his mighty hands pulsed a glowing sword of light.

What Rendolph wrestled against, Jace could not fathom. Na'tal's transformation turned him into a hideous contortion of flesh and limbs. The unearthly creature's skin was a deep reddish-hue, pulled tight over pulsing muscles. It stood five cubits high—a full head taller than Rendolph. Its head was crowned with horns curled like a ram's, its eyes turned an unearthly yellow, and fangs hung from its mouth. Its torso was wrapped in thick layers of muscles, which pulsed and pounded with each swing of the huge black sword held in the monster's giant hands. A jewel-studded sash ran across its chest. Its loins were covered by a short leather skirt, and its legs were beast-like, covered in thick hair. They were gnarled and twisted at odd angles in the shape of a horse's hind parts and ended in two cloven hooves.

Jace reeled back in horror, but Zax and Obban's grip, though gentle, held him firmly.

He looked over the masses of soldiers whose appearance had changed as well. Each soldier now resembled an unearthly being—some twisted creation of every man's fear in one form or another.

Some had fur—thick and smooth like that of a wolf—with long, protruding jaws to match. Their backs hunched over as they pawed their weapons, lifting their beastly snouts as if they could smell the growing fear in Jace's heart. Others had a smooth insect-like shell covering over their entire bodies. They clicked their mandibles in wanton anticipation of their prey, twitching every now and then. Some were too hideous to name and looked like some warped imagination from a man's nightmare. The horde stomped their cloven hooves or screeched horrible sounds from unearthly lungs, all the time drawing nearer and nearer.

The robed men laid Jace softly to the floor. The three made a circle around him. Only then did Jace notice that they had drawn their blades, each pulsing with a translucent light. Jace struggled to his feet. The air smelled thick to Jace, filled with an impending doom of dread and finality. His heart sunk as he realized there was no escape.

The rafters shook as the mighty Na'tal bellowed. With one clean sweep of his sword, he sent Rendolph stumbling into the wall. The force shattered the rock, and the rafters groaned against the shock. Rendolph fell to his knees, wasted and spent.

Na'tal laughed. It was a deep, rich chortling of satisfaction. He wiped a trickle of blood from his lips. His gigantic unearthly mass heaved with every breath he took. He stood over Rendolph, a great smile of satisfaction spreading across his demonic face.

"This is truly a magnificent moment!" He boomed, "Not only have I the pleasure of sacrificing this pitiful Keeper, but greater still, I have the satisfaction of slaying the mighty Rendolph, a champion of the Most High," He spat. "I shall savor this for an eternity."

Slowly, ever so slowly, Rendolph struggled to his feet. His body swayed, his every move a work in painful discipline. Finally, he spread his feet, lifting his great sword for the final onslaught.

The great hall shook and the pure ring of light pulsed. From its depths, a voice uttered, "There is no wisdom, no plan that can succeed against the Lord"

Na'tal slowed. He stretched his hand out in front of him, feeling the air within the few strides between he and his prey. He squared his body to Rendolph, leveled his sword, and lifted his head slightly, sniffing the air as if searching for something. After a moment, he advanced. As he neared Rendolph, he raised his sword. The blade arced downward, but stopped in a blaze of sparks, inches from Rendolph's head. Rendolph's sword was raised, and his eyes blazed with defiance. Na'tal leaned his body forward, hoping to crush Rendolph under his weight. As Na'tal pushed with all his might, Rendolph slowly muscled his sword away from him till the two blades were lifted high above their heads. Rendolph's body began to glow white hot, brighter than the sun, then brighter still until his face was unrecognizable. The light chased away the shadows. All who stood before it turned away, the purity too much for their eyes to bear.

There they stood before Jace, Rendolph a majestic blaze of glory and Na'tal blacker than the night. Their swords were locked high above their heads sparkling and crackling in blue-white light.

Only a moment passed and suddenly Na'tal was engulfed in crystal-blue flame. His massive body shook uncontrollably. Screams of sheer pain echoed throughout the grand hall. His body was raised above the heads of all who looked on as if by an unseen hand;

then it was propelled backward like a doll into the legions of soldiers.

The army stared, stunned by the fall of their master. Rendolph stumbled toward Jace, now drained from the fight. His stature was as Jace had first seen him, and he wondered if what he just saw was merely some trick of the eye. Zax and Obban tendered their commander, helping him keep his footing.

"Our work here is finished," said Rendolph, his voice filled with fatigue. "Let the Almighty be glorified. Now, let us leave this awful place."

But as Rendolph finished, the unthinkable happened. Behind the crowd of soldiers came a loud rumble. The earth shook and the rafters swayed. A shape reared its head behind them. A form moved—or what could be called a form—for its image was so black it did not succumb to the light. The soldiers parted before this hideous beast. It was long and moved with a fluid motion, arching its back as it came. It had no limbs, none that Jace could see, but on its back were a pair of curled wings folded close to the body. On their tips were hinged claws and as it moved, it steadied itself against the walls with these. Its neck was long and coiled upward to its head, which narrowed to a point. So dark was the creature, it swallowed the light, and though dark cannot glow, this creature pulsed. Absolute silence fell through the hall, the only sound the rasping of the being's voice, like rocks rubbing against each other.

Rendolph's face turned to stone. If Jace had thought his energy was spent, he doubted it now.

"Sa'vard, you hold no power here," he cried waving his hands wide, "This is a child of the Most High, and where he goes you cannot follow. You have no power in this."

"Bring me the boy," the creature rasped.

The vast multitudes of soldiers raised their bodies to full height and brandished their weapons. They pressed their ranks tightly, advancing toward the four robed warriors. As they closed the last few strides, they broke into a frenzied charge. Some fell while others climbed over them, their minds set on accomplishing the sole command of their dreaded lord. At the last moment, the four robed warriors threw their arms out in defiance. A flash of blue erupted around them, and the band of light over their heads thickened until it was nearly a solid disk.

The robed men turned to Jace. Two grabbed him by his arms, while Rendolph stood in front. All around them the blue barrier of sparkling light swirled sideways and though they tried, the unearthly beasts could not break through.

Jace heard the voice once more, clear and consuming: "Look unto me and be ye saved!"

The Keeper raised his head to the heavens. The disc pulsed and grew brighter still until its light consumed the hall. The hideous mob of soldiers reeled and fled from the powerful blaze. The forms of Jace's body and the four robed men around him were lost in its light. A sound of rushing wind filled the hall once more and the twisted, contorted minions of Sa'vard's army broke and hid their bodies in panic. None noticed the images of the robed warriors and the tattered prisoner blur, shimmer, and disappear. The light winked out and the wind went with it. The Mines of Shorn were once again flung into utter darkness and madness.

Only one being had not missed the young man's final moments. Sa'vard licked his forked tongue. This Keeper, this mortal would have to be shaped. His defeat would be all the sweeter now. All in time, though, all in time.

2

IN THE GARDEN

A SOFT BREEZE BLEW THROUGH THE MEADOW, rustling the leaves and caressing the grass. The birds chirped on the branches while they bobbed up and down in the fair wind. A doe and her fawn looked up from their grazing, distracted by a sound, then dipped their heads once more to the grass. Three more deer waded into the brook nearby, their tongues lapping the cool, life-sustaining water. The late morning sun cascaded on the scenery, bathing it in a soft, buttery yellow.

There was movement under the tree by the brook, and the creatures lazily watched while a young man slowly sat up, taking in his surroundings. He was tall, lean and bare from the waist up. His broad shoulders were covered with scars that stood out in the lazy sun. He was clothed only in coarse, brown woolen breeches. The man yawned and rubbed his eyes, taking in the surroundings, somewhat bemused and startled by all he saw.

Never had he remembered seeing such untainted beauty! The soft bubbling of the brook as the deer lazily munched the grass just a few strides away from where he sat—it was as if he was in a waking dream. He stood up and steadied himself on the tree. He could feel every notch and crevice of its texture. Every smell, though subtle, filled his lungs—the sweet fragrance of the meadow flowers, the lingering scent of pine in the woods around him, and even the water. All his senses drank in his surroundings.

Rolling meadows stretched for miles, dotted by a rainbow of wildflowers swaying in the breeze. Patches of forest and tall trees snaked across the fields. Deer grazed in the tall grass far off, a few here, some there. Off in the distance, in every direction stood snow capped mountains, their peaks glistening in the sun.

He had seen such places before, he thought, but never were the colors so vivid, nor the sounds so crisp, nor the scents so full. He watched, content to take in all he saw, touched, smelt, heard and tasted. He stood for a while, breathing deep full breaths, yet softly so as not to disturb his surroundings.

He noticed the doe lift up its head and look over its shoulder. Only then did he see the man who strode toward Jace, hands outstretched and palms down, skimming his hands along the grass as he came. He was dressed in a simple white robe, his hair falling to his shoulders. Even from this distance, the gentle smile that crossed his face could not be hidden under his beard. There was a regal air about him, yet he seemed approachable. Having seen him, the deer made their way toward him. The fawn jostled ahead, its tiny tail pointed high. It touched its muzzle to his palms, licking his hands affectionately. The man patted the fawn's head, scratching it behind the ears. Jace could hear him whisper something softly. The birds chirped excitedly as if welcoming an old friend. A soft golden finch alighted on his outstretched hand, whistled its praise and flew away. The parade of deer walked beside him as he came towards Jace.

"Welcome," he said. His voice was rich, and every word that fell from his tongue was a gift to the ears. "You have slept much. Would you care for some food?"

He waved his hand toward the tree and only then did Jace see the meal awaiting nearby.

"Where is this place?" said Jace. "I remember the mines, four men, flashes of light, but where—how did I get here?"

"You are still weary, friend. Come, eat and all shall be answered. There is much to explain."

The man sat before the meal as Jace lowered himself gently.

"How are your wounds?"

He touched his hands to his back and winced slightly. The wounds were there, freshly scarred over. He trembled as he ran his hands over each one remembering the place where he had received them. His legs were sore, but unbruised. His body was battered, and he could not recount the last time he ate. His mind raced with questions, and he opened his mouth to voice them, but the man was giving thanks for the bread and Jace dared not disturb him. When he opened his eyes, he broke the bread and offered Jace a piece.

"You can eat your fill, Jace, but eat slowly," said the man.

He dared not object. His body screamed for nourishment, and it was all he could do to calm his hunger while the man watched him with a steady gaze.

The food was splendid. An assortment of cheeses and fruits was laid before him. All were of excellent quality and seemed to provide instant healing to his body and soul. The bread was warm and soft, and its sweet subtle taste lingered a moment on his tongue after it was swallowed. The cheeses were smooth and melted in his mouth. Some were cool and mellow while others sharp and pungent, but all left him wanting more. The fruits were ripe and crisp, and cast a rainbow of colors before him. A plethora of apples, berries, and wild grapes beckoned him.

He ate, taking in each piece of nourishment as if it were his first and last. He reckoned that he was there for quite some time, though the sun barely crossed the sky. His stomach never felt full, nor did the food seem to diminish in number or quality. He ate long and heartily, with the man looking on and occasionally sampling the food.

When finished, Jace reclined lazily on the cool, soft grass and listened to the sounds of nature around him. He looked at the man seated before him. Who was he? How did he know him by name? Jace had never met one of noble birth, which this man must be, or his senses betrayed him and he was completely a fool. Still, this man seemed familiar, as if an old friend had come to talk to him after a long, winding journey.

"There are many questions in your eyes," said the man. "Some I can answer, but there are many that you must be content to let remain a mystery. First, tell me of this place you spoke of from whence you came. A horrible place, it seemed in your brief description, but you have peaked my interest."

The man seemed kind enough. He sat watching Jace with his clear eyes. He looked comfortable and at ease with Jace as they lay under the tree, but Jace felt differently. He did not trust anyone at first glance. Not after the Mines. Yes, the stranger seemed nice and put his mind at ease, but as he looked at him, he judged the man was not being honest with him. A look of suspicion passed over Jace's face, and he looked away.

The man's suggestion made Jace's skin bristle. He did not want to recount his horrible tale of the mines. The entrance to Sheol, many said, lived on only in tales told to little children, and there they were to remain. To be there, to know such a place existed in reality was unnerving at the least. That he had escaped it by some sheer act of the Maker and that there were many who remained firmly under the Mines' grasp—for it let no one go easily—left him with a supreme sense of guilt. Such a task of recounting his tale burdened him heavily, for he wished to let it pass on into forgetfulness but decided he would risk the pain to please the man who provided him with such a bounteous meal.

"My heart is heavy, sire," he said, addressing the noble in the high tongue. "To live through such a tale is unimaginable, but to conjure it into my memory once again is not something I relish. Yet, I can see that you are a man of wisdom and mean me no harm in your request. I will tell it then."

Jace went silent for a moment, letting his thoughts take him back many years before his journey began. So long ago it seemed, he thought to himself. Where to begin? He waded through his memories for that perfect moment that launched him on the path he was on. He still felt a twinge of uneasiness in speaking, but his gracious host waited patiently. Jace closed his eyes once more, conjuring up the image to the forefront of his mind. With a long sigh he opened his eyes and began his tale.

IT STARTED WITH HIS BONDING AS A KEEPER in the tower atop the peaks of the Withering Mountains. Since childhood he had claimed Yeshua as Lord and Ruler over his life. His bonding was a solemn public oath to carry out that promise whatever the cost.

The meaning of "Keeper" was threefold. First, one was sworn to uphold the commands of the Almighty and Yeshua: Keep yourselves in the Father's love as you wait for the mercy of our Lord Yeshua to bring you to eternal life. By obeying the first, a Keeper maintained unity and closeness with others and provided a witness to those who did not know Yeshua. Second, one was to make every effort to keep the unity of the Spirit through the bond of peace. Finally, the charges were sealed with a promise recorded from Yeshua's lips: "I tell you the truth, if anyone keeps my word, he will never see death."

The ceremony was a formality, an outward profession of something he had done at an early age in the privacy of his home. However, it was a special time in every Keeper's life when they proclaimed to all those around them that they had indeed made a very real decision to remain true to Yeshua throughout their life.

Afterwards, he had intensely studied the Song of the Ages, the written words of the Creator. After a final scrutinization of body, mind, and spirit, his teachers thought him ready to journey abroad, without supervision, into Emblom to seek those that did not know and had not heard the whispers of the saving grace of the Almighty's Son. He was given the task of journeying to Nadir in hopes of meeting someone there with further instructions. He was wary to tell this noble more, for it was a secret errand, one of which even he did not know the full details. He had been told it was to be kept that way, and in fact, that was the reason for his torture in the Mines.

Somewhere within the North Wood, his plans had gone awry. He had left the Northern Trade Route in hopes of keeping his whereabouts a mystery and to throw off any pursuers, for the Wood was home to a great many people. He had been there many times before, though never alone and never this far. Over a number of days, he lost all sense of direction. Coming to a hill where the trees thinned, he surveyed the land. Soon he realized he had headed too far south and was approaching the land of Eben. Everyone had warned him of its danger before he set out, for it was a vast plain with little cover. Many an eye would see him if he ventured onto its limitless, open wilderness. Many who should not see him, for it bordered the land of the Stygians and the Great River. Such a place harbored dangers for which he was ill prepared.

But Jace was stubborn and loathe to make right his mistake. He decided to set foot on the Eben wilderness, for there his steed would not be hindered by the trees of the North Wood. *Surely, the detour would shave days off of my journey*, he thought in his folly. He would follow the edge of the North Wood, and come nightfall, find shelter beneath its branches.

Days passed and Jace found the wilderness did not welcome travelers as he had assumed. The wilderness was a rolling land of hard, parched clay. Rains had their way in these parts, leaving great tears and splits in the land that cut across his path indiscriminately. The cold windy rains were only one of the many ills of this place. Food was scarce. Many a day Jace saw neither fowl nor beast.

"The Maker must have forgotten the Land of Eben when he blessed the earth with greenery and goodness," Jace said, at which his host stirred softly.

"It was not always thus, Jace. Many ages ago the land of Eben was wreathed in beauty and blessed mightily by the hand of the Most High. Its children were close to the Master and longed to please Him in all they did. But their pride increased and soon they worked solely for themselves, forgetting the very One who blessed them. In His wrath, Elohim swept His mighty hand over the land, scattering the people to the four winds. He cursed the land, and little has grown there since."

Jace looked at the man as he ended, choking on his last words. His eyes were distant as if he were reliving the very thing he spoke of. They were filled with sadness and his brow was creased in pain.

"It is as you say then," said Jace. "Forgive me, I did not know. But this troubles you, sir?"

"Alas, it does, but speak no more of it. Your story was on your lips, not mine, nor the tale of Eben. Forgive me for being so forward, Jace. Go on."

Jace stared openly at the man. Regal though he was, he seemed far away and distant. How old was he? What strange wisdom was this to know the histories of the very lands through which Jace had passed? There seemed to be more he would say, if given the chance, but much that pained him. The man was withdrawn, not letting on his whole nature, so Jace thought. He shook his head, *I have become suspicious in my travels*, he thought, *though it was not in my nature, it has become a tool I have found useful. I wonder what this man hides?*

"Forgive me, where was I?"

"The land of Eben," said the man sadly.

"Yes."

Jace recalled the land—being mindful to leave out the Maker's hand in the matter—and how devoid it was of fruit, beast, or fowl. He was hard pressed to find sustenance for him and his horse. His personal rations dwindled while half the day was spent wandering the cold, dreary, rain-soaked plain foraging for food. Progress came slowly, and as he neared the foothills, obstacles seemed the only thing this land had in abundance. Ravines rose up one after another. He led his horse down into them, steadying himself with his staff. The mud churned under his feet, and all too often, he found himself stumbling out of the way as his steed lurched down the steep sides. Thistles clawed at his soaked leggings and cloak; it seemed to be the only plant that was willing to make this land its home. Rocks barred his way within the jagged crevasses, and once out on the open plain stones would trip his tired legs. The journey was adding days instead of lessening his time, and he thought more than once of turning back into the North Wood. Soon he became hasty in his attempts to cross the plain. He looked for ways of staying atop the open expanse instead of scrambling up and down the great splits in the earth. He would run the entire length of some just so he did not have to challenge their steep slopes.

The days the rain lifted, the sun would beat down on the land. By mid morning, the earth was a parched, cracked wilderness of clay. Even after he had removed his cloak and loosened his shirt, his exhaustion and thirst were unbearable. By noon, he and his horse had to wait out the sun till evening when the sweltering heat subsided.

Sleep did not come easily, and he tossed and turned throughout the night. The air became cold and damp. More than once he awoke wrapped in his cloak, shivering in a steady, cold downpour. The ground was hard and unyielding. Brambles did not make a soft bed, and more than once he winced as a dried root stabbed him in his side. On a cloudless night, he would lay awake staring at the stars and listen. The silence on the plain was eerie. No sound drifted to his ears other than the soft panting of his steed. So passed the days in Eben.

Jace began to take increasingly greater chances. His haste drew him farther out onto the plain, and one evening, as twilight drew near, he turned his horse only to find that the North Wood was gone from view. He cursed the land and quickly collected his thoughts. In the distance he could see the foothills, which opened onto the Wanton Plain. If luck was with him, he could reach them by nightfall.

The man shifted again.

"Luck, you say? Is there such a thing? Does not the Creator hold all things in perfect balance?" he asked.

Jace was startled from his narration. His jaw dropped, and he narrowed his eyes at the man. "Once again, it is as you say. The Master holds the keys to doors that only He can open. Nay, luck exists only in folly, and even then it holds no power over our actions. May I go on?"

The man motioned for him to continue. Jace stood for a moment staring at the man. The slightest hint of a smile formed at the edges of his lips and then was gone. *Was this man goading me?* he wondered. He perceived that the noble wished to hear his story, but interjected his strange wisdom at inopportune times, almost as if there were a point he was trying to make in the subtlest of ways. *Perhaps this man mocks me,* he thought, *but why?*

He cleared his throat and began again. "Yes, the Maker had smiled on me." As Jace said these words, the man nodded in agreement, the slight curve of the lips coming once again.

Jace reached the foothills with light to spare and spent the remaining time searching for a resting place and gathering wood for a small fire. He had unwillingly given up the nightly comfort while traversing Eben, though he longed for a crisp fire to warm his toes. It had always fascinated him to watch the flames dance as the embers shimmered and glowed. The crackling and pops the fire made were almost like an added companion on his solitary journey. Though at the sound of the man stirring once more, Jace quickly added how the Maker's presence was always a comfort. The man nodded slowly, a twinkle in his eye.

That night as he settled down to rest safely off the plain and out of harm's way, he decided to light a fire—a small reward for completing the hardest leg of his journey. Once over the hills, he would head eastward, traveling unmolested out onto the Wanton Plain. It was clearly out of the way, but he figured it would be a small matter since he had traveled this far off course already. The remainder of his journey would be swift; the Wanton Plain was known for its lush unending sea of tall grass and mild breezes. Unlike the inland world that was known for its harsh winters and sweltering summers, the plain was temperate and was not known for such extreme weather. Though he had never been there before, he remembered his father telling him of the blue green grass, the herds of great beasts that roamed there, and the occasional fruit tree that marked the countless waterholes. He could almost feel the warm breeze brush though his hair as he meandered lazily toward his destination in perfect contentment. He yawned as he poked the fire. This task was not as difficult as his superiors had led him to believe. His roundabout journey would be worth the minor setbacks that had happened. His eyes dropped, and he smiled lazily, thinking of the coming days of wistfully riding northward to Nadir. His eyes closed, and he approached the point where thoughts and memories became dreams. He settled down for the night as the visions calmed his aching, tired body to sleep.

A cry in the distance stirred his unconsciousness. He rolled on his side, putting his hands under his face and stared into the darkness. There it was again. He sat up and scanned the plain in the night air. Somewhere out of Eben a low howl carried its way to his ears. He stood up and listened, thumbing his cloak. It was not a howl, nor was it the call of a horn. Its sound was low and ominous. It did not waiver, but carried on for an exorbitant amount of time. The sound raised the hairs on the back of his neck. Years spent growing up on a tiny farm had acquainted his ears with the sounds of nature. In all those years, never before had he heard such a sound. No person could make such a noise. No beast's breath could last so long or carry that far, at least none that he knew of. There was reason to fear. Whatever it was, he would not stay to meet it.

He kicked sand on the fire, now cursing his decision. Since he stepped on the soil of Eben, things had turned sour. He had spurned sound advice by his many superiors who had far greater knowledge of the world than he did. Eben was a land to be shunned. The reasons were not given, but Jace had a feeling they were many. Now something was out there, something that had seen the light from his tiny fire. He had met no person in Eben, seen no living creature, and heard no sound other than the steps of his feet and the panting of his horse.

Once he destroyed the fire, he roused his steed. After he had hitched his pack to the horse and secured his walking staff behind the saddle, he mounted and wheeled his horse, scanning the sky for Almaris, the unmoving star. Finding his bearings, he began to gallop across the hills. As he did, the sound came again. It seemed closer and more intense. The roan's ears pricked up; its eyes grew wider. She sped over the ground with haste, down the hill and then cut across an open field of grass. The horse clamored up the next hill, losing little speed, jumping over low shrubs and dodging trees as they loomed out of the darkness. As his horse topped the next rise, the call was answered from the north. Jace urged his horse onward, frantic to reach the open plain. He knew now he was pursued, but by what he could not imagine.

The pale moon in the sky cast a dim light on his surroundings. Hill after hill he climbed, the sounds coming ever closer. Finally, the hills gave way to a flat valley. His steed, now lathered in sweat, found new hope and bent its neck down as it pushed onward. Jace could not judge how far away the plain was, but this valley cut through the downs in a straight line towards the flat land. The moon was low in the sky and the first lights of dawn were beginning to show in the east. The treeless hills stood on in silence watching his flight.

Then he saw them. As he turned over his shoulder, three black shapes came striding down the hill. Their gait was frightening in the half-light of morning. They were not man, nor were they beasts. They ran on all fours, loping as they came. Their hind legs were crouched close to the ground as their arms steadied their swift approach. They were gaining on him at a maddening pace. He spun forward in his saddle and saw two more swooping down the hill to his left. They were covered in thick hair save for their chests, which pulsed with muscles as they moved closer. Their hairy arms ended in curled talons that clutched the ground. The skin on their faces was pulled taut over the bones beneath. Short muzzles protruded from them, and beady narrow eyes stared at him through the darkness. As they came, each man-beast would sniff the air. They were so close now that Jace could hear their panting and the soft jingling of the bone necklaces they wore, mementos of their victims.

He leaned back with one hand and unfastened his staff. The beasts could come as they may, but would not find him an easy prey. The three behind him were now only three or four horse-lengths away, their muzzles drenched in frothy spittle, their fangs casting an eerie grin in the twilight. They closed behind the mare's heels intent on knocking Jace down. He swung about in his saddle to face the night-creatures. The lead man-beast clawed at the horse's hind parts. Jace brought the staff high above his head and plunged it in a downward slant, landing squarely on the side of the beast's head. In mid-stride, the creature went limp with a muffled cry while the other two trampled the body of their comrade underfoot, the bloodlust now filling their eyes. Their low war-howl filled the morning air.

The call was answered yet again, first from the north, then from the west, while two calls rang out from the south. Jace spun around to see the two creatures from the hill fall in with those behind him. Two spread out to his left and right, coming alongside him, but keeping out of range of his staff. The two behind came closer. Jace fended them off with his staff while the two astride him sounded off with their low howls. He looked at the slopes waiting for their answer, then turned his head, once again to the enemy at hand. The creatures behind him drew back from him for a moment. Then with a short howl, one lunged high in the air above Jace and landed atop the horse's rear. The horse grunted under the weight and stumbled for a moment. Jace brought his staff into the beast's mid-section, and it tumbled from the horse, but it was too late. The two from the sides closed in, grappling the steed's front legs in their powerful jaws. The lone beast in the rear drove toward the crippled horse thrusting its arms at the hind parts.

Jace's mare tripped, throwing him off its back in a shower of rocks and dust. He threw the staff from his hands, bracing himself as he hit the ground, sliding a good ten paces. He turned in horror, watching his mount make a fruitless attempt to regain its footing. One creature pinned her to the ground from behind, another clutched the roan's throat between its jaws. The third mounted the beast and as he did, the horse gave out a piercing cry of fear and anguish. Her body was lost from view as the night-creatures huddled around her. Jace saw his mare struggle and kick a few moments more and then with a grunt go limp. He looked on as the beasts, caught in a spell of rabid hunger, ripped his horse apart. For an instant, he was frozen at the sight of absolute carnage. He scanned the area for a weapon to aid his attack and saw that his staff lay some paces away. He crouched and leapt for it.

At the sound, the beasts looked up from their morbid feast. They turned and stood growling low in defiance as they advanced on their new prey.

Jace stood, throwing back his cloak and spread his feet, letting his staff hang limply in his right hand like his Mentors had taught him. The three beasts spread out in a circle, licking their muzzles and growling intently. The one behind him charged first. Jace stepped to his left bringing the staff up with lightning speed, catching his assailant in the chin. His body fell, but the other two were on him. One cuffed him in the ear. His vision went hazy, and he stumbled forward. Another grabbed him by the throat, forcing him to his knees. He brought his right forearm down on the creature's wrist. The jarring of bone on bone sounded as the creature released him. Jace rolled back a few paces and brought himself to his knees. He sprung on the attacker to his left and kicked his legs out at the beast to his right. He caught him in the ribs and the creature dropped on all fours, laboring to breathe. He rolled with the other, tightening his hands around the creature's throat as it clawed at him in panic. He head-butt the thing and then rammed his elbow into its temple. The beast dropped to the ground.

The final one came to its feet in front of him. Jace kicked himself backward, anticipating the creature's charge and grabbed his staff. Instead the creature stood panting, then came to his full height. Thin and wiry it looked now in the budding gray light of dawn. It raised itself to its full height, eyeing Jace a moment as it wiped its grizzled muzzle. It sucked in its breath and tossed back its head, his howl high and shrill now, carrying over the soft hills. Jace cursed the creature—it was obviously calling for help. He charged the beast, striking it dead as he swung the staff in a wide horizontal blow, which landed with a crack at the crown of the creature's skull.

Jace stood. He dropped his staff to the ground. His shoulders heaved and his lungs were burning from the melee. He wiped his mouth and looked around the area, wondering how and where he would go from here.

His heart fell to his feet as he heard a low resonating howl which came from every direction. He heard another noise, a low rumble, and it grew louder as the howls came nearer. He looked as the beasts spilled over the hills around him from the north, then the south, and west. First only one or two appeared, and then came ten or more. Finally, like a bursting floodgate, the hills turned black with their numbers as they poured forth.

Jace turned eastward. He could see the blue-green fields of the Wanton Plain in the early morning light, some leagues away. Even if he reached the plain, it would be a futile effort; he could never turn aside this horde of animals. He turned westward again to greet them and the inevitable conclusion to his life. As the black mass churned toward him, his final thoughts were that he would never walk among the peaceful blue-green plains of the Wanton Plain. He lost consciousness as the tide of beasts crashed into him.

JACE STOPPED HIS NARRATION AND HUNG HIS HEAD. He stared blankly at his feet, sapped of all the strength that it took to retell his journey.

"That is the last of the open world I saw, the last things I remember before the mines," Jace said. He shuddered as he spoke the words, his brow beaded with sweat. His flight to the plains was a nightmare all its own, one he had forgotten in the midst of the mines. Still, it paled in comparison to them, for he had awoken from that nightmare, only to be flung into that of the Mines of Shorn, one from which there was no waking. He bent over clutching his shoulders, his body shivering as the past memories bubbled to the surface of his mind. The scene was out of place in these serene surroundings.

"Peace, Jace," the noble man said as he softly touched his shoulders. "Your tale was long and hard, full of anguish, sadness and defeat. What a price you have paid just to tell it! Rest a moment, for if any deserves a time of rest, it is one such as yourself. Peace."

With his final word, he touched Jace. Cool and soft were the man's hands. The touch was reassuring and calming as from a loving father or dear friend. His mere presence brought tranquility to Jace, and he swooned slightly as he laid himself on his side. Sleep crept over his body, and slowly his eyes closed.

His dreams were filled with memories long forgotten: his childhood innocence, running along the fresh-tilled fields near home, the warm fire his family sat around as the day waned, the gentle smile of his mother's approval, and the warm laugh of his father. The images danced in his head, one fading out as another took its place. Long, deep, and peaceful he slept, not afraid of tomorrow's worries or the present one's dangers. His spirit rested, content and satisfied.

He sighed softly and the sound nudged him awake. His eyes flickered open and he sat up. The noble sat before him as he had left him. The vast display of food had vanished from sight, but the sun had barely moved from its mid morning spot.

"My apologies, sire. Have I slept a day?"

"Nay, Jace. Time is different here, not a day as one would call a day. Nor an hour as one would have it. You have slept your fill, and that is what matters most," said the man.

"In truth, I am refreshed. But what is this trick where time stands still, and one sleeps his fill in a matter of moments?" asked Jace. He did not like things he did not understand, and his mind was always quick to wonder how things worked.

"This is a place somewhat removed from the world around us. It is called by many names. Some call it the Mountain, others have named it the Garden. Whatever title it bears, the purpose is the same. Here is a resting place away from all else," explained the man.

"But how am I come here? What brought me?"

"Some things cannot be explained within the realm of nature, Jace. Some things are left to be trusted upon wholly, though they cannot be understood at all. Such is as the Maker would have it."

"Then this is not a dream or an illusion from which I will wake?"

"Nay, this is reality as much as one can call it reality. But one cannot enter here, unless you are called."

"Then I will never truly understand what magic has been wrought in the creation of this place."

"Magic, indeed. Magic comes from man, or worse from the one who holds the world in sway. No, magic was not used in casting this place, nor illusions, nor tricks of old. The Most High—may His name be forever exalted—has touched this place with His blessing: no more and no less."

"Ah, a true place of wonderment, indeed, sir. And woe be to me, for I have seen it touched it, yea, dwelt in and supped in it. Me a wretch above all others."

"Why do you say such things, Jace?"

"My tale is not yet finished, sire, and though I am loath to speak of it, as I have said already, I feel compelled now to tell it, but to finish it in haste."

"Speak you, then," said the man reclining against the tree.

JACE COLLECTED HIS THOUGHTS AGAIN, this time without so much worry.

His trials of the Mines were far worse than his journey in Emblom, but he wanted to be done with the whole matter. The kindly noble, though mysterious and somewhat detached, had been a courteous audience for the most part and set Jace at ease. Still, what he was about to retell was the most hideous of experiences he had gone through. Jace folded his arms tightly across his body and began in a strained monotone.

He told of his waking, clasped in chains to the bare rock of the mines. The man listened to his tale of the many days spent there: the countless beatings and the slow, wearing away of his spiritual fervor. He told of his attempts to escape and the miserable results—how his hope seeped out of him with each passing hour.

Alas, he came to the end of his tale. He recounted in detail the confrontation with Na'tal, Du'mas, and the final attempt to break his will and turn his existence to the glory of Sa'vard. At these things the man listened intently, nodding and rubbing his chin pensively. Though he did not interrupt, his mouth opened and closed many times throughout the story, as if to interject or explain something Jace had not seen or understood. Jace told of the unexplainable wind, the flashes of light, the four men in white, and the shape-shifting of things around him. He recounted the voice that came from nowhere and everywhere, the pulsing disc of pure light, the transformation and fight of the ones named Na'tal and Rendolph, and of the eerie, formless creature that swallowed the light as his rescuers fled. Finally, he sat in exhaustion and silence, not knowing if what he had spoken was true or illusion, fancy or real. A deep pain was formed in his heart, and he hung his head from the man in shame.

TIME PASSED and then his host spoke.

"Much have you spoken of what few of the world have ever seen. I can tell you wrestle with questions, wondering if what you saw was real, but there is something else, is there not? Why the look of sadness and pain, Jace? What troubles you so deeply when you are here, away from the evil that entangled you and at peace in a land so fair? What is it?"

Curse this man, was there nothing he did not see? No matter how hard he tried to hide it, this man perceived all things as if he saw into his very soul. His insights were a mockery to secrets Jace wished to keep private. He did not want to explain himself, but he wanted to stand up to this noble, to show him that he was not afraid to meet a challenge or look at what he did not want to see. He rose up and looked in the man's eyes with contempt, lines of sorrow creasing his face. The words came to him, but thick they were and filled with emotion. His voice wavered, but he carried on.

"You have sat and listened with all the mockery of a peasant! How many times have you goaded me while I spoke, questioning my allegiance to Elohim and gaining pleasure from my short-sightedness. I took an oath, and though it seems ages ago, I can remember it like yesterday. My love for Him and my allegiance to Him were written and sealed upon my heart. But you question it as if I acted out of folly all along my journey. Why? Speak!"

As soon as the words left his mouth, Jace was sorry and ashamed that he had said them. The man was taken aback as if slapped across the face. Lines of anguish creased the look of sadness he gave Jace.

"Truly, these were not my intentions, Jace. I am sorry that you perceived them as such. Your allegiance to Him was never a question in the forefront of my mind. No, your story proves all the more how you love Him."

Jace turned away, his lip trembling, shaking his head, ashamed at his actions and what he had not told the man.

"What ails you now? Is not all made right?" questioned the noble.

"You don't understand," said Jace falling to his knees, his voice trembling on the point of collapse. "I spoke with my lips, but not with my heart when I said I would never turn from the Father. In earnestness, I had given up on Him long ago. The Mines spurred on my hopelessness, and I believed He had abandoned me to them forever. Now I see He was watching, helping, even with me all along. I failed Him! When everything came to a head, my trust wavered. I did not believe He was there; I thought He had forgotten me. I turned my back on Him who loved me so much. How can I bear to keep breathing? I have hurt the dearest friend I have."

"Jace, He loves you still—"

"Stop! How can you say such things? You who sit there and listen, do you know anything of what I have gone through?"

The man looked at Jace, and a tear rolled down his cheek. Jace saw nothing but love in his eyes. He stood and held out his hands to Jace turning his palms outward. Only then did Jace notice them. The scars in the man's hands were deep and piercing. Jace's eyes grew wide with astonishment, and he fell to his knees sobbing and trembling at the feet of his Lord.

"Kyrie!" He cried and then could say no more as the tears welled up within him.

Yeshua softly laid His hands on Jace's head as he wept openly.

"I was there, Jace. I was there all along."

3

AN EXPLANATION

However long Jace lay at his Master's feet, he could not tell. And when he looked in His eyes, Jace wept once more, for who could bear to look into the eyes of one they had called a beggar, only to realize they were standing in the presence of their Maker? Yeshua wrapped His arms around him. So firm was His hold, yet so compassionate and tender. Finally, he pulled Jace away, wiping his face.

"It had to be this way, Jace. I know it was almost more than you could bear, but that is the way it's always been. My Father and I have never stopped watching, never stopped caring for you. But you, like every man, must come to a place of realization—a place where you end and I begin, a place where you realize your attempts at success are futile without Me. Only then are you ready, and only then can I help. Come, there is so much to show you and so precious little time."

He put his hand on Jace's shoulder as the young man got to his feet. The food had given him strength, but his body was still weak from countless days of struggle. They walked across the meadow while the deer looked on. Their feet stirred up the scents of the wild flowers as a soft breeze moved from down the mountains. While they walked, Yeshua plucked a flower from its stem. He breathed deeply, letting its scent fill his lungs and smiled.

"This world was not always broken, Jace, nor the fellowship between the Most High and His people so distant. The world was whole then, a sight to behold. This place is just a glimpse of its former beauty."

He swept his arms over the surrounding fields and hills.

"Times were simple, then, before the Fall of Man. He knew only the fellowship he had with his Maker and found pleasure in it. All around him were signs of wonder and joy, reminders of his Master's power and love for him. He reveled in its beauty and worshipped in its peace. Even the beasts of the field and fowl of the air dwelt in harmony with man. There was no bad thing in all he saw, all was filled with balance and joy and life."

Jace nodded with a smile. The story of creation was known to all, but hearing it from the very lips of the One who made it filled him with a sense of awe. Yeshua spoke with such love and passion, telling how the Almighty gave light with just a word,, put the sun and moon in its place, and scattered the stars about the heavens. He told how the earth was formed and shaped in His hands and with His thoughts, how He separated the lands with vast bodies of water, crafted the mountains into magnificent chiseled peaks, dotted the hills with great trees which swayed in the winds, and spread large open plains for all of creation to share. He recounted the living creatures He had placed on His earth, smiling a little as He recalled each one—the great lion, the intrepid eagle, the graceful deer, the gentle dove, the ancient animals that graced the land with their giant masses, the mysterious creatures of the deep.

He beamed as He recalled how He took the earth and shaped it into man, breathing life into his being and watching with love and pride as he opened his eyes for the first time. He delighted watching man frolic about all of the creation that lay before him, walking with him in the cool of the evening and greeting him each morning with the first light of dawn. He told of the gift of a partner He bestowed on man, how his lifemate was formed not from the earth, nor from his foot, nor from his head, but from man's rib—a sign of equality and unity. They were created male and female, and their bond was like none the world had seen. Together, they were given the power to rule all that their Master had created. How he delighted in them and blessed them with everything he had, trusting them with dominion over all the earth.

"The bond of unity flowed throughout all of creation. It was pleasing to behold," said He with a smile.

"But Sa'vard, was not he at war with the Almighty even then?" asked Jace.

"There was a time when even Sa'vard himself and all his evil minions walked in fellowship with the Most High. He was a magnificent being, loved by all. The Creator set him above all else, save Himself and His Son; such was his beauty and wisdom. Alas, beauty and wisdom cannot waylay bitterness nor are they salves for power. Sa'vard's control begat arrogance, and in that arrogance, Sa'vard thought himself subject to no one. He believed himself worthy of the everlasting throne that only the Maker is able to rule from. In Sa'vard's might and wicked desire, he was tempted to stand in defiance against the Maker himself. But his haughtiness clouded his vision and judgment because no one is worthy, nor powerful, nor wise enough to take from the Father what He alone can have. In His wrath, He cast Sa'vard out of His presence, never to return. It was a pity that one so mighty and beautiful should turn from his Maker who loved him the most. A fateful day that was, for Sa'vard had led many astray. His followers, a third of the heavenly hosts, were cast out of Par'lael as well."

Yeshua's eyes were dark as He spoke, "Such is the fate of all who stand against the Almighty. Never has His standard fallen, nor His power failed!"

"This is truth, Lord. But Sa'vard was spared, was he not?"

"Sa'vard was exiled to this land, never to walk in holiness again. That was the Father's sovereign choice. Even now my Father uses him as an instrument to bring glory to Himself. Sa'vard fools himself, believing that he holds true power over all. Some have called him the Prince of the Air or the Ruler of this world. He rules, but only as a subject, not as lord. Instead he is subject to the Creator and a slave to his own selfish desires. His heart of hearts has become corrupt and downcast, but still he is mighty in strength and dominion. His power is weakened, but not crushed, or defeated—not yet. Though he holds sway over the earth, it is only as much as the Almighty lets him."

"Even now his power wanes. The day of the Lord approaches ever closer. Soon all must acknowledge the power and glory of My Father. On that day He will give me the throne that Sa'vard had thought was his and rule all creation. I will gather all His people, and they will worship my Father in His everlasting glory."

"Maranatha, Lord! We are ready, the earth awaits your return!" cried Jace.

"But it will not have it, Jace. Not yet. I wait for my Father to call me. He alone sets the time for the return of His Son. Fear not! On that day, many things shall happen. I shall come with all My mighty host and wrest the world from Sa'vard and his minions. On that day all shall know and see the Truth. My Father shall grant me rule over all things, and I shall dwell with my people who have My name written on their heads and in their hearts forever. This world will pass away, and my Father, the Creator of all, shall make a new heaven and new earth where all is whole and pure again. It will be as it was, and all My people shall live in peace, lifting up their hearts in praise to the Almighty and the Lamb. Then will the Song of the Ages be complete. All forms of wrong that separate man from Me shall be destroyed. Then will all dwell in perfect harmony as the Father planned. This place we see is only a shadow of what it once was and a sad representation of what is to come. The world will be made anew and rich blessings will flow unceasing from my Father's hands."

So vivid was the picture, that had Jace closed his eyes, he believed he would have seen it. Yeshua stood for a moment His eyes distant, a radiant smile upon his face, the breeze blowing through His hair and rippling across His robe. So mighty was He, even here adorned with only His simple robe, and yet love and power radiated from His being.

"Ah, how I long for that day even now," He said.

They walked farther on in silence. So peaceful was the day and their surroundings as they passed on. Across the rolling meadows they walked, and though they said little out loud, Jace's heart was filled with peace and contentment if only it meant staying in His Master's presence. The spoken words by Yeshua were comforting. He was fain to go on like this forever, here, in this place with the Savior of the world leading him. He had all but forgotten his former trials. They walked for many miles as the sun climbed into the sky. Its warmth filled the air, a reassuring warmth that winter was long away, but spoke of summer being also distant.

Presently, they arrived at the foot of the mountains. As Jace looked up, he shook his head. The mountains had seemed some leagues away, but they were already here. He turned and saw his Lord try to hide a smile under His beard. Then he remembered how time was not measured here as one would normally measure it. Slowly the feelings of confusion melted away and were replaced with acceptance. Yeshua turned to him motioning toward the heights.

"Atop these peaks many wonders are visible. I know you have almost forgotten the terrible ordeals you have gone through. It would be peace to let them lie and for some time we may, but there is a great deal to show you up on the heights of these mountains, if you will venture them with me."

Scale the mountains? His request seemed more like a command. Jace scanned the rocky crags: daunting they stood, waiting for his challenge. Suddenly, this place did not seem so welcoming or open as he had thought it only moments before. The mountains seemed to grow before his eyes, the chill peaks going stiff in defiance. He could imagine the many perils that awaited him, should he decide to climb. One loose stone, a weak grip, or poor footing was all it would take. He shivered, imagining the scenario: grabbing for a hold, slipping backward, his scream of hopelessness, and the sound of breaking bones as he landed on the jagged stones far below him. Was this truly worth it?

Yeshua asked the question almost nonchalantly. Did He not understand Jace's frailty? The fresh scars on Jace's back seemed to pulse in time with his fear. The Lord asked too much of him too soon. His stomach began to knot up and roll over and over. He could feel a buzzing in his ears as his vision started to stretch and blur. Surely, this was not a good idea.

"Is something wrong?" Jace heard Yeshua say through his hazy vision.

He looked at the mountains first, lurching to the right in his dizziness. Slowly, his eyes settled on Yeshua. His jaw hung limply as he worked to say something through his fear.

"To climb this with no rope? We need gear, don't we?" Jace asked, his breathing going shallow.

"All that you need will be provided for."

"My feet are bare...."

"The trail is soft."

"I'm just so weak...."

"Your strength does not only come from within, Jace."

"I'm still so tired...."

"Jace, " said Yeshua, looking him full in the face, "What is wrong?"

Jace sighed, hanging his head. He thumbed his britches for a moment and then looked at Yeshua. "Nothing, it's just ... it's just too much."

Yeshua put His hands on Jace's shoulders and gazed into his eyes. "I will be there, Jace. Could you ask for more than that?"

Ashamed Jace hung his head. "I'm sorry, Lord. I do not wish it. I can think of a hundred reasons why I would not mount these heights, but if You ask it, I shall follow You. You have done so much for me already."

With that, they set off. Jace had not noticed the trail that wove up the mountain, though it was right before his very eyes. He was glad his Master did not look back often, for he blushed several times at the ease with which their ascent took place. More than once he looked back. The trail was much easier to see from this height. He looked farther up the mountain. Funny, the trail was indistinguishable up ahead. But he could see the path as the Master marked it for him. Such is life itself, he thought, so much easier to see where you have been than where you are going. How it should always be this way! One cannot see where the path lies unless He follows the Master's footsteps. Up and up they went. Before long, they were well over halfway to the top.

Soon the way became rough and narrow. The trail had dwindled to a mere footpath, no wider than a small boy. The rocks crowded in on them, and more than once Jace found himself squeezing through tight places. At this height, only stunted plants and moss grew amidst the stones. The air was heavy and wet as they passed through the clouds. So thick it was that Jace could barely make out the shape of his Lord. The fog pressed in on them and seemed to blot out the dim noises of the birds and deer far below. Only the plodding of their feet stirred the silence. The going was slow, and more than once, Jace slipped on the wet moss. Every time, it seemed Yeshua was there in an instant to make sure he was not hurt.

The path came to an old bridge made of rope and wood planks. So long it was that it vanished in the fog. Yeshua beckoned him to follow. Jace lagged behind reluctantly and slowly went forward. The bridge creaked underneath him, the ropes stretching under his weight. As he made his way across the foggy chasm, a soft breeze rocked the bridge. Jace tightened his grip on the ropes as the bridge groaned. He did not like putting his trust in things he could not control. Nor did he enjoy heights, especially those to which there was no bottom. He closed his eyes and steadied himself. Breathing deeply, he swallowed and pushed on. He heard Yeshua call from a distance. As he slowly moved forward, Yeshua's form loomed out of the thick air. He welcomed Jace across the rickety span onto solid ground again. His reassuring touch calmed Jace once again.

"Only a little farther must we go. The air has thinned somewhat, hence we won't move on so quickly."

Jace smiled at the encouragement. Farther on they went, and the trail slowly began to rise again. The rocks were tight here, but they made for sure handholds on the steep path. Their going was slow and not only from the thin air. Their progress was meager, but deliberate. They moved with caution rather than speed, making sure their grip was secure and the rocks sound before they placed one foot in front of the other. Jace could see the sun trying to pierce the fog.

As they climbed, the fog gave way under the sun's persistence. Jace turned to look as he moved upward. He could see the summit fast approaching, the peak a welcoming sight. The view was amazing! All about him mountain peaks touched the sky. Their cliffs rose up from the clouds like jagged islands upon a white wispy sea. The sky was the deepest blue, devoid now of any clouds that usually dotted its expanse. The sun was a clean white orb balanced high in the heavens, smiling down on him. On the horizon, the moon was rising as a crescent sliver, another sight Jace had missed for quite some time. The air, though thin, was cool and crisp and sparked him with new vigor. No sound blemished these parts except a lone eagle's cry. Of any sound in creation, that fit his thoughts that moment:

> *He gives strength to the weary and increases the power of the weak ... those who hope in the Lord will renew their strength. They will soar on wings like eagles; they will run and not grow weary, they will walk and not be faint.*

That is what it feels like, Jace thought, *to soar tirelessly amidst such beauty, to be free and not faint, to live and not just be alive! Can I live that way? Have I lived like that? Am I living that way? I can and should and will! Why? Only one thing can bring me to that height: I must not only follow, I must place all my hope and trust in Him. This is my test for life - that I should daily live as one who hopes in the Lord!*

He smiled, looking up to Yeshua. Yeshua turned and held his gaze, a smile creasing His face.

"Yes, that is your test, Jace. And that is My promise. As I have been, so shall I ever be: faithful. Wherever you go from here, whatever circumstance may arise, know this: I will never leave you nor forsake you. You who have been called by My name and are mine. And if you abide in me as I abide in you, you will ask what you will, and it will be given to you."

Jace's journey was starting to make sense—not the mere climb up the hills, but his travels across the Great Wood, Eben, and the Mines. If only he had kept such a stout heart during those times, his Master would have been glorified all the more. If only he had let his Lord lead him on his journey, things would have been different. Maybe things would not have been so dim. Now the climb up the mountain was almost complete. He recalled how the high peaks were so foreboding, how he ventured up them, following his Lord in spite of his own reluctance and opposition. Could he have done this without Him? Would he have ever attempted it? How his Master was faithful to him every step of the way! Where He led, the path was easy to make out. If he stumbled, Yeshua, Son of the Most High, was always there. And when he thought he was alone in the thick fog, there was his Lord, only strides away, hidden from him one moment and visible the next as Jace followed where He had been.

"You must remember these things you have learned, Jace. The time is coming when I will not stand before you, but I still will lead you through your life. When you do not see Me, trust My promises. Let this time of fellowship be an encouragement and an example to you. Do not forget what I have done, nor how I have been faithful, for the time shall come when that will be the only thing you will be able to hold on to. Where you go, you will not see Me, but nonetheless, I will be there. And if you call on Me even then, I will keep you in Me."

Jace looked with love into his Savior's eyes. The words Yeshua spoke grieved him, for he did not desire to leave His presence. Still, Jace knew he must. He could see the pain in Yeshua's eyes. In that moment Jace knew that he would cause Him much sadness for his life would lead him down many roads, and he would stumble and fall many times before he saw his beloved Master's face once more. He took the words and stored them in his heart. A time would come when he would need them.

The final ascent went easily. Oh, the rocks still crowded the path, the air was thin, and Jace was very tired, but his spirit was lifted, knowing that his Savior had not given him an obstacle that he could not bear. Yes, it was too much for him alone, and the nearer they got to the peak, the more he found himself reaching out to his Lord's hands.

Finally, they mounted the summit. There Jace stood clinging to Yeshua in exhaustion, his knees buckling as he gasped for breath in the thin, cool air. He shielded his eyes from the sun above. The light shimmered off the clouds, blinding him for a moment.

"Behold my creation!" Yeshua spoke and His voice boomed with the air of sovereign authority. "Open your eyes, is not there delight in what I have wrought? Behold!"

Jace let his hands fall from his face. As he did, the clouds parted before him, and Jace looked upon the vast expanse of what was called the Garden. Beyond the horizon it stretched: rolling hills of the greenest green, spotted with proud pines here and tall oaks there, nothing but pure unblemished nature. He strained his eyes to the valley far below. The animals, now only specks to the eye, roamed freely about the land. Flocks of birds slowly drifted across the sky. There below and to his right some leagues away, he saw a stream cutting down from the north. It glistened in the light of midday, and he could see many creatures drinking from its waters.

He tossed back his head and laughed as he clung to his Lord. It was a laugh filled with joy and freedom, a simple expression of overwhelming peace from sharing this moment with the One he held so dear. That laugh was filled with wonder and thanksgiving for all his Creator had done for him. He saw now the trials from whence he came led a long, burdensome path to where he was now. He would have it no other way. His laugh carried far across the plain, and all the creatures who heard it nodded with agreement.

He turned to Yeshua whose face beamed with delight. He put His hand on his shoulder, and they stood for a time looking out on the Creator's goodness. At length, Yeshua sighed.

"This vision is peaceful, and I am loath to leave it. Now that we have gazed upon all that is good and fair, we must turn our minds to other things for I brought you here for a far greater purpose. Look once more on the land, Jace. Then we will begin."

Jace drank in his surroundings. He closed his eyes and listened to the tranquil silence and the soft distant sounds far below him. He felt the sun upon his face, bathing him in its warmth. At last he sighed.

"I am ready, Lord. What must You show me?"

"Where we are is far removed from the world around us, Jace. There, a battle still exists, not one apparent to the eyes and ears, but rather one seen by the heart and soul. For it is a battle between Sa'vard and I over the hearts of men. It is time now for you who once were innocent to such things to be shown the fullness with which this war exists."

YESHUA TOUCHED THE AIR BEFORE HIM. The air rippled, like one touching the water's surface. As it did, the sky blurred and darkened. Jace leaned forward, peering at the vision in front of him. Slowly, he began to make out shapes. A great forest came into view, its tall evergreens marching for miles to the horizon. The vision turned and Jace felt as if he were lifted on the wings of a great bird of the air. He lurched sideways and was restrained by Yeshua's arms. He looked off to his right and left only to see utter blackness illuminated for a few paces by the light from the vision. He stared at it again, and it was as if he were looking in through a house's lighted window during a moonless night.

The sky moved forward around him as they passed over the trees. Cottages sped by as they went. Some were tightly shut, their chimneys smoking. People stood outside, others were saddling their horses or feeding livestock. Jace could tell it was early morning, and the sun peeked over the horizon as if to say he were right.

"The North Wood," he murmured.

"Of course," Yeshua said, "But what lies beyond this great forest, Jace? What treasures or nightmares does it hide from curious eyes? Look and see."

He waved His hand across the air, and they sped farther west. The trees thinned, and they passed over high hills deep green with grass. Now and then ominous boulders showed their craggy faces amidst the gentle rolling hills. Jace knew this place from his studies. The land of the Stygians was known for its beauty throughout the world. Great were the people who dwelt there. There were said to be healers and craftsmen who worked as one with the land and in harmony with each other. Onward they went, flying over land so fair it rivaled all but the Garden with its beauty. The towns that passed underneath them seemed to melt into the hillsides. Roads were nothing more than cut grass, not paved as the great byways of the east.

The horizon gleamed, and Jace knew they were approaching the Great River. They shot over it and passed by sprawling cities bustling with commerce and great hulking masses of ships that moved slowly in the morning breeze. The towns were filled with merchants and craftsmen already busy in their morning routine. The harbor was no different. It was packed with vessels moored to the piers while others waited anxiously, stuffed to overflowing with their goods. The sight was there, then gone in a matter of moments.

The river stretched far ahead of them. As they went, its waters changed from a light, blue green spray to a dark grayish hue. Scattered vessels dotted the river, which was legendary in span. In some places its shores took a week to reach and here was not an exception. Its teeming waters gave life in many ways. The bounty of food that was pulled from its depths had no limits. Its welcome rains were the only source of showers in the inland world, and its water was as fresh as the mountain streams from whence it came. Even as the thoughts passed through his mind, he saw fishermen pulling in their first loads of the day.

Beyond the river a grayness loomed. The Clonesian Empire hurled towards them, and at once they flew over its shores piercing in to its heartland.

Yeshua explained the dark land to Jace. "This place has never seen true, pure sunlight since that fateful day many ages ago when Clonesious swore allegiance to Sa'vard and declared his lands forfeit. Now, the sun comes up, but its light only shows here as a dim orb. It is enough to keep trees and plants alive, but a constant reminder of how heavy Sa'vard's hand is in these parts. These people have long grown accustomed to the grayish sky, taking it for reality, not realizing the sun shows much brighter than this where Sa'vard's rule still wanes. They have forgotten what it was like to bask in its true brightness. Indeed, they do not walk in the Light at all."

Here was a place shrouded in secrecy. Only fleeting rumors and old tales were known to Jace. The Elders said he was too young to know the lore of such a place. Still, his ears had perked so much the more on the whispers and hearsays he had by chance overheard. To even think that such a place existed where laws were forgotten was unfathomable to Jace. Here, Yeshua's name was only spoken of in passing or over a mug of ale, and then only used as an oath or curse. People's hearts were as dull as the pale yellow sun that shown in their sky. Yes, they worked, it was said, but for what, they did not know. To what end they owed their meager existence, none knew.

Clonesians lived for one thing: themselves. All other thoughts were lost in a murky haze that was suffocated by their unquenchable endless desires. He had heard that every conceivable sin under the sun was commonplace among them. Some things he had heard whispered had flushed his face and turned his stomach. Thieving, burglary, and cheating were common practices, but these were only the beginning. Their every waking moment was bent in the pursuit of fulfilling their lustful thoughts, no matter the costs. No unity or sense of nationhood existed. It was a wonder the entire kingdom had not fallen apart. But dark were the rumors he had heard to the forces that kept the mighty empire from crumbling.

He watched this mysterious empire unfold before his very eyes. Before his ordeal, he might have considered a moment like this a genuine treat to his folly, like a taste of some forbidden sweet his mother would leave out, but much, much worse. Now, this land's connection to Sa'vard made his skin crawl. He set his jaw and peered hard at the vision, hoping to unmask the evil land and glean whatever insight he could use for good.

Sights flew by. The shoreline was seemingly empty, but as he looked, he saw mounted skirmishers patrolling the beaches in their dark armor. Over the first hills stretched a line of towers made of stone. The banner of the Clonesians snapped in the wind—a silver crown wreathed by an olive branch and crossed by three swords. The symbols boasted of a once proud and mighty kingdom, but meant little today for no such land of noble cause or justice existed. The fortifications were impressive. A great line of earthworks ran in front of and behind the towers. Masked archers watched in all directions from the tall buildings.

"The great earthen barriers still keep a watchful eye on the borders. But look! What do you see amidst the towers?"

Jace looked and saw great smoldering heaps of wood.

"These are used to light the sky at night for the watch is never blinded from the actions of its borders. But these towers serve a dual purpose. They see all and are not only meant to keep prying eyes out, but to keep its people in."

Jace nodded. The two lines of earthworks hinted at such, but subtle enough was the defenses that the people within did not notice.

Further on they moved. The impenetrable line of defenses yielded to a vast open plain. He noticed the telltale signs of smoke from early morning fires puffing out of chimneys. Tiny houses dotted the countryside and the green hills as they moved inland. The houses were peculiar here. The structures were wooden from the ground up, very different from Jace's plain, stone-walled, thatched-roofed cottage in the woods. Except for the pale gray color, the landscape looked strikingly similar to the Stygians. The grasses beyond the banks were browning, but then they were farther inland. The easterly winds left little moisture for the soil in these parts. But the Clonesians were inventive in their own right. Large wells had been dug, and ditches of irrigation crisscrossed the fields. These were tools of old, harkening back to the realm's former glory.

As they passed over the country, Yeshua poured out insight after insight of the place, "Citizens in this land have little to want. The harvest is toiled by endless amounts of workers who serve in the blistering inland heat. Ever a watchful eye is kept on them. Six masters watch over each party of thirty-six. The fields produce vast amounts of every kind of grain, vegetable, and fruit. In fact, they export the excess to the Stygians. Though the Stygians would deny such a thing, they are heavily dependent upon this trade, and in fact, they have prospered much from their close relations."

"Much of this looks normal to the untrained eye, Jace, but watch and see. Many a wandering eye passes over the black-cloaked men who stand apart from the crowds in the shadows. Do you see them? Passers by give them never a second glance. They have a secret purpose that none know for these are the servants of Sa'vard: ever present, but never noticed. Their task is to gauge order. They see all. Nothing escapes their watchful eyes. They are the ones who hold the keys of power in this chaotic land."

As Jace picked out their dark cowled forms, Yeshua went on:

"All forget the figure behind the merchants who keeps tabs on the daily routine. Eyes dismiss the dark figures in the shadows of the tavern, monitoring the day's business. None see them in the shadows as they walk the streets at night. Oh, they see, but do not truly understand. They are part of the world around them as much as the trees or the cobblestone roads. Clonesians give little care to what stands apart, as long as it does not interfere or threaten. But they are not privy to the power that these beings of evil hold over them. Long ago they remembered such, but Sa'vard charmed their minds by fulfilling every want they could imagine. Now Sa'vard keeps an iron grasp over this land, though none see it. Their wants and concerns are only for the moment, and Sa'vard entertains their lusts for that keeps the kingdom within his clutches."

The vision revealed many things. No more were they gliding above the trees. They walked through small villages, upon the farmlands, and into the very capital of Clonesia. What Jace saw dispelled all that he had previously known. True, Clonesians were selfish to the core and vastly narcissistic. When Jace had pictured the empire in his mind's eye, it was a smoldering, apocalyptic ruin where everyone lived in fear and killed for bread. What Yeshua had shown him was quite to the contrary. These people were well fed, some adorned in rich fabrics of the social elite. Others of the merchant class wore great jewels on their fingers and around their necks. Even the lowliest street urchin had a hearty smile of satisfaction on his face. Commoners bartered here as they would any place in Emblom. Jace saw no fights and no acts of mischief, at least none that was uncommon for such a place. People went about their daily tasks with order and even purpose. However, in spite of the normalities, Jace would not forget the Watchers, as they were called. If Yeshua had not pointed out these things, his impression of the country would have been boringly normal. Yet, the more he listened, the more he saw how heavy and open Sa'vard's hand was.

All this could not prepare him for what he saw next. A great circular mass rose up before them in the heart of the city. It was the flat brown of sandstone and stood out against the sky. Banners wreathed its heights and many people walked along its ramparts, going in and out of its numberless gates. Jace could hear a great cheering from within its walls.

"This is the great Kolosia of the people, where the throngs are entertained."

"I did not know man could build such things so massive and high," Jace said.

"Many years were spent in toil to build this, but it is now the heart of Sa'vard's power, the crowning achievement of his enchantment over the masses. People come here to witness many things, to be entranced, entertained, or to quench their desire for the macabre. Look!"

They rose up over the great circular structure and gazed down inside. Row after row of people stood cramped and staring down into the center of the giant ring. Some conversed amongst themselves like merchants dealing business. Others laughed and cajoled each other as they talked in the crowd. Families stood together. Fathers mumbled words in some deep discussion with each other while the mothers chatted away, all oblivious to their children that ran haphazardly in the aisles. Many stood with their eyes transfixed on the action below, their deep-throated cheers of anger and excitement rising in waves throughout the throng.

Jace turned his attention to the ground that was encompassed by the raucous throng. There, a small crowd of people stood in ragged clothes. They were ringed by a number of armed horsemen that prodded them out into the center of the circle. The crowd's cheers rose in anticipation. The prisoners huddled close together. Jace could make out men and women among them, some limped, others wore old tired faces, still others were as young as he, while some were younger. Many of their eyes bulged with fear, and Jace could see that their faces were swollen from crying—men and women alike. Some were hugging and sobbing on each other's shoulders. Many held hands. Then there were the few amongst them who stood tall and defiant with their gaze fixed in loathing upon the guards that encircled them.

Jace's heart seemed to sink where he stood. He had never heard mention of this in all the wild rumors. He could not tell what would happen to the small crowd of prisoners, but he sensed something horrid and evil was about to take place. He turned to his Master, ringing his hands, a look of bewilderment and fear upon his face. Yeshua's look was grim. His jaw clenched and fire blazed in His eyes.

"This is the height of Sa'vard's entertainment. The people you see below you have done no wrong, only questioned his authority. All are Keepers like yourself. Sa'vard hands them over to be sacrificed for his glory while the crowd looks on. He delights in torturing them before they die," Yeshua's voice grew low and hard, "He pleases his minions with the blood of the saints."

Jace shook his head, his eyes growing wide. The crowd's cheers rose higher, but Jace would not look at the vision now for fear of what he might see.

"Lord, why? Can't they be saved? You hold the power to keep them from harm. Surely You would not give glory to Sa'vard at the hands of Your people?"

"My people glorify me not by their circumstances, but by the attitude of their hearts. Sa'vard views this as a victory, but it is a sham. No one is guaranteed safety of the body, but I promise salvation of the soul. The witness that My people give to those around them, whether in life or death, gives Me victory. Those you see before you knew the price that would be paid to reach those that are lost, but they gladly embraced it. They knew the Truth: to die is gain."

"Still, Lord, they will die ..."

"Yes, Jace. This is the price that must be paid to reach those that have never heard nor seen Me. Still, there are times when others will hate and despise you. Did I not say that people would reject you because of Me? If they persecuted me, they will persecute you also. They will treat you this way because of my name. Fear not, Jace, these shall awake in glory on the shores of Par'lael. Though you and I shall weep for them, they shall be gathered unto Me and my Father in their resting place," as He spoke, His face twitched. He closed His eyes and bowed His head.

Jace could hear the crowd jeering, and then their shouting broke into a cry of shock and amazement. Somewhere under the roaring din he thought he heard the ragged prisoners singing a hymn in loud defiance. Their voices rose higher for a moment, wavered, and then were drowned by the throng's overwhelming cheer of satisfaction. Amidst the cheers he heard screams from the Kolosia's floor. His eyes caught sight of the fallen men and women in the center of the circle, and he turned away, knowing all too well what had happened. He brought his hands to his face and choked back a cry as the angry murmur of the mob died away.

When Yeshua lifted His head, Jace could see he had been weeping.

"Do not let their skin fool you, Jace. Their hearts are what you cannot see and those are as you have heard. Do not let their smiles or compliments disarm you; behind every word is a plan of deceit. Though they have moments of kindness, their thoughts never stray far from themselves for they are slaves to their own desires. Remember this, but remember even more that I love them. Though their hearts are hardened and their eyes are blinded, I sacrificed Myself for them also. My heart is grieved, lo, many of these whom we have seen have set their minds to themselves and will never know Me. Still, even amidst these people are those who would listen were someone to tell them My truth, which breaks all bonds. Though this is a dangerous task indeed, someone must...."

Yeshua waited a moment, letting Jace digest what he had seen and heard. Much of what Jace had been taught had been laid bare before his eyes. The grotesque nature of the true battle between Yeshua and Sa'vard and the dastardly lengths to which Sa'vard went were dreadfully revealed in one foul swoop. Jace's big eyes and the way he plucked his breeches spoke volumes of the conflicting emotions with which he wrestled. Moments passed, and Yeshua urged Jace from his swirling thoughts with a gentle touch.

"We must go, Jace. Time is short ,and still there is much more to show you. Come."

Yeshua touched the vision and again it rippled. When it cleared, they were speeding over the Great River as before. The sun was high in the air and made the dark water gleam. It was good to be out from under the shadow of Sa'vard. The river grew wider still, and before long, it filled the vision. They cut east over the Inland Basin, just short of the land of Eben and glided over dry land. Tall grass waved in the tranquil bay breeze as they crested over a stunted hill.

There they stood, looking down on a town, its structures fading into the hills around them. The simple streets of soft, short cut grass were filled with folks walking here and there. Though Jace saw great herds of sheep and cattle in the outlying fields, the lack of pack animals was apparent. What man could not carry with his own two hands, he put in great two-wheeled carts and hauled behind himself. People passed by in low-hushed voices, their clothing simple, but sturdy with a finely woven stitch. They greeted one another with warm smiles and soft salutations, each mindful to offer a helping hand if needed.

The town was spotless. No refuse piles hid around any alleyway. Streets wove lazily around the hillsides. Wildflowers lined them, and their scent wafted through the vision. Every low-roofed house was kept in immaculate condition. Fresh gardens welcomed guests. Women and men alike were seen sweeping what little dust was left out the front doors. Fresh baked pies sat in more than one window.

Jace scanned the buildings. These looked like simple, low-roofed cottages, their backs leaning into the hill behind them to preserve the heat and add extra storage. The houses had a craftsmanship that he had never seen before, and the quality was work fit for a king. Now he noticed the simple, yet ornate woodcarvings that bordered the windows. The windows themselves had six pains of glass with genuine pewter latches. On each door hung a solid brass knocker with the initials of the occupants. The thatched roofs hid thin metal "ditches" that ran the length of the structure.

Jace assumed they were gutters. He had heard of these rails that channeled water off the roof—quite expensive they were and only the most lucrative of traders of the east could furnish their houses with such. Every house was adorned with these simple, but extravagant fineries. The guttering ran off to a low trough on the house's side. Some scooped buckets out of the rain water, pouring it into their animals' feeding station while others took it inside to be used for cooking and cleaning, no doubt.

Other gadgets he saw, some he could even name. The site was incredible: simple and luxurious at the same time. Everything had its place—all the people moved in a sort of dance as they went about their daily business. There was a certain peace about the area, but something was strange.

"Are all towns like this?" He asked.

"Ah, the land of the Stygians. All are not so simple and well-cared for. Some are as peaceful, and some not quite as quiet. Others are a bit more forthright with their art and decadence. But, then, that is not what binds this land together. Stygians disagree on many things, hence the Union is not as strong as one would think. Yes, they are as different as their towns, I would say, but all agree on one thing. To be a Stygian means to live at peace. They all love their fellow man, more or less, and strive to live in harmony with all living things."

Yeshua drew in the sand at his feet as He spoke, "Before the Union, they let their differences be known to each other. Many a battle raged and many a house burned to rubble. Now, their common bond and pacifism unites them."

Jace rubbed his nose, "Lord, I am troubled. Is there not more than this? They practice love, more than some Keepers I know, but do they not know of the Maker? Surely He has blessed this land and those that are in it, for in no other place have I seen such beauty. Do they not worship and give thanks to You then?"

"The Almighty is the only One who blesses in truth, but even Sa'vard can conjure what seems to be good. I tell you the truth: His hand is at work here. As for the Stygians, they believe their salvation is found through what they have done. Oh, there are those who offer up praises to the Almighty and erect great structures in His name, but all have turned their backs on Him."

"How?"

"They treat with indifference the price I paid for their wrongs. They believe they can work their way into paradise by fulfilling great deeds while here on earth. They sell their possessions and live in poverty to prove their dedication, or they give alms to the needy each day. They never lift a hand against their fellow man and obey the Old Way with every waking breath."

"Lord, these actions put many Keepers to shame, for we rarely live a constant life of servitude."

"Yet, even the least of you has done more than these. I say that not out of anger, but pity. Sad it is that an arrow should fly so true, but still miss the mark. Indeed, they have missed it all. About them it is said, they have rejected the cornerstone. They have trampled the Son of the Almighty underfoot and treated My sacrifice with contempt. In doing this they have spurned the gift of My Father who loved them so that He sent Me to them. They mock the very One they claim to serve. Many of these do not know Me, many more have known and rejected Me, but all have fallen short."

They stood watching the scene a few moments more while the sun crept farther east. Jace's heart was torn for he longed to live in such a place where beauty abounded, and wars and heartache were only bygone memories. He knew this place was only fallacy. Yes, it was real enough, but the Song of the Ages spoke of wars and battles to come that would touch all the earth, even here.

Furthermore, the price was unimaginable. True, he could settle in the valley he saw before him, surrounding himself with every good thing, but then he would have to sacrifice everything that meant anything. He turned to Yeshua, his Master, his Savior, his Lord, his Friend. No, the price was not worth turning his back on the One he had come to know and love.

"We must go," Yeshua said again and touched the vision once more. The haze cleared, and there they stood floating over his homeland.

"It is as I remember it," said Jace as they left the North Wood and rose up the lofty plateau known to all as the Gap.

"You know this place and still, you have never traveled its whole. It is time for you to see with your eyes what you have only read about."

As Yeshua finished, they moved forward. Jace could see his house off in the west, a small cottage tucked in the depths of the forest. The surrounding area was well known to him. The trader's path that wound its way south, the small village placed in the clearing only miles from his home, the gentle brook with the swimming hole—he noted each one as they moved farther north.

"Some say this place is an anomaly," said Jace. "In ages past a giant unbroken mountain range ran east from the Lothian Plain to the sea. The Great River was a thin stream that dried during mid summer. In those times, Sa'vard and his host walked the land rarely unchallenged."

"Only the Land of Eben shone then as a light of the Almighty's eternal glory," replied Yeshua. "I believe you know the tale, Jace. The entire world was in darkness until the Almighty sent Me to offer My life as a sacrifice for all. This was done so the wrongs of the world might be atoned and all could come, if they chose, to a restored fellowship with the Almighty through my mediation."

A smile crossed Jace's face. The story never grew old. It brought joy to him now as it did when he first accepted Yeshua's gift as the only sacrifice that would pay for his wrongs and committed himself to follow Yeshua the rest of his life.

"When I left this world, it was changed forever. The vast range of peaks which separated Emblom from Sa'vard were torn asunder. A great plateau rose high for the entire world to see as a witness to My Father's power and a testimony to My great gift. There dwell My followers, all who dare call themselves Keepers," Yeshua said sweeping His hand over the vision, "This land is sacred. All who dwell here bear My name."

The land itself was not known for its beauty. It was a rugged place, not welcoming like Stygian land. The air was noticeably thinner here than most places, which made it hard to breathe. The soil was filled with stones in many areas which made farming grinding work. Some parts flooded after heavy rains, and the cold, dry nights during wintertime were well documented.

Yet, the Gap was also beautiful in its own rite. The mountain streams cut many a flowing brook through greatly wooded glades. Wildlife flourished in these densely forested regions more than anywhere else. Cascading falls dotted the areas around the mountains. Here, after every rainfall, beautiful rainbows were seen, a sight which was not so common in the rest of the world. The land was not a plateau as some would think. Yes, great flat expanses existed about the Gap, home mostly to large herds of beasts and wild horses, but the land had many rolling and jagged areas as well. Such variety of land and animal existed only here.

Keepers liked to say the land mimicked the life of any who chose to follow the One. Hard and toilsome it was, filled with many obstacles and trying times, and yet filled with sights and wonders that could only be a blessing from the Creator.

"You have heard of the many people who live here, I'm sure. Some ways they give praise are foreign to you, Jace, but they honor Me nonetheless. The people of the south-central region are quiet in their worship, wishing to honor me with reverence. Those to the North and East are bold and joyful in their praise. You will also find lone persons high in the mountains who offer their solitude and meditation in worship. All have claimed the Son as Lord. As each worships differently, so also do they strive to bear witness to My name in different ways. Many encourage each other with words, some with actions. Some go to the lands around them, teaching the Truth to all they encounter. Others spend much time in deep communion and meditation with the One. My Father finds joy in all these things."

They flew farther north now. Trees gave way to plains of low shrubs and lively herds, which gave way to trees again. They passed over streams, rolling hills, peaceful valleys, and broken plains.

Finally, they looked upon a great line of fortifications and earthworks, which stretched into to the west and east. The battlements were crawling with people going about a myriad of tasks. Archers scanned the great battle plain beyond the walls in silence. Groups of mounted pickets scouted the grounds, never going beyond bowshot. Soldiers, men and women, assembled behind the walls. Here troops snapped off their drills as the wind whipped around them. Over a ways, quartermasters oversaw the delivering of rations and weapons to the walls. Endless amounts of clothing, meats, grains, arrows, swords, and horses arrived to the front in a chaotic mess, which was nevertheless sorted through with a great deal of discipline and patience. Though the air about the front seemed to be busy with frantic anticipation, everyone involved went about their business with a sense of earnestness and diligence.

"This is a sight which many in the Gap know little of, or have forgotten its importance. This is the March, and it is here that the stand against Sa'vard remains an ever-watchful eye. If not for this, the entire land of Emblom would be overrun by the Bothian hordes and other minions of his."

"The Bothian hordes?"

Yeshua turned to Jace, "The same creatures of the night that carried you to the Mines of Shorn. They and those like them are the very hosts that Sa'vard led astray."

Jace rubbed the scars on his back. "Then it was real!"

"Where you were was not a dream."

"Na'tal, the men, the ring of light?"

"Yes. A great and wicked being is Na'tal, a chief over Sa'vard's forces. His goal was to break you, Jace, and he did, but you called on My name and I heard you. The four you saw are soldiers of the heavenly hosts sent to bring you here."

"I saw a being, Lord, menacing and shapeless. It swallowed up the light as it came."

"Do you fear this creature?"

"I can see it even now as I close my eyes. It was and is a fearful sight to behold."

"Be vigilant, Jace, for you looked upon Sa'vard. He comes in many forms, that one you saw is not his most hideous. Do not be afraid. Remain in Me, and he will not have his way. Remain in Me, but be on your guard."

"The Bothian hordes, Lord, what of them?"

"They serve Sa'vard's beck and call with a fervor that can only be matched by the zeal of the men and women of the Gap and the vigilance of the very hosts of heaven."

"I knew nothing of this," Jace said with a frown.

"And well you shouldn't. Only those Keepers whose walk is constant with their Savior have a hope to stand against such beings. Those who place their trust in anything else or waiver in their faith are easy prey for the Boths. You should know that by now."

Jace nodded slowly, remembering the Wanton Plain.

"The Gap has been silent for some time now. Sa'vard is gathering his forces. He is preparing to wage open war against My followers. This has never been done on such a scale."

"What will become of us, Lord? Will we fall?"

"Many may, Jace. The Song of the Ages bears instruction for all to follow. It holds the key to stand against Sa'vard. But as with those in the Kolosia, many may fall. The question is this then: will you stand? Will you stand if it meant you were hunted down for My name and forced to live in the hills and caves? Will you stand were it to cost you your life?"

"Lord, give me strength. If this is to be, I will need it. I know what You ask, and I know what it will cost, Lord. Yet I would never wish to have to live that way."

"And I would never wish it upon you, Jace, but what will be will be. Neither you nor I can change it, for it is My Father's plan that He had from the beginning. Hold then, to the Truth, which I have given you. Turn not to the right or to the left, but look only to Me and I will keep you."

"This I will do," said Jace.

"Come, then, for this is all I have to show you. Though we turn away from this vision, Jace, hold close to your heart all that you have seen and all that I have taught you. There is much that you will go through before I call you home, and you will need all the truths and promises that I have imparted upon you to guide you through your life."

As the vision dimmed, Jace looked around. They stood inside a modest cottage. Before them were a table and two chairs. On the table sat a plain loaf of bread, a pitcher, and two wooden mugs. Many candles lit the room. For the first time since Jace had been in the Garden, he felt truly tired. He wondered how late it was as he looked through the window into the night. Yeshua bid him sit, and Jace sat opposite his Master and Friend.

Yeshua bowed His head and Jace followed as He gave thanks for the simple meal. Yeshua broke the bread and offered Jace a piece.

"This is my body which was broken for you. Take and eat."

Jace bowed his head slightly and ate the bread in silence. Yeshua poured the two mugs of wine, and after He gave thanks he offered Jace his cup.

"This is my blood which I spilled for you. Drink."

Jace turned the cup up, drinking the rich wine. As he did, he was filled with awe at the symbolic meal and all that it conveyed about what Yeshua had done and would do for him. From his Lord's death long ago which met the penalty for all of Jace's wrongs to Yeshua's boundless expressions of love for him—for all of these and the promises he would glean in the future, he was forever grateful. He opened his mouth to give thanks. Yeshua nodded His head closing His eyes, already knowing all the thoughts of wonder, thanksgiving, and praise that ran through Jace's head.

"You will fall asleep soon and when you wake, you will find yourself within a day's walk of home."

Jace began to protest, but Yeshua lifted His hand.

"I know you don't want to go, Jace. When you leave, remember all that I have said. When the world presses in around you, think of Me and how much I love you. I will be waiting for you with open arms by my Father's side in Par'lael."

Jace wanted to speak, but the tears now flowed freely. He could stay here forever, but he knew Yeshua's words were true. He must leave.

"There is one more small gift I will bestow on you in your journey ahead, Jace. Come hither."

Jace came and knelt at Yeshua's feet, his tears flowed softly down his cheeks as he laid his head in his Master's lap. Jace felt Him lay His hands upon his wounded back. His touch was cool and calming. He felt Yeshua tremble and a cool sensation ran through Jace's body from his toes to the top of his head. Jace looked up into Yeshua's smile.

"Touch your wounds, Jace."

Jace ran his hands along his back and gave a cry in amazement. The wounds were gone! He looked into the eyes of Yeshua who smiled slightly.

"Live as I have lived, Jace. Share My love with those around you and never be ashamed to tell what I have done for you."

"I will miss you, Yeshua" Jace said, the tears falling, "Lo, I miss you even now."

Yeshua kissed him on his forehead and led him to the bed in the corner of the room. Jace lay there as sleep overtook him. His last sight was Yeshua standing over him, arms stretched wide, interceding for him to His Father.

4

THE GAP

Any moment now. The trees were thinning out. Only a little more. His heartbeat rang out with deep, heavy thrusts; climbing always had that effect on him. The path was well worn; he'd been there many times. The rich dank smell of the woods brought back so many memories. Here he used to play till sundown after he'd finished his household chores and completed his daily studies. Every child in the Gap had those whether they wanted them or not, but in time, he had grown to cherish both the menial labor and pouring over the rough parchments of the Song of the Ages.

Many trails wound through these woods. He smiled; he knew every one. They were a comfort to him when he needed a moment of freedom and solitude. He would melt into the woods for hours. There he was free from the rules of his parents, the endless power struggle between him and his siblings, and his duties as a son, brother, and friend. It was hard for him to set aside time for his long, traipsing visits underneath the trees, especially during harvest and First Days.

Like every person within the Gap, he was expected to do his part. Though he relished the hard labor of the fall, he knew it was his responsibility as one of two sons to help his father in the fields. Amoriah always got the household duties: she tidied up, helped her mother with the chickens, and occasionally milked the cow, although sometimes she forgot that.

Of course, the older they got, the more they were given to do. Each passing year brought another task to master and another chore to juggle. Being the second child, he had mixed feelings. He ached to be given the freedom and trust that his parents showed his older brother, but was always overcome with jealousy at how his younger sister lagged slowly behind him in age and responsibilities.

His older brother was a jewel and incredible role model. He took the weight of growing up solidly upon his shoulders with a sobriety that was cushioned with steady perseverance. Jace all but idolized his attitude and ways. He grew into manhood quickly and was soon the workhorse of the family. It was a pity to see him leave for East Haven and even more upsetting when the Council sent him out into the world. The family had leaned heavily on his brother and a part of each of them went off him with, it seemed. Jace had been anxious to fill his shoes and tried desperately to meet each task how he thought his brother would. He remembered what his father told him the first time he handed him the flail:

"It's all in the rhythm, son. Keep your back straight and spread your feet as wide as your hips. Put your arms into it, but not your back, mind you. This isn't a race, it's a job. You need to keep this up for an hour, at least. Above all else, remember, not too hard and not too soft. You need to shake the wheat out of the husk with your strokes, but don't bruise the stems. Nina's very picky about the hay she gets, and besides, bruised hay makes the mattresses smell too strong." With that, Sedd handed over the flail and swiftly made his way around the shed. It was the first light of morning, but they all had plenty of work to do. He remembered his brother's fluid motions with the stick, but could not emulate them no matter how hard he tried.

Of course, Jace was only seven years old at the time. The flail was tall and awkward in his hands, and he never found that magic rhythm his father told him about. By midday his hands were raw, and his arms felt as firm as water. His father flailed the rest of the hay for him, never chiding him about the bruised stems. In spite of all his father's warnings, Jace went to bed that night with a very sore back on a very pungent mattress.

HE SMILED AS HE WALKED ALONG. Those and other memories flitted through his mind as he approached home. He had never grown into his brother's shoes, but had carved out a niche in the family all his own. His light-hearted remarks and unique way of looking at situations made for plenty of laughs, and the long days flew by. The trip to the places of learning had come with joyous welcome on his part, for he was glad to be out in the world on his own, even though he hated to leave his family. The change left him free from the endless showdowns between him and his sister. Still, all his family was near and dear to him. He kept them in a special place in his heart and was ready to help them if ever they asked.

He stared at the woods. It seemed ages ago since he had taken this very trail down to the Northern Trade Route into the North Wood. What would his elders think of him coming back without a mount? What of Nadir and his unfinished journey? He stopped and leaned on a tall maple, balding now in the autumn air. What would his parents think? Did they know? He adjusted his cloak and shrugged his shoulders. It really didn't matter. It was out of his hands. Besides, what had Yeshua said? "Your journey has yet to begin. Remain in Me and all else will follow." That was it. What did the Master have in store for him? He shrugged again. That too was out of his hands.

The trail came to a shallow crest, and Jace looked about him. A stone's throw to his right, he could make out a ridge through the woods marked by a jagged line of rocks protruding out of the ground. A deer trail wound through the rocks, easily noticed despite the autumn leaves that covered it. To his left, the trail turned around a mound in the ground. That way led to one of the brooks that crisscrossed through these parts and passed behind his home. *If I hurry,* he thought, *I'll be able to surprise Mum before she puts out the clothes.* A thin smile crossed his lips; being home always brought out the mischief in him that his teachers tried so desperately to quench. Where else could he let his guard down if not here? He remembered Dorath and Hadran shaking their heads as his father told them one of his bravest endeavors.

"THREE EGGS OR WAS IT TWO?" his father had asked, looking over at Jace as he fronted the question. "I can never remember, but that's not what matters. Mailyn was inside working on her scandalous pumpkin tarts when this rascal sneaks in the back door without making a peep. She'd settled into her baker's mind and counted out the proper portions for everything. He comes in and whisks some eggs out from under her nose. Needless to say, Mailyn isn't in the habit of recounting, so she went on with her work. An hour later, those tarts came out of the oven, hard as wood. Mailyn was fit to kill a calf and there's Jace in back of the barn doubled over with glee."

Sedd looked over at Jace with a reproachful glance, but Jace could see a twinkle in his father's eyes. His Mentors looked like they bit into something sour until Sedd turned back his head and roared with laughter. The looks of discipline dropped from both their faces, and they joined in.

"This one takes after his father in the most despicable ways," said Hadran dryly.

Dorath shook a finger with light-hearted correction, "A game of fun is well to do, but don't go making bad habits. Did you take the consequences well?"

"One cord of wood for each egg, and a week's worth of help in the kitchen," said Jace with a grin.

"Well, was it two or three cords?"

"Two," he said eyeing his father with an innocent grin.

"And was it worth it, son?" asked Hadran.

"I'm still wondering that myself."

The three men shook their heads. They had watched him carefully as he grew from boy to young man. His grasp of the Song of the Ages was beyond his years, but his lack of regard for the norm was noted with dismay. His coming of age meant he had to be turned loose either way, and he was ordered to the East Haven for his final preparation.

When the time came, everyone stood, along with his Mum and Da, as he recited the vows of a Keeper: to love Yeshua with all your heart, soul, mind, and strength; to love thy neighbor as thyself; and to carry the Truth unashamedly to the utter ends of the world. There were many more vows that his teachers had impressed upon him, but these were paramount. He had been given his riding cloak then, a heavy, black woolen cloth that spoke of the populated sheep hills of the eastern region and was a sure sign that he was a Keeper. It was held together with a silver clasp—a finely shaped rendition of an open book with a sword lying across it , a symbol for the Song of the Ages.

His mother kissed and held him for a long time before he set out. She had brought with her an assortment of dried meats, bread and cheeses—only what their humble family could offer. Their eyes met and she touched his cheek. Yes, they had always had their differences, but the love they had for each other covered everything. He kissed her forehead and embraced her a final time, whispering in her ear that he would be safe and that he would always ask Yeshua to bless her each night. He remembered turning a final time to wave one last goodbye before he descended from the Gap. There his parents stood side by side, two tiny specks in the distance with their hands waving high as they held each other. That was the last he saw of them.

He remembered giving a short cry as he settled in for his first meal alone. The night crept in around him and the Wood seemed less hospitable than he recalled. It became clear how alone and helpless he was as he sat huddled under a tree with only his cloak for warmth. He reached into the sack his mother gave him and ate of the rations she had sent. He started when he saw what was buried in the bottom of the bag. There were three pumpkin tarts the shape of hearts his mum had wrapped for him with loving care. He smiled and shook his head. It was just another simple way she found to show him she cared. He leaned back against the tree. Suddenly the world was not so lonely. He knew that his mother was thinking of him.

How excited he was then, for his chance to see the world free from authority with only his wits and knowledge to guide him. *How young and naïve I was*, he thought with a cringe. It must not have been a year since he embarked on his journey, but he was different then. He shook his head absentmindedly peeling the tree bark off a young pine. No need to prolong the inevitable, he thought as he gathered up his cloak and made off through the crisp autumn air.

HE FOLLOWED THE STREAM around the bend, jumping over its rocks to his parents' pasture. The grass was thick, but brown and curled. Father must have turned Nina in already. He could see the three goats in the field eating in a huddle as he made his way to the top of the hill. There below him sat the crooked little cabin that he had called home all his life. Only a thin wisp of smoke said the cottage was not abandoned. He strode down the hill keeping close to the fence. The sun was well above the trees now. Shouldn't they be about their business? He jogged into the yard, mindful to steer wide of the chickens and cautiously stepped up to the door. As he came close, he heard the sound of voices inside. It sounded like his mother and father:

"It'll just have to be that way. I'm tired of repeating it. That is my final answer so take it, if you wish."

"Mai, be reasonable. There are other places. It's not right here. No one reaches out like they used to. I'm alone. Even you don't care—"

"Leave me out of this! It is your own fault. You sit and stew in a corner, moping and pleading for attention. You are never happy with what you get. You always want more. When will you ever stop thinking about anybody but yourself?"

"What are you speaking of? I've given my whole life for you and the children! Is it too much to ask for someone to care now and then? I thought you would, if anyone was supposed to. Isn't that what the Song of the Ages says?"

"Oh no, you don't! I'm tired of you twisting this around. You love to manipulate, but I have had enough. You are not going to pull me away from my friends just because you have none. You need to go somewhere. There are plenty of places in the Wood that would be glad to help you. They even have herbs you can take."

"I am not taking herbs!! The Almighty says He can heal me and He will!"

"Maybe that's why there are people in the Wood. Maybe He sent them here for you."

"Don't patronize me, Mai!"

"You're hopeless!"

"And you're ignorant!"

"Stop it!" a young girl screamed.

Jace rapped on the door. The house went silent. He heard the sound of dishes being moved. Something was dragged across the floor, and the door opened.

His father stood there, his brow dark and brooding. He was dressed just as Jace remembered him. A tight leather vest covered his chest. Underneath was his badly stained woolen shirt that he always seemed to be wearing. It had been patched and repatched until its shape had taken on the look of a patchwork quilt. His breeches were heavily stained with soil, and his boots were well worn. Sedd's frame betrayed the fact that he was a farmer. His thick, gnarled hands and broad shoulders made him good for a long day's labor.

Sedd was stout and only slightly shorter than Jace, but was of a much heavier build. His face had a timeless quality to Jace. His father's skin had a brownish pigment to it that hid the few wrinkles on his forehead and around the eyes. Jace admired his healthy complexion and how nicely his father had aged. His da's features softened when he saw who it was.

"Mai," he shouted, "it's Jace!"

His mother came to the door, a look of wonderment and longing in her eyes. She wore a dark blue skirt and a simple white, cotton shirt. It was none too exquisite and yet it had cost Jace's father a month's worth of wages. The family did not have many bright articles of clothing, and Jace always found his mum's outfit a treat for the eyes.

Mailyn was also of above average height. Though she did not have the presence that Jace or his father had when they walked into a room, she was tall in her own right, dwarfing most of the women in the nearby village. She was larger than a good many ladies and was always self-conscious that her clothes could only do so much to hide her disproportionate size. Her face was always kindly and though she was slightly older, her features were pretty. She usually wore a smile, and her laughter could be heard in even the noisiest of places. She started, threw her arms around her son, and gave him a hearty kiss.

"Jace, I … it's been so long," she said, kissing and hugging him again.

Jace put his hand on her head and rubbed her back softly. His mother always blew things out of proportion. "Ma, I'm fine. See?"

He stepped back, stretched out his arms and spun around to show them all that he was in one piece. He turned and saw Amoriah peering out from behind the threshold. His face broke into a smile, and he threw open his arms as she tackled him with a sisterly hug. For some reason youngsters seemed to think the harder one hugged the more love they showed.

"Ouch. Stop, Sis. That hurts!" He looked at his parents with a smile, "What are you feeding her anyway?" His sister stuck out her lip in mock strickenness. She leaned back on her mother, her big brown eyes dancing in merriment. They all stood there drinking him in.

Amoriah smiled happily. She stood almost as tall as her mother. Her dark hair was short and hung loosely above the shoulders. She had gotten her dark brown eyes from their father and her smooth skin from her mum. She wore a brown woolen dress that draped to her ankles. The last traces of childhood were slowly fading away from her. She had grown up since last he saw her, but she was still young enough to offer him a hug.

Mailyn's eyes were bloodshot. She wiped away her tears. He remembered her so tall and proud. Now she looked somewhat fragile and shaken, standing there in the doorway.

His father eyed him steadily. His gaze was always so deep and penetrating. He stood erect, his thick frame sidled up against the threshold. His face seemed taut and drawn.

"Is something wrong? I thought I heard shouting?" asked Jace suspiciously.

His mother's eyes bulged and she glanced briefly at Sedd. "Of course not, Jace. Will you look at that, we're letting all the heat right out of the door! Come on in and eat. You must be starving, running around this early in the morning without any food in your belly, I'm sure!"

His father clapped him on the shoulder as they went inside. "It's good to see you, Jace," he mumbled, pushing him back and looking him up and down.

"Will you look at him, Mia, he's taller than me now!" he said, seeming to notice for the first time. His eyes were troubled, but he took on a lighthearted tone as he spoke.

"Come on you two, the food is getting cold."

With that, everything seemed to fall into the morning routine he remembered. Jace and his family sat around the table and talked while they ate. The eggs washed down nicely with a long draught of cool brook water. He ate the muffins, careful to conserve the little jelly they had, but to be truthful, he wasn't very hungry. The three sat and listened as he told them of his trip through the Wood and seeing the fields of the Wanton Plain. All smiled and laughed, but Jace noticed the tightness under his father's and mother's eyes. They avoided each other's touch, but replaced their mutual disinterest with attention to their son's story.

His father clapped his hands. "Well, there's nothing like having a good meal to start the day. Let's see, the chickens need feeding, two fields still need to be plowed, and one could still use some gleaning. Jace, you came right on time, the Almighty certainly knows what He's doing. What do you say? Do you remember how to drive Nina?"

Jace threw up his arms. No sooner had he arrived than his father put him right back to work! To make matters worse, he offered him Nina of all things. Apparently it was never too late to plow the fields. Well, at least it was not summer, the sun could only beat down so hard. He rubbed his hands and blew into his fists.

"I was wondering if you were going to make it to midday before asking. I guess I have my answer," Jace said with a wry smile.

"That's the spirit! Come on then, I'll meet you out by the barn."

He rose to go out the door, but his mother held him back.

"He really missed you, Jace. Not just in the heart, he's been having trouble doing all this, what with Rae and you gone. Be easy on him, mind you. He's been tired and needs you more than he'll admit," she said rubbing his shoulder. She stood on her toes and kissed him on the cheek. "It's good to have you back."

"Hmmph! At least I'm old enough to do something besides dishes and baking," he said, flashing his eyes at his sister with a wicked grin. She stuck her tongue out at him as their mother pushed him out the door.

He spent the day guiding Nina through the loamy soil. His movements were jerky at first, but it all came back to him soon enough. The sun seemed to hang in the cool autumn air and just stay there. He stumbled many a time on the uneven soil, even falling once to be dragged a good many paces before he regained control of Nina. He could have grumbled many a time, but Jace found the work rather tranquil. Oh, it was not fun; he did not think he ever romanticized plowing, but it was simplistic. He enjoyed the steady walking, watching the hard gray earth yield the dark, rich soil. The falling and stumbling were minor setbacks compared to his journey, and he welcomed them as part of the labor. Still, the two fields were large, and Jace did not finish till well after sundown.

That night as he hung the leather harness behind the barn door, he offered a silent prayer of thanks to the Creator to be back among his family. He walked to the house, rubbing his neck and rolling his shoulders. His shirt was soaked with sweat, and his body was filled with tired muscles and kinks from a hard day's work. Opening the door, he was sure to keep his noise down since everyone was already asleep. He hung his cloak, washed his hands and went to bed in exhaustion, too tired to even exchange his clothes or rustle up anything to eat.

DESPITE HER HUSBAND'S PROTESTS, Mai let her son sleep in the next morning. All the humdrum and cacophony that went into a morning meal could not wake him. He lay there peacefully, a soft snore heard every now and then. Daybreak turned to morning and morning to work time, and even then Jace lay sound asleep. At last, he rolled on his side and opened his eyes.

He looked out the window and saw the familiar figures of two men standing outside talking to his father. Both were dismounted, but held their horses' reins in hand, occasionally patting their muzzles. Jace could not hear them but their gestures were animated, and they seemed to be discussing some matter of importance that they did not agree upon.

"Those fools are up to no good," said his mother giving him a sidelong glance while she worked some doughy mixture in a bowl. "They've been there half an hour now. A little longer and I'll put them all to work."

"Oh, I'm sore." Jace groaned as he yawned and stretched. He flung the covers off and patted his damp clothes. His throat was itchy and he stifled a rough cough.

"How many times have I warned you about sleeping in wet clothes?" chastised his mum. "It seems you've earned your sickness once again."

Jace climbed down from his bed and gave his mother a look of exasperation. He was 20 years old and still she treated him like a child. It was annoying. She tendered him with a warm mug of spiced tea and patted his forehead.

"Sleep well?"

"A fine sleep, fine indeed," Jace said, anxious to move away from his mum's criticism. "It's been ages when last I slept in so fine a bed."

His mother eyed him with a look of suspicion, "You haven't told us about all of your travels, have you?"

"More or less," he said, sipping his tea.

"Less I believe," she said with a frown.

"Mother, there's only so much I can tell over one meal. Besides, some things are meant to be kept in one's heart."

"No need to be fresh, young man," she said, shaking her spoon, "You're still young enough for the paddle."

He sighed and shook his head. Fully grown and still an infant in his mother's eyes. Would it ever end?

Sedd opened the door and motioned to Jace, "I need to talk to you outside, Jace. Be quick about it! Dorath and Hadran are waiting for us."

He pulled his cloak around him and fastened the clasp. As he stepped through the doorway, he coughed once more. His mother gave him another suspicious look as she went back to kneading her dough.

"Finally awake, I see," his father commented.

"Only in body, I'd say!"

Jace grinned at Dorath and Hadran who eyed him with wry smiles. His Mentors thrust their arms out and gave him two hearty handshakes.

"Your father says you returned yesterday."

He nodded his head looking at Sedd. They talked for a spell, asking politely about his trip. After the small talk subsided, Hadran and Dorath grew serious.

"We've come to get you, Jace. The Council wants you back in East Haven to finish your training. They said you would be here when we arrived. They have been waiting for you. You're to be packed and ready by noon."

"Well, this is a surprise!"

"No time to waste, your father will help you. Pack the usual. We'll ready your horse."

Jace raised a finger, turning toward Hadran. "Uh, about that. Umm, I came back here by foot."

Hadran gave him a quizzical look, "Then tell us where she is, and we'll fetch her."

Jace wanted to explain, but all he could do was let out a groan.

Hadran looked him up and down, arms folded, "I see. You'll have to explain it to the Council, then."

"Go easy on him, man. There's always a story behind each problem," said Dorath, giving Jace a warm smile.

Hadran and Dorath locked eyes. The two bristled as they stood in silence.

Sedd broke the tension. "This discussion can wait for another time. We'll go pack his things," He stabbed his finger at Hadran. "He rides with you," he said. He turned on his heel and stalked off.

Jace followed behind his father. They gathered his things without a word. Mailyn had already packed food for Jace, and though she was obviously upset at her son's quick departure, she stood on in somber silence. Sedd led his son to the yard where Hadran and Dorath sat atop their steeds.

"I entrust him into your care, gentlemen. Take care of him," Sedd spoke. He faced his son, "Whatever happens, remember this: Kyric Elcison—God be with you. Be quick to listen and slow to answer. Give an honest account of your actions, and Yeshua will bless you. Remember, you're there to learn. That takes priority." He touched his son on the cheek, "I love you. Hurry back."

Hadran pulled Jace up onto his steed. "We'll be there by morning," Hadran said to him. With that, they wheeled their horses towards the Withering Mountains and rode off. Hadran led the three out of the yard at a trot. They crossed the brook and were swallowed from view by the trees. From there they followed a trail that ran due east.

Hadran turned his head to the side. "Hold on, boy," he yelled and drove his heels into his mount's sides. The stallion jumped forward as Jace clutched at Hadran's waist.

The trail wove gently around the shady trees. It was a firm trail, well-worn and a main throughway in those parts, though the path was empty on that cool autumn day. As it widened, Hadran and Dorath spurred their horses onward. They rode through the afternoon and into the night, stopping only twice for short meals and a chance to water their mounts. The rapid pace was wearing on Jace, and he fought back fatigue as he ate his food. His cough had worsened the farther they rode, and sniffles and aches accompanied it with the setting sun. The beasts themselves were lathered when night fell, and Jace could see the steam rise off their bodies in the eerie twilight. He shivered—he had not ridden a horse since that night.

Jace's mind passed through the last day's events: the warm meals, gentle conversation, Nina, his mother's look of suspicion. She had known he hid a good part of his journey from her. It vexed him how one could be so keen on what was not said. But Jace had seen the look in her eyes when he asked of the commotion the first day he was home. It seemed each of them hid something from the other. He wondered what it was.

Onward they rode, ever eastward as night fell around them. The trees closed in on them but did not hinder their advance. Jace's tired mind saw strange, curved shapes watching them as they passed by. The night grew colder and Jace worked his numb fingers to keep a grip on his Mentor. Hadran drove his steed onward while Dorath rode at their side, watching Jace for signs of exhaustion.

They rode past midnight, and Jace worked to keep his eyes open and his mind alert. His growing sickness was not helping, and he silently wished just once that his mum had been wrong about sleeping in wet clothes. His eyes and imagination shifted the darkness around him into hideous formations akin to the Bothian Horde. He clutched Hadran's cloak and buried his face in its cloth, silently urging the horse to hurry and wishing the sun to rise. Many times he lurched sideways only to come to his senses at the last possible moment before he tumbled from the saddle. Hadran turned and scolded him each time, threatening more than once to elbow him in the ribs. At last he gave in and leaned his body on Hadran as his eyes slowly closed. His head bounced uncomfortably, but Jace did not care. At long last he heard Hadran give a low whistle through his muffled hearing and blinked. There before him was the first hint of morning as the sky turned a dull, cold gray. Jace wiped the sleep from his eyes and looked around.

The beautiful oaks and pines surrounding his home were replaced by a tangle of low-lying shrubs that dotted the rocky landscape. The trail climbed up the mountainside at a fairly steep grade. The forest lay some distance below them. They were now well above the tops of the trees, and Jace could see many leagues to the west. He pulled his cloak tightly over his shoulders as a blast of wind rolled down the mountainside. The gust sent Jace into a hacking spell. Hadran cackled at the invisible onslaught.

"Do you miss this place? Of course you don't. No one misses the weather at least. The bleak, rocky land, the never-ending blasts of wind that blow right through you, and the chill air that seeps through your bones. Once it's in there, no number of warm fires or meals will get the cold out of you. No matter, we're not here to frolic in the fields. This place is dedicated to learning, training you up in the teachings of the Song of the Ages, filling your heart with the Word of Elohim, and guarding your mind against all the ways of deceit which lead to death—if ever you forgot. All other wants and distractions have been pushed aside.

"Don't roll your eyes, boy! You can never be reminded enough. There are few places that offer such strict and pure instruction of Truth, and you should be mindful to take advantage of it!"

Hadran always had a way of filling the air with stoic resolve. Jace had lost count how many times he had told him these things. Yes, the words were true, as Jace had found out. True to the core, but he could do with a little less repetition. He knew Hadran meant the best for him, in spite of his callous nature. As the Song of the Ages said: a fool listens not to advice. He would listen to Hadran whenever he spoke, no matter how often he said the same thing.

Hadran was not a pretty sight. He stood tall as any other man, but his features were hard. His hands were thick and gnarled, like the rest of his body. His face was weathered from the many years of service at the cold wind-swept fortress of East Haven. More than one scar ran across his face, but they blended in with his aging skin. Despite the wrinkles, he was nearly the same age as Jace's father, and the two had grown up together.

Hadran had a permanent scowl. Students that he mentored or those that crossed him in the many courtyards always recalled the scowl and gave him a wide berth. Hadran was not known to stroll at leisure. He seemed to walk with a purpose, hunched forward with his neck slightly bent. If one could be said to stalk everywhere they went, it was Hadran. Jace had never seen him in anything other than his black riding clothes and cloak. This all added up to a menacing figure, if you did not know him. However, Jace had come to learn that that was simply Hadran.

They slowly wound their way up the rocky trail leaning in to the heavy gusts as they went. Halfway up the trail, they turned down an unmarked path: an old shepherd trail, Dorath had told him once with a wink. The mountains rose up to meet them, and the path looked like it would run straight into them. As they approached, a thin strip of blue split the heights in two.

Dorath turned and grinned at Jace as his jaw dropped. So tired he was, yet the sight still impressed him. The path was known to only a select few to guard its secrecy. Many paths ran throughout these parts, and one could get lost up here forever if they did not know their way. The chasm they were about to ride through was another story. You have to be nearly on top of it to see it, he remembered Dorath say once. It was some trick of the eye he could never quite figure out. Jace stared up its height to the blue sky far above. The chasm was the only entrance to East Haven, or so he was told. Its path was watched by a number of hidden sentries, and the fortress could be warned well in advance. When Jace had asked more, even Dorath gave him a stern look that curbed his interest.

They rode in silence for a league or so. His fitful naps on the journey and growing congestion added to his misery. Shivering and tired, Jace maintained a grip on Hadran as he fought to stay awake for just a little longer. Finally the chasm gave way to a broad, flat featureless rock. In the middle of the terrain atop a slightly raised hill stood the fortress of East Haven. Tiny figures could be seen moving atop its battlements.

East Haven had a long and rich history going back to early times when the Gap was first formed. Back then it was only a tower guarding the eastern flank of the highlands. As ages passed, buildings sprang up beside the Great Keep, as it came to be called. Walls were erected around them and soon East Haven was somewhat of a city. Yet, it housed no commerce, and no merchants peddled on its streets. It became a great place of learning—Hadran had not exaggerated when he mentioned it as such. Scholars from across the Gap studied within its walls. Every child within the Gap was obligated to complete their studies at such a place. East Haven was now many times greater than it once was.

Dorath had given him a brief overview of its layout when he originally had come to East Haven. At first glance, the countless buildings, hidden alleys, courtyards, and hallways seemed like a disorganized hash of things, but as he lived there, Jace began to make sense of it. Wall after wall ringed the Great Keep and the inlaying structures. Behind the thick outer wall were the soldiers' quarters. East Haven boasted a small garrison by regular standards. These men and women were used as a defense force, he believed. Since the city's size was substantial, there were a number of garrisons stationed throughout.

The soldiers hailed from all over the Gap. He had heard of the shepherds of the western highlands. From their region came the bowmen. They were said to be deadly with their weapons, and Jace had seen them keeping a constant vigil on the fortress battlements. A contingent of mounted knights also guarded East Haven. From what Jace had gathered, these were highly trained individuals who maintained ceremonial protection over the students. None had been told their exact number, but they could be heard practicing endlessly through the day to sharpen their skills. Other troops fluctuated in and out of the East Haven. Regular footsoldiers, swordsmen, and pikemen came and went from the place on a regular basis. Jace rarely saw these people whose business kept them to the outer parts of the fortress. Between his studies he had caught a glimpse of them once or twice. As they passed, students were told to stop and bow slightly as a sign of respect and gratitude. The soldiers usually gave a quick nod of the head in return as they went on their way.

The second wall housed goods and stores of every kind. The stables were located here also, but students were not permitted in this place unless they had official business.

The area was somewhat of a mystery, but Jace's roommate, Trel, used to joke that that was where the Mentors had all their fun.

The third wall contained lecture halls, a myriad of libraries, studies, and the Mentors' quarters. Jace remembered how awestruck he was to see aisle after aisle of books, the shelves sagging under their enormous weight. Like most children in the Gap, his father and mother had taught him to read and write at an early age. Still, he had never owned a book, nor seen the likes of row upon row of every conceivable parchment stuffing the shelves to overflowing. He had licked his lips while he imagined the wealth of knowledge that only one of these rooms housed.

The fourth wall contained students' quarters and the practice courtyards. It was here that he had spent the majority of time pouring over book after book as he went about his weary studies for hours on end. Students were also given lessons in basic soldiery and hand-to-hand combat. They were offered their choice of weapon to master, and unlike many, Jace had chosen the staff over the sword. They performed numerous drills, both individual and group formations. The art of horseback riding—both saddled and bareback—was pounded into every student.

There were many firsts for Jace at East Haven and riding was one which had taken him by complete surprise. He had tried to forget his lack of ability in that area. It had taken him several months to learn exactly how to sit atop a horse and handle the powerful beast that sat between his legs.

Survival skills of building shelter, finding water, hunting animals, and differentiating harmful and helpful plants and herbs were all taught in various classes. These were supplemental to the vast knowledge that every student was taught of the Song of the Ages, but he, like so many other Keepers, welcomed the teachings as a break from his studies. He had enjoyed them mostly because it reminded him of his home and the familiar woods in which he had spent so many hours.

The fifth and final wall housed the Great Keep: administration structures, the Council chambers and quarters, and probably his favorite place, the kitchens and dining halls. Some dismissed the food as mediocre and sub par, but Jace was delighted with the variety and selection that came with every meal. He had tasted things here that one just could not have growing up on a small farm in the woods. Jace resented those who turned up their noses at food he considered well beyond the quality that he grew up with. He did not care for certain students' haughty attitudes and still bore a deep grudge for those who thought themselves too good for "commoners" as himself. This always reminded him how even Keepers had a long list of social disparities that divided them.

The Council's chambers were a different matter. Their lights burned far into the late hours, and Jace had gone to sleep many a night before they were extinguished. He often wondered what deep hidden things they talked about. He and Trel would produce all kinds of imaginary scenarios that they were sure existed within its secret walls. For all any student knew, their imagination could well be the truth.

In reality, students knew nothing of the Council or its dealings. The Council was known to issue broad sweeping laws and mandates for the entire countryside. Their decrees affected everyone from the smallest cottage to the mighty fortress of East Haven. Here, the Council's decisions trickled down to the Mentors to whom were entrusted young Keepers like Jace. They were known to be men of great importance, steeped in the Song of the Ages, and fervent in prayer. What they said was hailed not as the word of the Master, but as something of great meaning nonetheless. Their thoughts came, after all, from hours of reflection in the Song, almost a constant meditation in the Spirit, and communion with Yeshua.

AS THE TRIO DREW NEARER to the walls, Jace could make out the flag of the Gap lifted high above the stronghold's inner tower through his cloudy, fatigued vision. The flag was the oldest of its kind. It bore a red cross on a square of blue in the upper left corner. The rest of the flag was snow white. Dorath had taught him its significance:

Red for the blood of our Lord that was spilled
On the cross so that scripture might be fulfilled
Blue for the majesty of Him who was slain
Who sits by the Throne and is coming again
White for the hearts who trust only in Him
As light shall they be and never grow dim.

It was the only sign of outward adornment for all of East Haven. Jace cocked an ear as a single herald sounded their approach in the bright morning air. They rode through the gates, never slowing their pace till they were safe behind the second layer of walls. As they reined in their horses, several squires rushed to attend them, helping them and their belongings off their horses. Jace nearly collapsed as he slumped off the horse.

"Gently with him, lads," said Dorath, throwing back his cloak and sliding off his horse. He came up and cupped his hands around Jace's face, looking into his eyes and rolling his head from side to side. Jace's eyes were barely open, and his breathing was shallow. Dorath frowned, knitted his eyebrows and turned away.

He marched over to Hadran grabbing him by the shoulder, "This boy is very near exhaustion! I told you we should have waited!"

"Unhand me!" Hadran snarled, stepping back. "You heard what they said! I had my orders! The boy is here now and will be well taken care of."

Dorath stepped close to Hadran, their noses almost touching, "I also have orders. So help me, Hadran, if he is harmed because of your stupidity, I'll—"

"Gentlemen! I see my arrival is right on time. You two have managed to survive the trip without tearing each other's eyes out. Where's the lad?" asked a tall, distinguished looking officer who had approached the arguing Mentors unseen.

Hadran and Dorath snapped to attention.

"Constable Wood. Jace is over there," said Dorath motioning towards the crowd of squires.

"Make a path, men! Let's see. Hmmm."

Constable Wood knelt beside Jace putting his hand to his breast, then feeling his forehead. He nodded calmly. "Take him to the Great Keep and see that the head physician puts him under his care. Tell him plenty of rest and water will do for now."

He turned to Hadran and Dorath eyeing the two of them. "On behalf of East Haven and the Council, I offer you thanks. We knew you both would not fail. Come, there is much to discuss, and both your presences are required in my chambers."

Dorath and Hadran exchanged measured looks, each adjusting their cloaks and then fell in behind the officer. They made their way through the streets of the city fortress while students and soldiers went about their appointed tasks. It was almost half an hour before they passed through the third wall and entered the constable's office. Being in a prominent position overseeing the students, he was granted a room high in the Mentors' buildings. The room offered a spectacular view of most of the city through its wide glass panes. Constable Wood waved his hand to the chairs in front of his desk.

"Have a seat, both of you," he said as he closed the door.

They chose their seats, waiting to sit down until the Constable had first done so, as was the custom. Hadran and Dorath had a hard time relaxing in the cushioned chairs because they both knew what was coming next.

Constable Wood cleared his throat and began. "Now that we are behind closed doors and through with our pleasantries, let me be candid. Were it not for the Council's decision, I would not have chosen the two of you for the same task, had my life depended on it. It is obvious to all how much each of you despises the other. I am disgusted that ones so steeped in the faith could be so cruel to their fellow brothers."

The man leveled his gaze at Dorath. "Dorath, your complaint was voiced before you left. The matter was resolved then, or should have been. Were you mistaken with what I said?" The Constable leaned forward, putting his hands on the desk. "Well?"

"Sir, no."

"Then where is your air of humility? Remember the epistles, which clearly state that we work as a common body, striving for a common good, Dorath. Remember your place when it comes to one of submission. Is that clear?"

Dorath nodded slowly keeping his eyes fixed on Constable Wood. His knuckles were white as he gripped the chair arms, wrestling with his feelings towards Hadran. Sometimes he could not help himself. It sickened him how Hadran pushed Jace with such an uncaring, selfish attitude through everything he did. It infuriated him that the Council would sit by and let Hadran have such free rein over one of his students, looking the other way when Hadran chose to discipline Jace however he saw fit. Dorath sat and fumed. No Mentor should have that right.

Constable Wood shifted the papers on his desk. He locked his eyes on Hadran who sat sunken in his chair with a dark scowl on his face.

"This is your last warning Hadran. You were given special responsibility for this mission because none know the trails as well as you. There was no one better qualified, and I personally recommended you. You succeeded our highest expectations. Perhaps that was a misguided judgment. I was the only one who thought you were ready to heed another's advice. Though you are both Jace's Mentors, Dorath was sent under you with the realization that you would be aware of his recommendations when making your decisions. Instead you willfully followed your own instincts, putting Jace's life at risk. Is this how one acts who keeps the title of Mentor?"

"No," Hadran admitted.

Constable Wood stared across his desk at Hadran who sat unflinching. He tapped his desk absentmindedly and sat back in his chair, rubbing his chin. Finally he leaned forward, folding his hands on his desk in a pensive stance.

"Hadran, few know all the perils and trials that the Master has seen you through. Fewer still have you confided in. The Almighty brought you here to teach others what He taught you. I tell you this as a friend who has grown up and seen much of what you have done. However, if you cannot shake this attitude of unaccountability, if you refuse other's counsel, then your work here is no good to us. It is no good to Him," he said pointing his finger above him. "You and Dorath have both expressed concern for Jace's maverick attitude. We all have seen his great potential. Many pass through these gates with his same problem. He is not the first. For his sake, we all need to convey an air of unity in the Spirit. We all had his problems once, and though he is a man, he is still impressionable. There are enough bad examples for him to follow without him looking at his two Mentors for the same. I have seen how he looks at both of you. You need to resolve the issues between yourselves; it threatens Jace's maturing and neither I, nor the Council, nor the Creator Himself will accept that. Is that clear?"

The two nodded.

"As for now, you are both on notice. Wash up and get some rest. As soon as Jace awakens, you stand before the Council with him."

The two rose and turned to leave.

"Sit down. There is one matter left to discuss," said the Constable holding an opened letter before him, the wax seal broken. "I received this only hours after you had left. Do you know what it is? Of course not. It's a letter explaining Rae's disappearance." The two did not flinch, but Counselor Wood could sense their growing uneasiness. "He hasn't reported in a year. He hasn't been seen in five months. I know you trained him well enough that he knows not to do such things. Still, no one knows where he is."

Constable Wood waved the letter in front of them. "This concerns me, and I suspect it does you too. Do you have anything to add? Any words of wisdom, perhaps."

The room was silent for a long time. Finally, for the first time, Hadran stirred. He leaned forward and coughed, "Does … does Jace know this?"

Constable Wood pursed his lips, "The Council thought it wise to keep this information private for the time being."

"Do you think that wise?" questioned Hadran.

"It does not matter. That is the Council's ruling and as you and I know, their decision is final."

Hadran snorted. "He will find out soon enough. Jace is a smart lad."

"There is no question about that, but the Council has other plans," ended Constable Wood curtly.

The three finished their meeting shortly and Hadran and Dorath went to their respective quarters, each pondering Constable Wood's words.

JACE LAY IN THE INFIRMARY all day. When he awoke, it was well past the eleventh hour and approaching midnight. The head physician laid his hand on Jace's forehead and smiled warmly.

"Welcome back, Jace. Rest for a moment."

Jace lay as the man pushed back his eyelids and peered at his pupils. He gently massaged Jace's throat and put an ear to his chest.

"It appears you're coming down with a fever, young man. Your head is hot, and I hear a slight wheezing in your chest. I'm going to recommend you take plenty of these hot herbs and keep your head warm," he said, helping Jace sip a warm cup of tea. The man sighed, "Alas, if I had my way, you would stay here for two weeks, but the Council wishes to see you immediately."

Jace groaned aloud. His head felt like jelly. He could sleep for a week and a day and still have no desire to face the Council. Slowly he shifted out of bed and wrapped his cloak about him. The healer gave him some herbs with simple instructions, and Jace listened as he rubbed his throbbing temples. He was given a light meal of steaming broth and warm bread before he was to meet with the Council. Afterwards, he rose reluctantly and stumbled out the infirmary door.

Hadran was waiting for him outside. He turned toward Jace and put a hand on his shoulder. Jace thought he saw a smile crease his face, and then it was gone.

"I— I'm glad you're all right," stammered Hadran.

Jace stared at him, not knowing what to say. It was not like Hadran to show affection. Hadran's features seemed softer and his scowl was not so dark. He wondered what had happened to him while he was asleep. They walked through empty courtyards and cut across streets. It had rained while Jace had slept, and the torchlight reflected off the wet cobblestones. They met Dorath outside the Council chambers. He gave Jace a reassuring smile.

"Be at peace, Jace. There's no need to fear. Be honest and tell the Council all that has happened. Remember the words of your father," he said rubbing the boy's back slightly.

The two Mentors pulled back the great oaken doors and followed Jace through. The three of them made their way down the hall, padding lightly on the stones. Only the quiet flames of the torches filled the muffled silence. They came to a set of red doors. Two men dressed in purple livery pulled back the doors, and Jace stared into the blackness beyond.

"Come in, Jace," a voice beckoned from within.

The three walked in and stood still. The room was very dim, lit only by a few small candles here and there. Jace could barely see, but he could tell the room was immense. The air was cool and rather moist from the rain, but he felt no drafts.

"Come closer."

He stepped forward a few paces. As his eyes adjusted to the dimness of the room, he could make out a long curved table before him. Behind it sat many men, silhouetted in the darkness.

"Tell us of your journey."

Jace rubbed his head and shifted his feet. He sighed slowly. It wasn't that long ago that he stared into the eyes of Yeshua as he poured out his tale to Him. It calmed him that His Master had listened intently, giving thought to all he had done. He was glad when Yeshua had affirmed him, reassuring him that in spite of his trials and the battles he had lost, he was still a follower: loved and sealed. This, above all else, calmed his fears as he cleared his throat and recited his tale once more to the unseen faces before him.

He left nothing unsaid, beginning from the time he waved his last good-bye and drove his mare into the Great Wood. He told of his errant choice to leave the Trader's Route and journey deeper into the forest. He recalled with disdain his willfulness to travel through Eben, to light a fire in the foothills, and his ill-fated flight from the Bothian Horde. Not a sound was made in the great room. No encouragement to continue or gasp of reproach. He licked his lips and went on. He recounted his waking in the depths of Sheol, his suffering at the hands of the guards, the hard walls and endless nights. He told them of his trial before Na'tal and stopped short of telling of the four men in white and the band of light.

Jace hung his head and thumbed his cloak. Would he be laughed at, or thrashed if he told them of the men, the light, Sa'vard and Yeshua. Would they think him crazy and make him leave—or worse lock him up as he was before?

"Go on"

Jace bit his lip. He closed his eyes and remembered Yeshua's face when he recognized His nail-pierced hands. The words from the Song of the Ages filled his head:

Whoever acknowledges me before men, I will also acknowledge him before my Father in heaven. But whoever disowns me before men, I will disown him before my Father in heaven.

Jace sighed a long, slow sigh. He tossed his hair back and stared at the faceless men. Slowly, he told them of the men in white. He told them of Rendolph and Na'tal's transformation. He explained the white-robed men, the voice from heaven, the eerie army of beasts, Zax, Torne, and Obban to the last detail. He explained how he woke in a valley of color and smell so vibrant that he thought he was in Par'lael. He spoke of Yeshua, His tender care and sympathy. He told them of the climb up the mountain and the visions he saw—of the vast world, the Kolosia, the Clonesian Empire, Stygian Union, the Gap, and the Northern Marches. He told them of the simple communion he had had with the Lord himself before he drifted off to sleep and awoke only miles from his parents' house. He gave each thing a detailed account, and when it was done he stood facing the table not knowing what to expect, nor what would become of him.

There was silence in the hall for quite some time, and Jace heard only the tiny flickering of the candles. At last the voice spoke.

"A great many things have happened to you. For much, we offer our sympathies. 'Twas not our plan to send you on your way only to be mauled by the Bothians and sentenced to the Mines of Shorn. We are but human and our knowledge limited, but we know the One who holds the world in His hands and we entrusted you into His care. In all our supplications and reflections, we knew the Creator had chosen you for this mission, Jace, though we did not know to what end. We can see, as you have learned, that He works for the good of those who love Him, who have been called according to His purpose.

"These things you have seen—do not be surprised. As Yeshua told you so shall we: You have not dreamt or imagined these things. Yeshua is real, and many if not all Keepers have had the experience of going to the Garden at one time or another in their lives. He laid bare the way of the world to you, and we affirm it is as He said.

"Such things are not common knowledge. Many do not see the world through the eyes of Him who created it. They choose ignorance over Truth and adopt an attitude of acceptance and toleration for the good as well as the evil that is in the world. Have a care to whom you speak such things, Jace. For not even all Keepers are mature enough to understand deep things as these.

"As for the loss of your horse, do not worry. You could not have saved her. She was given to you to help you on your way. None should bear you ill will for your loss for she was not yours. Neither was she ours to give for all blessings come for the Almighty."

Jace nodded in the darkness. He had not known what the Council would say, but he would not deny his Master and Lord again. He was encouraged by the Council's insights and affirmations, but would have believed what he saw despite their opinions.

"Thank you," he replied in a level tone.

"Jace, as Yeshua said, your journey has only begun. Since you have become well-versed in the Way, the Almighty can use you in greater ways yet. You are to journey to Nadir again. There you will meet one called Blynn. He will tell you more."

Hadran quickly stepped forward, "Brothers, this man is still recovering from his ride. He needs rest for he is showing signs of a fever."

"Arrangements have already been made," said the voice. "Before he sets off for Nadir, he must travel North to the Marches, carrying supplies. This will allow him time to recover and a chance to touch and feel what Yeshua has shown him. He will ride with you, Hadran, at midday. When he returns, he will gather provisions and set out for Nadir."

Jace bowed slightly.

The darkened men rose, "Go, Jace, and may the Lord bless and protect you as He has already. Our thoughts and intercessions to Yeshua are with you wherever He leads, only rely on Him and keep to the straight and narrow way that He commands."

Jace turned and followed his Mentors out of the chamber. He knew he should be excited, but his head was pounding heavily and he coughed a little. The Mentors eyed him, wishing to evaluate tonight's happenings with their pupil, then thought better of it. They walked him back to his room in the students' quarters. Everything was as he left it. Trel turned over and mumbled in his sleep as Jace fumbled in the dark over to his bed.

5

COMINGS AND GOINGS

The next day was First Day and all the students and Mentors assembled in the Great Keep at the break of dawn. They lifted up their voices in the chill air with songs and worship, giving thanks to the Almighty for all His blessings. The atmosphere was festive, yet reverent at the same time as all praised Elohim, Yeshua, and the Counselor.

The students had come from many places throughout the Gap. Some worshipped in strange ways to Jace and Trel. Some kneeled with eyes closed and hands folded while they sang while others raised their arms over their heads, waving opened hands with loud voices. Some jumped up and down, others danced in the aisles. Growing up in a small village, Jace had not been exposed to the many forms of praise. Some of the people made him feel strange. Their worship had originally been alien to him, and he still viewed some of their actions with uncertainty.

Each song they sang held unique meaning and sought to crystallize the feelings of one and all to their Lord and Savior. First Days were special in that the day was set aside as a time of complete focus on their relationship with Yeshua. Most everyone's favorite expression of thanksgiving was through music and singing. This hearkened back to their heritage of which the Song of the Ages spoke:

Praise the Lord. Praise Elohim in His sanctuary; praise Him in the mighty heavens. Praise Him for His acts of power; praise Him for His surpassing greatness. Praise Him with the sounding of the trumpet, praise Him with the harp and lyre, praise Him with tambourine and dancing, praise Him with the strings and flute, praise Him with the clash of cymbals, praise Him with resounding cymbals. Let everything that has breath praise the Lord.

Sometimes the songs were playful and rejoicing. Other times they were slow and reflective. Whichever form they were in or mood they took on, all served the same purpose: to bring any who listened to a point of awesome awareness of the Lord they served and to praise His name.

Today the song was a melodic chant. It had a calming effect on the listener, not because of its soothing fluctuations, but because of the words that brought the heart to gladness. Trel—rejoicing to have his old roommate back again—stood together with Jace, tall and still, singing slowly with the assembly. Their voices rose happily to a crescendo and echoed off the stone walls:

Blessed are You who sits on the Throne
And unto the Lamb who will draw us home
We lift up our voices and loudly we sing

Praises to You, our one offering
We come with our lives and talents we bring
And hail You as Lord, Yeshua our King.

They both recalled the scathing rebuke they received when they had snickered at some of the others during worship. It happened two summers earlier. Constable Bilscen had taken them outside the Keep in front of the entire assembly. There in the courtyard he had chastised them until the end of the service. He spoke in a voice that carried to all who passed by while Jace and Trel stood at attention, their faces red with embarrassment.

"Who are you to judge another's worship? Don't you know that Yeshua Himself says that we will worship Him in spirit and in truth? Your brothers and sisters are honoring Him because their hearts are in the right place. Their expressions are outward signs of how they feel in their hearts toward the very One who has saved them. When you mock their worship, you mock the One they praise."

Most of the one-sided conversation went through one ear and out the other, but Jace never forgot those few words. True, what he saw was immensely foreign to him. He had grown up mostly singing, sometimes only chanting, the ancient songs he read. Only when he had arrived at East Haven had he been introduced to the many forms in which people gave thanks to Elohim. The Constable's words stuck with him. Maybe it was the way he put it, or maybe it was the two weeks of stable duty that followed.

After the time of worship, the students and Mentors all sat down while one of the Constables stood to give the week's teaching. It was Constable Bilscen this time. Trel elbowed Jace and smirked. Jace grinned widely and nodded as the two remembered Bilscen's "talk." In spite of the stiff reprimand, Constable Bilscen was a genuine man and his services were always lively and readily applicable. Today he spoke from one of the epistles. This letter was written by Petra.

"Beware!" yelled Constable Bilscen in a fiery tone. "Beware your enemy, the one who prowls o'er the earth like a roaring lion seeking whom to consume! Resist him and stand! Stand in your faith! Kra'ken is powerful and his might stretches far and wide. We are not safe, even those who are within the Gap shall be tempted by his schemes. Let us never give up our stand against him. Hold to the truths Kyrie has taught us. Read daily His message. Confide in Him constantly for He shall keep you safe!"

Constable Bilscen paused to catch his breath and the hall was silent. Even in the cool autumn air he had to mop his forehead. Few of the students ever lost attention when he spoke, so animated was he. His voice rang throughout the hall like a bell, and none ever fell asleep. Jace scribbled in his journal many a note that service. His mind was quite focused, and he paid no attention to the wheezing in his throat or the dripping of his nose.

After the service, Hadran met him by the stables with his black riding cloak dancing in the morning breeze. Jace stared at the sorrel mare he held by the reins. She pawed the ground patiently and glanced sideways at him. Her muscles were toned and Jace could tell she was good for traveling many leagues.

"Try not to lose her this time," snorted Hadran. He examined his rust-colored stallion, checking to see if the gear was secure. The squires had done a good job, but Hadran still went over their work with a critical frown.

"You took your herbs, I hope? We won't be stopping again till late afternoon."

Jace nodded with a cough. He followed the healer's orders, though it didn't seem to be much help. He scanned the courtyard.

"Where's the supplies?"

"They left early this morning," Hadran said, rubbing his chin. He waved his hand so as not to be bothered. "We should meet up with them this afternoon."

Jace stood on in respectful silence while Hadran finished his inspection. He stepped back with another snort and looked at Jace.

"That will have to do," he said, squinting his eyes and running his hands through his hair. He led them in a short petition to their Maker, asking for a steadfast ride and safe passage. The two mounted their horses and were off.

They made their way through the outer wall and disappeared into the chasm with the sentries looking on. The air was crisp and calm, and the sunlight bright. There was no sound along the trail for few creatures lived in these parts, and those that did kept their distance. They trotted side by side without speaking. Only after they stepped on the trail heading down the mountains did Hadran break the silence.

"Was the Council all you expected and feared?" Hadran asked with a smug grin.

"I feel much better, now that that is over. I had never dreamed of meeting them face to face—but why the air of secrecy? Do they ever show their faces?"

"No, but they do not act that way out of folly. Long ago, the Council decided that they should remain hidden. They believed their wisdom would be for naught, and those who saw them would be distracted and abashed. They wanted their wisdom to reach the hearer untainted. The idea was to advise without offering extraneous disturbances in the process."

Jace looked up at the clear blue sky. Wisps of clouds dotted the horizon far to the west. "Where do the members come from?"

"The Council keeps its selection a mystery. They know that their position is both very prestigious as well as influential. Since elections are private, they are free from much political pressure and can be kept relatively free of bias," Hadran gave Jace a level gaze and then went on. "The Gap houses those who are called by His name, Jace, but that does not mean that we all act in harmony. Neither are there those who are above asserting their own agenda over the whole of this land. The actions of the Council are meant to keep the population safe from such individuals."

"Isn't there an air of favoritism? These men are a select group. Is it possible that their choices for future Council selections are slanted towards their own beliefs?"

Hadran snorted. "There's the rub. Some believe this to be the case and there has been much debate about it. There have been a number of times when the Council was threatened with dissolution by forces within and without, but they have emerged from them much stronger than before. People have their own opinions behind the reasons of the Council's resiliency, ranging from the possible to the absurd. From all my wanderings and knowledge, I can say this: the Council speaks wisdom from the Almighty. Never have I heard them utter something that is against what the Song of the Ages teaches. Their decisions are made after much debate and studying in His Word, as you well know.

"As for favoritism, I personally don't believe it exists. Council members are chosen from all over the Gap. Many of their beliefs may vary, but their fundamental truths are the same: Yeshua was and is the Almighty incarnate. He is by very nature deity. They, like all Keepers, believe that His sacrifice and death is the only way one can enter Par'lael. No one can approach the throne of the Almighty except through His mediation. His sacrifice took the place of and paid the penalty for our wrongs."

Jace sighed.

"I sense another lofty exhortation on our fundamental truths about to take place," he said wryly.

Hadran looked him up and down, his eyes squinting at Jace. He grew rather silent and that was when Jace knew he was in trouble.

"Fine," his Mentor said, adjusting his cloak. "It's been thoroughly engrained in that gourd atop your shoulders then. Very well, recount it to me."

Jace huffed. He had been gone just long enough to forget the sour games Hadran played to help teach him. He shook his head. He had walked right into this one.

"Well," Hadran said, lifting an eyebrow. "I'm waiting."

Jace sighed and began where Hadran left off. He would show him this time. He explained to his Mentor how the Song of the Ages was the infallible written truth that was inspired by the Almighty Himself. It was the only book written this way. The third point was the miraculous birth of Yeshua. He was not conceived by human means, nor did His life begin at that moment. He was the Alpha and Omega and lived since the beginning of time along with His Father and the Counselor. The points were, of course, accompanied by dozens of scripture. Beyond that Hadran had given Jace counter-scripture to the worldly arguments of the Stygians to memorize. The entire discourse ran nearly an hour, and though it was dry and lengthy, Jace felt extremely good about himself. Finally, Hadran yawned.

"Enough," he said, his mouth gaping wide. "We can go over the rest this afternoon."

"Does my speech bore you?" Jace replied with a smile.

Hadran shot a scowling look at him. "As a matter of fact, yes."

"But I've given it back to you nearly verbatim," said Jace, showing mock hurt.

"That is the whole reason, Jace! You act as if this were a game to be won instead of truth to apply. Did it ever occur to you that someday you'll need what I've taught you? There will come a time when you'll have to defend yourself using only what you know. I train Keepers to leave Emblom, not to hide in their mother's skirts the rest of their lives. I'm telling you these things to build up your defenses, boy," Hadran raged. His scowl was darker than usual as he went on. "Soon you will leave too. Will it be a game then?"

"I am sorry, Hadran," Jace whispered. "I never thought—"

"You never do, Jace! One day it will come back to haunt you."

Jace wilted under Hadran's hard stare. The man was obviously speaking from a world of insight. Suddenly he could see the hurt in Hadran's eyes, the fear that Jace was indeed soon to leave his tutelage. Jace hung his head in sorrow for he had treated his Mentor with shame. He turned away and shifted in his saddle.

Hadran sighed and rode on his way. Sometimes Jace truly acted like a little boy instead of a young man. There was so much he had to teach him, but so little time. There was never enough time.

By midmorning they had descended from the mountains and turned onto the main thoroughfare. Jace had finally apologized and, as always, Hadran had grunted his forgiveness. Their spirits lightened as they hit the open road.

As much as Jace wanted, Hadran would not let them take their rides above a cantor. *A pity that such a good flat road should be wasted,* Jace thought with a light smile. He loved to ride. There were few things he could think of that were more thrilling than hugging his horse as it surged forward on a flat straightaway. Horses seemed to be built to gallop. It was as if they were unleashed from their rider's orders when they were pricked to a furious pace. He loved the feel of the beast under him as it reveled in its freedom and labored with all its might to push itself farther and faster. He loved the wind in his hair. He shook his head. *What a pity.*

Midday approached and they stopped for a spell to eat a short meal and stretch their legs. Hadran watched him as they sat.

"You've changed since your return, Jace. Where is the carefree, fickle lad that first came to East Haven? Your eyes are distant now and withdrawn, if I may say so."

Jace stared ahead, chewing his bread in deep thought. He glanced at Hadran who eyed him steadily, waiting for his response. He wrinkled his brow and shook his head.

"There was a time when I thought the world so simple. Things were happier then, but that seems but a distant memory," he said sadly. He nodded, "I laughed then and enjoyed everything, but now ..." He shook his head slowly, "I will never forget that night, Hadran, nor the countless days that followed. Never in my darkest dreams had I imagined one could go through ... so much. There were things that happened there—things I will not talk about."

He hung his head, "Something was taken from me in that place. I know now that the world is not simple, but I would rather know the truth than to go on living a lie."

He was silent for a spell, then smiled slightly as his words trailed off. "You should have been there ... to where He took me. How can I begin to describe it?" He spread his arms, pointing at the surrounding view, "This world, with all its wonders and glories cannot compare to what I have seen. My heart is in another place now, and I am burdened to stay here in this tarnished world. You should have seen it."

"I have," said Hadran.

Jace blinked and turned to look at him.

"No words can do it justice, boy. If you tried, you would only do it a disservice, but you are right. It is the most beautiful thing one could ever see except Yeshua Himself."

As Jace stared at Hadran, the scowl fell from the Mentor's face. His eyes looked clear, and the lines and scars that marked his face seem to fade for a moment. Then the scowl was there again as Hadran rose up, looking at the sun.

"Come along, we can't sit here all day."

With that, they swung up onto their saddles again.

IT WAS APPROACHING DUSK when they met up with the supply wagons. The two slid off their horses, Jace inadvertently rubbing his hind parts. They had ridden a good four hours without a stop, and he stretched out his stiffness in the fading light.

He looked over the supplies. There before him stood three large wagons covered with goods. They were pulled off the byway into a clearing in the woods and were drawn up one beside the other. The wagons were tied down with canvas, but Jace could make out the bumps and shapes of chests and crates underneath. The teams of horses were off to the right, unhitched and resting. They ate noiselessly from their feedbags while tied to the trees. Beyond the wagons, a small fire was blazing and a few people huddled around it, talking in low voices. Hadran walked past him, leading the two horses and muttering under his breath about the poor time they made.

Jace shook his head and coughed. Hadran looked back over his shoulder as he walked away as if to remind Jace of the herbs he needed to take. Voices hushed as the men from the fire turned to see the newcomers. They nodded slightly and went back to their conversations.

Jace nodded to the men as he passed by the fire. They sat watching him curiously while he rustled in the underbrush with his back to the fire. Jace emerged with a short branch and sat down opposite the five men. He pulled his cup from his sack, poured some water from his flask, and sprinkled some herbs in the cup. Using the branch, he dangled the cup over the fire and waited for the water to warm. He licked his lips, staring at the large cast-iron pot that hung over the fire.

"You're too late, we ate more than an hour ago," barked a short, little man. He sat with his toes next to the fire, puffing slowly on a short pipe. His cloak was draped over his shoulders, and his bald head glistened in the fire light. He stared across the fire with his squinty blue eyes as the blaze fizzed and popped. "Supper's packed and we're off to bed in a bit. We need an early start tomorrow. You'll just have to wait till morning if you want some food."

"You'll give us what you have and like it!" boomed Hadran as he strode up to the fire. He looked at Jace and then nodded at the short man. "Dolpher always cooks more than he can eat. That cloak does little to hide the round belly he's blessed with."

"It's Dolmer to you, you gangly old man, and if you're referring to this," replied the stumpy man, pointing at his stomach, "that's where the meal's at!" With that the little man pulled back his cloak and thrust out his belly. Hadran creased his brow at the fellow, and then the two roared with laughter.

"Some things never change," said Dolmer, grasping Hadran's hand as he bowed slightly with a grin. "A wee bit tardy aren't you?" said he, looking up at Hadran. "That does no good for your mighty reputation."

Hadran smiled as best he could and clapped the man on his back, nearly knocking him over, "Enough banter, little man. We took the road easily. The lad is sick and we traveled at a modest pace. Yet, here we are and now we eat. Watch your cup, Jace."

Jace pulled the tin cup out of the fire. Its bottom glowed red hot and the water within bubbled violently. Jace sipped the liquid gingerly while Hadran sat and chatted with Dolmer and his crew. Dolmer passed them a bowl of stew as he went over his news. Jace wet his lips as the strong aroma of venison hit his nose. He ate slowly as Dolmer explained that they were carrying another train of supplies to the marches. This was their third trip this week. It was always the same: food, clothing, and arms. This region was less traveled than the west, but the fronts were clogged with goods coming in from all over the Gap.

"Things looked suspicious," said Dolmer, lowering his voice as he looked at Hadran. "The marches have been quiet for some time now and that never bodes well." Hadran shrugged his shoulders as he ate his stew.

"The marches themselves never bode well, be they quiet or not, but these things are out of our hands. What of Sturbin? Have his preparations gone smoothly?" asked Hadran.

"Well, no. Arthur is up to his old tricks again, stirring up trouble and what not."

"Not him!" Hadran growled, glancing at Jace and then turning to Dolmer. The little man blinked and then dropped his jaw, also looking his way. The matter seemed rather touchy and an awkward moment of silence passed while Dolmer changed the subject.

"It's hard to say. Everyone is busy up there. From the looks of it, it's a mindless ruckus, but then it always looks that way. You'll have to ask him yourself, if he has the time to speak with you."

The two talked late into the night. Jace fell asleep to their voices, for there was much news to be told and a great many fears loomed in the future. Hadran woke him before dawn for the day's trip. Jace had only to roll up his pack and strap it to his saddle. The rest of the party was ready and waited patiently.

The day passed uneventfully. Dolmer decided to skirt around Sage to make better time. The plain forest and wide byway was all that passed before their eyes the entire day.

The party kept to the same pace and Jace knew it was because of him. Hadran rode at the head of the column talking to Dolmer while Jace brought up the rear. Their conversation was animated, and more than once, Jace caught the two of them staring back at him. He knew they were talking about him, and they did little to hide it. If he hadn't known any better, he would have thought Hadran looked worried. Dolmer gave him a reassuring pat on the back and the party rode on.

The next morning, Hadran woke him the same as before. He noticed his wheezing and aches had subsided considerably as he trotted in the dark, cold morning. The sun revealed to them what Dolmer had said. The tiny town of Noll could be seen in the distance, but the road between them was packed with carts and wagons of every conceivable shape and size. It took them the better part of the day to get anywhere. Finally, a quartermaster directed them through, and they rode on to the front as the day came to an end.

When Dolmer's team parted ways with Jace and Hadran, the tiny man gave them each a reassuring touch on the shoulder. He jumped on his wagon and leaned toward Hadran, nodding and raising his eyebrows, as if to voice some unspoken word. Hadran pursed his lips and nodded firmly. With that the little man grinned, shoved his pipe in his mouth, and slapped the reins to his team.

The two were left alone in the bustling street. Hadran turned to Jace and beckoned him to follow. They made their way through the crowds, side-stepping a number of fast-moving carts and giving way to others. Beyond the crowds, they ventured amidst tiny shops and buildings. They passed smiths, coopers, tailors, and a myriad of other shops Jace could not identify. At last the cramped shops opened up, and they found themselves on the training grounds with countless troops. Formations snapped off drills, horsemen wheeled their mounts in precision lines, and pikemen and footsoldiers stepped in tight phalanx formations. Hadran walked quickly through the sea of men, and Jace followed at his heels in the fading light.

They came to a grand lodge and Jace recognized the wall behind it from Yeshua's vision. They went inside and were greeted by a rush of warm air. Jace looked around at the stark features. The building was akin to the Great Keep, though not as grand, with tiny rooms tucked out of the way in its corners. Torches cast long shadows on the smoky rafters above, and large woven murals hung from the beams against the walls. They depicted various scenes, all of which showed an army of white and silver armor in pitched battle against a neverending sea of black, shadowy figures. The soldiers rallied around the flag of the Gap, which waved defiantly in the wind. The hall itself could hold some 200 people easily. There in the center of the room stood a group of 30 soldiers. They ringed a man, listening intently to what he said.

The man was slightly taller than average, with a heavy build and thick hands. His burnished breastplate sparkled in the torchlight. His features were tan, and he had a strong jaw. As he spoke, his voice was loud and commanding. His words stirred the soldiers, and Jace could sense their eagerness. The helmets hid the faces of men and women alike. Jace listened as their leader spoke:

"Why do we hide in this place waiting for the inevitable? Did not He who leads us claim that we are soldiers? Let us take the fight to the enemy! With the Almighty's strength we can take back what was lost! Does not the Song say that we can quench all the fiery darts of the wicked one and that we are more than conquerors? Let us put these words into action!" The man's blade rang as he drew it from its sheath. Holding it over his head and pointing he yelled, "Let us go forth, to honor and victory!"

The crowd broke into a cheer, clapping their hands and shouting loudly. They raised their spears and swords, clapping and chanting. Their voices lowered as Hadran broke through the center of the ring. He walked close to the leader, his black cloak nearly touching the soldier's silvery breastplate. The crowd drew back and went silent.

"What is the meaning of this, Arthur?" shouted Hadran. "Get back to your post!" He spat, barely controlling his rage. "And take your troop with you."

The voices murmured in anger, and Arthur raised his hands for silence.

"We will not. Yeshua has given us a promise and we claim it. We have grown weary of watching and waiting while Sa'vard plots and schemes. We will go forth and wrest from his hand that which he took. We will be victorious and fight—not cowardly, only waiting for him to attack us again."

The crowd roared their approval raising their fists in support.

"You traitor! Why twist the words of the Song? It never says we should attack. Yeshua never said that either! Stand your ground, and having done all, stand firm, it says. Never attack. The battle belongs to the Lord." Hadran said, drawing himself up.

"You twist the Song in your own way, Hadran, but we will have none of it. We have seen His promise and will follow His call."

"You filthy worm!" Hadran seethed and grabbed Arthur, but was met at once by the points of drawn swords as the crowd stepped forward. Hadran slowly looked around and released Arthur.

"Sturbin will hear of this," he said through clenched teeth and walked out of the hall with Jace behind him.

They walked through the streets. People gave them a wide birth, for Hadran's scowl was darker than ever. They climbed the March Wall and made their way along its heights. Soldiers pointed Hadran to Sturbin and then melted away from his smoldering gaze.

They found him looking out at the wilderness and the darkness, the land Sa'vard had claimed long ago. He leaned on the parapet, his head slightly bent from years of age. His back sagged, but could not hide his authority or strength. Sturbin wore the white cloak of the March, one of the seven commanders that oversaw all its activities. His thick gray hair and well-groomed beard gave him an air of professionalism that added to his rank and office. As he turned to Hadran, Jace caught the glimpse of the highly polished breastplate on his chest. He could not help but glance at the mighty broadsword that hung at his side. Hadran approached Sturbin and bowed.

"I know why you are here, Hadran. You need not utter a word. We are of one spirit, like the Song commands us to be, agreeing in all things and putting unity in Him above our individual wants. This matter of Arthur, I have given it much thought," He spread his hands. "Arthur is like the wind. Try as I may, I could bring no sense to his soul. He is rebellious and will do what he wants, despite your wishes and mine, and even the Lord's commands. This has brought me sadness, for he should not be this way, but his heart has grown hardened, and he will do what he wants. Many people will mourn and suffer because of his actions."

There was a cheer from the gate below as a band of mounted cavalry rode out into the wilderness with their black riding cloaks flapping in the wind. Before they were swallowed by the shadows, Jace caught a glimpse of Arthur at the front of the column, his sword raised high, pointing into the night. Their shouts and cheers were heard long after they vanished into the the darkness.

Hadran fumed, "The strength of the March Wall has lessened with his absence, Sturbin. His troop was the best."

"That is true, but what would you have? A man's strength is no good if his heart is not. Perhaps his actions are for the better. Only the Maker knows," he sighed and shook his head. His eyes were filled with much sorrow. "Come, what is done cannot be undone. Let our thoughts turn to other things. I see you've brought the lad this time. Is he the one you say is filled with so much promise? Does he remember me? Come here, boy, and let me look on one that once I knew so well."

Jace stepped forward and looked at Sturbin. He hated that his superiors found the need to call him a boy when everyone knew he was a man, but the sudden surprise of Hadran's compliment made him ignore the comment. If Hadran felt this way, he certainly did not let it show. On the other hand, he did not recognize Sturbin from anywhere. He had never seen him, or so he thought. Yet, as the two stared at each other in the flickering torchlight, memories came back of a time long ago, where a younger, softer version of the man tendered him on his knee. He turned his head and peered sideways at Sturbin.

Yes, he had known him, long ago. As a boy, this man had visited his house with Hadran and Dorath. He had lived close by, and Jace remembered nights of eating in a quiet hall with his family, other people, and this man. Everyone had bowed their eyes when he had given thanks and listened to him as he had poured out truths from the Song of the Ages. They had joined voices in praise to Yeshua and then he was gone from Jace's memory. What was it he had said before he left?

"Paths lead to and fro,
Some come and others go.
But they all are intertwined
I am His and He is mine."

Jace uttered these old words with a thin smile on his face.

Sturbin smiled softly. *Yes, it was he.*

"Where there was a boy, there is now a man," said the commander, examining Jace. "Yeshua has cleaved us together again," he said grasping Jace's shoulders.

Sturbin led them to his quarters, a solitary room that overlooked the March Wall and the menace beyond. The room was surprisingly neat, if only very small. A tiny, unadorned desk was placed in front of the window. Beside it was a table and chairs in front of a small fire and on the other side, a humble cot. No other furnishings embellished this room, and Jace got the feeling that it was used very little. Sturbin waved to the table and the two settled only after Sturbin had moved the desk chair to sit with them.

The three talked for a while. Jace mostly listened while Sturbin and Hadran relayed information from their stations to each other. The conversation turned to Jace, and Sturbin looked deeply at him while Hadran told of his progress. He told the commander of Jace's journey, his failure, and the Mines of Shorn. Sturbin nodded patiently.

"There is little of this that I have not heard. But now, I would like to hear from the lips of him who has seen so much. What do you make of all your comings and goings?"

Jace shrugged his shoulders in a tired effort. "There is little Hadran has left unspoken."

"Tell me this then, Jace," said Sturbin, rubbing his chin, "The creatures you saw, were they real? These men that protected you, were they?"

Jace stared at Sturbin flatly, his features growing hard. "Yes."

Sturbin leaned back in his chair and gestured lazily at Jace. "You will see stranger things than these in your life, young man. Men are not the only creatures who inhabit the earth. Have a care for you may entertain heavenly beings without knowing so. Keep your wits about you, for Sa'vard's minions also roam this world freely now. The Bothian Horde is the least of your worries, some would say. His forces can take many forms. They can walk among the crowds, and none but the most wise can discern their nature. Even then, they have led many a well-intentioned Keeper down the wrong path. Be on your guard and never forget to test the spirits."

As Sturbin spoke, Jace remembered the shadowy figures in Clonesia. He shivered at the thought that he might not recognize the evil identity of a Watcher.

Sturbin nodded slowly, knowing the words had sunk in. He waited a moment, then changed the subject. "I can see the questions in your eyes. You remember me, but only from long ago and wonder now how I have come here."

At Jace's nod, he continued, "You will find a good many friends from your memories have found their way here in service of the March. All have come from different paths, but all for the same reason. When young and growing, they thought only of themselves and how the Maker could satisfy their needs. Now, many of them have come to realize their obligations to their Lord and Master. They choose to serve Him best by standing at the March of the Gap in protection of all Emblom. They do this to hold back the tides of Sa'vard. They are the ones who Yeshua has called to keep Sa'vard at bay in constant vigilance. Their stand is not so much with iron and steel but with sound hearts and intercession to the Most High."

It made sense to him now. The elders that were so common a sight to him in his younger years had come north to the March. Their years of growing up in truth had led them to a duty of service and defense. He leaned back and thought as faces floated across his mind: His first teacher, old Miss Pell, with her round, failing body and kindly spirit was probably here. Then there was Master Klim, tall, thin, and pale, who knew every scripture, but offered each one with a gentle tongue. Those and others were probably nearby. A genuine smile creased his face for the first time since he had returned home. How he wanted to see them all!

"Tomorrow, Jace," said Hadran, anticipating Jace's thoughts. "It's past midnight, and they're all most likely asleep now. First, rest and we'll meet them tomorrow."

He lifted a kettle from the fire and poured Jace a cup. Jace mixed the last of the herbs in it and sipped the bland liquid half-heartedly. Hadran readied the cot while Sturbin talked with him.

"Rest here tonight. The morning comes quickly."

Jace tossed uncomfortably on the hard cot for a few minutes. At last the herbs won him over, and he drifted off to the sounds of the crackling fire.

THE MORNING CAME, but he did not stir. By midmorning he came to his senses and sat up in his bed. Someone had rekindled the fire during the night, and a meager plate of cheese and bread sat on the table next to a pitcher of water. His clothes lay pressed and folded on the desk chair. He rose and dressed, eating while he looked out the window at the sentries on duty. It seemed rather odd that Hadran had left him alone this long. He shrugged his shoulders. He did not mind the momentary solitude and if Hadran was busy, maybe he could entertain himself.

Finished with breakfast, he went out the door and down the stairs. The scribe at the desk looked up from his work as Jace entered the room.

"Greetings Master Jace. Hadran left a message stating he would be on official business through most of the week. I am Eckalus. He has entrusted you to my care. Hadran only requires you offer your assistance to me for two hours each day. The rest of your time is to be spent familiarizing yourself with the March, its walls, and other structures, as well as the myriad of occupations that keep this place running and the task that each entails. You may sleep here each night. As your Mentor, Hadran expects an exceptional report by the end of the week. Now, having had a decent night's sleep compared to most, your work should be done by noon. Come."

He should have known something was amiss the moment he had seen his pressed clothes. Since Hadran had become his Mentor the first week at East Haven, he had rarely given Jace "idle time," as he called it. Jace grimaced slightly, sat down, and picked up a quill as the scribe showed him the task at hand. For the next two hours he poured over records, copying numerous items from book to book and making sure the numbers added up. The figures were amazing. Twenty carts, each one containing 100 pounds of cotton, were brought to Noll alone in the past week. That was one ton! Wood was floated down the Furbice River and had been marked at three tons per week. Perishables were even more astounding. Ten tons of beans and flour sat in storage even now. When Eckalus caught the look of surprise, he explained.

"The Gap houses a number of replenishable resources that can be readily harvested. Unfortunately, we can never have enough. Saddles break, clothes need stitching, horses must be reshod and given food—the list goes on. Here at Noll, the troops go through 500 pounds of flour a day and we're not even housing half the soldiers we could house. Imagine what would happen had we twice the army and raised their diet to full rations. The place would be a nightmare!"

As if it wasn't now, Jace thought. He shook his head in consternation. He understood the use of quartermasters and their function, and he was even thankful for their deeds, but he could not fully understand the amount of goods they were handling. *Better to leave it to those who do*, he thought. He finished his work by noon and the quiet scribe invited him to eat.

Eckalus and Jace made their way through the crowded streets and entered the area lodge. Here, they waited in line and received their midday rations. Eckalus seated them in the far corner of the great room as it slowly began to fill. He watched while soldiers entered from the far side, their breastplates and helms reflecting off the torches. He also noticed scribes and clerks line up, their common sackcloth outfits and ink-stained hands giving them away. Smiths with their leather aprons and soot-drenched faces stood next to clean-shirted tailors that eyed them graciously through their spectacles. Every type of artisan he knew stood shoulder to shoulder in line with soldiers, clericals, and quartermasters—all waiting patiently to receive their meal.

It stunned him how old the crowd was, despite Sturbin's warning. The faces of many an aged man passed him by, but few were those who were younger than his father. Even his father would seem a youth in this crowd, he thought. Eckalus watched him with a slight smile.

"It's always a treat to watch someone see the Marches for the first time," he said, eating his bread slowly. "Your eyes ask, 'Why are there so many aged?' if I'm not mistaken. Hadran didn't tell you?"

Jace shook his head, "Actually, Sturbin did, but it is one thing to hear of it, another to see."

Eckalus sighed and adjusted his spectacles, "The age of the soldiers seems to be getting older still. They have always been old, but now," he shook his head, "so few come to join them and take their place in defense of the land. This younger generation does not consider the paramount importance of the March," He gave Jace a stern look and went on. "Arthur and his company were the last who came that I can remember. They were very gifted, but very hard-headed. I have seen the worried look the soldiers give when they see their thinning ranks. They know their number is growing old and disappearing. They will miss Arthur's relative youth, if not his ways, when the time comes."

"But the Song of the Ages says the battle is the Lord's," Jace interjected. "Does it not matter then on the number of troops, but on His faithfulness?"

"That is true, Jace. My point is this: some believe that this matter of the March does not concern them. They believe only a select few are called here to serve this way. The Song, however, says no such thing. It makes no distinction of who should and shouldn't stand. We all have an obligation to serve in this way. Whether we choose to or not, then, is the question."

Jace nodded in agreement. He watched the crowd moving through the line as Eckalus explained the inner workings of this place. People could accomplish much with hardly a plan. Significant labors, however, required organization and a fair stroke of wisdom. The Gap had long held Sa'vard in check but only through extreme discipline. Yes, the Maker was the One who turned aside the enemy's advance, but part of Yeshua's legacy was for His people to stand against the Wicked One. The outline for this was taken directly from the Song of the Ages: His people must focus their hearts on Him, remain of one spirit in unity, give thanks without ceasing, and constantly guard their hearts through meditation in His Word. These were the seeds to success. Only then would their stalwart watch be fruitful. Only then would Sa'vard be kept at bay.

Of course, there were the material necessities to keep such an operation moving. Sa'vard waged war in many ways. The people of the Gap were taught at an early age that the battle that was waged in the spiritual plain was in the heavenly realms as well as in their minds. But all could also attest to the physical side also. Not everyone had faced the horrors of the Mines of Shorn, but one need look no further than the battle-scarred lands that stretched for leagues beyond the March Wall to see Sa'vard's handiwork. Not only must they keep their hearts and minds prepared, but their bodies as well. Hence, the importance of the quartermasters, clerks, artisans, and soldiers. All were important, needed, and respected. Everyone had their respective tasks which provided all the aspects that went into the defense of the March, keeping it safe and the watch prepared.

"I know you find no glory in my simple job of bookkeeping, Master Jace. Not many do. However strange and odd it seems to you, I hope you understand its importance. Children's memories are romanced by grand scenes of mounted soldiers rallying to defeat the armies of Sa'vard, but the reality is much different. They forget the lesser parts of

Yeshua's bride. Each person who is called by His name has a special task within the body of His believers. None should shirk it or be ashamed of the responsibility to that which He has called them to do. Each should respect the other, for we all work toward the same purpose of glorifying Yeshua and the Most High."

Jace frowned and looked about him at the faces that ate. Noble knights sat side by side with simple bookkeepers, wagoneers, and old women. They talked while they ate with smiles on their faces. Some patted each other on the back or offered a word of encouragement. The truth of Eckalus' words was plain to see.

They finished their food, while Jace scanned the crowd. His eyes focused on a wrinkled, old woman who stood by herself a few tables away. Many years of age had whittled away at her body and now she moved with a feeble, tired gait. Jace could tell she was in pain as she slowly lowered her round body into its seat. She sat exhausted and alone. Folding her hands over her food, she whispered her thanks to Yeshua. After lifting the pieces of bread to her mouth, she rolled them around, savoring each morsel. She sat contented with a warm-hearted smile across her face. Jace excused himself from Eckalus and walked up to her. He leaned down so she could hear above the noisy din.

"Miss Pell?" he asked.

"Yes, dear?" she answered, turning toward him. Her hair had thinned and her skin had grayed considerably, but Jace could never forget her simple dress and smile.

"Do you recognize me?"

"Come closer, dear."

He lowered himself, and they looked each other in the eye.

"Closer."

He leaned forward till he could feel her breath on his face. She reached out a hand and ran it slowly over his eyes, nose, and lips.

"She cannot see, my son. Her sight has left her for quite some time," said a tall thin man. His eyes were narrow and on his pinched nose hung a small pair of spectacles. He was dressed in a simple black overcoat and pants. "Can I help you?"

"Master Klim, don't you recognize Jace?" said Miss Pell, turning to the slender old man, a hand on Jace's arm to steady herself.

The man's mouth dropped open, and he worked to say something to cover his embarrassment.

"Won't you sit with us, lad?" His face had reddened considerably.

Jace slid in beside them and talked for a spell. It amazed him how easily his friends from the past opened up. He soon felt like he had returned to the age of seven as he sat there and listened to his first two teachers. He remembered the old stories they would tell him from the Song of the Ages: the rebellious prophet who was swallowed by an enormous fish, talking donkeys, the giant flood that covered the earth, the great man who destroyed a pagan temple with his bare hands, and the birth and life of their Lord, Yeshua. The three sat and talked long after the hall had emptied. Jace felt himself at ease among his old friends.

Though her eyes were blinded, Miss Pell remembered how he looked. She laughed as she told of his interesting mannerisms. She noted with a smile his strange outlook on life at such a young age. He always seemed to be wrapped up in his studies, she said, and was quite shy when it came to games and the young ladies. He always was nervous around others, especially the ladies.

Jace blushed while she spoke. He laughed when Master Klim turned away, obviously not used to this kind of banter. Miss Pell went on, glossing over the topic, but letting Jace know in no uncertain terms that it was high time he start thinking about a future woman to make his mate. Finally, the conversation died down and Master Klim stood to leave. He bent down to steady Miss Pell. She put her hand on his as she rose and turned to Jace.

"Since you're here for the remainder of the week, you'll have to pay us both a visit. Master Klim works in bookkeeping, and I am across the green in the infirmary. We do love our former students and friends stopping by, don't we Master Klim?" she said as she rubbed Master Klim's arm, smiling warmly.

He grunted softly. "It would be a pleasure, lad. I apologize again for mistaking you at first. You looked, well, changed, and I never can tell who I can trust these days," he ended, coughing loudly.

Jace thought about Master Klim's words, then waved him off good-naturedly, "You were only protecting those you love and questioning those you did not know. There's no need to apologize."

He walked the two older people out of the building and then made his way back to Sturbin's room.

AFTER JOURNALING HIS FINDINGS for Hadran's future report, he climbed to the March Wall. The writing had taking him several tedious hours, and the sun had long since set when he left Sturbin's study. A pair of guards barred his way at the head of the stairs.

"Show your papers and state your business, boy," one of them said gruffly. The soldier squinted suspiciously at Jace from under his helmet, licking his lips.

Jace quickly gave his business, making it clear the permission he had through both Hadran and Sturbin. The guards' eyes jumped at the last name, but they still crowded his way. When he did not offer any papers, Jace could see the grips on their spears tighten. He sensed their uneasiness and distrust and slowly backed away, turning to leave when he heard a voice behind the parapet.

"Grimly and Tover, let him pass."

The two turned and backed away. Sturbin looked down at him from above and he motioned for Jace to join him. Jace passed the guards who fidgeted nervously. The torchlight revealed their old haggard faces, and he suddenly noticed their feeble shuffle. The grips on their spears seemed more for support now than from suspicion. Jace eyed them with sadness—two old, tired men, willing to do their duty despite their frailty and fear. He met Sturbin looking over the wall into the night sky once more. He watched the darkness in deep thought. A series of flashes lit up the darkness far to the north. Jace jumped as the guards along the wall all began to speak out in a confused murmur.

"Our pickets lost sight of them early this morning," said Sturbin, keeping his eyes strained northward, "Arthur's troop had disappeared beyond the foothills some 20 leagues to the north. We thought that was the last we would see of them. Now, I'm not sure. I do not know what this sign means. Arthur, or some of his company may yet live, at least for the moment. No one who has ventured into Sa'vard's realm has ever returned. Still, where there is Yeshua, there is hope."

He looked at Jace. As he did, a low, rumbling wind passed over them. He braced himself against the wall. The soldiers shifted anxiously with fear, but they held their positions.

"It's a minor passing, Jace. The land beyond the Marches is never fully asleep. Some never get used to its rage. It is a sign of things to come, of the war between Yeshua and Sa'vard that one day must come to a head. It is a reminder that this world is not whole, that when Yeshua returns, all things will be made new. But the land beyond is awakening. Never before has there been such groanings, even in the stories from ancient days. The time draws ever nearer to our Savior's return.

"But presently, my thoughts and intercessions are for Arthur. Only Yeshua knows where he is now. Only Yeshua can save him." He glanced at Jace. "He is there, in your memories, Jace. He grew up with your father. I think he still harbors a deep hurt with what happened then. I do. It is sad how some can be bonded so tightly through the Master's work and yet become unraveled by personal sorrow. Arthur was a friend; he was one of my pupils. Though we saw things differently, we still loved our Lord. I fear for him now, if he still walks the earth. Sa'vard is ever active, but he saves his most hideous deeds for night, always at night."

Sturbin leaned against the parapet and hung his head, sighing deeply. Jace put a hand on his shoulder. It saddened him to see this man from his past losing hope. His memories of him were of a simple man with a tender smile and softly spoken words of wisdom. As he looked at Sturbin, he could see the weight of responsibility slowly crushing him and wearing him down.

"You have done so much, don't let things you cannot control steal your hope," Jace said. "I do not know Arthur, though he is in my memories, nor do I know the things that have happened to cause this rending of fellowship. What I have seen is your hurt and care. If these have been your actions all along, then you are not to blame. You could have done nothing, sir," he said, touching Sturbin reassuringly.

Sturbin lifted his head, looking Jace in the eyes. A warm smile creased his face and his weariness seemed to lift momentarily. "Alas, your words ring true. I can see why Hadran favors you so highly."

Jace gave him a quizzical look. If Hadran thought highly of him, he did not let it show. The endless errands Hadran sent him on and his curt responses gave no sign that he enjoyed Jace at all. Sturbin patted him softly on the back.

"Come, it seems we both have had a long day. Sleep would do us well. Tomorrow has enough problems of its own."

6

THE GATHERING

The week went by quickly and in spite of Jace's chores, he had plenty of time to browse the buildings, talk to the many people, and probe mysterious areas at his leisure. Eckalus was very respectful of his time and privacy. Jace often caught him smiling to himself as he watched Jace go about his investigations. He was always willing to offer valuable insights on the hidden workings of the March guards, the goods being brought in, and the intricacies of the relationships with the artisans, clerks, and troops. More than once Eckalus had critiqued his findings, correcting various points with a respectful tone.

"It is true that the March is the geostrategic point of entrance to all Emblom and separates Sa'vard's lands from that of common man. That is accurate, but we are not the 'protectors' of the land, Jace. Yeshua has left his legacy that we should 'stand in the Gap' against the evil one, but our strength lies in *His* faithfulness, not our might. I know I've tried to explain this before and made a poor go of it. Maybe it's just something you'll have to see for yourself."

Jace spent countless hours on the March Wall and questioned the troops. Many times he found them huddled around a raised firepit, pulling their white cloaks over their silver chainmail in the chill air. They seemed cautious of his questions at first. Rare was the young man who walked through the March unattended. Sturbin had written him a letter the day after they talked, and Jace found this opened a great many doors and relaxed many a wary eye. These were the elusive "papers" that he had been questioned about. He kept them in his shirt pocket throughout the day and left them on the table of Sturbin's room before he went to bed.

Of the many people, he found his interest peaked towards the soldiers. Maybe it was the child in him, mesmerized by the burnished swords and bright cloaks. Maybe it was the air of respect they seemed to command, or maybe it was that Jace did not recognize that everyone was treated with the same dignity as the ones he held in such high esteem. The troops, however, entertained his questions and childlike fawning. They met him with level stares, answering him politely, but never puffing up with pride.

Most of the troops were old, grey-headed folks like Grimly and Tover. They were not given to bouts of childish rage, nor did they show an abundance of emotion. They carried themselves with an air of professionalism that matched their polished armor and spotless white uniforms. As they spoke, their mail jingled quietly while they motioned to the land beyond the March Wall.

They told him how the land had become a wasteland whose soil brought forth nothing but various thorns and tangled vines that grew around twisted trees. Mounted pickets scouted this land, but rarely out of bowshot. These troops kept close watch on the gradual advance of the vegetation which some said had a mind of its own. Throughout the day people were seen scattered in small bands in the rolling hills with their backs bent to the ground as they pulled countless thorny roots from the soil. The work was hard and tiresome, and soldiers were regularly rotated from sentinel positions on the wall to join in this thankless, but all-important task. After all, what would become of the wall if the thorny mass ever imbedded itself in its cracks?

The scouts also offered an early warning to any advancement of Sa'vard's forces. The low hills to the north hid any visual hint of the movements beyond them, but there were other signs to look for. The shrubs seemed to grow at a speedier pace as an assault neared. Some plants gave different scents to herald their master's coming. After all, Sa'vard was called Prince of the Earth by his followers for a reason.

Many scratched their heads when Jace asked them how long it had been since the wall had suffered an attack of any size. It was old Grimly who shuffled forward and spoke of the attack in his father's father's time. Men nodded their heads in remembrance, and some gave a low whistle as Grimly went on.

The March Wall was farther north then, beyond the low hills and manned by many more troops than it was now. The land, which was known for its dryness, had been filled with rain that week when the heavens opened up. This made pruning difficult. When the sun finally showed its face, the thorns had surged forward with an added fury. As night settled, the troops were forced to abandon their work for the safety of the March Wall. That evening, the soldiers could hear the mass stirring as it anchored its roots between the stones. When morning arrived, the plants had a firm hold in the wall and try as they might, they could not be dislodged. As night approached, the soldiers were desperate to loose the vines' hold, knowing that the roots kept their scouts from providing a warning and would eventually pull down the wall.

In the early evening the order was given to set fire to the thorns. The plants hissed in the blaze, but as the flames rose higher, the soldiers noticed their mistake. Though the evil weeds yielded, they gave off a putrid, billowy smoke. The blaze caused the eyes to itch and made it hard to breathe, but worse, none could see beyond the thick barrier it created. The inferno burned on and soon grew out of control.

As the soldiers fought to extinguish the blaze in the darkness, Sa'vard launched his army. Out of the fires they came, their dark hideous shapes shining off the flames. Their bodies were like the black of shadows and one could make out neither eye nor mouth. Those that recalled the shapes said they were darker than the night, soaking up the light around them. Their bodies were smooth as a snake, yet without markings or garments. Others said they were shapeless, formless creatures that resembled black oil, shiny and fluid in their gait. They attacked with a frightening speed and purpose, spurred on by their master's will. Up the smoking vines they bounded and mounted the walls, taking many of the soldiers by surprise and force.

They made no sound as they advanced and overpowered the white-caped guards with sheer numbers. The guards' amazement at their thin, formless bodies gave way to surprise and fear as they realized the creatures' overwhelming strength. Seeing their defeat, the rest fled from their positions, leaving their comrades to perish amidst the fiery carnage and Sa'vard's bloodthirsty troops. The March Wall was lost that day and so were many soldiers of the Gap.

Grimly's voice cracked and he leaned heavily on his spear as he told how his grandfather was swallowed up by the shapeless host. Much was gone, but the price that was paid in blood was the greatest of tragedies. The soldiers around Grimly nodded in agreement, some patting the old man softly on his shoulders in comfort.

They had learned much that day. Ever since, the tangled mess was tended to with a sense of urgency. More than two-thirds of the March Wall ran parallel to the Furbice River now. If they suffered another full-scale assault, there was nowhere to retreat and the March would have to be abandoned in its entirety. The vines were never burned again, instead, great ditches were plowed in the soil and giant curved grapples attached to teams of oxen rent huge holes in the thorny fields. The weeds themselves were buried beneath the freshly plowed earth. This process took much longer and required substantial labor, but it was very successful and efficient. The March Wall had been built and remained where it was to this day because of years of disciplined perseverance. During the winter, they were able to reclaim much of the soil since even the hardiest vines did not grow in the harsh northern cold.

Jace had listened for hours as the guards talked. His fascination and hunger for these tales never ceased. How he longed to fight the good fight as these men and women! How glorious their tales and stout their hearts! Jace glossed over their sadness as they told of the many heart-breaking losses they suffered at the hands of Sa'vard. All had lost some close friend or relative. Their eyes spoke not of honor and glory, but of responsibility and duty to their Lord and King. Jace wrote of their exploits, history, and losses, but he couldn't quite capture the air of hurt, sorrow, and devotion that hung so heavily upon each soldier's heart. When he was done, he had come no closer to the enigmatic relationship that existed between the soldiers and the Almighty.

As much as he liked, he could not spend all his time on the wall. The week drew to a close, and he realized how little he knew about the rest of the March. He knew Hadran would not be pleased with his lopsided research. Hastily, he went about Noll and the outlying country to observe the distribution of goods and the work of the craftsmen.

Jace made his way through the maze of shops out into the busy streets of the town. The well-worn streets had not changed and were still a soup of dark mud that was crisscrossed by a thousand ruts. He quickly got tired of dodging the teams of horse-drawn carts and decided he'd had enough when one passed within hairs of his face. He stumbled backwards, landing with a dull plop down in the mixture and was liberally sprayed by the passing traffic as he worked to extract himself from the thick mud. Jace stood up, grumbling to himself while he tried to scrape the mud from his clothes. He trudged the rest of the way through town, paying little attention to the carts that kicked up filth since he was covered from head to toe already. As if to add to his growing misery, the clouds rolled in, hiding the sun, and a cold autumn wind began to blow. Shortly, he found himself on the outskirts of town, cold, wet, and dirty in the graying afternoon light. He followed the road which ran west.

The throughway began to firm up again as the shops and houses thinned out. He followed the road for some time until the city had dwindled to farmland. The soft, green hills were dotted with cattle and crisscrossed by dozens of fences. The road paralleled the hills, cutting into dense woods some distance down the path. As he approached, he could make out the sounds of men yelling and tools clinking and clanking deep within the shadows. He was soon swallowed up by the dark forest, and the sounds came closer. Soon the road emptied out into a large field.

Jace surveyed the scene in the gray afternoon. Giant wooden structures could be seen throughout the field with hundreds of men and women climbing about them. An occasional crack of the whip could be heard accenting the noisy camp as teamsters struggled to control their horses. The crews dragged heavy logs across the grass and were unhitched and fitted into place by bands of thick-muscled men. As he looked closer, he saw groups bracing wooden beams with great metal fittings that were pounded into place by a number of men and women. The scene reminded him of a thousand ants cleaning the carcass of some massive beast. He stared in awe at the fascinating construction.

Some of the structures towered into the sky, as tall as the battlements of East Haven. Others lay on their side and still others were strange assemblies of wood, rope, and metal. So bewildered was he that Jace paid little attention to the shouts and yells of some teamsters as he walked through the site.

Before he realized what was happening, giant arms wrapped around him, his neck snapped backward, and he was pushed to the ground. He shook the dizziness out of his head and peered up at the hulking man standing over him. He was not very tall, but his shoulders were exceptionally broad as was his entire body. He was dressed in simple workman's clothes. His leather apron, face, and shirt were drenched with perspiration and steam gently rose from his head in the cold air. Thick arms hung at his sides and he looked down at Jace with worry in his hazel eyes.

"I did not mean to startle you," the low voice boomed. "You didn't look like you saw the horses and one can not afford to second guess someone around here."

He motioned slowly to a pair of heavy workhorses only paces away. One was on its side with a few men around it. They had come to a sudden halt, reigning in hard and had broken their lashings. Their load—a giant log some fifty hands in length—lay at an odd angle. It had carved a deep gash in the ground and then rolled mere paces away from where he had been only moments before. Jace looked up at the stout man who stood towering over him, not believing he had almost been trampled by horses he had never even heard.

The man looked down at him gently and half whispered at him, "Are you alright?"

Before he had time to offer the man his thanks, another man shouted, "Where's the filthy bugger who did this? I'll thrash his hide and send him to work in the sheep hills for the rest of his miserable life!"

The large man turned to reveal a short, thin rat-of-a-man. The small cap atop his head could not hide the scowl smeared across his face that matched the frowning sky. He strode up to Jace with a look of determination. Had his savior not stepped in the way, he thought he would not have lived to see tomorrow.

The short fellow looked up at the hulking figure in front of him. A tense moment passed, then his features softened, and he slumped his shoulders. The large man put his thick hand on the fellow's shoulder as he sunk to his knees, his head in his hands.

"Lumphar, the day is almost to a close. Perhaps you should take an early leave," he suggested.

"It will never be done in time!" cried the little man. "Before we know it, winter will change to spring. Summer will be upon us and what then? We need more men. We need more of everything! Don't you see, Alaric? It is hopeless! We will never accomplish what we need to do."

Lumphar began to pitch sideways, but Alaric tenderly held him steady. He hugged the tiny man and gently rubbed his back.

"Your work for the day is finished. Go rest well tonight, friend, and when you do, enjoy a warm cup of tea for me and the lads who will still be toiling here. You have earned at least that much. Say a kind word to our Master for us. He will see us through, despite our apprehensions."

Alaric comforted the tiny man for a few moments more and then sent him on his way. Past him, Jace could see the horse on its side, struggling to get up. The men around it fought to keep it calm while others clutched at its reins. The horse began to bay a low, mournful sound. Alaric put his hands on his hips, shaking his head as he watched the action. He turned to Jace and stared at the ground.

"That was our second horse today and fifth of this week. Lumphar will have a fit when he finds out," he said gravely with his hands on his hips. He lifted his head and looked Jace sternly in the eyes. "Just what is a lad your age doing around here without supervision?"

Jace began to apologize, stumbling over his words and muttering under his breath. He fumbled through his shirt and pulled the letter from his pocket standing at attention while Alaric surveyed its contents. The man read slowly, looking up more than once. When he had finished, he handed Jace back his papers, a dark expression crossing his features.

"Have you read this?" asked Alaric, flicking the parchment in Jace's direction. Jace shook his head dumbfounded as he returned the paper to his shirt. "So, Sturbin has given you liberty to walk the March. But nowhere in there do I see permission to haplessly stroll while not minding your surroundings and nowhere do I see permission to lame a horse!" Alaric fumed, jabbing a finger at Jace.

Jace began to apologize, but the man cut him off with a flick of the wrist. He stood silent, letting his anger subside. He took a deep breath, thumbing his apron while deep in thought.

"Don't worry about the horse," he grumbled, wincing through clenched teeth. Jace could tell the man was pained by the loss, but leaned toward graciousness even amidst his hurt. Thank the Maker he had the letter! "These things are bound to happen despite the best precautions we have." He looked up at the darkening sky and sighed, "Three more hours of this and possibly a storm. No matter, we will work through it. Come let me show you around."

The two walked through the field while hundreds labored all around them. They came to one of the tall structures that stretched far into the sky. Alaric explained about the contraption slowly, but with great knowledge. The structures were divided into three categories. The tall tower they stood in front of reached into the sky and was a movable station. Those like it could be brought to an assigned area along the March Wall and erected in a matter of hours. Alaric threw open a small door at the base of the structure. Inside were a series of wooden gears, rope winches, and leaded counterweights that crossed over and through each other until it made him dizzy. Alaric's eyes shone with brightness as he told how the buildings expanded to twice or three times their original height by way of this assembly. With these, they would be able to see some leagues into the desolate land beyond.

"It will be hard to suffer another surprise attack so easily," Alaric said with a twinkle in his eye.

The next machine they came to was a long, wide wagon, bigger than any Jace had ever seen. The mammoth vehicle had huge wooden wheels with great pegs sticking out of them at odd angles. They circled around the side of the machine. It looked as though the thing carried giant sections of wooden fence as its cargo. Alaric described to him how the fencing slid down pairs of greased timbers and were driven into the ground three at a time with the force from what he called a counterweight-hammer. With only the pull of a lever, the machine could assemble fenced fortifications quickly and effectively for troops to fall back on, Alaric explained with a hint of pride in his voice.

They came to a small overseer's station and entered the building. The workers had already lit the oil lamps in the darkening sky. They climbed the stairs to the second floor and made their way onto the viewing platform. Torches had sprung up across the fields to light the furious work as night gathered in. Alaric pointed off to their right at a well-lit area where many people swarmed around yet another strange object. The thing looked similar to a giant bow, laid on its side. Underneath, a carriage structure ran the width of the bow. Jace watched as six men struggled to fit a massive log across the bow and a team of workmen slowly cranked the machine. Jace could see the bow bend and the line grow taut. A woman touched a torch to the log and with a "whoosh," flames sprang up along its length. Many shouted and the scene broke into confusion as people scattered for protection. Over the noise, Jace heard someone bark a command. There was a loud "click" and the fiery log was loosed, shooting out over the field. It bounced end over end to land in a clearing some distance away. Broken cheers rose up from underneath Jace and Alaric as people rushed to put out the burning javelin-log. Jace surveyed the damage, but Alaric only shook his head.

"That one will need more work," he said in a serious tone. "Perhaps some fletchings will do the trick," he said turning away. Alaric told him how the machine eventually would be able to fire "missiles" into groups of massed troops. These would hopefully break a charge or send it into chaos, at any rate. If successful, it could be the edge they needed along the March.

Jace shook his head. Only half of what he heard could he understand and of that, he comprehended little of its ramifications. Clearly something was going on here he knew little about. What of all these items of warfare? What army would they be used against? Were not those of the Gap peace-loving people, never lifting a hand in violence against anyone?

Alaric patted him on the shoulder with a smile in the twilight. Of course, they were. These inventions were to be moved to the March Wall once they had been completed. There they would be used in defense against Sa'vard and his armies.

Jace gave a puzzled look, "What of the Song where it says, we wrestle not against flesh and blood? Surely these enemies will not turn away from physical weapons."

Alaric thumbed his chin, his tongue clicking absentmindedly, "Your story says differently, Jace. Were not you subject to the Mines of Shorn?"

Jace's eyes grew wide and he worked his mouth. How had he known? Alaric waved him off. "You are not the only Keeper to have fallen to the Bothian Horde, nor will you be the last. Don't trouble yourself, that was all Sturbin divulged. Sometimes, Jace, spiritual forces manifest themselves in physical forms, don't you agree? It has not always been thus, nor is it common, but here along the March Wall, Sa'vard's minions have taken physical shape more oft than not."

"Even so," said Jace, "Surely victory does not rest in the hands of these weapons. That, at least, I can attest to. Does it not say, 'Some trust in chariots, but we trust in the name of the Lord?'"

Alaric nodded, cocking his head, and a sly look ran across his face, "You speak the truth, Jace, but what then? The Master does not call us to sit idly by either while the enemy approaches. Aye, the battle is in His hands, and He holds the keys of victory, but we must strive to do all that we can. We are told to constantly be on our guard instead of being idle or complacent."

Jace bit his lip. Something seemed amiss. The world was changing quickly, or what he thought the world was. Until then, he had considered the Mines his own personal struggle, unconnected to anything. Now, here he was at the forefront where the old ones said with a hard look in their eyes that Sa'vard and his forces entered the realm of the touchable. This was not the world he grew up in. He wrestled with what was real. Besides the old soldiers' stories, he had not seen even a stirring of life past the March Wall.

True, the thorns and vines, though hideous and foreboding, teemed with life. He had gone to sleep more than once to the ominous hissing of the plants as they grew during the dark when all else was still. If he had not seen the Bothian Horde or been rescued from the Mines of Shorn, he wondered if he would even have believed the old folk's talk. That and the fact that they trained with an attitude of purpose persuaded him that terrible things existed here that he knew nothing about. Surely, there was something to what they said. Still, it seemed almost unbelievable to him that he had grown up within a few days travel from this place that was so different from his simple home. It was hard to fathom that he had innocently matured in the Gap and been totally unaware of how close ultimate danger lurked from him and his family. How many who lived here truly understood what threatened them? He bit his lip, overwhelmed now that the true importance of this place was finally sinking in.

Alaric touched his shoulder, "So you see, when Sturbin found out that Lumphar and I had a few creative ideas, he gave us the liberty to expand on what was bouncing around in our heads. That was over a year ago. To have only one of my dreams made manifest would have been enough, but I am humbled. I would never have dreamed I would have seen all this," he said sweeping his arms in a grand gesture over the various tasks and constructions that continued as the sun dipped behind the trees.

Suddenly, Jace remembered Miss Pell. Hadran was scheduled to return tomorrow and Jace had not yet visited his childhood teacher! Hurriedly, he thanked Alaric for his courtesy, promising to pay for his earlier accident in the near future. Alaric let him go without a fuss, but looked rather hurt that he had not had more time to talk to his new friend.

Quickly, Jace wove his way through the field, mindful this time of the various hazards found in sites of labor. He made his way to the edge, then skirted around the rest of the site and up the road through the trees. Night had fallen, but Jace's eyes were used to the woods, and as the sounds of the craftsmen faded away, he jogged through the cool air without a care.

Before he knew it, he had come to the outskirts of Noll. The town had grown quiet since dusk. Most of the workers had turned in to spend time with their families and Jace trotted past lighted windows where sounds of warm conversation spilled out. The streets were void of the daylight bustle, and he stuck to one side of the muddy throughway. A thin mist fell from the sky and Jace gave a laugh at Alaric's keen weather-sense. He scampered past Master Klim's workplace, noticing the lights were out to his dismay. Jace would have to visit his spindly friend the next time Hadran brought him here.

By the time he reached the green, he had been running for the good part of an hour. He shuffled across the empty field, spotting the large, white infirmary at the far end. Stepping through the door, he pulled back his cloak and gave a look around. The giant hall was well-lit with clean-burning lamps instead of torches. The whitewashed walls and pristine, white beds that lined them contrasted sharply to the mud-churned streets of the town. Even here, there was an attitude of steady working. A myriad of women and a few men quietly walked about the room with determined faces. Immediately in front of him was a waiting area where a variety of rain-soaked craftsmen and soldiers sat patiently. A middle-aged man who must have been a cooper sat holding his arm close to his chest. A soldier dressed in the usual ceremonial white cloak sat silent, his right leg stretched out before him, a blank expression on his face. A woman before him cleared her throat.

"Can we help you?"

Jace turned to see a young lady that must have been close to his age standing behind a small desk. Her skin was fair and unblemished and her long auburn hair cascaded over her shoulders. She stood with her hands on her hips and head cocked to one side looking at the rain-soaked, sweaty-haired Keeper that blocked her doorway. There was a look of hurried consternation on her face and she asked Jace again in case he hadn't heard.

Jace gave her a long stare. His mouth hung open as he worked to form some audible speech. He was not very good at talking with women his age, and this one was quite pretty, if not the only one he had noticed since he had been at the March. After a moment of unintelligible noises, he gave up, thrusting his hand into his pocket once more to present Sturbin's letter which was now worn and soaked. The lady held it by the tips of her fingers, letting the water drip onto her desk as she eyed Jace with silent disdain. He shrugged his shoulders and grinned sheepishly, knowing what she was thinking.

Even in East Haven, all were taught of the infirmary's high need for cleanliness. He and Trel used to joke at how one could eat off their floor, but here and now, it seemed to be no laughing matter as he stood before the orderly. She laid the paper on her desk, giving Jace another smoldering look as she unfolded it. She pointed to an empty seat, not looking up from the letter and Jace quietly sat in his place. After a moment, her voice broke the silence.

"Master Jace?" she said, looking up from the letter. "This letter tells me nothing. Do you have a need to be here?"

"Well," he began, "I have come to pay Miss Pell a visit. She said I should stop by before the week was—"

"Have you looked around you?" the young lady interrupted, her eyes boiling and her voice none too quiet. "Miss Pell is very busy and as you can see, there are more people who are waiting for her expertise. Maybe you should come back in the morning when it's dry and you've had a—"

"That will do, Lashara," said Miss Pell, stepping out of a doorway into the hall. "This man has had an appointment due for some time, now. Besides, there is always time to see an old friend. Will you send him this way?"

Lashara stuck out her lower lip and clenched her jaw. She folded her arms and stood for a moment looking Jace up and down. Then she put out her arm, giving Jace his letter and pointed her chin in Miss Pell's direction with an emphatic, "Hmmph!"

Jace turned, not forgetting a slight bow of respect, and quickly walked to Miss Pell's room, glad to be through with the little parley.

Miss Pell welcomed him, stretching up to give him a warm hug, despite his wet clothes. "Pardon Lashara, Jace, she means only the best for the sick, but sometimes she forgets the humanity involved in her work."

Jace nodded, a bit bewildered by his new surroundings. This infirmary was not like the one at East Haven whose walls were grey, unadorned rock. Here, the white walls were tended with care. He noted the paintings that accented the walls as he entered the hall.

They gave the building a sense of welcome, although it was a bit sterile. He looked around at the spotlessly clean furnishings, beds, trays, and offices—all in perfect order—as he half-listened to Miss Pell's words. She brought a hand to his face, running it along his features once more. He apologized softly to her, and she shook her head with a smile.

"You have changed much and yet you are still the same," she said, her old wrinkled face forming a smile. "Tell me where you have been since last we met."

He walked her into her study. She seated herself in a chair and Jace sat on a short stool that was in the corner. He began to tell her his adventures this week—the many hours questioning the soldiers of the March, and old Grimly's story. She laughed heartily when he told of his filthy walk through Noll and listened intently as he spoke of Alaric and the curious machines.

"Many have said there is a menace beyond the walls, Miss Pell. They say Sa'vard's power is strong here and that his minions have been known to take shape," Jace said, pausing a moment. "Things used to be so simple when I was a boy on Da's farm. I could feed the chickens and goats, and walk Nina. I knew that they were animals and that the things I did gave way to consequences. There were no mysteries, and with that, I was satisfied." Jace sighed, flinging his arms wide in futility. "But now, I don't know, Miss Pell. I have heard many stories and been given many sober looks on account of my apprehensions. Tell me, Miss Pell, what of these stories and histories of the March Wall? Do they ring true? I am slow to believe that I grew up less than three days from this place yet unaware of the dangers it borders. I do not know these people, but if you speak of these things, I will know then that the truth has been told."

Miss Pell leaned back in her chair, her short, heavy frame causing it to creak. She worked her hands up and down the length of her lap and sat for a while, nodding slowly while she pondered her thoughts.

"Some things in the world are very hard to explain, Jace, and words do not do them justice. Before my sight left me, I would have sworn to you that what could not be seen could not be touched and what was seen could not possibly be affected physically by what wasn't. You knew me then, but even though I taught you on my knee, I could not grasp that the two worlds were intricately connected. I believed there was a defining point where they met, but they never crossed over into each other. Since I have come here, my sight has gone, but there is much I have come to understand. If you wander the world, people will think you a fool if you tell them what you are about to hear. Then again, they have never lived in these parts, mind you."

She stopped and frowned slightly, scratching her head, "When you left the Gap, what happened?"

Jace looked at her, taken aback by the question. He wanted to skirt around it, but knew what she was really asking. He shrugged his shoulders and started to tell her, but she waved him off.

"You see? How could you possibly explain what happened to you on your way to Nadir? The chase, the fight, beasts that moved as one herd to bring down their prey—things that none have ever seen—some say do not exist in all the world. What would you tell them when they laughed at your fairy tale, your stories of nightmarish creatures, pulsing lights, men that shifted to unspeakable shapes, and others dressed in white who kept whole armies at bay? What would you say, Jace? Do you think they would believe you?"

Jace narrowed his eyes and even though she could not see, Miss Pell felt the tension in the small room rise. No one liked being questioned and called a fool. But how did she know? He had only told his story to Yeshua and the Council. His mind raced with questions, but he let them pass and agreed with her, understanding the point she was making.

"Some things just cannot be explained, Jace, but rest assured that they are as true as what you have been through. One has never touched the sun, but all know that it is hot. You cannot clutch the wind, but we can all see its effects. Some things, though seemingly incomprehensible, cannot be explained away. One day you will see the reason we defend ourselves so harshly, but I hope that day will not be soon. Who knows? You may see stranger things than these before your life is over. The time of the Master's return draws nigh and even now there are signs of His coming."

He stared openly at his former teacher. In a matter of moments she had comforted his uncertainty, deflated his ego, and humbled his pride. This was not how he remembered her, but perhaps that was part of growing up. Everything she said made sense, though she had not given him a clear answer. He sat stunned while he pondered these things. Looking back on it, he would realize that he came to learn more about the March in her simple study than the entire week spent exploring.

Miss Pell gave a short laugh, "Do not be so easily disheartened, lad," she said, touching his knee. "You have undoubtedly found some answers to your questions, but even some questions will not be answered until the hereafter when we sit at Yeshua's feet in Par'lael. Maybe in another time, and another place the Maker would have chosen to do things differently, but for here and now, that is how He chooses to operate."

She leaned forward, the chair groaning loudly, "Now you must answer my question," she said, a subtle smile on her face, "What did you think of Lashara?"

Jace face grew bright red and if his jaw had not been attached, he would have surely had to pick it up off the floor.

"Miss Pell!" He stammered incredulously.

The old woman cackled, clapped her hands, then spread them wide in innocence.

"Allow an old lady her follies," she said with a disarming smile. "I do not mean to embarrass, nor to ridicule, only to know what is on your mind. You are approaching that age, you know."

Jace sighed and slumped forward, his arms on his knees. Sometimes, he wished the Song said nothing about honoring parents, elders, or the like, but Miss Pell was dear to him and he could see she truly meant no mischief. He struggled with his words at length, confiding that he had not had much experience in that sort of thing. Even though she asked only about Lashara, he knew what the underlying question was.

Yes, he found her attractive, if only in passing, but that meant little. Relationships were not built on such things, at least ones of consequence, and besides, he would most likely never see her again now that Hadran would arrive tomorrow morning and they would journey back to East Haven. At that, Miss Pell gave a strange expression, she brushed away a half-hidden smile by tweaking her nose and coughed loudly.

"Ah, to be young again and not know where life would take you," she said with mischief in her voice. Jace was not so sure that she had been entirely honest with him.

As the evening grew to a close, he thanked her once again. They said a short word to the Maker together, thanking Him for time well spent, for who knew when next they would meet and under what circumstances?

As Jace made his way past the front desk, he paused momentarily, a roguish idea popping into his head. He turned to face Lashara and bent down to the small lady, planting his dirty hands on her desk and soiling the papers underneath. He stared at her a moment with only the "drip, drip" of rainwater from his cloak illuminating the silence.

He looked her in the eyes with a blank expression and said with all the honesty he could muster, "It was a pleasure meeting you, my lady."

Lashara looked at him at length, her eyes softening for a moment and her mouth opening slightly. She started softly as Jace stood there, holding her gaze. Then a wicked grin spread over Jace's face as he rose to leave. Lashara looked over her desk at the muddy handprints and water that had ruined her records. When she looked up at Jace's grin, her stare could have melted iron. Jace bowed low and turned to leave, a certain satisfaction bubbling up inside him that he had teased such a pretty girl who had made him feel so ill at ease.

Then he felt it. The first piece hit him across the shoulder. He turned around in time to duck as a letter opener flew over his head, its sharp point spinning end over end out the darkened doorway. An inkwell hit him squarely in the mouth, leaving a dark, purple splotch that ran down his neck. The crowd in the waiting area gasped in shock, some letting out a laugh, others clapping their hands. While he crouched in disbelief, Lashara had picked up two paperweights, one a heavy orb of blown glass, the other, a jagged piece of shaped quartz. Jace spun and ran out the door into the night air under a hail of desk objects with the crowd in the room jeering loudly, and Lashara yelling half-intelligible phrases and threats of what would happen should they ever meet again.

Jace was only three blocks from Eckalus' shop when he stopped running. He slowed to ponder the situation, touching the wet ink on his neck. He lifted it to his nose, sniffing it absent-mindedly, a grin of impish joy, splitting his face. If only Trel were here. The prank was worthy of their most famous exploits! The look on the young girl's face was priceless—well worth the jeers and ink!

It was a pity he would never see her again. Though she was a bit cool and impetuous, she was quite a pretty thing to look at. Maybe it was even worth the hassle.

"Oh well," he sighed.

The office was strangely quiet as Jace made his way to the mirror. He immersed the washcloth in the water pan and dabbed the ink off his face and neck, watching himself in the glass. The liquid came off rather well, most of it anyway. After five minutes, he had given up scrubbing. He peered into the mirror, seeing only a thin bluish tint to the left side of his face, around his mouth, and on his neck. He shrugged his shoulders and headed up the stairs to bed.

A shower of light blinded him when he flung open the door to Sturbin's room. There by the fire sat Hadran and Sturbin talking quietly to a large man, his back turned toward Jace. The three looked up as Jace entered the doorway.

"Ho, boy, it's good to see you again," said Trel, tackling Jace to the floor. The young man tousled his friend's hair as Jace stared up at him in shock, a smile slowly forming on his lips.

"Trel!" he exclaimed, rolling him over and pinning him to the ground with a fierce hug. The two wrestled playfully for a moment, forgetting the others in the room. They stopped, both lying on their backs, hooting with laughter. He was not too old for such childish displays of youth. Jace had missed his friend dearly and only now realized the strength of their bond. Sturbin cleared his throat and the two propped themselves up with their elbows, exchanged glances and sprung to their feet at attention.

Sturbin and Hadran looked Jace up and down, the two noticing the slight bluish tint to his skin. Hadran snorted emphatically, his scowl dark as usual. Sturbin spoke first.

"By the looks of his skin, your pupil has some stories to tell, Hadran," the grey-haired commander said flatly. Jace's eyes widened—if his antics were revealed, Hadran would have his nose in books till Yeshua returned. Sturbin motioned the two boys to relax, and they followed him to the window.

Jace started to produce his written findings from his journal, but Hadran shook his head. His Mentor motioned him to silence while Sturbin began to speak.

"It seems, Jace, that the Council has a task for you," he said, handing Jace a sealed parchment. "Keep this with you, in case you forget my words. It bears essential instructions for your journey. The Council does not wish you to return to East Haven. Instead you are to travel to Nadir, once more—strictly keeping to the Northern Trade Route this time. There, you will meet with Dorath who has special instructions and a guide for you. Your party has been chosen for you, Jace. Nearly all are present, but the last should be here shortly. It seems the Council values your friendship with Trel also, though I trust the two of you will remember that this is not the scullery of East Haven, but that you will be traveling through the land of Emblom. A great many dangers exist, as you well know. Among them are some that are not so noticeable as that which you have already met. You will be followed by Alaric here, whom, it seems, you have already met. Couriers escorted him here moments before you arrived. He is very useful in the traditions of the east and has a great knowledge of the peoples of the land. He once was a student like yourself, but has spent much of his time recently here at the March Wall. I have faith you will lean towards his advice, for though you are in charge, he has been sent to offer his assistance and a wise man would take it. You leave immediately," Sturbin said, tossing Jace a small bag of gold.

Jace looked first at Sturbin, then at Hadran and then saw Alaric standing with them. All this seemed so sudden that it was hard to grasp. The boyish grin that he wore a moment ago was replaced by a firm expression that echoed his resolve. Despite his whimsical attitude when left for a time to his own devices, he understood the seriousness of the Council's missions and the countless hours of training at East Haven. This was what it was all about—to be sent out into a world that did not know his Master and Savior, to tell and show them about Him and His gift to the world.

He gathered his staff and belongings from the foot of the bed, glancing at Alaric. The man was dressed in deerskin breeches with a long woolen shirt that stretched across his chest. His black rider's cloak was flung in back of him, clasped about his neck by the familiar book and sword brooch. Underneath, a smooth riding vest had replaced his leather apron. From his belt hung a heavy double-bladed axe and large sword hung across his back disappearing under his pack. He simply nodded at Jace while thumbing his axe, a sober expression across his face.

Trel helped Jace with his things, smiling warmly at Jace as they all made their way down the stairs. Outside the office, the drizzle had turned to a steady pour, and Jace stayed with Sturbin and Hadran while Trel and Alaric went to fetch the horses. Hadran paced back and forth and turned to Jace to speak, but the look on his face was a tapestry of mixed emotions. He looked at Sturbin and the man nodded slowly. Hadran turned once more to Jace, and he cringed slightly as he spoke to him, his ever-present scowl glowering darkly.

"Sturbin and the Council have made their decision," he began, his voice trailing off as he fought for the proper words, "Theirs was not mine for reasons I cannot say. I know where you are going and begged them to have me lead you or at least take me in your party for safety's sake. There are things which you still know little about, though you are ready and have been ready to go to Emblom for some time. Have a care, boy," Hadran said hardly, but his voice was shaking now, "I have given to you all my knowledge and would have given you more had there been more time. The enemy will hunt you, this you know, but in more secret and devious ways then you can possibly imagine. Do not allow him a foothold, for when he does, then he will exploit it to its full extent."

Hadran handed him a small book, its cover cracked and worn and its pages giving off a musty smell. "Read this daily, for it will protect the very heart that Yeshua gave His life for."

Jace looked at the cover, its title in simple black lettering: The Song of the Ages. He gasped, for he had never owned a book, let alone a copy of the sacred Word. He raised his head to Hadran, a look of confusion on his face. Hadran stared back at Jace, his hard scowl unmoving. He flung his arms around the young man, hugging him fiercely. When he released him, Hadran's eyes were filled with tears, but he looked away. "Go now, boy, and may Elohim protect your steps."

Sturbin stepped forward, tenderly grasping Jace's shoulders.

"Before we go, let us bow our heads as we offer up our voices and hearts to our Master and Friend," he said, his voice thick with emotion. The three bowed their heads and draped their arms across each other's shoulders. Sturbin spoke, "Lord, as You have in ages past, protect us each, as we go now to our appointed tasks. Let us carry the light that You have stoked within our hearts to a world that is lost in darkness. Let us stand always against the powers of darkness that threaten to consume this world. When our feet falter and we have lost our way, let us remember that You have not forgotten us and that You have and will always hold us in the palm of Your mighty, unfailing hand. Let us honor You always in word and action. Go with us now, we ask, always in Your holy Name, Ieysa."

As Sturbin lead the two out the door into the downpour, he continued, "There is another the Council has seen fit to offer in assistance. You must give her proper respect, for though she is the only woman among your party, she has been versed in the Way. She has a gift for mending the body as Yeshua can mend the soul. Yield to her advice on all these matters."

Jace turned half-expecting to see Miss Pell atop one of the horses. Instead, a white horse pranced sideways in the soaking rain. Upon its back was a lady whose face was not unfamiliar to Jace. She looked at him, suppressed contempt barely hidden while she steadied her horse. Jace's face went white as Lashara brought her horse forward, edging close to Jace. She gave Jace a look of wrath, then turned her attention to Sturbin and Hadran.

"You expect me to ride with him?" She asked in a high-pitched squeal. Sturbin and Hadran looked at Jace and he grinned innocently, shrugging his shoulders as if to say he knew nothing of what she was talking about.

"The Lord requires it!" shouted Sturbin above the rain. Lashara let out a cry of entrapped consternation. She wheeled her horse and galloped away in frustration.

Jace mounted his horse along with Alaric and Trel who each gave him a questioning look. He cringed to all and then kicked his horse into a gallop in pursuit of Lashara. The others followed close behind.

Sturbin and Hadran stood alone, the rain coming down around them. "It appears the two have already met," said Hadran without a hint of sarcasm.

"The group will need more intercession than I thought," said Sturbin, and both retreated inside against the onslaught of the downpour.

7

ANOTHER PLAN

The starling hung on the leafless branch, clutching it in the windy buffet of the pouring rain. It watched the small party travel down the winding road towards the Northern Trade Route. The dim morning light brought another cold, rain-soaked day to the Gap. The streams were full, and some had crested their shores as they emptied into the North Wood farther south. The slopes had turned to an eroding sludge by now, and the bird watched the troop skitter haphazardly down the steep decline to lower ground. Their shouts and warnings carried to the tiny fowl, and it turned its head to catch the half-audible phrases before they were swept away in the rain's cacophony. It gave a deep throaty croon in the wretched weather and one of the members of the group—the large one—lifted his head, searching for the bird. The starling shook the rain from its wings and flew away before it was spotted among the thick forest branches.

It climbed high into the sky, making its way northward. Fighting the wind, it screeched angrily, flapping away as it bent into the gusts. It stayed below the clouds, looking here and there while keeping to its ponderous flight. It blinked at Jace's humble home in the small clearing surrounded by the tall pines and maples. Only the goats and pigs were outside—the goats lazily munching the grass, paying no heed to the watery sky or the howling wind. The pigs squealed loudly in the mud. Although cool, they were obviously enjoying the raucous fun. The only other hints of life were the thin wisps of smoke that snaked out of the chimney of the cottage, revealing that the family was nestled inside.

The tiny winged creature followed the northern byway, seeing the maze of trails that ran up into the mountains towards East Haven. By noon it had passed over Noll. The small town was congested even on this dismal day, the caravans stretching to the horizon. The bird flew past the shops, over the training grounds and over the March Wall without any turning an eye in wonder, for who noticed a single bird amidst a storm?

Farther on it flew, beyond the low hills, and over the endless sea of dread weeds and twisted, evil-looking trees that choked the soil. It passed beyond where any human eye cared to freely wander, into the depths of that unspeakable land. The weather was clear this far north, if only a bit colder. Patches of snow dotted the craggy landscape as day turned to night and a biting winter wind kicked up. Boulders of numerous sizes dotted the snowy, barren land, but even they were covered as the bird flew ever farther north. Finally, from horizon to horizon, the earth became a carpet of endless snow that stretched, unblemished, illuminated by the glowing full moon. The bird was just a speck amidst the sea of white, the smallest of spots that was nearly missed against the pure backdrop.

Far to the north, a shape rose up out of that endless sea. Slowly, it took form as the creature moved closer. Tall battlements of glistening white stretched toward the black sky, catching the moon's light and refracting it in every direction so the castle cast a certain glow. Its gate was open, the portcullis raised, though no creature great or small occupied its empty mouth. The thing looked as though it was made of ice, pure and unyielding, its towers never witness to attack, never knowing defeat or siege. The massive structure looked abandoned. Not a single light shone from its gaping windows as the starling circled high overhead.

The castle was not white. Layer after layer of ice clung to its walls and spires after many untold ages. The palace was built, in fact, of a dark, ancient stone, long ago. It could only be seen as one drew closer and stared beneath the frozen layers.

Finding what it sought, the bird dove downward, the ominous palace consuming its vision. At the last instant, the creature spread its wings, slowing its descent noticeably and came to rest gently on the sill of a wide, low window. The air around the opening danced from the heat within and, as the bird stared through, it could see that the place was indeed occupied.

The room spread out in every direction. Giant tapestries adorned the black stone, moving slightly in the heat. Beams of mellow-colored oak were crowned with a thin film of soot that covered the high ceilings. A large pit was sunk in the center of the room, its fire licking high into the rafters. At one end were two massive oaken doors banded in iron. They were flanked by ceremonial guards dressed in rich red livery with sashes of silver girdling their waists. Each stood tightly at attention, holding a wickedly curved halberd in one hand whose pole rested on the ground. The hall was grandly lit with its enormous fire pit chasing away the shadows. The air was comfortable enough, though several windows were flung open. The room suggested a haughty, unwelcome attitude of regal importance. Gilded lamps and chests dotted the ornate hall, and one might have thought that its undisturbed furnishings had rarely entertained guests.

Atop the dais, a youthful lad lounged lazily on the opulent throne. He was a striking figure, lavished in a bright, clean linen shirt and a fine, dyed woolen longcoat. His dark hose betrayed his lengthy legs and well-formed muscles. His face was spotless, his skin a healthy complexion that naturally complimented his rich, dark hair. The boy was not young, but instead a budding adolescent. He was obviously of noble birth and in the prime of life. His features were soft and non-threatening, but his looks could not hide his strong personality. Though boyishly handsome, he projected an air of knowledge bordering on arrogance. He looked like a lion, at ease in his home, but his eyes saw everything. He played with his sceptre while his steely blue eyes looked far away.

The bird gave a quick whistle and the noble stirred on his throne. He looked sideways at the creature, a thin smile forming on his lips as he motioned for the bird to come. The starling alighted on his outstretched palm and turned to eye the boy with curiosity.

"A visitor," the lad mused, his rich voice bright as the sun and filling the empty hall. He stroked the bird lightly, almost friendly, and whispered to it, "Little creature, tell me where you've been."

The bird chattered away, hopping up the man's arm, then fluttered down onto his lap. His little voice squawked loudly, growing deeper as it continued. The man bent forward as the bird carried on, listening closely while the thing chirped along. The bird jumped down the man's leg. Its voice grew louder still as it hopped onto the marble stone floor, turning to look at the prince without stopping its song. The creature's voice became deeper, its light song now a throaty yell. The lad looked on as the obnoxious speech continued, paying no mind to its grating tones.

As the bird's voice deepened, the creature stepped from side to side and flapped its wings. Its shape seemed to bulge slightly as it cackled away. Slowly, the tiny starling grew large, its voice never stopping, but growing low, almost hollow. It spread its wings and bent its back forward. Amidst its noisy speech, its wings touched the ground. The feathers melted away to reveal two curled hands. The bird's body turned fleshy and its spindly legs rippled into a man's haunches.

The man stood upright and the prince looked on approvingly. He snapped his fingers and two servants scurried forward and dressed his naked frame. They draped a fine embroidered emerald coat over his cambric shirt and carefully held white leggings aloft while the man stepped into them. As he finished closing the last of his buttons on his shirt, the servants brought him a heavily jeweled cane, though the man had no limp. His long face was well shaved and his grey eyes met the prince's stare. Finally, he smoothed his coat and stood erect, awaiting his master.

"A brilliant disguise, Du'mas," the prince said with a look of satisfaction.

The man bowed low, a subtle smile rounding his lips.

"Tell me, how goes our progress?" the prince asked off-handedly.

Du'mas cleared his throat, "The time draws nigh, sire. Your forces are ready and our numbers grow even as we speak. Soon the few who stand in our way will be crushed underneath the swelling tide of your imperial magnificence."

"And the boy? How is his 'progress'?"

Du'mas gleamed with excitement, "The plans are laid for his ruin. Even now he journeys towards his doom."

A smug smile floated across the prince's face. So long he had watched and waited. Now his time to rise and come into his own was near. All the centuries heaped on top of one another, and the countless ages of preparation would finally see their fruition.

"He journeys down the southern slopes, my lord. The rains have slowed him, but he marches on without a care. He suspects nothing," Du'mas paused then added, "He was given a company, highness, to aid in his advance. He does not travel alone. This is something we did not expect—"

The young noble waved him aside, "It is of no importance. You trouble yourself with details, Du'mas. How many times have these small bands amounted to anything of value?" asked the prince, his eyes still distant. He twirled his sceptre slowly with his right hand. "All too often they serve our purpose, or fall prey to the same things we've intended for only one of them. It is a pity the Council has not seen the error of their ways." He yawned. "I grow bored with the lack of sport it takes to nullify these Keepers. If only it were a challenge to make them succumb and submit, my appetite would be satisfied more easily."

Du'mas looked at his master. He nodded in agreement. The list was long which spoke of those in the Gap who had been won over, nullified, or crushed. How many times had the Council tried this puny tactic? Surrounding a Keeper with more of the same only meant more food for the feast. He licked his lips. Sa'vard always had an eloquent way of putting things in perspective.

"Even so, lord, he must be watched. The list is also long of those who have escaped your grasp, though the trap was set and painstakingly prepared."

Sa'vard laughed. The high tenor voice echoed off the black walls, filling the room. It was a sound of disdain which spoke of coming triumph. He stopped short and looked down his throne at the pacing messenger.

"Du'mas," he said rebukingly, "How many times have I told you? I have rarely lost one whom I have set out to ensnare. They may struggle and move about, like a fish who's tangled in a net, but as time marches on, their will is slowly whittled away until they come, almost pleadingly and submit to me, their new master. I have seen it time and time again."

"But the Mines, sire."

"The Mines of Shorn were but a stepping stone, Du'mas. Now the stakes are raised higher. Is the boy in Par'lael? Then he is not untouchable. My grasp will slowly close around him. That is all life is for these miserable Keepers: a slow downward spiral until they are finally made an example of one way or another. The boy has not escaped by any means. No, his trials have just begun," he said with an evil smile, his features growing darker.

Du'mas hated that face. He had always felt uncomfortable when his master assumed the shape of a fair and innocent boy. He had no sympathy in his heart for neither the old nor the young. However, the young proved to be won over with the simplest of ease, most more than willing to accept the presents that Sa'vard offered so readily. Yet, how strange it was to see a boy, whose image portrayed the very essence of freedom and love—the qualities the Creator intended for all men—talk with such menacing hatred and loathing. That evil grin set upon the face of a child always made his skin crawl. After centuries, he still had not gotten used to it.

It was one of Sa'vard's favorite forms for a number of reasons. First, he knew it made his servants feel on edge and he liked that. He could never let his commanders become too comfortable around him. There was a need to instill fear even within his troops. That always gave them a quickness to their actions and a fear of the unknown. It also reminded him of Yeshua, his eternal foe. Where Yeshua had "suffered the little children to come to him," Sa'vard had done the same. It always amazed him how the young ones freely accepted whatever he offered. If he could seduce them early, they remained his most certainly for eternity.

He grinned wickedly. In doing this he had beaten Yeshua at his own game. There were many other reasons, some quite personal and others fickle. Sometimes the form of a boyish, trustful, faultless looking lad seemed to be the epitome of his cause. To take one such as this and turn him into something completely narcissistic and wholly evil was exhilarating, a challenge, and a work of art. Sa'vard sighed softly as he thought of how few of his followers could completely appreciate the intricate labor involved in changing one's soul to follow its true desires.

Changing his train of thought, he recalled how the Creator had lied to all mankind, claiming that his son would set the world free. Free from what? Whereas Yeshua offered life filled with rules and boundaries, Sa'vard let man pick his path, free of inhibitions. He was the one who offered true freedom. All it required was their soul in exchange.

That mattered little. After all, that was what Yeshua wanted also. So, while Sa'vard offered freedom and fulfillment of every want and whim of the heart, Yeshua peddled rules and submission. What fool would accept slavery and limits when they could have freedom? His face twisted in revulsion. Only those self-righteous fools of the Gap were gullible enough to believe the lies the Creator told. They were the only ones who stood in his way.

He thought for a moment. Though the Gap's rebellion was a never-ending splinter in the palm of his hand, he had already subdued half the world. The Clonesian Empire was the pride and joy of his heart. What a glowing example of a people who prospered because they did what they wanted! Their occasional riots, looting, murder, thievery, debauchery, and the like showed that they were finally realizing their potential. Even now, their influence had begun to rub on the Stygians—those pious people who followed a collection of dead gods or a marred version of the Creator. He cared little for that. As long as they never fully knew the Creator and never paid homage to Yeshua's name or true nature, it did not matter what they did. He snickered, they were another gullible people to believe that mere actions would gain them acceptance into Par'lael. If they only knew.

He would never tell them the truth—why would he want to? That was not where he was or would ever be. If they only knew the true master they served, they would not want to go there either. As it would be, when the ages passed into eternity, they would follow him and his minions into his dwelling place forever.

He almost smiled at that. He could remember the fateful day when the Creator had banished him from Par'lael with Yeshua looking on. He remembered how the Creator, Yeshua, and the Holy Counselor had said that he and his followers would be sentenced to Scheil-duum, the unspeakable place, where fire and brimstone churned in an eternal lake of unimaginable pain and heat. It was like yesterday. He stood in defiance then, and his heart had grown only harder as time passed.

Things were not destined to be an unending struggle. He welcomed the beginning of the end, for he too knew the signs of the end times. These were the moments he had waited patiently for. As the time drew ever nearer, his preparations had moved forward without any resistance. The numbers of his army had swelled, his human trophies were many, and the Bothians once again roamed the night. The Watchers had carefully tweaked the Clonesian system to his design, allowing for all to be delighted, and the enormous Kolosia had brought an animal hunger to the population, with more of them under construction even now.

The Creator had made a mistake, however. Always, Sa'vard had been given limits to his destructive power and he accepted them with the futility of a caged beast while continuing to make progress in his plans. The Creator had let one thing slip. In the final war, he had promised to give Sa'vard what he had wanted all along. The season was near when the Creator would allow Sa'vard to wage open war against Yeshua's followers on a scale never before seen and challenge him personally for control of the world. The Creator should have banished him to the place he promised before the world came into existence. Now, since the beginning of time, he had devised his forces for that nearing moment. When the Creator gave him absolute freedom, he would rally his forces in the north and ignite the fire of the Clonesian Empire to envelope the world in his name. In the process, the followers of the Gap would be crushed and those that survived would provide entertainment for him and his people in the Kolosia. The Stygians would finally realize their fickle ways, and the erratic land of Emblom and the south-lying lands would either be subverted, subservient, or submissive. In the end, he would sail across the Unending Sea, destroy Par'lael and claim all of creation as his own. The grand scheme was appetizing at the least and would be unparalleled euphoria when accomplished.

He turned his thoughts now to the babbling idiot Du'mas who stood below him, trying unsuccessfully to show interest. His servant was loyal, but his rantings became somewhat tiring.

"... He is livid. After his confrontation with Rendolph, his wounds healed slowly, but he refuses to wait a moment longer," said Du'mas, apparently speaking of Na'tal. "I've tried to sooth his fragile nerves, but he would have none of it. Since then, he has stirred up discontent and raised quite a following in the Mines. I am surprised I got here before him. When I left, he said he was on his way."

As if on command, the oaken doors were thrown back, scattering the flimsy guards up against the walls. The noise shook the pillars and more than one tapestry kicked up on its end. Na'tal filled the doorway letting out a gigantic bellow. A thin trail of brimstone rose off his back as he entered the hall. His great cloven hoofs sounded on the stones while he crossed the floor, walking directly through the fire pit without so much as a wince. Na'tal rose up, overshadowing Du'mas. His red tinged body pulsed angrily, and his hands worked while spittle flowed slowly from his fanged mouth.

"Such displays of bravado do not shake me, Na'tal," Sa'vard said smugly. "State your business or leave my presence."

"Sa'vard, your followers demand your accounting!" Na'tal roared, his voice dripping with hatred. "I have paid the price for your insolence! The Keeper is gone or has that escaped your notice? Meanwhile, we dawdle here like fools while the Creator mocks us. Are we to continue on like nothing has happened or bend our backs once more under the scourge of your better?"

"Careful, slave," Sa'vard said reproachfully, "I can stomach insults through the millennia, but don't take well to challenges."

"There is no challenge," Na'tal stated gruffly, his voice losing some of its edge. "I demand an accounting, it is my right!"

"I answer to no one. You lost your rights the day you chose your leader," Sa'vard hissed. "How quickly the underling forgets his place in the order of things! Go back before I change my mind about you, Na'tal, and have you stripped of your flimsy title. There are a million worms with twice as much talent waiting to take your place!"

Na'tal looked like he had been slapped in the face. He blinked while his mouth hung open wordlessly. Only his low growl was heard. He stared up at Sa'vard. A measured look of defiance passed over his face and then he whirled about to leave. Sa'vard waited intentionally until Na'tal had turned.

"Wait!"

Na'tal stopped in his tracks and slowly turned around.

"My thoughts have changed. Perhaps you should stay a bit longer. There is a chance you might learn something useful," Sa'vard said, with a hint of a smile on his face.

Na'tal slowly made his way back to the dais. His smoldering look of fury clearly showed his displeasure with being told to enter or leave depending on his master's present state of mind. He stood watching Sa'vard hungrily, flexing his thick arms, waiting for the chance to challenge Sa'vard, but knowing he could not.

These were the moments Sa'vard most enjoyed. The delicate manipulation of his subjects—letting them know without a doubt where they stood in the order of things by catching them unawares or having them obey his every want and command. He believed Na'tal would have jumped up and down on his right foot for an hour had he some faint desire to see it done.

Sa'vard's emotions raced every time he witnessed this playing out of events. How he enjoyed putting his minions in their place, especially Na'tal.

Na'tal was stupid. He relied heavily on his brute strength and had no sense of timing and very little wit. He could never lead. Too often he failed to keep his emotions in check. Once his anger bested him, he was nothing more than a roaring torrent of power that demolished whatever happened to be before him.

It was Na'tal's arrogance and lack of vision which had made them lose the Keeper. How this had infuriated Sa'vard! But Na'tal had thrived in the Mines. His choice to put him there was a stroke of genius. Now after centuries of grooming, Na'tal had risen through the ranks and was a trusted servant, provided he was given some direction and made an example of every now and then. Sa'vard shook his head at his constant project. One day he would have to dispose of the creature. Then again maybe he could be brought to heel like Du'mas.

The two slaves eyed each other suspiciously. There was always the constant jockeying for position within his ranks. More than once Sa'vard had played one off against the other, another scheme he thoroughly enjoyed. The two were forced to work hand in hand, despite their near hatred, if only because they feared Sa'vard. He grinned ruefully. Who else could think of such things? No, there could only be one master.

He collected his thoughts momentarily while the two waited in submission. What had Du'mas said? Ah, yes, Rendolph. So, it was he that the Creator had sent in protection of this Keeper. Not only him, but Zax, Obban, and Torne, if his eyes had not deceived him. He would have to keep special watch out for them. Four of the Creator's heavenly host to match the party of four Keepers. He should have suspected.

It was not the first time that these beings had crossed his path. He could remember them from long ago when all creation had gathered around the emerald throne to worship the Creator before the beginning of time. Things were different then. He had grown to love the Creator then, and he remembered Rendolph, Zax, Torne, and Obban huddled near their Master as they sang out their praises. They were always quick to carry out his every command, no matter how small. The thought sickened him even now how they followed the Creator's words in blind acceptance.

Once the Creator had given him charge of all the hosts of heaven, he had come to the realization of the Master's weaknesses. Elohim could not possibly be all-powerful. That was why he had given Sa'vard so much control. Where there was lack of sovereignty, there was weakness, and where there was weakness, there was opportunity. He could not remember how long the thought had taken before it had crystallized into a scheme. With his leading and charisma, he had convinced a third of the heavenly host to follow him to liberate themselves, overthrow the Creator, and set up Sa'vard as the supreme ruler.

He remembered the look Rendolph and the others had given him while the Creator gave his sentence with Yeshua looking on. In the end, the loyalty of Sa'vard's minions would cost them. They would be the first of the Creator's followers that he would send from Par'lael. There they would dwell among the mortals awaiting the final days when they would bend their backs in submission to him forever.

So Rendolph had bested Na'tal. Good. Na'tal needed someone to show him his fallibility. For Na'tal to accept his physical defeat would take more than this. Na'tal was all but screaming for another chance to show his skills. Who knows? Before this scheme was carried out in full, Na'tal may get his wish. He turned to Du'mas, intentionally ignoring Na'tal for the moment.

"Explain to me the details of the northern forces."

Du'mas blinked and then slowly began, "Your hordes simply await your calling, sire. They have moved themselves just beyond the low-lying hills. Their outliers and scouts have probed the defenses in the moonless nights. They have reported that the walls are strong, but are poorly manned. There are some rumors of strange machines being made in a glade somewhere outside of one of the towns, but we have never found them. If we struck now it would surely be a victory."

"Victory without meaning is simply a squandering of resources. No, we wait until summer. There is a message I wish to send and I want the ears pricked to hear it. There will always be rumors, Du'mas. Have the Stalkers probe to the west and south, we have spent far too long searching the Eastern March. I doubt there is any surprise that we have not seen in these parts. What of our dear friends? How go the days of Sturbin and Hadran?"

"The old man grows weary, lord. He stays awake long into the night and is up before the first hints of morning light. His will is failing slowly, but he still commands the March Wall with much efficiency. Another thing," said Du'mas, licking his lips, "He lost Arthur."

Sa'vard's eyes brightened, "When?"

"Sometime a week ago. We're not sure when. He's been harrying our vanguard and wreaking havoc with our scouts, but nothing serious. It seems your plan worked."

"Of course, Du'mas. A light prod gets the horse underway. Most times, people only need some minor suggestion or mention of something scandalous. Usually, they do the rest themselves and before long, they are found walking swiftly down the path that I have set for them."

"Yes, but the hint was masterful. Rarely have I seen one take such little bits of malice and turn them into so much anger and self-righteousness."

"The Song of the Ages says many things, Du'mas," Sa'vard instructed. "Many people of the Gap read its pages religiously and more often than not fight about obscure passages of relative importance. If they can be divided on whether or not Yeshua draws them or they accept salvation through Yeshua, so much the better for me. Let them fight amongst themselves while the world is swallowed in my grasp. Arthur was ready to prove himself; I simply gave him the chance."

"Sturbin misses him and his troops, lord. Their flight severely weakened the March Wall's position. I believe Sturbin suspects something. He has ordered excess supplies into the towns and stepped up training as well. He has toyed with the idea of conscription."

Sa'vard clicked his tongue. "He is a worthy opponent at times. Let him have his follies for now. By the time we strike, he will be worn to the brink of incapability."

"Must we strike on the flank?"

"It is as I have said. And what of Hadran? How goes his progress?"

"He did not get his way at the Council. They decided to push the Keeper through to the mission despite his lack of training. Hadran was seething, but he refuses to openly oppose the Council's decisions still."

"It is only a matter of time. Hadran will never let a mistake go; it's not in his nature. Give him time. Keep his mind on the inefficiency of his superiors, and he will eventually turn, I have seen it all before."

"The present Council is strong, Master. Their actions, though inefficient now, may be the cause of much glory to Yeshua in the future if their plan succeeds."

Sa'vard delved his eyes into Du'mas. He had given him more than enough liberty to present his findings, now the fool used his freedom to voice his own opinions. Sa'vard sneered openly—how dare he question his authority! Du'mas was somewhat intelligent, but capable at best. How could he ever comprehend the complicated web that Sa'vard wove to ensnare the world? He held out his hand, twisting a pattern in the air.

"Kneel," he said, thrusting his fingers at Du'mas. The figure crumpled to his knees with barely a struggle. Du'mas looked at Sa'vard, fear welling up in his soul. He started to speak, but Sa'vard pointed his fingers again.

"Silence," he whispered and a strained hiss of air passed out of Du'mas' mouth. He closed his lips, his eyes darting back and forth in panic. He struggled noticeably, though Sa'vard's will held him in place.

Sa'vard twisted his face as Du'mas bent helplessly before him. He watched him for some time, delight filling his being at the effects of his power. He gazed at Na'tal, who had blanched considerably, challenging the underling for a confrontation. Na'tal stood staring straight ahead, only his lightened complexion and shallow breathing betrayed his anxiety. Sa'vard laughed at his minions. He spoke off-handedly to them, shifting while he lounged in the chair.

"You have both annoyed me today. Must I constantly toil with ones so much lesser than I?" He gave a great sigh and then began again with an air of indifference. "If things must be, then they must. It amazes me that you have such little faith, though you have seen my actions time and time again. Is there any human in all the world who holds such power?" he asked no one in particular. "Then surely none can stand in my way, no matter how much they prepare—be they Clonesians, Stygians, or even members of the Gap. Even the great Clonesius could not oppose me. You will watch and learn in the months to come as my plan unfolds, and when it is done, you both will see why I am the master."

He waved his hand once more and Du'mas and Na'tal were both forced prostrate at the foot of his dais, their groans clearly audible above the noise of the flames.

Sa'vard ignored them and continued, "Everyone has their faults, every creature, every being. Humans are no different. Some are susceptible to greed, or lust of every kind imaginable. Some simply want power, some gold. Others are content to be left alone to their own devices in rooms of secrecy. Still others do not know what they want. Everyone has some hidden want, some insatiable appetite that yearns to be filled on some animal level. I will turn over every hidden hunger, find each dark desire and feed it until that person has grown to rely on me.

"I will have Jace one way or another, perhaps his friends if they should interfere. Maybe I shall be entertained for a while as they offer up their puny resistance. Let them call upon their precious Yeshua, he can only offer them momentary protection. I will sift each one of them like wheat until they have glorified me one way or another."

He looked at the backs of his followers. A thin film of sweat formed on their bodies as they fought to breathe under the press of Sa'vard's will. He cocked his head to one side, a thought coming to mind.

"Perhaps it would be wise to let you in on my plans, one more, at least. You did not think you knew all my intentions, did you? The one whom I have personally nurtured will come to light very soon. This traitor will lead the Keepers down a path they will not want to go and take them far from the straight and narrow. His deeds will come to fruition soon enough. Then he will receive his due reward."

He stroked his scepter in thought, "The Creator is not the only one who is all-knowing or powerful. My spies have turned the world upside down and revealed every hidden part of man. The Bothian Horde snatches up the innocents during the dark of night, and my plans touch even the most decrepit beggar and innocent baby. My decisions that embarked me on a path bound for greatness long ago are approaching their point of germination. The seeds of hate and malice, pride and discontent, and every selfish hunger have grown now like a full-ripened fruit. These ideas which have laid dormant for so long take patience and care to carry out. Great ideas always take time and passion. Soon we will recognize them, soon. The words of the Song of the Ages are only boasts by ancient writers to the one they served. If they had known me, I would be their king."

Then with dark finality he said, "There are no prophecies, only signs. I control my own destiny."

He looked down at his groveling servants, their muffled cries begging him to release them. Slowly, he rose from the throne, his boyish head not taller than the chair. He looked around and found his scepter, sticking it in his jeweled belt. He stepped down the platform moving the two prostrate forms out of his way with an impetuous kick.

Sa'vard sauntered directly to the doors while Dum'as and Na'tal cried for him to return. He strolled through the fire pit, his heels sounding on the stones as he came out the other side. Thin trails of smoke swirled about his little body. They twisted around him as he walked, shrouding his figure in a smog. His silhouette through the smoke stretched and twisted. As the haze vanished, Sa'vard stood, a tall, dark man whose head nearly brushed the top of the doorway. His black leather boots were soft on the pavement, his rich velvet apparel a striking contrast to his earlier attire. His hair was dark and oiled closely against his scalp. His pocked face was set and determined on dark purposes only he knew. He walked down the hallway and almost as an afterthought, flicked his hands to release Na'tal and Dum'as as the hall doors slammed shut.

8

FARTHER ON

The rain was intolerable. It had not let up for over a week, and the shadowy sky matched the group's spirits. They awoke each morning cold and wet, and broke camp in the dreary weather with barely a word. Throughout the day they kept to single file on the horse paths lining the North Wood and maintained the same formation when they reached the Northern Trade Route. Jace had wanted to ride the steeds hard, but on Alaric's advice he kept the pace to a steady trot.

The weather had darkened Lashara's mood further and Jace's decision only added to her rage. She watched even the trade wagons pass them. Alaric had said it would save the horse's strength over time, but that idea did nothing to change their pace in the dismal weather. She had focused her anger on Jace and rode on in silence, giving any of them a piercing stare when they had tried to make small talk. Her air had affected them all and been an excuse for them to do little more than keep to the daily routine of riding until nightfall.

At camp, their fires were small and seemed to be a light without heat. The wood was soaked through and more often than not, it left their lungs and clothes filled with a wretched smoky stench that followed them the rest of the day. This melded nicely with the dank odor their woolen cloaks put off, but they had all been driven past the point of caring. Each person ended the day huddled and shivering next to their pitiful fire and somehow fell asleep, if only from pure exhaustion. Trel had the makings of a nasty cold and accented their trip with a fine assortment of coughs and wheezes that sounded more animal than human. So the days had passed for them all. The daily monotony left each of them alone with their thoughts and doubts about where they were headed and why they were there.

Trel let out a loud hacking spell. Despite the awful cold, nasty weather and bad company, he was in relatively good spirits. When he had been snatched from his studies and taken to the March Wall by Hadran, whom he dreaded, he had expected the worst, and so, to be on a trip with his good friend, away from his books, and on the open road had not seemed like such a bad experience.

He watched Jace's back as he rode directly behind him. His friend had seemed changed since he had left his schooling. He was more of a man now and less of a youth. Trel remembered his eyes—how sad and distant they seemed when they met in Sturbin's room—though his face had cracked into one of his famous grins when he realized who it was. He sat high in his saddle, glancing at the tall pines on either side of the highway. He looked pensive and alert, riding with a watchful eye as the sheets of rain poured over them. Trel noticed how he guided his palomino now with one hand easy on the reins while he relaxed his other on his thigh. Strange, he remembered Jace's first meeting with a horse and how it had not gone so smoothly. Yes, he had grown up.

Trel's thoughts turned inward as he rode, looking up at the clouds that hung low and brushed the tops of the pines. He was glad to be gone from East Haven. He could remember so many times, the night before his tests, asking the Master to come back and wishing so often that His return would spare him the misery of low marks. Maybe He had finally answered his cries in some strange way. Whatever it was, here he was now, stuck on a path he had not chosen with only his friend and two other strangers on some journey he knew nothing about. The unknown made him scared and in spite of being free from the watchful eye of his Mentors and the fearful expectation of his examinations, he wondered if he had overstepped his bounds.

He had always wanted to see the land outside of the Gap, his parents had brought him there at a very young age and he had never been to another place, though he had heard a great many tales and such. Now here he was and the thought frightened him more than anything else. The world seemed so big, and he felt swallowed up in its land the more he traveled. Here one could get lost rather easily and maybe worse. His imagination ran wild thinking of the horrors that potentially lurked around each corner.

The only thing that kept his anxiety at bay were the Mentors' teachings and the passages from the Song of the Ages he had committed to memory. They tumbled through his mind and he found himself mouthing the words as they passed one after another through his head. "The Lord is my shepherd, I shall not want." "...to Him who is able to keep you from falling..." "You are my hiding place." "The Lord is my light and my salvation, whom shall I fear?" The words came and went, but he always found himself returning to them when he seemed the least bit frightened. *I guess the Mentors knew what they were doing after all*, he thought reprovingly. Maybe he should have paid closer attention. He vowed silently, if he were to make it back to East Haven, he would throw himself wholly into his studies with as much passion as he could muster.

During the week he had thought often of the Master's decision to send him forth. He had heard the other students chatter about heroic stories of the men and women whom the Creator had sent into the world on appointed tasks. Some were great, others were of minor importance, but he had been firmly reminded that all were equal in the Almighty's eyes and served to advance His kingdom and bring Him glory, not themselves. Each person who was called should give their all to what they were called to do. He had no doubt his mission was serious, but how could he give something his all when he did not know what he was supposed to be doing? He shrugged his shoulders. Couldn't the world be just a little less complicated?

Lashara wiped the rain from her face as she watched Trel. His arms were making exaggerated motions and from the look of his back, he was talking to himself again. The boy had obviously fallen from the saddle at a very young age, maybe more than once. Jace kept dubious company indeed.

She snorted when she thought of him. There he was riding in the lead, his frame haughtily raised erected. She grew to like him less and less each day, always finding some new fault, if she watched long enough. He obviously did not know how to treat a lady, what could she expect of one of Hadran's pupils?

She despised everything Jace did. Oh, he did have a handsome face, but he was overconfident and lacked the seriousness needed for leading. That pretty twinkle in his eyes was clearly a sign of mischief and cunning that spoke volumes about his maturity. From their first meeting he had embarrassed her in front of the soldiers and craftsmen and in her place of work, no less! Then he had insulted her openly while he left. Now, she was forced to follow him on some fool errand of Hadran's, she was sure. The boy did not know proper manners, what else could he be ignorant of? She cringed, wondering when one of his lazy remarks would compromise the entire party's safety.

The heart of the matter was that Lashara was uncomfortable, and her anger towards Jace helped deflect her feelings. She enjoyed the safety of the Gap and though she reveled in the outdoors, she preferred the sanitary conditions of the infirmary. The wet and cold were things she would easily trade for bandaging a soldier's arm and encouraging some poor cobbler. This uneasiness was heightened by her new companions. She had never been so violently removed from her environment without a say in it and been surrounded by people she had not known. Furthermore, they were men—both rude and disgusting, as Jace and Trel had confirmed on a daily basis. The best she could hope for was that they would all leave her alone and consult her only in some dire situation.

The truth was, she did not know how to relate to men. Her closest friends were all women, and since Miss Pell had adopted her as her apprentice, she had found little time to garner relationships of any depth while working among the sick and hurting. Though the same age, Jace and Trel had proved to be nothing more than overgrown children and took turns teasing her with snide remarks around the campfire, or as they packed up each morning.

She admitted to herself that she could laugh and engage in a few ribs every now and then, but her profession required a high degree of thought. Teasing was a different matter entirely, and she abhorred the practice completely. It made her feel little and she refused to sink into trading insults, as men were so in the habit of doing. Many times people mistook her stand-offish attitude for prudish behavior, and though this upset her, she would have nothing to do with the silly games boys played. When she had finally let her guard down, she found some nasty trick or another the two had concocted waiting for her.

Her back was a prime example. It still scratched from the itching powder Jace and Trel had sprinkled down her shirt a day ago while she slept. After they had spent the day snickering at her, Alaric took the two into the woods on a small walk. When they returned, their faces were hard, and they did not look at her. Neither did Alaric. Now Alaric kept a watchful eye on the two as he brought up the rear behind Lashara. The big man was an exceptional tracker who now used his skills to mind the young men.

She did not know what to make of him. He talked little and was kindly to her, helping to pack her belongings and offering a friendly word now and then. He remained aloof from the rest of them for the most part. Maybe the difference in age made him feel uncomfortable, or maybe something else troubled his mind.

Lashara held her cloak tightly as another cold blast of wind and rain swept over the group. She looked at their surroundings in the cold afternoon. There was not much change of scenery, only the rutted brownish-yellow byway and the surrounding forest. The road was always there, trailing off to the east, but quickly vanishing in the steady rain. She had heard it ran all the way to the Unending Sea, but knew they would not go that far.

That, at least, was a comfort. The sea was vast and kept to its name. No man had ever crossed its depths and returned to tell the story, but its waves were rumored to end at the land of Par'lael, the paradise of the Almighty and home to His Son, Yeshua. There, all who had passed from this world and were called by His name awaited the day He would return and claim this land as His own. As the Song of the Ages taught, it was a land of unequaled beauty where those who were welcomed there lived forever in the very presence of Elohim. No tears of sadness touched their cheeks and no evil thing dwelt upon its shores. There was no hunger, strife, or pain, only the joy of praising their Savior for the rest of eternity. No man had returned from there, save one. All the Gap knew His name, the name of Yeshua. She was even told that people throughout Emblom and the other lands knew it, though they had forgotten His story and the price He paid to follow His Father's will and save any who called on Him. One day, He would return across the sea with all the heavenly host to command and establish His kingdom here forever. That was an image hard to imagine, but she smiled a faraway smile as she thought what it would be like.

It was much easier to enjoy that vision than the picture of the Unending Sea with its ceaseless waves churning and rolling as far as the eye could see. The thought made her stomach queasy. She had seen the water many times before; even ventured upon its waves at times to fish from its depths, but that was in her life before the Gap. She decided that the tapestries and pictures throughout the land did not do justice to its power or greatness. Even thinking about standing on a ship at sea made her insides clench and shift uneasily.

Lashara was not the least bit anxious at her journey so far. Maybe that was because she had lived outside the Gap until she had met Miss Pell. The lady had ridden into town, and word had spread quickly of the wise woman who was helping heal the sick. She used no tricks or deception like so many mystic healers in Emblom, only a mix of good roots and warm water, served by a warm hand and with a genuine smile.

There was something else about her Lashara noticed. Her actions were plain enough, but there was a sense of love that enveloped her every move. Whoever was placed before the old woman was showered with abundant affection and boundless caring. Such openness was uncommon in Emblom, and it piqued Lashara's interest in the bent little lady. It was easy to listen to her speak, and Lashara found herself drinking in the woman's words as she talked about the Creator, Yeshua, and His mighty plan to save all who would believe on His name and commit their lives to Him.

With complete trust, Lashara had followed the lady's wisdom, placed her heart and allegiance in Yeshua and journeyed with her to the Gap. Their common bond in the area of help and healing nurtured their companionship, and over the next four years she learned much about the Way.

She prided herself on her work and was encouraged by Miss Pell's astonishment at her improvement. The work was stimulating and required a great deal of concentration and attention to detail. Setting someone's bone was not the time to joke or be thinking about the finer workings of the universe.

She was one of the few young people who had not gone to East Haven to receive the proper formal training. Miss Pell and Hadran had an ongoing debate on that issue every time their paths crossed. The two seemed to take it well, neither one coming out the victor, but Lashara had a growing animosity toward Hadran that Miss Pell had chided her on. Now that he had finally won, or Miss Pell had acquiesced (it mattered not to her), she was downright livid. The Master had used her well at the infirmary, and she felt like she was being punished for something by being taken from the work she loved. She rode on in silence then, a myriad of questions bouncing through her head and her confidence shaken.

Jace guided his party off the road. They all dismounted under a large maple whose leaves had not yet fallen. The protection was a chance for them to remove their hoods and rub some warmth into their hands. Trel opened up his pack, distributing one of the many containers of dried fruit and nuts that weighed down his animal. The mix was good and made for a break from the cheeses, dried meats, and hard breads that he usually offered.

Jace had assigned his friend to handle the food stores, and the young man had not disappointed in providing an assortment of treats to break the daily humdrum of the past week. The others had all waited eagerly each meal to see what surprise Trel would produce from out of his bags. Whether his prankish attitude had subsided, or he had not noticed their anticipation, he presented the food with indifference and did not take advantage of the situation. Whatever the reason, it was a grateful change to his character that may have been prodded by his talk with Alaric.

The group washed down the food with water from their canteens. Trel took the time to examine the branches of the maple. He balanced on his tiptoes, sipping slowly while he drank from one of its leaves. Then his eyes bulged and he curled over, gagging when the liquid went down the wrong pipe. That brought on another of his hacking spells and soon Trel was wheezing and wiping his dripping nose on his sleeve. Lashara shook her head as she looked on and then guided the horses to graze on the far side of the tree's protection.

Jace took the break to consult Alaric on their journey. He unfolded the letter and scanned its contents once again.

"I wish the instructions were more descriptive. I hate loose ends," he shouted to the large man. They huddled close enough to hear each other's words in the downpour. "I expected Sturbin or Hadran to give me some other advice than what they told me before I left. This barely says anything," he said, slapping the wet letter.

"It says enough. Nadir is less than three more days ride, maybe only two, and if the weather clears, we could be there even sooner," replied Alaric loudly. "We're making good time and the letter mentions nothing about a hurry. I believe the Council only wishes for us to accomplish the task."

Jace frowned. He hated traveling at a snail's pace, and only did it because of Alaric. If the man could put dreams from his head to wood and iron like Jace had seen outside of Noll, Alaric knew more than him. It felt good to have someone to lean on for practical advice.

Jace shrugged, "The only thing seems to be to just keep moving."

Alaric patted Jace reassuringly, "We're doing fine. Nadir will be here before we know it. Perhaps tonight we should discuss our actions in the city. It is far larger than any settlement in the Gap. They have many traditions that are different than ours, and I would hate for us to disturb any local customs."

Jace nodded, "How much longer before sundown?"

Alaric stared at the sky for a moment and pursed his lips. "Two, maybe four hours. The days are getting shorter and the cloud cover doesn't help."

"We can do it then. Before we leave, let's glean some branches from this place, dried wood may be hard to come by with the darkening sky, and it's one less thing to worry over."

Alaric nodded approvingly and the party went to work. After a quarter hour they had gathered enough wood, stored it under their bags and were on their way, each pulling up their hoods against the rain.

Jace admired Alaric. The big man was never disturbed and provided stability to the group. Even when rebuking him and Trel, he had done it with understanding and respect that drove his point home hard. The talk had convicted Jace and even though it was not a punishment, he was left thinking more about other people's feelings.

The talk had also made him see how awful he had treated Lashara and he felt personally responsible for her distancing herself from the group. Before him, she carried herself with such confidence, and this made Jace feel nervous when approaching her. No wonder he felt the need to make light of the situation. He knew he owed her an apology, but felt it wise to lay low for now. The storm provided the perfect excuse for him not to talk to her, even though he knew she noticed.

The girl was a wonder to him. Out of all the group, he knew her the least, but felt that before this was all over he would have to know her very well. The thought scared him. No one had ever explained in detail how he should act or treat a woman except his father.

"Treat her like you would your mother," he could still hear him say, but not all women wanted to be treated the same way. His father had never explained those words and his brother had not helped him either.

He could remember Rae feeding his fantasies about strange and beautiful women. No long speech was needed, only occasional comments as a girl walked by them at East Haven. He heard his brother's friends talk about them countless times in low voices while eating their meals in the kitchen halls. They always hushed when the Mentors walked by, and that piqued Jace's interests even more. Not all that they said was wholesome and uplifting, and his ears burned red after hearing some of their words. If the Mentors had ever overheard half their comments, they would probably have been sentenced to the libraries until their heads had grayed.

Now Jace was confronted with starting a meaningful relationship with a woman with only these two major extremes to guide him. Instead, he chose to keep his mind focused on his mission, the letter, and the tattered Song of the Ages copy he kept close to his chest. Those seemed to waylay the errant thoughts of women that bounced inside his head and kept him busy enough to justify ignoring Lashara, though he found himself staring more and more at her long hair, blue eyes, and girlish figure. He cringed at that, shaking the thoughts out of his head. These feelings came and went, and were only at the forefront of his mind in the moments before he fell asleep.

The responsibility that had been squarely placed upon his shoulders consumed much of his thoughts. How the Council had decided that he should ever go out again was beyond him. His last trip being a disaster, he was determined not to make the same mistakes and attempted to take advantage of the people that had surrounded him.

He tried not to view himself as the leader, although he was clearly appointed that task. He found himself struggling with not letting the idea go to his head. It was fun to be the one to divide up certain functions—Trel the food, and Alaric the money, for instance, but he had always heard that leading was a job people relished because those people were forced to make decisions no one else wanted to. He hoped he would not be faced with such decisions.

Just in case, he tried to steal times to read from the Song of the Ages each day. They were usually odd times—late at night before sleep, or early in the morning while others packed up. He even read as he rode. Wherever or however he studied, it always lifted his spirits with the promises his Lord had for him.

These routines and the constant need to mull over the upcoming objectives freed his mind from most things, but his dreams were still filled with nightmares. Since his return, he had woken several times drenched with sweat, haunted by the images of the Mines, Du'mas, and Na'tal. His tormentors' faces hovered before him, and he could hear their voices and see the blank stares of the ever-present guards.

Being in enclosed rooms of any size for any length of time made him edgy also, but to sleep in one set him into panic. His only way to fall asleep in Sturbin's room was with either the window or door cracked open. That embarrassed him, but the light or moving air and noises of other human voices calmed his nerves as he went to bed. He still found himself waking, suffocating, thinking he was trapped in the Mines with the spaces closing in around him, only to find that he had twisted himself amidst his blankets.

He was relieved, to say the least, to sleep outside and be free from the tight, crushing ceilings and spaces, but this did nothing to rest his fear of the Bothian Horde. He found peace in the company of others, even if they were not ones he knew so well. As the dark settled, he huddled close to the fire and hoped he was not the last to fall asleep. More often than not, he lay awake late into the night, listening intently to every, coo of a bird, rush of wind, or snap of a twig. His fears were heightened by the long shadows that melded with the bending trees of the forest. The rain did not help either. Every sound or shift in movement threatened to change the world around him, and he half-expected to hear the low trumpeting bay of the Bothian Horde at any time.

The days after such restless sleeps were long and drawn out, and he felt more annoyed and impatient as they wore on. Yet, as night came again, he found himself too tired to resist his fatigue. Indeed, his mind seemed too tired to perpetuate its imaginary tricks. He constantly wrestled with his fears and found little solace from them. So, no matter where he went, the enemy always haunted him, and he pleaded to Yeshua that it would not get the best of him, though he feared it would sooner or later.

They rode their steeds unhurriedly eastward. Merchants' carts passed the travelers every so often. The bells of the reins bore little warning to their approach in the rain. The wet travelers let them by without a wave, each tightening their cloaks as the day dwindled to an end. Jace waited till his eyes could barely see before he signaled they set up camp. The road had widened out significantly, and they found they did not need to move entirely off the byway. Alaric pitched two oil lamps to mark their party's camp while the rest of the group unpacked their horses. Everyone handed Jace the wood they had gathered earlier and he started on the fire. Alaric had lent him his steel and flint and he was eager to have a go at it. Lashara was picketing the horses, and Trel unpacked the foodstuffs while skillfully avoiding her eyes.

Alaric joined Lashara and the two set a spot for the group's sleeping space. Hooking a branch with his axe, Alaric forced the limb to the ground. He drove a long iron stake through the limb, securing it firmly to the ground. He did the same with another branch while Lashara wrapped a blanket over the two trunks and tied them down to form a makeshift lean-to.

Jace found a large, flat rock and threw some underbrush on it in a neat pile. He draped his cloak over the heap, shielding it from the rain and struck the flint against the steel a couple times. The brush smoked softly and then licked to flames in a few moments. Quickly he added the smaller sticks and backed away as the fire took on its life. By the time everyone had finished their chores, the fire was a healthy light of yellow and orange flames. It seemed more inviting than last night's, and the crew settled around it warming their weary, stiff bodies. Then, as is if Yeshua were giving them an added blessing, the rain began to taper off.

Trel passed around the food, this time a double portion of jerky, while the others broke off pieces from the cheese and bread the group shared. Jace gave a short blessing over the food and thanked their Lord for the breaking weather, and they ate in silence, each hungrily consuming their food.

When all had settled, Alaric cleared his throat, his soft-spoken words, clearly audible since only the water dripped from the trees.

"It is possible we will reach Nadir tomorrow," he said picking up a good-sized rock to grind his axe. "Now that the weather is lifting and the road has widened, I expect a rise in traffic. With your permission, Jace, I would share what we may see, so as to prepare us for some differences in the city."

Jace nodded for Alaric to begin and he picked up his axe, grinding it slowly, while he thought out all the anomalies the others might find surprising in Nadir. When he thought of one, he stopped his grinding and talked to the three, being mindful to look them in the eyes to make sure they paid attention, especially the men.

Jace had never been taught in such a way, and he found the informal manner in which it was presented relaxing and entertaining. Alaric spoke slowly, making each word clear and letting it rest in all their minds that they might weigh what he said.

Nadir's inhabitants were not like those in the Gap, he explained. Some could be trusted, but others could not. Though they found things to swear by and oaths to take, there were few who lived there that believed in the Creator and followed His Son. As such, he warned them to be mindful when approached for alms or by merchants and other peddlers.

Nadir was a town of riches and the people were proud of their land. It straddled the river Eisel and was a city built on trade and commerce. Merchants and peddlers of every kind flocked along the Northern Trade Route to buy and sell in the marketplace and at their fairs. Goods were shipped up and down the Eisel River and distributed along the steppe all the way to the Unending Sea. The economy of Nadir was largely merchant-based, but the town had a good many nobles and serfs.

Trel and Jace raised their eyes at the word of "noble," obviously excited to see those of pure birth, but Alaric deflated them. These were men as normal as any. Their titles meant little in the eyes of Yeshua, but they should be given proper respect the same as any man. The quizzical look the two gave when Alaric mentioned "serfs" made Lashara shudder—how little did these fools know? Maybe it would be better to gag them and drag them into town, unannounced. She sighed, if only that were an option.

Lashara listened to Alaric at first, but soon got bored with his warnings. She was not trying to be impolite. Most of it she had heard or seen already, the area being close to her birthplace. Some things of the darker nature, Alaric conveniently left out, but Jace and Trel sat and listened in amazement nonetheless.

Yes, Nadir was the jewel of the Northern states some said, and so it was, but she remembered other things. Not all who lived within the city were rich. Not all could afford the finer luxuries. The city's discrepancy in social classes was glossed over or maybe forgotten as were the awful living conditions to all but the highest classes of society.

She had only been to Nadir four times, mostly to buy food with her mother. They were special times, and she had found the markets filled with all sorts of trinkets and toys that glittered in the sun. Some booths contained clothes from far off places whose fabrics were delicate and much softer than her woolen dress. Oh, how she yearned to own such stitched finery. She and her mother would take much of the day looking at the many clothes that they would never own. They only frequented the markets in the southern half of the city, away from the decadent houses of the merchants and the palace of the ruling magistrate. Prices were intolerable even there, and her mother could only afford one ham, two chickens, and some essentials that could not be garnered from their farm. The purchases were just enough to alleviate some of the household drudgery and allow her and her mother to work the fields during harvest time. Lashara's eyes grew heavy and soon she drifted off to sleep, the memories of her and her mother's journey through the large city ushering her to rest.

Alaric continued his talk, letting the young lady rest for tomorrow. Jace and Trel snickered, watching Lashara sleep with her mouth opened wide, breathing softly, but also listened respectfully to their elder. The conversation turned once more to Yeshua and the Gap.

"People in Nadir do not care much for the Gap. To them, it is a lowly land filled with beggars and simpletons. They feel the people keep to themselves, thinking themselves better than the outside world, and often use us as the butt of their jokes," said Alaric, grinding his axe softly. "What they know of us is partly our own doing, but we must have a care to remember that these people know neither us nor our Lord. Their minds are filled with rumors they've heard that are often twisted by Sa'vard. I think we should let most of their remarks pass, answering only if one is genuinely interested in hearing what we have to say."

Jace's eyes narrowed. He was not sure what Alaric was getting at, but the man's words made him feel uneasy. "Are you saying we will be made fun of?"

"No," he said softly. "Not directly, but people will mock our heritage and Lord. That is a common practice."

"I don't think I like that at all," said Jace flexing his fists, ready to fight.

"Neither do I, Jace. None of us should, but we must pick and choose our battles. Sometimes people are looking to goad us into smearing the name of our Lord by plucking our nerves. The best thing to do is walk away and ask Yeshua to reveal Himself to them. Remember that we may be the only Keepers they will ever see."

Jace said nothing, but he disagreed with Alaric. After all he had been through, would he tolerate someone mocking his Savior? How could he let someone do this to his Lord and say nothing in return? That was a situation he would have to remedy he thought, rubbing his staff.

Alaric watched Jace across the fire. He noted how the young man touched his staff and pursed his lips. He would have to keep a close eye on him in the city. Jace showed subtle signs of a temper that could flare out of control, and that could have far-reaching repercussions not only for them, but for the reputation of all Keepers.

He switched to sharpening his sword. Although the weapons were not for show, they were not his first choice to solve a problem either. Lumphar once told him never to think with his sword, and those words had guided him through many a trying time. The high-strung little fellow had been placed in charge of production in Alaric's absence. Alaric hoped his nerves were holding up to the tense atmosphere in the labor yards. Lumphar was very smart and knew the projects would have a direct impact on the success of the Gap's defense, but still Alaric hoped that he would not lose his cool as the summer approached.

The long, hot summers usually found the March under some form of attack or probing measure. For some reason Sa'vard preferred to launch his campaigns in the heat. Sturbin perceived that next summer would find the Gap under pressure and ordered Alaric and Lumphar to speed up their efforts. There had been a debate about the actions they should take, and he had heard that the zealous Arthur had removed his support from Sturbin. He shook his head. Now, when people needed to pull together was when they found reason to separate. If they were not careful, the fragile unity that bound all people of the Gap would be lost, and there would be no one left to defend against Sa'vard or stay his advance into Emblom.

Of course he was worried. Alaric had left his wife and child under Sturbin's protection. The thought of being away and what could happen always loomed before him. His inventions and their crystallization into workable platforms had consumed much of his time, but his wife and child just could not be replaced.

What were they doing now, he wondered as he stared up at the sky. The clouds were parting, and he could see the stars clearly for the first time in more than a week. His lovely wife was probably just tucking their newborn in. Alaric pictured it in his mind—Nadine was rocking their toddler in her arms while humming some lullaby. He adored the way Melanin's head bobbed from side to side when she fell asleep. Nadine would kiss their child, gently settling her into bed and ask softly for Yeshua's blessing over her after she had gone to sleep.

The blessing of their baby was nothing but a miracle. They had always hoped for one and tried so many times over the years to have a child of their own but finally had given up. After that, they had simply enjoyed what the Almighty had blessed them with, careful to nurture their relationship and strengthen it as best they could. Life had been wonderful, and Melanin had been a joy and surprise that was beyond what they had hoped for.

Alaric and Nadine had struggled with their new family—he remained hard at work until nightfall, and she persevered in the new role of mother. Life was not perfect—no one's was—but they found it was the little things that made life fulfilling.

Now, here they were leagues apart, and he could only trust Yeshua to keep them safe. Alaric was not angry, he knew there was a purpose behind his calling to this journey, even though he must sacrifice his time with those he loved. It was the least he could do and it would never repay Yeshua's sacrifice to him, but he would be a fool to admit that he was at peace with being apart from Nadine and little Melanin. This was another test of his faith—would he trust the Lord to take care of those he loved, or would he constantly worry even though he truly could not protect his family against Sa'vard?

Unlike Arthur, he did not question the Council's decisions. There were always those who criticized leaders, and the Council's actions were always a source of gossip, unfortunately. As he saw it, the Almighty had called certain people to certain tasks. Since they were called by the Creator, it was obvious and apparent that their actions were blessed. There were always times when he did not agree with their decisions, but that was only his opinion. He was not in their position, nor had he been given their task, and so it seemed foolish to criticize those who had.

After Alaric had finished sharing with them about Nadir, Jace and Trel decided to curl up for the evening. They had rolled out their mats already and each said a silent word of thanks to the Creator before turning their backs to the fire. Trel's soft wheezes could be heard above the crackle of the flames, but Jace thumbed through the pages of the Song of the Ages for a while before sleep overtook him as well. His snores complimented Trel's buzzing chest and joined with the fire in a unique nighttime symphony.

A smile crossed Alaric's face. The two young men reminded him of himself at that age. Not much good came when the two combined forces, and he had waited until finally pulling them aside for his talk. They seemed like good enough lads. It was a comfort to know that East Haven still produced such good quality pupils. Still, Alaric knew that one reason he had been chosen was to keep the two in check and preserve the unity of the group.

How many times Alaric had ventured from the Gap, he could not say. The missions had always made him a bit excited. Sometimes he led and other times he came in support. He enjoyed seeing how the Almighty gathered people of such different backgrounds and used each of them in a special way each time. Even now he could see some of the ways the party's members had complemented each other.

With his sword finished, Alaric laid the weapons by his mat, wrapping them each in an oiled cloth. Tomorrow would prove interesting and he might as well get some sleep instead of thinking about all the scenarios that might occur. He pulled his blanket over his shoulders staring at the orange flames quietly dancing in the cool night air. The sound soothed him, and he spoke a quick word of thanks to the Maker for their safety and joy of serving Him. He gave into sleep, not minding the wet, squishy soil that he had become so accustomed to in their short adventure.

9

NADIR

The dull yellow sun greeted the Keepers that morning with a cold, crisp wind in the blue sky. More than one of them groaned, pulling their blankets tightly over their bodies in hopes of catching those final undisturbed moments of sleep. The fire had gone out during the night and smoldered while ashes blew about the campsite.

Jace blinked in the morning light, rolling at an odd angle to catch a view of the camp. The horses stood in a line, whipping their tails against the wind. One of them whinnied their impatience and hunger. He turned his head up and to the right, seeing Trel rummaging through the packs for breakfast. His friend's eyes searched the bags thoroughly. Despite his cough and sniffles, Trel was a morning person through and through, and nothing could change that.

With as much silence as he could muster, Trel was setting down the morning rations. He unstrapped some pots from his mount and started lowering them to the ground, but the horse sauntered to the side. Trel grabbed the pack with one hand and the pots with the other, but the whole mass gave way and scattered loudly about the ground. He gave an embarrassed grin as the other three looked up from the fire with cool glances, their sleep disturbed. Sullenly, Trel began placing the pots one inside the other, the metal rattling and banging.

With a vent of frustration, Jace threw back his covers stretched and rose to his feet. He walked over and helped Trel with a frown that complemented his messy hair. Trel nodded his thanks, knowing Jace abhorred mornings. Jace put on a good face, but would have slept till noon if the Mentors allowed it. Trel lowered his head to hide his smile.

The others were awake now. Alaric slowly nursed the fire to life while Lashara stared blankly at the sky, refusing to get up. She knew she could not lay there forever, but hated to start the day as well. Jace and Trel laughed softly, intentionally raising the noise of their work, but, with a look from Alaric, instantly lowered their volume. By the time they had finished, Lashara was up and about, leading the horses a little ways from the camp. Jace watched her holding his horse by its muzzle. The large creature dwarfed the little lady. She spoke softly to it and rubbed its fur gently with her tiny hands. Somehow her features did not seem so rigid and mean as the sun reflected off her skin and the wind played with her hair. She laughed quietly and kissed the horse on the nose. When she caught Jace staring, her features hardened, and she turned on her heel and walked away.

Jace felt annoyed. Did she have to be like that? How was he ever supposed to talk to her if she did not even allow him the time of day? There were other emotions bubbling through him as well and one in particular he had never felt before. It was a warm feeling that started at his toes and rose to the top of his head. The emotion always came on when he looked Lashara's way and grew as he watched. A lump would form in his throat and his mouth would get dry. If he looked long enough, his face would get red and his speech would start to fumble. He dismissed it. It was something he did not understand and did not have time to ponder.

Trel decided it was beans and bacon for breakfast. The four ate heartily, knowing that today would be a long day. Jace hoped they could cover lost ground, now that the rain had lifted. He even hoped they would be inside the city's gates before nightfall.

He chewed on the beans doing his best to picture the magnificent city he had heard so much of. Were there spires that stretched to the sky, topped by pennants that fluttered in the breeze? What must it feel like to brave the bustle of the crowds each day as one passed through the marketplaces of the city? How could people afford to live in a place, supported by only the weight of gold in their pockets? Would he see soldiers and knights, or perhaps even a noble or two? What did a palace look like, he wondered. He let his thoughts paint the picture, carrying him away while he ate.

The other three were busy discussing duties and things that would happen today, each warming their hands by the fire every now and then. They were all excited, except for Alaric, of course, who met the day like any other. He made a mental list of the things he hoped to accomplish and then set about to do them. Trel was buzzing with anticipation and began cleaning the pots as soon as the last morsel of bacon was lifted from the pan. Lashara hoped to begin, if only so she could trade the cold, damp surface of the ground for the hard, leather of the saddle. She could never stay too long on either and was looking forward to possibly trading both for the comfort of a bed before the sun set.

By the time the group broke camp, it had been light for a good while, but the sun was still below the trees. They rode eastward in their usual single file: Jace in the lead, Trel next, and then Lashara, with Alaric bringing up the rear. The weather had turned a blustery cold, the wind swinging the tall maples and pines about. Jace leaned into the wind, frowning grimly. He urged his horse forward, setting the pace slightly higher. If it was possible to see Nadir today, he did not want to pass up the opportunity.

The ground had drained well, but the highway was still a pool of mud. The horses' feet made sucking sounds as they trotted along the road. Time passed slowly and was marked by Trel's steady spells of coughing and wheezing. All the birds had flown south for the winter and nary a sound was made in the forest besides the wandering travelers.

Jace plucked a handful of leaves from a low-lying branch. Their colors had turned different shades of red, green, and yellow, and he played with them in the pale sunlight. He liked the change in seasons. There were some places, he was told, where the weather stayed the same year round. *What a bore it must be to live in such a place,* he thought.

Change was good, he always said, but he was not looking forward to the upcoming winter. Many of his folks loved the cold, saying that it was easier to get warm in the winter than to stay cool in summer, but he would never see it that way. He all but despised wintertime with its long nights, frigid days, and leafless forests. Everything seemed to die in that season, and it made him melancholy.

Then there was the cold. No matter how he bundled up, the chilly air always found its way through to his skin. It would blow down his shirt through the neck, or up his sleeves, even finding its way up into his leggings. The wind was unbearable. His layers of clothing never stopped the gusts, which always seemed to blow right through his body and take his breath away, leaving his face tight and frozen. No, he could certainly do without the winter.

He tossed away the leaves, upset that he would see less and less of them until spring. Soon they would be finished with the letter's commands. They were supposed to meet

Dorath in a tavern named The Two Swans. Jace could not wait to see the kindly Mentor again. Hadran shaped by force, constantly pushing Jace to do more than he thought possible, but Dorath taught by encouragement. Jace felt like Dorath was there with him while he learned a new truth or insight, whereas he always seemed in a state of perpetual catch-up with Hadran.

The lean Mentor was slightly shorter than Hadran, but stout with an ever-present smile upon his face. His eyes were a light green and graced a face that was still lively and young despite the man's years. Dorath usually wore light deerskin leggings and a soft woolen shirt. He made it a point to keep up a clean appearance, hoping his students would follow suit, but never shunned anyone who didn't. Pupils only hid from Dorath when they were ashamed of the wrongs they had done. In spite of their fears, he always admonished them with a gentle word and never in public. More than a few hailed Dorath as their favorite Mentor, and Trel was personally ecstatic to know that they were to meet up with him soon. That was all the letter said and all the orders Jace remembered. Somewhere within the enormous city they were to meet one person in some insignificant meeting place. Jace sighed. Once again he would have to trust another member of his team to lead, for these were strange lands to him. He read the letter again, seeing if he had missed some hidden meaning.

As the sun crept through the sky and they went westward, signs of civilization began to crop up. They passed a number of highway markers telling the distance to neighboring towns. Every now and then a cottage or inn popped up alongside the road, and Jace saw more than one pair of horses resting in its stables. They made good time, and by midafternoon, the trees began to thin out. Jace could see a good ways over the rolling farmlands and dotted patches of forest. A steady stream of merchants' wagons marked the highway's path through the countryside.

With each passing step, the party's excitement grew. Trel was anxious to spur his horse forward. Lashara began to think more and more of relaxing in a hot bath and cleaning out her tangled, unkempt hair. A thin smile crept across Jace's face. Part of him could not wait to see Nadir, some of him was interested in the next place Yeshua would take them and still more of him simply enjoyed the freedom of the open road.

Alaric, on the other hand, was edgy. He was more concerned with the reaction of the party to the multitude of differences in Nadir as opposed to the Gap. There were many things he had not told them and some he was sure he had forgotten. He hoped that their time in the city would be a growing experience and one of learning, but he was aware that there were a number of things that could or would offend the group. What would happen then?

They traveled on for another hour at a steady trot, passing a number of cottages and a handful of farmhouses. By now the ground had soaked up the rain and the well-traveled path had beaten the mud into submission. The wild vines that laced the fenced farmland lent a sweet smell to the group's progress.

Their chatter was broken up by a rumbling behind them. Jace turned back to see a group of horsemen coming over the last shallow hill along the road. At the forefront rode six knights, their highly polished steel catching the sun as they came. They rode with their lances high, their tips carrying the house colors for whom they rode. Their war horses thundered down the road, churning up great chunks of earth. Their breath heaved swirls of vapor in the cold. Behind them rode a man and lady, their dark silken clothes and heavy riding cloaks offset by the beautiful white stallion and mare they rode. Their saddles were laced with gold and the bells on their reins made sure those on the byway cleared a path for them.

The group stood aside while the cavalcade passed. Jace watched in awe while Trel was nearly euphoric with excitement. Alaric measured them with only a steady gaze, but Lashara eyed them smugly as they went by. The mounted knights and nobles rode on without a nod or salute of recognition and disappeared over the next hill.

One thing Lashara had never quite been able to get over was the animosity between commoner and king, vassal and lord. The two classes despised each other; the former needing the protection of the latter, while the latter depended on the labor of the former. If it weren't for this symbiotic relationship, the city and its surrounding lands would have dissolved into a bloody feud long ago. As it was, the two groups tolerated each other out of pure necessity, neither giving the other more than it was due.

Despite Lashara's feelings, Jace was caught up in the moment and he urged them on, galloping over the next hill. He reined in hard, looking down at the valley below him. There was Nadir, straddling the River Eisel which curved southeast to the horizon. The city covered most of the valley and ended at the surrounding hills which were dotted with farms and outlying houses. The grey stone walls clearly marked the great municipality, and the sun shone upon them as it neared its setting. In the middle of the city, off to the right along the river rose up what could only be the palace. A number of pennants fluttered from its towers, and its grand design was more thrilling than Jace had imagined. He stood, taking in the scene for a moment, not noticing those beside him.

Trel's breath was short and he wheezed loudly. To him, the city was like a dream and he felt as though the journey itself was worth it, even if he were to turn around now and head back to his schooling. He rubbed his hands, fighting off the chill of the day, not quite sure of what was next.

"The city's gates close at sundown."

Jace turned to see that it was Lashara who spoke. He stared at her, not knowing what to say and afraid that she might take any sign for an excuse to lay into him.

"Well, are we going to stay here till Yeshua comes?"

Jace was about to let her lead when the young lady spun her horse around shaking her head, kicked the beast into a cantor and descended into the valley. He grimaced and nudged his horse after her.

There was a long line of wagons and carts that stood outside the city, waiting to be inspected before they could enter in. Nadir regulated their commerce tediously, taxing the merchants heavily and searching meticulously for contraband. Inside the gate, hawkers and merchants stood by their booths, catching the last business of the day. The streets were overflowing with people, and their shouts and yelling spilled over the walls in the early evening hour. The city guards eyed the four travelers with suspicion. One unshaven soldier licked his lips while gaping openly at Lashara. The look made Jace's blood boil for some reason, but Lashara merely smiled in return.

The guard approached her, his heavy eyes unashamedly taking in Lashara's entire body.

"How many?" he asked slowly, preferring to address her rather than look over the group himself.

"Only four, sir. We've had a long day's ride and wish to patronize the fabled city of the North."

The guard laughed shortly, eyeing the woman lustfully.

"Everyone says such things. We have too many commoners and not enough merchants. Perhaps there is something you care to give that could persuade me otherwise," the man said, his arm slowly reaching towards Lashara's thigh.

Before the man could go further, Lashara gracefully dropped a few coins into the palm of his hand and he looked up, stunned. Blinking at the coins, he showed his teeth in a yellow grin and motioned the four through the gates.

Jace followed behind Lashara red-faced, but as soon as they passed beyond earshot, he blocked his horse in front of her.

"What are you doing?" he sputtered furiously, "Did you see the way he looked at you? You were in danger and he could have accosted you!"

Lashara's jaw dropped and her cheeks flushed a rosy red while she stared into Jace's confused eyes. She then gave him a steely gaze and waved him off.

"It's a common practice for the gatehouse guards to get more than they deserve and want far more than they can have."

"But you bribed him and he wanted to, he wanted to..." Jace's voice trailed off as his face turned even redder.

Lashara fixed him with a stare to melt iron.

"What he asked for he would never have gotten," she said, and wheeled away.

"Where are you going?" he yelled in consternation.

"To The Two Swans, of course," she replied over her shoulder. "Care to follow or do you want to argue for another hour? Some inns close rather early here, and I'm sure they are no exception."

Jace looked at Trel and Alaric. Trel shook his head and rolled his eyes. Jace let out a long breath and the three followed her, negotiating the noisy crowds. Even in the waning early evening, the streets were packed to the limit. People stood in the way, oblivious to the heavy traffic of horses, wagons, carts, animals, knights, and nobles. Jace caught a glimpse of a lady, reclining on her lift, barking orders to her servants to push her through the market. The servant's faces were grave, and they bullied their way through, kicking those less fortunate to be caught in their path. A fight almost ensued and suddenly militia and mounted soldiers were around the noble, prodding the mass back with their spears and short swords. People grudgingly gave way, many plainly showing their hatred of the social elite upon their faces.

Trel and Jace took note of the incident, deciding to go around the volatile place. Both shook their heads in sadness, seeing the disparity that existed, but did not get involved in the ordeal. *Such hatred and inequality would never had happened in the Gap*, Trel thought to himself.

Among the crowds were richly colored merchants that stood out from the lower classes. At first, their bright clothing mesmerized Jace. Their finely woven outfits consisted of deep indigo doublets, brocaded dresses of royal purple, and double-stitched tunics that were mostly cream in color. The merchants' garments looked highly personalized, although Jace could not make out one rich man from another.

As he watched them, he noticed a distinct group of individuals that stood out from the rest. They were diminutive in height and walked around the crowds instead of through them. They kept their noses high and rarely looked at the scenery around them. They seemed unaware of others and did not offer so much as a word to those they passed. The peculiar merchants were always dressed in drab colors, and though they bore themselves with the utmost importance, their garments were not flashy by any means.

Their facial features were quite unlike the Nadirians whose soft, pale skin and rounded faces looked like they were all related. These quiet men and women had angular faces and bronze skin. Their hooked noses and dark eyes and hair stood out from the lighter features of the people they passed. The distinctly different people acted aloof from the rest of the Nadirians and kept to themselves. They were obviously not from these parts.

Jace remembered Alaric saying something about these people. They were the Oncan'lar, the wandering pariah that had once populated the Land of Eben. Alaric had said they were Elohim's chosen people. They had followed Him, but when Yeshua had walked among them, they had rejected him outright. They did not believe that He was the chosen one, called to restore their people. Now the Oncan'lar walked the earth as outcasts. All lands despised them and their strange customs.

They were, however, exceedingly good at the businesses they had established, and the authorities regarded them as prized sources of income. Nadirians, as well as other cities, viewed them with thinly veiled contempt. They were seen as the leeches of society—people who did not have a home of their own, who had no loyalty except to themselves. The townspeople tolerated their odd habits only for the sake of their business. Alaric also had told him that the Song of the Ages said they would be cleaved to Yeshua in the end times, but that remained to be seen.

All the crowds seemed caught up in their own personal affairs, and Jace had to skirt several areas where there just wasn't room for him and his steed. Eventually he lost sight of Lashara and had to go down back alleys to catch up to her. High walls kept the narrow places dark and musty. The horses' hooves clicked loudly on the cobblestone pavement in the eerie light as night settled. They moved along, wary of what was hidden in the shadows. Putrid steam hung in the air, wafting slowly from open heaps of refuse. Unlike East Haven, Nadir had no sewage. Apparently society here had not found a constructive way to treat their waste. Lingering odors of various natures mingled with the sweet, sickly smell of the large trash piles. Trel could not stop his hacking and wheezing that was encouraged by the strange scents that bothered him.

Jace wrinkled his nose in the fading light. He could see forms moving about the garbage. It dawned on him that they were people, huddled and bent over the trash, sifting through its contents for something to eat, wear, or use. The people were dressed in little more than rags, and their faces had dark smudges crisscrossing them. A number of children clung close to their mothers and fathers; the older ones helped their parents examine the smelly, heaping waste.

"These are the homeless and destitute that live in the shadows," said Alaric quietly as they picked their way through the dark. "The city fails to acknowledge them, and even the lowest commoner would not lift a finger to help one."

"Can't they go anywhere?" asked Trel in a whisper. "Surely there are other places where they could live better lives."

"They know no other life," said Alaric sorrowfully. "Many have lived here for generations, subsisting off what others throw away. People tolerate them as long as they keep to the back streets."

"How can Yeshua change this?" asked Jace incredulously, keeping his voice low.

"This is not His fault. The Maker loves even these. Sadly, this is a product of man's folly. Things were not like this before the Fall of Man when all creation dwelt in harmony. Then there was no poor or needy. So shall it be again on the day of Yeshua's return when all is made new."

Jace and Trel nodded. Their hearts went out to those before them, but realizing they could do nothing about it at the present, they moved on silently. Each said a short word to the Almighty to protect and bless those they saw. They promised not to forget them, like so many had already, and should the situation present itself, they were determined to lend them a warm, helping hand.

They passed through a number of alleys and finally spilled out into a wide square teeming with people. Torches were starting to be lit and the light bounced off the crowds. People's faces flickered in the glow of the lamps. They cast long shadows back down the alley from whence Jace and his friends had come.

At the forefront of the square was a large, raised platform on which stood a man, dressed in fine merchant's clothes, his deep blue robes swaying while his hands moved sporadically. People were huddled in tight around the platform, many shouting with their hands raised. Some held slips of paper, others raised coins of silver and gold which gleamed in the torchlight. Another man stood behind a podium with a short hammer and pointed at members of the crowd, banging the gavel every so often on the wood in front of him.

Jace scanned the crowd. His eyes caught a movement of white far on the other side of the square. Lashara stood in the shadows, mounted on her white mare. Jace could see that her attention was focused on the action around the platform. She did not look pleased and was plucking her cloak with one hand while she held her saddle with the other. Her knuckles were white, her jaw was clenched, and her eyes were fixed in a thin, dangerous squint that Jace had never seen before. Along with Trel and Alaric, he made his way over to her. Jace wondered what had caused her anger while he approached. As they pulled up alongside her, Trel tapped his shoulder, anxiously pointing at the merchant and the platform.

There, behind the wealthy man was a row of men and women. Their clothes were filthy and they were bound together by the shackles ringing their necks. The chains passed from one of them to the next. They stood feeble and dejected, many staring blankly ahead, making no sign at the taunts of the crowd. The mob's yelling turned to jeers as one of the prisoners was unchained and brought forward by a thick-muscled man. He carried a whip and flayed it across the dirty man's back as he stumbled forward. Stifling a cry, the man fell to his knees and was heaved to his feet by his master. He was kicked in the back and straightened upward, wincing in pain.

"Slaves," said Lashara darkly, her features going livid.

Jace gave a troubled look. He had never heard the word before, but was highly perplexed by what he had seen. Lashara explained it to him shortly, never taking her eyes off the man being paraded before the crowd.

"The merchant travels through many lands trading people for money. By the looks of his clothes, he's rather good at it."

"Who would be willing enough to sell themselves?" Jace wondered aloud.

"No one," said Lashara flatly. "The men and women are found out in the open, alone. They are taken far away and sold in different places where no one will recognize them. That way slave traders can argue legitimacy since authorities can't prove it was kidnapping. They brand the people they've taken on the left shoulder with their personal seal. Once done, the person is considered no more than property. I've heard that the more zealous businessmen have taken whole houses in the middle of the night, the family waking up with chains around their necks."

"What happens to them?"

Lashara shrugged. "Usually they are bought and sold individually. Slaves are very expensive, and families rarely are bought as a whole. Since traders go to great lengths to get slaves, they charge a hefty price, but if they are caught, they pay with their lives. No matter how bad the morals of Emblom are, they do not tolerate kidnapping."

"Why don't the slaves just run away."

Lashara looked him up and down. Her eyes were mixed with surprise and hatred. "Do you know what a merchant does to a runaway slave he catches? Of course not. Let me just say that the punishment keeps any from thinking of freedom. Harboring slaves or helping them escape is also forbidden. A slavetrader has certain rights, after all, and can bring those he thinks are guilty of such acts to the local magistrate. Since most authorities side with the merchant to begin with, the outcome is usually in their favor. No one ever attempts such acts though."

"Why?"

"The punishment is death," she said flatly.

Jace gasped, but went on with his questions, "If countries know that traders steal citizens in the first place, why don't they outlaw slavery as a whole?"

"Profit! Besides the fact that branding makes the person a permanent slave, slave guilds also are the strongest forces in the city and have many supporters. Some places tried to do away with them, but the guilds were too deeply rooted then. The city and guild eventually came to a compromise: slavery is highly taxed and so the cities profit from the trade as well. People don't seem to notice the wrongs around them when their purses are a little fatter." Her eyes were ringed with sadness, hurt, and anger as she finished.

"To the man with the green smock!" roared the merchant behind the podium, pounding his hammer. The crowd cheered as the dirty man was led off stage to be handed over to his new owner.

The companions' hearts sank at what happened next. A family of four was the final offering of the day. They were led forward to the edge of the platform and the crowd jeered in fury, its hunger renewed. The mother was weeping openly. Her tiny son clung to her ragged dress and she held her baby girl close to her chest. The father was led forward, futilely struggling against two of the merchant's men. His voice gave hoarse protests, and the crowd drowned him out, urged on by the display of rebellion.

"An extraordinary chance, my friends!" yelled the merchant. "Where will you find such fine specimens to work in your fields, your stables, your houses?"

"Look at their flesh, the man is as strong as an ox, is he not?" The merchant stood for a moment, letting the husband's voice fill the air with pleading until one of his captors knocked him unconscious with a blow to the head. The crowd laughed raucously, some clapping their approval.

"The mother has a stiff back and even the lad and baby show promise. Surely they are worthy of a decent price. What shall we start at? Do I hear any for three gold pieces?"

The crowd's voice grew to a hush. Many waved their arms angrily, the price too steep for them. Only the higher nobles could afford the family, but there were a number of them in the crowd and soon the bidding was in a frenzy. The commoners oohed and aahed as the fee for the slaves rose higher and yet higher.

Jace's mind worked furiously. *There must be something I can do*, he thought, and he looked around in agitation. He turned to Alaric, pointing at him.

"How much is in the money bag?" he questioned.

"Twelve, maybe fifteen pounds," said Alaric, not catching on.

"All gold?"

"Yes," he said and then he gave a look of shock. "Jace, think a moment—"

"Give it to me," Jace commanded.

Alaric started to argue, but Jace was urgent now; the price was going higher, but the bids were becoming more and more infrequent.

"Give it to me!" He nearly shouted to Alaric. Stunned, Alaric reached into his saddle bag, throwing the heavy gold to Jace.

Jace nearly fell off his horse, knocked off balance from the weight of the money. He quickly judged how much he held and nudged his horse forward, into the torchlight. He raised the bag high over his head with both hands and opened his voice into a bellow.

"Fifteen pounds of gold!"

The crowd's buzzing soon died away to absolute silence. Many turned their heads, some giving a low whistle. The hushed nobles stared at Jace in annoyance, knowing their chance to purchase the prized family was dashed. The merchant stood, his mouth hanging open for a moment and then he recovered. With no more bids to be heard, the other merchant slammed his gavel down.

"Fifteen pounds, gold!" he yelled, and the crowd erupted with cheers of glee. Jace moved his mount forward, the mass respectfully giving way, some even bowing low. Alaric, Trel, and Lashara followed slowly in a single file. The group was led around the platform to claim their prize.

He knew he could not save them all, but Jace was comforted knowing that he had changed the lives of a few for the better. This must have been the reason Yeshua had given them the gold. He had no idea what he would do with them, but they would be better off, no matter where they were. Jace slid down from the beast, carrying the gold while some people tapped their congratulations on his shoulders. He edged forward to the merchant who eyed the bag hungrily.

Alaric was trying to tell him something, but Jace was busy signing papers while the merchant weighed the gold. He looked up as the slaves he bought were ushered before him. The husband and wife bowed their thanks to Jace with kindhearted smiles and tears in their eyes for their family was still intact. He could feel Alaric once again tapping his shoulder while he started to speak to them, but he was interrupted by the angry merchant.

"What is this!" said the man, baring his teeth in hatred. He was standing over the open bag looking Jace in the eyes with a twisted frown. He flung some of the coins at Jace, showering him about the head and shoulders. Some rattled off his skull and Jace turned and stared down at the ugly little man.

"What mockery is this?" He challenged, cutting his eyes at the man. The man shoved the money under his nose.

"Gap coins!" He spat, pointing at the raised seal squarely planted in the middle of them. "We don't take these here, and we don't do business with Gappers," he said throwing the coins on the ground.

Jace leaned forward and planted his hands on the merchant's table. The man had turned his back to him, talking to the merchant behind him. When the man turned to face him, Jace caught a glimpse of the person behind the merchant. He was dressed in black and his cloak covered his face. Jace could see no features beneath the hood, but knew instantly that the creature was staring directly at him. He froze and time seemed to stand still while the two held each other's gaze. He could feel the creature's will probing his soul, looking for some weakness to open and spread out through into his mind. The feeling sent chills up his spine as Jace realized he was only paces away from a Watcher; a servant of Sa'vard, in Nadir.

His hand reached beneath his cloak and rested upon the Song of the Ages which was warm and almost pulsed within his grasp. The icy feeling was there for a moment longer until Jace's senses cleared. The warm book seemed to flood his mind with verse after verse from the Song, focusing his thoughts on Yeshua and the Almighty, slamming the door on the Watcher's probing.

He turned to the merchant whose voice rose higher now, causing some of the crowd to turn his way. The Watcher stood over the tradesman, whispering softly into his ear. The man's temper grew as he spoke and a large number of the crowd pushed in around him, their faces twisted as they eyed the four Keepers. Jace spoke above the growing murmur, not noticing Alaric steadily tapping on his shoulders now.

"My money is as good as any. Take it and melt it down, if you wish, but these people are mine," he said with a tone of finality.

The merchant stood now, flanked by four of his henchmen. Jace looked around, realizing the man meant to keep the gold and the slaves. He sneered at him, realizing he had been cheated and lunged across the table in fury at the merchant. His fist hit him in the chin awkwardly, and Jace doubled him over with another blow to the stomach. The two collapsed on the ground and the henchmen swarmed over them, grabbing and kicking at Jace.

He realized that he was trapped and now fought to escape the four thugs on top of him while they clutched at his clothes. He could hear the shouts from the crowd around him, but could not see what was happening. Suddenly, Alaric was there, his large frame tossing the henchmen aside like they were dry leaves instead of grown men. He yanked Jace by the collar and dragged him away. Lashara and Trel were mounted, their horses blocking the mob from attacking Jace. Trel was kicking men in the shoulders who came too close, his short sword in one hand. Their bodies spun around and were flung back into the mass of people. Lashara had produced a thin dagger from some hidden fold in her clothes and was waving the blade in the air menacingly. Alaric flung himself on his horse, clutching Jace who let out a painful cry as the thugs pushed the slave family away.

The mob was coming over the side of the platform, now, while others pushed toward Lashara and Trel, causing the stage to buckle. Alaric gave a whistle and Lashara and Trel abandoned their efforts as the crowd rolled forward. The Watcher stood unmoving behind them. The three galloped headlong behind the platform bursting through wagons and sending goods flying. Jace hung close to the ground, still manhandled by Alaric's grip while they plunged through the streets. He could see Trel, a wild look in his eyes as he held the reins of Jace's trailing horse. Lashara rode, a look of angry determination on her face, her hair bouncing about her shoulders. The streets had thinned out and the party soon outdistanced the mob. They made a dozen turns, however, before coming to a safe halt. Alaric released Jace and the three climbed down, puffing from excitement. Jace turned on Alaric.

"You should have protected me instead of fleeing like a child!" he said heatedly. He towered significantly over the shorter man, his accusations flying, "That family was counting on us to rescue them and bring them to the Gap. Why else would Yeshua have given us the gold we never spent? Now both are gone because YOU decided to take charge of a situation that could have brought glory to Him and rescued four others!"

"You bumbling idiot!" Lashara snapped, coming up beside Alaric in his defense. "If it weren't for him, you would still be squashed by those guards, and we would all be thrown in the city dungeon. You owe Alaric your life!"

"I apologize for usurping your position, Jace," said Alaric humbly. "From my eyes, the environment was unraveling rather quickly and we had little time to make a decision before we were overwhelmed by force. Where would we have been then?"

"You overstep your bounds, Alaric. You also, Lashara. Didn't you hear Sturbin or are your ears already losing their sense?" Jace retorted. Alaric winced under Jace's stabbing remarks, but he held his ground, his face showing no emotions. He only looked into Jace's eyes.

"Did you see it?" the man said in a level tone, his voice laced with discipline and fear.

Jace breathed in, ready to launch another tirade, but stopped. Alaric was right. He could understand that now. He nodded slowly. The Watcher had hung back from the confusion and anarchy that it had caused, preferring to orchestrate the events from a safe distance, but there was no denying the creature had been there.

Jace shook noticeably, recalling the faceless stare the creature had given him while searching his thoughts to plant seeds of doubt and trouble. Yeshua and Sturbin had both said he would see strange things once he left the Gap and he had been taken off guard. It was only by the Almighty's divine plan that his hand had gone to the battered copy of the Song of the Ages he carried. The action had guarded his mind against the creature's attack, turning his thoughts to his Master and erasing his doubts and fears.

Instead of calmly leaving the scene, he had lashed out, causing his anger to fuel the creature's plan. If it weren't for Alaric's quick actions and steady thinking, the situation would have deteriorated further and landed them only Yeshua knows where. He bowed his head, his shoulders slumping.

"They were so innocent and meek," he said distantly. "I thought if only we could save one from the crowd, things would be different. The merchants who had taken those people…the awful things they must have gone through. I can still see the looks in their eyes."

He looked up at Alaric, spreading his hands, "I was only trying to help them. Now everything is gone."

Alaric touched his shoulders reassuringly, "Your intentions were pure, Jace. That is what matters. That is what Yeshua sees."

Jace looked at the party. Alaric stood, watching him. Lashara stuck out her lower lip, her dissatisfaction clearly evident. Trel was wild-eyed with fear, taken aback by the awful surprise.

"This is all my fault," said Jace, "I apologize to each of you for putting myself in harm's way, not remembering that in doing so, I did the same to you."

Alaric nodded his forgiveness. Trel only stood, breathing heavily, his congestion causing a high whistle to come from deep within his chest. He blinked at Jace, recognizing the words he spoke, but was still fighting back the fears of the ordeal they had gone through.

Lashara glared at him. Jace had a habit of opening his mouth before he thought, and his accusations stung her still. She stared him down with her cruelest look and thumbed the dagger hidden beneath her cloak. She would think a while before offering her forgiveness. She turned away and mounted her horse with a sniff.

"The sun is nearly set. I suggest we make our way to The Two Swans," she said coolly.

"Where is that?" Jace asked awkwardly.

Lashara pointed down the street without a word. The party climbed onto their steeds and followed her down the now deserted lane. Though the streets were mostly vacant, the city was still very much awake. Noisy crowds spilled out of taverns and well-lit shops revealed people finishing up their labor for the day. A troop of mounted soldiers were clearing up the remaining people on the streets, enforcing the curfew that existed within the walled city. Lashara greeted them warmly and they let the party pass—more than one soldier eyeing the maiden.

Jace felt dejected. Even though they had survived the day, they had no gold to exchange for meals and lodging. He could only blame himself for the day's mishaps and resigned himself to eating whatever they could find. Hopefully the innkeeper would let them rest for the night in the sitting room.

They came to the front of The Two Swans and the four of them stared at the building. Its design was grand, taking up a fair portion of the side of the street before it turned around the corner. The architecture was unlike the practical buildings of the Gap. The dark maple framing was carved with a great many weaves and waves that curled around the windows and doors. The gold and blue accents around each of these gave the place a welcome feeling that was complimented from the flags that hung from the three floors above the parlor. The main entrance was open and a steady drone of conversation came out of the commonplace.

Alaric turned his head at the sign, inspecting it closely. He squinted at the two birds, frowning and thought. Suddenly, his eyes widened and he gave a start.

"Wait here," he said, slipping down from the saddle.

The three waited uneasily, each knowing that they could only barter with the gear they had for whatever they could get. Jace looked at his two companions who were lost in their own thoughts. Moments passed and their beasts pranced impatiently.

"I wonder what he's doing," he thought out loud.

"Hush," Lashara said curtly. She looked him up and down and then turned away.

Jace let out a huff. No matter how he tried to talk to her, she cut him off. He could almost feel the tension building over the days and his mistakes seem to compound the animosity that existed between the two of them. If he was to be a gentleman, he would have to begin with her forgiveness. He gathered his courage, gave a quiet cough and began.

"Well, this is the end of our escapade, it seems. I don't know what's in store for us now...." he let his voice trail off, hoping for a response, but neither one of them answered. He raised his voice higher, talking wistfully, "I have never been in a city, as you have probably guessed. I'm a little scared, but it looks like the Master has led us through safely—"

"Will you please shut up!" Lashara said over her shoulder.

Jace dropped his mouth and looked over at Trel who motioned for him to let it pass. Jace clenched his jaw and knitted his eyebrows. Fine, if Lashara wanted to keep to herself, let her, he was growing tired of making her feel comfortable, anyhow. He turned his horse around, purposefully edging Trel between him and his new adversary. He didn't know why Yeshua or the Council had seen fit for Lashara to join them. Maybe it was someone's sick humor or maybe the Council just did not know what they were doing.

Jace resorted to talking to his friend. The two eyed the sign carefully. It was suspended from a bronze hanger out over the entrance. The painting showed two swans facing each other. Their wings were extended and their necks were intertwined. With their beaks they grasped an olive branch together in the universal sign of hospitality. What was it that made Alaric jump, they wondered. While they stared, Alaric exited the building, his face showing the slightest bit of relief.

"We can bring our horses around back. Let the stable hands wash them down and tell them to feed them proper rations. They've been underfed for the last few days and deserve a reward," he said, tossing them each a wooden marker. "These are vouchers and good for whatever is served tonight and your rooms as well."

He turned to Lashara. "We will sleep in the same room tonight, but the housemaster has prepared a separate room for you, if you wish. He has ordered a hot bath which should be ready after your meal. He also extends his greetings, my lady."

Lashara gave a look of astonishment which quickly vanished. She dismounted and led the horses around back with a newfound bounce in her step. It was Jace's turn to sniff in agitation. He and Trel watched her leave and then turned to Alaric with their questions. The man simply bid them follow as he walked up the inn's steps.

They entered the main hall and were instantly hit with the smell of fine food which set their mouths watering. This was mixed with sweat and smoke that always seemed to accompany such places. The room was filled to capacity, and they had to squeeze through people and around tables as Alaric led them into the room. Guests seemed to be friendly, compared to the mob they had encountered, and most did not turn when Jace and Trel pushed through. The ones that did only gave a quick look at Alaric's large frame and then went back to their business.

The large man led them to a booth tucked out of the way in an obscure corner of the room. The table was stained with many years of use and the benches' high backs gave the place added privacy. At the table sat Dorath, his tanned breeches and finely pressed shirt standing out sharply against the darker clothes of the inn's rabble. His cloak was draped on the corner of the booth, as was his polished sword which hung from a simple leather baldric. He hugged his two pupils and shook Alaric's hand warmly, motioning for the Keepers to sit. He watched them with his warm smile as they crammed into the small space.

Trel's fear melted away and only the closeness of his surroundings kept him from jumping up and down in excitement. They huddled into the booth and there were smiles all around the table.

"I'm glad to see you are all safely here," the Mentor said, his clear voice cutting through the din of the room.

A serving girl arrived and set down a battered pitcher and mugs. They all showed their tokens and she nodded politely, vanishing into the crowd. Jace began to ask a question, but Dorath motioned for him to wait until the meal had ended. Moments later the lady came back setting down a plate in front of each of them. It was heaped high with cuts of meat and potatoes swimming in thick brown gravy. A mound of stewed carrots and greens rose up from the other side. Steam rose off the dishes into their travel worn faces, and Trel and Jace gripped their forks with anticipation while Dorath blessed the food. The two dove into their dishes, only tasting the food after it was down their throats. Somewhere in the backs of their minds they remembered that they had not eaten since the morning, and the happenings of the day had worked up their already ravished appetites.

Dorath and Alaric ate slowly, watching the young men devour their food. They finished their plates well before their elders and waited, half-embarrassed when the serving girl asked if they wished for seconds. The two watched Dorath who gave a slight nod and the dishes were removed from the table. They were replaced shortly by more of the steaming goodness.

Jace and Trel leaned back after their third plate, their hunger getting the best of them. They decided it was best to fill their stomachs, each wondering how they would pay for the food with no coins to their name. Only Dorath's welcome smile and Alaric's indifference told them everything would turn out fine. When the two men had finished, they moved their plates out of the way, each mopping their mouths in turn and then throwing the napkins on the dishes. The woman came once again and before they knew it, the table was cleared, save for the pitcher and mugs.

"It would seem there has been some distress in your travels," said Dorath, kindly offering the question to Jace. He nodded shortly and told his Mentor their mishaps, the dangerous encounter with the Watcher, his responsibility of losing the money placed within his keeping and the slaves that he could not free. The soft-hearted Mentor nodded understandingly.

"Greater men have faired far worse, Jace. Remember that you will never save yourself from a Watcher, but keep your heart on Yeshua and the promises of the Creator and they will flee from your presence like the night before the dawn," he pursed his lips and went on, "Even so, you should not stay here long. The Son of the Wicked knows you are here now and will set his forces to delay your progress. Too many times Keepers are caught up in confrontation with his forces and forget the priority of their objectives. I hope you will learn from their mistakes instead of making the same."

"As Alaric said, you have done well considering all. I wanted to commend you: you've come a long ways since your early years of at East Haven. It seems you can do more than ride a horse, which some of us never expected in the first place," he said, casting a smile at Trel.

Jace smiled also. Dorath's light-hearted remarks always took the sting out of any chastisement and reassured his efforts. He felt his burden lift slightly. The money would never be replaced and he had learned from the event, as well as the tough travel from the Gap. They had arrived safely and now, somehow were sitting here in the fellowship of their Mentor. They talked for a while, each enjoying the company that only comes after a task is accomplished. Trel and Jace grew easier as the night went on. Even Alaric gave a laugh now and then, and they sat for a good while exchanging information and telling everything they had learned during their adventure.

After a while, the talk dwindled. Dorath loosened his shirt and drew himself up, marking the turn in conversation to serious issues. The table grew quiet and their attention focused on him.

"You have marked the end of your first journey, Jace. The Council will hear of this with much happiness. Hadran and I had no doubt that you would accomplish such, and I am glad to see that you took advantage of those in your party and readily offered apologies when you were in the wrong. Our Lord has blessed and protected you, and I am sure that your faith has grown because of this."

He stopped momentarily and produced a sealed letter which bore the Gap's insignia of the book and the sword. The document was weighty as he dropped it in Jace's hands. "Of course, this is only the beginning of your task, my friend. The Council thought it best to send you here before you were told the full extent of your journey."

Jace leaned back, troubled. Dorath was never uncomfortable speaking, but now he wrung his hands, stopping several times before he went on. "We all love you, Jace. Hadran and I have looked after you as your father said. We did not agree with the Council's decision to send you here, but part of being a Keeper is respecting the unity of the whole. In doing that, we did our individual tasks, though we each despised doing them."

He took a breath, leaning forward and put his hand on Jace, looking him in the eye, "This is about Rae. He's been missing since we last sent you out. We only know that he was somewhere in the Clonesian Empire."

Jace's heart sank. He had known something was amiss. He should have seen it coming from the moment Hadran said his uneasy good-byes. He looked at Dorath, not knowing what to say.

His only brother was very dear to him. Rae had raised him when his father was gone in his childhood, always certain to keep him safe from harm. They had each looked out for one another while growing up, vowing to come to the other's aid no matter the cost.

Now he was gone. Too many questions flooded his mind, and suddenly it didn't seem so important where he would sleep tonight. He only looked at Dorath, a lump catching his voice in his throat. Dorath shook his head, encouragingly.

"We don't know what happened, Jace, it's that simple. He could been side-tracked. There is no sign or evidence that he was apprehended, and I do not believe he was bested. Hadran and I raised him also and we don't produce cowards," he said, his voice going hard. "There are more questions now than answers. For all we know, he could have simply forgotten to return," but Jace knew that was a lie.

He caught his breath, imagining the worst possible. He could see his brother, alone in the midst of some rabble of a city, hurt and tired. He hoped it wasn't so as he fought off the fears. Doing his best to remain calm, he looked at Dorath.

"What does the Council say?" he asked levelly.

Dorath exhaled, his sigh heard even above the noisy chatter of the hall. "They asked for you."

He nodded slowly; it was what he expected. Their journey seemed to have little purpose until now. "What must I do?"

Dorath opened his hands, "Do what you can. You must travel to the Clonesian Empire and find your brother. If he is alive—and I know he is—tell him the Council needs him back at East Haven immediately."

Jace almost lost his breath at the impossible task, but Dorath waved him off, pointing at the letter in Jace's hands. "These are the final correspondences we have had with Rae. Perhaps they contain some clue to his whereabouts. There is also a detailed map that our scouts have compiled of the land between here and the Great River. It should help speed your advance. We have also provided you with a cart loaded with supplies and enough coin to purchase any lodgings or fares that you encounter—not to worry, it's Nadirian gold, good throughout the world," he said with a wink when Jace voiced his objections.

Jace caught the wry smile beneath Dorath's thin beard. So the gold had been a test. He nodded, finally understanding. He could never have bought the slaves and the Council knew it. It was, however, a test to see how he would use the money allotted him. He was somewhat comforted knowing he had used it in hopes of freeing people, despite the devastating results. Perhaps his actions had far-reaching effects he would never know about.

"There is one more instrument we have to aid you," Dorath said, motioning at the darkened corner of the booth. A creature leaned out of the shadows, its black cloak covering its head. Jace and Trel clutched each other's arms for a moment before the man pulled his hood back to reveal a greasy face. His skin was olive complexion in the dim light and a thin beard outlined his dirty face. Black hair was cut close against the man's scalp. The strands were so gangly they looked pasted flat against his head. He wore nothing but black clothes, his dark, heavy wool the same shade of his rider's cloak. About his neck was a simple clasp, but Jace's keen eyes noted it was not the symbol of the Gap. The man grimaced at Jace and shoved a pipe in his mouth, lighting it without asking. He turned and spat against the adjacent wall, eyeing the four of them with an ugly glare. Dorath introduced the man.

"This is Blynn and he hails from the Clonesian Empire. Don't let his appearance fool you, he grew up in the Gap and has undergone the rigors of East Haven. He prefers to dress lazily, shall we say, which is a custom of some in the Empire, and I have been unable to break him of it. He serves as a guide to our Keepers, assisting them among the Clonesians. Although he no longer serves on missions, he hails Yeshua as Lord and I personally vouch for him." Blynn grunted and eyed the Keepers, fixing his gaze on Alaric who returned it unflinchingly.

"Blynn was the last to see Rae, and we're hoping that once you cross the Great River, he can pick up your brother's trail easily."

Jace looked at Blynn and smiled. Dorath was an excellent judge of character. Anyone he vouched for was certainly a friend of his. Blynn nodded curtly, turning to focus his attention on his pipe.

The five of them sat for a while in uncomfortable silence, the dangers of the coming journey looming over their heads. Dorath took the pitcher and poured a drink into the mugs. The liquid was dark and foamed over the short cups. He handed one to each of them and sipped the liquid gingerly.

Jace gulped the drink and spit it out his mouth the next instant. The liquid had an awful taste and stung his throat. He wiped his mouth and looked at the bottom of his mug. Dorath set his drink down and cleaned up the wet table.

"So, you have never tasted ale?" he asked Jace who shook his head in return. "The city dumps its refuse in the Eisel, poisoning its own water. Were you to drink it, you would come down with a nasty fever, if you lived long enough."

The Mentor lifted his cup, "This is the only way they can drink it safely, he said, taking another sip. "It tastes wretched, but it keeps one from parching the throat. I took the opportunity to fill your water bags, but good water is not offered in the city and the housemaster would wring my neck if he knew that I had a supply so close to his hands."

"Don't drink too much of it, mind you," said Alaric. "It will set your head to spinning if you've never had it before. Remember we are not to be drunk on wine, but to be filled with the Spirit."

"Well spoken, Alaric," Dorath said, "But the Song also says we are to have a little wine with our food. If the lads can stomach it and it does not offend you, let them drink for a spell. There is no other beverage in this place, and you will have to conserve your waterskins for the journey ahead."

Alaric nodded reluctantly and Jace sipped the drink once more. He forced the liquid down his throat, trying not to think about it and soon got enough to satisfy his thirst. Pushing the cup away from him, he sat while Blynn, Dorath, and Alaric drank another mug slowly. The five of them talked as the night passed.

Lashara had not finished her bathing, or at least he had not seen her. He was quite glad with that, but soon found the need to turn in as well. He and Trel rose to leave and Dorath called after them.

"You are welcome to stay at the inn for a day before you set out, but remember the Watcher and start as soon as you are rested. The owner is a brother of sorts," he said with a grin, "and always provides wonderful hospitality. Keep your wits about you, rely on those who are with you, and remember the Counselor has gone out ahead of you to prepare your way. We will be with you in spirit, and Jace," he said, waiting for him to turn around, "Mend your relationship with Lashara soon; the Lord will use her in ways you will never imagine."

Jace blushed at the admonition and bowed to his Mentor. Trel followed him through the hall, and they wearily made their way up the stairs. A servant showed them to their room and they thanked him as they closed the door. Each fell into bed, not caring to remove their garments. They lay awake only long enough to realize that Lashara was still bathing in the next room, humming softly. The mattresses felt like clouds after sleeping over a week on the hard earth and soon Jace and Trel drifted to sleep, paying no attention to the sounds of Lashara in her room.

10

ON THEIR WAY

A cold draft of air woke Jace from the window he had opened the night before. Its gentle breeze allowed him to tolerate the enclosed area. He yawned and stretched, looking about the room at his companion's beds.

The one next to him was a disheveled mass of Trel's twisted bedsheets. He was probably off wandering the city as the group made their final preparations to leave. Alaric sat at the small desk in the corner hunched over a ragged book. His leggings were clean and his shirt unwrinkled, complementing his freshly shaven face. He looked like he had been awake for a good hour or two.

"What are you reading?" Jace asked curiously.

"I am finishing the epistle of Corinth," he said without moving.

Ah, Corinth, Jace thought. The letter had countless tidbits of wisdom. Some of its passages were his favorite. There was the section that told of the Counselor's ability to reveal the Almighty's plans through meditation of the scriptures, one which explained the Creator's unending wisdom, the part on encouragement of unity in all things, practical application for marriage, spiritual freedom, and of course, the great passage on love.

Alaric put his book away, saying a short word of thanksgiving to the Almighty. Jace watched him. The man always projected an attitude of calm stability. He had never spoken out of turn and was never one to be whipped into a frenzy. In fact, Jace had never seen him give in to an emotion since they had met. The two of them were very different in that way. He yawned once more and sat up.

"How did you know that this place would give us lodging without payment?" he asked the big man.

Alaric shrugged, "I did not know until we stood outside the inn. Come, let me show you."

Jace got dressed. A new pair of clothes were folded neatly at the base of his bed and gave off a warm, light aroma that was quite unlike the wet, worn smell of the ones he had on the day before. He splashed his face with water at the basin on the nightstand, and the two made their way outside.

The inn was empty and only a few men lingered by the fire, stretching their legs in relaxation. Jace had not seen any sign of Trel, Lashara, or Blynn and wondered where they had gone off to. The inn's door was opened and the two went outside into the late morning sun. Even in the cool air, people filled the street with a buzz. They shouted their goods, their breath billowing out of their mouths like angry chimneys. A few booths had been set up even at this narrow turn in the city, and traffic fought to move against the crowds that stood around them. Jace could see two mounted militia eyeing the growing congestion, they seemed disinterested so long as the people still moved and there were no arguments. Alaric turned and pointed to the inn's sign, his hands moving in explanation.

"Long ago, Keepers were under heavy persecution. During those dark times, they maintained their safety by a custom they used to identify who they were. When two met, one would draw an arch in the ground at his feet," he said, tracing a line on the cobblestone as an example. "If the other was a follower of Yeshua, he would respond by drawing another arch connected to the first. The symbol was a simple drawing of a fish and an easy way to identify others who followed the Almighty. The custom has been passed down and is used even today to tell other Keepers they are welcome, though the symbol has become hidden more discreetly."

Alaric pointed at The Two Swans, their graceful bodies and ornate features looking like an ordinary sign to Jace. "Turn your head and examine their necks," said Alaric. "Tell me what you see."

Jace did what he was told. For a moment, the picture looked the same and then he saw it. The interwoven necks looked exactly like the symbol Alaric had described and Jace gasped in astonishment.

Alaric drew close and spoke softly, "The housemaster is a Keeper and has lived here for some time. By using this means of communication, he is able to maintain his secrecy while helping others in an area where people are not too fond of us. When I saw the symbol, I immediately talked to him. He was more than willing to meet our needs. Such is the way of the Almighty: when we are at the ends of our means, He is there to carry us further," he ended with a smile.

The two went back inside and sat at a table to outline the day ahead. While they talked, a maid served them a small meal of warm bread and cheese. They ate slowly while they decided what to do.

Dorath had left the inn after Jace turned in. He was traveling straight back to the Gap on some urgent mission he would not talk about and only bid the party not to become complacent in their stay.

The other three were about the city, collecting certain supplies for the journey ahead. Trel, as always, had gone over their food stores and went out to purchase some extra provisions. Lashara had decided to occupy her time with clothing, making sure that the party had extra garments for the coming winter months. Blynn said nothing to the group, but apparently had left to get some things for the horses and spare parts for their cart, in case the road proved too difficult.

Alaric said little, but Jace got the feeling he was suspicious about the shady man. Jace had his own feelings on the matter, but decided to trust Dorath's judgment: he had obviously known him far longer than anyone else.

Alaric was restless and wanted to leave the moment the party was assembled. He was troubled they had seen a Watcher this far east and wanted to leave before the creature found where they were. The Creator was omnipresent and all-knowing, but Sa'vard or one of his minions would find them sooner or later. It was only a matter of time before the creature scoured the entire city. Who knows what problems would arise then? Nadirians loathed the Gap already. The Watcher could stir their hatred into an unending malice as they had seen with the mob. He thought it wise to maintain one step ahead of it, keeping them free from much unwanted trouble and spurring them on to their objective. Jace agreed and the two of them went upstairs to gather their things before the others came back.

When they were finished, they went back down to the common room. Trel and

Lashara had returned and were anxious to share their findings with the group. They walked out back to the courtyard where the cart was being readied.

Lashara rummaged through the wagon, pulling out the shirts and leggings she had bought. She had purchased other goods more suitable to her profession, but the fabrics seemed a more intriguing find. Her eyes sparkled as she held them aloft for all to see. Eagerly she explained the subtle qualities of each fabric, not noticing how the men listened to her with apathy. The three men nodded politely, trying to show their enthusiasm as well. Despite her efforts, Lashara's best attempt to open up to her new friends only proved their different interests.

Trel refused to show them his treats. He did not wish anyone's hunger to be a hindrance. Showing each of them the delicacies he had bought would only wet their appetites and let their minds wander when they had to be focused on the days ahead. The more they prodded him to reveal his hidden treasures, the stronger he refrained from showing them until they all turned their attention to other things.

They were busy strapping the last of their goods to the cart and checking their horse's saddles when Blynn burst into the courtyard. His greasy hair was a mess and his skin was beaded with sweat. He ran down the stairs to the cart, making little effort to hide his worry.

"We must leave immediately!" he exclaimed loudly, "I have seen it! The creature is in the marketplace down the street. He is coming this way with a dozen militia," he stammered.

The stable hands peered around corners to view the anxious party, more than one hearing their conversation. Jace motioned for Blynn to lower his voice with a look of annoyance. Blynn did not seem to care and carried on.

"If we don't leave, they will be here any moment; they may be here even now!" he all but shouted, his eyes wide. A clamor arose in the front room of The Two Swans. Jace could hear the commotion growing as several of the serving girls voiced their surprise and a voice that could only be the housemaster joined in with his disapproval. The sound of furniture being turned over was followed by footsteps running upstairs. Blynn turned toward the building, a look of fear in his eyes. Jace stood still, his hand beneath his cloak, grasped tightly around the Song of the Ages and letting his thoughts focus on his Lord. Somewhere in a corner of his mind, Jace felt something searching him. Behind it lay a cold feeling of utter fear and hopelessness. That was all he needed to make his decision.

"To the horses!" He commanded and jumped on his mare. He wheeled her around as the others made for theirs. Trel scrambled aboard the cart with Blynn. Lashara had grabbed the reins of his horse while Alaric mounted his charger. They scanned the courtyard frantically. The only visible exit led to the street, which was beginning to fill with soldiers. The horses whinnied anxiously as the troops poured down the entrance and into the courtyard. Jace loosed the staff from his saddle and turned his horse toward the troops.

"There is another way out!" Blynn yelled.

Jace stopped and turned toward the man, whose features were wide with fright. He was pointing to the stables in hysteria. The soldiers had formed into a phalanx and were marching slowly across the square, their swords unsheathed and lowered.

Jace turned toward the troops. The five of them could fight their way through and lose the militia in the crowds, but it was almost certain there were more of them waiting in the street beyond. He turned toward Blynn, afraid to trust the dirty man, but having little choice. He nodded and Blynn slapped the reins hard.

The cart shot forward into the stables and out the other side as the others followed. As Jace ducked into the building, he turned back, seeing a black-cloaked figure standing in an open window of the inn. He could feel the waves of fear and anger passing over him as the Watcher saw his prey slip through his fingers once again.

Jace turned his head from the faceless stare and stayed close behind the others. Blynn took them recklessly through the streets, and people darted out of their path while they charged by. He turned into the alleyways and led them south through the city. They emptied out on a street running parallel to the river and Blynn slowed to a canter. He led them hastily over a bridge and they made their way through the streets toward the city gates.

Jace paid little attention to his surroundings, but looked back a number of times. It seemed they had outdistanced the soldiers, but still he listened for a trumpet to alert the city gates.

Moments passed and no alarm was raised. The soldiers must have been hired thugs, he reasoned, and turned his attention to Blynn. The man's face was a work in perspiration as he rode, hardly checking to see if the rest followed him. Trel clung by his side, his eyes fearful and his knuckles white.

They continued through the city, gaining the gates before noon. The tower guards eyed the group suspiciously as they went through Blynn's papers. He had stated that they were merchants traveling south and the guards conversed with each other, debating whether they should inspect the contents of the cart. Blynn cleared his throat nervously, dropping a few coins in each of their hands. The habit was not something Jace approved of, but in the present circumstances, he knew they needed haste. The guards folded their arms and let the party pass.

Blynn drove them south over the outlying farmlands until Nadir was lost in the cloudy autumn haze. He then turned east without a word and led the troop off the main road. The flatlands of the river basin changed to rolling hills that soon became dotted with trees. They traveled for hours, letting the sun go down; knowing that time was paramount. The more distance put between them and the city would be more of a chance to lose their pursuers. Blynn led them on a back road that twisted around several hills into the thickening North Wood.

They traveled late into the night, the chill air keeping the travelers awake. By moonlight, the road was hardly noticeable, but Blynn knew where he was and pushed them onward. Only the dull thud of the horses' hooves and sound of their breath cut the quiet night. The bells on their reins had been put away when they turned off the road, and Jace lost track of time while the moon hung suspended in the sky.

Finally, Blynn reined in the cart. It was well after midnight and the party gathered around him closely. His voice was less frightened, but his eyes bulged in the moonlight.

"This place looks good enough for tonight," he said, pointing to a dark thicket off the road. "It will provide ample protection from prying eyes and shield us from the wind. We can stay here for a few hours while some sleep and the others stand watch," he said, his tone more a statement than a question.

No one questioned the ugly man, thankful that he had led their escape. They had never seen one so filthy who hailed Yeshua as Lord of their life. It was an unwritten rule that Keepers dressed in a clean manner.

On First Days, people went out of their way to dress their best. Jace had heard it had something to do with presenting your finest appearance while in the presence of the Creator. Though this was only an outward act, it showed the Keepers' obedience and love for their Lord.

Blynn's appearance was homely and his clothes gave off the odor of smoke and sweat. He never seemed to mind and did not show the slightest concern for how he looked. The others shied away from him and his coarse ways, each asking how he let himself sink to such conditions. Whatever the reason, his appearance and attitude left them feeling he went out of his way to stay dirty.

Blynn led them quietly into the dark underbrush. The party dismounted, hushing their tired steeds. Without a word, most of them fell asleep. The ground was littered with sticks and roots, but to the sleepy individuals, they were as soft as the beds of The Two Swans. Only Alaric stayed awake with Blynn. The two sat in silence, peering out at the forest around them. Hours passed slowly and nothing stirred. Eventually, Alaric succumbed to fatigue and only Blynn remained to guard the five of them. He sat on his haunches motionless, his body becoming one with the shadows.

Though he did not move, Jace's sleep was troubled. He dreamt of the chase from Nadir while surrounded by soldiers at every turn. The men wore evil grimaces and reached out to tear him from his horse. He was alone in the dream, separated from his friends and frightened. Rolling hills stretched as far as he could see. The land was empty and there was no place to hide.

Overhead was a blood red sky. The light came from everywhere though no sun shone above. All he could do was spur his beast onward. Men seemed to melt up from the ground as he rode, their awful grins mocking his hopelessness. Their faces were contorted in evil, dark grimaces that spoke of awful purpose. He looked behind him and saw numberless soldiers on his heels. Their bodies twisted into a thousand loping creatures, and he watched while his pursuers turned into the Bothian Horde. He could feel the stare of the Watcher just beyond his vision. The creature laughed at his efforts, the sound bouncing inside Jace's head. He cried out to the Creator and Yeshua to rescue him, but no reply came and he rode on.

Jace started from his sleep. Darkness had enveloped him, his breathing sounding loud against the surrounding silence. Blynn cursed at him to keep quiet. The man's form was barely seen in the shadows. How long had he been watching over them, Jace could not tell. He looked at the man who gave no apology for his obscene outburst. The two stared at each other in the blackness.

Jace let the comment pass and calmed his breathing. Curses and swearing were viewed by his Mentors as indecent behavior. Marked passages in the Song of the Ages confirmed their arguments, but Jace figured it was not the time or place to confront Blynn about his wrongs. Everyone had things to work on, and it was clear that Blynn had his share.

Instead, Jace questioned him about their passage. What route would they take to the Clonesian Empire? How would they cross the Great River? Had they thrown off their pursuers? How long would their journey take? He whispered his queries to Blynn politely.

Blynn brushed him off, giving only a curt "Hush" in reply. Jace sat for some time in the night, boredom eventually getting the best of him, and he fell back to sleep.

Almost as soon as Jace had closed his eyes, Blynn woke the party. Trel and Lashara groaned softly as Blynn shook them. Jace was perturbed, having finally found the chance for a decent rest. Alaric untied the horses and walked them out onto the trail while Blynn guided the cart.

It was still dark and they kept to the path. Lashara figured it was a few hours before dawn. She did not know where the strange man was headed, but from her knowledge and the lay of the land, they were cutting through the North Wood. Blynn had taken control and the thought lifted her spirits, even in the cold night. It was time that someone stood up to Jace. The young man was arrogant and did not seem to learn any other way. Blynn was unsightly, but he had done a masterful job at deflating the pompous Keeper. He could do no worse than Jace's debacle at Nadir.

She flinched when she realized Jace was right beside her. His blue eyes glinted in the dark. The last time he had been this close to her was in the infirmary. There he had disgraced her in front of their peers and she had never forgiven him, but now, his face was different. He looked at her, his eyes deep and steady. No boyish grin was on his face, only a solemn stare. The two brought up the rear of the group, and Jace used the chance to talk to her in a low voice.

"I wanted to ask your forgiveness, Lashara," he began slowly. "I have treated you rather poorly since we met, and the thought has troubled me. I know it was not right of me. You did nothing to deserve it. I was acting like a fool and have been ashamed to admit it. I do not know how to mend what I have broken, and I know this will not do, but I hope that it is the beginning of repairing all that I have done."

Lashara eyed him suspiciously in the moonlight. The last time he had been so honest, it had been a front for concealing his tricks. She wanted to respond in anger and knew she had the right, but also knew the Song of the Ages commanded forgiveness. He had apologized in front of everyone before, but she had thought it was a ploy to gain acceptance, using the group to pressure her answer. Now here alone, he seemed to genuinely care that he had hurt her. There was no air of arrogance or self-righteousness. Instead his figure betrayed his nervous vulnerability. Lashara decided to give him a chance.

There were times Jace had shown good qualities. He had tried to talk earnestly to her several times before. He had almost bought the slave family their freedom, and put the safety of the group over his desire to fight the soldiers when they were in the courtyard. Lashara could see qualities in him that might prove promising.

She wanted desperately to have someone in the group she could talk to. Alaric was kind, but he was much older and spoke little. Trel was a bit scatterbrained and immature and Blynn was, well, Blynn. She looked at Jace and nodded her forgiveness.

The tension in his body melted away and he sagged noticeably in the moonlight. Being honest had always been one of his better characteristics, he thought, but talking to ladies was not. Dorath had urged him to talk to Lashara, and he had viewed the confrontation with supreme reluctance, though he knew he must approach her. Now that Lashara had forgiven him, he felt easier, but kept it in the back of his mind to give her due respect from now on.

It took the better part of two months to cross the North Wood. The going was slow and soon the trail Blynn was using faded into nothingness. The woods were thick. Its tall pines, elms, oaks, and maples melded with a tangle of underbrush of small bushes, trees, and bracken. Several times a day they had to skirt around fallen trunks. Rock formations jutted out of the ground at odd angles that made footing difficult and hampered the progress of their burdened cart.

Various streams ran throughout the Wood, carving small ravines steep enough to keep the cart from fording. Once or twice they had to disassemble the wagon, move the goods across the terrain by hand, and manhandle the cart down one side and up the other. Blynn made up for his lack of strength by positioning while Alaric heaved the cart out of sheer will. Jace and Trel joined in, but Alaric had asked Lashara to mind the horses. His years on the farm did not go to waste as Jace struggled with his end. Trel's wiry frame proved sufficient, and he helped Jace steady the wagon with success.

The operation would take most of the day and leave the group hungry and tired. Trel would always lift their spirits with some surprise of his own that he had found in Nadir and cooked it to perfection. The troop's appetite was always satisfied, and they all went to bed with a healthy load in their bellies.

Once Blynn was sure that the Watcher had lost their scent, he decided to ease up on the pace, giving the crew a much needed rest. The action did not go unnoticed and the other members soon realized that Blynn was not all that bad. Some of them compared him to Hadran—solitary, with a hard exterior, whose feelings of care were locked deep inside of him. Others did not categorize him so easily. Alaric noted his anger that was not unlike Jace's, the unquestioning air with which he ordered people to and fro, and the obscenities that dropped from his mouth every so often. Whatever their feelings were about the dirty man, they were all thankful for his skills of navigation and the routine concern he seemed to show.

Jace had not forgotten his brother and found his thoughts turning to him throughout the month. He had read the letters Dorath gave him. The first entries were long and detailed, portraying an attitude of diligence and pride in his work. Rae stated often how he could see the Maker working in his life and in those around him.

These depictions were less and less frequent as the letters continued. They finally ended in short summaries of where he was and nothing more. Jace read the letters with a troubled spirit. The things his brother had not written were the things that bothered him the most.

He knew his brother was filled with passion and sympathy; he had witnessed it countless times growing up. He remembered the time he had gotten back from his work in the field. Deep sobs were coming from their cottage and as he made his way through the door, he saw his mother holding Rae close to her bosom. At their feet lay a bird, its wings laying in an awkward position and its tiny chest unmoving. The creature had fallen from a tree learning to fly, and Rae had raced home with it in hopes of healing its wounds. Realizing there was nothing he could do and watching the life slip from its body brought Rae to tears. He cried for an hour with Mum consoling him in her arms.

The image was one of many Jace could conjure up, and a perfect example of how Rae went out of his way to help those in need. These memories were rather different than the picture the letters painted, and he was left with an uneasy feeling in his stomach. What danger had befallen his brother in the Clonesian Empire? He wondered if he would even find him again as he watched Blynn riding in the cart in front of him.

Their entire mission rested with the filthy man. Jace did not know if he liked that, but he hoped nonetheless that the Master would guard their advance and give Blynn the ability to lead them to success. After all, what mattered most was finding Rae and bringing him to safety, not the dynamics of the group.

The feelings grated on Jace and he found himself talking to Lashara to keep his mind off his brother. The diminutive girl was meek in her responses and said very little, but she listened with an unmatched intensity Jace had never seen. Her attitude reminded him much of Miss Pell and he could clearly see the influence the woman had played on her life. He found himself enjoying her company and made time each day to ride by her side. Lashara was a beauty and at first he found himself stammering as he spoke to her, but her gentle voice and welcome attitude encouraged his efforts.

Lashara looked forward to Jace's conversations. Once he had decided to stop teasing and act like a man, he was not that bad a person. She watched him while he talked. His simple features hid nothing and she found herself staring at him. He would only stutter and look away until she begged him to continue. His timid actions with her were not something she had seen before and were quite different from the cockiness and overconfidence that she had first seen in him. She found herself attracted to the tall man, and as the days passed, the fact that he was Hadran's pupil did not seem so bad to her.

Lashara was not the only one he talked to. Jace made it a point to converse with every person in the party if they were feeling up to it. Since he clearly was not the leader during this leg of their journey, he thought it his duty to engage in pleasantries. Small talk always brought relief from the boredom that inescapedly crept into such long travels.

Though quiet, Alaric was willing to speak and Jace found his insights complemented his own. The two of them talked for many hours about their families and their relationship with Yeshua. Alaric and Jace would always ponder the Song of the Ages, questioning each other on the truths it contained. Their conversation was healthy, and they never argued over their differences. Each seemed to sharpen the other's understanding of the scriptures, and they would laugh good-naturedly to themselves of the things they discovered.

Jace would venture forward to talk with Trel and carry on loudly, though Blynn would eye them with disdain. The two enjoyed ribbing each other and would trade insults throughout the day. The change was welcome from the suffocating attitude that they were accustomed to in East Haven. Each of them needed their studies, they agreed on that, but they needed the chance to be free of such labor and have fun also.

Trel was glad to be rescued from the monotony of riding with the wordless Blynn. The man grimaced even when he rode with the pipe stuck between his lips. That changed as time went on. The smell of the pipe was soothing and Blynn even let the boy try a puff or two when the others weren't looking.

This did little to improve the cough that Trel was just getting over, but he felt a strange acceptance when Blynn offered him the instrument. The man even cracked a smile when Trel doubled-over and sputtered frantically after inhaling it for the first time. Blynn gave a raucous laugh and clapped him on the back.

The two of them would talk for short spells. Blynn's shady character fed the mischief that Trel was born with. They would talk about things that Trel knew were unacceptable, but the thrill of speaking the unthinkable within earshot of others was overpowering to Trel. Blynn's views on cheating and stealing were questionable, to say the least, and Trel found himself agreeing with him. The man would show him passages from the Song of the Ages and how they were outdated and old.

"Sometimes there are situations that are not mentioned in this book, and we have to figure things out for ourselves," Blynn would say in his grating voice. "Take bribing the gatehouse guards, for instance. It may be wrong, but Yeshua possesses boundless grace to His followers, even if they stumble every now and then. The Song says little on bribery and so we must decide what is best in certain circumstances. Though it is a questionable business, if we had not given them money, we would still be at Nadir and the Watcher would surely have found us, taking us to who knows where."

Trel shivered at being in the clutches of the Watcher. The argument seemed logical to him, and he nodded, dumbfounded. Blynn brimmed with confidence, and even though his thoughts were not entirely pure, Trel dared not question the man for fear of what would happen. So he rode, letting Blynn talk as he saw fit and listened with curiosity. Blynn's thoughts on everything were skewed from what Trel had been taught at East Haven, but his arguments were laced with scripture from the Song of the Ages and so Trel let it pass.

Every now and then, the conversation would turn toward the opposite sex. Blynn would never wholly say what was on his mind, but Trel figured out quite easily what it was when the man would turn to look back at Lashara and lick his lips lustfully. Trel was not blind either. Lashara was a pretty thing to look at and though Jace had obviously warmed up to her, he could look at her and admire her from afar as a striking young woman.

Blynn, on the other hand, stared way too long and the looks he gave disturbed Trel. When he caught Trel watching him, he would shrug it off with some dirty remark and tap the reins lightly.

All in all, Trel liked the man. He knew someone would have to confront him sooner or later about the things he noticed, but for now he kept to small talk in hopes of cementing their relationship.

On lazier days Blynn would hand over the reins to Trel and teach him the finer art of driving a team of horses. It was something he had not learned in his studies, and encouraged by Blynn's steady teaching, he soon found he was a natural at it. Blynn would let Trel guide the horses for a time while he took short naps. The two became quick friends, if only because no one else would talk to Blynn.

Night fell early in the afternoon, now that they were in the dead of winter. Most traveling took place in the warmer months and those that attempted journeys in the winter found the task long and arduous. The party set camp early each day, not wishing to brave the cold, starless dark, since the danger of pursuits had passed. They would spend a good deal of time encircled around a blazing fire while each took turns at entertainment.

Lashara produced a reeded flute from her saddlebags and would play softly while the others listened. The tunes were mellow and gentle, like the warm breeze through the summer trees. It would take each of them back to memories of innocence and times when things were much more simple. Her tunes were not all slow or melancholy, and if the mood struck her, she would play a dancing melody or a jig. The men followed along clapping, and sometimes Jace and Trel would dance together providing a good laugh for all.

Other nights Trel and Jace would practice with their weapons. They constantly argued over which was the better—the sword or staff—and would take to arms over the matter on occasion. The fights were non-lethal, each trying more to improve their skills than to hurt the other.

Jace, of course, preferred the staff. Though it required both hands, its heavy oak felt sure and the balanced object had a long reach and fearsome blow. Many overlooked the staff as an oversized walking stick, and he declared that one could bring it almost anywhere without raising an eye, unlike a sword.

Trel naturally leaned toward the short sword. He liked the feel of steel in his hands. The sharp ring it produced always seemed to heighten his senses. Though significantly shorter in reach, the sword was lighter and quicker and sharper.

The two would put on a fine show in front of the others. Since selecting their primary weapon was one of the first things a Keeper did at East Haven, Jace and Trel had years of practice and were very capable with their instruments.

Each would toy with the other, hoping to catch them in a mistake or lull them into a trap. Jace liked to use his staff as a defensive weapon. The long piece of oak deflected Trel's blows easily. The action was strategic. The staff made an excellent defense and could be then swung around to provide a counterblow, depending on how it was held.

Trel was always infuriated by this move. Rarely had he gotten past the staff only to lose his balance and get a rap on the back from Jace. Once, he had tangled his arm between the oak and Jace's body, and Jace had nearly broken his arm. That had made him cautious ever since, but he knew that if he bided his time, eventually Jace would get bored with giving ground. The Mentors had always taught them that fights, as well as battles and wars, were won with patience.

One fine night, the two again put on their mock battle. Jace had harangued Trel about the soup he cooked and he jumped at the chance to challenge him. The chill air was downright biting, and the sparks twirled up from the fire and were chased away by the wind. They pulled their cloaks off and backed away from the blaze while their audience turned to eye the battle.

Jace clutched the staff vertically, but before Alaric gave the signal to begin, Trel wrapped his knuckles with the flat of his blade. Surprised, Jace let go, and with a sly grin Trel laid into him. Jace stumbled back, his footsteps muffled in the fresh fallen snow. He regained his composure and set about dodging Trel's attack preparing for his counter. Jace side-stepped his friend and jabbed his staff at Trel's feet. Trel was ready and jumped, swinging his sword over his head. Jace rolled, the singing blade landing less than a pace away from his head and he looked up with a grin of his own. He shot out his legs, tripping Trel and the two struggled to their feet. They eyed each other, breathing heavily, their audience clapping in amusement.

The fight lasted fairly long. Neither could better the other, and their faces lined with sweat despite the cold. Each thrust was turned aside easily, the other used to his partner's moves after all their years together. Subtle mistakes were capitalized on, but quickly reconciled, and the attacker became the defender a number of times. The two's movements were more of a finely orchestrated dance than a brutish street fight, and their faces showed their obvious delight. In their intense concentration, they seemed to forget the others were even there.

At length, the two let out a burst of furious blows. Their attacks were quick and each face was set in determination. They came in close to each other, one dodging out, the other going in, and still both remained standing. Finally, they separated, each breathing heavily, steam rising off their bodies. Lashara and Alaric applauded while Jace and Trel caught their breath.

"Suppose it were real?" came the scratchy voice of Blynn. He eyed the two young men smugly. "Can you do it when it counts?"

Trel shrugged, "Our Mentors taught us to disable. We are not to harm those whom we fight, even if there is just cause. Our blows may render our attackers unconscious, but we would not bring someone to death, not on purpose: 'For we wrestle not against flesh and blood, but against principalities, against powers, against rulers of darkness of this world, against spiritual wickedness in high places.'"

Blynn turned to Jace, "And you, boy, what would you do?"

"The same," replied Jace curtly. Blynn's question was almost a challenge. He did not care much for Blynn's attitude, his curses, his provoking glare, or the stench of smoke that hovered around the man. If it weren't for their common bond, Jace would probably have nothing to do with him. He was rough, and his haughty stares always seemed to be hiding some dark secret or private joke.

Blynn knocked the ashes from his pipe and set it down by the fire. He stood up, unclasped his cloak, and strode to where the lads were. His walk was confident as he looked the two Keepers up and down. As Blynn faced him, Jace saw the sword at his side. It was a thin blade, highly polished and of good steel. The silvery metal stood out against Blynn's black clothes.

"Show me," he said, thrusting his chin at Jace challengingly.

Lashara started and Alaric stood to his feet, but Blynn motioned for them to sit. He explained that this was simply for show, though his features said otherwise.

Jace gripped his staff and waited for Trel to sit with his friends. Slowly, Blynn drew his blade, the metal rasping on his baldric, and pointed it at Jace. He bowed his head slightly and the two circled each other.

It did not take long for Jace to discern that the dirty man was a seasoned swordsman. He walked lightly, keeping his balance, while waving his sword. The picture of the haggard fellow prancing like a cat looked rather comical. They weaved about each other, both preparing to strike.

Jace let out a series of blows, testing Blynn's defenses. The swordsman knocked them away nonchalantly, nodding his approval. The two circled once more, and Jace tried again with little success. Blynn laughed this time, his dark chortling making the night seem colder. The man rose up, turning his sword arm at Jace and returned the assault.

It suddenly occurred to Jace how tired he was. Trel's silly game had worn him out, and the stiff wind seeped his strength. He fought off Blynn's frenzied attack, giving him lots of ground. Blynn smiled at him and walked to flank him. Jace leveled his staff, twirling it to rest at his side. They stalked each other again, their bodies coming together.

Blynn's sword rang on the staff as Jace deflected the blow. He side-stepped the man lashing with the pole, but Blynn caught the staff under his arm, pulling Jace off balance with a mighty heave. Jace stumbled forward, losing his grip and tumbled away from Blynn. The others let out a gasp, as Blynn stabbed the ground about his feet while Jace rolled away. Blynn threw the staff away and followed Jace, leveling his sword at the young man as he scrambled away. A shadow passed over his face and for an instant, Jace thought he saw the cowled visage of the Watcher. He came on and only a thin smile curved around his lips as he marched towards Jace.

"Stop!" Lashara yelled, standing to her feet.

Blynn's sword was at Jace's throat and he eyed the young man with a cold stare. Then he relaxed and turned towards the fire.

"For fun," he explained in an innocent tone. He turned to Jace and offered him his hand. The menacing look was gone and Jace had wondered if his mind had played a trick on him. He took Blynn's hand warily and was pulled to his feet.

Blynn patted his back reassuringly. "A fine sport," he rasped, "Better luck next time."

"There's no such thing as luck," Jace mumbled. He threw his cloak across his shoulders, picked up his staff, and he stalked off to the horses.

The three eyed Blynn warily. Lashara was frowning, her hands hidden under her cloak. Trel's eyes were big and confused, wondering what Blynn would have done had the fight continued just a few moments longer. Alaric was still as a rock and remained seated, but his dark eyes watched Blynn unblinkingly.

"That was mean and cruel," Lashara said, as Blynn walked toward the fire. "We don't fight to injure, Blynn, or have you been away from the Gap so long you've forgotten?"

Blynn whirled on Lashara, his face hard. His muscles pulsed under his greasy skin and he eyed her threateningly. "Where we are going, girl, we may have to be mean and cruel! Nadir is nothing compared to the Clonesian Empire! Rae may be fine, but he may also be hurt or captured. We may have to use force, despite your apprehensions!"

"You're not in charge, Blynn!" she shouted at him.

"No? And where would you go without me? What would you do?" he grated. "My ways may not meet your approval, but they work. That is why Dorath chose me."

Alaric stepped in between them, his face staunch and grim. He drew close to Blynn and held his arm that had been dangerously pawing his sword. He looked into the man's eyes silently and then turned to stare at Lashara. She turned away, ashamed she had spoken in anger.

"The Spirit leads," he said softly. "We are but followers, the Spirit leads. The Master has gathered us all for a reason, and we must cling to the task. Don't allow Sa'vard a foothold or he will tear us all apart," he said for all of them to hear.

He relaxed slightly and backed away from Blynn. "It has been a long day. Let us rest and travel on in the morning," he said and then turned to Blynn. "Yeshua has placed us in your care. Do Him honor."

The man sneered and walked off into the darkness.

11

THE GREAT RIVER

The previous night left a bitter taste in all their mouths, and the dawn found the party's moods just as sour. They ate quietly around the fire and were off shortly with few words spoken. Trel took his place half-heartedly beside Blynn whose rough exterior seemed threatening now. He watched him out of the corner of his eye as he rode, casting a nervous smile when Blynn turned his way. The man had never apologized for his actions, and Trel wondered if he had misjudged him.

Trel was not slow, nor was he stupid. If anything, he was accepting, depending on others until they proved otherwise. In the Gap, order and safety depended on one trusting their superiors. The attitude had been ingrained in him. Staring at Blynn, he thought maybe it was wise to view new acquaintances with a bit more skepticism.

After some gentle prodding, Jace had returned to the fireside the previous night. Alaric had spoken to him at length and he had finally returned and immediately went to sleep.

Blynn had returned silently during the middle of the night. Lashara was keeping watch with Alaric, the two taking turns poking the fire. The shimmering coals always intrigued her, and she watched them change from orange to yellow to silver and back again. Every now and then, one of them scanned the darkness for signs of Blynn. They talked in whispers, careful not to wake Jace and Trel. Blynn appeared suddenly, sitting across from them in the shadows. His silent stare and grimy complexion did nothing to mask his contempt. He eyed them for some time before throwing his cloak about himself and bundling up for sleep. Lashara was highly upset at the wormish man, but she heeded Alaric who told her things would be better in the morning.

Along with the bitterness, they awoke to find fresh snow on the ground. The white stuff did little to lift their moods and they stalked about the camp quietly, getting a slow start in the knee-deep powder.

Their travel was slow the next couple weeks. The low-hanging clouds dropped the soft flakes unceasingly, and before long, the North Wood became an untraversable forest of white. Try as they may, the group could only muster three leagues per day and that with a supreme effort. Jace did not see a trail, but Blynn seemed to mark his directions carefully, moving them ever west.

Since the incident with Blynn, Jace had become more solitary. He had never liked losing or being embarrassed, especially when he put forth a gallant attempt, and the thrashing Blynn had given him had made him ashamed that he could not best the man whom he was quickly learning to despise. It was more than that though. Blynn's actions had scared him. The man had seemed intent on harming him, and try as he may, he could not erase that horrible blank stare and the shadow that had passed over him when he had held him on the ground at sword point. He wondered what Dorath's purpose was in assigning Blynn to their party.

It bothered him further that he could not see Yeshua's handiwork in the matter. He argued with himself that the four of them could have found their way across the Great River. They could have even hunted down and found his brother. Jace convinced himself that Blynn's talents would only benefit the group in a minor way. If the decision were his, they could have gotten along fine without Blynn. He rode on at the rear of the party, murmuring to himself about all the angles of their journey that he had seen and questioning what the future might bring.

Alaric, Trel, and Lashara were worried about their friend and cast glances back at him throughout the days. They all spoke softly to each other long after Jace had slept about what could be done to encourage him and debated whether or not they could continue in this fashion. Trel and Lashara were anxious to confront Jace, or console him, but Alaric believed they should let his grief run its course. There were things that Jace must wrestle against that they could not help him with, he told them. It was prudent to let the man reason out his problems and be ready if he should ask for their support. And so they waited and watched him—Lashara and Trel biding their time for the moment when Jace would snap out of his melancholy state.

The dead of winter found them all at the edge of the North Wood, gazing at the boundary of the Stygian Union beyond. The land was fair and even as they stood being battered by a chilly northeast wind and blowing to warm their frostbitten hands, they could not help but smile on a land so blessed. The ground gently sloped to the Great River from the Northern Wood. Its tranquil rolling hills were marked by free-roaming cattle and other beasts that pawed through the snow to the grass beneath. The wind kicked up particles of ice from the ground, cutting the visibility down considerably, and the party leaned into the gusts on top of their steeds. Alaric's warhorse kicked the ground impatiently and they set off west with the cart in the lead.

As they passed through the rolling terrain, Trel could make out trails of smoke rising out of the land around them. He stared into the wind and saw that houses were built into the sides of hills. The land was quiet. No one came out to greet them in the howling wind and they passed through it quickly.

At the day's end, Blynn stopped them in front of a large hill. Lashara gave Alaric a quizzical look as Blynn jumped off the cart. He vanished into the gusting snow and the lot of them stood wondering where he had gone. He returned followed by a short, round fellow who was wrapped in a heavy cloak up to his chin. A small cap was thrust on his weather-beaten head with two flaps protecting his ears from the ice. The red-faced man examined the group, frowning openly at the horses and turned and bowed to Blynn. Blynn held his hands up to give something to the rotund fellow who shook his head hastily and ran back into the wind. Blynn yelled above the wind and pointed for the others to follow. He led them around the hill into a short, narrow ravine. The others followed him through a door that was built into the side of the earth. Once inside, they shook off their frozen clothes and shards of ice fell to the floor.

Jace examined where Blynn had led them. They were in some large room that looked very similar to a tavern with a peculiar domed ceiling. In the corner was a blazing fire where one old man was dozing in a high-backed chair. Tables were neatly cleaned with chairs pulled up underneath them. The floor was spotless, its high-gloss shine reflecting the fire's glare. A short counter stood in front of them with a door at either end that led to the kitchen. Various shaped glasses decorated the shelves behind the counter, each filled with a different colored liquid. One of the doors opened and the red-faced little man entered. He was shaking snow from his cap and wiping melted ice from his round head.

The man talked to Blynn excitedly, pointing to the other end of the room and motioning for the party to sit at one of the tables. Their hands touched and Jace saw the man hurriedly stuff a handful of coins into his deep pockets.

They sat down at the table and the man disappeared behind the doors. The party shuffled noisily into their chairs, listening to the crackle of the hearth and the lazy snoring of the old man. It had been the first time since Nadir that the party had sat on anything besides their saddles or the frozen earth. Suddenly, the door opened and the old man gave a start. In entered the red-faced host accompanied by three serving girls. They carried a platter of food in each hand and filled the table with an assortment of hot roasts, warm potatoes, cabbage, and ripe vegetables that looked strangely out of place in the middle of winter. The smells filled the room, and even the old man peered at them from his chair at the enticing aromas.

Their host said a short blessing and bowed, letting the party assuage their hunger. They ate trying to keep their ravenous appetites from overcoming their manners. The food was tender, fresh, piping hot, and felt perfect after the long winter days they had recently experienced. Trel's skills with a fire and a few pots were extraordinary, but still no match against a well provisioned inn. Jace and Trel sawed huge chunks of venison and pheasant from the table, stifling a belch every now and then. Alaric paced himself, eating an assortment of vegetables that were balanced by a healthy portion of meat and potatoes. Lashara picked at the cool fruits, cheeses and vegetables, eating a fair share of peppers, tomatoes, and greens. She was not terribly hungry and could not eat a full course meal if she tried. Blynn ate with disinterest, looking at the rafters in pensive thought. The others shook their heads at the strange man's behavior and continued their gorging. When they settled back, they saw their efforts made barely a dent in the food presented them. They sat, rubbing their bellies and washing their food down with cold ice water.

Women came and took their food away while they nodded their thanks. Trel stretched his arms and broke the silence, voicing his questions about this and that to Blynn. The man only stared at him. Alaric offered his answers instead.

"We have arrived in the outskirts of the Stygian Union, a loose alignment of states that runs the length of the Great River," he spoke softly, hoping to keep the sleepy old man from hearing. "People here are friendly and many go out of their way to show acts of kindness, as we've already seen. Their works are admirable and they are peace-loving people. Still, we must all keep our minds in this place. We are nearer now to the border of the Clonesian Empire and Sa'vard's Watchers are said to be extremely active in these parts. Keep your wits about you, and do not make a scene. Remember, our goal is specific and we must not compromise it for now," he said, looking long at Jace.

"Stygians are kind people, but even they do not worship the Almighty in truth and spirit, for if they did, they would have honored Yeshua and moved to the Gap. There is very little hostility here, but they frown on many of our practices. I do not think it wise to hide our identities, if asked, nor do I think it wrong not to share our beliefs with any. Who knows? Maybe we shall plant a seed for Yeshua to harvest, but still we must lean toward caution."

"How do you mean?" asked Lashara.

Alaric pointed out their host who had frowned when he saw their horses. "Stygians believe in unity of all things above all else. They strive to live in harmony with nature. The host was rather upset seeing our horses shod and used to haul us and other goods. They are highly agitated by any such action, for they believe it aggravates the natural balance of things."

"But the Song clearly says that man has dominion over the earth and everything in it. The Maker gave us everything in the earth to use as we see fit. Isn't the Stygian belief, then kind of, well, stupid?" said Trel wrinkling his nose and speaking just a little too loudly. The old man turned from the fire and stared not too kindly at the group. Alaric went on in a whisper.

"You will find, Master Trel, that a great many things others hold in high regard mean little to nothing in our Master's eyes. In spite of this, we must respect their customs, for that may provide a means to share with them Yeshua's sacrifice. I suggest we travel the rest of the way by foot," he said practically. Blynn, who had been sitting in silence, burst out in surprise.

"Walk to the Great River by foot?" He yelled. "Why do such a thing when we have fresh steeds to ride and carry our goods? No, we move on and change nothing," he said without waiting for debate.

The old man turned now, staring harshly at their table. He was obviously irritated at their volume, but more so at their conversation, having pieced it together with what he overheard. Jace went to the old man and kneeled down to him. He muttered his apologies in a low voice and then went back to the table while the old fellow fell back to sleep.

The group watched, waiting for his decision on how they would continue. Jace mulled it over, weighing the consequences of each action. The choice was easy enough since going horseless would glorify the Almighty. This would show their respect for the Stygians and serve as a basis for explaining their beliefs. Riding about the country would only infuriate all who saw them. If he had learned anything from Nadir, he knew that led quickly to disaster.

He looked about the table. Trel and Lashara watched him expectantly. They waited for him to go against Blynn's wishes so they could laugh as he watched his iron grip of power transfer to Jace's hands. Alaric sat expressionless and tense, knowing that the decision was a chance for Jace to take command and renew his self-esteem. Jace's eyes came to rest on Blynn at the end of the table. The dirty man challenged him with a dark frown, shaking his head slightly. Jace froze looking at his cold stare. He cowered against him, letting out a long sigh.

"Well?" said Blynn haughtily.

"Blynn has done a decent job thus far. If he wishes to continue however he pleases without listening to sound advice, let his actions be on his own head."

An audible sigh of frustration let out from Lashara and Trel while Blynn bowed mockingly. He stared back at Jace arrogantly.

"Just as long as he takes us to Rae," Jace said, his voice steely. Blynn's eyes wrinkled slightly, and the two held each other's gaze. It did not bother Jace so much that Blynn wanted control. Jace could give him that, so long as the man did what he was told.

They left the table, each going to the rooms that Blynn had purchased without asking for advice or permission. He had obtained a separate room for each individual, and they looked into each area, amazed at the richness that went into the decorations. They were exquisite compared to the practical houses of the Gap and the chambers of East Haven. Each was furnished with different beds and chairs of the highest quality. The dark maple and mahogany that accented the rooms were inlaid with gold designs. Oil paintings hung on the walls, their colors warming the lavishly decorated rooms. Each had its own fireplace that was straddled by two chairs and a finely woven rug.

Lashara's room had a gigantic wooden object that Jace and Trel found curious. Its face was lined with a number of drawers. Lashara looked at her clueless friends, explaining that it was a dresser and held clothing and other objects. The two scratched their heads. Having grown up with only two sets of clothes, they were baffled that one had need of such a thing.

The rooms had no windows, since they were nestled into the heart of the hill to conserve heat. They were, however, spacious and ornate and left the party breathless. Despite their luster, the gnawing fear of the Mines of Shorn still clutched at Jace, and he flung his door open wide to ease his dread of closed spaces. Their belongings had been brought discreetly to their chambers while they ate and even Jace settled in for the most comfortable sleep he had had in nearly two months.

IT TOOK MORE THAN TWO WEEKS TRAVEL from the inn for them to reach the Great River. Winter had not let up. This added to the fact that all except Blynn had dismounted from their steeds and traversed the land by foot severely hampered their progress. Jace was glad that many of the Stygians stayed inside, for he was embarrassed that Blynn did not follow their customs. He knew the party stuck out sorely against the snow, and it was plain that though they were not mounted they were working their horses rather vigorously.

The going was slow and Alaric used his warhorse to carve giant troughs in the snow for the others to follow through. Blynn was angry with their slow advance and let his curses carry across the countryside. Trel blushed at the obscenities as he rode by the man, and Alaric turned back a number of times, showing his obvious disapproval. Jace and Lashara walked behind the cart, paying little attention to the muffled screams of Blynn, absorbed in their own conversation.

He could not help but notice Lashara's rosy cheeks, full lips, and white skin that stood out against her flowing hair. Her features seemed to light up the world around him, in spite of the foul weather, and he caught himself staring openly at her. She would blush slightly, fluttering her lashes. It was strange that this was the same woman that months before had ordered Jace out of her work under a hail of objects. He stifled a smile remembering the warm ink on his neck and then thought twice about bringing up the memory.

Her companionship was comforting, and he found himself wanting more than simple friendship as he pondered their relationship late each night. He would read long passages from the Song of the Ages prior to falling asleep, but would lie awake in his knapsack afterwards thinking of the little lady.

The land was a gentle downward slope that spurred their pace. The curving country was dotted with groves of tress here and there that stuck out against the snowladen surface. When the weather broke, the scenery was cold and clear with a taste of sea hanging in the air. It was not the salt-smell that told of the ocean, but a pungent water odor that wafted over the hills. They could hear the call of birds far to the west, and soon saw giant gulls with speckled wings flying high in the air.

The port city of Samilon was nestled in a protected cove at the base of the hills. Its sprawling commerce was marked by hundreds of ships moored far out into the fresh water of its harbor. Dozens of tall-masted cogs and schooners lined its wharf. There were no empty piers, and the docks were crawling with traders unloading their ships. The city was not walled and its inhabitants spilled over onto the surrounding hills. Here, at least, the roads were cleared of snow, which was melting now as the days neared spring. The paving was a modest sprinkling of gravel that rose up as the countryside disappeared.

The party continued to walk their horses. Only the stubborn Blynn kept his beasts tied to the cart, lashing them every now and then to the dismay of many a local. They saw several frown at Blynn's behavior, but none approached to admonish or greet them and they passed unmolested.

The houses on the outskirts of town were akin to the inn they stayed at. Many had only a wooden face that was sunk into the hill behind in the fashion of their land, but all were well-kept and conveyed a cheery openness to passers-by. Families swept what little dust was in their abodes and tinkered with the multi-paned windows that were a hallmark of the Stygians. The strange guttering that Jace had seen in Yeshua's vision made a quiet gurgling sound as it carried away the melting snow.

The sun breaking through the clouds seemed to make the city come alive, and shops flung open their doors and raised their signs as the party made their way into the city. The merchants and artisans had well-crafted wooden houses that stood along the road. Though their homes were built into the hills, places of business and trade were freestanding structures. Jace reasoned this was to accommodate guests who were uneasy with the style of Stygian homes. The Stygians seemed more than willing to adopt the traditional structures that the rest of the world used.

The closer one moved to the interior of the city, the more wooden and stone houses one saw. After a while no sign of "homes in the hills" (as Trel called them) were seen at all. Blynn took them directly to the wharf, and they followed him through the maze of busy merchants and dockhands that filled the place.

The merchants Jace saw looked no different to him at first. Their clothes were of a different cut, but they moved and acted the same way as the ones he had met in Nadir. All of them seemed agitated and bent on the one thing that consumed any who were in business: making profit. They paid little mind to Jace's band of travelers, only viewing them as an obstacle to unloading their goods. A number of them swore angrily at him as he dodged around their work, keeping his sights on Blynn.

The vulgarity made him uneasy. It was something that was rarely heard, if ever, in the Gap. Whenever one had slipped from someone's mouth, there was a quick apology. He was sure he had heard his leaders say one once, but these were mostly spoken out of anger or in the heat of the moment and excused the moment they were said. Unlike them, the merchants strung their obscenities one after the other, and all but Lashara and Blynn cringed or blushed. Lashara had lived outside Nadir and though she found these words unbecoming, she had heard their use quite frequently while growing up. Blynn, on the other hand, viewed them with indifference, his mind on his own goals.

The traders and merchants that lined the dock were somehow different than those of Nadir. Without anyone telling him, he knew they were from the Clonesian Empire. This was the only obvious explanation since that was the only country bordering the Stygian Union to the west.

The atmosphere about them was unlike any he had met. Where the merchants in Nadir had been outright selfish, the Clonesians were focused on the business at hand. They flew into rages at anything that did not suit their plans and were quick to flog their hired hands.

Jace watched while one merchant oversaw the unloading of his ship. A number of overloaded pallets were being hoisted down the side of the vessel. The merchant was yelling harshly at his dockhands, despite their best efforts. It was clear they were doing the best they could and struggled with the heavy pallets that held countless goods from across the vast river. One of the teamsters was urging his group hard with a short whip, and all of them were sweating in the cold wind. A rope got tangled in the mooring lines and the pallet dipped to one side. The crew gave a shout and their hands worked furiously to correct the mistake, but the pallet leaned farther. It suddenly crashed to the dock with a deafening sound, its contents scattering in a light smoke.

The white-faced merchant ran down the plank and surveyed the damage, turning to eye the teamsters malevolently. Their leader backed away with fright, and the merchant tore the short whip from his hand. He beat the man repeatedly while he held his hands up in defense. The merchant did not stop though the man cried out for mercy. The whip tore his clothes to shreds and still the merchant flayed his body which was soon a crisscross pattern of blood. The man went silent and the merchant looked around for something else to vent his frustration upon at the irreparable damage to his materials.

He turned his wrath on the dockhands who scattered in every direction. One poor soul was not fast enough and got caught between his employer and the ship. Jace turned away as the man let out scream after scream that was only silenced by the staccato of the whip. The actions sickened him and he thought seriously about intervening before remembering Alaric's stiff warning. He forced himself to move on and tried to forget the injustice he had just witnessed.

These occurrences were commonplace on the dock. For every livid merchant there was an equal number of selfish dockhands. Jace saw many of the crew looting the very goods they transported. One merchant was thrown overboard into the icy bay and another was stripped of his fine garments to be left in only his underclothes. They reminded Jace of what Yeshua had said, but he still found himself wrestling with many emotions. The regard for life among the Clonesians was little if any and their lack of respect was likewise. It surprised him that the wharf did not turn into complete anarchy, but this was only due to the threat of the awful cruelty that Jace saw all around him.

He could not imagine how callous one had to be to treat life so indifferently. He could not understand how anyone, even if they were not raised in the Gap, could explain their justification for nearly killing someone who had only made a mistake or caused an accident. However awful it seemed to Jace, their Stygian counterparts ignored the Clonesians' demeanor and welcomed them and their business.

Blynn led them down the wharf to a large wooden ship. Its hull was sleek and narrow and three masts were mounted atop its deck. The prow was decorated with the figurehead of a scantily clad lady that held a spear high in one hand. Farther down the vessel were the words "Crest Cutter" written in large scrolling letters. A number of dockhands were busy scrubbing the deck, checking moorings, and climbing about the masts. The vessel itself rose up and down in the deep, cold waters of the Great River, conveying its need to be out on the open waves.

Blynn stopped the cart at the ship's gangplank and walked aboard. The sailors were deep in their work and failed to notice him until he climbed the raised platform in the stern and approached the captain. He looked Blynn up and down arrogantly and they began to talk with rapid gestures. Jace could see that Blynn was arguing a price for their passage and by the looks of both of them, he was getting the better of the captain. The two shook hands and Blynn passed down the gangplank.

"The captain has granted us passage aboard his worthy vessel," he said, giving a sour look back at the man. "His price was decent, but we must make haste. They are readying their ship to leave at noon."

He told the party of his plans as if they were set in stone. Passages aboard ships were notoriously high with merchants paying all but their soul to move their goods across the water. For this reason, Blynn wanted to sell everything and travel light. The cart was merely a disguise, and they did not need a year's supply of food or clothing. The gold they received in return for their sales could be used to purchase themselves other horses in the Clonesian Empire. At that, Lashara and Alaric bristled.

"We will not sell our steeds, Blynn," Lashara said coolly, rubbing her horse's nose. "There must be some other way."

"That is the best way," he said, not caring to look at her.

"No," said Alaric flatly.

Blynn's back stiffened at his words and he then faced Alaric, his greasy face doing its best to show an air of serenity.

"You can sell the goods," Alaric remarked, "but Jace and I will find some other means for the horses."

"Suit yourself," Blynn said with a shrug. He fitted a small pack across his shoulders and disappeared into the crowd.

"I do not like that man," Lashara seethed, watching him leave. Alaric stared at her and she said no more.

The four of them knocked heads about their problem and soon decided on a course of action. They agreed to split up to find means of stabling their animals until their return. Jace and Alaric would venture into the city, and Trel and Lashara would scour the wharf. Alaric passed out enough gold for all of them to make reservations, should they find a suitable place with conditions to their liking. Once again, he warned them of cheats and swindlers and told them to keep vouchers of their purchase.

By noon, Jace had found a spot three blocks from the wharf whose accommodations met their criteria. He purchased a voucher and the four of them said good-bye to their horses for the time being. They made their way back to the Crest Cutter and found Blynn with a look of satisfaction on his face.

"I got twice what it was worth," he boasted about the cart. "Half the clothes were moth-ridden, but he took my word they were fine silks without venturing a peek."

Alaric only shook his head. After encouraging the others not to cheat or swindle, here was Blynn providing a perfect example. He did not like it, but hoped the others would catch his deceit without Alaric criticizing him.

They made their way aboard the ship, and Blynn paid half the passage up front. A cabin boy led them to their rooms which were once again far too extravagant and a waste of their resources. Jace was fuming and ready to confront Blynn for his unilateral decisions, but Alaric persuaded him not to.

"We need him now more than ever and if he decides to use your anger as a reason not to help us, precious time will be lost in finding Rae," the large man said quietly.

Alaric was right and Jace moped about the deck while they waited to get underway. He hated having his hands tied especially since Blynn took full advantage of it time and time again.

By midafternoon, the Crest Cutter set out. The dock hands cast off the mooring lines and climbed aboard. Sailors lifted the anchor and sang a sea shanty while they went to work preparing the sails:

A friend of the ocean is a friend to me,
With nary a song or whim.
We laugh and we sing and we toil on the wings
And if he dies, we drink to him.

There be fine tales of the ladies and whales
And many a thing in the sea,
But if ever you saw the greatest of all
Have heart lads, 'tis only me.

Cast off the bow line and set for the sun
Live long, be happy and free,
And when I die, don't lift me on high,
But bury me deep in the sea.
'Tis where I'm happy and free
Have heart lads, 'tis only me.

The tune was pretty, but when Trel pondered the words, he soon realized the errors it hid. The words alluded that life ended with death and that one should live how they pleased without reservation. From his studies, Trel remembered this was the heart of every Clonesian belief, and it contradicted everything the Song of the Ages proclaimed. He decided not to sing the song in the future.

The Crest Cutter moved along quickly. Captain Meld, as he was called, was a master sailor and found plenty of power to move the big ship even in the breezeless afternoon. The boat sliced through the waves, true to its name, and they were soon around the cove and out on the open water. After a few hours the land disappeared behind them, and they were left with only waves and seagulls to look at. While the ship rocked smoothly in the deep waters, Trel and Jace made a game of seeing who could keep their balance without moving their feet on the shifting deck.

They enjoyed themselves thoroughly for the remainder of the day. Strong gusts of cold air eventually drove them below decks, and they found plenty of places to explore when the crew was too busy to rebuke their curiosity. Their cabin boy was a few years younger than them and happy to lead them around. That evening found them on the deck again, braving the wind as the sun neared the water's edge. The sight was like something neither of them had seen before. They stared in awe as the burning circle collided with its reflection and sank below the surface of the waves.

Jace turned and saw Lashara leaning on a banister. She was not looking at the sun, however, and she gripped the side of the ship with her trembling arms. Her eyes were closed and her face was a light shade of green. Jace walked over to her, careful to keep his balance on the rocking ship.

"Beautiful sunset," he commented happily. "In all my short years have I never seen one so pretty."

"Shhh," she said thickly with her eyes still closed. She seemed to be ignoring him and so he stood by her side her awhile. He looked her up and down while she stood rigid and breathing shallow.

"Are you feeling alright?" he finally asked her.

"Shut up!" she said. She fluttered her eyes and then closed them again. "I'm sorry, it's just, your talking—it only makes it worse."

"Oh," he said, dumbfounded. He stood by her a little longer and then realized she was not going to say anything more. He moved away softly and found Trel. He was sitting with the cabin boy and the two were watching while Alaric sharpened his broadsword. The young lad was examining Alaric's work and sat listening as he explained the nature of the world.

"Of course not," he was saying. "The Creator planned this place with knowledge and wisdom that we can see all around us. The sun rises in the east and sets in the west each day. The fish of the sea feed off plants and we feed off the fish. Storms drop their rain on the plants and the sun makes them grow. There are signs of an awesome design all around us that this world could not possibly have sprouted without meaning. Such a place would not have such fine inner workings."

The boy folded his hands and thought for a spell. It was clear he had never heard of the Creator and never thought of His hand at work in the world before. He scratched his face and bit his lip. A thousand questions seemed to bounce around inside his small head. The boy was intent on listening as Alaric talked with him some more. Jace and Trel watched as his features changed and his knitted brow was replaced by wonder. He looked as if he was seeing the world around him for the first time.

"Wirmal, get back to work!" came Captain Meld's angry words.

The boy ducked his head just in time to avoid a thrown glass bottle. It bounced across the deck and over the railing. Wirmal scuttled away and the captain scowled at them. By the captain's side stood Blynn, his greasy skin nearly giving off a glow in the setting sun. He was dressed in a fine, brown suede jacket and a light blue shirt. His thin silver rapier dangled from his waist. He grinned at the three of them sardonically and turned and followed the captain. The two walked to the other side of the bridge, staying close beside each other in conversation.

What Jace had just witnessed made him uncomfortable. Everyone knew that Blynn was rough and not exactly a shining example of a follower of Yeshua. They had almost accepted that this was the way he would be and they would just have to deal with him, but seeing him walking with the captain made him wonder. The men spoke and cajoled each other for all to see. One may have mistaken them for long lost brothers.

The party's rooms were separate from the sailors, but they still had not seen much of Blynn. He had taken up residence in a cabin adjacent to the captain's quarters and walked the ship with him. The two were always dressed in expensive clothes that marked their station above the rest of the sailors and guests. Blynn gave the party little attention. The group wondered if he had forgotten about them. Now seeing Blynn and Captain Meld together made them wonder just what dangerous game Blynn was playing.

They had all been upset by the displays of cruelty on the docks. Their captain was also capable of such things, no doubt, as his actions toward Wirmal suggested. If Blynn accepted Clonesians so freely, what could be said about the man's nature? No good could come of bad company, Hadran always said, and the idea of Blynn and the captain's cordiality made them like the man even less.

They went to bed early that night. The supper was a humble meal of cooked fish and a boiled potato. The food was bland and the fish was rather bony, but the company was glad to eat the meals given them.

Jace went to his cabin and laid his cloak in the tiny closet space. The room was smaller than the tavern's and far less furnished, but enormous compared to the bunk spaces that housed the crew. Still, he cringed in the small space. He had counted out the dimensions of the room—five strides by three. The eerie similarity to the size of his cell in the Mines of Shorn did little to quell his fear of closed spaces.

The first time someone had shut his door to the room, he nearly passed out in panic. The room seemed to stretch and shift, and his breathing went shallow in the stifling cabin air. He crawled his way to the door, keeping his eyes closed and felt for the hinge. The sudden rush of air was all he needed to calm his beating heart. Air aboard the ship was all the same: thick and hot with an odd assortment of fish, sweat, and other not-so-fine smells, but to him, the gush of hot air meant nothing less than freedom.

After he had done his customary propping of the door, his nerves calmed noticeably. He took and read the Song of the Ages, huddling close to the dim light of his solitary candle. The passage was from the letter to Philippi and clearly stated Yeshua's deity:

Who, being in the form of Elohim,
Thought it not robbery to be equal with Him:
But made himself of no reputation,
and took upon him the form of a servant,
and was made in the likeness of man:
And being found in fashion as a man,
he humbled himself, and became obedient unto death,
even death of the cross.
Wherefore the Almighty also hath highly exalted him,
and given him a name which is above every name:
That at the name of Yeshua every knee should bow,
of things in heaven, and things in earth, and things under the earth:
And that every tongue should confess that Yeshua is Lord,
to the glory of his Father, Elohim.

Jace had read this particular passage several times before. Sometimes he skimmed through it, not noticing half the jewels hidden in each line. Other times he poured over it, dissecting the hidden meaning behind each phrase.

Now, as he sat alone in the cabin swaying to the rocking of the ship and thought about how they were steadily moving toward the most dreaded place on earth, the passage gave new hope and meaning to his journey. All the earth one day would declare the praise that was rightly due Yeshua. All creatures under the earth—be they Du'mas, Na'tal, or even Sa'vard himself—would declare the same. In that time, the truth would be revealed, and no one would be able to rationalize or explain away his Savior's glory, no matter how powerful or strong they were.

In that moment, an unexplainable calm came over him. Yeshua, the Almighty's Son, the name that was above all others, had blessed their journey and was watching over them each step of the way. Jace had no need to fear. He knew in his humanness that he would forget the promise that had been revealed to him right then, but he thanked his Master in the solitude of the night for comforting him at this moment and in this way.

He laid the book on the shelf over his bed and took out the map and the letters from Rae. These were nowhere near as precious as the Song of the Ages, but he felt inclined to hide them nonetheless. Should someone find the book, he was more than willing to proclaim his allegiance to Yeshua, but if someone found the important documents, there was no telling what effects it would have on Rae, the party, or the freedom with which they could move about the country. He stuffed the papers under his mattress, smoothing them out so they rested flatly on the boards beneath. When he departed the ship, he would retrieve the documents, but for now, they would be kept in a place that only he knew of. He tidied his room, folded his garments in the corner, and settled to bed in his underclothes. He drifted off to sleep, stirring only to the cries of the seasick Lashara three rooms down.

BY THE END OF THE WEEK, they had made their way far into the Inland Basin. The weather here had the beginnings of spring, and a cool breeze played with the sails all week.

Jace and Trel stood at the prow counting the whitecaps in boredom. Sea life had grown rather dull for the two, and they walked about the ship with nothing to do. Whenever the captain saw Wirmal approaching them or Alaric, he shooed him off to some task below decks. The party felt ostracized from the crew, but were fed properly and left alone as long as they stayed out of the way. Lashara had stayed below decks for most of the voyage. She had resorted to locking herself in her cabin, and she could be heard groaning in sickness even when the sea wasn't too rough.

The air was crisp and Jace drank in the sun as it broached the surface of the waves. He was not a morning person, but on Trel's insistence he had climbed out of bed to watch the sunrise. The sky had changed from a cold, uninviting grey to a brilliant white after passing through every color in between. *The sight was well worth it,* Jace thought as he wiped the grains of sleep from his eyes. Trel was standing next to him watching the water's transformation with glee. Jace could only shake his head, wondering where his friend found the boundless energy to meet the day wide awake.

The hours passed uneventfully until late afternoon. Alaric sat with them by the main mast and produced a bag of round stones, many of which were brightly colored. He dumped them on the floor at their feet, and Trel and Jace eagerly gathered around him while he explained his game. Each player took three of the larger stones. He then cleared the rest away and tossed a handful of smaller stones within their small circle.

The object was simple. Each player used their large stones to hit the smaller rocks. If they succeeded in hitting a rock, they kept it. If they missed, they lost one of the three large stones. If a player hit more than one rock, they kept each one touched. The one with the most rocks was the winner even if they lost all their larger stones.

They drew lots and Jace began. He rolled his stone into the rocks hitting three tightly bunched together. Alaric gave a grunt at the beginner's success. He picked up his stone hitting two himself. As the game went on, the rocks became harder to hit and each shift of the ship made their stones roll wide. Jace was never good at fine aim and he lost his three stones all in a row. Alaric had two stones, but Trel took to the game having twice as many stones as Alaric. The game finished shortly, and Trel gave a foolish grin at winning his first time playing. Though the object and rules were easy, the game was challenging, and they played well into evening. Only a shout from the lookout interrupted their sport.

The lookout shouted again and Jace could clearly hear him cry the signal for land. A collective sigh of relief was felt across the Crest Cutter. Captain Meld urged his crew to trim the sails sharply and keep their eyes open for shoals and reefs. Blynn stood at the captain's side watching him as he went over the operations of his ship critically and paid little attention to the underlings around him as they scurried out of his way. When a few of them blocked his path, Blynn gave them each an evil look, threatening to kick anyone that did not get out of his way.

The three Keepers watched with disgust at Blynn's actions and then turned back to their game. After a supper of salted fish and biscuits, Trel and Alaric went topside while Jace checked on Lashara. They could see the mainland now, a deep blackness that stood out against the starry sky. Fires twinkled on the quiet shore, and the two stared at the land as they leaned on the banister.

"Is it truly as awful as the Mentors say?" Trel asked, turning toward Alaric.

"You will have to see for yourself, lad," said Alaric softly. "At first glance, this land looks much like any other place we've been, Trel, but as we move farther inland, you will see marked differences. Clonesians are proud people and will use any excuse to start trouble, take advantage of you, or worse...."

Trel cringed as Alaric let his words trail off into the unknown. He did not like Captain Meld and if he was anything like a Clonesian was supposed to be, they would be in for a tough time. He could only imagine a place where people had forsaken the Creator in exchange for momentary freedom of their temporary, mortal lives. Now, the possibility that he must walk amidst these people and live in their land for some time made his stomach roll.

He knew Yeshua had died for them and put that in the forefront of his mind as he prepared to venture into the Clonesian Empire. His attitude toward these people he had never met was not one of despise and hatred, but rather sadness mixed with a loss of hope. How could he relate to these who did not even honor their Maker? How could he begin to tell them of the One who loved them so that He sacrificed Himself in their place? Was their any hope that just one of them would receive Yeshua after they had rejected Him their entire lives? Trel did not know what would happen and only wished for expediency in their journey. He hoped they would find Rae swiftly and return to the Gap before the week was out.

As he and Alaric watched the land slowly approach, Trel's thoughts went over his feelings about where they were headed. Jace and Alaric had both furnished him with tidbits of information on the Clonesians. He knew his curiosity would never be satisfied until he met these people and faced his fears. He would have to wait and see how he handled each predicament and met each new problem. Maybe his actions would give them the chance to tell others about their Savior. Maybe someone would be open to listen to them.

He was worried about Blynn. His one-time friend had distanced himself from the rest of them. Their journey ashore would at least make Blynn leave the influence of Captain Meld. Hopefully, Blynn would renew his relationships with the four of them. They needed him to find Rae, but Trel also wanted Blynn to know that they cared for him as well. The signs Trel had seen aboard the ship did not bode well for Blynn's witness to others about his allegiance to Yeshua. Trel scratched his ears wondering what course Blynn would choose to take among the Clonesians.

He lowered his head and looked at the black water. How he longed now to be back at East Haven, safe at his studies! What had Yeshua seen in him to send him some place so hostile? He pulled his cloak about his shoulders. Giving himself over to the will of his Savior was always a struggle. This place would be a proving ground for them all.

12

THE CLONESIAN EMPIRE

Jace awoke to the soft lapping of the waves against the ship. The deck boards creaked noisily overhead as the crew went about their work. The rocking of the ship had stopped, and Jace flung his covers aside, remembering they had seen land yesterday. He dressed quickly, pulling his leather boots on in haste. Throwing his cloak about his shoulders, he went to the cabin's small mirror and patted down his hair. While making his way through the Crest Cutter, Jace ran into Alaric, Trel, and Lashara. The three were dressed and carried their gear on their shoulders and weapons in hand. They eyed Jace up and down.

"Where have you been?" Trel asked.

"In my quarters," he replied.

"Did you just wake up?" Lashara asked with raised eyebrows.

"Of course," he said, wondering if his hair and rumpled clothes looked that bad.

The group looked at him with big eyes. Captain Meld had sounded the morning meal three hours ago and ordered all passengers to be off his ship in a quarter hour.

He was not too pleased at the Keepers. He had recognized their cloak clasps halfway through the journey and was angry that Blynn had hidden the origin of his guests from him. If he had known, he would never have given them passage and threatened to throw them overboard while they slept that morning. Blynn had soothed the captain's feelings and paid more than triple the price of their earlier fare. Ironically, the cost was exactly what he had cheated the merchants out of for the sale of his cart. The action had put Blynn in a sour mood, but eased the captain's hatred. Captain Meld had ordered the five of them to pack and be off before midmorning or suffer the consequences. The warning bell tolled for all passengers to disembark, as if to hurry the group along.

The four of them separated. Lashara and Trel took Alaric's gear while he went with Jace to help him pack. Trel almost collapsed under the weight of Alaric's mighty broadsword and heavy axe, but Lashara steadied his feet as they struggled to the deck. Jace stifled a laugh as he turned away from the two. Trel looked like a drunken mushroom stumbling up the stairs, his thin body weighed down by the large heap of Alaric's things.

Alaric and Jace ran back to his room and threw his goods into his pack. He held the pack open while Alaric swept whole shelves clean with his arms. Jace watched as Alaric set about the room swiftly. The speed at which the large man moved was most impressive. Jace had to jump out of his way more than once. When it was stuffed, Alaric wrapped the pack about his shoulders and grabbed Jace's staff. They looked about the room for any things they could have missed, then slammed the door and ran topside.

No sooner had they stepped foot on the deck than the final bell rang. They hurried across the gangplank to be met by Captain Meld and his men. He held up a gauntleted hand, motioning for the two of them to stop.

"The bell has sounded and anything left aboard my ship is forfeit to me by right!" he declared for all to hear.

Jace and Alaric pulled up short by the captain, stunned at his words. They had never heard of such a law and did not know what to do. Lashara and Trel looked at them safely from the dock. They were worried and their faces were ashen with fear as the words hit them. Blynn stepped forward from the dock.

"What treachery is this, Meld? We've paid more than you're due!" He spat, his greasy features growing threatening. The animosity that now existed between them was quite apparent, and the two stared hard at each other. Blynn stood close by the captain, his face twisting in rage.

Meld held his ground, two of his crew flanking out beside him in case of any trouble. Blynn scoffed at them and turned his attention back to the captain.

"Let them go!" he said flatly.

"I wouldn't dream of it, Blynn. Unless, there is something you can offer in exchange," he said, his eyes looking at the bag of gold that hung from Blynn's side and then resting on Lashara. Blynn threw back his cloak, and tapped his rapier gently.

"Let them go."

Captain Meld opened his mouth in shock and then hardened his jaw. His eyes smoldered.

"You wouldn't!"

"Oh, but I would," Blynn said hungrily.

Meld's eyes hardened again and he snapped his fingers. The two guards spread out, brandishing their swords while Jace and Alaric watched helplessly from the gangplank. They waved their weapons low to the ground, watching Blynn cautiously. The dirty man seemed not to notice and continued to hold Meld's gaze. Meld also had drawn his sword: a heavy blade with a jeweled hilt that showed the merchant's crest on the pommel. It glittered sharply in the morning sun as he leveled it at Blynn.

Blynn surveyed the three, taking each in carefully. He flexed his shoulders and shook his head lazily from side to side. His face seemed filled with anticipation and his fingers twitched excitedly. He spread his feet and leaned forward, ready to spring into action.

One of the ruffians lunged at him forcefully, thrusting his sword forward and off balance. Blynn sidestepped and brought his fist down atop the man's neck. The sailor stumbled forward and turned slowly, shaking his dazed head and rubbing his shoulder. Meld and the other man jumped at Blynn in fury, their blades pointed as they lunged.

In a flash, Blynn spun away from them, drawing his sword. Meld and his crony shied back a moment and then dove at him again. Blynn's point seemed to move in a whip-like fashion, and he knocked the blades away with ease. An exuberant hate was etched on his face, and he smiled darkly as he parried the swords to his sides. While his hands moved deftly, his feet danced on the dock in perfect balance. The other henchmen recovered from his blow and clumsily joined the fray.

As Jace watched, he realized Blynn was a much better swordsman than he had shown himself to be in the forest. Though the blades sang about the filthy man's head, he used his sword and shifted his body to avoid every blow or turn it away. Those on the dock hardly cast a glance at the melee, either feigning disinterest or refusing to be associated with such behavior. Jace got the feeling, however, that they had all seen plenty of these altercations before.

Captain Meld was clearly the best swordsman of the three attackers. The two sailors charged at Blynn with brutish blows and off-balance lunges and were showing signs of fatigue already. They kept Blynn busy while Meld hung back and joined in with well-aimed thrusts from his heavy sword. Meld was patient and waited his chances. His eyes blazed with scorn and revenge from Blynn's betrayal and deceit.

Finally, Blynn pushed his advance. He drove into the three, scattering them with his blows. His lips were peeled back as he laid about them in wrath. His focused attacks were quick, and he lashed his adversaries with lightning thrusts and slashes. A look of shock and then fear that Jace had seen once before filled the men's faces as they frantically dodged Blynn's blade.

Blynn went to work with expert precision. Though Jace never fully saw his blade, a nick appeared suddenly here and there about the sailor's shoulders. Their efforts became slower as they fought to keep their swords raised. Blynn's horrible features were twisted in rage, and he renewed his spearing and cutting with speed Jace had never seen. The sailors fell back, holding their blades ever lower, and even Meld fought to keep his composure.

The sailor to Blynn's left pushed aside his attack but was too slow to bring his blade back around. Blynn drove his sword clean through the man's shoulder, twisting the blade as he drew it out and setting about the swordsman to his right. The wounded swordsman yelped in pain as his blade clattered to the ground. He clutched his shoulder and fell to his knees. Blynn drove the others back a ways and then turned on the injured sailor, driving his sword through his other shoulder at an odd angle. He pulled the blade upward, causing the man to come to his feet as he howled in pain. The sailor's eyes rolled back in his head and he slumped unconsciously forward.

Seeing this, the others drove forward in anger and fear, but this was what Blynn wanted. Meld and his cohort now lashed at Blynn with unfocused malice, their wide blows leaving them unprotected. Blynn dodged aside and struck out with his sword, sinking it through the other sailor's leg. The man fell to one knee, turning and stumbling to bring his blade to bear, but Blynn had already struck again. It landed on the man's forearm with an awful crunch and his sword sprang loose from his hand. The man leaned forward, steadying his body with his broken arm and crying out in agony. The sounds of the wounded seemed only to heighten Blynn's bloodlust and he swept aside Captain Meld's attacks, piercing the sailor at his feet after each one. After the man collapsed, he turned his rage on the captain.

Meld's face grew stern and he fought Blynn with stoic composure. Blynn laid about the man with practice, goading the captain to attack. Finally, Meld lunged. His blade was well-aimed, but only slightly lower than it should have been. Blynn easily turned the sword aside, looping the blade around his own. The maneuver jarred Meld's sword from his hands and it spun away down the dock. Meld fell to his knees, pleading for mercy, but Blynn lifted the captain's head with the tip of his blade.

"You should have taken the fair price when you had the chance, Meld. Now your time has run out."

Blynn drew his sword back and prepared to strike, but Lashara's scream cut him short. He turned and looked first at Lashara and Trel, then at Alaric and Jace. Alaric's gaze was dark with disapproval, and Blynn lowered his blade to the ground. He backed away from the sobbing captain and gave a short, mocking bow.

"Remember this," he hissed. "There will come a time when I shall collect my debt of mercy," he said and turned toward Lashara and Trel.

Alaric and Jace made their way over and around the disgraced captain and through the moaning sailors. They caught up to Blynn who was walking quickly down the dock, trying to get away before the local garrison was alerted. He turned past a shop, going down a narrow alley and then turned back on to a main street. After several moments, he turned down a side street again and twisted around a number of smaller roads. The crowds were large here, even away from the docks, and Blynn motioned for the four of them to follow him closely and not get lost.

After his nerves had calmed, Jace went over Blynn's encounter on the docks. The more he digested it, the more incensed he became. One of the first rules his Mentors had taught him was not to harm another person. Jace had struggled with the belief and still did, but his teachers constantly reminded him of his actions. Even if his life depended on it, he was to hold another life sacred. Yeshua had died for all men. One should never presume that he was the means for removing another's soul from them. Keepers represented Yeshua Himself, and so must always convey the actions of their Savior.

Consequently, Blynn's actions were disastrous. He had gone out of his way to harm another person. It did not matter that they were Clonesians. Yeshua had died for all men, and so all men were to be respected. Jace thought up a number of alternative endings that would have led to a far less violent conclusion.

He caught up to Blynn and began to voice his complaints, but he was shushed rudely as their guide led them further from the wharf. By noon, they were well on the other side of the city and Jace had had enough. He did not care how it turned out, the man had done enough damage already and had to be stopped. His selfish attitude and questionable actions coupled with his disregard for rules and human life had gone too far. Finally, Jace confronted their guide, planting his feet in his way. Blynn almost bowled him over before halting directly in his face. The two stared at each other, Blynn's face growing livid.

"You need to answer for yourself, Blynn," Jace said loudly. "You have continued to do whatever you wish without a care for others or following Yeshua's guidance. When Wirmal was disciplined, you laughed at him, you all but removed yourself from us aboard the ship, you have cheated and bribed others, and now you have attacked and seriously wounded two of Captain Meld's crew—all of which goes against the teachings of Yeshua and the Song of the Ages!"

Hearing talk of Yeshua, a number of people on the street slowed. Their stares were icy and many of them thumbed their swords, which everyone seemed to carry. The fairway grew noticeably quiet and Blynn led them a healthy distance down a side street. When he was far enough away, he turned on Jace.

"You stupid boy!" he said in a strangled tone. "Your foolish acts and disregard will get the whole lot of us killed or worse yet!"

"I don't care anymore, Blynn!" Jace retorted. "Your actions are despicable and you need to make yourself right, or we will venture on without you. I would rather spend twice as long looking for Rae than tolerating your behavior or pretending to look the other way any longer."

"Don't tempt me!" Blynn spat, rising up in Jace's face. "The only reason I continue to humor you is because of my word. You owe me your life, or maybe I should have let

Captain Meld have his way with you. Perhaps you wish to go against Dorath's commands and strike out on your own? Go ahead," he said, flinging his arm in the direction of the road, "You will never find your brother, if you even last a day here."

Jace felt about his clothes for the map and letters that would help point him to his brother. They were clear proof that he did not need Blynn. Once Blynn saw them, he would have no choice but to acquiesce or be dismissed.

Jace's anger turned to dismay as he fumbled through his shirt, pants, and then his pack. The map and the letters from Rae were not there. He groaned loudly, gritting his teeth at his loss. The documents were back on the Crest Cutter, neatly tucked underneath his bed. There was no way he could retrieve them if he wanted to, Blynn's actions had assured that. The tables had once again turned in Blynn's favor, and Jace hung his head knowing they had no choice left but to follow wherever the contemptuous man said. He seethed openly at him, wishing their paths had never crossed.

Blynn's white lips drew back in a smile and he leaned forward. "What were you going to say?" He questioned Jace with a rueful grin. He paused in triumph as Jace stood with his head lowered in anguish.

"Dorath was right, you just don't know when to take orders," he said, clicking his tongue. He stood over Jace, waiting till he raised his head. When he spoke, Blynn's voice was a whisper of hatred. "If you cross me again, I will leave you and your filthy band to rot in this place. Clonesians can smell fear and four lowly Keepers would be no match for them. I will take you to Rae, but after that, we are finished," he said and walked away.

The others huddled around Jace whose body trembled softly. They had heard some of the words Blynn had said, but his threats and promises had escaped their ears. Alaric and Trel stood nearby dumbfounded, not knowing what to say or tell Jace. Lashara reached out to him, touching Jace on the shoulders. He flinched under her soft touch and when Jace turned upwards, tears streamed down his face.

"I hate that man—" he choked through clenched teeth and then lowered his head in quiet sobs. The hopelessness of the situation had drained him. The fight in the woods with Blynn had cemented his feelings about the man, but still he had tried with all his heart to obey Dorath. He had gone out of his way to make him feel welcome and hidden his feelings for the sake of the group.

Blynn, on the other hand, had taken every opportunity to publicly demean Jace. It had broken his confidence and made him feel worthless. Only the others' subtle encouragement had restored his fragile self-esteem.

Blynn made it a point to show that he was both the leader and indispensable to the party. The way he flaunted his authority and knowledge of what they did not know had at first plucked Jace's nerves. Blynn never offered thanks or a kind word to any of them and had made every effort on the ship to show others he was all but one of them.

He wanted so much to leave the iron yoke that Blynn had put over the group, but every time he did, Blynn roped them in again. No matter how much he tried, Blynn's actions always seemed to be one step ahead of them, and they were left with nowhere to turn, but to continue following the shady, despicable character. It did not make sense. Jace was filled with a suffocating rage. He could not understand how Yeshua could possibly be glorified through Blynn or how it was a blessing to remain in his company.

When he had thought of traveling the world to tell others about Yeshua in the presence of other Keepers, he had pictured a time of rejoicing and happiness where all of them were of like minds. The wedge between Blynn and himself was aggravating and unjustified. He had tried to appease him, but the man was never satisfied with his role, and now that they had stepped foot on foreign soil, his animosity toward them all seemed to grow exponentially.

Alaric, Trel, and Lashara huddled around Jace as he wept softly, not knowing what else to do, or where to go. Finally, Jace looked at them again. His face was red and his eyes were puffy.

"This will not get better, will it?" he asked each of them.

Lashara tightened her lips, not daring to speak. Alaric and Trel looked about them, wishing to look anywhere, but into their friend's eyes. Each fought their own feelings of dismay. None could think of an encouraging word.

Trel reached out his hands to those beside him.

"No, not here," Jace said, looking back out at the street and the crowd that had dispersed. He led them farther down the alley to an alcove in the wall where they huddled close, out of sight of any passersby. He grasped his friends' hands in his, holding back his tears and began to call upon Yeshua.

Each of them spoke in turn. Their petitions were quiet but earnest, and each muttered their agreements as they spoke to their heavenly Father. They honestly voiced their bitterness with Blynn and asked for guidance in the matter. Each admitted their doubts about their journey and asked Yeshua to put them back in His will again. They continued for the better part of an hour, until they found no need to say anything more, knowing the Counselor knew what they meant. A wave of peace washed over their hearts, and they knew the Master had heard their cries. They opened their eyes and looked around.

The sky had darkened slightly, though it was nearly noon. Jace looked overhead at the clouds that were a pale white, as if all warmth had been sucked from their shapes. Everywhere he looked, the color was the same. The buildings were leeched of their beauty. The stucco walls they saw were dry and plain. None were in disrepair, but neither were the shades as vibrant as they had seemed before. The dull light made everything less alive than they had first seen.

Even the rich colors of the merchants walking by the alley were faded with a dim lifeless tint. The clothes they wore were the same and the elegant fabrics and jewelry about their necks and arms were still far beyond what any of the Keepers could afford. Under the pale light, however, all the finery and glamour did not seem as enticing as it had at first.

People on the street acted much the same as any place of commerce, but there was something different. As aboard the ship, the local merchants, craftsman, soldiers, and commoners had a tangible coldness that hung about them. The harsh stares that they had noticed were not only directed at them but also each other. The air about the entire city seemed to sit with an edgy tenseness that seemed like it would shatter if provoked. The party walked slowly back out into the crowded street, surveying the world and how differently it had changed since they called upon Yeshua.

"The Creator has opened our eyes to the truth of this place," Alaric said softly.

It's true, thought Trel. When Lashara and he had waited on the docks, they had been overwhelmed by the regal air in the city. Everywhere they turned, new fancies and delights beckoned to them. Jugglers in fine outfits entertained large crowds. Extravagant smells of cooking wafted through the markets. Hawkers and merchants sold everything from playful trinkets to horses and livestock. Wherever the two had looked, more amusements had popped up to offer a variety of entertainment, all of which seemed to cater to their every desire. The port was alive with activity that tantalized their eyes and tugged at their souls.

Now, all around them, they could see shrouded men standing at corners of buildings or out-of-the-way places. They stood motionless, and those that passed them neither greeted them nor talked to them. The pale sun seemed to flee from these figures. Their cloaks soaked up the light, and no reflection of their bodies painted the ground at their feet. The mysterious dark shadows hovered everywhere the Keepers turned their eyes, gauging the activity and monitoring the city. None seemed to see the Watchers but them, and the foul shadows went about their tasks with a hideous purpose.

Jace could hear a subtle whispering in his ears that was barely audible. The sound came from every direction—a low murmur of chanting that filled the fair. At times it rose in volume and then dipped to a whisper. The longer Jace listened to the song of the Watchers, the more he lusted after his surroundings. His vision fluctuated between that of a brilliantly decorated city where the sun shown gloriously to the pale lifeless color that he had seen long ago in Yeshua's vision. He steeled himself and walked on, drowning the deathly melody by reciting verse after verse from the Song of the Ages.

The Keepers recoiled at the site of the Watchers. Only Alaric, in his years in Yeshua's service, had seen so many before. The rest followed his lead, keeping their eyes close to the ground and their thoughts on the Almighty.

The Watchers paid them little mind. Maybe they had not recognized the Keepers, or perhaps they were preoccupied with the crowds under their spell. Whatever the reason, they walked past the shadowless creatures without incident.

The four of them wandered through the streets aimlessly, hoping to catch site of Blynn. The city was flat and sprawled out for miles in every direction. It was a mirror image of Samilon, its business also coming from the shipping across the Inland Basin. Folk here were curt, of course, and kept their beady eyes pointed straight ahead. They gave Jace and the party suspicious glances and a wide berth. Their dark woolen cloaks stood out against the colorful fabrics of the city, and they stuffed them in their packs to avoid attention.

The air here was dry and significantly hot for early spring. As the dull sun crept into the sky, the heat made the air shimmer, and the party had to stop to refill their waterskins every few city streets they past. Jace and Trel loosened the ties on their cotton shirts, letting the air pass across their skin. Lashara looked on jealously at their exposed chests and rolled up her sleeves instead. The going was slow, and they rested in the hot shade of the roofs of the buildings.

The Clonesian Empire was rumored to have one of the largest standing armies in the world. The Mentors at East Haven told about the country's vast wealth and how it enabled their emperor to field a large number of troops almost continually. He could do this because of the heavy dependence on slave labor, tremendous efficiency of their farmlands, a steady trade with the Stygians, and sheer strength of arms. Civilians only spoke the best of their ruler, which was due in large part to the imperial presence that was visible everywhere one went.

Rows of mounted soldiers marched through the city and pikemen stood at every corner. An invisible barrier went out before the troops, and the sea of commoners parted for them as they paraded through the market with stern faces. The mounted troops rode with chainmail hauberks falling to their thighs. Their faces were covered with slatted helms, and they watched the crowds through them with sharp eyes. The footsoldiers seemed more idle, shifting on their feet as they surveyed the crowd. They were armed mostly with short swords, an occasional buckler, and the fearsome halberd. The heavy bladed spear also had a gruesome axe at its tip that was known to inflict horrible wounds. The militia stood about in fives, sometimes tens, striding here and there, but stiffened noticeably when their superiors rode by.

Off to one side, Jace could see an officer, marked by a plumed helmet and red vest, questioning a group of merchants. The looks on their faces were fearful as they answered rapidly to the soldier. One of the merchants was waving his hands, pointing about him in disarray. A man approached him on foot from behind the officer which Jace could clearly see was Captain Meld. He limped slightly and listened to the merchant intently, scanning the crowd for Blynn or the Keepers. The party slipped by unnoticed and continued rapidly through the streets.

Like Nadir, everything here had a price. Merchants shooed them away when they realized they would not buy anything, and housemasters ushered them angrily outside when they saw the party would not even buy a drink.

The truth was Blynn had kept the money purse when he stormed off. Alaric had a few coins of his own, and Trel and Lashara found some after rummaging through their packs, but between them all they had precious few. They decided to save what they had, spending only what they needed frugally and haggling the hawkers down to the very last copper. It came to their attention that the street vendors and hawkers had the lowest prices on goods. They did not bother patronizing the finer shops of the merchants after that.

The merchants were rather happy the four of them did not enter their stores. Their guild had regulations that bad attire by the clients was bad for business and their reputation. Commoners were swiftly thrown out of such establishments, and though the merchants did not know what to make of the Keepers in their strange clothing of the Gap, they threw them out as well. The hawkers were more than willing to trade and saw the merchants' loss as their gain.

Anything and everything was used for currency. When a vendor, by chance, saw the game of shiny stones Alaric carried, his eyes grew as big as plates. After first offering the entire bag to fill their waterskins, Alaric whittled the man down to one stone. When the deal was done, the man held the stone close to his dirty face, turning it around in the pale sunlight. A look of wonder spread across his face and he broke into a giant grin, showing a number of missing teeth. Apparently polished stones were a rarity in these parts, and the party soon realized that they had more to offer than they once thought.

By late afternoon, they found Blynn. He was standing outside a rundown tavern talking to several of the local riff-raff. They were smiling at his new purchase: a well-to-do cart led by two heavy draft horses. The cart itself was carved with inlaid wood. Gilded accents ran down the fenders and the seats. The reins were fastened neatly to an iron handle and the rider's bench was stitched cushioned velvet with a hardy bronze brake by the side. The cart was covered by heavy canvas with gold embroidery. Its bed was spacious and loaded with foodstuffs, fabrics, and various metal ornaments and decorations held in brightly wrapped boxes of outrageously expensive paper. Blynn hovered over the cart, showing all his proud possession.

"...sold to me for ten gold and three coppers," he was saying. "The man had no choice but to buy it after I told him of the proof I had. No wife likes finding her husband in such a precarious position, after all."

The men laughed and cheered for Blynn, raising their mugs high. A number of them lurched and stumbled in the late afternoon sun. They were obviously drunk but carried on in their loud voices.

Blynn grew stern when he saw the party approaching and dispersed the crowd with a shower of coins. The men reached for the shiny objects at their feet, pushing and shoving those nearest out of their way. Those that grabbed the coins stumbled inside the tavern to buy another drink. Blynn watched them leave, a sardonic smile on his face.

"I didn't expect you for another day," he said to the four of them mockingly. He stood by his cart while the party piled in, avoiding his smug frown. Only Alaric lifted his face to look him in the eyes and Blynn stepped back slightly. An unspoken admonishment passed between the two, and Blynn tightened his jaw in defiance when Alaric turned his back.

He climbed aboard and backed the cart away from the tavern. The peculiar punishment he had given them was somewhat childish, but they kept quiet since there was little else they could do. Their wandering through the city had proved to each of them how lost they were without their repugnant guide, and they accepted his "kindness" now with a hidden loathing. They rode on through the streets quietly and passed the city gates in the fading sun.

This time there was no bribery of the tower guards. The soldiers didn't move as the cart exited their station out into the flatlands. Their hauberks and shields caught the light of the setting sun as they stood ominously still on the battlements of the walled city.

Trel watched Blynn closely. Since the change in light, his olive-colored skin had changed to a pallid white. His sullen, pale face had a look of unspoken fear. He stared straight ahead as they passed under the portcullis and tapped the reins nervously. Blynn's lack of confidence spoke volumes about the pecking-order of the Clonesians. No matter how wealthy or powerful one was, the ultimate power was in the hands of the kingdom's military that, combined with the ever-present Watchers, kept a stranglehold on the population's resentments.

It was true that Blynn was scared. Those secrets that he had kept from the party would not be revealed until it was too late, but he could not hide the terror he had for the soldiers. Clonesians were fearfully militant, and their selfish attitudes had a way of provoking clashes of any magnitude from a private scuffle to an all out war between nations. Blynn's long service within the Clonesian Empire made him painfully aware of this whenever he was in the vicinity of, or under the gaze of the army. He could not hide his fear of them and cringed inwardly, knowing that his sign of weakness might cause the others to take advantage of him.

Lashara saw the scowl that Blynn tried to hide from everyone else. It was not that apparent, but the slight shiver of his arms gave him away. She knew he was frightened and wondered why. The man had too many secrets. Clearly he had been hiding something from the rest of them. It pricked her nerves that she had not found out what it was. All this time from Nadir, through the North Wood, across the Stygian Union, and over the Inland Basin, she had watched him and pondered his secret. There was something about him she could not put her finger on, and she eyed him sideways in the evening light.

With the sunset, most of them settled in for the night. Trel and Lashara sprawled out among the packages, and after Blynn scalded them for rumpling a box, they fell asleep in the mess. The ride was not too comfortable. The road, though flat, was filled with ruts and bumps. Somehow they managed to find sleep despite the jostling of the cart, the crunching of the packages and sacks, and the smell from Blynn's pipe smoke.

Alaric and Jace hung out the back of the cart. They had lowered the gate at the guardhouse and now sat with their legs dangled over the edge in the night. When the heat had lifted, the lowlands came to life in the evening air. A chorus of frogs, crickets, and strange loud flies that Jace had never heard before sang as the stars appeared. The area to either side of the road must have been marshes, Jace guessed, and every now and then a musty, dank smell came up on the thick humid breeze.

In spite of everything, Jace was happy and grinned openly. He loved the road, the countryside, seeing the moon and stars, and hearing the wild noises that filled the night. It did not matter that they were in the Clonesian Empire, or that they still rode with Blynn. Times like these—when the night came alive with life and all nature made a melody of its own—could not be spoiled by the things he had gone through that day. These were the moments when he felt Yeshua's presence watching over him. Jace closed his eyes for a moment and listened to the noises in silence.

Alaric had taken out his axe and sword. Tonight, he only oiled the blades, letting nature continue its chorus undisturbed. He watched Jace take in his surroundings. Somehow the young man could heal the deepest wounds he had by the simplest means. It made him happy that the lad was feeling fine after the awful run-ins he had had with Blynn. His remarkable ability to bounce back from such circumstances was noteworthy. Jace turned to Alaric and beamed.

"Sometimes, there are moments in life that stand out from those around them."

Alaric simply nodded at the Jace's observation. He thanked the Maker that fleeting moments like these could be used to quicken the spirit.

The two of them turned their attention to the horizon as the sky darkened. The outline of the city was clearly evident on the flat plain. Even now it took up a fair portion of the horizon. Off in the distance, lights bounced off the low-hanging clouds. They were evenly spaced in the distance, and Jace questioned Alaric on their meaning.

"The coastal watchfires of the Clonesians," Alaric muttered with disapproval.

Jace gave a short gasp. He had forgotten the towers and fires from Yeshua's vision and had not seen the structures as they disembarked from the Crest Cutter. Alaric surmised that the reason he had not seen any in the city was because of its commercial aspect. The fancies of the city served as an enticement to traders and adventurers stepping foot on Clonesian soil for the first time. The watchtowers, on the other hand, herded the newcomers, keeping them from asking too many questions and becoming too curious while Sa'vard's Watchers worked their spell of enchantment. Jace grimaced as he eyed their glow. He judged the lights were well over ten leagues away and stared in amazement at their brightness. The clouds hung silently, their orange underbellies marking where each watchfire stood.

Jace quickly forgot his carefree air and pondered the ramifications of the watchtowers. They were a clear reminder that this land was both hostile and unwelcome to Keepers. He looked over at Alaric who was oiling his blades. He felt an intense urge to find Rae that very moment and flee from the Clonesian Empire before dawn, but knew that was impossible. He sat impatiently swinging his legs on the back of the cart, hoping Blynn would hurry them to their destination.

Once they found Rae, he was sure to return. Jace knew his brother. Nothing could keep them apart and he was not an unreasonable man. As soon as he realized his mistakes and the urgent need they had for him back home, he would return without any trouble. Jace was delighted at the prospect of meeting his brother over the next few days.

A thought suddenly occurred to him and he interrupted Alaric.

"The watchfires, Alaric," said Jace. The man lifted his face and turned to him. "Yeshua told me they keep people from leaving the Clonesian Empire."

Alaric nodded. He knew their dark purpose, but Jace was flustered.

"If they keep one from leaving, how will we return to the Gap?" he cried in dismay.

Alaric lowered his head to his oiling. He rubbed the cloth down his broadsword and wiped the excess oil from the blade, raising it aloft in the darkness. He inspected his work, not seeming to hear Jace's question. Jace fumed, his anxiety even more pronounced. He was getting ready to ask again when Alaric calmly laid his weapon down, wrapped it patiently in its cloth, and pursed his lips.

"That is in the Maker's hands, Jace," he said quite plainly.

Jace's eyes opened wide. Alaric's patience infuriated Jace sometimes. How could he sit there and so matter-of-factly address the issue with such a statement? Alaric turned to Jace, a thin smile plainly evident in the moonlight.

"We will just have to wait and see, my friend," he said, giving Jace a reassuring touch on the shoulder. "You must learn to trust Him," he chided Jace. "He has sent us on this journey, not Dorath, Hadran, or the Council. He has gathered each one of us for a specific reason, even Blynn, I'm afraid. Though I do not have the answers, I am not deterred. I know the One who does and I place my faith in Him."

Jace looked at his friend, stunned. He obviously had thought of their predicament long ago. Jace knew he would have to trust his Savior on things he did not understand, but the thought still perplexed him. How could he rest without knowing the answer to so blatant an obstacle that threatened their path?

"You must sleep now," Alaric said, as if he had heard Jace's thoughts. Jace looked at him in agitation. "You have had enough for one day, Jace. Don't worry about tomorrow; it has enough problems of its own."

Jace gave Alaric a wry look and then climbed into the back of the cart. Alaric was right again, but it did little to calm Jace's anxiety. He lay awake for sometime, listening to the night noises while the cart lurched on the flat dirt road before he fell asleep.

13

THE SEARCH FOR RAE

The jostling of the cart that lulled the Keepers to sleep awoke them the next morning. Blynn had driven them straight through the night, his fear of the soldiers getting the best of him. Alaric turned from his station on the back of the cart and nodded as the other three roused themselves to meet the day.

They climbed to the rear of the cart and spread out a blanket while Trel rummaged through his belongings. The biscuits, dried meat, and cheese they had for breakfast was a treat. Jace and Lashara looked at their friend suspiciously. Neither of them could figure out how Trel could come up with such extravagant meals and still have enough room to fit all those things into his packs.

Trel merely gave a sly smile and winked at them. As long as they were happy, they really couldn't complain, and Trel didn't see any reason in explaining his secrets when they weren't needed. He did his best to lounge amongst the packages as the cart bounced along through the day.

The party stared out at their new surroundings. Their vision had reverted back, and the pale light was nowhere to be found. The sun was shining above the trees and they scanned the land around them. They were still on the broad, flat plain that bordered the Inland Basin, though the city was nowhere to be seen. All about them were green fields that ran in every direction in a checkerboard pattern. Low trees marked their edge where deep ditches of water flowed between the fields.

The dikes were wider than Jace remembered. The ancient waterways had small barges that were moored by certain fields. Droves of people were filling them with produce while others pushed the large flat boats about the waterways with tall poles. The barges were then tied to piers beside the roads and were unloaded onto a caravan of wagons that dispersed in every direction. Some carts moved back towards the city, others up the coastline, and still others moved farther inland. The task was overseen by a number of ugly looking men with whips and a fair amount of mounted soldiers and pikemen. Thin stone towers dotted the fields. Jace could see masked archers in them keeping a watchful eye on the operations below them. They held their bows tightly, each having an arrow knocked and a full quiver at their side. The task was monumental and the party could only guess at how many men, women, soldiers, and merchants were spread out on the miles of fields around them.

Lashara was eyeing the men with whips contemptuously.

"Slavemasters," she sneered.

Her observation made something click in Jace's head. He finally understood how far-reaching the influence of the Clonesian Empire extended. The slave trade was not some separate entity that was alive on its own. Its power sprung here where its usefulness came to fruition. The endless free labor was the sole reason that the Clonesian Empire could continue to function with such opulence and power. How fitting that the decadence and splendor that Sa'vard had created was traced back to so hideous a profession.

He looked around and saw for the first time the different people in the fields. Some were tall and thin, like himself. Others were shorter and thick-muscled like Alaric. Some were women, he even saw children among the rows of vegetables, grains, and fruit. Still others were dark-skinned people that Jace had never seen before. The slaves seemed to be gathered from every realm. His heart went out to them as they moved along. Injustices filled the world and some, if not all, would remain until Yeshua returned.

THE DAYS PASSED BY SLOWLY. Gradually the land changed from the low-lying country to rolling hills. As they moved westward, the grass browned. The trees thinned out and the short, dry wasteland steadily took over. The vegetation withered to near nothing and only stunted, twisted shrubs and clumps of tall grass dotted the bleak terrain.

Every now and then, Jace and Trel spotted a caravan of merchants or a column of soldiers marching along a far off road, but the distances here were long, and they met few travelers on their path. The weather became blazing hot during the day and was substantially colder at night. Each of them took out their cloaks and wrapped themselves in extra clothes when the sun disappeared. The loose soil kicked up dust freely, and the sand got into all their belongings and several of Blynn's goods. Blynn kept the cart at a slow pace over the hills, more careful to move safely through the wilderness than to be done with the place.

The landscape reminded Trel of East Haven, and he wondered what his friends were up to back at the fortress turned institute. It was most certainly approaching spring. The winter that year had probably been bitter cold, and Hadran must have had a joyous time in the notoriously bleak weather. Trel did not miss the winters of that desolate place. The stone walls were always freezing and the place was filled with drafts. Even after the Mentors had given him his cloak, he had remained cold. He remembered walking through the halls, his hands freezing and his toes numb. The memory seemed very distant in this land, and he found it hard to believe as he wiped his sweaty face.

The outposts they passed here were nothing more than a handful of rundown houses around a plain, dusty courtyard. Blynn stopped long enough for them to fill their waterskins and purchase supplies before getting back on the dusty road. The man had not said anything to them since they left the city and watched them silently from atop the cart while they went about their business there. He gave no sign of communication and more than once Trel and Jace had to chase down the cart as it moved out of the outpost. His actions got them angry, but they refused to talk to Blynn and huddled next to Lashara and Alaric in the back of the cart.

The four of them had organized the cart to their liking, much to Blynn's dismay. They had neatly built a wall between them and Blynn with the goods that were spread throughout the cart, keeping the softer ones for pillows and cushions. The barrier rose more than halfway up the sides of the cart and even Blynn seemed to welcome the lack of socialization between him and the others. Lashara and Alaric had fastened their two cloaks to the back of the cart and the drape kept the cabin cool. It was rather spacious, everything considered, and comfortable also. At night, the two of them would remove their cloaks to bundle up in and let down the back plank for anyone to dangle their feet out, if they wished. They rode that way through the wasteland and the days plodded by.

By the end of the month, they had traveled far into the interior of the Empire and the land had changed again. One morning, they awoke to a cool breeze upon their faces. The sun was high in the sky and, out the back of the cart, the wasteland was showing signs of green. Over the course of the day, the land changed dramatically. The grade of the land had risen steadily upward over the past few weeks and though they had not known it, they had been climbing. They crested the gentle slope and the land opened up before them.

Blynn turned the cart along the ridge and the rear opening caught the two vastly different environments in one picture. To the east were the bland, dry wastelands they had just crossed where the irrigation fields of the Inland Basin had not yet traversed. To the west were the rolling plains of the Clonesian heartlands. Gigantic forests spread over the land, their dark green patches separating the open countryside. Towns of wooden houses dotted the plain, and herds of untamed horses and other large beasts roamed where they wished. Jace could see thousands of troops here and there, their spear points and armor reflecting off the sun. Garrisons of soldiers were spaced out evenly on the roads and byways, and a number of the troops were drilling in the cool summer morning, their bodies like ants in their tight formations. Two huge cities oversaw the plain, one to the south, the other in the north. Their gated walls sat atop massive hills, and their towers and pinnacles dominated the land around them. Far to the north, Jace could see the Clonesian Heights in a haze. The sight was foreboding, for he knew the Lothian Plain, the unprotected flatlands that led into Sa'vard's realm were in that direction.

Even at this distance, he recognized the northern city as Clonesia, the capital of the sprawling Empire, and the crown jewel of Sa'vard's earthly victory. The view was astounding, even though the city itself must have been some 20 leagues away. It was enormous in size and had outgrown its walls several times. Its population spilled over them, marked by houses that ringed the giant hill and spread into the valley around it. In the center of the city jutted out the imperial palace. Its walls were a gleaming silver. The flags on its towers were not noticeable this far away, but the regal structure was clearly evident.

In the heart of the city, directly opposite the palace sat the Kolosia. Its tanned walls were innocently displayed, but Jace trembled, knowing what hid within them. He could almost hear the screams and cries of his fellow Keepers and the innocents who had met their fate there.

The city far to the south was an enigma to Jace. He did not remember it from his vision. Its walls stood staunchly on the high plateau it occupied. It was nowhere near as majestic or grand as Clonesia, but was a gem in its own rite and far larger than Nadir. The stark buildings of its inhabitants contrasted sharply against the garish opulence of Clonesia. No notable structure rose from within its walls, save one. A gray obelisk, unlike the rest of Clonesian architecture, rose up from the urban sprawl. The stone structure dwarfed the rest of the city. Only the imperial palace and the Kolosia were built in its fashion. This was the Belazian Keep. It marked the home of the Commander General of the Clonesian military, who answered directly to the emperor. The city of Trailaden was the capital of the southern provinces, and was only slightly smaller than Clonesia. Throngs of military marched in and out of the city, and the party looked on with awe at the might of the Clonesians.

Blynn turned his cart towards Trailaden, making his way slowly down the slope that descended into the Inner Plain. Despite its immensity, the city was nearly two days away and the party made themselves ready for the last leg of their journey.

They went over their belongings the remainder of the day, making sure their goods were secure and organized. Trel gathered up his pots and pans, examining them for extra scratches, dings, and bends. The objects had made it this far in surprisingly good shape, and Trel smiled in satisfaction as he packed them away. The food stuffs were in good order and he made sure all were well-placed for maximum storage.

Lashara had brought along a pouch of herbs and a handful of bottled medicines that none of the other Keepers knew about. They were her most prized possessions, given to her by Miss Pell. She had mixed feelings about not using them, but was glad they had remained secure throughout their trip. They were worth far more than the cart and all the goods that Blynn had cheated his friend out of. Lashara was glad that the greedy man had never known that she kept such rarities hidden.

They each did one last check of their weapons. They would be little use against an army, but they wanted to be ready in case there was some minor altercation within the heart of the city that the military forces were not involved in. Alaric stowed his axe and broadsword against the wall of the cart next to Jace's staff. Trel lashed his short sword to his pack, and Lashara gave her dagger a look before sheathing it and tucking it back under her belt.

They grew fidgety throughout the day and woke early the next morning. None of them knew what to expect in Trailaden. The military of the Clonesians was unlike that of the Gap. The latter was of necessity while the former almost put on a show. Their smart salutes that they gave each other and well-polished armor had few scratches or dents and seemed more suited toward the parade than the battlefield.

None of them had any doubt about the army's abilities. They had seen their movement in the port city and watched them drilling as they came down into the valley. The world knew far and wide of their exploits and the unsurpassed might of the Clonesian army. Some of the Constables at East Haven believed the Clonesian armies could swallow the entire continent, if ever they were roused. Although Keepers the world over gave them their due respect, they knew the forces of the Gap were far more important. The Clonesian army could quell any person, but only the Keepers stood in defense against Sa'vard. Furthermore, any fool could hold a sword. The Keepers wondered what drove the troops to preserve such rigor if they did not fight against the forces of Sa'vard. What greater foes could one have?

They entered the city well after nightfall. It was not what they expected. The streets were quiet and still. Few moved about them, save for their cart and the soldiers. An occasional one or two people walked along the darkened streets, but they were obviously off-duty soldiers and kept to their business. The roads were clean and void of traffic, litter, and riff-raff. No overly loud noise came from the buildings. The taverns and inns were ordered to keep their doors shut and only the sound of steam rising from the sewage holes greeted their entrance.

A few blocks from the gates, Blynn pulled up on the reins of the horses. He came around the back and shook the Keepers awake.

"Get up," he said curtly.

They yawned and got their things. When they climbed out of the cart, they looked around, confused. There was no inn or tavern in sight and they turned to question Blynn.

"We're stopping here?" Trel asked, scratching his ear. "Where shall we sleep?"

"Wherever you want," Blynn said, pushing the back gate of his cart closed. "I have fulfilled my word and taken you as far as I will."

"You were supposed to take us to Rae," Jace said stepping forward accusingly.

"I have!" Blynn said angrily. "Rae is within this city. Even if I knew more I could not get close to him. It's a military city, and soldiers do not mix with commoners," he said, twisting his pale lips.

"Rae is a soldier?" Jace said, startled.

"I don't know," Blynn said tiredly. "When Dorath asked me, I told him I knew where he was, not his lifestyle or personal preferences," he said in disgust. "He is here and that's all I know."

"You can't just leave us, Blynn," Lashara said. "We have no idea where we are."

"Trailaden, of course," he said with a wicked smirk and jumped on the cart.

"Aren't you forgetting something, Blynn?" Alaric asked, stretching out his hand.

Blynn stared at him, a look of fear on his face for a moment, and then he shrugged his shoulders.

"No."

"The moneybag, Blynn."

Blynn shifted in his seat, like he'd been stung. He looked back at Alaric, but made no movement to give him their gold.

"It's mine," He said selfishly. "Dorath said I could keep it as payment for my troubles."

"I highly doubt that, Blynn," said Alaric quietly.

"You can't prove otherwise, can you?" he challenged.

Alaric looked at him flatly and sighed.

"No. Do you give your word in Yeshua's honor that this is what Dorath said?"

Blynn stared at the Keeper sardonically.

"Absolutely," he said flatly.

He was lying. Everyone knew he was lying, but they could do nothing to prove his falsehood. The impish man looked the four of them over smugly. He lashed the reins to leave, but Alaric was holding the horses. He shook his head at Blynn quietly.

"Let go Alaric, or I'll run you down," he said slowly. Alaric only stood and stared him back. It occurred to Jace how frightened of the muscular man Blynn was. He froze, lowering the reins, his face growing whiter in the lamplight of the cart.

"This is a military city!" he rasped. "With one word, I can have a company of horsemen here. They do not care about words and oaths, and they would be happy to have their way with four Keepers who hail from the Gap. All they would see are four petty thieves assaulting a merchant. They would throw you in the lowest dungeon and forget about you before the sun rose. No one would come to the rescue of four Keepers in this city, especially so late at night."

Alaric shifted, weighing the threats. He let the reins slip from his hands and backed away.

"Whatever happened to you, Blynn?" he asked sincerely. "Where was the man that Dorath vouched for at Nadir? What allegiance do you have?"

"Out of my way!" Blynn spat.

"Please, Blynn!" Jace said, stepping forward. "Name your price! There must be something we have, something we can give to make you help us further."

Blynn paused for a moment, a cruel smile forming on his lips. They could only imagine the thoughts that ran through his head at the open invitation. Then he stiffened and stared ahead, not even turning to entertain Jace's plea. He motioned to leave, but Alaric cut him off.

"Go, if you must," he said, drawing close to the cart, "but know that if you leave, we do not want to see your face again. You have been given every opportunity to honor Yeshua and you have chosen instead to layer insult upon injury on all of us. If you leave, you have shown your true colors, Blynn, and revealed that you are not what you say you are. A Keeper would have compassion, goodness, selflessness, honesty, and patience—none of which I see in you."

Blynn shook under the hail of accusations, but said nothing. He turned to leave, but then stopped.

"There are many people far and wide that I have seen. Some claim one thing, others another. Some have hearts of gold, but do nothing. Others are the most selfish people you could imagine, but do wondrous deeds. You act as if you know which one I am. Don't presume to know my heart!" He spat at Alaric and slapped the reins hard.

The cart sounded on the cobblestone street and disappeared into the night. They were left in total darkness. The party watched as the cart's lamp dwindled into the distance. The shadows closed in around them. A great burden seemed to lift from the group even as the cart's sound muffled and then was gone. Hopefully, they had seen the last of Blynn, and they let out a collective sigh of relief.

Sadly, their situation had changed little. They were still in a foreign town with no guide and very little coin. The warm air seemed suddenly colder and they looked at the heavy outlines of the strange wooden buildings in the dark. They huddled around each other, none daring to be the first to speak in so desperate a situation.

Trel let his packs slide to the ground with a clatter that shattered the silence.

"Shush!" said Lashara.

"Don't 'shush' me!" he said quietly. "Give me a hand. No, not there. Put it here. Now hold this," he said, pausing in the dark. "And this."

"My hand's already full!"

"Well put it in your other hand!" he whispered in exasperation. "There. Give me a moment," he said putting something metal on the ground loudly. "Now give me the first thing I gave you. No not that, the first thing!" he said to Lashara.

The rest of them waited patiently while Trel tinkered with the objects in front of him. They could hear him tapping metal lightly and turn a rusty knob with a squeak. A rasping sound followed with the sound of several small objects lightly hitting the pavement. Trel growled and they heard him fumble around in the dark. They heard a pop and a small flame appeared. He brought the fire low to the ground, holding it next to something and the air around them grew light. Trel fidgeted on the pavement with the lamp's wick, squeaking the knob again and then put the glass casing over the flame.

"How did you do that?" Lashara asked, amazed.

"Matches," he said. The group had never heard of such a thing and Trel showed the group exactly how they worked. He spryly plucked a thin piece of wood from the cobblestones and held it close to the flame. The wood flared to life and he gave it to Lashara who pinched it with her fingers. She examined it as it burned to the tip and its flame dimmed.

"Ouch!" she said, dropping the burnt twig.

Trel pulled the lantern off the ground, lifting it to his face. The others eyed him suspiciously, his sly grin flickering in the glow of the flames.

"I bought it in Nadir. It only cost a silver, but the man gave it to me for half a loaf of bread. I thought it might come in handy and the man threw in the matches along with it."

Alaric shook his head in disapproval at Trel's secrecy, but the wiry young man spread his free hand innocently. "Have I been a disappointment, or should I put it back?"

Jace nudged his friend good naturedly, and Trel's grin grew wider. They picked up their things and headed down the street. They followed the road for several minutes. A number of times they had to duck into a side alley and dim the flame as a patrol passed them. The going was slow and they walked with measured steps on the bumpy road.

None of them talked as they went along. They did not know what they were looking for and so they stumbled through the night. Trailaden was rather peaceful in the still darkness. No one was about the city now and only an occasional wood-paneled storefront or house showed dimly lit candles inside. There were no sounds in the dark streets, not even the cry of a stray cat. They saw no Watchers, but knew Sa'vard's minions followed their progress as they slowly crept through the city. The ever present whisper of the Watchers had not ceased since they entered the Clonesian Empire, but each of them had learned to ignore it in their own way.

Trel and Alaric recited verses from the Song of the Ages. Alaric meditated over each phrase, saying a short word of thanks to Yeshua after he was done, but Trel fumbled through his fearfully. He clung to each verse, wishing the sound would go away and whispered fervently to Yeshua when no verse came to mind. *At least with all this practice, I'll pass East Haven's exams with ease,* he thought wryly.

Lashara meditated quietly on all Yeshua had done for her. She did not know much of the Song of the Ages, only the stories Miss Pell had taught her. Between her thoughts she reflected on the narrations that her teacher and friend had told her. She found comfort in Yeshua's sermon on the mountain and the Almighty leading His people through the wilderness. The stories comforted her and kept her memories close to the Gap and all that was pure.

Jace never let his hand stray far from the copy of the Song that Hadran had given him. He kept it close to his chest, thumbing it when he grew tense. He quietly hummed the tunes of the hymns that he had learned in East Haven, careful not to let the others hear. He considered each of the promises put to tune that sprang up in his head:

I'll never leave your side.
In Me, always abide.
Turn not away,
Never to stray,
And I'll be your guide.

Listen to the voice that is calling.
The one that will lead you home.
Draw near to Me,
Look and you'll see,
You're never alone.

All you who rest, draw nigh.
Come to Me, I am here.
I am the Lamb.
Holy, I AM
There's no need to fear.

In spite of the deadly singsong of the Watchers that threatened to entice him, Jace found his own praises to the Almighty uplifting him amidst his circumstances. The party moved on through the night, curiously joyful despite a clear goal or destination.

At length they came to a small shop at the end of the street. It was not the first dead end they had encountered, and they were about to turn around when Jace stopped them. Something about the shop seemed strange and though he thought he should leave, he motioned for Trel to cast more light on the storefront.

The building was nondescript. Its simple wooden design was a copy of more elaborate merchant shops. The double rows of glass windows were cluttered with stacks of parchments and inkwells, put there out of necessity rather than decoration. Jace looked at the shop sign which marked the store as a printing press of some sort. The Pen and Quill it read. The letters were finely written in wide scrolling form and a quill feather hung over them, dripping into an inkwell. He ran up to the shop, climbed the railing and looked into the windows.

"Jace, what are you doing?" Lashara squealed.

"There's someone in there," he said holding his face close to the window. "The light is very faint. They must be in a back room."

"Well, get away, they're sure to spot you!" she said angrily.

Jace rapped noisily on the door and Lashara squealed again.

"Don't do that! We'll get thrown in the dungeon for sure!"

"Someone's coming," said Alaric. He was standing farther down the street close against the houses. "We'd better leave very soon."

A shadow came to the door, set down their candle and fumbled with the lock. The door opened and an older man blocked the entryway. His salt and pepper hair was thinning and on his thick nose sat a small pair of spectacles. He was in his night clothes and his disheveled hair hinted that he had been woken up by the banging. His deep frown and dark set eyes said he was not too happy, and he looked sternly at Jace in the single light of his candle.

"Pardon me, sir, but my friends and I have need of a room..." Jace said, his voice trailing off.

"What good is that to me?" the man said bluntly, his tone not too kind.

Jace stammered. Things were not going as he had thought.

"Let's go, Jace," Lashara said, apologizing to the man as she tugged at Jace's arm.

"We need to go now," said Alaric, striding back to the shop. The sound of approaching horses was clear now and torchlight spilled around the bend of the street.

Jace turned back to the man. He thought quickly and spoke again.

"Uh, there must be some mistake," He said, "Is there someone else I can talk to, an apprentice perhaps?"

The man stared at him hard and slammed the door shut. His light vanished into the back of his office and then winked out.

"Great," Lashara blurted, "Now we're caught for sure. Can we still make a run of it, Alaric?"

"It's possible," he stated.

"No, we wait here," said Jace.

Lashara spun on him and Alaric turned also, his brow knitted in confusion.

"Trust me, Alaric, we wait."

Alaric shrugged indifferently and leaned against the wall. Trel had turned the wick of his lamp down to nothing in hopes that whoever was coming would turn back around, but the light and the horses came closer. Trel and Lashara stood by Alaric, trying to melt into the wall. Only Jace stood on the stairs of the shop, waiting at the door.

The patrol came around the bend of the street. In the lead hovered a dark shadow, close to the ground. It was dressed in a tattered cloak that hid its face. Its arms beckoned for the soldiers behind to follow. The Watcher floated down the street in ominous slowness, blocking the Keepers' escape. The rasping whisper of the creature's song rose in volume as it approached, filling the ears of the Keepers. It stood some distance down the street, raising and pointing for the soldiers to encircle the four of them.

The hooves on the pavement punctuated the night. The soldiers were dressed in dark green vests. They bounced lightly atop their mounts, their swords dangling at their waists. Each of them held a spear thrust into place on the side of their saddle. The officer in the middle held a lantern that dangled in front of the troop from a long pole attached to his horse. The eight mounts reined in beside the Keepers and stood. Their visors were pulled over their faces and the gambesons they wore creaked noisily under their vests. They flexed their leather gauntlets and their chargers snorted impatiently. The officer nudged his beast forward.

"What business have you at this hour?" he questioned the four of them.

Alaric stepped forward to explain, but Jace cut him off.

"We have lost our way through the city, sir, but have found our home. We thank you for your assistance."

Alaric glanced at Jace, his eyes hard as he backed against the wall. Jace turned and motioned for the guards to leave.

"We will wait for you to enter your house under our protection," the captain said, "One can never be too safe in the city, after all."

Jace patted his clothes and threw up his arms, "It seems I've lost my key, gentlemen," he said, shaking his head foolishly. He saw the faces of his party tighten at his last remark as he began the dangerous game of bluffing the guards. The officer was silent and then spoke.

"Perhaps a simple knock on the door will bring someone. That is, if all of your friends have lost their keys as well," the captain said provokingly.

The others shrugged their shoulders and scratched their heads, preferring to play the fools in the deepening scenario. Jace nodded his agreement at the officer's advice and turned back toward the door. He gave four swift knocks to the door and waited in silence. He turned back toward the soldiers, giving a nervous laugh and waited. A light flickered in the back of the shop and slowly made its way through the rooms. The door opened once again and a short, young lady squinted in the glare of the lamp.

The officer waited while the woman's eyes adjusted and then asked her if she knew her visitors. Her eyes swept the scene, curiously lingering around the bend of the street. She scrutinized each of them slowly, her gaze falling last on Jace. She then turned to the captain and replied in a very level tone:

"Yes, sir. These are my guests whom I have been waiting for."

She fixed her eyes on the captain and went on.

"I thank you for finding them, this is an awful time to be out at night, and your protection will not go unnoticed."

Jace's face dropped in astonishment and surprise, but he recovered in time to nod his thanks. The captain bowed slightly while Jace and the other three Keepers entered the shop. The lady bowed to the soldiers and then closed the door behind her, latching the bolt.

She stared at the four of them, her face serene. She waited for the soldiers to leave and then motioned for them to follow her through the shop. She led them down a narrow hall, opening the door at the end and stepped down a set of stairs. The stairs opened out into a shallow basement. Various furniture and large stacks of paper were crammed into rows on the rock floor. The air was surprisingly cool.

The lady turned to the four of them. She held a green shawl across her shoulders with one hand. Her white gown spilled onto the floor, covering her feet. The tips of her fingers were smudged with ink stains. About her waist was strapped a small dagger that was thrust under her belt. She did not try to to hide it and made sure the four of them were well aware she had one. Jace could see clearly now that she was not a youth, but middle-aged. She was strikingly beautiful, however, though she looked them up and down with a hard stare. Her face was lined from many years of hard work, and her hair was rolled up neatly into a bun.

"You have some explaining to do," she said quietly.

The five of them stood silently in the low basement. None of them knew how to begin, and all of them eventually turned their eyes to Jace who had gotten them into this mess. He looked about them with embarrassment, scratching the woolen cloak about his neck. He cleared his throat, throwing up his arms.

"This is the Pen and Quill, is it not?" he asked.

"Any fool can read the sign," the lady said coolly. She moved her hand from her shawl to her dagger.

Jace watched her nervously. He did not know how to explain his actions and the movement of the lady only made it worse. He stumbled over his words.

"We're here to...I knocked in hopes that, ummm...we're searching for someone and —" He stared at the lady whose features had not changed. She flicked the blade from her waist and held it to his neck before he could blink.

"This city has enough trouble without me letting it through the front door. State your business or I'll throw you all out in the street," she said looking at Jace and motioning for the others to keep their distance.

"We're travelers," he started. He could feel the cold blade nestled tightly under his chin and swallowed. "We come from the North in search of a friend."

"Where," she asked him levelly.

"From across the Great River," he dodged.

She jerked the dagger slightly and tightened her eyes.

"Where."

Jace swallowed again. The situation left him little choice and he blurted it out.

"The Gap."

The Keepers started and the lady's eyes widened only slightly, but she went on.

"What is you purpose here?"

"We're searching for a friend. We were told he is within the walls of the city and have come to find him. I saw your shop and the sign, the curl of the last letter and thought you might be of some help," he said. Raising his hands slightly, he drew an arch on the rock floor with his foot.

The lady stood unchanged and then silently moved her foot in an arch on the ground, completing the shape of the fish. She slid the blade back under her belt and stepped away, her features relaxing.

"One can never be sure in these parts," she said quietly. "I saw the clasp on your cloak, but even then, one is not truly a follower of Yeshua."

"But we're Keepers, my lady," he replied.

"Of course you are," she said primly, "But even that does not guarantee your loyalty to Yeshua."

Jace was offended by her comment, but understood what she meant. After their journey with Blynn, he realized that one could say they were Yeshua's, but leave doubt, or even prove otherwise by their actions. He spoke to the lady, wishing to ease her suspicions.

"I made the choice as a young boy to accept Yeshua's gift of salvation and claim Him as Lord of my life. Ever since, I have followed His teachings written in the Song of the Ages. We were sent here by the Council in hopes of finding a Keeper who has gone silent. Our travels have taken us far from home and through many dangers. I have been told that shops and homes bearing 'the symbol' would offer help to any Keeper in need."

"Well spoken," said the lady. She eyed him briefly and then sighed. "This Keeper must be of some importance for you to come so far into so dangerous a land."

"He is my brother," said Jace quietly.

The lady nodded and touched his cheek, a look of sympathy on her face.

"My name is Shereel. All that I can do and all that is within my power is yours. I give you my word as a follower and Keeper of the Most High and His Blessed Son, Yeshua."

14

THE END IN SIGHT

The other three gasped in shock. They looked at Jace, their brows knitted and arms crossed. He returned their angry stares with a guilty grin.

"I wasn't sure of the sign," he began, "so I figured it best to tell you afterwards."

Lashara gave him a smoldering look. She took it personally that Jace had not communicated his findings to her. "Thank you so much for your concern," she said under her breath.

"The four of you are very brave to come this far into the Clonesian Empire," said Shereel. "Trailaden is crawling with Watchers. How many have you seen besides the one that led the patrol?"

"You saw it?" asked Jace with astonishment. Shereel only gave him a quick, formal nod. *Of course she saw*, he thought, *the Creator has cleared her vision.*

"More than we can count," Trel answered. "The ones we don't see mark their presence with their tempting whispers. I've been reciting verse after verse from the Song since we stepped foot on Clonesian soil. It's all I could do to keep from fleeing the city."

"Don't ever stop," Shereel said, "Now that the Watchers know you are here, they have only to wait until you lower your defenses. Only by keeping your hearts and minds in Yeshua will you gain protection. Expect your quest to become more difficult as you continue."

Trel groaned at her words. It was what he feared she would say. Now that his suspicions were confirmed, he suddenly felt drained. From the looks of his friend's faces, Shereel's terse comments had sunk into their hearts also. They steeled themselves and waited for her to go on. Instead, she lowered her candle and gave them a short summary of the shop.

The Pen and the Quill indeed had the fish symbol that Alaric had once shown Jace. It was not apparent at first, but Shereel confirmed that the curl of the last letter had a hidden meaning. The store was much larger than it appeared. Its quaint front, where all the work was done, was stuffy and unorganized. The papers and odd assortment of inkwells, quills, and stamps that sat in the window spilled over onto the counters and tabletops.

A large, bulky wooden table was the centerpiece of the store. It was a strange device, having a tall wooden frame over its flat surface that housed a fixed wooden slab. A large screw was attached to the slab and ran up into the wooden frame. The surface of the table had line after line of metal rails to fit rubber stamps securely into place. These stamps ranged from letters to intricate symbols or designs. They were then rubbed with a thick black powder and brushed with a dark smelly liquid. A sheet of thick parchment was placed securely on the upper slab and cranked into place on the stamp-filled, ink-soaked surface beneath. The operation took all day, but when finished, produced four sheets of beautifully designed paper with heavy lettering.

The process was very expensive. Most merchants and nobles could not afford to employ the services of the store, but if one could do business with the Pen and Quill, they received an elaborately designed print that was also a substantial work of art. The costs were enough to support an entire crew of apprentices and well-paid craftsman.

Despite its exorbitant prices, the Pen and Quill was stocked with a high volume of orders from most places. The nobles used the printing press to order everything from royal decrees to wedding invitations for relatives, which kept the small shop busy well into the night. Merchants also patronized the city's only printing press. Since hawkers and street vendors were frowned upon in the city, the business fell largely to them. They preferred to have their stores' inventory and its prices displayed on the extraordinarily decorated, highly expensive parchment that only the Pen and Quill produced. Since the patrols had all but eradicated thieving and burglary, most shops comfortably hung the parchments in their windows for all to see.

The storefront was a hectic place, but its recesses were another story. The upper rooms were living quarters for the owner, his family, a foreman, a number of craftsman, and apprentices. The ground level housed the administrative offices and storage, but the sublevel was what piqued Jace's interest. The open basement, though immense, made him queasy and light-headed, and he fought to maintain his composure while Shereel led them about. As he struggled with his fear of enclosed areas and underground places, he noted the vast expanse of the hidden rooms. The main space they were in was a storage of some sorts for the heavier equipment and spare parts for the machinery. Most of the objects were out of use and quite old. The party walked with light steps into the silent chamber, but still managed to stir up a fair amount of dust. The thick air only heightened Jace's nausea, and Trel's coughing and wheezing from the dust only encouraged it.

Shereel led them past the equipment to a number of interconnecting rooms. Several long passageways ran off into the darkness and Jace could hear the sound of dripping water far in the distance. Shereel explained that the rooms were a series of passageways that were woven throughout the city. Originally, they had been designed for storage. Corrupt merchants and shop owners had added the interconnecting passageways to smuggle untaxed goods into the city. The tunnels were rumored to run throughout Trailaden and perhaps a large part of the Empire. When others like Shereel had uncovered their existence, they used them as a haven for Keepers or refugees who were trying to flee from the Clonesian Empire. Both would most certainly be put to death if their whereabouts were exposed. The secret of the underground maze was closely kept among the few Keepers that lived under the watchful eye of the Belazian Keep.

She calmly told the story as she led them about the tunnels. It was strange that they had found a Keeper inside the Clonesian Empire at all, let alone Trailaden of all places, and they listened to her knowledge as if their life depended on it.

Shereel was the head apprentice who worked in the printing press and lived with three other ladies. She was very different from Blynn, and once they had gotten past the awkward situation in the basement and her skill with her dagger, she had opened up to them like a flower in spring. Her manner, though inviting and calm, was laced with a touch of coldness. She had lived in the Clonesian Empire for some 20 years and had fought to keep her guard up against the surveillance of the soldiers and the suspicious stares of everyone else in the city. The years of persecution had left their mark, and she apologized for her withdrawn demeanor, reminding them often how joyful she was to be among her spiritual brothers and sister.

The room where she led them was painted a flat grey with no adornments. It was simply four walls, a ceiling, and a floor. She motioned for her guests to put their things down and make themselves comfortable. When morning came, either she or someone else would lead them out of the tunnels, and they could begin their search for Jace's brother. Whoever arrived, they were told to remain silent, letting the person explain their presence to the merchant or store-owner from whose shop they would emerge and not talk until they were safely out on the street.

The measures were precautionary and a safeguard to protect both them and their guides. Clonesians were rather taken with the suspicious acts of foreigners and jumped at the chance to alert the guards to the presence of illegal activity. There were rewards for doing this, and it helped to quell such actions. Keepers, besides being hated, were also a pricey reward. The emperor had put a price on every Keeper's head and, if found, they and anyone connected to their presence would be taken off to prison. Whole houses had been torched because of this, said Shereel bleakly.

Keepers were despised, not just for their place of origin, but mostly because of what they represented. In ages past, many had openly proclaimed the truth in the streets, even in the capital of Clonesia. What they spoke had been reprehensible to the Clonesians, and the crowds quickly became violent toward all who hailed from the Gap.

Clonesians, above all, wanted to do whatever they desired. Sa'vard had used this attitude to furnish them with anything their hearts wanted. The empire had become subjugated to him through these means and was a ready example for the Mentors at East Haven of Sa'vard's deception and persuasive techniques. When Keepers came and spoke of the Almighty's power, Yeshua, and how there was no other way for any Clonesian to come to Him except to acknowledge what Yeshua had done for them, claim Him as their personal Lord, and relinquish their wrong and selfish desires, Clonesia went into an uproar. Most did not care about the Almighty and those that did could not stomach that the Song of the Ages told them they would perish if they did not change. They killed many Keepers in a kingdom-wide persecution, and those that were left had been forced to go into hiding. Now the remaining Keepers could only eke out their existence cautiously, venturing to tell the truth only after they had known a person for some time and then they spoke almost in riddles. If their kindness should backfire, they would be taken away in the middle of the night, never to be heard from again. Even mentioning the Gap was cause for a public lashing, imprisonment, or death.

Shereel turned to leave, and Trel lit his lantern. She reminded them again that danger was ever-present in the Clonesian Empire, even underground. They were told to keep their voices to a whisper and not stray into other rooms, lest they become lost in the endless maze forever. She said a soft word to Yeshua for them all before she left and offered her hopes that Jace find his brother soon.

The party rolled out their blankets and went to bed by the dim glow of Trel's lantern. The steady, far-off dripping they heard in the tunnels lulled them to sleep, and after a short while, only Jace remained awake. He sat huddled in a corner with his knees pulled up. Cold sweat ran down his back and he fought to control his breathing.

The blank floor and walls reminded him of his cell in the Mines. He could sense the mass of the earth crushing down on the ceiling over him. The ceiling was supporting untold amounts of weight from the ground above. The walls themselves seemed to close in around him, suffocating him as they stretched and elongated in his vision. Their smooth walls mocked him, watching silently and waiting for him to cave in under his fear. The constant dripping uncovered memories that he had long thought hidden: his countless time pacing his cell, the beatings he faced, and the dreaded look of death he had seen from Na'tal. He shivered at the haunting images, comforted only from his narrow escape by the men in white. The steady whisper of the Watcher's voices throughout the city seemed to grow to a shattering roar in the underground tomb. Try as he may, he could not drown their voices from his ears and he buried his head in his lap in fear.

Lashara awoke from her sleep, turning to look at the small flame of the lantern. She could see Jace curled up in the corner, the flames flickering off his shivering body. She rolled over and watched him carefully.

"Jace!" she said in a loud whisper. The sound, as soft as it was, bounced about the room and echoed down the tunnels. Jace snapped his head up, throwing his arms against the walls. His face was pallid and his eyes searched the room with a look of delusion. Lashara said his name again and his eyes focused on her. His breathing was still shallow and Lashara crept up to him, examining him closely.

"Make it stop!" he cried between gasps and then sobbed into his lap. He clutched his head and rolled back and forth.

Lashara gently lowered his hands and lifted his head. She touched his chest and felt his breathing. The symptoms were common to other soldiers she had seen. Some deep-seated trauma had fixed itself in Jace's head, and though she did not know its origin, she knew how to treat it.

Miss Pell had taught her the proper doses and mixture. Quietly, she lifted the pouch of herbs from her bags and uncorked one of the bottles. She poured some water into her wooden cup and mixed a sprinkle of dried leaves with two drops of another liquid. The mixture bubbled and hissed quietly as she stirred it, and she lifted it to her nose to see if she had added the proper portions. The water was warm with a sweet smell and she held it close to Jace's lips.

"Drink this," she whispered, helping him swallow the warm liquid.

The drink went down well enough and he shook his head moaning slightly. Its reaction did not take long and he slumped loosely against the wall. She lowered him to the floor, propping a rolled shirt under his head. His breathing grew deep. She wrapped his shivering body in an extra blanket and curled up to sleep on her bedroll.

Jace was able to escape the torment of the darkened halls, the dripping, and whispers, but his slumber brought on dark dreams that he could not shake. He found himself standing alone near the center of Trailaden. All about him circled thousands of armor-clad warriors. They marched about the city with blank eyes, blocking his search for his brother. They were being driven by hundreds of Watchers, their formless cloaks pointing down one street and then another, commanding the troops to scour the city. All the while their lethal whispers rasped tempting suggestions to the soldiers, locking the men under their control in a hypnotic trance. Jace ran from them, going from building to building, concealing himself under boxes, around corners, and behind doors. There seemed to be nowhere to hide and many times he found himself alone and out in the middle of the street. Soldiers only had to look up from their fervent searching and they would see him. He would run by them, his feet heavy and dreamily slow, despite his best efforts to make them go faster. The Watchers would hiss their warnings to the troops. They would catch a glimpse of him at the last moment as he turned a corner, desperately searching for a way to escape the horrible city. He found himself running in circles, and no matter where he turned, he could not escape those that hunted for him.

In the very center of the square was a stake firmly planted in the ground. A crowd of soldiers were busy milling around the courtyard, waiting for some meeting. Jace huddled in the shadows to watch, transfixed as his brother was led out into the center of the square. His face was downcast, his arms and legs were shackled, and he limped badly. The soldiers threw him against the stake, tying his hands behind his back and to the post. They heaped branches and sticks close to his body, burying him to his waist. Jace looked about him for any sign of freeing Rae. The square was gated and he watched through the bars as his brother fought to free himself while the soldiers lit the wood. He could see Rae yelling at him as the flames rose around him. Jace shook against the gate furiously, but it did not move.

"Hold him down! Jace, Jace, can you hear us?"

Jace clutched at the unmoving shadows, trying to free himself and save Rae. He flailed his arms wildly, but he could not free himself.

"Jace, Jace! It's me!"

Jace shook himself while the shapes took focus. Alaric was standing over him, his thick arms pinning him to the ground. Lashara and Trel were crowded around him with deep lines of worry on their faces. He stopped his waving and lowered his arms to the floor. His clothes were drenched with sweat and he felt exhausted. He caught his breath while Alaric climbed off him.

"What happened?" Jace asked. His speech was slurred and he raised his head sluggishly.

"You were dreaming," said Lashara. She sat with her cloak draped about her and looked extremely vexed. "You kept muttering things about Rae and Watchers, but we couldn't get you to wake up."

"I'm so tired."

"I gave you a potion. Don't you remember? What is the matter, Jace? If something is wrong, you should tell us," she said.

Jace sighed. "I saw my brother," he said, "He was being led to his death in the center of the city. There were soldiers and Watchers all around him. I tried to save him, but I couldn't reach him," he trailed off, trying to forget the sight of the fire and his brother's screams.

They pondered the dream. Finally, Alaric grabbed his shoulder. "It was a dream, Jace. Learn from it, but don't dwell on it. The enemy is trying to plant doubt in your mind. Rae is fine. Remember, Yeshua brought us here, and He will lead us through. We start the search for Rae today."

A woman stepped forward from the corner of the room. She was dressed in a blue woven skirt that fell to her ankles and a simple brown overcoat. She looked very similar to Shereel and though she did not tell her name, Jace guessed the two were somehow related. The woman had a small dagger strapped under her belt and her fingertips also were stained with several shades of ink. Seeing that Jace was better, she ordered the four of them to get their things. She stood quietly out of the way while they packed in the solitary light of Trel's lantern.

Once they were ready, she led them out one of the doorways and down several twisting passages. The air turned cooler and the steady dripping grew louder. Jace could feel a soft breeze coming from the direction they walked and, much to his disliking, felt as if they were descending into the earth. He swallowed hard as they delved deeper. Before long, the lady led them into a wide room with a high ceiling. Large pillars that were spaced every ten strides supported the ceiling. The top of the large room creaked often, signaling a fair amount of work taking place on the floor above. The space was spotless and had the furnishings of a substantial wine cellar on one side and an office space on the other. Thinking of Shereel's tale, Jace wondered if the wine was legitimate or smuggled. Many lamps were housed on the walls.

When all had entered, the young woman called for Alaric and Trel's assistance. The two of them moved a large bookcase over the doorway and the little lady and Lashara heaped boxes around it. Jace watched while they hid the doorway. The lady put the finishing touches on the well-made disguise. She laid a wooden plank along the wall to the side. Reaching her hands from out of her pockets, she scattered the boxes and bookcase with a fine dust. After smoothing her skirt, she examined her handiwork and turned away. The room looked remarkably ordinary now, and they followed the silent woman up the winding stairs to the noise above.

The room was a wide, open workspace. A myriad of women sat before countless looms and spinning wheels, turning out fabric and working the yarn into cloth. Dozens of women dipped the fresh spun yarn into large vats of brightly colored liquid. Others hoisted the wet fabric to dry while the liquid ran back into the oversized tanks of dye. One level overhead, a number of soldiers watched the activity. The work was surprisingly organized and the ladies moved about with minimal noise.

A man who must have been the owner or lead craftsman hung over the upstairs banister. He was dressed in a tight-fitting gray doublet with dark leggings and high boots. His long, black hair was tied in a knot and ran down his back. A thin mustache covered his lip and offset his weathered features. He watched the work with a cross expression, eyeing the labor down his hooked nosed and making sure his profit was not lost.

As soon as the party emerged from the cellar and into plain view, his attention was on them. He watched the five of them weave their way across the floor like a hawk. Before they could reach the doorway, his voice cut through the work.

"Cleaning the stalls does not take that long, Clarissa. Your labor, or lack thereof, has set me back at least half an hour in wages."

His smooth tenor voice went through the crowd like a razor. At the sound, all work ground to a halt and the women on the floor looked at Clarissa and the party with dread. Their foreman was notorious for his scathing inquisitions, and his anger came down hardest on those that cost him profit. He walked close to the railing and came down the stairs, never losing sight of them for more than an instant. A fair share of the seamstresses were trembling at his approach and backed away discreetly. It was never a good sign when the overseer stepped onto the work floor. He made his way through the drying fabrics and silent looms, followed closely by four soldiers carrying short swords. Coming to stand beside Clarissa, he towered over her and eyed those that were with her.

"My lord," she began meekly. "The stalls have been clean for half an hour now. I was about to come in when these four approached the stables from a side street asking for the local garrison. I would have ordered them around, but they declared their business urgent and so I brought them through the shop. I know my lord is a kindly man and would not interrupt official business, so I took the liberty of escorting them myself."

The man looked at them down his nose, gauging their demeanor and then turned his attention to his apprentice.

"Who else saw this exchange?"

"None, my lord. You sent only me to clean the stables, choosing to keep the rest of your workers on the floor ."

"Don't insult me, woman! I know my own commands. Where is their documentation?"

"Their matter is most urgent, so they were not given the proper papers, but they did give me this," she said, handing the foreman a small note. It was simply folded and he unwrapped the string binding and read its contents.

Jace and the rest of them held their breath while the man went over the letter. It was tattered and worn and looked barely official. Its ink was badly smudged, but it did bear the seal of some minor noble near the blemished signature. The man wrinkled his face at the worn document and stared at the five of them suspiciously. He folded up the letter and handed it back to their escort.

"Who gave you authority to think, Clarissa? Next time someone approaches my property, report to me immediately or I will have you whipped!" A deathly hush fell over the room at the foreman's words. He said them loud enough for all to hear. His threats were clearly unshaped promises and Clarissa turned a pale white. She bowed low and made her way out the door.

"Be back before nightfall! I will not leave the doors unlocked again. If you happen to come back too late, I will have a surprise in the morning for you that even your fellow workers will fear!" He yelled at her as she trotted swiftly out into the open street.

The day was clear and the sky was a bright blue with little splotches of clouds. It was going to be hot although there still was a cool breeze wafting up from the plain below them. The streets were filled with a midmorning bustle. Merchants had opened their shops some time before, and businessmen were upon the streets now, mixed with the military presence and steady stream of carts with goods from across the land. The streets were void of hawkers and their booths, leaving Jace with an eerie feeling in the absence of their noise.

Trailaden had a very tight feel and a no-nonsense attitude permeated the city. People walked without greeting each other, and Jace saw no exchange of pleasantries at all. None cared to look at each other, save to give a suspicious look up and down before passing quickly onto whatever task they had. The attitude stemmed from more than just the overwhelming military nature of the city, Jace suspected, and he kept his eyes to himself and head down.

Clarissa walked straight ahead for a number of blocks, only turning around after they had gone well away from her place of employment. When she turned to look at the Keepers, they could see that she was highly distraught. Her face was white with fear and her lips had an almost imperceptible tremble. Her dye-soaked fingertips held the note she had given the foreman tightly, and her eyes darted back and forth at the people that passed them by.

"I fear my lord's suspicions are mounting too high. I will not be much more use in these matters until I have gained back his good favor," she said to herself. "You must follow me closely, the guards watch the streets for ones like us, and their superiors have been known to send whole patrols of them to round us up in broad daylight."

The funny way she said "superiors" made Jace's neck prickle. Clarissa was surely talking of the Watchers. It set them all on edge to know they were in danger even here on so ordinary a day. The four of them nodded back their agreements to stay near their guide.

She did not take them to the local garrison, but instead to an unsightly tavern. It was nestled down a side street that was dark even on so fine an afternoon. The building was in disrepair. Half the sign dangled from its post, broken in two. What was left of it was burnt and unreadable. The strange wooden shingles that adorned every Clonesian house were missing in a number of places, and the door opened and shut on rusty hinges.

"This is a favorite watering hole for a number of military outfits. Stay here as long as you like. You can purchase rooms or sleep at one of the tables, if you don't mind the noise. The owner does not care as long as you pay up front." She drew close and her voice dropped to a whisper as she stared into Jace's eyes, "This place has a bad reputation. I suggest as soon as you find your brother, you make haste to remove yourselves from the city. It is bad enough that places like this exist without frequenting their establishments. When you leave, exit through the western gate. It is the least monitored in the city, and its soldiers are usually drunk or asleep."

She ventured to leave and then thrust the worn paper into Jace's hands.

"You'll need this if you're stopped. It is a forged copy of an official document. Give this to any who ask."

"What does the letter say?" Jace asked quietly.

"The letter is smudged badly, but it doesn't matter. Authorities only care about the seal and the signature at the bottom," She put her hands to her mouth and then pointed at the letter with a twinkle in her eye, "Actually, the letter is a recipe for tomato stew," she said with a wink.

Jace sputtered and grinned. He thanked Clarissa for her help and she bustled away. They gathered their things and entered the run-down tavern, taking a darkened booth in a rear corner on the second floor. It was neatly tucked out of the way and provided an ample view of the doorway and a large part of the lower floor. Their table was greasy and littered with crumbs. Lashara stepped on something gooey that stuck to her sandals, and she gave a disgusted look as they put their things on the benches.

The tavern was empty and the party waited patiently for the soldiers to stumble through the door as they finished their patrols. They sampled the food while they waited, which was burnt and slimy. Only Jace and Trel stomached their meals while Alaric and Lashara resorted to Trel's food stores.

By early evening, the place was packed with troops, their different colored vests marking the many outfits that frequented the tavern. The noise grew louder as the night went on, and several of the soldiers drank more than they could handle. The party watched as they stumbled and spilled their mugs on their fellow friends. Occasionally a rowdy song broke out and the four blushed at the contents of its verses.

They took turns watching the door. The troops all looked the same to Lashara, but Jace eyed every one of them closely. None of them looked like his brother, though the soldiers who came in were of every shape and size.

Finally, Jace saw him. His hair was shaved close in the uniform likeness of the military, and he walked with an air of surety. His features had changed from the soft rounded face of a boy to the stark angular face of a man. His shoulders were broad and his frame was more muscular since last Jace had seen him. He was a whole head shorter than Jace, but the resemblance was clear. His clear blue eyes stood out against his brown gambeson and he saluted to several officers as he made his way through the crowd. Trel and Lashara looked at the two brothers and their remarkable likeness.

A flood of memories came back to Jace as he watched Rae. He did not look angry or upset. Neither did he seem in any danger like in Jace's dream. In fact, if Jace had not known of the Council's decision, read Rae's letters, or seen and felt the dangers in the Clonesian Empire, he would have thought his brother at home. Indeed, Rae seemed at ease in his surroundings, shaking his comrades hands and buying several of his friends a round of drinks. They cheered at his hospitality, slapping him on the back, and Rae nodded back with a modest grin.

Rae had not seen his brother. Jace moved to meet him, but Alaric pushed him back into his seat. He waited until he had Jace's full attention and then began.

"Be careful, Jace. Your words could have an awful effect on your brother and his friends. You must choose them wisely and not be angry with their results," he said, waiting for Jace to acknowledge hearing before he went on. "There is nothing else the rest of us can do now. We will be here watching and interceding to the Almighty for your success."

Trel and Lashara nodded at Jace. They patted him softly on the hands, motioning him to go. He rose slowly and walked through the tavern.

Rae was surrounded by his company and Jace excused himself, making his way up to his brother. He received a number of hard stares from the troops as they looked at his strange cloak and garb. He paid them no mind and moved beside his brother, lightly tapping him on the shoulder.

Rae spun around quickly, bringing up his fists. He crouched defensively before seeing who it was and peered at his brother between clenched hands. As he recognized Jace, his arms dropped and he relaxed. His eyes went soft and a brief moment passed before Rae embraced him. He threw his arms around him, nearly suffocating Jace in a bear hug while the soldiers around him laughed.

"Jace? What on earth are you doing here?" yelled Rae above the noise. He stepped back and looked at his brother, a smile of pleasant surprise painted on his face.

"I came here to see you," said Jace, but before he had time to explain, Rae went on.

"A toast!" he bellowed, springing up onto his table. He raised his mug high and the crowd grew quiet. "To renewed friendships and my long, lost brother."

The tavern roared its approval and tilted back their drinks. Rae stepped down and slapped his brother on the back. Someone began to strum a song on a stringed instrument and several soldiers joined in. Their singing was sloppy and they held each other up as the tune went on. Despite their bleary eyes and the lingering smell of inebriation that hung everywhere, the tavern's occupants seemed to be enjoying themselves. Rae hugged his brother about the shoulders and motioned for him to follow him outside. Jace looked at his party waving his hand that he was alright and stepped out after Rae.

The sun had just set and deep purple clouds hung over the thin space between the roofs of the shops. The stifling summer heat of the interior of the Empire was fading away with the onset of night. The two brothers sniffed the cooling air as a number of shops' lanterns were lit in the dusk. Troops of soldiers were flooding down the alley in small groups, and Jace could tell the noise of the tavern would soon spill out into the street. Rae turned to Jace, a gleam in his eye and a sly look about his lips. He had seen that look before. It was a telltale sign of Rae's more mischievous side preparing to take over.

"The night is young, boy, what do you say? Would you like the short tour of the city, or skip to the chase and see my garrison?" he asked roughly, spitting onto the curb of the street. That was one bad habit Jace had conveniently forgotten about Rae, but he still looked fondly as his older brother cajoled him.

"I've seen most of the city," he lied, "How about you show me your place?" he asked.

Rae caught Jace's meaning and grabbed his brother by the head before he could get away. He tussled his hair and then kissed him soundly on the crown. "I missed you, boy!" he grinned, slapping his younger brother hard on the back. With just a few familiar phrases and boyish roughing, the two brothers had cut through months of separation. They traded sly looks and set off for another adventure.

Rae led them back down the street. They took several turns and soon Jace had lost all sense of direction. They passed by a number of soldiers. Rae gave them quick nods of recognition or a curt wave. Jace beamed with pride when a small group of them halted in front of Rae, each giving a crisp salute as he passed their line. Rae simply walked by, barely noticing the exchange.

Apparently, his brother had accrued some rank at his station. Though Jace was quite surprised finding his brother in the services of the Clonesian Empire, he was nevertheless happy that Rae had successfully risen through the ranks in such a short time.

Dusk soon turned to darkness and even though it was well past curfew, the streets were alive with people. After examining many of them, Jace realized they were mostly young men and by their short hair and confident step, they were soldiers of the Empire like Rae. They past several Watchers, but Jace was accustomed to their presence now, although he did not let down his guard.

A thick shadow loomed out of the darkness and for a moment, Jace's heart stopped. The Belazian Keep seemed to stretch into the clouds. This close, its solid granite walls disappeared into the night sky. High above, Jace could see torches lining the parapet. They seemed to hover in midair and he gaped openly at the mammoth structure as the soldiers passed him by.

"Come on," Rae said, tapping his brother on the shoulder. "Don't dally on the open streets alone."

"It's quite safe, Rae, look at all these soldiers," he said.

"I know," said his brother stopping short, "Do you see anyone else up here?"

Jace shook his head.

"That's because the troops would have their way with them. Some only lose their money, but a number of soldiers consider it good sport to beat the commoners, should they be so unfortunate as to be found alone this close to the Belazian Keep. They keep order over the city, but nobody keeps order over them."

Jace touched his lips, dumbfounded at Rae's perfunctory answer.

"Not to worry," Rae said, pulling his stunned brother along by the cloak, "As long as you stick close, you're under my protection."

Jace stiffened and then followed his brother, although a bit woodenly.

They circled around the Keep, drawing close to the fortress until it loomed almost directly overhead. Rae led them into a three story bunker. It was akin to the fortress on a much smaller scale with hard stone walls and small, slatted windows. The main hall was stark, bare of all decoration except the regimental banners of the three outfits it housed. These hung over the mustering pit. Up the stairs, the quarters and offices were housed in a formal row by row arrangement. Small common rooms for the commanding officers and quartermasters were on the ends. The officer's quarters were small rooms that sat side by side down the length of the building. The top floor was dedicated to the bunking of the common troops, and Rae strolled through the open area before leading Jace back down to his room.

Jace was left alone momentarily while Rae went to change out of his uniform. He surveyed his brother's quarters. Rae was a junior officer and as such, his office and study were combined into one room. He did not have to share his living space like the lower troops, but also had various tasks to perform after his patrols. With rank came privileges, but also responsibilities. His space, though small, was rather lush and made Sturbin's meager dwelling look like a cowpen. The granite exterior of the bunker was nowhere to be found. Lavish stained mahogany walls were furnished with a great many awards and commendations. Flags and pendants draped above his desk denoted the pride in his accomplishments. Everywhere Jace looked, Rae had souvenirs of his service sitting atop stately furniture. Books on his duties, or reminders of his obligations to the Clonesian Empire filled every space, but still the room projected an air of tidy opulence. Jace searched, but could find no clue or sign of Rae's former life in the Gap or hint of his charge as a Keeper.

When he entered, Rae was wearing a double-stitched overcoat on top of a finely combed cotton doublet. The shirt was pressed and starched and its white fabric glowed in the light of the lanterns. The raised buttons were rounded onyx encircled with gold. The matching pendant on his left breast reflected darkly against the light. Rae's hose was similar to the finest merchant's weave Jace had seen only once before in Nadir. Golden thread ran lengthwise down his pants in a ribbon that was wider than Jace's thumb. His overcoat was pulled tight against his shoulders, showing Rae's muscular frame.

"That must have cost pretty," said Jace with a low whistle.

"Indeed," said his brother, with the mock air of a nobleman. "This shirt comes from the lower waters of the Neft River. The overcoat is from the Northern Steppe region of Emblom, and the leggings were purchased from a Stygian merchant. The entire outfit took many months to assemble and tailor, but I will not tell you how much it was," he said, with an artful look in his eye.

Instead, Rae swung open the door of his closet to reveal a substantial wardrobe of even finer clothing. Dark vests and coats were stuffed in beside rich-colored shirts of every shade and cut. His hose were neatly folded in several small piles. The material could have kept Jace and Rae's entire family comfortable for the rest of their lives. In a corner of the closet Jace spied Rae's coarse woolen riding cloak of the Gap hidden nearly out of sight in a crumpled mess. As Jace looked at the elegant fabrics and the cloak thrown in the corner, he felt an unexplainable rift beginning to form between them.

Rae moved a portion of his collectibles and pulled out the chair from his study. He motioned for Jace to make himself comfortable on the bed while he sat facing him. He was at ease in his quarters and lounged in the oaken chair like a king. Jace stared about the room amazed at the collection his brother had amassed, but hid his concern and questions about Rae's former letters to the Council. He decided it best to play it safe with simple small talk.

"You've done well for yourself, Rae," he said genuinely.

Rae took the compliment with modesty. "I've put no more into my work than any other man. The Clonesians pride themselves on uniform discipline, and it seems I fit nicely into their mold."

"Don't be silly," Jace laughed, "You've obviously gotten where you are quite fast. I've seen the faces of the soldiers. Half of them are your age, a fair share are older than you and those are the ones that salute you. You've surpassed a number of senior soldiers to gain your position, I'm sure. You've done exceptional, Rae, since last I saw you," he finished, hoping Rae would take the opportunity to discuss the Gap and his reasons for his failed communication.

"Thank you," Rae grunted. The two sat silently. Jace wondered if Rae had caught his elusive statement or if he was not even listening. Rae fidgeted with the things on his shelves. There were leaded figures in the shapes of soldiers lined up in formation, and small plaques were fitted beside numberless medals and ribbons.

"What are those?" Jace asked, pointing at two blue and green ribbons that draped over an award.

"They're from some campaign in the southern boundaries of the Empire," Rae said off-handedly. Jace picked up on the story and soon got his brother talking of his adventures.

Rae had been all over the Empire, it seemed. While he had been laboring under Hadran, Rae was gallivanting across leagues of open plains with the Clonesian pikeman or holed-up in maneuvers far to the south of Trailaden under the watchful eyes of his superiors.

He told Jace of many sights. His commanders had led him through many a harrowing journey and through countless campaigns. He picked up mementos, telling the story behind each one, setting it down and then moving onto the next: the crystal rivers that led to the low marshlands where flies were as big as a man's fist, tales of vast herds of strange creatures that dwarfed whole squadrons of dragoons, and the fine women that were found in every town from here to the marshes and across to the Great Sea.

At mention of them, Jace blushed furiously. The sly grin Rae gave his brother was strikingly similar to the looks he gave when he talked of the young ladies at East Haven. Jace's own rise from boyhood had taught him much. He could guess clearly the deeper meaning when Rae told of spending long hours with countless women as night turned to morning.

The statement brought up guilty thoughts that he had had of Lashara in the past. He pushed them back out of his mind and focused on what Rae was saying. True, Jace had had these thoughts. His father had told him that every boy had them at one time or another, but Jace had kept his feelings in check, knowing that to act on them would dishonor his Lord and blemish his soul. Now, here was his brother openly confessing immoral relations with other women and doing so quite comfortably.

He thought of Blynn's behavior for a moment and his loose line of rationality for his actions. His brother seemed to be taking the same course of action as his former guide, first seemingly cutting off communication to other Keepers, and then making his own choices despite what the Song of the Ages said to the contrary. The thoughts made him wary, but he steeled himself and listened again, trying to think of some way to broach the subject of Rae's change in behavior.

"Does it bother you that we weren't brought up that way, Rae? We were taught to treat women with respect and dignity. What would Mum or Da say about your actions now?" Jace questioned. He was about to mention Hadran's opinions on the matter, but then remembered Clarissa's and Shereel's warnings to be discreet.

Rae jerked under the accusations by his brother. He looked at Jace, his eyes big and pensive. A cloud seemed to lift from them for a moment, but then his face grew dark and he smiled cunningly.

"None of them are here, are they?" he said frankly. He let his voice and the repercussions of what he said trail off. No, their parents weren't here. Neither was anyone else. It was only he and his brother. Jace thought of pressing the issue, but Rae stared him down, waiting to see if he would continue. Jace withered under his gaze.

"No, they're not," he confided quietly.

Rae nodded slowly, his lips growing wide with a look of freedom. He continued on, telling Jace more of his stories, spurred on by the lack of confrontation. Jace stared at his brother as he poured over countless acts of things that were in blatant conflict with the teachings of the Creator. He talked with ease, sprinkling his language with obscenities at his choosing, even using Yeshua's name vainly until Jace lost count. He rambled on without any hint that he thought his actions unbecoming a Keeper or dishonorable to their Master. Jace did his best to listen respectfully.

Though Rae considered himself more upright than most soldiers, he had done a small amount of lying and cheating to further his promotions. When others weren't looking, he had stolen from the garrison stores large numbers of goods and sold them to his troops for a profit or to local merchants for personal favors. The acts had made those under his command fiercely loyal to him. He was praised for his soldiers' high morale and staunch brotherhood. The noteworthy cohesiveness of his troops earned him first choice when promotions came. He neatly rationalized that the unity he cultivated justified his wayward decisions.

Every officer he knew stole. Others murdered merchants that owed them coin or even their own troops when no one was around. As long as they weren't caught outright, their actions were overlooked. A good officer was valued, and his colleagues turned their heads at questionable behavior, as long as there was no solid proof of indecency.

Rae considered most of these actions below his code of chivalry. In fact, he did not stoop to a large number of habits that most officers followed. His actions were nonetheless wrong when gauged against Yeshua's teachings and questionable even by Emblom's standards.

Rae was not a heavy drinker, not to Jace's knowledge anyway. He shied away from gambling, the customary drawing of lots, and harsh betting that accompanied many officer's meetings. These and other forms of frivolous or selfish behavior were not high on Rae's lists of actions. Cheating and stealing were not the tools of choice in his daily decisions and he rarely resorted to these actions at all. He had participated in nearly every lewd act or questionable behavior mentioned, but was not noted for any overindulgence in any one lifestyle compared to his peers. Still, his actions alluded to a track record of blossoming impurity and a heedless concern for staying on the straight and narrow. However, Rae's actions stood out among his peers.

In fact, Rae's level of decency and high conduct had been noted among the other officers, even copied. He handed Jace a decree on a finely printed document, commending his upstanding citizenship and high standards. Jace noted the Pen and Quills' handiwork and signature multihued ink that was raised above the page. At the bottom in sweeping penmanship was the signature of the Commander General of the Clonesian Empire, thanking Rae personally for his level of service and commitment. His raised seal of an eagle head was marked in thick black wax.

Rae's life was seemingly exemplary. It was extraordinary how far he had risen in so short a time. His awards and commendations all pointed to a budding career in the Clonesian army that would flourish in due time. The underlying lifestyle that he had taken up, however, was what concerned Jace. Obviously, he had higher standards than most Clonesians. He should, since they were modeled after the Song of the Ages, but they paled in comparison to the bar of excellence Yeshua had set for all to follow.

It did not matter that Rae could not reach Yeshua's standards, no one could. What mattered was that Rae had let his morals slip to attainable levels. This, however, was merely the beginning. Rae seemed at ease with his lifestyle in the Clonesian Empire, content to revel amongst his fine clothing, excellent living conditions, sexual conquests, and hoping to amass even further material wealth in the future. He seemed undeterred that he had turned his back on Yeshua and the responsibility to live as if he were answerable to Him, and instead lived a lifestyle of one who did not claim allegiance to the Almighty. Jace did not see any hunger in Rae's eyes to leave and return to the Gap, to dwell among fellow followers of the Most High, or to reconcile his failing relationship with Yeshua. There was precious little that he saw that marked Rae as a Keeper at all.

The two of them talked well into the night. Rae seemed content to open up to his brother, laying his actions bare, despite Jace's looks of distaste at Rae's questionable way of living. It seemed incomprehensible to Jace how one could follow anything other than what the Song of the Ages said after they had been shown its wisdom. He found it hard to believe that anyone could possibly assert there was a better life to follow than the one Yeshua promised. Rae went on, not paying much attention to Jace's wry stares or the indifference he gave Rae's adventures now. His stories did not provide the same spark of excitement that Jace remembered growing up.

Back then, Rae's misadventures and sneaky mischief had given Jace a rush that was indescribable. He had hung on Rae's every word and thought his brother the hero as he outwitted their parents or other authority figures. Rae's accounts were filled with deeds that were every boy's dream of performing but all would dismiss attempting for fear of getting caught. The accomplishments ranged from sneaking the last sweet from under Mum's nose to leaving their cottage in the dead of night to meet some young damsel. Whatever it was, Rae was the best at beating the odds and keeping his actions secret from his parents. The dignity with which he took his lumps when caught had only added to his reputation in Jace's eyes.

Jace had long since ceased to view these acts with high regard. He had often wished he had done half the outrageous antics his brother had, but had understood the ideas were far out of his reach long ago. As he immersed himself in his studies and came to know what it was to be a Keeper and follower of Yeshua, he realized his brother's actions were only clever disguises of common rebelliousness. He had wrestled with the fact that he worshiped his brother, in spite of his downfalls, and fought to change this.

Now, Rae's adventures seemed nothing more than other ways to be disobedient. They certainly did not glorify Yeshua or the Creator and served only to magnify Rae's selfish ambitions. Jace did not see Rae as some egotistical maniac, wholly bent on his own ambitions, but the more Rae talked it was obvious that Rae had taken to the road suiting his own desires instead of following Yeshua.

It suddenly occurred to Jace that he had been up for almost a day straight. The nightmares of the night before had left him drained. The day had plodded on without rest until he had seen Rae. Now that they were well into the night, his eyes sunk slowly to the droning of his brother's voice. Rae shook him awake.

"I can see you've had a long day yourself," he said good naturedly. "You can rest on my bed tonight, if you'd like."

"I shouldn't," Jace objected. "I have friends waiting back at the tavern for me. I should probably be heading back."

Rae gave him a flat stare for a moment. Rae stewed for a while, thinking of the possible company Jace traveled with, but his brother remained silent. He slapped his hands on his thighs and stood up, offering Jace a hand.

"Well, we'd better be off then. The tavern is more than an hour away. We should get going, if either of us wants to get any sleep before sunrise."

Jace rubbed the cobwebs from his eyes while Rae slipped out to change. He thought of the conversation they had had, thinking of a way to enter into the real reason he was there. He whispered that the Creator would provide a means for him to broach the subject easily. Rae seemed nice enough and Jace shook off his apprehensions about opening up to his brother. Alaric's encouragement that Yeshua would not forsake the plan that He had given them put Jace's mind at ease that he could be honest and frank with Rae once and for all.

Rae returned shortly and they started out the garrison. The place was void of all life; either all had turned in earlier that night or were out in the city and up to no good. They left the building unimpeded and made their way swiftly through the city. The air had grown significantly cooler than the blistering heat of the day, and cold blasts of wind met them around every corner. The heavy wool of Jace's cloak kept the wind at bay, but Rae shivered noticeably in his sleek clothes.

"This reminds me of an autumn at home," Jace said offhandedly.

Rae grunted an agreement, leaning into the gusts. "I don't miss that place much," he said. They walked on for a couple streets in silence.

"How are Mum and Da?" he asked, turning back to talk to Jace.

"Alright. They miss you dearly. Da never says so and Mum would never come right out and say it, but I can see it in their eyes. Even Amoriah does," he waited a moment, hoping for a response from Rae, but his brother only kept walking. He changed his approach and went on. "Da could use you at the cottage. Nina's got a few more years of use before Da sets her out to pasture, but he isn't any younger and working the fields is hard labor," he stopped to adjust his cloak. "Amoriah's grown past my waist and helps Mum some. They were all quiet when I saw them last. I suspect something is amiss between Mum and Da."

"That doesn't surprise me," Rae grumbled. He stalked on through the city, mindful to stay to the sides of the street.

"Do you ever think about anyone else, Rae? Dorath or Hadran, perhaps?"

Rae spit on the curb. "I try not to," he said shortly and moved on.

Jace caught up to him and pressed the opening. "Why not?" he asked, trying his best to sound innocent.

Rae stopped and looked off into the distance. He smoothed his coat and thought a moment, folding his hands behind his back. "When I left, I knew I would never return home. Something always told me that that was not where I was supposed to be," he spread his hands, taking in the buildings. "My path led me here and I decided to try my hand at different things. Finally, I found my way into conscription and quickly rose through the ranks. Here, I fit in. Here, I am at home. I can finally do the things I have always wanted with no one to judge or question my decisions. I like it. It feels good to finally do what I want without anyone telling me it is forbidden."

"But it is, whether someone says so or not, Rae. You and I both know that. The things you have said—the things you have done—we both know our Master teaches us not to do them despite what everybody else says. No matter how genuine the world's façade may seem to appear, we know the truth of our actions in light of the One."

Rae was silent. His body was turned from the streetlamps and stood darkened in the shadows. The air was ominously quiet as Jace waited for Rae's response.

"Do you know how big the world is?" his brother asked. "I've wondered many times. I've seen mountains so high, their peaks are lost in the clouds, valleys wide enough to hold ten thousand legions, and seas so deep they would drown entire cities. It goes on and on. I've never seen the end of it, but one thing I do know: the world is big enough to hold everyone's opinion. Some believe there is no ultimate being watching the world go around," he said, sweeping his hands in the air. "Others believe whoever made this land now sits somewhere, watching us from afar. Still others believe whoever or whatever made or created all this is almost close enough to be touched and to hear and to hear us—"

"That's all good and well, Rae, but you know what we believe," Jace interjected, a tad annoyed. "Whatever anyone else says does not matter. What we have been taught is not a lie."

"I have heard a thousand different ways and in-betweens. Who are you to say what is right or wrong?" Jace started to answer, but Rae went on, "Some believe we are all there is. Others believe we were made for a purpose. Stygians say we can worship the person who made everything we see any way we choose. Emblom says something different. Even where we grew up, we were taught something else."

Rae turned to Jace. His features were like stone, and when he spoke, his voice was harsh and bordered on loathing. "I was forced to follow one way without anyone laying all these paths before me. If things had been different, maybe I would have gone down another road, but I chose to accept Yeshua," he said in a whisper, making sure those that passed them did not hear. "Now, I want to live my own way. Yes, what I am doing may be wrong in someone's eyes, but it is my choice and it feels good."

Jace looked at his brother's shadow in the dim light. "It doesn't have to be like this, Rae," he said quietly.

Rae stiffened in the darkness. "I'll take you back to your friends now."

He turned and Jace followed him slowly the rest of the way. Jace mulled over Rae's words as they went along, fighting the wind as it tore at his cloak. The more he poured over Rae's answers, the more questions came to mind. Jace had been shocked at the awful turn of events.

Rae's anger had surprised him. He had been consumed with the danger of their journey and had not thought about the all-important moments of talking with his brother. He told himself that he had dismissed Rae's letters as depression instead of a willful disobedience. In doing so, he had led himself to believe that all he simply had to do was tell Rae it was time to come home and he would follow. He could see how ludicrous a strategy that had been now.

The two walked down the streets for several more blocks. The air had grown tight between them, and Jace could feel his brother slipping away the closer they got to the tavern. Somewhere in the distance, he could hear a low buzzing and the longer they walked, the more it grew. The buzzing soon turned to a low hum, and the hum became the rising and falling of a bubbling mass of conversation. The shops and buildings were darkened, but Jace recognized that they were now very close to the tavern.

As he fought to create some final ultimatum to offer his brother, they rounded the corner and strolled down the alleyway to the tavern. The street was packed and as they turned around the bend, the full force of the noise hit Jace's ears. The peaceful quiet of Trailaden that lay over the rest of the city was nowhere to be found. Strings of lanterns hung lazily from the second story awnings across the narrow road. The light revealed the teeming crowd that packed the street. Manly faces of the young and old filled the alley. All were dressed in superb outfits like Rae had on; their military apparel traded for the finer garments of the higher social classes. The men were clean-shaven and well dressed.

Jace also saw a fair amount of women mingled among their ranks. The ladies were obviously civilian. He gaped at their suggestive outfits, turning different shades of red as he passed through the crowd. Jace had no idea where they came from, but soon understood, as he watched their glowing feminine stares, why this place was such a watering hole for the troops. They clutched at Jace as he walked by, asking him to stay for a while and fondling his hair. If he weren't under such duress, he would have thought seriously about entertaining a few of their suggestions. After all, there scents and stares called to his masculine nature, but Rae was pushing through the crowd and Jace fought hard to keep up with him. The stench of ale was mixed with heavy scents of perfume and musk in the tight quarters to produce a funny smell that lingered in the crowd. The chill air of the empty streets was gone, and Jace found himself sweating amidst the throngs of people.

The inside of the tavern was less crowded, but still full. Only the area by the entrance was packed, and Jace gagged when one of the older men turned and blew a strong whiff of pipe smoke in his face. The air was filled with the stuff and caused a thick haze to swirl over the booths and tables. Rae led them to the center of the tavern where several of his comrades from earlier remained. Three or four sat slumped in their chairs and a number of women clung to the soldiers. More than one had two on each arm and they flocked to Jace and Rae as the two drew close to Rae's comrades.

Jace spotted his friends in the upper corner, but turned his head slightly and the three remained seated. Trel sat anxiously watching Jace, his eyes wide. Lashara's steady gaze narrowed as three women surrounded Jace, whispering in his ears and rubbing his shoulders. He pushed their hands away, but they groped about him, until he finally shooed them off. Lashara's stare softened and Jace blushed innocently. He turned to Rae whose back was facing him and drew close to his ear.

"Can we talk privately?" Jace asked loudly. Though the crowd was thinned, the noise was still heavy. Rae led them up the stairs to where Jace's party sat, sitting in the booth diagonally to their right. He stared at Jace, his features hard and expression taut.

Jace sat across from him nervously. Rae was a tough shell to crack and once he was slighted, he was impossible to assuage. Jace knew he had to try and so, with much chagrin, he began to speak.

"I have been sent by the Council, Rae," he said just loudly enough to be heard over the raucous crowd. "They told me how you had stopped communication. I couldn't believe it when they told me, but I read the letters."

Rae flinched as Jace finished. He looked like he'd been hit and his face twitched angrily. "Who gave you permission to go through my private correspondences to the Council? Those were not written for you to go fumbling through at your leisure!" he bellowed angrily.

"They showed them to me, Rae! Hadran sent me to Dorath, and he handed them over into my care by permission of the Council."

"Those were not yours!"

"I know," he said soothingly, "but they wanted to prepare me with whatever they had so I could talk intelligently with you when the time came."

"You tricked me, Jace! You didn't come here to see me! You only wanted to put another feather in your cap for your Mentor's approval!" Rae roared.

Jace was stung at his brothers accusations. If Rae had only been there and known how he had been lulled into the mission through trickery! "I do care about you! Do you think I would have come all this way if I didn't? You don't even know half the things I have gone through," he shouted back, "and I went through them so I could see you!"

Their voices had picked up a fair number of listeners and those around them turned to hear their heated debate. Jace's party watched as men stared. Those below pointed up at them and lowered their conversation to catch what the brothers were saying. Some pulled their friends in from the street to watch the two. Lashara froze with dread as first one Watcher came through the door, then another. Soon a steady stream of soldiers and Watchers were tumbling through the entrance as word of a brewing fight broke out. As Rae and Jace locked horns, their actions slowly filled the lower floor with curious onlookers. Alaric and Trel tried desperately to give Jace a discreet sign, but his temper had been pricked by Rae's accusations.

"I've been following the Way since I left home, making sure my heart remained pure, and hoping you were safe and nothing had happened to you, only to come and find you looking like this!" he said, flicking his fingers disdainfully at Rae's clothes. "You clothe yourself in frippery and count your worldly accomplishments as great prizes when you should have remained loyal to the Maker! Where is your sense of chivalry or have you traded your spiritual duty for comfortable surroundings? I expected to come here and find you fighting the good fight, not living like this. You have shamed not only your family and our friends, but also the Lord you claimed to follow! You only seem to follow the Creator when it suits you until it goes against your own desires instead of standing firm like the Song of the Ages says!"

"And you manipulate the scriptures to judge me!" Rae roared, his face red. "Whatever happened to 'Judge not, lest ye be judged?' If you really were half the Keeper you claim to be, you would love and respect me. You would accept me for who I am and let me do what I want!"

"When was the last time you ever read the Song, Rae? You're only quoting it now to suit your own beliefs! Accountability is a cornerstone to being a Keeper. We are not called to accept one another's actions when their lifestyle openly conflicts with Yeshua's commands! Yet, you have traded His sacrifice for just that!"

The room was hushed and filled to overflowing. All ears strained to hear the conversation which was plainly heard well into the street. Jace and Rae were caught up in their anger and were unaware of those around them.

Lashara's ears, however, were filled with a roaring sing-song of the Watcher's deadly chant. Along with Alaric and Trel she quickly forgot Jace's attempt to coerce his brother and strained to keep from drowning in the torrent of the Watcher's whispers. They fought even to breathe as the shapeless wraiths circled the tavern, floating amongst the crowd that was transfixed on Rae and Jace.

Much of what Jace and Rae had said made little sense to the Clonesians, but the majority of them had picked up on such words as "Keeper," "Yeshua," and the "Song of the Ages." These words, mixed with the Watcher's song, were enough to plant the seeds of anger and loathing for all who dared call themselves by Yeshua's name. As they listened to Rae and Jace, and the Watcher's vile words, their hearts turned black and they seethed with hatred.

Rae looked at Jace. His features were pulled taut and he trembled with rage. He did not see his brother before him, but a self-righteous man who hid behind words he had learned in his upbringing instead of fighting against Rae on the open plain of rationality. He embodied all that Rae had despised: the authority of accountability, the lack of tolerance, compromise, and freedom to pursue his desires. Who could see his heart but the Maker Himself, and so there should be only One who should judge him.

Jace's anger smoldered behind his temper. How could he be betrayed by one he had grown up alongside and so dearly loved? Rae was a Keeper. His personal feelings put aside, Rae was called to submit and follow Yeshua and His commands. No, Jace could not judge Rae's heart, but he could question his actions. It infuriated him that Rae chose to throw in his face any accusation he could instead of answering for his own actions. The deepest hurt, however, came from the fact that Rae chose to follow his own selfish ways, despite the fact that they belittled Yeshua and His sacrifice. His actions and lack of desire to change his ways left Rae little choice but to choose between acquiescing, which would save his relationship with his brother but would go against Yeshua's teachings, or shunning him, following his Lord's commands and losing his brother. It was an awful choice and he blamed his brother that he had tried to force him into submission.

He remembered not so long ago when he had turned his back on Yeshua, only to be received into His grace again after repenting of his actions. He could still see his Savior welcoming him with a loving embrace with His scarred hands. To willingly turn his back on his Master again was not an option. Furthermore, Jace was affronted that Rae encouraged, even commanded him to do so.

There was only one question to ask. One final question to seal their fates. One question that he had needed to ask all along. He looked into Rae's eyes and cleared his throat. He stood up and spoke, his voice filling the hall.

"Will you choose to follow Yeshua and turn from your ways?"

Rae looked at his brother, his face a work of stone. He trembled slightly, his body on the verge of springing on Jace and tearing him to pieces. Somewhere through his hatred, he heard his brother's question. It seemed odd that Jace had not known the answer. Every fiber of Rae's being was forced into the words he uttered. They came out of his mouth like a river breaking its dam.

"I am my own master. I have made the choice to follow no one, neither friends, nor family, nor any other authority on the earth, under it, or from above. Were Yeshua Himself to come down and ask me likewise, so also would be my answer."

15

A TRAP IS SET

Lashara, Trel, and Alaric had moved as close to Jace as the crowd allowed. While the tension mounted, the tavern had filled to overflowing. People had taken up every bit of the place, squeezing in until there was only room enough to stand. The looks on their faces ranged from hollow submission, enthralled in the Watcher's song, to scorching hatred, recognizing the identity of the Keeper in their midst. Jace's three friends had pushed close to him and Rae with the rest of the soldiers and stood only arm's length from the two of them. The building was quiet, all listening to the words of the two brothers. Everyone could hear them except for Lashara, Trel, and Alaric.

Lashara could see Jace's lips moving. His gestures of rage and hurt were clearly etched upon his face, which was red and twisted. She only watched with detached interest, more concerned for her own safety and the torrent of noise that drowned out all other sounds. The Watchers' chants had grown to a horrible buzzing that left no room for thought. She stood almost to the point of tears from the overwhelming concentration she maintained. Only her extreme focus on her Savior kept her from being swept away in the sea of sounds. She watched as Jace shook his head. Rae gripped the table in return, his muscles pulsing with checked hatred. The two eyed each other disdainfully, trading verbal jabs and questions that neither agreed with.

The vocal lashings continued and the drumming in Lashara's ears shifted from a heavy buzzing to a powerful rush like the sound of a mighty waterfall. The noise made her feel as if she were moving and she struggled to keep her footing. The chorus of chants swelled, rising in pitch and suddenly stopped as if all who heard it had arrived at some mysterious destination. The stillness that accompanied it was deafening and she rubbed her ears, afraid she had lost her hearing for good. Then she heard Jace and Rae, their voices tight and drawn, one challenging, the other unshakable.

"Will you choose to follow Yeshua and turn from your ways?"

"I am my own master. I have made the choice to follow no one, neither friend, nor family, nor any other authority on the earth, under it, or from above. Were Yeshua Himself to come down and ask me likewise, so also would be my answer."

The instant the answer was given, a heavy click sounded as if a great key had slid into a hole and unlocked some unknown door. Lashara looked around, confused. The Watchers' song had hushed and the room was left in complete silence, though Sa'vard's minions were still present. Then, in a voice that was near to death, she heard them clear as a bell. The command consumed her head as the Watchers' lifted their arms in unison and pointed at Jace. When they spoke, the sound pierced into Lashara and she gasped, clutching at Trel.

"Bring us the Keeper."

The room seemed to spin as action sprang from everywhere at once. The Keepers lurched on their feet and the mass of loathing soldiers surged forward. Their hands strained for Jace as they enveloped his table. They swarmed over him and Rae, collapsing the booth under their weight and losing Jace in a sea of hands. The crowd had loosed like a bowstring, and before Lashara recovered, the men had pushed the other Keepers away and were carrying Jace down the stairs. Lashara could hear his cries mingling with the low booming yells of the crowd, his anger and betrayal filling the tavern with a shrill pang.

Alaric and Trel were suddenly around Lashara, pushing back the mob. Alaric's huge arms swept his axe back and forth moving the crowd away. Those that weren't so fortunate, he clubbed with the flat of his blade. Trel also pummeled those that boxed them in. The mass scattered before them, many fleeing the two armed men. None had weapons, save the three of them and the crowd bulged away from them. They made a path through the mayhem, following close behind Jace and his captors.

Jace was held high above the mob. The soldiers had tied him in his own cloak, and he fought to free himself as they drove him out of the tavern. He could see his friends carving a hole in the crowd behind him, but the soldiers moved about him like a torrent and he was swept out into the street.

He could also see Rae watching him from high above where they sat only moments before. His face was ashen and he watched Jace with a mixture of scorn and pity as people pushed about him. He called to Rae and his party, but they each seemed to be caught up in their own affairs.

The mob carried him out into the alley. Their hands were all about him, and their voices were full of an angry hatred he had never seen before. The Watchers flanked the mob, pointing them out into the street. Their enticing song had dwindled to a soft chatter, like the sound of rain. The frenzied mass did not need much prodding or direction and obeyed the hideously quiet words of their masters. Several of the mob had collected torches, others long knives or short spears. They loudly surged out into the street. The shops that were not wakened by the tavern's ruckus before now turned their lamps on. Merchants and laymen both leaned out their bedrooms, catching a glimpse of the mass as they paraded Jace through the city.

Jace could see the dark of night changing to morning gray in the sky high above him. He did not know where the crowd was taking him, but he struggled furiously. The soldiers laughed at his attempts, mocking him. Some poked or prodded their spears into his back while the rest held him up in the air. His anger toward Rae had not calmed and he focused it on his captors. He lashed out at them the only way he could—with a stream of obscenities. The crowd looked at him, stunned for a moment that a Keeper would say such things and then laughed again while they renewed their efforts. Jace kicked and rolled, but try as he may, the large mob moved unceasingly toward whatever cruel conclusion they had in mind.

After awhile, Trel and the others had to stop. The mass had swirled around them, not giving way. Spent and exhausted, they lost Jace and his captors around one of the numerous bends in the street. They stood on the corner, watching as stragglers of the mob ran by them. Alaric lowered his axe, depleted. Trel and Lashara caught their breath. They regrouped as the shouts drifted away from them.

Trel was the first to recover. He went about gathering up his pack. The nimble man stood to his feet, crossed the street and vanished down an alley. Lashara and Alaric swung their gear on their shoulders and followed after him.

Trel moved along the vacant alleys listening quietly to the mob's vulgar shouts and cheers. It was the only sound in the city at this waking hour and left its imprint on the silence like a hot iron. They watched his quick, wiry frame dart in and out of the shadows while they fought to keep up. Moving silently down the darkened roads, they kept quiet, stopping every now and then to see if they were nearing the crowd's vicinity.

The tidy side streets made it easy to move and the party soon caught up to Jace's assailants. Finally, the party caught a glimpse of the mob two streets over. They ran ahead of them, turning again to cut them off.

A squad of mounted troops nearly bowled them over. The three Keepers scattered while the soldiers reined in their steeds. In a flash, the small troop surrounded them, lowering their short spears. Their chargers nickered and stomped the pavement. Trel and Alaric lowered their weapons to the ground and threw their hands up.

The sergeant kicked his mount forward, his helmet glinting in the lamplight. He leaned toward the three of them and pulled back his visor. The man's gauntlets were layered with metal plates atop the leather. Studs of iron protruded from the knuckles. His vest was black as midnight, but as Lashara looked closer, she saw the visage of a proud eagle head splayed across the man's chest. The mob's cries were fading into the early morning. The sergeant lifted his head, following their sound.

"Where are your papers?" He questioned sternly. A deep pink scar ran down his chin and it pulsed angrily as he spoke.

Lashara stepped forward, smoothing her cloak. She swallowed, trying to steady her breathing. Doing her best to remain calm, she addressed the man:

"We are following the crowd, sire. They are having a celebration of sorts, but we lost them in the streets. We did not want to miss them and thought it best to move quickly through the alleys. Our band nearly caught up to them, when we ran into your men. We apologize for our actions and will be on our way—"

"I do not care of your comings or goings. Nor do I care what hour you walk the city," he said gruffly. "You failed to answer my question," he said, waiting shortly. "Do I have to repeat it?"

The three of them looked at each other. Alaric and Trel gave her a discouraged shrug; they were all out of ideas. She turned to the leader and threw up her hands.

"Bind them," he said. The sergeant looked at them with a muted expression. His eyes were flat black coals that bore into each of them.

Two of his men slid down their horses while the others kept their spears low. They moved towards the three Keepers, casting a fearful glance at Alaric. He began to resist, drawing back from the guards, his eyes blazing.

"It would be wise for you to calm your friends, Miss," the sergeant said pertly to Lashara. "My men have been up all night and things have been known to happen to those we run into in the wee hours of the morn."

The rest of his men laughed softly, their features drawn. They watched the Keepers testily, hoping they would give them some excuse to step down from their saddles. A moment of confrontation passed before Lashara stepped in. She strode up to Alaric and whispered something in his ear. His shoulders sunk and he put out his hands. The guards tied them all without incident and roped them closely to their saddles. They nudged their horses into a trot, watching with cruel smiles as the Keepers stumbled to keep up with the pace.

They led them through the city. The sky took on a deep blue hue in the light of morning and soon dawn began to appear in the east. The air was bitter cold, unlike midday, but even so, the three of them sweat as they ran behind the soldiers. A cool air traveled through the streets of Trailaden, urging them to maintain their pace.

The soldiers lashed them onward for half an hour. They drove them inward to the heart of the city, making sure they were pushed to their limits. There were certain rules they had to abide by, since their sergeant was present, but he let them try the envelope of decency every now and then. They watched the Keepers, openly laughing as their faces beaded with sweat and fatigue.

They dipped down a depression in one of the streets and Lashara lost her footing. The guards dragged her halfway down the road before yanking her to her feet none too nicely. When she recovered, her leggings were shredded and the skin underneath was ripped and red. She fought to continue, but her right leg gave way and she fell again. The soldiers didn't bother to pick her up this time and she slid for a good hundred paces.

Alaric pulled her up, his face set in stone. He had hardly perspired and Lashara thought he could run like this all day, if need be. The large man steadied her as they ran. He looked troubled, however, and did not speak a word.

When she looked up, she could see a massive stone fortress catching the rising sun. Its granite walls shown with hundreds of bow slits and its ramparts were lined with bright flags and masked archers. If her circumstances were different, Lashara might have taken the whole thing in with awe, but for now, the Belazian Keep was a place of foreboding.

The soldiers rode under the structure's portcullis, moving the Keepers past pikemen that paid them no mind. They stopped at the horse pens, and slid down from their saddles, untying their prisoners, but keeping their bonds in place. A number of squires and men-at-arms ran up and led their mounts away as others took their weapons and gear.

Alaric watched his things go. His cheek pulsed and his eyes were dangerously small, but he kept quiet and followed his captors. He did not care for Clonesians and he certainly didn't care for his treatment. They needed to find Jace. This place and its strange customs only served to retain them while his trail faded. One guard cuffed him in the ear and several laughed. They liked the sport of antagonizing those that could not fight back. Others took turns pushing Lashara and Trel as they fumbled through the courtyard.

The prisoners were led through a pair of large doors banded in bronze with deep sunken iron images of an eagle emblazoned in their center. The hall was lined with torches that dripped a greasy mess on the floor beneath them. The air became musty as they moved farther into the Keep. The soldiers guided them through another darkened hall and then they walked down a long flight of twisting stairs. Lashara could hear the sounds of chains and high-pitched cries for mercy coming from the depths. She walked slowly, but her guard prodded her forward.

Finally, the stairs came to an end and they passed by a series of barred cells on their right and large metal doors to their left. Behind the gates huddled skinny men, their frail bodies and long beards shivering in the damp air. Puddles of water mixed with straw matted the cell floors. She could see small mounds of what appeared to be food thrown onto the hay. Apparently, the inmates were not even given plates with their meal, Lashara reasoned. Some of them watched the new prisoners with beady eyes, others sat mumbling things to themselves while they rocked back and forth in their wretched surroundings.

She did not know what horrors hid behind the iron doors on the other side of the hall. Cries of agony and fear mixed with grating metal and slaps of leather came through the small eyeholes. One of the doors opened down the hall and a thick man with a hideous black mask stepped out of the room. Lashara's eyes bulged, but she kept her face forward, not daring to look into the room. She could see only twitching movement out of the corner of her eye and heard the sounds of chains and a muffled cry of fear that rose and fell in time with the clinking. She fought back tears, but kept her head level.

Trel, on the other hand, had made the mistake of staring past the opened door. What he saw made his heart quiver. What terror awaited him and his comrades? He began muttering a quiet stream of verses, pining softly to the Creator for his friends and those around him. His attempts at maintaining his sanity were not enough and he could feel his heart sink with despair even as he mumbled the words to his Savior.

The guards led them to the end of the hall where they were thrown into separate cells to await their trial. Lashara fell face down in the straw, whimpering as the guards slammed her cell shut. She rolled over and straightened, her hands still tied behind her back. She could hear the echoing of the guard's boots as they walked away. The torches made heavy shadows about the room, and provided little comfort in the macabre dungeon. She pushed her way to the cell's gate and looked at those across from her.

A decrepit old man was chained to the wall opposite her. His arms dangled over his head, which was slumped forward. She shook her head at the man whose chest rose slowly up and down. How could anyone sleep in this place?

The crack of a whip sounded and a cry of pain filled the dungeon. She saw movement from another cell. Trel was curled up on his side. His chest was pulsing quickly and his legs twitched with each scream that echoed through the halls. He had buried his face in the straw and was chanting half-heard phrases over and over again. She called out his name in the torchlight.

Trel bolted upright, looking about the place with quick movements. Straw clung to his hair and flopped against his cheek as he flicked his head back and forth. He saw Lashara and his face twisted on the verge of hopelessness. He pushed his head up against the cell gate, working his lips in exasperation.

"Where's Alaric?" she asked Trel.

His eyes darted to the stall next to her, his lips trembling as he fought back sobs. Lashara narrowed her gaze at him. He would break soon, if he was left much longer in this place. She shuffled to her knees, watching her friend. Looking him in the eyes, she relaxed her features, portraying a serenity that she did not feel. Someone needed to be brave and she was willing to put on a show of strength to give her friend hope.

"Don't lose faith, Trel! The Master knows what He's doing and will see us safely through this place. Just hold out a little longer and we will be home and free."

Trel looked at her numbly. Her words seemed true enough, but he could see through her hard exterior to the hopelessness that hid beneath. He hung his head, falling back against the wall. They were doomed.

The man to the right of Trel stirred. He coughed loudly and spat into the straw at his feet.

"Your savior cannot hear you here!" he said in a voice like iron on flint. "Call to him if you must, but it will go unanswered." He raised his wrinkled head and stared wickedly at Lashara. One of his eyes rolled lazily in its socket while he cleared his throat. Through his grizzly beard, he gave her a crooked grin. When his voice began, it sounded like an old man offering sound wisdom to any who would listen.

"I was your age when I last saw the sun. I tried every possible way to escape, but was brought here over and over again. There is nothing in the world that can save you from the Belazian dungeons."

"Then you do not know our Master," boomed Alaric from the cell next to Lashara. She heard him shift in the hay and push his head close to the barred gate. "Thousands of our friends have been in such places. They have persevered and carried on the legacy of faith in our Lord, Yeshua. If it is our fate to do the same, then we will meet our task in His honor."

"Yeshua," the old man said, turning the word over in his mind. "I've heard that name before...long ago. There were many I remember who were imprisoned here in years past. They spoke the name you now say. I dare not utter their stories."

"Tell us, old man," Alaric muttered. He eyed his mocker wearily.

Lashara and Trel also shifted in their cells, their interests peaked at the mention of other Keepers from this man's past. After a moment of pensive contemplation, their cell-mate began. The sounds around them seemed to fade away as the old man spoke.

He told of long ago when he had been sentenced to this place for cheating an officer out of a proper meal. The army had certain laws they forgot when outsiders crossed their paths and to them, everyone was an outsider. The man was taken into the dungeon as a young lad to rot in the bowels of the earth while friends and family forgot about him through the years.

His heart had fallen to despair until one prisoner was thrown into the cell opposite him. His new inmate bore the same black cloak he noticed on Lashara with a silver clasp about the neck. The clasp seemed very important to the prisoner and he hid it each time the guards came to torture him. When he was shut behind the iron doors, his cries filled the dungeon.

"He would only repeat one word over and over," the old man said pensively.

"Yeshua."

The others stirred in their cells. How long it had been since this had happened, they did not know, but the thought gave them hope that others like them had stood true.

"What happened to him?" Trel asked. He had somehow worked the bonds free and now gripped the bars with both hands.

"He died many years ago," the man sighed. "Before he passed, we used to talk late into the night, when the soldiers had left us alone. He told me that others would come bearing the marks he bore and saying the same things he had said. He said if I should listen to them with my whole heart, they would give me something that no mortal could take away."

"At first, I believed him, but as time wore on, I took it as the ravings of a madman. Now, the pages have turned and I look at his words fulfilled," he said, giving Lashara and Alaric a piercing stare with his wandering eye.

"I have thought for many years of what the man once said to me. Here, alone in my cell, with only the shell of my body proof that I still live, I have wondered what thing cannot be seized from me that has not been taken already? I have wrestled with what I would do if given the opportunity to meet those that he claimed would come to me," he said unblinkingly. "Do you know what this man spoke of?"

The man's question hung in the air. All other sounds faded away from the Keepers ears. Somewhere, far away they could here the tortured cries and screams of a dungeon, but they seemed so distant from where they were at the moment. A blossom of hope filled within each of their souls as they mulled over the man's question. The simple fact that this prisoner had not heard the Almighty's plan for his life and Yeshua's supreme sacrifice and lordship were unfathomable to them all. They turned to him, ready to share with the old man the gift of salvation that Yeshua had made possible.

There amidst the horrors of the Belazian Keep in the depths of the dungeon where despair and dying dwelt, they told the old man of the Creator. They detailed His loving plan of sending His Son to earth to die for everyone's wrongs. They shared how He was sacrificed, buried, and rose again, victorious over death and wrong, and now dwelt in Par'lael at the right side of His Father's throne. They told how, if anyone confess with their mouth that Yeshua is Lord of their life and believe in their heart of hearts that the Almighty raised him from the dead, they would be saved and have an everlasting relationship with Him.

The old man looked dumbfounded at the Keepers. He had never heard anything remotely close to what they spoke of. Somehow, he knew what they were saying was true. The actions of the man he had encountered long ago testified to a faith that was deeper than what could be seen by human eyes. All the time that he had spent between then and now, had served to harden these facts. Countless numbers of men had entered the dungeon strong and unafraid, only to be reduced to rubble and tears. None had withstood the pain and trials unscathed, save the man he had once met. Though the soldiers beat him hard and often, he had not lost hope and his faith did not waiver. Now he could see the Truth to which the man had clung.

The old man turned toward the Keepers. His leathery skin was filthy and his hair was matted with hay and dirt. His unkempt beard and wandering eye would have made any man look on him with contempt, but the Keepers did not see his exterior. He asked them slowly what he must do to claim as his own these treasures they spoke of and have a relationship with the Son of the Most High. The Keepers led him through a simple and yet profound petition to the Creator where the man accepted all that Yeshua had done for him and vowed to live the rest of his life for the glory of the Lamb.

All opened their eyes, calm smiles filling their faces. In the middle of the hall between the four cells, the air was stirring. There was no wind or breeze and no sound filled their ears. Nonetheless the air shimmered and spun with an iridescent glow. Flashes of light shook the dungeon, but only in the eyes of the Keepers. They all bowed their heads as the light caved inward, forming an image of a dove suspended in midair. Its wings pointed downward and its skin shown a silvery white that pulsed in time with their beating hearts. They sat in awe at the image, transfixed as it hovered. As they watched, a voice filled their minds. Its sound was like a thousand bells and the ringing of praise mixed into one melody. They listened to what was said, peace filling their souls.

> *For the Almighty did not send His Son into the world to condemn the world, but to save the world through Him. Whoever believes in Him is not condemned. I tell you the truth, whoever hears my word and believes him who sent me has eternal life and will not be condemned for he has crossed over from death to life. Do not let you hearts be troubled. You believe in the Almighty, believe also in Me. In My Father's house are many mansions; if it were not so, I would have told you. I am going there to prepare a place for you. And if I go to prepare a place for you, I will come back and take you to be with me that you may also be where I am. I tell you the truth, if anyone keeps my word, he will never see death.*

The light pulsed again and the image of the dove grew brighter. Its form disappeared in glorious light, which shifted and spun. The area flashed and pulsed, growing dimmer and as it faded away, a calming peace filled the four prisoners hearts even as the sounds of reality filtered back through their ears.

What they had witnessed was beyond amazement. They sagged against their cell walls, their spirits spent from the holy encounter. The Counselor had come to their need to quicken their spirits with a miraculous light and words of hope from the Song of the Ages. Each of them lay still with their thoughts, tranquility filling their souls. None said a word for the rest of the day. They fell into a deep sleep that brought only peaceful dreams and a vision of an iridescent dove and soothing words.

LASHARA AWOKE to the sound of her cell being opened. She was heaved to her feet and thrust against the walls. A guard checked her bonds and then pulled her out into the hall. Alaric and Trel were waiting, each of them accompanied by two soldiers. The guards had found Trel's bonds hidden in the hay and had not been too pleased with their findings. His face was badly bruised and streams of blood ran from his nose and left ear. He looked away from Lashara, ashamed.

"Move!" the guards yelled, kicking Lashara in the knee. She fell to the ground and they kicked her in her temple. She let out a cry and the guards laughed. Stars spun in her vision and they pulled her to her feet as they marched her out of the dungeon.

"Fear not, friends," came a voice from behind them, "The Lord has saved me! Your presence here has not been in vain! Should I not see you in this life, we shall meet on the shores of Par'lael."

"Silence, Bartemus!" a guard said to the Keepers' one-time friend, banging his cell with his short sword. "Crazy old fool."

As they walked past the cell, he began to sing a happy melody that filled the dungeon. It was clear to all that he sang to Yeshua and the Almighty, but the guards ignored him and moved to the exit. They led the Keepers past the cells and torture chambers, climbing the stairs from which they had descended.

"Someone must want you badly," one soldier said gruffly. "I've never heard of being removed after only spending one night in prison."

"Keep quiet, Blaven," said another. "They don't need to know any more than they're told. I'll make sure you get demoted if you say another word."

Blaven and the rest of the guards continued on in silence. They were led out into the courtyard and covered their faces in the bright sun. The light had grown thin again and bore the taint of Sa'vard's hand. From its height, Alaric judged it was approaching noon. In spite of its pale glow, it still hurt their eyes. They were shoved aboard a cart and each fastened into a set of stocks. The wooden frame held their head and hands while they stood for all to see. They rode through the city streets, careful to keep their footing while the public hurled jeers and insults at them.

The ride was not easy. The cart pitched from side to side, shaking their bodies and even Alaric stumbled more than once. Each time they fell, the wooden frames choked their necks and they stood up, gasping for breath while onlookers laughed at their punishment. Since it was noon, the commoners were strolling about, and they entertained themselves by pelting the Keepers with objects. The cart soon became drenched with a pasty assortment of bruised fruits and splattered vegetables, which made the cart all the more slippery. Every now and then, someone would throw a blunt piece of wood or jagged pottery at them. It did not take long for their faces to become scratched and bruised. Pretty soon, no one could tell them apart.

The gauntlet was dreadful. Around every corner, a crowd waited for them. Some held signs that echoed in large letters their distaste of the Keepers. They ranted and roared as the cart passed them by, the younger ones following them for several blocks. All joined in their public mockery. Merchants stood side by side with commoners and craftsman, children and women. Their faces were red with anger and they clenched their fists, shouting at the three. Word must have gotten out of their passage and whereabouts. The whole city seemed to be aware of their presence, and all those who had idle time turned out to egg on their demise.

Though his eyes had been almost swollen shut from the beatings, Trel could hear that they were approaching some square or marketplace. The groups they passed grew louder and more defiant. Before long, the streets were lined with a continual stream of people on both sides. Trel could hear strong yells coming from some ways away.

Alaric was in the lead stock, as chance would have it. What Trel could hear, he saw. The crowds were not only larger, but filled with a significant number of soldiers. Some were mounted, others stood in small groups on foot. They were dressed in ceremonial garb and made the turnout seem more like a parade than a trial. He watched as the cart slowly moved under an archway and entered an oversized square.

The area was filled with throngs of people. Some watched solemn faced, but most of them cheered as they caught sight of the cart. Children ran about the pavement with long streamers in their hands while their parents threw everything from rotten fruits and rancid meat to old shoes and rusted nails. In the middle of the square was a raised platform and someone was standing proudly with a rope around his neck. Those at the base of the stand chanted in unison their hatred at the individual who seemed not to notice them.

The cart drew close to the platform and lurched to a halt. As it stopped, a swarm of enraged men and women consumed the cart, threatening to pull it over. The Keepers swayed in their stocks as it angled heavily to one side. Lashara tried desperately to shake the hands that reached to pull her down. She kicked the air frantically, hoping the mob would back away.

For the first time since they entered the Empire, she was glad to see soldiers. They circled the crowd and violently removed them from the cart's vicinity. One poor commoner's rage turned to screams as he clutched his side. A soldier had clipped him with his pike and he doubled over. His friends dragged him away to see what damage had been done.

The pikemen formed a solid wall around the cart, leveling their weapons outward. Two sergeants climbed aboard and unlocked the three of them from their stocks. They urged them up the stairs on the side of the platform where a black masked, bare-chested man was waiting for them. When they appeared atop the stage, the crowd filled the square with a cheer, raising their hands in delight. Three other masked men moved the Keepers to center-stage and faced them toward the mob. The square went wild.

They stood beside the man Alaric had seen. He was a full head taller than Alaric and dwarfed even Trel. His frame was thin, if only because of his height. He stood defiantly, silently showing the crowd his will. He turned and looked at the Keepers. His face was bludgeoned and split in several places. Alaric could barely make out his eyes underneath the cuts and purpled skin. It's a wonder his nose isn't broken, he thought. Surprisingly, the man turned and parted his swollen lips in his best smile.

"So glad you could make it," he said flatly.

"Jace!" Alaric said stunned. Jace laughed at his large friend. For once he had gotten some other response than his soft, tempered remarks. The reaction was priceless, even under the circumstances.

"What kept you so long? I've been here since sunrise."

"We had a minor set back," said Trel, turning his beaten face to his friend with a grin. Lashara looked at both of them. She had believed Trel's flogging had been severe, but when she examined Jace, she counted him blessed to still be among the living. She reached over and touched his face tenderly, only then realizing that her hands were the only ones left unbound. Jace winced slightly, but did not back away. The two stared at each other, an unspoken affection passing between them.

The crowd began to quiet and the four looked out. A man saddled in a white steed pranced before the masses. He had raised his saber high into the sky. A squad of pikemen flanked him as did a ceremonial procession of archers, swordsmen, men-at-arms, and dragoons. Their garb was silver with a blackened vest.

Their leader was dressed in midnight suede. His hair was oiled and his beard was clipped close to his skin. His black cape flapped about his mount and when he turned his horse, the Keepers could see the blackened eagle head upon his chest, lined in silver. He eyed the Keepers disdainfully, turning his steed back to the crowd.

"Behold the price of allegiance!" the Commander General of the Clonesian Empire bellowed. His horse rose on its hind parts and he pointed his sword at the Keepers. The crowd roared emphatically and the troops snapped to parade rest.

"But allegiance to whom?" he shouted, pointing his sword at Jace. "All know the penalty for swearing fealty to something other than the Empire! But most of all, all know the penalty for paying homage to Yeshua."

At the mention of His name, the crowd fell silent. The children dropped their streamers. Those that were engaged in idle banter hushed to listen.

"This man is guilty of these things!" he roared and the crowd voiced their agreement. "For that, he must pay the ultimate price!"

A cheer rose up into the sky. The little ones waved their ribbons wildly as the crowd began to chant with rage. At the front of the square, the mob was parting. A small entourage of swordsmen separated the mass, and a captain walked forward toward the Commander General. The two traded words heatedly until the captain produced a sealed parchment. The mounted figure tore the paper open and read its contents swiftly. Seeing this, the crowd grew quiet and murmured with confusion. The Commander General ushered the party to the side of the stage, a look of annoyance upon his face.

"It appears more mightier things are yet to come!" the Commander General spoke. "An accusation has been laid before me, sealed and supported by Clonesious himself."

The crowd's confusion turned to boos. They had turned out to see a hanging, at least a whipping and were in no mood to witness mere verbal sparring. The captain and his troop climbed onto the platform, their presence marked loudly with groans and rampant disapproval. He walked to the center of the stage followed by six shining knights in gleaming armor and a number of hard-eyed sergeants. Upon their chest was a silver crown wreathed by an olive branch and crossed by three swords—the seal of the Clonesian Empire and the personal mark of the house of King Clonesious. They strode up to the Keepers, their armor punctuating their steps as they fanned out across the stage.

"Is she the one?" the captain said formally, pointing at Lashara. She cocked her head at the officer, not understanding his question.

The soldiers parted and a man stepped forward. He was dressed in rich black and pranced toward the Keepers with pride. At his side hung a silver rapier, which dangled lightly as he moved. His pasty skin glowed in the pale sun and his lips curled with vengeance. The man's body was cleaner since last they saw him and his hair was now oiled in the manner of the higher classes. Blynn stared at the Keepers, his face twisted in an evil smile.

"It is she," he said reaching out and caressing Lashara's face. She pulled back and eyed Blynn angrily. Blynn tossed his head back in laughter and sneered contemptuously, "But there is only one way to know for certain," he said commandingly. "Hold her!"

A knight stepped forward and clutched each of Lashara's arms, spinning her back to the crowd. Blynn reached out and grabbed her neckline with both hands while Lashara struggled. He pulled hard, ripping the shirt to the waist and stepped back. The crowd cried their approval as Blynn pointed at her skin triumphantly. There on her left shoulder was a deep scar that looked like three circles laid on top of each other. Blynn turned her to the crowd, pointing at the brand that was unmistakable in the bright sun. They fell to a hush, letting what they saw sink into their minds.

"A runaway slave!" said the Commander General. He turned to the crowd shouting it again. The mob shouted back, their faces livid. All knew the penalty for such an act. No matter which land one was in, the sentence was the same: death for all those involved.

"These are who I suspected," said Blynn, squinting at the Keepers. "They took her from me long ago and brought her to the Gap," he said, spitting at their feet. "It's no wonder I couldn't track her! I lost her for several months, but brought the others here. I found them stowed away on a ship that had departed from Samilon. Once they landed, they stole a cart from some rich merchant and traveled here under a disguise."

The Commander General looked at Blynn as he weighed the accusation. Alaric, Trel and Jace stood silent, stunned at Blynn's sudden betrayal. Jace thought he had seen the last of the unsightly man, not believing he would dare show his impish figure in their presence after what he had done to them. He let the incriminations stand, not knowing how to counter what had been said.

Of course, the statements were false, or were they? He could not explain away their origins from the Gap, nor could he say Lashara had not lived there. And what of her scar, her brand that clearly marked her as a slave? How could he possibly say she wasn't one? As for Samilon and the stolen cart, he didn't know what to say. He had trusted Blynn paid their passage and purchased the cart, albeit he basically cheated the poor merchant in the process. Whatever happened, it was Blynn's word against theirs. The fact that they were viewed already as guilty because they were Keepers left them little room for leeway. Jace's head swam with questions as his world collapsed in around him.

He looked up only to find their former guide staring back at him. Blynn stood tall, his subtle smile conveying his victory. He folded his arms as the crowd's shouts grew, taking in the public ridicule in his gloating. It suddenly occurred to Jace that he possibly had been played all along. They may have followed Blynn here only to be led into a trap. The thought made Jace's skin crawl and his lips trembled in anger. He looked at Blynn, flexing his fists.

"You traitor!" he yelled, charging him.

Blynn stepped back while Jace ran at him. Before Jace could reach him, the rope around his throat snapped tight and he fell backwards on the stage. The mob whooped in laughter as he fought to catch his breath. Two of the masked henchmen pulled him to his feet. Jace locked eyes with Blynn, the two delving their stares into each other while the crowd urged them to fight. Blynn threw back his head and laughed.

"Not yet, Keeper," he snarled, saying it loud enough that all could hear him. "Not yet."

He turned to the Commander General who nodded his head. The leader raised his hands, quieting the crowd.

"There is a problem," he said. The crowd hushed as he laid his issue at their feet. "On one hand, we have a slave girl, taken away from her master and harbored asylum in the Gap of all places. This is a legal matter punishable to all parties by instant death. On the other hand—"

The mass roared its approval. The Keepers exchanged glances while the Commander General silenced the crowd again.

"On the other hand, we have the matter of treason! All who stand before you are Keepers, confirmed by the account of the slave master, and have therefore sworn fealty to someone other than our great emperor and king!"

There was silence. The crowd was still as he spoke, listening intently to the accusations laid before them. Though their appetites had been whipped into a voracious lust for blood, they now followed through with what the Commander General spoke of. A number of them sat pensively weighing the plight they were asked to solve.

"What shall it be?" thundered the General. "Shall we let our desire for torment be quenched now," a loud cheer rippled through the crowd, "or shall we send them to Clonesia?"

At this, the crowd jumped to their feet. They let their voices out, shouting in barbaric hunger. The ladies rattled their tambourines and the children danced with their ribbons. The Keepers looked at the chaos in strange disbelief. Alaric and Jace wondered what had driven these people so far from the Truth that they yearned for violence and cruelty. Trel stood, shocked that the roars of approval were for his demise. He did not know exactly what lay in Clonesia, but he knew somehow that it was not better than his present scenario. Lashara only stood clutching her torn shirt in stunned silence.

"Onward to Clonesia!" roared the Commander. The crowd grew louder, shaking the square with their cheers. The Keepers stared in amazement, as if it wasn't possible. It seemed the whole city of Trailaden rejoiced at the Commander's decision. They stood atop the platform, exposed to all the mob's wrath and fury while the henchmen and knights led them away. Blynn looked on, his face filled with ghastly delight.

Jace scanned the crowd a final time before he was led down the stairs. Though he didn't see him, he knew Rae was watching from somewhere. He stood a moment, hoping to catch one final glimpse of his brother's face, but the henchmen yanked his rope and he stumbled down the stairs.

They were thrown into a cart. Its floor was lined with straw. A grid of wooden bars kept the Keepers from jumping out while providing all those outside the ability to taunt the Keepers anyway they pleased. As the gate slammed shut and the cart backed away, Jace felt the mighty grip of Sa'vard closing in around the four of them.

16

THE CITY OF FEARS

The cart wound through the streets of Trailaden. Its pace was slow and a large group of commoners and merchants followed the wagon. They took turns shouting a variety of insults at the Keepers and slandering them and their Savior. When they finally ran out of words, they began showering the cart with objects. There was nowhere to hide and soon all of them were covered in splattered tomatoes, rotten cabbage, potatoes, and old fruits. When the mob ran out of these, they picked up whatever they could find.

Jace covered Lashara with his cloak. The two fell on the hay and Trel and Alaric shielded them as the crowd pelted them with shoes and sticks. The soldiers lining the street stood back only watching the mayhem. They made sure that it was focused on the cart and did not spread to an all out riot or looting. The people soon turned to other tactics. They crowded in around the cart. Several of them thrust their staffs through the cage, driving them into the Keepers as hard as they could. They began to throw other things besides garbage and old food. Jace buried his head as a stone whizzed by, hairs from his face.

The mob's shouts were deafening. Jace cradled Lashara's head in protection as the crowd rocked the cart. She let out short screams as they closed in around them, clutching Jace tightly as she cried. Jace could hear dull thuds hitting Trel and Alaric as the attackers threw any rock they could find. The two grunted, covering their heads as the stones landed about their face and chest. Some people were prying cobblestones from the pavement, heaving them at the cart. The wooden cage surrounding them cracked and splintered as the mob crushed the wagon inward. They could hear the groaning of the floorboards as they warped and shifted.

The soldiers pushed the chaos back. Slowly, a path formed through the sea of people and the cart lurched forward. A captain, his plumed helmet showing, ordered his troop to flank the prisoners as they moved along the road. The wagon eased down the street while the guards checked the crowd. The action moved the cart along, but did little to quell the anger of the mob. The floor of the cart was raised so the Keepers stood on a platform that overlooked the people. Their jeering never ceased as the cart laboriously made its way through the city.

In an hour, much of the riff-raff had diffused off the streets. The energy of the possible hanging had dissipated and the men and women went back to work. Some were still very excited, and Jace heard a number of them say they were packing their things immediately to head to Clonesia. He knew what was most likely in store for him and his fellow comrades, but he did not have the will to tell them. They rode in silence, wiping their faces and checking their wounds before huddling quietly in the straw.

Soon after, the soldiers dispersed and only the children followed the wagon. Their teasing was relentless. They seemed to have boundless words and insults to fling at the four prisoners and did so with heated expressions. They walked about the cart taking turns wrapping the wooden cage. The girls said things that were reproachful even in an adult's eyes. The boys mostly threw stones. Every now and then one would come close enough to spit on them. They would then run away while the others laughed loudly. Somewhere deep within their flawed character was a rebellion towards the Creator that Jace had never thought possible in ones so young.

A great many of them were dressed in colorful garments of silk and brocaded velvet. The young ladies' hair had been pulled up and many of their parents had taken the time to curl it as well. The lads were dressed in fine cotton doublets with different colored hose and matching shoes. They were a healthy looking lot, but altogether fiery and indignant.

It seemed very strange to Jace that ones so little were so taken with malice. Instead of growing weary of their incessant ridicule, Jace observed them for a good while. He wondered how they could become so enamored with hatred that they could perpetuate their actions for so long. He refused to believe that they were simply products of their parents' influence. What deep-seated hole in their souls allowed them to be so? As soon as he thought the question, he knew the answer. Looking into their eyes, it became clear what Yeshua had told him so very long ago. These children had probably lived their entire lives without knowing the true nature of the Creator.

He watched them silently from the corner of the cage. He forgot all that had happened to him and his companions in those moments. Only feelings of sympathy and sorrow for those small, wayward people filled his being. How he wished he had the time to talk to them. If circumstances were different, he would take each one of them aside and tell them the truth. How he wished he could whisk them away to the Gap and teach them the Almighty's goodness. Were it possible, he would take them through the vision his Master had shown him so long ago. He shook his head while they ranted on: this may be the only time in their lives they will ever see followers of Yeshua. *What a shame that they did not take advantage of the opportunity*, he thought.

The children finally grew bored of their hateful games, realizing the Keepers would not be provoked. They gave up and the cart moved down the vacant streets unheeded. Most of the city had apparently turned out at the square and the streets were unnaturally quiet. Jace studied the sky. They were winding northward down some smooth byway where the stones had just been reset. Rae had told him about the maintenance that went into the sophisticated roadways while they had walked about the city the night before.

He sighed. So much had happened since then. So much had fallen to shambles in so short a time. Now, the four of them were most certainly headed to their doom, and Rae, well, he would go on living the way he wanted.

The thought made him angry. How should his brother reap unending rewards and find safety for turning his back on Yeshua while he and his friends must suffer for being His servants? The Clonesian Empire was a world flipped on its head, as far as he could tell, where the righteous were persecuted and the wicked made to prosper. Oh, he did not count himself blameless be any means, but he did strive to live a life of purity. *What a horrible price we must pay for our convictions,* he thought, his mind forming the looming image of the Kolosia.

It was strange that he viewed his world with such detachment. After all, his face was battered, his body was in pain, he had lost his brother, perhaps forever, his friends were hurt, and Yeshua's influence was nowhere to be seen. Furthermore, they were very likely on their way to death for the amusement of some king and country's warped sense of morality. His quirky thinking allowed him to cope with his trials, he mused. He sniffed, playing with the straw while he thought how he did the same thing when we had been locked in the Mines of Shorn.

Part of him liked how he could do this—think about situations as if he were not in the midst of them. Another part of him said it was wrong. Every now and then, he had the sneaking suspicion that he was pushing his feelings down inside—the emotions he never wanted to discuss. Those feelings had bubbled to the surface at inopportune times: his anger at Alaric when he had lost their purse and the slave family in Nadir, his animosity toward Blynn on the way through the Stygian Union, the blatancy with which he voiced his concerns of Rae's actions. His temper had always made his predicament worse. Maybe that was why he had developed this unconscious form of avoidance, never dealing with his emotions as they came about.

He shrugged off his daydreaming. If it worked, why bother it? Even his Mentors and father had complimented him on how durable he was when faced with turmoil. They were always impressed with his outlook. It was good, he reasoned, to keep this attitude.

Before he knew it, the cart had exited through the city gates. It was working its way down the high slope of the city and northward into the interior plain. Jace looked up in time to catch the sun setting over the eastern line of mountains. The scene filled him with a sense of foreboding as night chased away the daylight, but he shook it off. The others had fallen asleep and lay still while the cart bounced down the steep path. He had never seen them looking so bad and felt pity towards them that they had undergone such beatings because of his actions. Even Alaric looked worn and bruised, but he had kept quiet. The man was an ox and could take punishment enough for two men, but the guards had heaped a fair amount on him nonetheless.

Trel and Lashara were another story. Trel looked like he could hardly walk, and his light skin was almost translucent from not eating. If anything, he was glad that they had been given a cart so Trel could keep off his feet. He was afraid his friend would not be able to absorb much more than he had, but was impressed that he had taken so much already. Still, he put on a good face and his wry grin was always an encouragement through even the harshest of treatments.

He could not bring himself to look at Lashara. The lady had transformed completely since he had met her. Nowhere to be found was the cool, business-like woman he had met in the Gap. Her lofty remarks at his mistakes and standoff nature to the rest of them had undergone substantial changes since then. She had opened up to all of them, allowing herself to become vulnerable and even letting Trel and Jace tease her on their journey. Now, she had been reduced to a shriveled mass of hysteria. She kept her back to all of them, clutching her bare shoulders and tattered shirt. Jace had covered her with his cloak, but she had not moved. He thought she pretended to be asleep, but he had seen and heard her muffled sobs while the cart moved along.

The sounds nearly broke his heart. Of all of them, she had opened up to him the most. He had found joy in knowing that there was someone he could talk to so easily, someone that cared about his presence and offered her advice in a straightforward manner. He had grown to see her, not just as a member of the party, but as a friend and beautiful young woman. The fact that she was a former slave meant nothing to him. It had surprised him, but everybody had dark mysteries they kept hidden from others. Somehow, her secret, or rather the unveiling of it, had changed her distinctly.

The sky turned gray and then night fell. The cart rode on down the highway into the dark. Somehow, the driver kept the wagon on the path. Most likely, he had driven this route with caged cargo such as Jace for many years. The idea sickened him as he thought of the countless number of others who had undergone the same things that he now was going through. The land of the Clonesians was treacherous. Oh, it was beautiful to the eye and filled with the object of every want under the sun, but all of it hid the fact that it was a dangerous quagmire to Keepers and hostile to Yeshua.

Somewhere between his passing thoughts and the rhythmic bouncing of the wagon, Jace's eyes had ceased to stay open. He slumped up against the corner of the cage while his head sloshed from side to side. The cool chill of night began to seep into his bones, but his fatigue and boredom won him over.

He curled up on the hay, nestling his head in the straw as he drifted asleep. His dreams were filled with his simple life in the Gap: his tiny cottage, Nina's gentle nuzzling while she chewed her cud, Mum's fresh baked bread on the counter, and Amoriah's adoring gaze. He reminisced of his da's sure hands and quiet tone guiding him through the dozens of tasks about the farm and lending him truths that pointed him towards a greater relationship with his Lord.

The dreams were jolted from him when the cart stopped. Jace squinted his eyes in the torchlight that surrounded them. Their wagon had stopped outside some small building. Its structure stood alone in the night, lit up by several lamps that were marked around its grounds. It was a two-story inn with several darkened windows. The pitch-covered wood was black and lent a faint burnt smell to the area.

The inn was silent. Only the jingling of wind chimes hidden from view could be heard as the air stirred about the place. Jace could see a few bodies moving around inside, but the rest must have been asleep. The silhouettes were facing each other and their hands were moving fast. The shorter one waved an arm to the other and the two disappeared from view.

A faint light split the front doors as the driver came out from the inn followed by three men. Two of them were carrying short swords and clutched at their thin velvet shirts. They hunched over in the cool breeze. Jace could see the frowns on their faces as they approached the cart. They looked perturbed that they had been ordered out in the chill air this late at night. The other was dressed in a leather tunic with tan boots that made no sound. He walked directly behind the driver with a light step. As he came closer, Jace heard the quiet clinking of coin in his pockets. He eyed the cart, casting a suspicious look at the prisoners.

"More lambs to the slaughter, eh?" he said with a wry laugh. "Move it off to the side, but keep it far enough away from the house. They have a queer air about them," the man said staring at their cloaks. "Keep the cart in the light, I want my men to be able to see them, should they be up to any mischief. You know the trouble we've had with their lot before."

He came close and shook the cage. "Double check that the gate is locked, I don't want them stealing my chickens," he said and turned to leave.

"Keepers," he muttered distastefully under his breath and walked away.

The driver gave them a smug look before climbing on the wagon. He was old and frail, but the contemptuous aura he emanated told he cared next to nothing for his cargo. He stopped the cart where he was told, checking the latch on the cage before unhitching the horses to take them to warmer stables. Jace watched him leave. He was a short man, gnarled and bent. His frame was large, rotund even, and he walked with a limp. He didn't give the prisoners a second glance and vanished behind the inn.

Jace couldn't sleep as the night grew colder. He didn't know how his companions could sleep. Maybe he could if he hadn't been privy to their final destination. The innkeeper was right, they had little hope for their rescue or vindication. There was no way they would see their homeland or loved ones again. It reminded him of the questions Yeshua had asked him. Would he shirk the path with which Yeshua had for his life, or would he relinquish his vows under pressure in the final moments? He had been in that situation only once before and even he did not know how he would react this time.

The lamplight flickered in the wind. He could hear the metal chimes somewhere playing in the air. A door creaked as it slammed open and shut, but no other noises interrupted the dark night. Off to the side of the inn stood a small wooden hut. A single candle shown through the window.

At the table inside sat the two guards. One rested lazily. His feet were propped up and his chair leaned back against the wall. His was sleeping soundly with his head resting against the back of the chair. The other guard was staring directly back at Jace. Even at this distance, the candle glinted off his beady eyes. He sat with his hands folded, unflinching save for the sliver of wood that he chewed in his mouth. Jace deliberately put his back to the man and straightened his shoulders in a show of defiance. The guards had unbound his hands when they threw him in the cart, but they were numbing in the cold and he awkwardly positioned himself after several attempts. He did not care for being treated like an animal or a caged beast.

He rubbed his shoulders as the wind picked up. His thin shirt offered no protection in the cold. He almost wished he had not given Lashara his woolen cloak, but then, looking down on her, he thought differently. She was sleeping now, her body rising and settling slowly with each breath. It was fitting that she kept the cloak. If that's all it took to give her comfort, it was worth the shivering he had to tolerate. Somehow, he finally fell asleep, but it was the restless slumber that only one has when they know they're approaching some impending doom.

The morning was filled with a dense fog that hid most of the lowlands. The pale sun was almost unnoticeable through the thick haze. The sentries had both fallen asleep halfway through the night. The one looked like he hadn't moved from his reclined position in the chair while the other was spread over the table. The two stirred as the innkeeper came out of the house, banging the door shut loudly. One looked about him blankly, then tapped his partner. The two patted down their hair and straightened their disheveled clothing. One took out his sword and began to oil it while the other doused the still burning candle and straightened up the guardhouse. They did this all with surprising speed and deftness, making next to no noise. No doubt they had many years of practice.

The innkeeper entered the station just as the guards both sat down at the table donning passive looks that said they were about their business. Their employer eyed them with an angry grimace and began to fume.

"How long?" he merely asked. His muffled words carried to the cart across the silent grounds. The innkeeper's look was dark, but the guards paid him no mind. They sat as if they hadn't heard.

"You aren't worth the stew I feed you! So help me, if ever I catch the two of you lazing around, I'll thrash the lot of you! It's a wonder you lasted as long as you did in the king's service. If it weren't for your mother and the good graces that come from who knows where, I would have thrown you out long ago! It's a pity she had to drag you into my life, but I'll get my worth out of you, if it kills you."

The guards still ignored the man whose agitation began to grow. He took a large board that was propped up beside the door. Brandishing the object with both hands he spoke again. This time, he was heard quite clearly throughout the yard.

"Get out of this building," he seethed. "There's a dozen things to do besides breathing air and taking up good space. Go!"

As he finished, he brought the plank down on the table and the two men jumped up like a flock of quail. The man laid about them with the plank as they ran to the door. The first one got away with just a glancing blow to the shoulders, but the innkeeper caught the second one cleanly on the head. The board gave a loud crack as it landed on his crown and he fell forward into a mud puddle outside the door. The sound woke the other Keepers who looked at the altercation in silence. The one guard kept running until he was well behind the inn and beginning his daily chores. The innkeeper came out of the guardhouse and surveyed his handiwork, kicking the limp body none too softly.

"He can rest for awhile," he said to no one in particular. "When he comes to, maybe he'll think twice about falling asleep on watch."

The innkeeper sauntered off and left the man face down in the mud. The cruel display left the Keepers aghast that one could treat their children so, but they said nothing for fear of retaliation. It was but one more act of violence in a land gone wrong. They watched helplessly as the young man laid unconscious, his blood mixing with the dirt. Outside the city, away from the beauty and glamour, men felt no need to gloss over their intents and actions. The Clonesian Empire's attitudes were laid bare with obvious poignancy. No one cared to lace their words with respect or flowery speech. Their selfish ways and careless regard for anyone was painfully noticeable.

Trel could not believe he had just seen a man killed right before his eyes. He relaxed slightly when he saw the young man was only unconscious, but he was still moved by his injury. If he had known he would suffer such wounds, he would have somehow kept the man awake. The guard sat up slowly, rubbing his head. Trel beckoned him to come closer so he could inspect the wound, but the man scoffed, kicked a shower of gravel at them and walked away tendering his head.

Alaric sat in the corner. He was like an immovable boulder, but they all knew he was stewing. His mind was set on the terrible scene he had witnessed. A heavy hand leads to deceit while encouragement exudes diligence. The innkeeper should have expected the animosity and discouragement that his sons showed him. Their actions were furthered by his punishments. Should Alaric treat the workers in the Gap with the same disregard, morale would suffer, and the defenses would never be finished in time. People needed healthy amounts of encouragement with small doses of discipline, not the other way around. It vexed him that leaders should abuse their power that was not theirs to begin with.

Alaric thought about how all authorities that exist have been established by the Almighty. No matter how awful the innkeeper, or how skewed the governmental policies of the Clonesian Empire, the Almighty had established their power to begin with. That was the one reason that kept him from reducing the cart to pieces and fleeing during the night. That decision would likely get him nowhere, but he remained submissive, not for lack of hope, but because of his unwavering faith in the Song of the Ages.

Since it was the inerrant word of the Creator, passed on to the hands of men, it was infallible. He had banked his life on its testimony, applicability, and durability in all situations. Since it said all authorities were set in place by the Most High, he trusted it, heaping undue pain and misery upon himself if only because the Song said he should submit to the proper governing bodies.

This was his conviction. Others may have turned and ran or formed some conspiracy and sabotage to quicken their flight back to the Gap. He, however, believed His Lord was mightier than this. Should He want, his Master could call down fire from the heavens and consume their surroundings to save His followers and bring glory to His name. Things of that nature had not been done in countless ages, but that did not sway Alaric's faith. His reasoning was that this was where his Master wanted him at this moment and he was content to follow Him.

It did not mean he did not doubt the Father. He constantly wrestled with his questions. He had been through far too much to stay his anxieties, but those times had served to further his faith that the Almighty had a purpose behind every joyous occasion and hapless trial. He had ceased long ago to worry heavily upon these things. Yeshua had brought him through so much that each new hardship caused him to focus on his Lord and Savior before he had seen the miracles the situations produced.

The results were not only continual peace, but a keen sense that no matter what happened, nothing was overlooked by his Master. He found that if he sat back and watched each case unfold before his eyes, he could see the Almighty at work in everything that happened in his life. This was the outlook he strove to keep even in their present situation.

He had, however, never conquered his human nature. This led to bouts of fear that seized him whenever his focus strayed. Were he to forget what he could not see and dwell upon his circumstance, he would fall just as surely as Petra had sunk below the waves when he doubted Yeshua. On these occasions, he had wrestled in his loneliness, turning to everything but his Master. His actions had left him despondent and afraid, but no matter how long he had wallowed in despair, he had always crawled back to his Savior and Lord with renewed focus.

Alaric was so deep in thought that when he finished, the fog had lifted and they were well on their way into the day. The sun burned down on them and their throats became parched. It occurred to him that they had had nothing to drink or eat since they had been imprisoned. The thought made him all the more hungry, and his stomach began to growl. He liked to eat so a substantial meal was always a welcomed sight that he never passed up. The sweltering weather only made it worse and soon he began to turn the idea of hot vittles and a cool flask of water over and over in his mind.

The others sat motionless throughout the day. They too had noticed their bodies' calls for nourishment, but they were too tired to care. The bruises Jace and Trel had received had grown darker and made them feel sore today. Neither of them moved much. When they did, it was always followed with horrible wincing and a grimace to match. Both their heads throbbed and Trel's ribs hurt. It was hard for him to breathe terribly deep, but he was afraid to ask Lashara to look at it.

The little lady huddled in the far corner and hadn't removed the cloak Jace had given her the night before. She was pulled up in the same position with her back to the group, breathing softly. They heard faint cries coming from her corner, but could not tell if it was simply their imagination. Halfway through the day, she removed the cloak from her head, but made no other movement. When Jace had stood to his feet to scan the plain stretching out around them, he noticed she was weaving the straw back and forth through her fingers, but he said nothing. He began to worry about her, fearing that she would curl up inside herself once more if something wasn't done soon, but he let it pass for the time being.

They said little while the day went on. Each watched the landscape pass, viewing the trees and hills with little interest. The land was drab, but it reminded Jace of what the Wanton Plain may have looked like. The gentle hills were only covered in grass and the occasional tree was all that broke their monotony.

All of them were thinking about what lay in Clonesia. Those that knew sat in brooding silence while those that didn't let their imagination run rampant. There was not much to say, and they conserved their energy, not knowing when they would receive their next meal, if any at all.

Trel took to counting the number of hills they passed. The journey was slow and the slopes soft enough that he had no problem keeping track. He only counted the ones he went over, but added the others as well when he realized the cart went around most of them. He imagined they were traveling over the giant heads of earthmen who were balding, save for their grassy scalps. Those nearest their path were void of anything except the short green grass. Farther off, the hills were dotted with trees. Some had dark patches of forest and others were simply boulders and weeds.

An occasional house was spotted. Some were well kept, but most were rotted and abandoned. Boredom kept Trel's mind wandering and he had to start his counting over three times. He finally gave up after losing track again, but his grand total was somewhere around two hundred thirty-seven.

Jace spread out in the hay with his head pointed to the skies. He made the time pass by watching the clouds. The shapes were always changing and none were exactly the same. He enjoyed the giant poofy ones that hung suspended in midair. The massive, steel gray ones seemed to weigh more than he could fathom and he pondered how they could stay afloat in the sky. They had a golden sheen painted on their backs where the sun touched them. He used to liken them to animals and beasts, but as he grew older, he simply enjoyed them for what they were. Some hung low in the sky and sped across the land rapidly. He would watch them slowly break apart or twist into different shapes as they vanished from view. As the day went on, the sky grew clear and there weren't many for him to look at. Instead, he was left to watch the wispy ones high up in the air. They looked like faint brush strokes on a blue canvas. He fancied that the Creator painted these throughout the day for ones such as he to look at. The images set him at ease as he stared at them through the gridded roof of the wagon.

They traveled for eight more days before they reached Clonesia. The third day found them still out in the interior plain amidst the flat, dry hills. They had not eaten or drank at all and their stomachs were long past telling them so. The driver pulled the cart up next to a low sitting lodge and walked inside. In a few moments, he came out leading a small procession of soldiers. Jace sat up to watch while the others laid about him. The guards were dressed in leather jerkins and milled around. Many were unshaven and unkempt. They were sweating profusely in the heat, and their stench wafted through the wagon as they crowded around the cart. The driver explained to the crew the cart's destination and the soldiers nodded, their ears perking up in interest.

"By the end of the week we'll be there," he said, scratching his stubbly chin. "They should be ready for entertainment no more than three days after we arrive. As you can see they're worse for wear, but don't let that fool you. Some of their lot have been known to fight tenaciously while others were said to take a fair amount of punishment. Either way, they will last long enough to provide amusement that will be talked about for some time."

The driver rubbed his chest in thought, then spoke to the crowd, "What do you say? The last bunch bid heavily on the small one and a fair number on the large beast in the middle. Have you any wagers?"

One of the soldiers spoke up gruffly, "They all look pitiful. I believe only the giant will be worth considering after the first bout. My coin's on him, if any of them," he said handing the driver a handful of his money.

"Ah," said the driver clicking his tongue and nodding, "It would seem so, I'm afraid, and many have thought like you, but I have watched them. The tall one can fight. Look at his bruises and that glowering he gives us. I have seen him in action and he has much promise. My bet's on him, if you care to know," he said, lifting a stick to prod at Jace.

Jace batted it away angrily and then snatched at it. The driver pulled it back and the soldiers murmured their approval. They began handing the man wads of their earnings, hoping Jace's tenacity would last in Clonesia. Jace stared at them menacingly. He hated being goaded. As soon as he was out of this cage, he would show them what he was made of. The soldiers walked away, laughing at his show of force. One turned to give them an off-handed comment.

"We'll see if they last in the Kolosia," he said. "I've heard it reduces grown men to babies and babies to rubbish. I wish I was there for the sport."

The driver waited by his cart while one of the soldiers came back out. He was carrying a large pail in each hand. One sloshed a trail of water over its sides. Flies hovered over the other. The driver opened a small gate in the caged wagon and the soldier put both inside. The guard went back into the lodge and the driver climbed up on the cart and urged the horses on their way.

Slowly the rest of the party came alive. Jace went over to the two metal buckets. In one was water that had turned a murky brown. The interior of the bucket was rusted and mud swirled about the liquid. The Keepers licked their parched lips in thirst. The bucket was extremely full and they were too weak to lift it. They took turns shoving their heads unashamedly into the water and drinking their fill. They sat back, wiping their faces and smiling at each other.

The other pail was filled with bones. They were not well-eaten and sizable chunks of meat clung to them. The four licked their lips and they dipped their hands deep into the pot one after the other. Trel went first, reaching for a thick loin bone. As he pulled it out, the flies flew around him in madness. He shooed them off and went into the corner to eat. The meat was hard with a greenish tint. It smelled horrible to all except the four of them who were starving. They sunk their teeth into the half-chewed meat as if it were a delicacy. They ate to their heart's content, polishing off the bones and then drinking another fair share of water. After they were done, they lounged lazily on the hay as if they were kings and queens. The weather seemed to be a bit milder and the sky a bit more blue with food in their bellies.

The rancid meat and rusted water seemed to rejuvenate their spirits. They became animated to the point of tiny conversation while they moved ever closer to Clonesia. They commented on the fair land about their eyes. Though none seemed to think so, they all affirmed that it was. They talked of their living conditions, which weren't so bad. Oh yes, they agreed, the cart was a fine cart and the hay was fresh. Everything was dandy, they said, but they avoided what was truly on their minds. Finally Trel turned to Jace.

"What did the guards mean by all that talk of Clonesia?" he asked.

It was the words Jace had dreaded hearing and he played dumb. "What do you mean?"

"Come, Jace. Didn't you hear them? The first place we stopped said we were 'sheep to the slaughter'. When we stopped today, the driver was making wagers like we were going to fight."

"What about that word he said?" asked Lashara quietly. They looked at her and her eyes darted away. She played with the hay, acting like she hadn't said a word.

Trel scratched his chin, "She's right. What was it that guard said? The Krimlesia?"

"The Kolosia," Jace blurted out.

"That's it!" Trel said snapping his fingers.

"I don't know, and even if I did I wouldn't tell you," Jace said kicking the hay and then turning around.

"What are you hiding, Jace? Is there something you're not telling us? You know I'll find it out."

"Stop pestering me, Trel. It's for your own good."

"Pestering? I haven't started pestering. That's a good idea though. I don't like secrets, Jace, none of us do," Trel said, getting loud. He lowered his voice. "You were supposed to be honest with us, remember, or are you going to start taking after Blynn?"

Jace whirled around. The look he gave Trel told him he had gone too far. Jace's fingers twitched and he stood like stone against the cage. "Take it back."

"No."

"I can stand your prodding and ignorance, Trel, but that is over the line. You may have come with me and gone through countless hardships on my behalf, but I am the one who has lost more than anyone. You did not have to come and quite frankly, if I had known you would be like this, I would not have let you. I don't need your foolish words."

"So help me, Jace," Trel said standing to his feet. "Your head's gotten bigger the farther we've gone on. You have no right to keep us in the dark, especially if it threatens us. If I have to, I'll thrash it out of you."

"Don't be a dolt," Jace said, swatting a fly away. "I'm nearly twice your weight. I'm not saying a word yet and that's final."

"Tell him, Jace."

The two looked at Alaric whose face was drawn and rigid. He looked up into Jace's eyes. "We're all headed to the same place, not you only. The young man and Lashara have a right to know."

Jace began to object, but Alaric cut him off. "If you don't tell them, I will."

Jace started to tell them, but his voice broke. He turned away and lowered his head. He couldn't bear to tell his friends that they were going to their deaths because of his decisions. He closed his eyes, trying to muffle his cries and keep his body from shaking. He waved for Alaric to continue as he stood facing out at the world around them.

"Clonesia is the capital of everything west of the Great River," he heard Alaric say. "It was a mighty fortress in its time. Army after army would throw themselves against it, hoping to destroy it, but never succeeded. It has stood almost since the beginning of time like some vast symbol of all of man's truest aspirations and highest deeds. Clonesious was the mightiest man that ever lived and all knelt before him. At one time over three quarters of the earth were under his sway, but that could not stop the inevitable.

"When Sa'vard brought his forces to bear, he laid waste to the city and tore the throne room to shreds, demanding Clonesious' fealty. The mighty king had no choice and now all his lands are forfeit to the Ruler of Darkness. To cement his power, Sa'vard built the Kolosia. It was and is the symbol of his sovereignty and a monument to the dark side of man. Sa'vard has used this gigantic building as a place to entertain the throngs of Clonesians in the most depraved ways their souls desired. More Keepers have met their fate there than any place in history."

Trel and Lashara gasped. "Does that mean... Are you sure that is where we are headed?"

"You heard for yourself," said Alaric in a chilling monotone.

"We're going to die? Jace, how could you?" Trel yelled, running at him. Alaric was up in a flash, his thick arms grappling Trel and moving him away from Jace. "We're all going to die because of you!" he spat in anger. "You wouldn't even 'fess up to it, you coward!"

Jace bowed his head, trying to blot out Trel's words. No matter how he tried, they stuck to his soul. He knew all too well what would happen. Trel was right. If he had done something different, maybe they wouldn't have gotten involved.

Alaric pinned the hysterical Trel to the cage, squaring him up until he calmed down.

"Jace didn't do this, Trel," he said, a touch of heat in his voice. "There are forces at work here bigger than mere men. Sa'vard wants us removed from this place and will stop at nothing to get what he wants," he said, shoving Trel once to give the words substance.

Trel looked stunned at Alaric and then at Jace. "I'm sorry," he said, "I didn't know.

"Of course you did," said Jace pointedly to Trel.

"Yes, it's just— It's so much easier to pin the blame on something I can see. Sa'vard has us between two stones it seems," he said, letting out a deep breath.

"That does not mean we're doomed," said Alaric forcefully. "Anything can happen before we get there. Stranger things have happened even on the floor of the Kolosia."

"Spare us, Alaric!" shouted Jace. "All those things have happened long ago. There's precious little we have to look forward to."

"Your not believing, Jace, doesn't mean it won't happen."

"If anybody knows that, it is I. I've talked to Yeshua, Alaric. He told me—" but he couldn't go on. They waited for him to gather himself and he continued. Jace looked them each in the eyes before he spoke. "He asked me if I would be willing to lay down my life for His glory. What do you think is going to happen? Why would He ask me something like that if only to prepare me for my future?"

Alaric was silent, but when he spoke, his words were slow and measured. "I do not know, Jace. Yeshua is wise beyond men's comprehension. Maybe He asked you so as to change your focus. Perhaps He did it to open your eyes to the severity of our actions. Then again, maybe He was doing like you say. Whatever His reason, we're still alive," he said, looking at each of them. "We mustn't give up just yet, neither should we disintegrate into a hopeless group of underlings. We serve the Master of the living, let us never forget that."

Jace and Trel starred at each other for a long spell. A gleam began to form in their eyes and they grinned a mischievous smile as if they were reminded of a secret that the whole Empire knew nothing about. They came together and apologized, clasping each other in a healthy embrace. Alaric and Lashara stood and when the two separated, they rejoiced anew for their Master's protection, and asked for direction and strength for whatever may befall them in the city of fears.

17

TO THE DUNGEON

Two more days came and went rather plainly. The cart meandered ahead and the Keepers soon found themselves hungry again. The sun seemed to stay in the sky forever, and its blistering heat was inescapable. At night, the air turned to a dry chill. The driver left them outside and unprotected while he slept in the nearest lodge or pitched a thick canvas tent with a warm fire inside. Morning would find the Keepers shivering and huddled close together to conserve body heat.

The driver had heard of their peculiar custom of petitioning the Creator. He could never comprehend how anyone in their right mind could converse with something or someone that was not there. True, he would talk to his departed wife every so often, but it was more out of tradition than earnestly thinking she was listening. Most people in the Clonesian Empire believed in only the here and now and the mystics that didn't kept their opinions to themselves. He ignored the Keepers' words outwardly, but noted their change in spirit.

This sickened him. He, like any good Clonesian, despised all that Keepers stood for. Their smiles and whistling, singing and chanting of praises to their Master were annoying and absurd. He was not impressed at all with their sudden change of attitude. Secretly, he hoped he would be one of the lucky few to have a seat near the Kolosia floor on the day these boisterous idiots met their Maker. They would die and be no more just like the one they followed. It would be a pleasure to see their faith that seemed so unshakable fizzle into nothingness when they realized their Lord would not save them.

What led Gappers to believe in something that was not there? He had heard a multitude of their explanations. Most of them babbled, unable to explain to him exactly who, what, or why they followed this being they called the Almighty, Yeshua, or whatever He was. The fact that they couldn't even explain it made him all the more skeptical until he had nothing but contempt for their frivolous ways.

He took to mocking them if they got too loud. When they were asleep, he would throw water on them or poke them sharply with a long stick. He cackled even louder when he saw he had aggravated them. The tall one was especially easy to provoke, and the driver took certain pleasure in whittling down his spirits. He directed his jibes and mocking toward the man. At first, Jace would bless him in the funny way of the Gap, but as they went on, he only answered the driver's remarks with silence.

On one occasion, the little old man grew excessively brash. The Keepers had taken to their strange conversation each afternoon when the sun was the hottest. The man would punctuate their earnest pleas with a slew of comments.

"There's nobody else here except me and the horses," he'd say condescendingly, or simply, "It will never help."

This did not deter the Keepers and they went about whispering quietly to their Lord or singing together. The third day came and so did their usual time of meditation. They began by holding hands and bowing their heads close to the hay, which by now was a pungent, sticky mess. They started softly enough so the driver would not interrupt their pleas. By the time he heard them, they were well into their worship, offering thanks and supplications to their unseen lord.

The driver would toss an insult to them. His favorite was to make a derogatory jingle out of Yeshua's name. This always seemed to incense the Keepers and it tickled him to no end.

While they continued, the clear blue sky began to grow dark. Dark clouds covered the horizon in the west and a steady breeze drove them toward the lone wagon. Before the end of the hour, the clouds had blotted out the sun and the wind was blowing the tall grass on its side. The driver leaned into the gusts, holding his rider's cap on his head with one hand while he held the reins with the other. His horses whinnied nervously as the storm came on. The Keepers stood together in the center of the cage lifting their voices above the wind. They never opened their eyes and stood content as the storm winds formed around them. Great drops of rain began to fall around the cart.

At first the rain was intermittent and the driver thought it would blow over. He saw he was wrong when he looked off to the west and saw the rains, marching like some transparent phantom across the rolling grasslands. They formed a solid sheet of dark gray that glistened in the dim afternoon light. They came on quickly and there was nothing the Keepers or the driver could do as the wave of water crashed into them. In one moment the gentle pitter-patter had turned to a torrential downpour. The sound was like a thousand drums beating while flashes of golden lightening filled the sky.

The driver hunched over, spurring the horses onward. It was strange to him that so violent a storm had come from the west, where unending desert was instead of the east, toward the Great River. It had just so happened that the storm hit when he was directly between the two nearest lodgings. They were both half a day's ride and he considered for a moment before pressing on. As loud as the beating of the rains were, he could still make out the words of the Keepers every now and then as they offered their continual blessings and praises.

Then it happened. The noise came from everywhere at once. It was not as overpowering as the pelting of the rain, nor as thundering as the crashes of lightening, but it was one of the most fearsome sounds anyone could hear when caught in the open with a downpour.

At first there was the occasional thud. Then, before he knew it, hail was falling down around them like frozen fists, hammering the earth into submission. The icy stones were larger than a man's head and came down in a fearsome shower while the lightening flashed. The driver looked over just in time to see a tree split straight down the middle under the ceaseless blows. Bolts of white light were marking the trees on both sides of the road and the horses rolled their eyes in terror. In only heartbeats, the tall grass had been reduced to a tattered carpet of swarthy green fibers, matted down as far as the eye could see. Everywhere he looked, the frantic man saw complete carnage.

Then, as if in a dream, he noticed. Though the land was destroyed and everything flattened by the awful frozen stones, the cart, horses, and cage were untouched. The scene was surreal as the horses trudged on through the rain at their feet. The driver saw an invisible barrier that encircled the cart. No hailstones entered its bounds, save for the shower of rain that poured down on them. He started in awe, but then caught again the sound of the Keepers' praises. He half turned to say something and then thought a moment, his heart filling with rage. He gave a crazed cackle turning to the four prisoners.

"Is this the best you can do?" he yelled above the storm, turning to laugh at the onslaught. "Your lord may cause fire and wind, or ice and rain to block our paths, but it will not keep you from your deaths! I have taken countless others of your kind down the same path thousands of times before! You will be no different! Your master holds no power here!"

As if in response, the rain let up. The storm was gone almost as quickly as it had appeared. The rumbling of thunder faded into the east and the rain diminished to nothingness. The air was left with a cool dryness that was quite out of place for the region, season, and time of day. Before the hour passed, the wind had died down and an unearthly quiet settled over the land. Only the rivulets of rain water and flattened devastation were proof of the intense storm that had taken place. The driver looked back at them. His lips were curled with malice and he spat his hatred at them.

"It always rains when you Keepers are under my care. Do you think this was all that special?" he said waving his hand at the destruction everywhere. "It is not proof of your lord, nor is it cause enough for me to turn around."

Trel jutted his chin out. "You can't explain away the hail," he said shaking his drenched head.

"There is some practical explanation for everything," the man scoffed, although he looked a bit unsure. "It doesn't matter. If whomever you are talking to was real, your cage would be opened and you would be free. Your lord can't even do that."

"Perhaps," said Alaric stepping forward. He rubbed his arms down, checking his wet hands, as if to see for himself that the rain was real. "Perhaps our Lord has made this a sign for you. He has shown His power and spared you so that you could honor Him and set us free."

The driver stood up on the riding bench, eyeing the four of them. He didn't like suggestions from prisoners telling him what to do. He mulled through what he had seen in his mind.

"No," he said. "If there was a being with that much power, he would not spare any that were not his own. This was some random occurrence that was entertaining, but coincidental nonetheless. It's related to nothing in particular."

"I wonder if you would have thought differently, had the circle been any smaller," said Jace. He rubbed his chin considering the alternative sizes. "It could have surrounded only the cart, but that would have most definitely killed the horses. What if it had only enveloped the cage and those inside it, would your mind be changed then?" he said, letting his eyes rest on the driver as he finished.

The driver turned white. Nothing could have survived a hailstorm. Ice that size would have struck a man dead. It occurred to him suddenly that he had been only inches away from death itself. The thought made him tremble and he looked at the Keepers.

Jace lips quivered slightly. The man was on the verge of a connection with Yeshua and Jace began to smile. Seeing the beaming face of the Keeper, the driver turned livid. He shot his gnarled hand through the cage and grabbed Jace around the throat pulling him up against the grid. The man had surprising strength, and Jace tried to catch his breath as the man's grip tightened around his throat. The driver smiled as the Keeper choked, clawing at his burly arm.

"Where is your lord now?" he seethed, throwing Jace back into the others. He could have choked him then and there, further proof to him that this Yeshua did not exist. The young man gasped, coughing on all fours. The driver looked at them narrowly as they gathered around their friend. They seemed so courageous one moment and pitiful the next. "I have seen all I care of you and your hidden lord," he said and sat down, slapping the reins hard.

While Lashara and Trel comforted Jace, Alaric strode up to the front of the cage.

"Be careful what you say," he said in his usual quietness. "As surely as I stand before you, there will come a time when our Lord will reveal Himself. He cannot be kept away by a simpleton's words. You may yet see the Creator of the universe do something that will shock you to the core."

The driver said nothing, but his back stiffened slightly. He tapped the reins and yelled harshly at his horses. He never uttered another word to them and the Keepers kept to themselves in their caged cell.

For the next two days, the massive hill of Clonesia filled their view. Its walls ringed the hill several times and its populous spilled out over the plain around the city for two leagues in every direction. The sun made the walls of the city a golden brown. The two dominant structures that they had seen from a distance when entering the interior plain shot up into the sky, dwarfing the city, and casting a long shadow onto the plain. The silver castle of King Clonesious shown like a diamond amidst the city: its gleaming walls welcoming all to the heart of the Empire.

"I recognize the palace," Trel said good-naturedly, "But what is that?" he asked, pointing to the giant brown stadia that stood opposite it.

The Kolosia took up most of what was left of the crown of the hill. Only its monolithic stature kept the castle from shining over the plain unchallenged. Its tan walls stood ominously for all to see. At mention of its name, Trel turned white. He and Lashara had not expected some awesome fortress they would be taken to. They thought the Kolosia was the name for some grand square or green where the Clonesians congregated on rare occasions. The name and the building struck the two of them with fear and they hushed themselves as they entered the city.

All the inhabitants of Clonesia felt secure under the shadow of the two great buildings and viewed them as kin monuments to the power and wealth that made their country great. Where one was the sign of unquestionable power and authority, the other was a reminder of all the amenities that could be afforded a country that was steeped in wealth. No other land boasted objects so enormous, nor ruled with so sovereign a hand, nor had riches and might that flowed so freely. Clonesians were proud and those within the capital walked with an open haughtiness when showing an outsider their glorious city of cities.

The cart was lost in the activity that swirled about the city. Streets were overflowing with markets and goods from every conceivable land. The wondrous smells mingled together and the Keepers drooled openly as they passed stands and booths filled with every imaginable delicacy under the sun. Colorful fruits and vegetables were stacked to overflowing, hordes of breads and pastries beckoned the eye, and meats from a myriad of beast, fish, and foul were packed in mountains of ice! From where they found enough ice in so hot a land to fill the numberless stands that lined the streets, Trel had no idea. It seemed anything that could be purchased was sold and bought here with equal flair. Brightly woven fabrics of every design clung to men's and women's bodies as they went in shop after shop to purchase goods. All wore garments of such finery, they would be considered noble in any other country. A great many of the inhabitants had coin to spare. It seemed the city itself oozed everything. Coin was not in shortage either.

The usual mix of people that comprised every city was there: merchants, hawkers, tradesmen, commoners, social elites, and soldiers bumped into each other wherever they went. Even small bands of the Oncan'lar flowed through the mass of citizens. There were others that Jace had never seen before. Wealthy aristocrats and tight-faced diplomats rubbed shoulders with the regular blend of society. It was not so different as Jace was used to, but it was on such a massive scale that to call it grand would have been an insult. He could not imagine there being a place that was larger or filled with more things than were within this giant city.

He and Trel ogled at everything they saw, pointing at mysterious objects and opulent houses that caught their eyes like they were little children. Their behavior was unlike any prisoner the city had seen, but it paid them as much attention as any other cart carrying caged goods. The two of them thought they could get lost in the sights, sounds, and smells of the city for years, if given the opportunity.

The streets were lined with olive trees. This, of course, was one of the Empire's imperial symbols, which adorned their beloved flag and helped remind them of the peace that could exist among all. Somehow slaves were overlooked in this construct. It was ironic as well that the city was so taken with the Kolosia and what went on within its walls.

The olive tree evergreens grew well in the dry climate, despite the excessive heat. Their thick, low trunks branched off into a wide, shady canopy. The short, almond shaped leaves were a silver-brown and among them sprung white, fragrant flowers. Some were adorned with fruit, which weighed the branches down slightly. Little children would climb the trees, gathering the black and green prizes and collect them for the highest bidder. These cherished trees shaded the causeways and were a pleasant feature to the capital.

Only after a long spell were the young men brought back to reality when they noticed Alaric and Lashara lying quietly in the hay. They settled down also, resting their bodies and turning their thoughts to why they were here. For the remainder of their trip, they closed their eyes and focused on what Yeshua would have them do. They opened their hearts to the Counselor's leading, letting them be searched and cleaned according to His convictions. They sat quietly while the deafening sounds of the city filled their ears.

All their belongings had been taken from them long ago, but Jace had kept one thing hidden. Somehow, the priceless copy of the Song of the Ages that Hadran had given him had been overlooked. He now thumbed through its pages, letting the Counselor lead him as he meditated on the words of the Most High. He was not shaken by the approaching outcome, but was highly apprehensive of what would happen. Despite Alaric's feelings of confidence and surety that Yeshua would provide an escape amidst their persecution, Jace's heart had sunk to second-guessing the finality of their situation. He knew that their singing and intercession meant little it they did not hold up under the trial they were about to face. He whispered his cries to Yeshua and listened to what the Counselor had to say through the Song of the Ages, but he was all but sure of their outcome and accepted it with stoic plodding.

They moved through the city, but instead of heading to the Kolosia, they were taken before the castle of King Clonesious. There, in a huge square outside the palace, they were put into stocks for the rest of the day. Some held the feet and hands in awkward positions and others held only the head and arms like the ones in Trailaden. Whatever the case, each one was uncomfortable and required the Keepers to hold themselves upright. After awhile, they became sore from the constant strain on their muscles. The courtyard was mostly empty and those that walked by them didn't give them much notice in the arid capital. They sat looking forward while their faces became drenched with sweat as heat rose from the dark cobblestones.

Each of Jace's party had been given a chain to wear around their necks. At its base hung the familiar symbol of an open book with a sword laid across it. It was polished steel and blazed in the sun for all to see, marking the four of them as members of the Gap. Those that saw them gave a range of responses. Some spit on the ground and cast reproachful stares in their direction. Some yelled in hatred across the square, letting their disapproval be heard by all. The party took the verbal assaults with stiff resolve. They were used to the reactions of the Clonesians by now, and despite how much it bothered them, they kept their mouths shut under the remarks of the people that noticed their origins. It was always saddening to know that the very people who decried their presence could have heard of Yeshua's amazing plan for their lives had things been different. Instead, they turned their thoughts inward while the Clonesians ridiculed them.

They were not the only ones held to the contraptions. The square, which was more of a circle, was ringed with prisoners of every age and nationality, both men and women. Some looked like they had been there for days. Their backs were humped and they hung their heads down sullenly. Others darted their wide eyes back and forth with fright. All who entered the square were free to heckle and tease them as much as they wanted, but they could not touch or throw objects in their direction. This left the square rather clean, spotless in fact.

Guards were dotted throughout the promenade behind the prisoners. Jace had ventured to make a sound, but was cuffed readily on the back of the head with the pommel of a sword. The guard barked an order and they sat there quietly, watching the sun work its way slowly across the sky.

By the end of the day, the square began to fill with people who lounged against the far walls. Others came in and spread short blankets on the stones, letting their families sit down. Jace sensed a growing readiness for something to happen and waited with an inward reluctance at what would occur. As the sun ducked its face behind the buildings and the shadows stretched to cover the square, two trumpets were sounded high in the palace. The prisoners that could craned their necks upward to a balcony that overlooked the square. Some ways up, the royal family came into view and the crowd cheered while the king raised his hands for silence.

"As there is a time for everything," he began while the crowd quieted down, "there is a time for such as this."

Those below him yelled their agreement.

"So, let the whippings begin."

At his command, a crack of the whip sounded at either end of the prisoners. Jace saw one masked guard at each end raking the captives with thrash after thrash. Their bodies shuddered and their heads bobbed in time with the whip. Those in the audience "oohed" and "ahhed" as they watched the punishment. The guards worked their way towards the middle of the lot with methodical precision. The ones nearest the outside of the half-circle must have been used to the whippings and as the guards approached the middle, more cries and screams came from those under their flaying. The crowd began to clap their approval at the sounds of the discipline. When a prisoner let out a painful cry, a number of them would cheer or raise their fists in commendation at the work of the guards.

Many of the crowd rose to stand as the guards came to the middle where the Keepers were. The shorter men and women stood on their tiptoes, trying to catch some visual reaction at what the Keepers would do. Jace tightened his jaw, hearing the whip coil back behind him. Its force nearly took the breath out of him and he staggered under its blow. He fought for air as the soldier readied to strike again. The next blow forced all the air from Jace lungs and he coughed hard. Those in the crowd murmured angrily, waiting for a sharper reaction.

They got it moments later when Lashara cried out down the line. Her shirt was ripped to pieces already and the whip sliced through her skin. The crowd cheered their agreements as her painful screams cut through them. The audience clapped heartily raising their fists in time with the beatings.

The scene was not unlike the Mines of Shorn where Jace had stood before Na'tal. Instead, King Clonesious looked on over an army of angry Clonesians. Jace's body rippled with pain. His back seemed to be on fire. He hung limply after it was over, only hearing faintly the grunts and shouts through clenched teeth Alaric and Trel gave as they fought to control the pain.

When it was done, the crowd and the king dispersed with hardly a word. Public beatings were much more commonplace here than in Trailaden and the population seemed to view the work with mild excitement. The tradition seemed to be a ritual that all went through with mediocre emotions. Most went away with empty souls, having enjoyed the moment, but thirsting for something more to quench their appetites.

The prisoners tendered their wounds into the night. The cool air was a welcome ending to the day and they sat amidst a chorus of moans. Many of them drifted to sleep leaving their agony behind to wake them in the morning.

Long after the sun had set and the square was empty, the sound of hooves broke through the night. A long train of wagons lined the courtyard and one by one the prisoners were tossed into them half awake. Jace let his arms hang out through the cage of the cart while those around him stood. The trip was rough and the prisoners jostled about the wagon. One couldn't help hitting another person's wounds and the people in the midnight procession groaned as the cart rocked along the road bouncing their aching bodies into each other.

They were led to a dark street that opened into a small dead end. Soldiers pulled the prisoners out of the vehicles and stood them in line. They were shackled in the torchlight and led through a pair of heavy iron doors that were sunken into the rock wall at the end of the road. The walls inside were carved stone. Torches lined the hallway and the group walked in without a sound. The passage curled downward into the earth and Jace stumbled along blindly as he fought to keep calm in the narrow surroundings. The clinking of their chains and people's breathing seemed to grow unbearably loud. He closed his eyes, pursed his lips, and let out slow, long breaths hoping to sooth his fears of enclosed spaces.

The carved sandstone hall opened into a series of caves where hundreds of prisoners were chained to the walls in a minimum of clothes. The soldiers took each person and clasped their hands and feet, chaining them like the others, some face forward, some face to the wall. They vanished swiftly as they finished their work and the prisoners were left alone to stare at each other in the dim light. The caverns was a giant cell with only a single door on one end. Its black exterior and tiny, barred metal window was their only representation of freedom that all who could see it focused on.

The prison was Jace's own private horror. He clung to the wall with his chains raised high over his head as he perspired in the dungeon. The space was rather roomy, as jails were concerned, but it felt like a tiny enclosure hidden under uncountable layers of rock. Cold sweat ran down his back and he trembled, paying little attention to anything else that happened around him. Flashes of the dark, endless passages of the Mines of Shorn flooded through his mind. Everywhere he turned, he could feel the steamy heat flowing through the caves. The rock seemed his personal tomb. Even the prisoners seemed to resemble the twisted forms of his captors. He hung his head, fighting hard to calm his labored breathing and forced himself to think of all the pure and good things that his life had been filled with, but to no avail. Instead, he kept himself to a whimper in the cavernous depths under the mountain of Clonesia.

Those around him hung for hours in silence. The dripping of water filled the vast network of caves and they listened as time went by. Someone began to hum somewhere. His humming turned to singing and his voice echoed off the cavern walls. At first, it was an odd, unwanted noise. The sound that came from the old man's lungs was horribly off tune and out of place. *Who could sing at a time like this*, Jace thought. *Why couldn't he be left alone with his thoughts?* As he began to listen to the singer's words, his mind changed and he sat pensively as the man went on. The tune was melancholy and slow, but it spoke of something deep that could not be moved despite the turmoils of life:

There I stand, alone again
My shame laid bare in my sea of sin.
Am I alone in agony?
Is no one to rescue me?
How long do I cry out to thee
to come and heal my misery?
Alas, alas, you hear my call
As I beseech thee, Lord of all.

I have strayed and lost my heart.
I've stumbled and I've played the part
Where I, the fool, was called to rise
And sing a song of compromise.
Did you hear how I was true,
And labored on to honor You?
Alas, alas, you heard my call
As I beseeched the Lord of all.

And if I come to some jagged place,
Will I still be given grace
As I leave this world in haste
And stand at last to see Your face?
I will laugh and sing to thee!
My Lord eternal ever be.
Alas, alas, you heard my call,
As I beseech the Lord of all.

Now when all is said and done,
I will look back and see I've won.
For though my trials cave me in,
I did all to honor Him.
I shall stand in eternal glory
Praising Him with my sweet story.
For I did answer to His call
And claimed Him as my Lord of all.

The song trailed off into momentary silence. Jace could hear the soft sound of sobs mingling with the steady dripping of water. Many of the prisoners hid their faces, their shoulders trembling in sorrow. Even those that didn't know the meaning behind the singer's words were moved to tears, so clear were his emotions and heartfelt plea. In the solitude of their hearts, all came to the conclusion that if they did not have what this man spoke of, they needed to make amends with someone to receive it. There was little hope for anything else.

"That was beautiful," one said.

"Here, here, let him continue his song," said another.

"Alas, that is the end," said the voice of the old man somewhere in the cavern. The sound of his voice echoed clearly off the walls for all to hear. Even so, his voice sounded happy, even relieved.

"It is fine, Bartemus, your words are encouragement enough," said a young lady.

That name stirred something in Alaric and he asked it to be repeated again. "I must ask you if you were alone in some prison before," he said staring at the walls in search of the owner of the voice.

"Yea, I have been in prison most of my life. I fear I am no acquaintance to one who sounds as youthful as you."

"That is likely," Alaric agreed, "Even if you were not, my friends and I are alien to these parts and would never have crossed paths with you. However, we were thrown in prison several days ago. We knew one whose name you bear, though only briefly in passing."

When the man spoke next, his voice wavered on the edge of hope. "Could there be three of you who say such a thing?" Trel and Lashara also gave voice with their agreement.

"It is I friends! The Bartemus whom you led to your Savior!"

The three Keepers were filled with emotion and gave glad tidings to their friend in so bleak a place. "I have remained true to our Lord and have never stopped interceding to Him on your behalf! What a joy it is to join in fellowship once again with those I hold so dear!" he exclaimed, his voice breaking.

The Keepers encouraged him all the more and they spoke candidly in the cavernous expanse. After all their petitions to Yeshua, they were still frightened and uneasy, but hearing Bartemus' voice again calmed them somewhat. The man whose repugnant exterior and condescending words had at first taken them aback now softened their troubled hearts in the gloomy caverns. At length, other voices sprouted from the silence of the cell.

"If you know our brother and friend, surely you know us," echoed two feminine voices from far away.

The voices of Shereel and Clarissa were like silver on crystal. They hearkened to

Jace like memories from of the past. He could never forget the two brave women who risked their lives to help him find his brother in Trailaden. They sounded timid and worn, but fought to keep their courage in the despairing surroundings. Each of them told how, after the party had left, the Commander General had ordered the city scoured and the remaining Keepers hunted down. Every stone was overturned and every house and workshop interrogated in search of any who dared call Yeshua their Lord. They had all been rounded up before the day's end and were flogged and beaten, much like Jace's group, before being moved north to Clonesia. They ended their stories with heavy sighs.

"We could not bring ourselves to turn our backs on Yeshua, after all that He means to us," they cried. "And so, we are here to honor him before the throngs of Clonesia."

Bartemus said the same. "Count it joy, my friends to suffer for our Lord. He did no less for us."

All of their hearts were heavy, but they rejoiced nonetheless. They would all die together as a sign of their love for their Savior. Many of those around them were confused by the strange way the Keepers talked. They had never heard "Yeshua" or "the Gap' spoken of with such reverence. Some of the prisoners mocked them, laughing at their strange behavior and fruitless hope. Then, there were those that listened to their conversation with a strange curiosity, spellbound at how these men and women of far different cultures were so unified. They were alarmed that these people could be so sure and unafraid in the midst of such overwhelming doom. They kept silent, but listened intently.

Jace cringed inwardly at the words of Shereel and Clarissa who helped him what seemed like ages ago. How many lives had he brought to an end by having them assist him on his mission? And for what? There was nothing to show for their efforts—Rae was lost and Jace's party captured. Would they all die in vain? As if it could not get worse, another voice floated through the cave. It was low and humbled, but rich. The voice spoke of a once proud man who had been broken.

"I have lived in the Gap most of my life," at his tone, all grew quiet. His words were a mixture of confession and many years of hard-earned wisdom. "As I grew from a spiritual infant to one who relied on Yeshua, I learned to despise all the workings of Sa'vard."

Many voices barked agreement

"His teachings are lies. Though his power is vast and none can hold a candle to the riches he has amassed, they are ringed with deception. I grew to hate him all the more for the dreadful trick he has played on the hearts of men," the trickling of water was the only other sound, but still he went on, "I vowed to pour my heart and strength into becoming a mighty soldier in the ways of Yeshua. I swore to guard myself in His power and lean on His direction."

Other voices echoed their approval. When the man went on, his voice turned painfully quiet, "Like a fool, I sought to break the back of Sa'vard on my own. I rallied others around me, turned my back on those that failed to follow and drove forth, deep into the heart of Sa'vard's lair. His forces drew back from us and I began to think us victorious, and my actions justified. But like any of Sa'vard's masterpieces, his trick took us by surprise. He waited until we had ventured deeply into his lands until he struck.

"There was no way for us to escape and we were cut off from those we had once spurned, the very ones that could have helped us in our hour of need. I believed our actions lost and that we would all die that day, but Sa'vard had more dreadful plans than I could imagine. He drove us slowly across his lair for many days and nights, never stopping even after we collapsed. Each sunrise was a waking nightmare and the nights were filled with incomparable torment.

"The days turned to months and still we went on. Our hearts began to despair and we cried out for death and even then, Sa'vard laughed and prodded us forward. By the melting of the snow, we entered the Lothian Plain and were handed over to the Clonesians. They brought us here to wait for some wicked scheme, some evil purpose to be fulfilled. Here, I and my crew have waited since, enduring the hardships of the dungeon and the flaying of the guards each day.

"Never before have I wished for death. But, through all the journeys that took me far from home, kin and even from my Master, I have learned the error of my ways. The unity of the Spirit binds us all together. We should never think so highly of ourselves as to disown those who call themselves by Yeshua's name and yet do not see eye to eye with us. We should always put the purpose of our Master before our own designs and accept humbleness for His name instead of glory for ourselves. I count it a privilege to be amongst those I do not know in body, but am one with in the Spirit. Should the time come, I will count it a blessing and honor to make my final stand with you all before resting in Par'lael."

His voice ended and only the faint moving of water was left. None said a word as if some of what was said had been on all their minds in one form or another. They focused their hearts for a time, seeing that they were clean and ready should they meet the Maker even now.

Jace's mind, however, raced with anxiety. The cavernous prison was a tomb that would crush in on him if he gave it a chance. While the other prisoners reflected on the words of the aged man, Jace was thinking of something, anything to take his mind off the suffocating air of the caves. He had followed the man's journey and something clicked in his head. Instead of remaining still, he broke the silence, offering up his question.

"Your name?" was all he could muster to ask without revealing his fright. He hoped it would be enough to stir the man to answer. The response was a single word:

"Arthur."

18

THE FOILED PLAN

A flood of emotions filled him as he wrestled with what he heard. Images from days gone by broke through his fears that strangled his breath. He saw the Gap and the March Wall spread out before him. Hadran and Sturbin stood by his sides as he watched a group of mighty soldiers with shining armor ride into Sa'vard's lair. They were gone from view in a matter of moments and Jace followed the two older men away.

The memory winked out and Jace came to. The man he had seen ride off for dead that fateful day on the March Wall was alive even now! Sturbin's prized pupil had been shown grace from above and lived to pass on knowledge to them all. Jace did not know what to say next, but it was Alaric who spoke instead.

"We also have journeyed long and hard," he said softly. "Our road has taken us from one end of the earth to the other. Many things have happened for which we were not prepared and though we have faced hardship, betrayal and all kinds of deception, we have each remained true to the One. We count it an honor ourselves to join you, Bartemus, Clarissa, Shereel, and Arthur, and if it be the final chapter or only the beginning of another journey, we live together that Yeshua may be proud of our actions."

Arthur placed Alaric's voice as another Keeper that he had known. The two spoke at length while all listened. They traded memories of long ago when times were better. The scenes they painted filled those that listened with peace and love like only the Master could. They spoke of friends gone by, and wives and children they missed. Each had left their family on their errands and it saddened them that they might not see them again. Instead of staying to that possibility, they spoke of their deep love and commitment for their families, wondering what their wives were doing just then and how their children must have changed since they were gone. They reminisced of Hadran and Sturbin, Miss Pell, Master Klim, Eckalus, Tover, Dorath, Grimly, Dolmer and others. All who listened realized that the Gap was a vast interconnected family that was bound together by the love of this Yeshua and His Father, the Creator.

Alaric could not forget of poor old Lumphar at work on his projects. Hopefully, he was near completion of the instruments that would insure the safety of the Gap. If he was successful, there would be little to fear from Sa'vard's probing, he reasoned. The thoughts seemed to ease his doubts even then.

The two finished by talking of Sturbin, their kindly hearted commander. Arthur was ashamed at how he had left his Mentor and friend. He wished he could tell him how sorry he was for all he had done. Alaric encouraged him, saying one day they would meet and somehow erase all the barriers that had built up between them. They talked some more, smiling and laughing of their adventures with loved ones and of their fellowship that could not be broken. Oh to be back among friends, each of them sighed.

Time passed and none could tell whether night or morning was upon them. It truly did not matter here in the lonesome solitude deep beneath the earth. They hung suspended from their chains, each with their own thoughts. When one had something to say, they would blurt it out, letting it bounce off the walls. Sometimes another faceless voice would respond, or the statement would fade into nothingness as what was said echoed away. No contact came through the iron door. Prisoners would take to staring at it, willing it to open or move at any moment. Some would whisper descriptions of their favorite meals and morsels, chanting them in a never-ending singsong in hopes that their dreams would be made a reality. Over time, the drudgery melted away at Jace, and he could hear more than one person let out a crazed cackle in the darkness. Time stood still and for how long they stood there was any man's guess.

When Jace was almost convinced that they were left there to rot, a faint sound came from the other side of the door. Men's voices approached and Jace could hear someone sorting through a set of metal keys. The caverns came alive with voices, and men and women faced the door in a mixture of excitement and morbid expectation. The door grated open and light burst through the opening, shining brightly on the feeble prisoners. People yelled at the guards, some cursing and ordering them to extinguish their flames.

The soldiers laughed at their crude behavior. They wasted no time spreading throughout the caves blatantly shining their torches in people's faces. Those who were brave or stupid enough to voice their anger were slapped.

Jace saw one prisoner kick a guard in the knee. The man dropped his torch and grabbed his leg while the prisoner shot his legs out again. The soldier crawled away. Recovering from his shock, he picked up his torch and turned on the man. He danced around the prisoner while the thin figure kicked the air about the guard. The guard shot his arm forward, thrusting the torch to the man's skin. The prisoner let out a howl and tried to shake the torch off him, but the guard pushed the flames closer and the man blacked out. Jace features grew grim seeing that the prisoner was Trel.

In the confusion, Jace could see some of the guards unchaining prisoners and leading them roughly towards the large opening in front of the door. They held their bonds close behind their backs and the decrepit men and women walked with an air of despondency. Two soldiers pulled Jace's chains from the walls and shoved him forward along with the others. They yelled and hit him as he stumbled to the foyer of the prison. As he was pushed ahead with those around him, he saw the faces of Trel and Clarissa, Arthur and others being led into the torchlight. He was brought to his knees in the struggle and ordered to wait.

The soldiers finally brought the cell to order. While the commotion died down and those that were flogged nursed their wounds, a small procession was led into the caves. Five shining knights came first, fanning out and studying those around them. They had their hands near their swords and they watched the walls and prisoners sharply. When the area was secured, they motioned for the remaining people to enter the cavern.

A lady ducked her head as one of the guards assisted her through the small doorway and then knelt with everyone else in the prison. She wore a rich purple dress. The garment was studded with pearls and silver fabric wove an intricate design about her bosom and waist. The arms flared at the shoulders and trailed down to the hands. The gown itself traced the outline of the woman's body from head to toe. Its fabric, though dark, was fitted tightly against the skin leaving very little to the imagination. Her dark features were set against smooth white skin and accented with the faint touches of rouge. She walked with the air of royalty, observing the prison and all those in it with discretion and disregard like only a member of the upper class could. The knights that circled around her conveyed an air of disdain for the lowly men and women tied to the walls.

A slim man followed behind her. His face was hard to see in the flickering light and he stole from view, keeping behind the noblewoman and her retainers. The guards shoved the line of prisoners forward. Their leader stood off to the side and bowed low, addressing the beautiful woman.

"These are the ones you requested, your highness," he said in a thin scowling tone. "The last ones arrived two days ago. They are a pitiful lot, but I am sure you'll get your worth out of them," he said, kicking the nearest prisoner.

The lady said nothing. She took a small fan and with a single motion, flicked it open and began waving the air over her face and neck.

"I thought we ordered the dungeons made cool before her grace's arrival," said one of the knights. "Where are the chairs and table she ordered? What pitiful accommodations you give to her highness, the princess!" he yelled accusingly at the guards. They flinched away at the anger in his voice. He let the statements hang in the air before going on.

"Let us continue and speed our passage from this miserable place," he said turning to the man behind him. "These are the ones you requested, are they not?"

The man stepped into the torchlight. He was indeed slim, but he carried himself with perfect balance and checked authority. His sharp suede cloak and midnight shirt and hoes ate up the light around him as he looked up and down the line of prisoners. His greasy, pale face nodded approvingly at the Keepers kneeling before him.

"Blynn!" said Jace loathingly through clenched teeth.

The man looked at him shortly and cocked his head at him arrogantly.

"Is that a way to begin a meeting?" he asked grandly.

"Get out of here!" Jace spat at him, but the ratty man ignored him and paced down the line staring at the prisoners.

"They are," he said with feigned indifference, patting his riding gloves against his thigh. "I thought it wise to expound upon my little scheme before sending them on their way. This is the most proper way as we have agreed, don't you think?" he asked looking back at the princess.

She nodded her head and he went on. "Bring the four I mentioned."

Two arms pulled Jace to his feet and he was thrust forward. They planted the prisoners side by side. Jace knew without looking that he stood with Trel, Alaric, and Lashara.

"Haven't we done this before?" said Trel comically in the gloomy surroundings.

"Silence!" Blynn said, backhanding Trel. The young man turned his head away and then stared vehemently at his one time friend.

"I could easily walk away and leave you to die without ever offering an explanation for my actions! I am only here because her majesty commands it, and I can see the opportunities that may arise from it," he said staring at the princess with a surreptitious gleam in his eye.

"Spare us, Blynn, you came only to gloat," said Alaric quietly. Blynn turned to Alaric, but the man held his gaze with a calm defiance. The pasty figure threw his arms wide.

"You have me there, Alaric," he mocked him, "but I'll continue nonetheless."

He composed himself and went on. "I am not a slave trader—"

"No, you're just a traitor!" yelled Jace.

Blynn ignored him, "—and have never been in my life. Instead, I've eked out a small existence running dangerous loads of Keepers into the Clonesian Empire and Stygian Union for a very long time. The work was hard and the pay was abysmal. However, I resigned myself to it for years on end and gained the trust of a good many people, including your friend, Dorath," he said, smiling wickedly at Jace. "The way they heaped praise upon praise for my courageous work made me feel rather important, at first, but that soon rubbed off. It did very little to save my life, if I were to get caught by the proper authorities," he said, glancing at the noblewoman guiltily.

"I grew tired of the work," he said matter-of-factly. "It gave me no pleasure and certainly did not save my skin. After awhile the praises soon began to sound the same and I needed more than just a kindly word for my actions. After all, I deserved something greater—I was running life-threatening missions everyday of my life and for what? For a simple 'thank you' only to be turned back out to do the same work again? No, I needed something more.

"The Clonesians had suspicions of my actions, and though they never did find me out, they kept a close watch on my movements. When I was filled to the brim with occupational misery and a lack of direction, only then did they talk to me. I was approached with a certain offer that grew more tantalizing the more I pondered it.'

Blynn did his usual prancing while he walked. He strutted up in front of the Keepers with an attitude of control and easiness that was out of place in the dungeon. Since the tables had turned and there was no need for disguising his malice, he walked among them with ease. All the cards were in his favor.

The more Jace watched him, the greater his contempt for his actions grew. All the wretched things Blynn had done and the horrible things he had put them through and accused them of made his blood boil. For him to stand before them like this and speak to them in such condescending tones, as if he was explaining some simple game instead of how and why their lives should end was incredulous. He watched the man he had trusted and followed, the one who had led them through Nadir with a Watcher on their heals, found shelter for them in the snowy landscape of the Stygian Union, and negotiated a safe passage to the Clonesian Empire only to give them up for dead at the hands of those who had turned their backs on Yeshua. He could care less why the man had done these things and more than once wrestled the two guards that held him tight, hoping to throw himself at the man who claimed to follow his Lord. Even so, Jace found himself listening to the man through the rising river of hatred that flowed through his mind.

"It came to me as we were crossing the Stygian Union," he was saying. "One night, I happened to spy Lashara while she was alone in her room. To be sure, I wasn't certain if what I saw was true, or if my mind was playing tricks in the faint glow of the candle light, but as she turned her back to the door and took off her shirt, I saw about her left shoulder the undeniable mark of a slave."

The way he said the words was cruel and he spat on the ground in dissatisfaction, "I thought to myself, 'how can this be true?' How could a slave have gotten away and lived forever within the Gap? Why then, would she happen to be riding back under my care to a place so filled with malice for those like her who had run away? Try as I may, I could find no reason, and then it occurred to me: I didn't have to. The fact that one so young had been entrusted to me, one with such a deep, dark secret, was a welcome chance for me to become free of my bonds. I began to devise a plan that would release me from any former obligation and send me to freedom at last."

He turned and stared directly at the four of them. He opened his arms to them as if they were his belongings, "Some view runaway slaves as worse than Keepers and here I had both in my hands! Were it not for such a blind stroke of fate, I would have gone on my way, but it must have been for some reason that these prize possessions had fallen into my lap."

"You turned your back on us, Blynn!" yelled Jace. "It was not a coincidence, we were supposed to trust you! Worse than that, you turned your back on Yeshua! You could have helped us, but now we're condemned! I will never forget what you did to us, or my brother!"

"Slow down, slow down," he purred, laughing gently at Jace's growing fury. "Your brother had turned his back on his Lord way before you or I entered the picture—or did you really think you could have diverted him back to his former responsibilities? I knew him for a good four years and saw how the Clonesian Empire slowly whittled away at his beliefs and trust in Yeshua. And what of this coincidence, do you really believe that too? Really, Jace, there is more at work than just the Creator. Sa'vard also devises his plan with a passion and vengeance that can be seen all too clearly at work in the Clonesian Empire. He has been preparing this day for some time, I was merely the vessel he used to bring it to full circle."

"You fool!" cried Jace, lunging at Blynn.

He stepped back, shaking his head and laughing, "Really, Jace, after all you've been through, you should learn to harness that temper of yours," he said disapprovingly, "It's led you and your party down many a wayward road all too quickly, I must say, and played particularly well to Sa'vard's advantage."

"Why?" said Jace, "Why have you done these things?"

The look Blynn gave him was as if he had been struck. "Look around you, lad!" he said disbelieving, "Look where you are!"

Jace turned slightly to eye the walls of the caves.

"Look at me!" yelled Blynn. "Is there any reason I would trade my place for yours? Never! Sa'vard has offered me riches untold, all I had to do was take his hand. Why live poor and afraid when I can live like this," he said flourishing his cloak to show his luxurious clothes.

"We leave this earth to be in the presence of the Most High, but all you have to look forward to is an impending destiny with Sa'vard," said Alaric without turning away his calm gaze.

"Poor, misguided Alaric," Blynn said, "Always ready to be the fool for his Savior. Do you really think the loving Creator would turn me away? I asked Him to come into my life long ago. He is like a doting father who would do anything to keep the union between those He loves. He wouldn't turn me away. But, if His promises are true, then where are my blessings? Where is my life of happiness and peace? What does it matter if I choose differently after that, anyway? He accepts even the prodigals. And if He does not accept me, what then? I've switched allegiances to Sa'vard, even now. He has offered me my riches and has already blessed me more than my former master. I only look forward with delight to what good things he holds for me in the future."

"You've lost, Blynn," Alaric said. "No good can come from an agreement with the Father of Lies."

Blynn curled his lips in thinly veiled hatred at the four. "Think you so? Then let us put Sa'vard's promises to the test, shall we not?" he said, motioning for the guards to bring them forward. He raised his voice, so all could hear him. "The first promise Sa'vard gave to me was that these Keepers would bow at my feet! Let us see if he holds true to his words." A murmur broke out in the caves as the prisoners questioned the test. Keepers would never bow to any, but Yeshua and the Creator.

Blynn gave the signal and the guards forced the Keepers to their knees. The crowds shouted raucously, saying that Yeshua was dead, but some saw the false actions for what they truly were. Blynn nodded and the guards bent the prisoners to the ground. Their faces were rubbed into the sandstone as they struggled without success to rise.

"This is no victory, Blynn. You can move our bodies however you want, but our hearts will not be changed!"

Blynn strode over to Jace as he finished his words. The young Keeper's endless prodding of the truth sickened Blynn and he lashed out at him. He brought the heel of his foot crashing down on Jace's cheek. Jace heard the bone crack and when he opened his eyes, he was blinded momentarily. Blynn commanded them to be brought to their knees and he looked them up and down.

"So, you cannot be broken, but you can be goaded," he retorted to the Keepers. "Bring the lady here!"

One of the guards brought Lashara close to Blynn and he stroked her hair gently. Lashara's eyes were wide. She had said next to nothing since her last encounter with Blynn and now eyed him openly with fear. Her eyes darted over the man and she shuddered when his hand touched her face.

Jace watched lividly as Blynn had his way with her before his eyes. He fought to pull free of the guards, "Don't touch her!" he said, his words dripping with venom. Blynn smiled at him provokingly.

"It appears I've struck a chord, Elidal," he said to the princess. He ran his fingers through Lashara's hair, breathing in her scent deeply. "The dreadful thing about being a slave is that they have no rights," Blynn explained dreamily, brushing her hair. "I can imagine all the horrible things one could do to you without ever being chastised," he whispered to Lashara.

As he spoke, his pale hands moved slowly down her hair to her exposed neck and back. He ran his fingers over her skin and eyed her covetously. Lashara closed her eyes and whimpered under the man's iron grip. All the emotions of slavery that she had hid from others and herself behind her hard exterior slowly oozed into the forefront of her mind. Tears ran down her face as Blynn's selfish hands ran over her body. He turned her to face him.

"The more I looked at you, the more I saw a diamond in the rough. Even for a slave, you have traits that would make you pleasing to any man. Be mine and I alone will keep you from Sa'vard and the fate that must befall all Keepers in the Clonesian Empire!" he finished by embracing her hard and forcing a kiss upon her lips.

She struggled weakly, letting out short screams. Somehow she got one hand free and clawed Blynn across the face. He let out a roar and clutched the wound. Blood trickled down his face and he towered over her. With one swoop, he backhanded her and she toppled to the floor. Blynn strode up to her to finish the job.

Jace pulled fiercely at his captors. "No! Don't touch her! I'll kill you! I'll kill you, Blynn!" he screamed.

"Jace, no!" roared Alaric.

Lashara's limp body lay before him. Blynn stopped over her, lifting his head and finally grasping Jace's words. A look of sudden recognition spread over his face and then turned to euphoric delight.

"So, you will," he said breathlessly. He tossed his head back with laughter. "I believe you will, or at least die trying!"

The nimble man eyed Jace and his friends contemptuously. He kicked Lashara hard in the ribs and laughed again. Then, with a grand flourish of his cape, he turned and left. "Remember your words, Jace," he cried after him, his voice filled with laughter and prodding, "Remember your words!"

The knights led the Princess Elidal out and the guards tied the Keepers back against the walls. The prisoners yelled at the guards, banging their chains as they went about their work. The three Keepers did not put up much fight, nor did the other Keepers who had been brought forward before the queen. Jace watched as two guards pulled Lashara's loose body up from the floor and strung her to the wall. Her head dangled, but she was breathing.

He turned and watched Blynn as he left the dungeon. The man would pay for his treachery one day. All that he had done would not go unpunished, even if Jace was the one who had to destroy him, it would be done. His heart sank to a depth of bitterness and anger that he had never known.

He did not notice the guards leave, nor his friends shout their motivations for him to stay true. He had already sunk beyond their help. From that meeting onward, Jace set his mind to how he would dismantle the one called Blynn. He pushed all words from the Song of the Ages out of his mind and ignored all cries of reason from the other Keepers. Each morning and late into the night, Jace thought nothing except how he would destroy him. With each slash of the whip, each beating from the guards, each peaceful phrase of Yeshua's that bounced off the cavern walls, every hateful comment from those that didn't know the Creator—everything became fuel that he used to burn his eternal hatred for Blynn.

Somehow this man was to blame for the failure of not apprehending Rae. If not in full than in part. What mattered was that Rae would fall further out of harmony with Yeshua now that he had made his choice.

The harsh parting of ways between them and Blynn in Trailaden was one thing. If it had been merely that, Jace would have been fine and he was, until their next meeting. Blynn's half-lies had cost him precious moments with his brother. He could have had a second chance to talk to him, had the mob died down and left him beaten in some alley, but the city soldiers had swooped him up at Blynn's accusations and taken him off to the heart of the Belazian Keep. There, he had been put under punishments and torture that rivaled that of the Mines of Shorn! He had awoken early the next day surprised to be alive. Finding out that Blynn had indeed played them all along and was in collusion with Sa'vard made him sick. He had been so trusting and open, lending himself wholeheartedly to any who hailed from the Gap. The treachery that Blynn had laid on them was unforgivable in Jace's eyes and he swore he would reconcile the man's mistakes with his life.

A GOOD TWO WEEKS PASSED before anything broke the daily routine of jailing and beating. In that time, the dungeon was stacked to overflowing as prisoner after prisoner filled the place. The endless caverns felt like a sauna with the bodies stacked tightly together. Extra hooks had been drilled in the ceiling and prisoners were strung by their chains in rows that stretched zig-zagged all through the caves.

These were not any ordinary prisoners. In the dim light and unbreathable stuffiness, one after the other would shout out their proclamation that Yeshua was their Lord. It surprised Trel that so many Keepers had infiltrated the Clonesian Empire. The Mentors had impressed upon him that the place was impregnable and absolutely impossible for a Keeper to remain there for any amount of time. Either they did not know what they were talking about, or they had lied to him in hopes of keeping some vast secret from common knowledge, Trel thought as he looked over the mass of prisoners. Either way, what was true was not what he had been taught.

The Keepers were of every possible occupation and class that Trel could think of. Some were tailors and smiths, some were merchants, some were dressed in rags that had once been extravagant garments of the social elite. It amazed Trel that the Clonesian Empire—that staunch monolith of a nation—was so filled with Keepers! Of course, after whatever happened that the Empire had planned for them, there would probably be few left, if any that existed in the land at all.

Some hours after their whippings and the sun had gone down, they were rounded up. The jail door opened and like any other time, the dungeon broke into madness. The prisoners were pulled out of the caves in great strands of chains that jingled as they made their way around the curling passages to the surface of the city. They were piled into giant wood-covered wagons with thin slits for breathing-holes out of the roof. The carts were packed so tight that one had no choice but to stand. The big wagons heaved and lurched forward as their teams of 16 horses gradually picked up speed.

The train of prisoners rode for what seemed like hours, twisting and turning through the city at a steady pace. When they finally stopped, the cart broke into disorder. People were sick of the tight space and struggled to move. Their shouts grew louder and then turned to cries. All along the walls of the cart, tiny spear holes had been placed. To quiet down the prisoners, the guards stabbed them at random until they were silent. The back of the wagon was then opened and they filed out into a courtyard.

Jace could not tell how many carts of prisoners there were. Some wagons were leaving as he stepped out, while others reined in to take their place. The mass of captives was led through a double-barred gate of iron that swung open silently in the moonlight. They walked through another courtyard and then down into a low passage that led to a series of large cells. Here, the prisoners were unchained and thrown into the pens to wait again.

Trel looked about the jail. A wide pathway separated the rows of holding cells. Greasy smoke trailed off torches that lined the hall. The floor was a carpet of straw spread over hard-packed dirt. The high ceiling was a single slab of brown granite that was filled with some kind of mortar to seal it to the walls.

As the last of the pens was filled, the place began to quiet down and most of the prisoners fell back to sleep or talked in low voices. The air was cooler here and the pens were open, allowing one to spread out or walk as they pleased. This was a luxury Trel had missed and he sauntered through the crowd, stepping over and around those who preferred to sit. He ran his fingers along the iron bars while he rubbed his wounds, letting his eyes wander over everyone in his cell.

As he picked his way through the crowd, it occurred to him that all those around him were Keepers. Their soft-spoken encouragement and sympathy betrayed their origins from the Gap. No Clonesian, no matter how altruistic, could suffer such actions. In truth, the Clonesian dungeons had been emptied of all Keepers. Those that stood before Trel were the entire population of Keepers that existed in all of the Clonesian Empire.

At last, he saw Alaric. The burly man came up to him rubbing his wrists. "It feels good to be free of the cuffs, if not the dungeon. Although this will do, I suppose," he said with a smile, looking about the jail and nodding his head as if to say he had a choice in the matter.

The light-hearted joking was not something Trel was used to from the big man, especially under such desperate conditions. He reasoned that the change of scenery had altered Alaric's spirits as well. A quick look around said he was not the only one. Those that were still awake talked with low voices, smiling and talking with each other in friendly ways. The air about the place was filled with relief.

"Come, I've found the others," he said, leading Trel back against the far wall.

Lashara sat with her head between her knees. She did not look up as Trel approached but rocked back and forth with her hands folded over her head. Her shirt—what was left of it—hung loosely around her neck with a makeshift knot. She was left with the decency of a covered bosom, but her back and the whip marks were exposed for all to see along with the ugly brand of three circles that marked her as a slave. Trel looked at her with pity.

Jace stood off further down the wall. His back was turned to them and he plucked at the stone angrily. He said nothing and gave no sign of acknowledgement to Trel.

"I'm surprised he even followed me over here," said Alaric, pointing at Jace. "He hasn't said a word since our meeting with, well, you know and just sits there brooding. At least we're all together."

Trel nodded slowly. After all they had been through, they were still together. Another man sat close by. He was rather tall with a frame almost as thick as Alaric's. His skin was tan and his jaw was set. He looked at Trel unblinkingly. His eyes were ringed with fatigue.

"May I present to you, Arthur," Alaric said to Trel. The man rose to his feet grasping Trel's arm and nearly pulling it off with his big hands. "There are few men that I would trust with my life, but this is one."

The dark man nodded slightly and turned to Trel. "There are trying times ahead," his voice boomed. It was not as deep as Alaric's, but rich and full nonetheless. He exchanged pleasantries with Trel and then talked with Alaric. "I have found most of my party in this cell, but some are across the passage. We should talk at length about what will happen when the time comes."

The cloaked phrases left Trel confused, but then his eyes widened. "Are we—" he began loudly, then lowered his voice to a dead whisper, "—are we in the Kolosia?"

Alaric surveyed the ceiling, as if the answer were hidden in the rock. "From what I can tell, Trel," he said simply. "There are very few buildings made from rock in the Clonesian Empire and this has the look of the tan structure we saw coming into the city."

Trel started and Alaric shushed him. "There's no need to be alarmed. We've no idea why we're here or what will happen over the next several hours."

"Several hours?"

"They never wheel the captives in until the day of their action," he explained. "Don't fall apart, Trel. There's no reason to."

Trel stared at the two strong men. His breath had suddenly gone shallow and he started to panic. "Before the sun sets, we'll be dead!"

"Shush, Trel!" said Alaric. His features grew serious and he stepped up to the young man. "Prepare yourself for whatever may happen. Some things may take shape that we've never expected and I don't want your faith to be shaken." He turned to Arthur. "Whatever happens, I want you and Lashara to stay close by this man, Trel. Do you understand me? Stop looking at everything, but me!"

Trel started to voice his growing fears, but Alaric cut him short. "I can't take care of all of you, Trel. You'll have to trust me. Stay close to Arthur and his men, they'll know what to do."

"Where will you be?" Trel asked on the verge of hysteria.

Alaric spoke, his voice hard as nails, "Some things need to be taken care of very delicately," he said, his eyes boring into Jace's back.

The sunlight was nowhere to be found, but certain sounds filtered down through the stone to the holding pens. People pricked their ears as the volumes rose. It must have been early morning and the first far-off noises were those of the merchants. The Kolosia was in the center of the city, the market district to be exact, and the noises grew to a low rumble. Trel could picture the scenes of the early morning mayhem as the streets slowly became congested and then overflowed with the daily traffic. He could almost hear the sounds of commoners bartering with merchants and hawkers shouting out their goods as carts and soldiers tried to push their ways through the solid wall of people. It almost sounded fun or carefree, and made Trel wonder if any of them cared about what would happen to all the Keepers that were locked beneath the city with him.

The commotion grew louder through the day and by noon the prisoners had grown restless. News of the Kolosia had spread among them, and those that knew the routine of the guards had dropped hints that something would happen to all of them today. Over the hour, soldiers poured into the large passageway that separated the cells. They were dressed in ceremonial garb. Brightly ornamented vests with the royal coat of arms decorated their chests. Their polished steel helms and breastplates cast a fearsome presence over the caged captives. Bands of thick leather gauntlets were woven around each forearm and they had matching greaves that covered their shins.

As they assembled, several jailers in sackcloth ran to open the pens and the prisoners began to stir. Loud drums were beating out a menacing rhythm in the distance and the soldiers sat in an eerie silence. The ringing of the keys and rusted creaking of the iron cage doors were the only sounds that punctuated the hallway. As the jailers forced all the prisoners out into the open at once, mass hysteria set in. The crowds drove forward out into the hallway, pushing and buckling as they forced their way through the small opening. Some of them turned to run away from the guards, but as they looked down the long hallway, they panicked. Another group of guards equal in size and strength stood at the ready. The two groups sandwiched the unarmed prisoners between them.

A wave of hopelessness and dread seemed to wash over the crowd. Older women fell to their knees clutching their rags in a torrent of tears. Grown men stood together, their faces gaunt with the knowledge that they were about to be led on a death march. The mass of captives let out a wretched cry of anguish as the guards stood, their shields locked in formation and their swords drawn by their sides. Slowly, the phalanx of soldiers nearest Trel began to drive the crowd forward. At first, they stood still in shock, and then the crowd rippled forward, like a herd of frightened cattle. The guards down the hall moved to flank the captives as they led them up the wide set of stairs at the far end of the passage. The group marched in time with the soldiers, the more able-bodied carrying the men and women who refused to move from their mountain of tears. The large mass swarmed inside their barrier like a herd of caged beasts being taken to the slaughter.

They entered out into the sunlight and as the searing orb burned down on them, a loud cheer broke out from the throng that awaited their emergence from the holding pits. A shower of streamers and shimmering bits of paper were tossed in the air from the rooftops of the houses that lined the pathway to the Kolosia. The entire city was packed tight with a multitude of visitors that had come to see the entertainment that the Keepers would provide. They jammed the streets and only the mounted cavalry kept them from consuming the prisoners in their excitement. The main thoroughfare they took was lined with brightly colored pennants and banners. The crowds cheered and hooted, pressing in around the Keepers and following them as they marched through the city.

The parade plodded on and it took them more than an hour to reach the Kolosia. Their holding cell was actually a low-lying building that could not be seen around the surrounding houses. It stood several blocks away from the Kolosia and served as a staging ground for the prisoners that would be transported there.

Trel did not notice it until its giant shadow blocked the sun. The throngs had nearly crushed the Keepers, and he had to fight them back with the soldiers a number of times. As the sky darkened, he looked up to see the colossal structure over him. Jace had only time to count six levels, but there were at least twice that many. He could see hundreds of people looking out of the myriad of windows and arches that ran up the outer face. The top was lined with flags and people hung over the edge waving and shouting happily to the Keepers below. The Kolosia looked as if it would topple over, it was so high, and he reeled back in terror. The guards and mob continued to push him forward so he had no choice but to continue on.

He was brought to a square lined with heavily armed soldiers and dragoons. They held the masses back as the Keepers stumbled in weary and worn from their forced walk. More than just the women were crying now. Trel heard loud horrible cries and pleas to Yeshua and the Creator as the guards prodded the stragglers through the gates and led them within the confines of the Kolosia. He kept close to Arthur as they made their way past stables and warehouses. This was the slave entrance to the Kolosia, but he could clearly hear a growing rumble as they journeyed through the inner spaces.

They were taken to a shop filled with every conceivable piece of armament Trel could think of. Whereas the Gap equipped its basic soldier with mostly swords, staffs, and the common bow and arrow, this place was filled with hundreds of weapons, some he had never before seen. There was the long slender pole with a fine metal point called a pike. He believed there was a lance standing next to it. He also saw large hammers with strange curved blades at the end and long rods with combination heads on them for piercing or cleaving. There were dreadful objects—a short rod with a spiked ball at the end, heavy handled hammers with spikes, and a handle that was attached to a spiked ball by a short chain. There were helmets and armor of every size and shape. He recognized some older pieces from the Clonesian gentry and others from the Nadirian tower guards. The objects were displayed on long wooden tables and watched sternly by dirty men with scowling eyes.

"Take anything you desire. Better for you to die in glory than go weeping to the grave," they challenged. More than one Keeper before the table was arming himself. Trel noticed how their eyes seemed to glow with hope as they handled weapon after weapon. Somehow, material protection always calmed an individual. Trel refused the offer, and followed Arthur and Lašhara. She had taken to crying again and hung her head low in shame. Trel patted her with compassion, but she flinched away.

They came upon Jace and Alaric as the hundreds of Keepers milled about the area. The men and women had calmed in the weapons shop, seeing one last hope for their life and honor. He could see, however, that Jace and Alaric had been having a heated discussion. Alaric propped himself against the table. His arms were folded and he fumed openly while Jace picked up one sword after another. He studied each, weighing the balance, tang, and strength of the blades. A look of disgust was on Alaric's face as Jace stroked the weapons, ignoring the big man.

"He won't listen," said Alaric looking at Arthur. "I've spoken to him ten times already. His mind is made up."

"This is fruitless, Jace. Why do you persist?" Arthur asked. His face was etched with worry and pain. Jace went on, moving down the line, sorting through the blades. "This is not how Yeshua would have us end our lives with futile blows of violence before we stand on the shores of Par'lael. Do you want your last act to be one that grieves your Master? It does no good, lad. Trust me, I know," he said resting his big hands on Jace's shoulder.

"Stow it," Jace said sharply, brushing the hand off him and picking up another sword with his right hand.

"Jace what are you doing? You can't even use a sword," Trel said.

"My father was a fine swordsman," he barked. "He taught me a thing or two before I went to East Haven."

"Look at the good it did him," Arthur remarked.

Jace whipped the sword around, bringing it within inches of Arthur's neck. He looked coldly into his eyes. "Don't dishonor my father," he said in a dangerously low voice.

"You don't want to do this Jace," Arthur said, lightly removing the blade from his shoulder. Trel got the feeling he was talking about more than the momentary threat.

"It's my choice," he said flatly. He examined the sword he held in his hand. After a dozen well aimed swipes he nodded to the man behind the table.

"An excellent choice," the filthy man said, cracking a smile of brown, rotted teeth.

Jace turned on his heel and made his way to the exit of the building. The three men followed close behind him with Lashara in tow.

"What are you doing?" Trel asked openly.

"I have a job to finish," Jace said.

Trel's eyes widened in realization. "Have you lost it? Blynn is quick with a blade. Even I would have lost that fight in the woods. He'll kill you, Jace, or don't you remember?"

"Then I'll die trying!" Jace roared, turning on his friends, his emotions raw. "Or didn't you hear?"

The outfitter gave the last Keeper her weapon and she disappeared through the crowd. There were a fair number of men and women armed, and Alaric and Arthur looked at them sadly.

"It was not supposed to be like this," they said. "We were never supposed to lift a hand against our fellow man. Sa'vard is truly at work in this place."

As if to emphasize his point, Alaric pointed at the opening of the armory. There, tucked closely against the threshold on either side were two cloaked Watchers, their faceless forms watched the nervous Keepers. Somewhere in the back of his mind, Trel heard a steady laughter. The crowd was gathered up and prodded into the low-hanging passage.

The guards brought them to a barred gate. Jailers stood on either side tying the Keepers together by two's. Arthur was bonded to one of his party, and Trel and Lashara were tied together. As Yeshua would have it, Alaric happened to draw close when Jace went through the gates. The two passed through it and were tied to each other by a long heavy rope. Jace straightened his back as Alaric gave him a long pleading glance. Neither said a word to each other as they walked away.

The guards stopped them all while the rest were tied. They stood before a large wooden gate with heavy metal hinges and bronze handles. From beyond it came the pulsing sound of voices in a steady rhythm. Trel looked back and surveyed the lot of them. They were a rag-tag group of men and women now, emaciated and worn to the bone. They must have been over 800 strong, but he got the feeling that no matter how many there were, they were doomed. Their faces were taut and they looked ready to flee. Though many were armed, they still cast long looks of fear and sadness. All of them knew they would not leave this place.

There was a loud grating of metal on metal, and the doors began to swing outward. Blinding sunlight splashed their faces, and they shielded their arms over their eyes as the soldiers behind them pushed them forward. As Trel's eyes began to adjust, he looked around in awe. The Kolosia floor was a flat, sandy surface. Poles circled the arena and armored soldiers on golden gilded chariots weaved between them, waving their spears. The horses had plumes on their heads and ran with a proud step as their driver guided them, holding the reins tightly. Painted targets hung from the poles, and as the chariots swung around them, the spearman would stick them to the cheers of the crowd.

An honor guard was dismissing from the middle of the ring. Their armor sparkled in the sun. They carried heavy drums and a rainbow of flags and marched to a steady cadence. They let out an ominous beat as they exited from the arena floor. Flagbearers lined the circle. Trel saw the coat of arms of the Commander General and a myriad of others that represented all the provinces of the vast country.

The flag of the Empire was draped from a second floor balcony and when Trel squinted his eyes in that direction, he could see the royal family taking their seats. King Clonesious was seating his wife and Princess Elidal sat behind them. To the right of her was seated none other than Blynn himself. Trel turned away, his stomach filling with nausea. The lengths Blynn had gone to entrap them and the revelation of his intense selfish motives sickened him.

The sound in the arena was deafening. The Kolosia was built like a funnel and all the noise filtered down to the middle. The Keepers stood in the epicenter and the force of the crowd hit them like a gale. All around them, the Kolosia was packed with the masses of Clonesians who roared at the sight of the hated prisoners. Their rolling cheers and the sound of the drums stormed the ears of the Keepers.

There was another noise that Trel could hear. It weaved through the wild yelling of the throng like a silvery needle and though it was barely noticeable, it was unmistakably clear. It was the death-chant of the Watchers that Trel saw dotted throughout the vast Kolosia. He was not the only one who saw them. As they looked around, other Keepers tugged at the shoulders of those by their side pointing out the deadly apparitions in horror.

A door slid open along the Kolosia wall, and black horsemen galloped out to meet the crowd of prisoners. The crowd cheered and the Watchers screamed as the masked horsemen prodded the captors into the very center of the ring, circling them with their spears lowered threateningly. Suddenly they stopped and wheeled their steeds. They faced the banner of King Clonesious, pointing their spears in his direction. The crowd's voices dwindled to a low murmur as the king rose to address his people.

"Our country has bled as century after century has passed!" His bold voice echoed clearly throughout the place. The crowd listened, their hearts pulsing and their emotions on edge. "A vile parasite has lived within our borders, secretly stealing away our children and friends in the darkness of the night. Year after year we have lived without action against these despicable people! We have turned the other cheek as they have taken from us what is rightfully ours and corrupted the future of the Empire. It is time, my brothers and sisters, to rid ourselves of this festering wound once and for all! Today we destroy forever the sickness that has for so long hampered our progress. Today, we wipe away the memory that for so long has haunted our dreams. Today we shall seal the destiny of the Keepers!"

The place let loose with a mighty roar, and the king held his scepter out to the guards that had lined the Kolosia floor as he spoke. As they stepped to the side, masked henchmen ran out to the center of ring. The black horsemen lowered their spears at those Keepers who made ready to meet the henchmen with their swords. They were held in check as they waited for the masked figures to approach their group.

Arthur tapped Trel on the shoulder and tilted his head to the side. The young man motioned to Lashara, and they trailed close behind Arthur as he pushed his way to the middle of the Keepers.

"Stay close!" he said quietly.

The Keepers began to grow agitated as the henchmen came near; they backed away only to be met by the spears of the horsemen. Panic filled them and they swirled in a roiling circle as the henchmen reached in, pulling out one and then another. The Keepers screamed, much to the delight of the crowd who returned their fearful cries with chants of mockery and applause.

The ten who had been taken were tied to the poles around the ring. Other masked jailers came out to pile large amounts of wood around their feet to the roar of the onlookers. The stadium became filled with an air of expectation as all knew what was about to happen. Men and women fell to their knees letting out great sobs of anguish as they watched ones they knew be bound to the stakes. They looked on helplessly as the jailers went about their work and the silent horsemen corralled them in place.

It must have been Bartemus who started it. His rough, off-pitch voice had become quite recognizable in the short time Trel had known him. While many wept and cried at the sight of their friends, Bartemus' lone voice cut through the crowd. He sang a bright tune to the Maker that carried above the sadness. One by one, others joined him as they watched their comrades. The tears turned to joy in the midst of the incredible adversity they faced, and the stunned crowd listened at the strange melody coming from the Kolosia floor.

Hearing the song, the Keepers tied to the stake lifted their heads. Their looks of distress melted away as they too picked up the cheerful hymn. They sang as the jailers went about their work. They continued even as the logs around them were lit with fire. They did not stop as the flames grew higher around them, licking threateningly at their bare skin. Those trapped by the horsemen sang even as tears streamed down their faces and they watched.

The crowd was stupefied at what they saw. Rarely had the voices of the Keepers reached so high. None could remember when they had withstood their torture with such courageous faces. For a brief moment, it seemed their eyes had been made to see, and they watched the macabre action on the Kolosia floor with hurt and pity. A large part of the crowds began to show their discontent with what they saw. Booing and pleading filled the arena.

The Watcher's chants swelled in the Keepers' ears and they watched as others shouted their hatred angrily at them. The masses in the Kolosia seemed to ponder amongst themselves how they should view the scenery. The grumbling for mercy was equally matched with roars for the action to continue.

All it took was the single cry. A young Keeper, no more than half Trel's age let out a scream of pain and fear as the flames closed in around her. That was all it took for the pleas to be drowned out by ferocious shouts of vengeance. The scream was followed by the hungry bellowing of the crowd as the Watchers filled their prey with their song. They hurled insults and slanderous words at the Keepers as the flames licked higher. They watched with twisted pleasure as the flames consumed the bodies of the ten Keepers. The other prisoners still sang, but it was lost under the mountain of cheers.

The horsemen lifted their spears and turned their steeds. They kicked them hard and galloped around the Keepers as the masses chanted excitedly. Suddenly, they wheeled their horses to the edges of the ring and the crowd roared their approval, holding their breath at what would happen next.

Not all of the Keepers sang. Those on the edge of the timid crowd gripped their swords with anger. As the horsemen pulled away, they raised them up, prepared to meet whatever came their way with defiance. As the horsemen pulled in behind the line of soldiers, those that were armed charged out from the middle of the ring. Their shouts of contempt lifted above the noise of the crowd as they ran to meet the swordsmen. Some Keepers held back, holding their swords with wild eyes, not knowing if they should charge or stay.

The line of Keepers was halfway to the wall. King Clonesious raised his scepter again and the soldiers turned their bodies. Clonesian masked archers sifted out from behind their ranks and stood with their bows drawn at the ready. The charging Keepers checked themselves for a moment, seeing their mistake and then let out a cry as they flew to meet the bowmen.

The king let his scepter drop and the archers took aim. Their arrows couldn't help but hit their targets that were no more than ten paces away. The line of Keepers seemed to waiver and crumble under their fire and the audience went crazy with delight. Without stopping, they began shooting their arrows into the mass of Keepers. Their numbers shrank rapidly as the arrows buzzed into the crowd.

Jace stood as those around him faltered and dropped. He dodged as the darts sailed by his head only to sink into those behind him. One glanced off his arm to land harmlessly in the crowd. A man in front of him spun around, his eyes wide. He clutched Jace's arms, a look of wonder and pain upon his face. A shaft was buried deep in his belly and he sunk slowly to the ground. The tight ball of Keepers seemed to peel back like layers of an onion as row after row of them fell dead under the hail of arrows.

Jace turned to face the archers. His dark mood was menacing and he walked forward to meet the bowmen. The rope on his left arm tightened and he looked back at Alaric.

"Don't do it, Jace!" he yelled above the chaos.

Jace turned back toward the archers and pulled hard on the rope. Alaric stumbled out after him and they stood on the edge of the circle. The archers had stopped their deathly volley and Jace lifted his sword for all to see. The crowd was in a frenzy now, raising their hands and jumping in time to the beating of unseen drums. They chanted their hatred. When they saw Jace, they focused their threats, yelling curses and swears down on him. He stood with Alaric at his side, the two of them several paces away from the group. He looked around for the thin, pasty figure that was lost in the crowd. While the crowd mocked his small form he shouted into them at the top of his lungs.

"Blynn! Come out and face me! Meet me like a man, you coward!" he yelled waving his sword above his head. The crowd began to roar at him and still he stood, walking about the circle, waiting for his challenge to be met.

A solitary figure jumped down by the banner of the Empire. He rose to his feet, wiping his clothes, and pulling back his cloak. The shadows seemed to hover around his black form as the sun hid behind the clouds. He pranced out to Jace and the crowd cheered wildly. The two stood to meet each other. Blynn gave Jace a mocking bow and Jace returned it with a rude flick of his sword. A thin smile shown on Blynn's face and he eyed the Keeper disdainfully.

"So here we are, at last," he said above the noise. "Tell me Jace, do you really think you have a chance?"

"Let's find out," he said menacingly.

Alaric drew close to Jace. "You can still turn away, Jace. There's no need to do this. It proves nothing and only feeds into the glory of Sa'vard."

Blynn scoffed.

"He's right, you know. There's always more room in the Creator's kingdom for another coward. He wouldn't even suffer two to come," said Blynn eyeing Alaric also.

Jace tugged at his bond, but Alaric held him tight.

"If I have to, I'll force you, Jace," Alaric said, his voice quiet, but his eyes filled with determination. "Don't make me."

Jace stared at the man. He had always been so kind and giving, never using his power in hatred. Even now he waited for Jace to make the decision his own. Jace could see the right path in his mind through his anger, but the fire of revenge burned brighter. Alaric stood unmoving, but Jace had made up his mind as well. He gave a swift tug on the rope, bringing it to its full length and swung his sword, cleaving it a few lengths shy of Alaric's wrist. The large man looked at him with a dumbfounded expression and Jace drove the hilt of his sword into Alaric's head. Alaric fell to the ground unconscious and Jace turned on Blynn. He held his sword low as the crowd roared deafeningly in their ears.

"Now," he whispered, "Let's do this."

Blynn turned to the king and bowed, saluting with his sword. The king nodded his approval and Blynn brought his blade to bear. Jace snickered evilly and lunged at the cat-liked man. Blynn danced away at the testing blows, his face filled with delight. He let his blade play with Jace's, walking to his right and then his left. The two stared at each other: Jace glowering openly at Blynn while the man smiled condescendingly in return.

The small group of Keepers huddled off to the side watching the action with the rest of the Kolosia. There were less than fifty of them left now and they stood dazed as the swords ringed off each other. Trel looked at Jace numbly. His friend was indeed gifted with a sword, but the look in his eyes was terrible to behold.

Blynn came at Jace with a combination of blows. Jace deflected them easily, but stumbled as he retreated backwards. Blynn swiped his blade at Jace's body as he rolled off to the side. The sword landed a hand away from his head. Jace caught a glimpse of the fury on Blynn's face as he pushed his advantage. He came to his knees and ducked as Blynn's sword flew over his head.

Jace drove out his sword and Blynn jumped back. His look of fury was replaced with fret while he became the defender. Jace worked first on the inside and then moved to the outside of Blynn's barrier. His sword flashed over Blynn's arm slicing the dark embroidery that ran along it. The two stopped and Blynn looked down at the hole and the thin line of blood that began to soak through the material. He stared at Jace, first showing his worry and then commending him.

"It's nice to have a token before I send you on your way," he said with a smile.

Jace swung the sword over his head and then jabbed at him. He knew the man was trying to antagonize him and he fought to focus his attack around his welling hatred. Blynn let Jace move nearly inside his perimeter, hoping it would lure him into a false sense of security. The action nearly worked and Blynn caught the flat of Jace's blade under his arm. He hit Jace squarely in the mouth and sent him reeling backward. The move was very similar to what had happened in the forest, but the sword slid out from under Blynn's arm as Jace backed away.

Jace clutched at his mouth with his left hand as he held up his guard with his right. The blow had sent stars through his vision and he struggled to see Blynn's pressing attack. Blynn sensed the advantage and thrust his sword deep into Jace's defenses. The tip caught Jace in the right side, below the ribs and he sucked in his breath as the blade sunk a whole hand into his belly. Blynn twisted the blade and wrenched it out at an odd angle, leaving Jace with a gaping wound.

He looked down and fingered the hole while Blynn stood back surveying his handiwork. His face twisted into a grin seeing the damage he had done.

"That will leave a mark, my friend," he said, clicking his tongue and giving Jace a gruesome smile.

Jace stepped forward with a series of blows, clutching his side. It hurt to breathe too heavily, and he stood back, letting the action come to him. Blynn noted Jace's strategy and took to slowly wearing him down. First, he took to attacking him from the sides so that Jace would have to turn to meet him. The extra effort made Jace labor his breathing even more, but he kept his guard up. His face was filled with hatred and he turned aside Blynn's blows, despite his weakening state. Blynn then varied his advance with a barrage of high and low attacks. Jace winced each time he raised his sword and Blynn used this to his advantage. He kept at Jace, using powerful blows to the high right and left and circling around him, always keeping him moving. Jace's defenses began to deteriorate rapidly, but he remained on his feet, every now and then lunging out with a sudden attack.

The aggressive flurries caught Blynn off guard, and he was left with a number of nicks and cuts. On one attempt, Jace knocked Blynn's blade away with a powerful blow and then sunk his own deep into the man's thigh. The wound left Blynn with a nasty limp, but Jace's cuts were mortal.

As the fight progressed, the tide turned in Blynn's favor. The blows mounted on his side, and Jace received a fair amount of punishment. Blynn took to methodically wounding him, leaving him with sizeable gashes on his arms and legs. He forced his way inside and struck Jace with another blow to the midsection in almost the same spot.

The blow caused Jace to drop his sword. He fell to one knee, backing away as the crowd cheered for Blynn to finish him off. Instead, Blynn threw away his sword. He grabbed Jace by the hair and brought him to his knees. All the roaring of the crowd and the chanting of the Watchers seemed to be etched into Blynn's face. He struck Jace's head with his backhand and then laid into him with closed fists. The maniacal flurry of Blynn's punches turned Jace's face into a bloody pulp.

Jace held up his hands at first, warding off the tirade, but his resistance spurred Blynn on all the more. A blow to his face rattled his jaw and his head swam in confusion. His arms slumped to his sides, allowing Blynn's fists to rain down on him unchecked. He could see Blynn's arms landing about his face, but the actions were somehow disconnected as he looked through his dazed vision.

At last, Blynn relented and Jace fell backward on the ground. His cheek was split and his eyes were almost swollen shut. Blynn stood over him as the crowd cheered wildly, holding up his hands for the Kolosia to grow louder. They did and Blynn laid into Jace again, kicking his wounded side and cracking several of his ribs.

Jace rolled his head in the sand. He recognized the man over him, but he had forgotten his name. All the hatred and malice seemed to seep out of his body and he gave the man a spent look, cracking his face in a simple smile. Through the pain, Jace knew that this was the end, and he seemed to welcome the sounds of the crowd and the strange man's hatred as he raised his sword high above his head. The cries and the picture of the angry man slowly faded from view as Jace gave into the serenity that swam around him.

Blynn's rage had filled every fiber of his being and he raised his sword for the final blow. The peaceful look on Jace's face only quickened Blynn's fury. He took a breath, hearing the cries of the Kolosia, and then drove his blade downward. The blade met sand and as Blynn looked up, Jace's body was pulled away. Alaric reeled in the sandy rope tied to Jace's hand and then pitched the young man on his back. He stumbled back to the tiny group of Keepers in the center of the arena.

Blynn roared in anger and pulled his sword from the sand. The guards that had for so long stood near the wall now moved out into the circle, enveloping the Keepers slowly.

As Alaric reached the group, the Keepers began to sing again, this time at the top of their voices. The crowd now screamed their hatred, urging the soldiers and Blynn to cut them down where they stood. The guards raced in, but stopped short.

Throughout the Kolosia, the dark clouds had rolled back and suddenly a shaft of light pierced the shadowy arena floor. It shone directly overhead, landing about the Keepers with a clean, sparkling brilliance that the Clonesians had never seen before. The throngs hushed, staring at the thin beam.

All that saw it had never seen light so bright and wondrous. They were momentarily spellbound by the beam and its color. At first, the bloodthirsty mob recoiled in panic, but as the spell passed, they turned their gaze upon it once more. It was more glorious than anything of value within their entire land. Their hearts seemed to call out to it, yearning for it as if there was some hole within them that was meant to be filled by only that which stood before them. They gaped at the light and only after a long glance did they realize the others that stood between the soldiers, Blynn, and the Keepers.

They looked plain enough. The crowd had to look twice. Their commonplace stance and their numbers were not overbearing, but as the crowd examined them closer, they were drawn to the hosts' garments. They seemed to be made out of pure light, radiating outward and cast all gloom and darkness away. The entire Kolosia began to shake with fear at the unearthly figures and their strange arrival.

The soldiers stopped in fear. They dropped their weapons and stood in place. Blynn stared, as if seeing them for the first time. He lowered his sword to the ground and looked dumbfounded as the men in white spread out.

A voice filled the Kolosia. It was not loud or booming, nor did it shake the rafters. It was rather still and small, but the words it spoke went straight to the hearts of all who heard:

The eternal One is your refuge, and underneath are the everlasting arms. He is your shield and helper and your glorious sword. Your enemies will cower before you, and you will trample down their high places.

The men in white spread out their hands, forming an unbroken circle around the Keepers. The huddled troop looked on. They had stopped their singing and now watched as the white robed men knelt with their eyes closed. The space between them and the soldiers began to flicker with sparks of white and blue. It grew until a solid band of crackling light formed and expanded around their circle.

The Clonesian soldiers recoiled from the supernatural flame and turned to leave, but the Watchers were all around them now, pressing in on the band of Keepers. They swooped down on the unsuspecting prisoners, clogging the air of the Kolosia and shrieking with horrid malevolence. The soldiers flinched from them, and the masses in the stands seemed to see the cloaked figures now for what they truly were as the spotless light revealed their hideous nature. The cowled phantoms pointed at the Keepers and their robed rescuers, hissing their commands for the soldiers to assault the flames. Those that tried were thrown backwards or fell unconscious at the wall of light.

The men in white turned to the Keepers, forming a tight circle around them and grasping their hands once again. All sound crackled with silence as the Kolosia floor ignited with blinding color. The white host's bodies burned brightly and all those in the Kolosia turned away as the light exploded through the city. As the untainted flame faded from view and the wall of white and blue fire dissipated, the crowd wiped their eyes and looked at the center of the arena floor.

Where the cowering mass of Keepers had stood was a giant hole, neatly bored into the earth. Its edge was smooth like glass and no one dared touch it. Where the bodies of fallen Keepers had littered the ground now lay empty sand. The pillars of still burning wood were void of any hint of a martyr's body.

The crowd was shaken at the unexplained sight. To where had the unexplained host escaped? Where had they come from? Was it possible for so large a throng of people to slip away from the Clonesian military? Could their emperor and King have summoned them for this elaborate hoax? Was it possible? Was it real?

They hurried out of the Kolosia in frightened silence. Over the days, their king and other dignitaries tried to explain what had happened. The masses that had seen it somehow did not trust any of the interpretations that their governing superiors gave them. They did, however, try desperately to forget its occurrence and somehow conveniently forgot the fearful sight of the Watchers and the undeniable words of the voice from the heavens.

19

FLIGHT

He knew his hands were there, but he could not see them. No matter how close he waved them to his face, they were not evident. He knew they must be there—he could feel the air moving, but the darkness still frightened him. There was heavy breathing all around him as the group nestled close together in the darkness. They were quiet after all that had happened, none daring to speak the first word.

Trel could hear somebody whispering quietly. The words were below the range of understanding, but the rhythmic clicking of the man's voice had to mean something. It continued on for several heartbeats, but the more he listened, the less he understood it. He could hear others doing the same, in fact there must have been a veritable chorus of people conducting the whispering chant in the darkness. It made the place seem filled with a bunch of tiny insects.

Finally, the voices stopped and there was only the steady sound of breathing again. Then, all around him, he heard the voices of men speak a single word:

"Ieysa!"

The cave slowly filled with a clear blue light. It hovered in front of the passage before them; a shining sphere that pulsed and quivered. The band of Keepers hushed as the light winked into view. The white clothed men that they had seen on the Kolosia floor stood all around them, and many of the Keepers fell with their faces to the ground in fright.

Their leader stepped forward. He was nondescript like the rest of the men, save for the brown hair which fell loosely to his shoulders and the crimson sash that ran across his chest. He spoke and his rich voice seemed to sooth the listeners instantly.

"Do not be afraid," he said calmly. "Arise, for we are but servants of the El Elyon. The Maker has sent us to lead you out of danger along paths that few men know."

His steady eyes ran over the tattered band. He studied their dirty faces and worried expressions with ease, portraying an air of confidence that stilled the fears of the Keepers. They stood and listened to the man as he went on.

"The Master has bid us speed you from this place in all haste. We travel to the Great River. Many of you are wounded and old and will not keep the pace that is set. Do not worry. We are under the Almighty's protection and influence. No matter the road, we shall prevail."

As if to emphasize his point, the other men stepped forward. Their faces were plain and they listened to their leader intently. They approached each Keeper lifting up their tired arms and passing their hands over the coarse bonds. The caves filled with a quiet clamor as the ropes fell off the Keepers. Many of them stared openly at the white robed men, rubbing their wrists. The men nodded passively in return and turned back to their leader.

He explained the route they would take, traveling by day and night through the caves. The journey was long and speed was of the utmost importance. He encouraged all who heard to take heart and not be discouraged, for if their hearts and minds remained on Yeshua, nothing would impede their progress. When he was finished, the Keepers and the men in white made ready to leave.

Over half of the group was injured in one form or another. There were also a fair number of elderly among them whose tired, old bodies looked like they could not walk 20 paces. Trel judged that 50 or so Keepers would not be able to keep their pace for more than a quarter hour.

His own body was severely burned from the time in the dungeons of Clonesia. His back was laced with whips marks like his fellow Keepers. He had narrowly missed an arrow on the floor of the Kolosia and was covered with a number of scratches, bruises, and lacerations. Besides that, his nerves were frayed from their harrowing ordeal. If anything, he was in the same predicament as the elderly and wondered if he too could make the journey.

Alaric, Lashara, and Arthur were all huddled around the still body of Jace. He was covered with bruises and caked blood. His breathing was shallow and blood poured openly from his side. His skin was white and he did not open his eyes. The look of Alaric was grave as he watched his friend's body fight to stay alive. The white robed leader stood over them.

"His body has suffered immensely, but Jace will finish the race," he said mysteriously. He pulled a pouch from his robe and placed it before Lashara. "You will need to use the gifts the Creator has given you to quicken your friend."

Lashara flinched as the man laid the small sack in front of her. She gave a timid look up at the man and turned to the pouch reluctantly, untying its leather strap. She started as she laid out its contents. They were her herbs and potions that the dungeon guards had taken from her! To her surprise, all were there. She turned to thank the robed man who nodded his head in recognition. Lashara's deft fingers began to sort through the items at her feet.

Quickly, she made a poultice that would cover the wound. She poured some liquid over it that fizzed in the stillness of the cave. Cupping it in her hands, she applied it to the hole in Jace's side, making sure it was completely covered and firm before packing her things.

Jace winced in his sleep, groaning when Lashara touched him. The five of them watched as his breathing began to grow deeper. His skin filled with a healthy shade of blood before their eyes and his expression seemed more relaxed. Alaric and Trel stared at Lashara. She was truly gifted in the art of care for the wounded. They gazed at her with looks of awe.

The white robed man gently gathered up Jace's body in his arms. He hung limply, his arms and head dangling out as the stout man cradled him. Another robed man came up to him as he turned to leave.

"Rendolph, the group is ready," he said.

"Then let us depart," Rendolph commanded.

All around him, Trel watched as the feeble band made ready to leave. The Keepers stood wiping their hands expectantly in the blue light of the orb. Any that struggled found one of the strange, white robed men instantly at their side to steady their feet. The party was a mixture of dirty Keepers in rags that were tendered by these men dressed in stunning pristine garments.

Two of the men took the lead and the Keepers began to follow. All were quiet and moved through the caves without a word. Water and lichen made the rocks slippery and the Keepers stumbled forward supported by the men. Their protectors said nothing, but smiled reassuringly and pointed the group through the passages.

The mysterious orb that lit the caves hovered ahead of them. It never traveled too far ahead, nor went too slow. The light from the little object left no crevice hidden and no passage unlit. Trel stared at the tiny miracle, absolutely mesmerized as it led them down the winding, endless caves. *His word is a lamp unto my feet and a light unto my path*, he thought as he watched the orb hovering before them. After a while, he realized the white robed men did not lead, they simply followed the direction of the light. Time seemed to stand still, and they walked for hours without stopping.

The journey reminded him of the great Exodus that Moeisha and the Chosen had made out of the oppressed land of slavery. There, the presence of the Maker had gone out before them, leading them as a cloud by day and a pillar of fire by night. The similarity was astounding and he felt akin to the old story, having some understanding what they may have been feeling.

The walk through the caves seemed to be a dream. He knew it was real, all of his senses told him so, yet it seemed removed and out of place. Since he had left East Haven his world had turned surreal. The more he thought about it, the harder it was to believe that he had traveled across Emblom, through the Stygian Union and into the heart of the Clonesian Empire. He had lived out the stories and adventures that he had only read about in his studies. In truth, they were not as pleasant as the tales he had read. His scarred back and bruised face vouched for that, but it was still unfathomable that he and his friends had come so far in so little time.

Was it better than keeping to his studies at East Haven? He did not know. He admired life on the open road in spite of the awful weather, bland food, and enmity that people had for those from the Gap. He could do without the whippings, beatings, and blows to the head, and would be happy for the rest of his days if he did not see another Watcher. Somehow, he couldn't bring himself to say he would never have gone. He knew that was not his decision anyhow.

However the Master saw fit to use him, he must obey. It was more than a command passed down from his Mentors now. He realized that his journey was to glorify his Maker and to bring honor to Yeshua. He understood now what Clarissa and Shereel had meant when they said they could not turn their backs on Yeshua after all He had done for them. Were he to have fallen in the Kolosia, it would yet have been worthwhile.

Where he was at the moment continued to be hard for him to comprehend. A day had not gone by since he had been in the Kolosia facing certain death. A day before that, he was locked in a cavernous dungeon bigger than the caves he was in at the moment and considerably more destitute than any place he had seen yet. Before that, he was traveling by cart in the Inland Basin toward certain doom with only his party and their faith in Yeshua as guidance. The list went on and on in a whirlwind of memories and feelings. He could not make sense of the events that he had gone through even now in the stillness of the caves. Somehow, he reasoned, this journey was not yet over.

The men in white were another story. He did not deny their heavenly origin, nor did he question their leadership in the caves. They were trustworthy. There was no question that they were sent from the Creator Himself. Where else could such powerful forces come from to combat the Lord of the Night?

Their actions on the Kolosia floor had left an indelible mark in his mind. He shuddered, remembering the dread whispers of the Watchers as they ordered the soldiers to kill them. They stood only paces away, separated from Trel and the Keepers by the dazzling, translucent barrier of light and the expressionless men in white. They were so close that Trel could hear their breathing and see the colors of the soldiers' eyes. It was hard to grasp just how near he had come to death.

He was left with little choice but to trust the men in white, but something bothered him still. He could not quite put his finger on it. Perhaps it was that he struggled with reality itself. He had read nearly all the stories of the Song of the Ages—how the Creator had done His most astounding miracles in the face of adversity. He always seemed to hold back until there was no other way for victory except through His intervention and made it absolutely clear that what had been done was from His hands alone. Trel had read it time and time again and had enjoyed it. It had always comforted him that the Creator in the Song of the Ages was the same Creator that he had pledged his life to. He rejoiced that this Yeshua written about within the Song of the Ages was the very Yeshua that was at work in the world today.

He had listened and believed all of what his Mentors had told him, but somehow missed the mark. Could it be that the Creator and His holy Son, Yeshua still worked the same way today as they had long ago? Maybe that is what he struggled with. Yes, he was sure that was it. All this time, he had observed what was written within the Song of the Ages, but never connected with the overwhelming truth: he was part of the plan that had existed from the beginning. The stories that existed in Song of the Ages were not some detached piece of history that only showed who the Creator was, they were a marker for where He had been. He had never stopped working in the world. Trel had been caught up in His wonderful work all along. It finally hit him as he stared at the glistening robes of his guides that he was in one of those stories. He had become part of the great history of the Almighty at work in the world. He had witnessed the awesome power of His Master in action. He had been swept up in the great battle between Sa'vard and the Most High that had existed since the beginning of time. The Song of the Ages was alive! It was not a silent book of some ancient Being that had long removed Himself from the world. It was a testament of what He had done and what He could and would do to reach the hearts of men and save them from the evil grip of Sa'vard!

A smile began to form on Trel's face. How could he have missed it all this time? How suddenly Yeshua had become so much more real to Him! Here he was walking with his Lord's host whom He had commanded to come and protect His Chosen. He began to walk with a lighter step, his spirit renewed by the gem the Counselor had revealed to him. He felt he could go on forever and began to sing praises in his heart to Yeshua.

The caves were still ominous and foreboding. Their massive holes and eternal halls seemed to swallow up his puny form. He had grown uneasy since he lost his sense of direction and only knew they were somewhere underneath the Clonesian Empire.

Despite his lack of control, the circumstances were rather peaceful. He was calmed knowing that his Lord had cared for him so deeply that He had sent a small army of His servants to clear a path for him and lead him to safer pastures. He walked quietly in the small company, resting in the knowledge that the Almighty was in control.

But some things did not make sense. As he sauntered on with happiness in his heart and a quiet humming on his lips, his thoughts turned to those who were not there. He remembered how large the group of Keepers were that entered the Kolosia. They had filled all the holding pens and marched out onto the arena floor nearly 1000 strong. Looking around, he noticed for the first time how pitifully few of them that were left. So many of them seemed so much older now. Where they had gone into the Kolosia with rejoicing and defiance, now they struggled in sadness, their bodies leeched of strength.

Why had so many fallen? Better yet, why were so few saved from death? What was the Almighty's reasoning in letting one Keeper live and another die? Why was he spared while so many had died in such horrible ways? Why were some killed with the bow and others burned at the stake? He floundered as repressed images and sounds of the Kolosia toppled down on him. He could see the arrows shooting by him in a blur of light, missing him by hand lengths only to sink into others that stood by his side. The crowd had melted away like wheat under the sickle as the volley of arrows slew whole rows of them at once. He could hear the sickening sound of their buzzing and the dull thud as the arrows hit their targets. He could hear the scream of the Keeper at the stake—only a child—as the flames took her life and the crowd mocked her pain with jeers. The memories sickened him and he stopped in the passage and groped the wall.

He wretched while others passed him by, keeping himself up by gripping the wall. The memories were too much for him to bear. He wiped his mouth on his arm and propped himself up against the wall, putting his hands on his battered knees. As tears choked his vision, he watched the others move by him. He let them fall unashamedly as many in the group had done already.

One of the silent guardians turned aside and stopped. He stood back waiting for Trel to present himself and ask for assistance. Trel smoothed his ragged clothes in an effort to act like everything was under control. He took a deep breath and turned to the man. The white robed figure approached him silently, offering a hand and bringing Trel to his feet. He looked Trel over without a word and beckoned for him to continue down the path. The two walked behind the party keeping some distance between them and the group.

"Your heart is troubled greatly, Trel," said the man in a low voice. He watched the young Keeper in the light of the orb. "Many questions have filled your mind and though you cling to the Master's call, you cannot make sense of what has happened over the past days."

"No," he agreed, his voice nearly breaking. "So much loss, so much hurt..."

The man in white walked next to him, not saying anything for a while. His face was ageless. All Trel could say with confidence was that he was a man removed from boyhood. His features were unwrinkled and his brown hair was not graying, but there was an air of eternal maturity that graced his presence. He walked quietly, his bare feet never slipping or losing balance on the craggy surface of the caves. Trel caught sight of the slim sword that was strapped close to his waist. His round eyes conveyed a sense of brotherly love and sincere concern as he looked at Trel.

"Yes," the man said. "Sa'vard would boast of a victory on such a day. Yet, his hopes to crush all the Keepers within the Clonesian Empire have been thwarted. He did not accomplish what he set out to do, nor did the Keepers that fell honor him. They died as the Chosen, never turning from their faith in Yeshua even in their greatest trial. Instead, they glorified Him before the throngs of the Kolosia. Clonesians will be hard pressed to forget the courage with which the Keepers fell, nor will they be able to explain away the disappearance of those that survived, but this is not what troubles you, is it?"

"No, sir," he said formally. "I understand what has taken place. I see the reasons behind the sacrifices of my brothers and sisters. I realize how the Almighty has gained glory for all that has happened. It's just, the people that died were real, their families and loved ones... we will all mourn their loss and grieve for days to come. Their bodies will rot within the Clonesian Empire instead of being honored for their bravery and their loyalty to our Lord."

"What is the body but a shell that comes and goes with the fleeting of time?" said the man. "But our Lord has not overlooked such minor things, Trel. Rest easy, for their bodies will not be desecrated. Yeshua has gathered their souls in Par'lael and hidden their bodies in a secret place to await His return. They shall not be harmed."

They walked along for a while and the man turned to him again. "Some things will weigh heavy on your heart, Trel. You may wish for an answer that will calm all your questions and rest your pain. Yet, you may never receive any such explanation. Whatever happens, remember this: hold true to Yeshua's teaching. Many things will never have meaning on earth, but eternal Yeshua knows even the innermost workings of life's mysteries. When all His family is assembled in Par'lael, then shall the puzzles of life be revealed. What we see in part shall be seen in full, but for now, rest in the truth that He knows what must be done."

Trel nodded, knowing that the man's words were true. They comforted his questions, and he laid them aside as they made their way through the wet, rocky caverns. Small streams of water were everywhere along the passages and the Keepers hopped over them. Some spread out across the cave's floor in a hundred interconnecting rivulets and the group sloshed through them, supported by the white robed men.

The rocks themselves were multihued and lent a unique backdrop to the scenery. Chunks of brown speckled granite stuck out of dark basaltic rock. The combination was like nothing Trel had ever seen. Quartz glittered in the light of the orb, its colors ranging from crystal white to royal amethyst. A thin sprinkling of gems gave a whimsical accent to the black caves. The effect turned the craggy overhangs and low-lying ceiling into a vast, far-reaching sky that was dotted with a thousand twinkling stars.

The caves themselves were not as empty and lifeless as Trel had first thought. Thin films of blue and green algae floated on the surface of shallow lakes. Their clear water said they that had not been disturbed in years. Trel could see small schools of fish darting close to the shore and odd shelled creatures delving into the crevices of the craggy rocks. Iridescent moss clung about the walls of the caves. The fungus glowed blue in the wake of the orb's passing. Trel looked back into the darkness to see the caves shining with the quiet, muffled lighting of the moss. No large creatures inhabited these caves, or at least they did not approach the party. There was little noise, but the constant trickling of water lent a tranquil effect to the silent journey.

Rendolph remained true to his word, allowing the Keepers only time enough to brush their feet off and drink from the waterskins. They traveled at a moderate pace, winding through the bleak scenery. Trel lost count of the hours which turned into days, maybe weeks as far as he knew. Strangely enough, the group felt no need to sleep and though they were tired, they somehow managed to maintain the orb's steady pace.

Trel hung at the rear of the group. He felt the need to be alone for some reason, if only to muddle through his thoughts. The man who had talked with him gave him distance, turning every now and then to make sure Trel did not lag too far behind. At last, Trel gave up his thinking and plodded on in the rocky terrain.

While he trotted along, Clarissa and Shereel drifted back to meet him. They remembered him, of course, and met him with fatigued smiles as they ducked through a low section of cave. They covered their heads with the tattered shawls they had managed to save after all they had been through and helped each other along.

Now that Trel saw them side by side, he couldn't help but notice their similarities. Clarissa was younger, her features were softer and her hair hung loosely down her back. Her voice was breathy, and she gave short embarrassed laughs when she stumbled over a rock. Shereel was the older, and though her features were more angular and hardened, they lent an exquisite chiseled beauty to her face. Her hair still remained up in the bun that she had worn when Trel had first met her. She helped her sister along with quiet words of encouragement, but did not say much else. Their two faces had several cuts and a large purple bruise covered Clarissa's right cheek. The backs of their dresses were ripped to shreds from the strokes of the whip, and they winced several times as they hunched over in the caves. Trel tried not to stare at their wounds without feeling pity and smiled warmly when they caught him looking.

The two sisters had recovered surprisingly from their circumstances. Though they had not seen anything but the city streets in years or been anywhere remotely close in comparison to where they were now, they continued on with a tenacity that betrayed their humbled exteriors. They were, after all, brought up in the Gap and had studied under the same tutelage and lessons that every man, woman, and child must go through before they left East Haven or any of the other places of learning.

In truth, they had grown up on the western escarpment overlooking the Feeding Plain. Since childhood, they had helped their father with the family flocks, trading their wool with the settlements below for butter, milk, and eggs. They only bought what they could afford and could not make and so became proficient at the art of thrifty behavior. They learned from their father how to whittle a branch into a bow, tell the signs of an oncoming storm, and sense when one of the sheep was sick. Their mother taught them how to mend a torn hem, weave a cloak, stitch, cook, and clean.

By adolescence Shereel and Clarissa had been charged with regular household duties and watched over their younger brothers and sisters. The hard life of the mountain shepherdess and bitter weather of the hills had shaped them into two hardy ladies whose beauty was as natural as the hills themselves. They had good heads about them, and their Mentors quickly noticed their unusual ability to persevere under extreme circumstances. That and their love for even the most lost individual made them perfect candidates for what the Council had asked them to do.

After several missions to the Clonesian Empire, they felt Yeshua's leading to establish a discreet presence within its borders. They had infused the Empire with a network of Keepers that secretly watched for opportunities to share of Yeshua under the dangerous presence of the Watchers.

Like Trel, they had their own list of questions. They were much like his, and though they could come up with no supreme answer as to why they had been saved from the doom of the Kolosia, they counted it all as part of Yeshua's gracious plan for their lives. They shed their tears for their fallen friends, comforted each other in their loss, and gathered themselves up to continue on the journey their Master had for them. The attitude had been instilled in them that they must run the race set before them, looking to Yeshua (and His example), who despising the shame endured the cross, and is set down at the right hand of the throne of the Almighty. Whenever their strength failed them, they considered

Him who bore such things so that they would not lose heart. As they had said countless times before: Yeshua had done so much for them, they could never turn their backs on him.

They drew close to Trel as the caves narrowed.

"I had no idea there were so many passages that existed underneath this kingdom," said Shereel in amazement. She looked Trel up and down and went on, "I have seen similar tunnels at the far ends of Trailaden and heard of others like them under Clonesia itself. Perhaps they are all networked somehow. If that is true, we could bring a flood of Keepers into the Empire without people ever knowing."

Trel stared at her, his eyes large, "Yeshua, help me, I will never go back! I hope I've seen the last of that place!"

Shereel pursed her lips, "Perhaps you have, Trel, but then again, were your Master to call you, would you be as faithful to Him as He is to you?"

She gave him a penetrating stare and he shrugged helplessly, "I suppose I'd have little choice, then. All Keepers go where He leads—they should, at least. That is part of our vows, is it not?"

Shereel nodded. "Of course, but there are many even now who shirk their duty or sidestep wholehearted action. They justify their complacency with small tithes and encouragements, never leaving the Gap to tarry for the Savior in hostile lands." She rubbed her thin hand where a substantial cut was and crouched under a precipice that jutted out. "Could you imagine what would happen were everyone of us who live in the Gap, who bask in the glory of Yeshua, who know the Truth—if we were to rise up for the glory of our Master and spread the word to the nations before us? How the harvest fields would overflow!"

"Or we would be cut to pieces," Trel said looking her in the eyes. "Clonesians would throw us in jail as soon as they discovered our origins. We would then be hauled off to the Kolosia without a word." He could imagine the devastation of his friends and family were they to travel en masse to the Clonesian Empire. *Sheep to the slaughter*, he thought. Shereel turned to him, her eyes hard.

"Where is your faith?" she asked bitterly. She took it quite personally that there were those who lived free from harm in the Gap while she and her sister faced death each day only because of what they believed.

"Have a heart, Shereel," said Clarissa. "The Master has called each of us for a different purpose. Some are destined to walk through the flames while others must attend to the home fires. It is not Trel's decision, but our Lord's. Would you blame Him?" she asked her sister.

Shereel stomped off ahead of them, leaving the two alone behind the party. It was obvious the two saw things differently. Trel saw both their arguments. There were particular things Yeshua had called each Keeper to do. Shereel and Clarissa's passion was clearly for the Clonesians.

He also understood Shereel's complaint. All too often the members of the Gap had kept to themselves. This had cost them, and the world around them had given into the rumors that the whole of them were a selfish lot that was of little use. Besides dispelling the myth, Keepers had an obligation to tell all countries of Yeshua's gift to all nations. His sacrifice had covered over the wrongs of all who chose to accept Him and claim Him as their Lord. Shereel was right, many of them kept to themselves, safe and comfortable in the Gap, instead of paying the price for sharing what they knew to be true.

Clarissa watched him mulling over these things. "I'm sorry about Shereel," she said as they walked. "She tends to forget the edge in her voice, but she does have a heart of gold. I've tried to tell her many times, but some people have things they will struggle with all their lives."

Trel waved her off. "It is alright. We've all been through plenty recently. Hopefully her pain will subside."

"It always does. She'll apologize to you before the day's through, whenever that is," she said, looking around as if to spot the sun.

Trel laughed and they walked on. Of the two sisters, Clarissa was the talker. Her friendly conversation was comforting and filled the hole that Trel had since Jace had withdrawn from the rest of them. He worried about his friend, but Lashara had done her work and Arthur and Alaric seemed to think he would be fine. He worried about Lashara also and soon found himself opening up to Clarissa about his companions.

Clarissa was not only an avid talker, but a very good listener. She let Trel know she was paying attention with plenty of eye contact and nods of the head. Her verbal affirmations were never too few, which encouraged him to speak instead of bogging down the conversation. He spoke of their journey, Blynn's treachery and Jace's defeat. Clarissa was touched with how much Trel cared for his friend. At length the subject turned to Rae.

"How is Jace's brother?" Clarissa asked pointedly. "Is he here?" she asked, looking around.

"No. We don't know where he is. The last we saw of him, he had relinquished his allegiance to Yeshua and stated firmly that he would remain in the Empire." Trel let out a long sigh. "I think Jace took it pretty hard. He is his only brother. He's looked up to him his whole life. To have him turn his back on all that Jace has known must have hurt him deeply," he finished, shaking his head.

"I'm sorry to hear of it," Clarissa said, genuinely pained. "Things will happen and still we must go on. Jace will get over it somehow."

Trel nodded, but he did not believe her. Jace would hold what happened close to his heart for a long time.

After another long spell of walking in the caves, Bartemus took up his singing. The tune was not heavy, nor was it frivolous. It was a walking song made for a time such as this. The old man always seemed to have a melody for every occasion. As his worn, scratchy voice bounced throughout the caverns, more people joined in. Trel never quite got the words, but the rhythm was what was important. It provided the perfect timing for a steady pace and fit in nicely with the speed of the orb. The group marched onward, letting their voices sink to a whisper or grow to a hefty bellow as they sang in the solitude of the caves.

Finally, Rendolph turned around. He still held Jace whose bruised body slept peacefully in the man's arms. His face was serene and he did not seemed perturbed in the least at their boisterous melody. He ushered them to gather around and spoke to them with caution.

"We are nearing the edge of the Clonesian Empire. Soon we will travel under the Great River and be free of this place." The crowd murmured in anticipation, but Rendolph hushed them politely.

"Our next leg is marked with danger. We shall be delving deeper into the earth and all must keep in single file and remain on their toes. This part of the caves is guarded and we will have to be silent or risk revealing ourselves to the Clonesians. Let us move onward."

All idle chatter fell away as they began to walk. The passage began to curl downward. The tunnel grew narrow and the group had no choice but to follow one behind the other and slowly pick their way down the steep incline.

Trel's attention was focused on the path, and he started when he looked up. The low ceiling had pulled away and the right wall had disappeared. The black above him was genuine darkness, and he grew dizzy as he looked out into the night at his side. The orb's light only shone bright enough for them to see their immediate surroundings, making him feel lost in the size of the large chasm into which they descended.

Heights were not something that bothered Trel, but as he peered downward over the edge, he grew rather uneasy. He clutched the far left wall, leaning into it and moved stiffly one step at a time. By now, many in the party had made Trel's discovery and he watched as their backs stiffened in front of him. The men in white guided them downward and people clung to them now with white knuckles.

By the time they reached the bottom, everyone was sweating profusely. Rendolph let them stop and calm themselves while he and his men gathered for discussion. Trel squinted into the darkness above him, but the shape of the giant cave was hidden under the blanket of darkness. It felt incredibly open, but Trel could only guess at its measurements. He sat and waited while the men in white made their decision.

Again they took up their things and moved out. They crossed out onto the cave floor. Here, there were only walls of amorphous blackness that limited their vision. Trel had grown accustomed to the tight tunnels of the caves and he felt uncomfortable in this large room's expanse. There was no life here—no gentle glow of moss or algae, no skittering of tiny shelled creatures—only thin pools of water lay on the black, lifeless rock. All sound was swallowed up in the vast darkness that surrounded them.

Hours passed and still the cave went on. Up ahead, Trel thought he saw the glow of torchlight. As they approached, it was undeniable, and the crowd of Keepers tiptoed ahead. They came to the edge of a cliff where the rock stopped short and, looking down saw a thin string of torches in another cavern some levels below. There were shapes moving along the line and Trel could make out what looked like soldiers in soiled uniforms and rusted armor.

As they made their way quietly onto the sunken floor, Trel could see their ugly faces. How long they had lived underground, he did not know. The torches seemed to be the only thing marking the outpost and the barrier of the Great River.

In all honesty, the outpost was the Empire's only official recognition of the smuggling that went on beneath their lands. They had sent small bands of soldiers to guard the entryways and map the underlying maze of caves in an effort to tax some of the trade of the smugglers. The actions were noteworthy, but hopelessly flawed. There were a myriad of caves leading into the Empire, and the smugglers knew every one.

Instead of bypassing the guarded entrances altogether, they had formed a consortium and drew lots to see who would journey through the taxed portions of the caves. The choice allowed for the majority of smugglers to pass unmolested through the secret entrances and kept the Clonesian Empire satisfied that they had quelled a large part of the smugglers' business.

In return the Clonesian Empire did not see any further need to waste valuable troops and resources on the underground layer. The two forces had come to a happy medium in the caves, with each one of them thinking that they had fully exploited the other.

The floor of the cavern was filled with boulders. The group hid behind these, passing in a large circle around the soldiers. The guards were much too noisy and only seemed interested in consuming the Imperial ale which was stockpiled in large quantities about their camp. Their loud laughter mixed with cursing said that they had already had more than any normal man should. Though the orb blazed brightly, none of the soldiers noticed it.

They, like any lost soul, were hampered by what they thought to be real. Their eyes were closed to the power of the Almighty that lit the caverns around them. They could only see that which their minds said was true, and so to them, the caves were dark save for the dim, oily light of their torches.

A minor problem existed, however. The outpost line stretched across the lone exit of the cave. To leave, one had to saunter directly through the camp. Rendolph straightened his body and motioned for some of his men to come near him. He laid Jace next to Arthur and Alaric, commanding them to watch over him. Stepping out from behind the rocks, Rendolph approached the camp followed by three of his men.

To the guards, the men seemed to come out of the darkness. They were dressed like any other merchants with their sackcloth clothes and dirty faces. A strong odor permeated the air around them and the soldiers wrinkled their noses with open disgust.

"We have come to pay the fare," the lead one said with a perfect Clonesian accent. He sifted through his dingy clothes and pulled out a heavy pouch of coins.

The guards leaned forward. The dirty merchant had their attention now. He loosened the leather bag and dumped a handful of coins into his hands. They spilled over and fell on the ground at his feet in a shower of golden, jingling raindrops on the rocky surface of the cave. The guards' faces twitched as they watched the man's friends pick up the coins. What the merchant held in his hands could feed a small town for a month and his bag was less than half empty. The soldiers stood on the edge of their toes watching the man greedily.

He stepped forward to the table and began paying the taxes. First were the border fees to and from their place of trade. The goods came next and the grubby teamster behind the merchant pulled a long list from his pocket. The poor fool had smuggled in fruits! After a sizeable portion of his bag had exchanged owners, the guards stood up to inspect his wagons. He waved his arms over his head sullenly and his carriers and packmen nudged his carts into the outpost. They were in great disrepair and the soldiers' faces lit up with glee. Worn vehicles were charged extra since they spent more time on the roads and stopped up traffic. By the time the merchant had paid for his goods, his passage, and the wagons, his bag was next to empty.

The guards thanked him kindly and the wagons moved through the outpost. The feebleminded merchants waved happily to the guards who returned the waves good-naturedly. What simpleton had thought the need to smuggle fruits through the borders of the Empire?

The soldiers went back to their drinking and laughed in the darkness long after the carts had faded from view. They would not forget the mindless merchant who had traveled the long dangerous road under the Clonesian Empire for a load of apples and grapes! As they laughed over another cask of ale, the Keepers and the men in white jostled away in the darkness.

20

THE JOURNEY HOME

"What just happened?" asked Trel breathlessly. They had been moving a good while and it was all he could manage in between breaths. The people around him looked ready to collapse and more than one elderly Keeper was clinging desperately to the men in white. No one answered him as they kept walking through the night. His lungs burned and his heart felt ready to burst. The orb blazed away and the men in white continued on breathing lightly.

At last, Rendolph and his men halted, and the Keepers fell to the ground breathing heavily. The white robed men went about the group, offering waterskins and hard biscuits to everyone. While the hungry crowd ate their fill, the men watched them, making sure each was well-fed. They were not on the verge of collapsing, the men in white noted, despite how they felt. They had, however, been traveling for over a week and deserved a rest even in spite of the quickening from the Almighty.

Over the course of the journey, Jace's mind had been alive with dark dreams. His wounds had burned in his nightmares and images of Watchers hovered over him. Low moans had carried from his dreams through his mouth and into the caves around him as he evaded the Watchers and cried out in the pain of his wounds. Rendolph muffled his sighs, whispering words and promises from Yeshua each time a bout of anguish crossed his lips. They had to halt several times on account of Jace after they crossed through the camp of the Clonesian guards. Rendolph had stopped and ordered Lashara to examine him. The others gathered around him, always expecting the worst, but Lashara had only said that he was working through his pain, and his wounds were sealing themselves.

In his mind's eye, Jace's brother stood before him. He reached out his hand to him through the cloud of Watchers but failed to touch him. Rae's expression was smug and though he didn't turn away, he watched arrogantly as Jace tried without success to pull him through the gale of Watchers. Sa'vard's minions laughed at Jace, taunting him to try again, vowing they would never relinquish his brother. He cried and snatched at his image, but Rae remained unmoved, his face never showing the faintest sign of hope or sorrow. Whenever Jace stuck his hand through the Watchers, his skin lit up like hot oil and he screeched in anguish, clutching his arm while the Watchers mocked him.

This scene faded from view only to be replaced by other horrors. Sometimes he stood in the throne room of Na'tal undergoing the same persecution before the throngs of unearthly soldiers. The whippings would light up his back and his body would shake in the arms of Rendolph. He would look up to see Na'tal's face as it twisted into the form of one of the guards in the dungeon or the dirty pale face of Blynn. He would then find his arms free and a sword in his hand. He and Blynn would stand alone in the Kolosia fighting while the sun rose and set, only to rise again. Blynn would cut him, but he would not bleed, though the wounds made him cry out in pain. The man would beat him until he had thought he would die. Every time, it ended the same with Blynn standing over him, his black shadowy figure looking like the image of a Watcher. A piercing light would burn him away, and Yeshua would stand before him, His scarred hands outstretched to greet Jace as deep breathes of life filled his lungs. He would open his eyes only to find darkness and the cave of the Mines of Shorn again. These and other nameless, horrible images cycled through his dreams in a never-ending river of fear and chaos.

Rendolph urged the group to rest. He and Lashara sat near Jace's still sleeping body. The young woman ran her fingers through his hair while she touched his head to check for signs of a fever. Her face was stern as she performed her skills. This eased Trel who had grown saddened at Lashara's retreat into herself. She said nothing to anyone and ran directly behind Rendolph with one of the men in white at her side. These she didn't even talk to and only came to Jace when Rendolph called her. The rest of the time, she sat apart from the group with her back to the crowd, rocking back and forth on her knees. The signs did not bode well for Lashara, and Trel silently said a word to Yeshua for her.

Several times he had approached her, but she refused to speak to him and backed away. After giving up, he had asked Alaric to talk with her, but she only listened to him with a blank expression while staring into the darkness. Blynn's abuse and the revelation of her secret past to everyone had changed her forever. Trel watched her from afar, hoping and wishing that she would somehow work through her pain. It seemed they all wrestled with deep-seated issues, and the solitude of the caves only magnified them.

Trel took another draught of water. The substance was cool and instantly perked his senses. This was no earthly liquid. They had lived off nothing but it and the simple loaves of bread the men in white passed out every time they stopped. No matter how far they had gone, the meal always quenched their thirst immediately. It reminded him how Yeshua had said He was the bread of life and gave everlasting water that all who drink it would never thirst again. The signs of their Lord were ever constant around these men and seemed to affirm any misgivings any had about their connection with Yeshua.

Trel's mind lingered on the scene at the outpost. He couldn't make sense of how the Clonesian soldiers had let 50 Keepers walk directly through their camp smiling and waving at them as they watched them go. He turned it over in his mind and shook his head. The man in white that had talked to him before sat off to his side and Trel motioned for him to come near. He voiced his question again. The man looked at him, his face smooth and expressionless.

"The soldiers saw what they wanted to see," he said as if explaining the obvious. "Their eyes are forever blinded by their greed for Sa'vard has hold of their hearts. They have given themselves over to their own temptations long ago and only persisted in their lifestyle in our presence."

"Well, that explains everything," Trel said, throwing up his hands. He had no idea what the man had just said. The man only looked at him and folded his hands on his lap. He began again, using his fingers to articulate his meanings.

"The guards were greedy. When we approached, Yeshua caused them to see a caravan of hapless merchants whose pockets were ripe for the taking. They saw none of the Almighty's host. The Keepers appeared to them as a train of wagons, worn and run-down. When they were finished, their pockets were full of good gold coin and they waved happily as we passed through their border."

"You tricked them?" Trel asked.

The man shook his head. "No. As the Song of the Ages says: He handed them over to their own selfish desires. They were not tricked, but they were not made to see either."

"Why?"

"As His Word says: 'Therefore the Almighty gave them over in the sinful desires of their hearts.' They exchanged truth for a lie, and worshiped and served created things rather than the Creator, who is forever to be praised. According to His Word, they were not tricked. They made the choice long ago what they would see and what they would refuse to acknowledge."

"But the Creator could have used the time as an opportunity to reveal Himself," he said confused.

"That is my Master's decision, not mine," the man said, "There is a time for everything, He says. This was a time when He used their folly to advance the safety of His people. Only our Master knows the nature of every man's heart. His plan is just, Trel."

Trel was shocked. He did not understand why Yeshua had not performed some miracle to peel back the shrouded vision of the guards and set them free as well. Why had He done such things in the Kolosia, but not in the caves? The man in white patted him reassuringly on the shoulder.

"Do not worry, Trel. Our Master is not finished with them yet. Perhaps it is His will that we should meet them again only to save them from themselves."

Trel nodded and let the matter drop. He could only ponder the deep thoughts of life for so long before his head began to spin. If he wanted, he could prop himself in a corner somewhere and question even simple logic until Yeshua came back. That would do no good, he thought and decided to be on his way.

Besides, he had heard of strange men who had taken to this already. Their findings had produced half-senile rantings that made sense to only the most delusional of men. Still, somehow these men had produced a following in some parts and gained great respect. It drove home what the man in white had told Trel. People were so willing to trade the truth for a lie.

Rendolph walked to the center of the group. The orb rose over him, casting its warm light over the worn travelers as they ate and drank. The leader lifted his hands for attention and quiet.

"We are now nearly finished with the leg of this journey that we have begun," he boomed. "Let us gather our things and move on, knowing that Yeshua has guided our path with success. Each man must help those around him. Encourage your sisters and brothers whose strength is weary so that they may not lose heart."

He turned and scooped up Jace in his arms. Everyone clamored to their feet, depleted and drained, but ready to be done with the dark caves. They spread out in the wide tunnel and gathered their efforts for one last push to relative safety and freedom. The orb of light drifted to the lead and they began their march. At first the pace was slow and they glided steadily through the caverns. They passed strange formations of rock that shifted in the light as they went by. The basalt had been replaced by white speckled granite with thick bands of shiny gray that streaked horizontally across its surface. The rock was significantly lighter and lifted the Keepers even as their strained muscles worked to continue.

They passed through a low section of cave where rocks were strewn about them. Alaric and Arthur stood at its narrow exit helping people through. The pace had quickened and the group thinned out as people staggered to keep up. The cool dryness of the caves had grown substantially humid as the path crept slowly through the caves. The tunnel had narrowed once more and warm blasts of air reached the Keepers whose clothes began to fill with sweat. The orb had dimmed considerably and now people could see a shifting light at the far end of the narrow tunnel.

"We are still some distance below the surface," said the man in white at Trel's side. He told their whereabouts with placid narration as he moved quickly over the rocks. "We are now approaching the chasm of the Great River, a tunnel which the Creator has carved of old. The cave's roof is frozen water. It is cooled by the pressure of the earth and transformed into the water table beneath. It is a sight to behold, a marvel which has not yet left the world."

The remote light drew toward them as they ran toward it. Its shifting colors swirled through different hues of white, blue, and green. A slow roar was building in their ears as they approached and the breeze had grown to a forceful wind of water-soaked air that choked the Keepers. They slipped and stumbled on the wet rocks only to be heaved up by the white robed men and urged onward.

Up ahead, Trel could hear shouting over the building roar. As he picked his way over the slippery rock, the tunnel was blocked with Keepers who stood catching their breath. Rendolph had stopped the group and was asking for Lashara. Trel flopped against the wall, sinking to the wet rocks and caught his breath.

While the troop had been running, Jace's consciousness slowly took shape. He opened his eyes to the rhythmic padding of Rendolph's feet. His head sloshed forward toward the darkened tunnel. As his eyes focused, he could see the spinning light at its end coming closer with each breath. He looked up to see the massive form of the white robed figure. The man seemed vaguely familiar to him. His brown hair fell over his smooth face and each breath he took was deliberate yet fast. The imagery was peaceful with the dank air and building noise filling the rest of his mental picture. He rested his head back as Rendolph chanced to look down on him.

"Am I in Par'lael?" he asked through parched lips that seemed strangely out of place in the humid air. It was not the proper question to ask for even if the mysterious bubbling light at the end of the tunnel was the land of His Savior, he was not yet there.

Rendolph halted in mid-stride. His face never showed a hint of fear, sadness, or joy as he laid Jace softly on the rocky surface. He called for Lashara to come forward and then turned back to answer Jace's question.

"Peace, Jace," he said and the command washed away all apprehensions that were beginning to root in Jace's soul. "You have been asleep for over a week and must still your weakened body before we go on."

All sound was blotted out for the moment except for the man's words. Jace could see the shadows of people on the edge of his vision. They must be his loved ones ready to welcome him through the gates into Yeshua's kingdom. He turned to them, his breathing growing fast with anticipation. He could see Alaric and Arthur in the front of the crowd. Others pushed in behind them to look at Jace. He was sure he would recognize them if he chose to look their way, but was content to look on the faces of his two friends. They had been through so much and he cast a smile of relief and happiness at them. They returned his gaze with eyes filled with worry and crowded in around him. The crowd parted and Lashara stepped forward and kneeled next to Jace. Her cool hands ran along his forehead as she studied his face, careful not to look him in the eyes. Streams of fire ran over his body as she tenderly touched his side where the poultice held.

"He is fine," she said woodenly and rose.

The large man crouched down, the red sash on his shoulder draping loosely across his chest. He lifted a waterskin to Jace.

"Drink," he commanded and Jace took several swallows before catching his breath. The cool water pulsed through his body running through every fiber and rejuvenating his spirit. With an extreme effort, he propped himself up on his elbows and took in the caverns for the first time.

"Where am I?" he asked, at a loss for words as he studied the craggy rock. He noticed at last the huddled mass of emaciated Keepers and the hovering blue-white orb above his head. Their faces were dirty and they looked at him through gaunt eyes filled with hope.

Rendolph spoke and as he did, the memories came flooding back to Jace. They flew by him at a rapid pace: Trailaden, the caves, the tavern, the mob, the caged wagon, furious storm, Clonesia, the Imperial Palace, the whippings, the dungeon. At the end of the visions, the Kolosia and all its meaning slammed into him with the full force of a storm: the shouts, soldiers, arrows, swords, the massacre, Blynn, and darkness. He felt like he had been run over by a team of horses and gasped in panic. Rendolph gripped him hard and Jace settled back against the rock.

The man looked Jace in the eyes. With descriptive fashion, he gave a summary of where they were, keeping his voice low so as to calm the frail man. The matter took a short while and the crowd of Keepers that had gathered took up spots to rest as word shifted among them that Jace had finally woken. Relief fell over the group for many had feared that the sole man Rendolph carried in his arms would surely fade from this life to the next. When Rendolph had finished, Jace looked around.

It suddenly hit him how far below the earth they were. The crushing fear that had filled him ever since the Mines of Shorn slowly suffocated his soul. All the associations that he had with such places began to consume his mind with terror. He fought to breathe and clutched Rendolph fiercely. Rendolph held him while Jace buried his face in the man's chest.

"I can't; I can't," he said over and over again as his breathes grew more shallow. The roaring noise in the passageway and the damp air choked him as he squeezed his eyes shut. He could feel the pounding of the rocks around him, mocking his fear and threatening to topple in his world should he flinch away from their prying stares.

"You must, Jace," whispered Rendolph in his ear. "Your friends will not go on without you. You must journey on or they will not continue."

Somewhere behind the group came a piercing cry. It ran through the group and cut through the roar of the low passage. The Keepers turned to each other murmuring their discontent. The men in white looked about them, their hands moving to the hilts of their swords. It came again and somehow the group knew it was closer. Its shrill voice could only have been that of the Watchers.

"Rendolph, the enemy has found us! He has unleashed his dogs to hunt us down even as we near our haven!"

Rendolph looked up at the man over him. Both their faces were calm, but urgency was in their eyes.

"Dispatch a force behind us, Obban. Yeshua has entrusted these into our care, and by His might, we will not lose a single one. Hurry!"

Obban rushed off into the crowd, shouting for others of his kind to follow him. The roof of the cave shook and several fragments of rocks scattered on the ground. The vibrations sent the Keepers into a panic and screams erupted through the crowd as they looked about them in terror. Rendolph motioned for Lashara again.

"Prepare something for Jace," he said quietly. He drew his sword and lifted it over his head. The blade glinted off the light of the orb which pulsed with vengeance. "We must move quickly! Carry the wounded and follow closely!"

Lashara had given Jace something and his body sprawled limply on the floor. Alaric and Arthur grabbed him to his feet and pulled his arms across their shoulders. The roof shook again and the piercing screams howled now as they moved toward the Keepers. Far behind them, the group could see thin shades of darkness swirling down the passageway. The forms swam towards them with frightening speed.

A buzzing sound filled the ears of the Keepers and the orb flashed for them to follow. The crowd sprang into a run, clamoring over the rocks at a maddening pace. They splashed through the puddles at their feet, spraying the walls with a shower of water. Despite the overwhelming chaos, the elderly and wounded were helped by dozens of Keepers and white robed men. The rear guard of Obban's men closed in behind them with their swords drawn and their eyes ever roaming the advancing shadows as they retreated.

The group burst into the next cavern, the sudden light spilling from the ceiling. Its roof was a solid sheet of ice, unbelievably thick and clear as the sky. The depths of the Great River churned above it, painting the giant hall with vivid blue and greenish shades that danced over the walls. Far over the waters, the sun pierced the depths. Giant shapes of unnamable sea creatures blotted out great portions of light and filled the endless cavern with hundreds of shadows. The ceiling dripped with water which ran in rivulets over the smooth flat surface of the cave and emptied at the corners of the room into the water table. In some places the water had left large cone deposits on the floor of the cave which jutted upward like giant teeth. The wind had stilled and the air sat laden with water. The roar that had seemed loud in the tunnel filled the cave.

The Keepers spread out onto the floor of the cavern following the light as it weaved through the rows of stone teeth. The room shook, but the sound was consumed in the turbulence that filled the space. They threaded their way around the stones, followed by the men in white who stepped quickly while taking time to look back. As the Keepers ran, the far edge of the room slowly rolled back and they halted on a sharp precipice overlooking a vast river of churning white. A crystal bridge of ice spanned its width, the broad structure somehow frozen despite the humid temperature of the cavern.

Rendolph lifted his sword waving it high for the Keepers to follow the orb across the river. The crowd sprinted across the bridge slipping and sliding on its surface as they faltered across it. It was long and wide and set low to the raging river, but kept its form and was surprisingly stable. Trel looked back in time to see the Watchers spill out of the passage behind them. Their gray, shapeless forms were translucent shadows that hovered next to the ceiling of ice.

They filled the far side of the cavern, assembling into a roiling swarm of blackness. Trel stiffened at the sight of the Watchers. They looked like some rolling thundercloud that slowly moved forward. He could not begin to count their number. A Keeper tugged on his arm and he pried his eyes off the sight and ran as fast as he could. The group was almost to the far edge of the span now, but as Trel looked back, the loathsome cloud was bubbling towards them.

The mass was slowly overtaking them. The Keeper's faces blanched as the thousands of Watchers that circled overhead drowned out the sound of the river with their high-pitched death-chant. They hung back as the orb blazed away. Some swooped low while Obban and his men swatted at their darting forms.

All the Keepers were across the bridge now and plunged toward the small, thin opening at the far side of the cavern. The Watchers dove at them, coming low and raking the group wantonly with their lifeless claws. Obban and his men spread out waving their weapons high while the Watchers danced away only to cave in on them again.

The group began to separate. Several of the older and more wounded struggled to keep up, their strength spent. Trel ran to help Clarissa who had tripped on her tattered dress. Obban and his men encircled them while the robed men in the forward group drew their weapons. The first group piled through the small doorway, running through the thinly lit passage beyond. The men in white formed a tight barrier around those that had fallen, pointing their blades out as the formless host swirled overhead.

The first group had all disappeared through the narrow passage. Rendolph blocked the doorway, drawing his blade. As the last of the first crowd of Keepers ran through, the pulsing orb stopped and then turned toward the crouching mass of Keepers. Their bodies were flooded over by a growing blackness of Watchers. The orb blazed with fury and shot toward the fallen company. The light burned over the Keepers and the Watchers recoiled, screeching in hatred.

Keepers and white robed men came to their feet and raced toward the tunnel. Even as they did, the orb winked out and the cave was left with what little light came from the water and could be sifted through the boiling cloud of transparent Watchers. They churned and made ready to dive on the small band of Keepers and men in white that eyed the black cloud above them with unflinching weapons.

The moment before they launched their attack, even as they gathered to strike, all sound muffled from the room. The torrential river, the screams of the Watchers, even the breathing of the Keepers faded to nothingness. Trel and Clarissa stopped as did the rest of the Keepers and their escorts. The mass of Watchers hovered about the ceiling of the cave expectantly. Heartbeats passed and nothing happened. The Watchers looked hungrily at the Keepers, their formless shapes chattering away, though no sound came from them. The Keepers backed toward the tunnel slowly, and then ran as the Watchers watched in stunned anger.

The thundercloud moved to strike again and as they did, a shining image exploded through the cavern with white-hot fire. There between the Keepers and Watchers stood a flaming sword, its jeweled hilt pointed menacingly at the Watchers. All along the blade dripped flames of shimmering blue and white fire. The Watchers swirled before the sword fearfully while the last of the Keepers retreated into the passageway one after the other. The men in white followed each of them, lowering their weapons as they strode into the tunnel. Rendolph was the last to leave, eyeing the swarming mass of Watchers disdainfully and then turning down the small passageway.

The blazing sword lowered itself to the threshold of the doorway. Its flames never quenched and its light never dimmed. The mass of Watchers howled in anger at the power of Yeshua. The blade spun on its pommel into a dizzying blur. It meshed into a single form of metal and flame, its image expanding and beating. Finally, its shape shattered into darkness and the Watchers dove toward the doorway even as the light faded.

When the light burned away, the Watchers stopped short, screaming in fury. The sword had been replaced with a smooth obelisk that ran flush with the cavern wall. Its form fit perfect with the passage of the doorway, leaving not the tiniest of gaps for the Watchers to penetrate into the tunnel beyond.

THE KEEPERS STOOD IN THE DARKNESS of the thin passageway directly on the other side of the rock. The terrible screech of the Watchers filled their ears and the walls shook as Sa'vard's servants threw themselves repeatedly against the obelisk in vain. The Keepers stood for a moment breathing shallowly and listening to the horrible cries in the black tunnel. The Watchers shook the walls of the caves and bellowed furiously for several moments while the Keepers held each other closely. At last their cries subsided and the group was left in the silent darkness.

A light was struck up ahead and the yellow glow of a torch filled the tight hallway. The light revealed the Keepers were packed together. Slowly they moved down the passage at Rendolph's command. The tunnel was quiet. No water dripped down its walls. Trel felt the floor of the passage slowly turn upward toward the surface. The hard basalt rock was soon replaced with dark, moist silt on either side. The cool earth filled the Keepers lungs with the dank smell of forested soil. They traveled quietly through the cramped tunnel, climbing ever closer to the surface.

It took them over half a day to reach open air. When they did, the sun was just setting through the forest around them. The lot of them gave long sighs, letting their alleviation show clearly upon their faces. A number of them kissed the leaf-strewn forest floor symbolically, not wiping their lips as they hugged one another in gladness. The celebration lasted until the sun had set and the white robed men were content to prop themselves against a tree trunk, or sit on a rock while the Keepers rejoiced. They followed Bartemus' lead as he broke into song, singing praise to Yeshua for seeing them through to some other land besides the dreaded Clonesian Empire. Their voices weaved through the leaves and carried on the wind to be lost in the wood around them.

After much rejoicing and gentle touches, the Keepers turned to their escort. Rendolph pushed himself off the trunk he had leaned on and brushed his robe. He raised his torch for the party to see him.

"Our Lord has led you through trials you dared not dream possible," he said serenely. A number of Keepers echoed their agreements. "Still, the road leads on. The race is not finished. You must follow me through the night to a place the Master has prepared for us."

The Keepers set their faces. Their time of worship had been a welcome stop, but they knew they must continue on. They joined the men in white, taking the small meal of nourishing bread and satisfying water before they followed the men through the trees.

Judging from the shape of the trees and gentle hills he had seen before the sun set, they were somewhere in the northern part of the Stygian Union. The air was much warmer here than when Trel had left the place. Though there was no hint of blue in the west, there was the slightest trace of cool dampness from the Great Sea on his lips. The forest was far less traveled than the section Trel and his party had come through. He only noted tiny cottage houselights shining far out in the rolling hills as they walked through the trees.

The night sounds of the wood filled the air. These were not as foreign as the lowland noises of the Clonesian Empire. Though they were not in the Gap, much of the animals sounded remarkably akin to those on the high plateau. Trel could hear the low song of the midnight thrush somewhere in a thicket. It was accompanied by the soft whooping of an owl. A thousand crickets chirped their agreement from the hills off to the west. As they moved quietly through the trees, Trel also heard the sound of deer moving through the deep woods, snapping branches and rustling the leaves. It always seemed the farther they were from men, the more in tune nature seemed to be. One day the rift between man and beast would be righted and they would sing in unison to the Almighty.

The night passed slowly, but the Keepers drank it in as if it were all new. Indeed, for Bartemus, it was. Even the night sky was somehow brighter than the bland sunlight of the Clonesian Empire. His ears took in each sound of nature's symphony and each unshackled step was a treasure he kept in his heart. The touch of the trees, the warm breeze, sounds of the leaves, and the general openness of the land all echoed the overwhelming sense of freedom within his soul. The world around him unfolded before his senses, and he walked through the forest in a state of awe.

After an hour, the moon showed itself. Its more than half full shape was low to the horizon and a cloudy orange. The Keepers whispered in astonishment as its beams fell among the branches. The glowing sphere was something many had forgotten in so short a time, and they cast long glances up at the sphere as it rose above the forest. The light cast friendly shadows over the ground and Rendolph extinguished his torch.

He led them all through the night and into the next day. The warm, humid air coming off the Great River was cooled and dried by the forest. They were in no hurry and Rendolph set a mild pace that even the elderly had no trouble keeping. Many of them talked at first, but as the night wore on, they were content to keep to themselves, cherishing their first real taste of liberty and letting the Counselor attend to their spirits. They padded through the woods, a part of the world around them, and the animals only lifted their heads in recognition at the caravan that passed by.

The night seemed to pass quickly. As dawn came, they found themselves trudging through harder lands that were a bit more hilly. Pointed rocks poked their heads through the surface like some giant turtle. Trees clung to them at odd angles, providing a loose canopy that showed plenty of sky. Trel looked back to see the Keepers spread out in a long line over the terrain. They were climbing their way over the rocky surface, making their way steadily up and over the rugged hills of the area. Most of them skittered cautiously around the boulders in their rags. Their bare feet and hands were no match for the jagged, rough land that they found themselves in.

They capped a rise that was fairly clear of trees. Off to the east, the sun was rising over a line of hazy blue. That was all Trel could see of the Great River. The flatlands and Stygian hills gave way to the vast forest they were in. The Stygian Union looked as smooth as a table compared to the robust hills of the North Wood. To the north jutted the Gap Plateau. It was over two days ride away, but its mass dwarfed the land around it. It was flanked far in the west by the white-covered Clonesian Heights. Trel fancied he could see the flat gray stone of the Withering Mountains off to the east. An audible gasp was heard by all as they saw their homeland, and many of their eyes filled with tears of pride and longing.

After several calculations, Trel deduced that they had somehow made miraculous time, passing some 15 leagues through the broken country in the course of one night! All he could do was shake his head. The Maker had once again provided them with uncanny proof of His amazing power. There was now no doubt in his mind that they were safe from the dreaded hunt of the Watchers. A general sense of relief spread over the party as a number of them realized the same.

By midday, they had reached their destination. After the treeless hill, the land dipped again into a gorge that cut north-northwest. The sun was nearing its apex, but the glen kept them cool as they trudged onward. At the end of the ravine, the forest merged into a glade of tall grass dotted with a rainbow of wildflowers that lifted their petals to catch the sun. The party stopped at the edge of the meadow, amazed at what they saw.

A herd of horses roamed over the field, nickering to each other in the cool air and munching grass. Rendolph and his men beckoned for the Keepers to follow, and they made their way toward the horses. Several lifted their heads from the grass and watched the newcomers. One by one, the horses began to move toward the band of people. Their tails were pointed high and they brayed their welcome. As they came closer, they spread out, each moving to their individual master. Trel held his breath as a steed walked his way. Its rusted brown coat and strong frame drifted effortlessly through the grass. The beast gave Trel a gentle stare and nuzzled his head in recognition.

He backed away and looked at the animal, studying his markings. Unmistakably, it was his horse, the very one he had left in Samilon! Wonders never ceased! The Keepers bubbled with excitement as they cried out at their animals. A number of them patted their steed's noses lovingly. Lashara clasped the neck of her white mare in affection. Alaric and Arthur each ran their hands down their warhorses' backs, checking their flanks and hooves for wear. Clarissa and Shereel had matching dappled packhorses that they looked over with fierce pride.

The men in white led them to the far edge of the clearing. In neat piles were spread fresh garments and foodstuffs. The horses led them instinctively to bundles, as if they had been waiting to show their owners some secret thing they had found on their own. Trel let out a cry as he saw his worn leather pack, and mended cloak and clothes. He strapped his short sword to his side and tore the pack open. His pots spilled out in a cacophony of clangs and he looked up with his signature grin at those around him.

No one noticed him as they reached about their goods, lost in amazement that their things that they had given up for gone were back in their possession. Alaric was latching his huge broadsword across his back. He finished strapping his heavy-bladed axe to his side and inspected the two weapons with a critical brow of satisfaction. Lashara was gathering her things in silence. She threw her cloak over her shoulders, covering her tattered shirt and checked her pack. Inside were more of her supplies that had been taken from her in Trailaden. She placed the small leather pouch Rendolph had given her among her other things and sat with a growing smile across her lips.

Trel watched her with relief. The added joy of receiving their lost things over their safe passage from the Clonesian Empire had infused Lashara with a deep sense of contentment. The timid appearance and melancholy shell that had marked her since the dungeons melted away, and she lifted her head with renewed happiness. She lay back, planting her hands in the grass and took in the scenery with the eyes of a child. A smile of finality hung on her lips, which seemed to say that her secret past that she was so ashamed held no power over her now. She closed her eyes, letting the sun drench her fair skin. Her mare nuzzled her face and she opened her eyes and gave her a short laugh. Trel smiled inwardly, thanking Yeshua and knowing that Lashara would be alright.

The Keepers saddled their horses and strapped their goods to the animals. Their faces beamed with something more than hope now, and they chattered to each other excitedly about where they were headed. Several pointed northward to the Gap and their home, looks of hurry and readiness on their faces. They helped each other with their things, making sure all were organized and the weight of their belongings was evenly distributed among their steeds. Finally, all were ready and they turned to Rendolph for their next task. The man stood at the front of the glade, his composure ever reflecting the faithfulness and unchanging attitude of his Master. He eyed the group expectantly and waited until they were all quiet.

"This marks the parting of our paths. We have accomplished the Almighty's plan and led you, His children, out of harm's way. May His name be forever praised for the wonders and great things He has done for you. May you never forget His love, nor cease to call on His name in times of trouble. When hope has failed is when your Father does His most amazing works. Journey homeward now, and may the speed of the Father send you on your way. We must depart, for there are other of His children who need His help and guidance. May you lift them up when you call on Yeshua, knowing that the Almighty will bring them through as He has already done for you."

The men in white gathered around Rendolph. Arthur and Alaric strode forward to offer their gratitude to the white robed figures, but Rendolph shunned them.

"Do not honor us like the heathens who know not the One whom we serve," he said loudly. "We work for the glory of the Most High. If you honor any, honor Him."

With that, the white soldiers stepped back. They looked at the Keepers with tranquility, knowing that their Lord's Chosen were momentarily safe from Sa'vard's grasp. The men stood close together, their robes catching the full light of the sun. As the Keepers looked on, their forms began to glow. The light around them began to twinkle and swirl as if the air had turned to liquid. The forms of the men distorted through the light, growing bright until only the dancing, glistening air could be seen. When it subsided, the white robed men were gone. A sound of mighty wings pushing through the air filled the Keepers ears, but as they looked about, the meadow was empty except for themselves.

21

TROUBLE BREWING

They stood for some time in silence. None dared to interrupt the moment, for fear they would spoil the silence. The loss of the men in white affected them deeply. Several of them stared with dumbfounded expressions as the shimmering dissipated and the scene around them turned boringly normal. They each pondered all the actions and miracles they had witnessed. Their wariness of their protector-guides had been replaced with a growing dependence through their journey, and now the Keepers found themselves painfully alone.

The situation seemed awkward at best. None of them figured their companionship with the host of the Most High to end so abruptly. Something seemed to be torn from their vicinity which could not be replaced by earthly means. It was not their guardians, but rather the Being they represented. The men in white were servants of the Almighty, Yeshua's Father, and a clear sign of the unending love that the Father had for His Chosen. Their departure somehow lengthened the link between Par'lael and their world.

Arthur turned around. He had traded his prisoner's rags for a long shirt of silver chainmail that hung to mid-thigh. Woolen breeches covered his legs and black deerskin riding boots were on his feet. His leather gauntlets were pulled over two bright metal cuffs that circled his wrists. A giant broadsword was thrown over his back, and he carried a javelin in his left hand. His face was covered by a steel helm that hung low across the eyes with a flat noseguard separating his features. His appearance had totally changed from when Trel had seen him in the Kolosia. He faced the group with a stern grimace, his figure emanating superb strength. The words he spoke came from years of hardship, but they were also laced with heart and conviction.

"Friends," he said loudly, "nothing has changed. Though Yeshua's host has vanished from our sight, our Lord is still at work about the world. I count it an honor that He would bless me with the ability to see His mighty hand at work in so intricate a fashion within my life. I will not let the legacy of our fallen comrades go for naught, nor will I allow Yeshua's efforts to guard my soul go unrepaid. He has sealed me, and so do I owe Him all the days that lie before me. Let us ride, then to our home and see how we may serve the Almighty there and bring glory to Yeshua for all He has done for us."

With that, he swung atop his charger and raised his javelin, wheeling his mount and pointing north to the Gap Plateau that loomed over the trees.

"Onward to home!" he cried and spurred his steed into the forest.

The Keepers climbed up their horses and followed Arthur into the woods. Their spirits were high and they urged their beasts forward, their excitement rising as they neared the border of their home. The land was rough and they cut through many a stream and around craggy hills in search of a path. Alaric rode beside Arthur and the two consulted with Clarissa and Shereel over the direction and quickest way to true north.

The sisters would take turns scouting ahead of the party. Their light packhorses coupled with their shepherdess skills made them excellent trackers. The caravan moved onward, their progress only hindered by the lay of the land. The going was slow and more than once they had to lead their mounts over the unforgiving terrain by foot. A number of trees blocked their path, their dead masses sprawling out over the ground. Loose rocks provided poor footing and the sloping hills grew steep and unrelenting. The party stayed to their task, keeping quiet and moving along despite the obstacles that popped out at them around every corner.

Jace lagged at the rear keeping to himself and mulling over various thoughts and stages of the journey. He was extremely weak from the awful fight with Blynn. Still, he was strong enough to mount and ride the steed Hadran had given him at East Haven. He rubbed his wounds half-heartedly as he recounted his foggy memories. The flight to the Great River was a blur. Lashara's potions and his wounds made the memory of the trek spotty. He remembered bits and pieces of the dark caves—the Watchers, the crystal bridge, and Rendolph carrying his broken body. The fragments formed some macabre memory that made little sense. He stowed the images away and went on to deeper things.

Unlike his friends, his mood had turned sour. As they drew closer to home, his thoughts turned more and more to all the aspects of his failed journey he had passed through. How would he explain to the Council how he had lost Rae? How could he look into the eyes of his family and tell them that his brother had made the choice to leave them and Yeshua for his own personal follies? The underlying turmoil that filled his soul was a private anguish that he shared with no one.

That night, they settled down, and while many of the party fell right to sleep, Jace lay awake, alone with his questions and hurts. He leaned against a skinny birch and nestled his backside into a wedge between two roots. His sadness at the loss of his brother was only matched by his bitterness toward Blynn. The dirty, pale man was everything Jace had come to despise. All the arguments that were contrary to Yeshua's teaching were wrapped up in the traitor. His acceptance to willingly turn away from Yeshua and spurn the safety of others for his own selfish motives was hauntingly similar to his brother's own decisions. Both of them went against everything Jace had grown to believe.

Furthermore, Blynn had played off Jace's faults and used Jace's pride to lure him out into the open. He had flaunted his abilities to all and used his knowledge to assert his station and power within their small party. Blynn had toyed with him in the forest and arrogantly proved that Jace was no match for him in a solitary duel. His actions of cunning and deceit had maligned the image of what a Keeper should be from Nadir to Trailaden. He had betrayed the Keepers with an unmatched petulance that showed no regard for their lives or Yeshua, and sided with the Clonesians and Sa'vard without remorse. He had taken the affection that Jace had for Lashara and used it to whip Jace into a deep-seated anger. All his subtle efforts had poked and prodded Jace down a path of Sa'vard's choosing that he had not seen until after it was all said and done. The man had goaded him into finally accepting his unspoken challenge and nearly taken his life in the process.

For some unknown reason, the outcome had hurt Jace deeply. Personally, he had been bested by Blynn in every way and on every level. Physically, Blynn had quelled him, nullified his attacks, and nearly killed him. Emotionally, he had used Jace's feelings to launch him down a path toward his own demise. Spiritually, he had given in to Blynn's demands and shirked Yeshua's commands. The facts had left Jace ashamed and despondently bitter. He stewed as the night continued, content to take all consequences of the mistakes personally and hiding his embarrassment and shame. Instead of going to his friends and apologizing to them for his wayward actions that lead them to the Kolosia, asking their forgiveness for his lack of self-control, thanking them for their kindness, and offering his need for support and comfort, he chose to isolate himself as a means of punishment, allowing his emotional and spiritual wounds to fester.

He had sold himself on the belief that good would always conquer evil on every occasion. Since Blynn was inherently evil, as best as he could tell, he argued that he would most certainly emerge victorious if he confronted him. The fact that he had lost had shaken his foundational theory. He refused to accept solace for his defeat, but knew deep down that this belief had been flawed from the beginning.

He sat staring into the darkness as he continued pondering. It was Dorath's fault. Jace had trusted him as if he were his own father. His overly accepting Mentor had been fooled by Blynn and carelessly vouched for the man, putting the entire party at risk. On the other hand, maybe Dorath had not been fooled. Surely Jace's Mentor was wise enough to see behind Blynn's façade. Then again, perhaps his laziness and assumptions had been a large reason for the disaster of their journey. It was Dorath's fault that he had not paid closer attention and scrutinized Blynn further on his loyalties.

Instead, he had sent Jace and his group merrily into the Clonesian Empire on the wings of a harpy. Their mission was doomed from the beginning. Dorath's simplemindedness and lack of probing had basically handed Jace, Lashara, Trel, Alaric, and every other Keeper in the Clonesian Empire over to Sa'vard before their journey began.

Jace bubbled over with fury. If ever he were to meet his one-time Mentor again, he would rectify the situation permanently. He would bring Dorath before the Council, strip him of all his honors and parade him before all the pupils of East Haven to voice how he had grieved Jace and caused him to suffer because he failed to look fully into Blynn's dark soul. Jace hid these thoughts deep within him, letting them ooze into his bitterness as a salve to replace his shame.

The morning found him propped up against the same tree he had sat near when the sun set. The party slowly came alive as the bright morning sun peeked its head over the trees and down into the hollow space they had holed up in overnight.

Trel shot up, flipping off his cloak. The air had been cool for a summer night, but it was not cold enough for the man to huddle underneath layers of clothing. Trel's actions agitated Jace for some reason, and he eyed his friend haughtily as he began rummaging through his packs. Once again, he spilled his pans out across the campsite, not caring to look up from his work despite the groans of those who fought for those few precious moments of sleep before the day began in earnest. Trel began sorting his army of pots and pans in a neat row near the crackling fire.

Shereel had tended the blaze most of the night and sat on the opposite side scrutinizing Trel dubiously as he scrambled back and forth. The thin man dipped into his packs and pulled out a handsome salted pork butt of substantial size. Five grand loaves of crusted bread were removed and laid on a blanket far enough away to keep the ashes from blowing over them. Trel went to work, depositing the meat in a cast-iron pot. He snatched the bubbling kettle that was over the fire and poured nearly all of the hot water out of it and into his pot. He then laid the empty kettle on the ground and pulled up the pot onto the stand over the fire with both hands. It was heavy and a fair amount of water sloshed on the hot coals, much to Shereel's dismay. She cast a glowering look of disapproval at him, and he returned it with a sly wink, turning his attention back to his meat.

Trel stood back and watched the liquid settle. Soon a thin film of salty foam rose to the surface of the pot and wisps of heated vapor swirled over the water. Trel placed a lid over the container and went about stowing his other pans into his packs.

The scent of the meat soon filled the camp. Men and women alike licked their lips as they went about readying their gear for the day's ride. Many of them had traded their clothes for sturdier garments they had found in the glade yesterday. They paraded about the clearing like a small settlement amidst the forest. Jace sniffed at them. They seemed so content and in their element whereas they had been fearful to the point of tears only days before in the Kolosia. He watched them from his alcove in the tree with a smug look and a frown.

Most, if not all of them were dressed well. Their clothes were not flaring or boisterous with color like the merchants of Nadir, but subdued and hardy like the Gap itself. The band of Keepers marched about in muted shades of gray, tan, and a curious dull blue. Though the fabrics boasted no outward attraction, they were high-quality nonetheless. Arthur's brilliant chainmail shirt stood out loudly against the somber array of colors.

Only Bartemus was left in his filthy rags. Since he had never been beyond the Clonesian Empire, no other clothes were waiting for him when the troop had entered the meadow. He did not show any sign of remorse and marched about the camp with a large smile that showed through his grizzly carpet of whiskers. All clapped him on the back and the women gave him many a brotherly peck on the cheek. He was well known now for the melodies that flowed from his lips without end in all occasions, giving thanks to Yeshua. The group had all heard his story—his meeting with Alaric, Lashara, and Trel—and had befriended the happy fellow as if he were family. Indeed he was.

Jace watched all this from his sullen corner. Finally, he propped himself up from the tree and made his way into the crowd. It was time he got on with the day, no matter how much he loathed it. He limped to his things and pulled a fresh set of clothes from out of his pack, latched it closed and turned away. Seeing the scraggly head over by the horses, he went up and tapped the man on the shoulder.

Bartemus turned around and jumped, taken aback by Jace's height. The man was smaller than a women and thinner than Trel. Jace's lanky frame made him look like a child and he stared up at Jace with his lazy eye giving him a quizzical look. Jace towered over him.

"Here," he said, thrusting the clean clothes at the little man. Bartemus looked first at the clothes and then back at Jace.

"You can wear them, if you'd like," he said shortly.

The man cocked his head to one side and then his face peeled back into his huge smile through his grizzly beard. He took the neatly folded clothes softly as if they were fragile to the touch. His eyes drank in the gray woven wool as if it were made of pure gold. When he looked back at Jace, his lips were trembling, and he flung his arms around him tightly in a thankful embrace.

Jace let out a howl. He staggered to his side, lifting his shirt and touching the poultice. The wound was soft and burned underneath his skin. He turned to Bartemus, his brow knitted, but then erased his anger as the man flinched away.

The poor man was most likely thrashed for doing something like that back among the Clonesians, he thought and softened his features. Bartemus came closer, kneeling to the ground and sniveled a line of apologies. The man was on the verge of tears, his fear rising up within him. Jace put his hand on the man's head reassuringly.

"I'm fine," he grumbled. Bartemus came to his feet still giving Jace a questionable stare, but Jace reassured him again. The man patted him gently, bowed low, and thanked Jace for his gift before darting into the crowd.

When Jace turned to leave, Lashara stood in his way. Her back was hunched slightly, and she looked away in disgrace. She flicked her eyes at him and then moved close, reaching her hands out to check the wound. Her cool fingers touched around his side and he winced slightly as she poked at his ribs. He waited woodenly while she probed his cut. Finally, he backed away.

"I'm fine," he said again, but as she moved to make a closer inspection, he put his hand out to stop her and stalked off. Lashara watched him leave with a look of longing and pity and then went back to her work.

Alaric and Arthur watched the exchange. They had been monitoring Jace over the previous days, making sure that he had not suffered any harm. They had not overlooked the lack of carefree attitude that was his trademark, nor his introverted behavior and laconic communication. Trel had approached them several times of his worry for his friend, and they made it a point to have him watched by one of the party every day. They knew he was hiding something deep within and waited, hoping he would share it with the rest of them.

Lashara was also a concern of no small importance. Others besides Trel had noted the return of her shyness and many were troubled by her timid actions. They had hoped her spirits would improve with her responsibility for Jace's cuts, but whenever she was around him she grew quiet and rigid. She had been happy to see her horse and overwhelmed that her priceless herbs had been saved from harm's way. For the most part she was notably relaxed, but quite the opposite whenever she attended Jace.

The smell of the pork said it was done, and the Keepers circled around the fire as Trel put the finishing touches to the meal. He had added some beans he had soaked the night before to the mixture, and the smells fused together into a harmonious scent that set the mouth watering. They waited expectantly while he stirred the pot and tasted the beans to see if they were finished. He smacked his lips while everyone watched, embellishing his motions and dramatizing it as best he could. He paused then and looked into the air, working something out in his head and then frowned and put the lid back on the pot. Everyone fumed and some threw up their hands knowing they would have to wait just a little longer for the meal. Trel lowered his head and snickered to himself. Something had gotten into him since the Kolosia. For some odd reason, in a childish sort of way, he had come to secretly enjoy keeping people's desires hostage until the last possible moment.

When the meal was ready, the Keepers formed a line and Trel filled their mugs to the top and cut them a large piece of bread. The line went slow and he asked Shereel to help him hurry the group along. She took the ladle and then gave Trel a long, flat stare when he removed it from her hand and gingerly placed the knife in it instead. She paused and then settled herself in front of the bread and began hacking away at it. Apparently, Trel's commandeering of the cooking had touched a nerve in the older woman, but he didn't seem to notice.

The meal was scrumptious and only a few had room for seconds. There were less than three ladles of beans and meat left and Trel mixed this in with the horse feed and gave it to a beautiful sorrel mare at random. The horse licked the pot clean, blinking peacefully at Trel while he rubbed her muzzle. Afterwards, he asked Arthur and Alaric to clean up. The two were more than willing to help the young cook. They looked rather silly—Arthur in his chainmail and Alaric in his burly leather riding vest —as they cleaned out the pots and folded up Trel's blanket. The work went quickly and by the time they were finished, everyone else was ready to leave.

They saddled up and disappeared into the woods. Clarrisa had found a deer trail earlier that morning, and they spread out in a single file along its path. The trail curled through the woods, which were ominously quiet. They rode on for the better part of an hour weaving through the trees. The soft trail beneath them was void of twigs and branches, and the horses made only a low drum on the earth.

A superb acrid stench crept up their nostrils through the trees as the land to the west of them began to dip away. The forest thinned out and they could see over a vast area of low-lying swamps. Clumps of weeds and islands separated the myriad shallow waterways and channels. Lone cypress trees dotted the swamp here and there. The wetland stretched all the way to the base of the Gap and vanished in the west at the foot of the Clonesian Heights. Even this late in the morning, a thin cloud of mist hovered over the moist region.

It was alive with all kinds of creatures. The insects and frogs sang loudly in the late morning, welcoming the heat. Their buzzing drifted into the forest, providing the only noise in these parts. As Jace looked out over the marsh, he could see giant birds flapping their wings while they skimmed the tall grass looking for food. They would travel over the water, alighting on the nearest tree, scattering others of their kind and look over their new domain from the high perch. The view looked miserable to Jace, if only because of his despondent attitude. Some of the party, besides Bartemus, had never seen a swamp and looked on the putrid, unmoving water with awe.

Arthur brought the group to a halt and summoned Shereel and Clarissa close to him and Alaric. They looked out over the swamp and whispered to each other in low voices. Alaric and the sisters were pointing off into the lowlands while Arthur was shaking his head adamantly and motioning at the trees. His hands moved in a wide arc, but Clarissa and Shereel watched him with quiet, accusing eyes. At last the four of them separated and spoke to the group.

"It is plain that we are nearly home," said Arthur loudly. The Keepers bristled excitedly as he went on. "From here, we will cross through the Lars Swamp. This area is known to some of us and should find us through in a hurry. We must stay close, following the horse in front of us with great care. There are no creatures here to have a worry for, but one wrong step could plunge a steed into the water or get them stuck in the thick silt beneath. If this happens, the animal is as good as dead. There is no way to pry it loose once the swamp has lodged its hold. Have a care."

He gave one last look at the North Wood and nudged his mount to a walk down the steady grade toward the swamp. Shereel and Clarissa fanned out in front of him eyeing the tall grass for the best possible route to begin. Their eyes were well trained and could see some distance even through the haze that hung over the marshland. The party slowed while they examined the swamps. All creatures near them had suddenly cut off their fervent singing and only the sound of the wetland symphony could be heard in the deep interior of the grass.

Shereel gave a low whistle to Clarissa, signalled slightly with her hands, and kicked her steed down the slope and into the grass. Clarissa followed her at a canter and the party stepped up to a trot at Arthur's command. The grass was dotted with low shrubs and stunted pines and oaks, but soon they crossed the last of the trees. From there on out, the ground began to get progressively spongy. The horses hooves began to make a sucking sound with each step, and several of them wobbled unsteadily and rolled their eyes at the shifting terrain.

Jace hung his head, watching the horse in front of him. Pools of water began to fill the hoof prints as they walked. The mounted Keepers easily trampled the ground around them and by the time the last one past, the horses had blazed a trail through the swarthy grass. Only the occasional gentle cry of the huge birds echoing through the background noise of the swamps broke the monotony. The awful stench of the weeds and soil filled the party's noses with its full force as they went deeper into the swamps. Ever so slowly, the sun began to burn away the fog of the swamp. The land provided no shade and the air filled with a suffocating humidity as the sun beat down on them. Jace set his shoulders and sighed. It was going to be a very long day.

He had heard Clarissa mention to Trel that they might come this way. Trel had seemed dismayed, but Clarissa was rather exuberant at the prospect. Her voice had filled with a chattery excitement as she told about the swamps.

"It's rather a beautiful place, Trel," she commented lightly. "It is, in fact, a broken tributary from the Great River that empties into no single body of water. Instead, the water seeps through the ground into the water table. It takes a while getting used to, but it's actually a very peaceful place. My father would take Shereel and I down from the highlands and we would fish the narrow channels at the edge of the Gap. They're filled with all sorts of small fish and some can grow quite large. I'll admit the water's a little bit deeper there, and the smell is a little less pungent, but it gives you the same effect."

Trel grunted his thrill at seeing the place.

"Oh stop it," she said, patting Trel on the arm with a smile. "There's also a hidden secret to the Lars Swamp. The Elders told me Yeshua created the place to deter the Clonesians from ever entering the Gap. Everyone knows that it separates the Gap from the Great River. Stygians are immobile; they don't take the time to go around such obstacles. Emblom thinks the world stops at the North Wood, but there have been rumors of people trying to follow Keepers into the Gap. Some of that's foo-foo anyway: it doesn't matter how well you know someone, only Keepers live in the Gap. Everyone else who's tried to live there without Yeshua's blessing has up and moved before the change of a season."

"Still," she said, putting a finger to her lips and returning to her point, "the swamp was created to keep people out of the Gap. It's Yeshua's way of protecting us from the countries that wish to destroy His people." Her face turned dark and she lowered her voice. "A number of Clonesians have said how, if it weren't for the Lars Swamp, they would have crossed the Great River and crushed the Gap centuries ago. To mount an organized assault through the swamp or the North Wood has been beyond Clonesian logistics. These are the reasons Yeshua put them there and that is the reason I will never stop thanking Him for such a place."

Trel let the conversation dwindle and then changed the subject. The argument sounded credible, though Hadran or Dorath had never told Jace of it. Jace sniffed at the thought of his gullible Mentor and then thought more about the swamp. What Clarissa said did make sense. Jace sighed. Despite his misgivings, he had to admit that the Lars Swamp was necessary for the safety of the Gap. He looked off into the marsh as the day went by.

Huge flies came out during the afternoon. They buzzed the Keepers faces and bit more than one person about their arms and neck. They seemed to enjoy the heat and flew in large groups over the tall grass. Jace had been told that bugs were too small to have a mind of their own, but the flies attacked the Keepers with a zealous, concerted effort he had not seen in so small an animal. The Keepers and their horses seemed to make too large a target for the swarm to pass up. Their large wings made a frightful noise as they landed on their prey. They could bite through the thinner garments and wasted no time showing the demoralized group they could do so.

Finally, Shereel stopped the party. A number of them let out murmurs to keep going, but she paid them no heed, jumped down from her horse and moved close to the nearest channel. While the group watched, she hiked up her dress, trudged out into the water up to her knees, and thrust her hand below the still surface. She pulled a large clump of firm clay from the channel and began breaking it apart. Smearing it over her hands and face, she walked back to the Keepers. The smell of the dirt was overpowering and several of the Keepers flung their cloaks about their faces and pulled their horses away.

"The swarms are attracted to our scent," she said in a voice like iron. "The mud covers up our fragrance and keeps the flies off the skin."

Finishing her short explanation, she turned around and started lathering her horse with the awful smelling silt. One by one, the group dismounted from their horses and started doing the same. The stench was almost unbearable, but as they rubbed it into their pores and covered themselves—many from head to toe—its power began to lose its effect. Almost immediately the flies retreated to the tall grass and the Keepers never had much trouble with them again. They climbed up onto their horses when they had finished and moved deeper into the swamp.

The vultures watched the caravan move slowly through their territory. The peculiar mud-covered figures with their two arms, six legs, and two heads did not look appetizing enough for a closer look and they ignored them the rest of their journey. In fact, the swamp itself seemed to accept the Keepers atop their horses as another one of its dejected inhabitants. The large, unearthly flies hovered about them, landing on their mud-laden clothes every now and then, but never biting. They seemed more curious than anything. The rich silt truly covered up their smell with its own, and the frogs and insects continued to sing until the Keepers were directly on top of them.

Only the sun bothered them now. Its golden light scorched the party as they picked their way ever so slowly through the swamp. The buzzing of the insects heightened as the day went on, mimicking the humid furnace. The air was so water-laden it was nearly unbreathable. The clothes of the Keepers were soaked through by midday. They had to stop every hour to smear more mud on their skin and their horses. Several of them, despite drinking their fair share of water, swayed in exhaustion on their saddles. Shereel made them stop while she and Lashara tended the elderly, making sure their aged bodies were surviving the thick heat as they went. The going was laborious and they lost all sense of time and direction in the monotonous landscape.

By sunset the group was over halfway through the swamp. They slumped from their saddles and stumbled over the soft earth as they settled in for the evening. Many of them were too tired to help. In all honesty, the group only picketed their horses, ate a short meal of dried meat and bread, and rapped themselves in their cloaks as they went to bed. They were sick of the swamp and only Clarissa and a few others stayed up in the heavy heat, listening to the night sounds and counting the stars.

Shereel sat next to Arthur and Alaric. It had been her decision to enter the swamps. Only her firm persuasion had kept them from traveling the rest of the way through the

North Wood. The route would have been shorter, but it was steeper and not suitable for the elderly and injured. She did not like the idea of trouncing through the woods directly through the Gap. Maybe it was her heightened sense of caution from living in the Clonesian Empire, but she felt the need to throw off any would-be pursuers from their course. She had been followed before and though her sister felt the rumors were "foo-foo" as she put it, they both had seen what a little extra prudence could do for their safety. She was not willing to subject herself, nor the others, to false protection when simple measures could be taken to provide it.

The swamp would take care of all that. Whereas forests were accepting of nearly every individual, most people found it repulsive to even enter Lars Swamp. Few, if any journeyed through it. The stench that loomed about the place was only suitable for the most down-trodden of persons and the nabbing flies were a constant menace to those who would not smother themselves in the filth from the bottom of the water. Their decision may have cost them an extra day, but it would all but guarantee that they remained unmolested from outsiders. The last thing they needed was to be captured again.

Jace's sleep was fitful. All day long, he had kept to himself. People seemed to recognize his somber mood and only Lashara bothered him to check on his wounds. He let her do her business without putting up a fight, but he did not talk and only murmured his thanks when she was done. For some reason, she would not look him in the eyes, but he only noted it in passing. The woman would have to deal with her own problems. Whatever pain she had, it was nothing compared to his.

He knew he had to speak to her or someone for that matter. Something inside of him told him it was no good for him to bottle up his anger and resentment for so long. He thought constantly of the botched mission, his personal failure to restore Rae to Yeshua, the public defeat at the hands of Blynn, and Dorath's betrayal. The memories made his mood dark and he paid little attention to anyone else, even Lashara.

Every time she came around, he tried to work himself up to talk to her. He would cast short glances at her while she checked the poultice, reapplying it if need be. Every now and then their eyes would meet and both of them would turn away quickly. He knew he should say something, but did not know how to begin. Try as he may, he could not work through his ocean of consuming feelings. An awful lump would form in his throat, and he found his mind would turn as mushy as the soil beneath his feet. Instead of opening up, he found it easier to keep quiet and wallow inside himself.

No, it was not good, but there was a certain comfort that went into his solitary struggle. As long as people knew there was something wrong with him, but never its full extent, he felt safe. It was better for them to know he was upset than for him to lay bare all his rage, malice, grief, and hurt that was slowly consuming his soul. *They would surely reject me if they knew how bitter I was*, he thought to himself. *Conduct unbecoming a Keeper,* he mused with a facetious grin.

Lashara slept no easier. Her journey was clearly different from anyone else's. No one had the awful scar to bear that told of the shameful existence of being a former slave. She had kept it hidden from so many for so long. Only Miss Pell had fully known her origins. The old lady had seen them by chance one night as they made their way to the Gap. That was before her vision had gone and she had questioned Lashara with honesty and love. When discovered, Lashara hid her head in shame. Miss Peel touched her back comfortingly.

"There is nothing to be ashamed of, child," she said. Love and sorrow poured out through her voice as she tried to comprehend what the girl must have been feeling. "The mark on your skin is not on your soul. We were all slaves once: slaves to our own desires and selfish attitudes. Just remember that if any should take to ridiculing you of your past. Your mark is a symbol of where you have been, not who you are. Now you are alive in Yeshua, free from the bonds of slavery both within and without! There is no reason for you to be shameful of such a thing!"

The old lady always made Lashara feel like she was worth the world. Miss Pell never called the ugly scar a brand, and this somehow alleviated most of the trauma that went along with it. Only because of her actions did Lashara have any confidence in herself. Over the years, their bond had grown until the two were as close as a mother and child, but no one else in the Gap knew of her shame. For her to be exposed in public and paraded before the Clonesians and the Keepers for her heritage was more than she could bare. In that moment, all the memories of her former life had returned to her.

The lord of the manor had not been nice to her and her family. He took most of their food that they produced with their hands, leaving them with only a fifth of their produce. It was a wonder their family had survived.

Lashara's family was almost always behind in their production, and their master would take it out on them physically. Her mother adored Lashara and the master knew this. He would beat her within breaths of her short life and leave her for dead in the manor courtyard while her mother and father would huddle around her to see if she was still alive. The punishment was without end and the master found any excuse to attack the helpless child. He would admonish her in public, heaping the wrongs of her whole family upon the little girl.

Of all the punishments, he never hit her above the shoulders. He claimed she had the most beautiful face and reminded her parents on occasion that he had the power to sell her for a hefty price if they did not meet his demands.

At nights, the master would come looking for her after he had filled himself with more ale than any man should have. He would invite the child to spend the night within his house to the horror of her family. Lashara would be returned the following day with a blank stare and say nothing. When her parents touched her, she would flinch away. No one dared ask her about what had happened, and she pushed the memories as far from her as any child could.

The worst of it was the eternal circle of it all. Lashara had been trapped in a life of slavery with no means of escape. When Miss Pell came, she had lied to the poor woman and stowed away in the lady's wagon as she left for the Gap. When the woman had found her, she pleaded with her not to send her back. The following night, Miss Pell had seen the mark on Lashara's back. That had all but sealed her fate and Miss Pell had whisked her away from her nightmarish ordeal to the safety of the Gap. She had given her heart and soul to Yeshua the day they had crossed the Gap border, and her origins had been her and the old lady's secret ever since.

It was true what Blynn had said then, though he had placed the blame on the wrong people. Any person in their right mind would not have faulted Miss Pell for what she had done, except for the Clonesians and slave traders. They were always concerned about their precious laws, materials, and wealth instead of the person. When Blynn had touched her, she could feel the touch of her former master reach out from her dark past through the years of all her freedom. The situation had left her cold and lifeless. Only the rejuvenating walk with the Lord's host, the return of her things, and the promise of returning to the Gap and Miss Pell had provided a seed of hope in her soul that had been numbed by the sudden memories.

Over the days it had stifled all guilt she had of her past, except whenever she was in Jace's presence. His flat stares and cool demeanor were easy to read. He became wooden to her touch. The hints in his body language were obvious in their meaning. She did not fault the man for shunning her. It is what she thought would happen if anyone found out her past.

It hurt nonetheless. There had been a fondness between them that had the potential for something more. Now, that was replaced with sadness and left an empty hole in her being that none of the other Keepers could fill.

Jace was the only one in the party that she had grown comfortable with. The lack of his friendship and his blatant decisions to ignore her again and again cut her to the core. She only wished he would flush out his thoughts to her and be done with it instead of acting like she didn't exist. He had no idea what she had gone through or what he was putting her through.

The next day was only worse. As if it couldn't get hotter, the sun proved them wrong. There was no mist for the heat to burn off. Instead, the beetles and crickets began singing their song at the first hint of daylight. There was some large bug which gave off a horrendous buzzing while the day marched on. Clarissa had told Trel that the sound always hinted that the day would be downright grievous. She was right. Even the mud burned as the party lathered down their bodies. Many of their clothes had not dried from the previous day and they began to weigh down on their bodies. The air above the swamp rippled with heat.

There was not the slightest stirring of air to soothe the Keepers who were exhausted even before they swung up onto their saddles. Many slumped on their horses, laying across their backs and guiding them with little care for their safety. Arthur and Alaric had to ride back constantly and encourage them to keep alert and fight off their weakness. The advice seemed hollow, but somehow they made it through the day.

On the second morning in the swamps, they reached the edge of the Gap. The party was tired beyond measure and only mumbled their relief at passing through the two-day sauna. It was as Clarissa had described. The grass was taller here, no doubt due to the deeper waters. The air seemed dryer, if only from the fact that they were out of the midst of the swamp. A cool breeze rolled down from the Gap and flowed through the party. The air seemed refreshingly light and smelled subtly sweet.

On the outskirts of the swamp, they came to a winding path that cut through the plateau's side. After feeding their horses and themselves, they attacked the slope with added fervor. There was no place to stop along this side of the Gap and once they began, they continued on to the top. It took them well into the afternoon to crest the top, and once they were there, they were met with an unexpected surprise.

The Feeding Plain spread out before them, its flat, lush grass dotted by herds of horses, cattle, and sheep. The air here was noticeably cooler—not parched, but not stuffy and humid either. It still shimmered with the heat of summer. The sun, though bright, touched the earth with a dry heat that was not the least bit leeching like the Lars Swamp. The view was phenomenal. Out of all the places the group had been, their hearts calmed with a certain awe as they looked on the land in which Yeshua had called them to live.

The view was broken by a strange line of tall posts that ran east to west across the plain. White strips of linen were attached to their tops and fluttered in the warm breeze.

The wind blew through chimes that were draped on a taut rope that ran to each stake. The sounds that came from them were light and fleeting, but Arthur, Alaric, Shereel and a number of the older Keepers looked at them with grave faces.

Shereel and Arthur kicked their horses up to the row of posts. They each gave a long frown at the objects as they examined them. Shereel circled her horse around one of the posts and stepped back, looking down the line. Arthur rode close to one, stood in his stirrups and pulled the linen off one of the poles. He rode up to Shereel and handed it to her. She turned it over in her hands and the two conferred with each other softly. Their faces were grim and they stood away from the group so none could catch their words. All of them waited in silence—the summer breeze and the breathy jingle of the chimes were the only sounds that came from the windswept plain.

Finally, Arthur and Shereel brought their horses forward. Their faces were set and the two rode directly through the crowd to Jace who sat looking at the grass pensively.

"Do you know what this means?" asked Arthur, his voice laced with fear as he gave Jace the cloth.

Jace blinked at the big man and took the fine strip of linen. There was nothing unique about the fabric. It looked well made, as if it belonged in the grand hall of a fine noble instead of attached to a post in the middle of the Feeding Plain. No markings were on the cloth and its texture was that of common linen. Jace could find no hidden meaning in the object and handed it back to Arthur, shaking his head.

"We need to speak with your father and mother," boomed Arthur. There was a heavy look about his eyes, and the words carried with them a multitude of hidden meanings. He drew his charger close to Jace. "It is very urgent."

Jace jut his lower lip out in pensive contemplation. He had been wrapped in his own sullen thoughts while the troop had traveled up the plateau and was paying little attention to what was going on. He did not see any danger in telling the man the whereabouts of his home. He raised his hand to the east, pointing it low over the grassy flatlands. Arthur looked hard at Jace and then gave a quick nod and whirled his great horse about, pulling it up on its hind legs.

"There has been a Calling!" he bellowed to all. A number of them gave a collective gasp. "Many of you know what that means. We ask those who don't know to ride with us, and those that do to make for their homes. We must ride harder still for time is not on our side!"

He raised a short war horn from his chest and brought it to his mouth. Three sharp blasts he gave from the horn and then kicked his steed into a gallop. The party separated in confusion as many of them split off in numerous directions and others followed Shereel and Arthur. Several of them were riding hard straight out into the plain, their bodies bouncing around as they fought to keep on their saddles. The herds of deer and cattle separated before the Keepers as they dashed out onto the flatlands. Jace saw many elderly riders and injured men and women also flogging their horses as fast as they would go. At least 30 of them spread out onto the plain, going a number of places. Some turned their steeds to the Western Highlands, others rode toward Dreffen and the Lambling River and a few pointed towards the headwaters of the Furbice and to Aider. Jace turned his steed as the group disintegrated. He could see none of his party and stood there for a moment, removed from his surroundings.

"Jace! Move!"

He spun around while Alaric and Trel called to him as they darted by on their horses.

They were bent low in the saddle and galloped eastward after Shereel and Arthur. Jace knitted his brows and frowned at his friends. He twisted his face in determination and slapped his mare hard. She jumped into a run, nearly throwing Jace from her back. He clenched his jaw as the jolt sent pains through his wound and his cracked ribs. He grabbed the reins of his horse and followed behind his friends as ten or fifteen of them stretched out in a thin line moving eastward.

The dispersion of the Keepers had taken only moments and now they split apart into small groups as the sun fled to the horizon. Jace lost sight of the Keepers that were moving north. He clutched his reins and hugged the horse with his legs. The Feeding Plain was perfect for fast travel. The Keepers and their mounts sped across the ground making great time. When the sun had dipped behind the Clonesian Heights and the shadows melded into one another, Alaric stopped the small group. They had been riding for a good three hours and their horses heaved to a stop, panting badly. The riders and their mounts drooped their heads in exhaustion as they stopped for the stragglers. A few swung down from their saddles and went about the party offering their waterskins and dried meat. Most of them consumed the food and liquid slowly. Shereel and Alaric made sure that everyone, including those that protested, put something in their bellies.

They waited until all of them had eaten, and then Arthur gave the order to ride again. Jace had little time to wonder why they were traveling with all possible speed to his house. It took most of his strength to stay in the saddle. Even though the Feeding Plain was flat, the jostling in the saddle did not encourage pondering such extraneous ideas.

The going was consistent, but his battered body found the riding rough. Each thump on the saddle shocked his body, sending pains through his wounds. His rump was numbed well before midnight and his head began to ache as he strained to keep his full attention on the matters at hand.

Shereel halted the party only twice during the night. The moon was full and its light cast a luminous glow on the open grasslands. There was no fear of danger among the Keepers and they rode as fast as their horses allowed them. The older woman went about the group with Clarissa and Lashara making sure that no one was suffering from excessive fatigue. They all checked the scratches and wounds of the people. Jace's physical ailments were the worst out of any of them, and they left his care to Lashara. She tended him quietly and they moved onward.

Arthur watched the ladies with growing impatience. It seemed whatever had stirred the man's emotions had set him on edge. Only Shereel, Clarissa, and Alaric had reflected the same attitude of the armored warrior. They all seemed very pensive, and moved about the party with purpose and a sense of expediency. Each time the party stopped, their four faces looked bleak and they did not spare any extra time before they ordered the group to move.

Lashara viewed their behavior with concerned suspicion. Those four Keepers seemed to be the oldest of the group and clearly the most knowledgeable of what was happening. They spoke in hushed voices each time the party stopped, but she could see the worry in their eyes. Lashara had no idea why they were headed for Jace's house of all places. The four of them had acted strange ever since they had laid eyes on the linen pennons and heard the glistening chimes. Ever since, they seemed tight and ready to explode.

Lashara shied away from them and only dismounted when Shereel said to. Her face was like iron and she viewed the other Keepers with a locked jaw. She spoke in curt, cutting orders, and all knew to stay out of her way, unless absolutely necessary.

After nearly two days of riding, the party halted. Almost half the Keepers looked white as sheets and swayed in their saddles with far away stares. Shereel approached Lashara and pulled her aside.

"I need your help," she said. Her words were short, but there was a look of pleading in her eyes. "The will of the party is crumbling. If we don't do something soon, people will start falling from their saddles and we will be forced to walk."

"Let them rest," Lashara replied as she wiped the fatigue from her own eyes.

Shereel shook her head. "There is no time. We need to make all possible haste or something dreadful will happen," she took Lashara's hand in hers, grasping it tightly. "Please, Lashara, there must be something else you can do."

Lashara frowned and then took the bag of herbs and potions from her pack. She poured a dark liquid into her water and stuffed three brownish leaves down the spout of the waterskin. She swirled the pouch gingerly and tied it to her waist.

"Stop again in an hour and the drink will be ready."

Shereel nodded her thanks to Lashara, clasped her hand and walked off. They rode cautiously for the next hour. When Shereel stopped the party, Lashara went about the group, letting each member drink a large swallow of her liquid. The potion seemed sweet with a tinge of acidity to it.

Jace puckered slightly as he handed it back to Lashara. After a few moments, he felt significantly different. The sleep that had tugged at him from behind his eyes for so long had suddenly been washed away. The headache in his forehead vanished and all other aches from his body subsided. He stiffened his back and rubbed his nose, blinking his eyes several times, now fully alert. He could see others of the party doing the same. Lashara had given a few drops to the horses as well and the beasts stirred restlessly. A small grin of satisfaction fluttered over Lashara's face as she exchanged glances with Shereel. The short lady turned to Arthur, nodded, and the troop was off again.

They reached Jace's cottage by noon of the fourth day. Lashara had needed to make only one more batch of the funny tasting liquid. The drink had kept them awake and vibrant and their horses' strength renewed. Only once did they have to stop and that was because someone's pack had come undone. As the trees came to an end, they slowed and walked across the stream. On the other side, they entered the pasture of Jace's home as he had done so long ago. The grass was tall now, its thick, lush blades dotted by wildflowers and several large weeds. The goats in the field did not look up as the Keepers topped the rise to look down on Jace's house. The gray, stone structure with its thatched roof looked smaller than Jace had remembered it.

He frowned. Something was wrong. The chickens pecked the ground by the front door, clucking anxiously as their heads bobbed up and down. Everything looked tidy. The barn doors were shut and his da's tools were neatly stacked against the sides of the shed. He could hear the low whine of Nina in some field on the other side of the house. Things seemed to be in order and though the grass was a tad overgrown, it was no cause for alarm.

Then he noticed it. There was no smoke. Mum's ever-present fire was not crackling from inside the house and no puffs of gray came from the chimney. Something was definitely amiss. Mum kept the fire on noon and night and even in the dead of summer, its thin, wispy tendrils could still be seen lazily rising out of the house. Jace started as he looked at the dormant scene. A hundred things could have gone wrong, and he fought the urge to rush down the hill and bumble into another trap.

Alaric motioned for the party to take cover behind the hill. They kept their voices low, careful not to disturb the goats and retreated out of sight. Arthur and Alaric slid from their saddles and slipped into the woods noiselessly while Shereel held their horses' reins. Jace climbed down into the grass and wormed his way to the top of the hill. He peered at the cottage through the blades and sat motionless, waiting to see what Alaric and Arthur would do. The moments passed in silence and the sun seemed to hang in the air.

As Jace sat hardly breathing, he suddenly caught sight of movements among the trees at the edges of the forest. Arthur and Alaric appeared from out of the woods. Alaric hugged the barn wall while Arthur ran in a low crouch to the base of the cottage. Both moved like trained soldiers. Jace was surprised at their speed and deftness for such large men. They poked their heads around the corners of the buildings, motioning to the other with short flicks of their hands.

Alaric nodded to Arthur. The big man rolled quietly around the corner of the house. Keeping his back against the wall, he moved his way under the window and sat next to the door. Amazingly, the giant man with all his chainmail and armor did not make a sound. Alaric had produced a stout wooden bow and had knocked an arrow in place. He peered around the corner of the shed, showing Arthur that he was armed and nodded to him. Arthur slid the broadsword from his back and slowly rose, to his feet keeping flat against the stone wall.

He nodded back to Alaric and then with one quick motion, turned and crushed the door in with a single blow. The door shattered into pieces and Arthur disappeared through its opening with his sword raised. The chickens scattered away, a few of them fluttering to waist level as they retreated to the far side of the house. Alaric spun around the barn and lowered his bow in a motionless crouch, eyeing the windows and surrounding objects.

Moments passed in what seemed like an eternity. There was no sound from within the cottage and Jace began to think the worst. Alaric sat with his bow taut, waiting for Arthur to voice his need or shoot any intruders, if it was a trap. Finally, Arthur emerged from the house. He grasped his sword in one hand and a thin, crisp strip of linen in the other. He pulled his helmet off his head and motioned for Alaric to lower his bow. The man came up to Arthur and the two talked quietly.

Jace came to his feet and broke into a run. Behind him, Shereel was screaming for him to stay, but his emotions had gotten the better of him and he ran down the hill fearing the worst. He collapsed to his knees in front of Alaric and Arthur and caught his breath. The rest of the mounted Keepers pulled in behind him.

"Where is my family?" Jace said clutching his burning side and breathing weakly.

Alaric and Arthur turned to him, their faces drawn and worried.

"Jace, they are gone."

22

THE END OF A JOURNEY

Jace looked at the two of them, his face a mixture of confusion and sorrow. He could not make sense of what Arthur had said. Had the rest of his family deserted him like Rae had? Was he left all alone now? His head was spinning with questions and he suddenly felt dizzy. He clutched his wound tenderly as he stared at the men in bewilderment.

They watched them, their faces bleak. Shereel walked up to them and snatched the linen strip from their hands. Her lips were set into an exasperated frown and she looked it over before turning her wrath on Jace.

"You should not have ran down the hill," she snapped, her voice filled with rebuke. "Did you not hear me, or are you just as rebellious as your father?"

The words pricked Jace. "My safety is not your concern!" he retorted. "If my family were in distress, I would be the first in their defense, no matter what you said!"

Alaric stepped between the two, but Shereel moved around him. "Your trust in your own decisions is foolish, boy! If you don't listen to other's advice, you've no business being a Keeper!"

"That is fine by me!" Jace yelled, but Alaric pushed him away from the older woman.

"Shereel, go tend the horses," he said bluntly. She lifted her head indignantly at him, but his eyes bored into her. She threw the linen down on the ground and stalked off into the crowd.

Alaric watched her leave and then turned on Jace. "You know she's right, lad, we had not cleared the area and you could have stumbled into serious trouble—"

"I'll take my chances!" Jace fumed. He did not like being ordered around where his family was concerned even if it was for his safety. The fact that people were treating him like a second-rate farmhand irked him so and he lashed out defiantly. He could fend for himself quite well without the need for a thousand nannies.

Alaric touched his shoulders gently and brought him close to Arthur who had picked up the linen. He fondled the piece of fabric while the two men started to tell the message behind it.

Jace did not feel well. His head was spinning and his hands went clammy. He did not hear what they said as they explained.

They hadn't gotten far when Lashara burst between the two of them and ran to Jace. She pushed him away forcefully and before he knew what was going on, her hands were on him. She had undone his shirt, poking around his wound and feeling his hands and forehead.

"You should not have done that!" she practically shrieked in admonishment. Her eyes were big and a look of worry was on her face—mixed with something else—as she examined him. She looked him in the eyes for only a moment as she went about her work.

"I have not been tending you all this time for you to go gallivanting off on some fool's errand to maim yourself as you please," she said harshly.

Jace looked down on the tiny lady sternly. He stuffed his shirt back into his breeches. His jaw pulsed angrily and he backed away, wrenching Lashara's hands from his face.

"I am fine!" he roared to everyone at once. He pushed Lashara out of the way and began to walk off with a scowl. He hadn't gone three paces when the dizziness overtook him and he fell to the ground.

Arthur and Alaric were by his side in an instant. Jace's skin was stark white and his eyes rolled lazily in their sockets. Alaric called for Lashara to come, but when he looked back at her, the little woman's eyes were filled with tears and she ran off into the woods. Trel jumped down from his horse and ran after her, followed close behind by Bartemus.

Alaric shouted again and Shereel came running from out of the horses with a small satchel and a bundled up blanket. She dropped in front of Jace, her face unemotional as she examined the unconscious man who had had it out with her moments before. She pulled his shirt up roughly, exposing his ribs and abdomen. Jace's cracked ribs were black and blue underneath his skin and the poultice had come loose from the wound. The bandage was soaked with blood, which ran down into his breeches. His breathing was shallow and his body sagged limply on the ground.

"He has lost a lot of blood," Shereel said hollowly as her hands ran over her things. She tore the blanket in two. One half, she folded quickly and propped under Jace's head. She tore the other half again into long strips, working furiously and then spilled out the contents of her satchel. She fumbled through her things, pulling out a large wooden bowl and spoon and dumped several scoops of powder into it. In a smaller cup, she poured a syrupy liquid and a handful of herbs. She then added a fair amount of water to the powder and hurriedly stirred it into a paste. She mixed the syrup and herbs into the paste and spread the amalgamation out over the strips of blanket.

Once finished, she wiped the wound clean, pouring water into the wound and swabbing a piece of linen deep into the gaping hole in Jace's belly. Jace groaned loudly and his arms and legs thrashed weakly on the ground.

"Hold him down!" Shereel said curtly to the Arthur and Alaric. She plugged the hole with a clean cloth and skillfully laid the poultice-laden strips across Jace's chest. Careful to overlap them, she finished by pressing them down firmly. Jace arched his neck as Alaric and Arthur held his limbs in place. After several moments passed, Shereel ordered the boy brought to a sitting position. She wrapped the blanket tightly across the fresh poultice and bruised ribs and had him gently lowered onto the ground. His breathing was shallow, and his skin was still a pasty white.

The three Keepers watched him for a while. The rest of the group had dismounted and were milling about the courtyard of Jace's family farm. Lashara's potion was wearing off, and several of them dozed on the ground, letting their horses walk where they pleased. Trel and Bartemus emerged from the woods, holding Lashara up between them by her arms. Her face was spattered with tears and she hung her head while the two brought her into the farmyard. They held her close, whispering soft encouragements in her ears.

"We will need a pallet," Shereel said shortly, eyeing Lashara and then turning to Alaric and Arthur. Deep circles were under her eyes showing the strain of the several days of their journey. She said no more and lay beside Jace while the two men picked up their weapons and went out into the woods.

Shereel patted Jace's head gently. She knew that the young man was wrestling with a myriad of problems and had chosen to take his confusion out on her, despite the fact that she had nothing to do with his inner turmoil. Such was the way of some people. Even older Keepers had done the same, and though Shereel did not like bearing the brunt of anyone's fury, especially if she was not to blame, she understood Jace's actions, however misguided and immature they were. Now that her own anger at Jace had subsided, she viewed the young man as a poor injured person, both in body and soul. No one liked being seen as that, especially a man, and it had taken a strong dose of her self-control not to call out Jace for what he was. The boy would realize his shortcomings soon enough without her saying so. Hopefully, he would begin to make amends for all that he had done.

The repercussions for his actions were already beginning to show. Looking off at the group that huddled around Lashara, Shereel could see some taking place. She knew there was some unspoken bond that existed between Lashara and Jace. It must have hurt the little woman that Jace had snubbed her with such open disregard. It was plain to see that Lashara had taken the matter to heart, and Jace seemed to be the only one who was unaware of the hurt he had produced. Shereel knew that he had not willfully done this or planned such injurious actions, but he had done it just the same. If he were truly willing to take responsibility, he would make peace with Lashara as soon as he crawled out of his cistern of self-pity.

Shereel rose and walked through the party of Keepers. There were less than 20 of them now, including Bartemus, Clarissa, Trel, Lashara, Alaric, and Arthur. The rest must have been from Arthur's party. She and her sister had chosen to ride with Alaric and Arthur instead of dispersing to their own home. Their leadership and guidance along with their medicinal skills had only added to the party's speed and health.

Altogether, the group was not bad off. All of the elderly had gone to one place or another. Most of them had spurred their way to Aider. There were no young or sick among them, save for Jace, Lashara, and Trel, and only minor cuts and bruises decorated the troop. Most of their wounds had healed on their walk through the caves and the swelling of their bruises had eased to only amorphously dark splotches on their skin now that they had come through Lars Swamp.

For some mysterious reason, Jace's wound had not healed. Though Lashara had tended it with more possible care than it ever deserved, it had remained almost as deep and open as when Jace had first received it. In many ways, it was like the problems Jace held on to. Its festering and constant oozing was akin to the troubles Jace held locked within him. If only he relinquished his pain, apologized to those around him, and got on with life, maybe his wound would also heal.

Shereel entertained the idea momentarily. She knew of some Keepers who swore that physical sickness was inherently linked to spiritual wrongs. Though she did not discount that Yeshua could work this way to open the eyes of the sickly to their spiritual shortcomings, she did not believe that every wound and injury was connected to a spiritual fault of the person. With Jace, it remained to be seen. She knew his cut should have been nearly healed by now. There may have been some relation between it and his spiritual sickness, but if there was, she could not help him. She dismissed the idea and went to help Alaric and Arthur in the woods.

The two men were just coming out of the forest when she met them. They were hauling two huge branches and stopped while Shereel checked out their work. Rough-hewn maple was not the strongest wood in the world, but it would suffice for where they needed to go. Arthur and Alaric began pruning the limbs of the smaller branches as she pulled another blanket from her pack. With their help, she lashed the blanket to the logs making a large sling for Jace's body. The logs were then tied firmly to the saddle of Jace's mare. After reinforcing the pallet with another blanket, they gingerly laid Jace between the logs and covered him with his cloak. Lashara reluctantly gave him another drink and he fell asleep even as they set off.

Shereel and Clarissa rode at the front with Arthur and Alaric. They led the party over the creek, being careful to lift Jace's pallet above the water. They walked slowly through the woods on one of the thin deer trails that wound through the forest. The group had filled their waterskins at the creek and journeyed through the warm canopy at a crawl. The travel was slow and once again, their progress depended on Jace.

Most of the party did not mind, but Lashara grew annoyed that Jace's every actions garnered so much attention. The entire journey seemed to revolve around the man, and she found herself reverting to her old view of Jace as a peevish man who cared for no one but himself. He could not help his wounds, but he did always seem to sicken at the most dramatic of times. She was tired of constantly caring for him when he did not give any thanks in return. The servile role that she had been assigned was made all the more trying by Jace's lack of appreciation for those around him.

Lashara's sadness and pity at the boy had turned to dismissal. They all had suffered hurts of various natures and degrees. No one had escaped the Clonesian Empire and the Kolosia without a mark of some kind. Even the happy-go-lucky Trel was pensive and withdrawn. Besides his burns, a cloud of sobriety muffled the spark of the carefree life that was always about him. Everyone had overcome their trials and the pull of Sa'vard that threatened to drag them down to despair. Even Lashara had thrown off the melancholy tug at her soul and strove to go on with her life. Their circumstances had not changed, but they all had made the decision to move on. Their joy was an attitude and a choice that they made to follow in spite of the obstacles they had and were continuing to go through.

The next day, they had traded the forest for the thoroughfare. The hard-packed dirt and the wide road was much more suitable than the muddled swamps and the grasses of the Feeding Plain for travel. Lashara could tell that they were traveling northward, she assumed, to the March. No one had told her, in fact, the group had remained very stoic. Arthur and Shereel's attitude dominated the party and their serious demeanors told the Keepers that something ominous was about to take place. They were all filled with a sense of resignation and rode in groups of twos and threes saying next to nothing.

The weather teetered on the edge of heat as the dead of summer tried its best to bend its will on the Gap. None of them were miserable, but the air was noticeably hot for these parts. The trees that bordered the road were cut back far enough that the thoroughfare was not shaded. Full sun fell on their backs and necks for much of the day, and though the heat of the Clonesian Empire was significantly more trying, the Keepers still found the traveling quite laborious.

Jace's bandage had taken hold. Shereel had relieved Lashara of her tasks to Jace and had taken over watching the slumbering man. She kept him full of her strange potions which subdued him and let him sleep. He rode in his pallet, his eyes closed and breathing deeply. No matter how rough the road or loud the conversation got, he remained fast asleep and oblivious to those around him. Lashara enjoyed this and for the first time in a long time found the journey free from anyone else's burdens but her own.

There were no signs of anyone. After three days on the highway, they had not run into a single party or wagon train going to or from the March. Lashara had heard that the road was continually busy and found the stillness of the empty thoroughfare rather disturbing. The leaders had not told them anything of this mysterious "Calling" that had occurred. She had deduced that it was connected to the strips of linen they had found along the way. Every now and then they saw one hanging on a nearby tree, its sheer white contrasting sharply against the green leaves.

Apparently, all the Keepers had been rallied to their homes in some grand muster that affected them all. Lashara had not been able to figure anything beyond that, and the usually boisterous Clarissa and soft-spoken Alaric had remained tight-lipped about the whole affair. She could not think of anything so vast that it would cause the whole of the Gap to draw up their arms. Try as she may, she was stumped. She discarded all her ideas and hopelessly rode northward to whatever was waiting for them.

By the week's end, they passed through Sage. The streets of the tiny town were vacant. All the low-sitting cottages and shops were either boarded up or sat with their windows and doors gaping wide at the band as they passed by. Curtains hung out the cottage windows and the doors slapped open and shut in the sultry wind that swirled through the streets of the abandoned town. Carts were propped neatly by their houses. Chickens strutted in the streets and pigs and livestock stood watching the Keepers in their pens as they moved through the town. Nothing stirred. Sage looked as if its inhabitants had fizzled away leaving behind everything except their horses.

The only sign of activity were the large tracks that were carved through the roads. Dozens of grooved cart ruts and thousands of hoof prints filled the streets marking some major exodus that had occurred no more than five days prior. The impression had turned the highway into a river of clumped soil. A dark swath of earth ran through the town pointing west to Dredger's Lake and Hedge. Another larger track cut north to Noll. The path spilled over the highway and into the surrounding fields leaving the crops and grasses flattened in a quarter-mile path that stretched to the horizon.

The younger Keepers viewed Sage and the heavy tracks with dark apprehension that teetered on the edge of fear. Their faces were pale and thoughts of the worst possible unknowns streamed through their heads. They sat atop their mounts like stiff reeds, unemotional and afraid of what would come next. Their horses whinnied restlessly and gave a low baying that was eerily uncommon for so large an animal. The sound drew the nerves of the Keepers as tight as a drum, and they ventured northward uneasily.

Only the four older Keepers eyed the town with any real indifference. It was if they had expected it to be that way, and though they did not say, their unchanged attitude helped settle the minds of the others. White strips of linen hung from many a door and window, but the four Keepers did not bother to inspect them anymore. They rode through the tiny village without stopping and camped in its outlying fields that night.

The night sky came on with a haze that blotted out the moon, leaving only a smeared yellow light in its place. There was no sound of creatures—wild or domesticated—that cut through the dark. Only the low cry of the horses carried through the party from their pickets, but Shereel and Arthur ignored them and the younger Keepers did their best to follow their example.

Not many of the party slept. Instead, they sat in a circle around the small fire and stared at the dim light that reflected off the clouds to the north. It cast a glow over much of the land, and the Keepers watched it without saying a word.

Jace showed signs of coming out of his stupor early in the morning. What few Keepers had drifted off to sleep were woken again by his fitful moans while it was still dark. Shereel refused to give him any more of her drinks saying only that it was time for him to catch his senses. Most of the party did not sleep and they set out early that day before the sun had risen.

By early afternoon, Jace was quite coherent. He had given up his low howling and had traded it instead for stark silence. He sat in his pallet, staring straight ahead, wide awake and as ornery as ever. No one dared approach him, and he was left to whatever bitter thoughts ran through his head. Shereel had ordered him to remain in the sling and when he tried to disobey, Alaric and Arthur forcefully strapped him down. This did little to quell his dark mood and he stewed openly.

Shereel had also given orders for no one to bother the young man. They needed no further advice to avoid him and left him alone. The day after, she discarded the pallet and let him ride on his horse. His legs were stiff and he managed to climb into his saddle after the third try. Though he swooned weakly from side to side and clutched the reins with white knuckles, he did not let go and Shereel let the stubborn man stay mounted.

Jace was pensive and was heard muttering to himself as he rode at the rear of the party. The Keepers watched him carefully, not knowing what his actions would be. For the most part, he did not partake of their company and refused Trel's meals. Late at night they would catch him uttering the names of "Blynn," "Rae," and "Dorath" contemptuously.

Now that he was mounted, Shereel let them move along at a trot. She constantly looked back to see how Jace was fairing and changed the pace accordingly. When the group would stop, she would take Jace aside and nearly force a snack down his throat. Everyone knew he needed food, but the petulant man had staunchly opposed all but the harshest of instructions. His attitude left the group sour and an air of growing resentment toward him filled the party as they neared the March.

The next afternoon, Noll could be seen on the horizon. Its buildings looked ordinary, but its appearance had changed somehow. Its outskirts to the north were crawling with what could only be seen as masses of dark lumps at this distance. The sky was blue and the many thin trails of smoke that lifted from the city were clearly evident against its backdrop. The younger Keepers pointed out the gray columns anxiously as signs of life. Whatever was happening, the answer lay at the base of the vertical clouds. The party cantered the last few miles into the city.

The wide highway of churned soil converged on the town. They began to hear the chorus of various noises as they approached its houses. A thousand differing sounds came from the far side of the city. As they weaved their way between its shops and dwellings they began to pick out certain ones. A host of shrill voices filtered through the chaos, calling out a sharp string of commands and reminders. They could make out the dull monotone of quartermasters as they read off their cargo. There was the sound of rhythmic marching, a thunder of galloping horses, and clamoring of metal and chainmail that added to the cacophony. The strain of rope on wood and creaking of slow carts rounded out the rest of the sounds. Beyond the hollers and shouts could be heard the steady clinking of metal and slow whirring of gears and other contraptions.

The buildings divided slowly as they rode forward and the Keepers were left with a broad picture of what the noises had alluded to all along. The sight was set on a monstrous scale. From the central square of Noll to the base of the March Wall was a solid mass of people. They rippled and pushed like a living sea, shouting and moving each to his or her own destination, but maintaining their discipline. As much as Trel could guess, there were well over 3000 men and women in plain view, not counting the ones that were hidden beyond the woods to the west and inside the auxiliary structures and staging halls. Most of the buildings had been stripped away and moved elsewhere to support the mustering of troops. Only the necessary structures remained. It was as if every conceivable person within the Gap had been planted before their eyes. The Keepers took in the view with awe.

As they looked, the band of Keepers could make out certain areas and groups. Where the north side of the town had been were large depots of goods that stretched for some ways. Clothing was heaped in long wagons, neatly folded and separated by size and function. Small huts of seamstresses stood beside the heaps of fabric, churning out apparel and mending cloaks. Foodstuffs and perishables were crammed into covered carts and kept in shady areas beside the huts. Raw goods of lumber and the like sat in large, secured stacks on the trampled soil. Curious tanks composed of wood and pitch housed a leather bladder that stored enormous reserves of water. Weapons mostly of the sword and bow nature stood neatly in polished rows next to helmets, shields, breastplates, and chainmail in their respective lines.

The quartermasters bellowed their orders to an army of porters and teamsters. They loaded stocks of goods into a line of carts and wagons that were then sent into the crowds to various positions along the March Wall. The group of logistical geniuses looked frazzled, but did their jobs with uncommon expediency and urged the teamsters and porters to move frantically. They poured over the fields of goods, loading one cart after another.

The supply station gave way to hoards of troops and soldiers. These groups jostled about as they moved their columns from one place to the next. Clarissa made out banners marking several contingents of troops from the foothills of the Withering Mountains and hardy axeman from the southern woodlands. She gave a short cry and waved to a band of archers from the Western Highlands. The group did not see her and marched on their way through the crowd to the immediate western flank of the March Wall.

Most of the troops bore regimental patches on their gray cloaks, but here and there were small pockets of gleaming armored knights, snaking columns of pikemen, and phalanxes of shielded swordsmen. These stood out against the rest of the crowd not only by their bright flags and uniforms, but also their discipline seemed higher than the rest of the common soldiers. These were the tower guards of East Haven and other hidden places of learning that dotted the Gap. They were the only standing army within the Gap besides the common troops that watched the Marches. Only in times of dreadful trouble were they to be pulled away from their fortresses, for without them, the places of learning were left undefended.

Trel started, recognizing Constable Bilscen leading a column of knights on a dappled stallion. The Constable from East Haven was dressed in silver chainmail and looked rather odd as he held his sword high, pointing his column around a group of pikemen with a grim look and leading them farther eastward.

Artisans and craftsmen darted around the soldiers. Each was on some solitary mission of upkeep that was no doubt vital to the assemblage of troops. In a chance stoppage from his brooding, Jace caught the hunched form of Eckalus moving about the field adjusting his spectacles as he clutched a sheaf of papers tightly against his chest. The clerk huffed as he scurried through the far side of the crowd and disappeared into a low lodge guarded by two spearmen. He seemed very distraught as he entered, and Jace wondered what had marred the man's life this time.

The March Wall, what could be seen of it far across the field, was lined with a significant amount of soldiers. They leaned on their spears and gazed over the wall. Whatever was beyond that wall was left to the imagination of the Keepers, and they struggled to keep their hearts from jumping up out of their throats. Archers and spearmen climbed the ramparts, slowly filling the thick wall with troops. As garrisons took up their positions, they staked their banners in their posts.

At the base of the wall were strange machines that were hidden behind some of the houses and lashed with large canvas covers over their forms. A number of men and women crawled over the machines. A thin, short little man was in front of one of the objects supervising its placement. He looked as if he was jittering away endlessly and ran about waving his hands with exaggerated signs of annoyance. The people slowly positioned the heavy object carefully while a number of curious soldiers, artisans, and clerks looked on at the activity.

The Calling had indeed affected all the inhabitants of the Gap, and though Jace's band had been one of the last to reach Noll, the mustering was still terribly disorganized. There was a sense of hurried preparation that one finds right before an unspeakable storm. All around them, the air was sizzling with tension and urgency. They watched at the madness as more and more troops continually poured in from the west. Flats of raw materials were being deposited in their respective lots and carts were streaming in from the central hills and Furbice basin to replace those that had left. All the figures that Jace had jotted down during his time with Eckalus suddenly leapt to life as he looked at the stored goods. The sight was staggering and the actions mesmerizing, but Arthur and Alaric pulled him and the others away.

They pushed through the crowd making a long diagonal cut through the churning body of men and women to the thin line of houses that stood near the March Wall. As they negotiated the teeming mass, word began to spread of their arrival. Jace's motley crew was made up of people from all over the Gap and a number of soldiers and craftsmen recognized at least one face or another in his group. Shereel and Clarissa seemed to have a reputation among the people of the Western Highlands. Those that saw them halted their columns, nodding slowly with respect and waving the women and their party through. Shereel tilted her head slightly in acknowledgement to the men and women while Clarissa simply blushed and let out little laughs of embarrassment.

None had forgotten the flare with which Arthur had left the Gap and word spread like wildfire that he and his troop had mysteriously returned. Though people gawked openly at his arrival, he returned their stares without any hint of his former arrogance.

Despite their relatively speedy travel, it took a long time to journey through the mess. It still took them nearly two hours to cross through the reserve materials, expanded parade ground, and the thin line of buildings at the base of the March Wall. Finally, they stumbled on what Alaric was looking for.

As chance would have it, they ran into Hadran while milling through the makeshift headquarters near the wall. He was stalking off to some unknown place with his ever-present scowl when he ran into the group. He looked up at Alaric, knit his eyebrows and frowned in vexation, as if to show them that their arrival was long overdo. His piercing eyes were not surprised, and they traveled over the group and rested on Arthur. The scowl on his face grew darker and he turned back to Alaric.

"Took your precious time coming back didn't you?" he asked gruffly.

"It's nice to see you too," boomed Alaric softly.

Hadran shifted on his feet and drew close to Alaric, his eyes growing soft. "Is the boy with you?"

Alaric looked at him and gave a short nod, not showing the least bit of emotion.

"Follow me," he said.

The group trailed behind him as he turned around, his scowl angry with frustration.

"Not you," he said to Shereel and Clarissa, "and certainly not you," he added thrusting a finger at Arthur and his friends. "Only the boy and his party."

Jace came forward followed by Lashara and Trel. Alaric waited for them to pass and then brought up the rear. Arthur looked stricken by Hadran's remark and leaned sadly in his saddle. The rest of the group waited while Hadran led Jace's party through the crowd.

They came to the low-sitting lodge that Jace had seen Eckalus enter some time ago. The guards snapped to attention and Hadran waved them still with a low growl. He stalked into the hall, not turning back to see if his four patrons were keeping up. The travel-worn Keepers stumbled in behind Hadran into the lodge. The main hall was brimming with people who huddled together speaking in low muffled voices. On each post hung three torches, their oily flames providing the only light in the big room. The air was tense and the murmur of voices did not hide the strained emotions that filled the hall.

Everyone was dressed in important clothing which clearly marked their stations. The warriors were all dressed in chainmail, leather gambesons, or some other armor. Clerks wore their tight-fitting surcoat. Artisans had either thick leather aprons or rolled-up sleeves with smudged shirts. No one was wearing the casual day-to-day garb that most Keepers wore when at home, however, there was a decent amount of troops who had not discarded their black woolen riding cloaks. Everyone's face and attitude matched their clothing: they all had a professional demeanor and listened to each other with very serious, weighted expressions.

Hadran escorted them to the back of the hall where the crowd was thinned out. A broad table sat against the wall. Maps and parchments were spread out across it and many officers and aides were gathered around the table listening to a tall, gray-headed man who was leaned over the papers.

"What about Aider?" he was asking.

A clerk stepped forward and pointed toward the map, "Reports have been streaming in since this morning. Korbin has retreated his main force across the Furbice and burned the bridge. Those that were trapped formed up farther down the river and are holding the shallows while he sends reinforcements. He's also dispatched a guard to his west so that no one escapes into the hills."

"How long will it take for the reinforcements?"

"At least a day," said the clerk. "Most of the horses that pulled into Aider were lame. The Keepers had to travel down river by foot under a hail of arrows."

The man paused. "And Loffel? Have Ferian and Wendyce survived?"

Another clerk cleared her throat and everyone turned toward her as she stepped forward. "Their forces said they took the brunt of the attack. They repulsed the early stages yesterday and have fought on into the morning. The last message we received said the city was torn apart, but the enemy has not gotten through. They could offer no assistance.

All their forces suffered immense casualties and they are now using their reserves to protect the March while they care for their wounded."

Everyone was silent.

"So it's just us then, isn't it?" he gave a huff and tapped the table. "Sa'vard has played us all along. We spread our forces out exactly like he wanted. We gave in to his plans. No one thought he would mass his main attack on the eastern flank," he looked at the officers as he spoke, "We all thought that impossible and didn't give it a second thought. Instead of asking for Yeshua's guidance, we've trusted our own judgments and wisdom. Even the Council was deceived."

A number of them shifted at the man's accusation, but their faces said he spoke the truth. They waited while he thought. Hadran cleared his throat and the man's head rose.

He turned to meet Hadran and Jace saw that it was Sturbin. His gleaming silver breastplate and white cloak made him look akin to the Lord's host. His jeweled broadsword hung heavily at his side. He was bent a little more and his eyes had deep circles of fatigue underneath them. His thick gray hair and beard could not hide the added creases in his skin he had acquired since Jace had last seen him. He looked worn, almost frail, but when Jace looked in his eyes, he saw the iron will the man still had. Jace gave the customary nod of respect and went to grasp the man's hand.

Instead, Sturbin embraced him in a fierce hug, holding him for a moment. He patted him on the back and then pulled him away, looking him over. His look was of a dear father seeing his son for the first time after a weary journey. He nodded slowly and put a hand on Jace's shoulder.

"We had feared the worst for you, Jace. We had received reports until you crossed over into the Clonesian Empire. Your parents and many of us have spent endless nights interceding to Yeshua on your behalf. It is good to see you and your crew are safe," he said softly and then raised his voice, "but now all can see that the Master was watching over you and your party all along. Let this be a sign in our troubled times that all is not lost and that Yeshua still works miracles even in the darkest of hours."

The men and women around him seemed to notice the four Keepers in their riding cloaks for the first time. They let out a sigh of awe and a glimmer of hope ran through the room.

"Take heart, my brothers and sisters!" said Sturbin. "Our Lord Yeshua has led these through untold trials. He most assuredly can see us through ours!"

Voices began to rise in volume as word passed through the hall that Jace's party had returned. A number of them stared openly at the tall lad and his friends that stood by his side.

Jace looked in the ocean of faces before him, but one seemed to flood out all the rest. Dorath stepped out from the crowd and began to walk toward Jace with open arms. As always, the man wore his light colored clothing and a well-groomed beard. On his face was a welcome smile that was on the verge of tears. He almost ran to meet Jace.

When Jace saw the man, something clicked. The crowd seemed to disappear and the space between Jace and his former Mentor seemed to expand. He could see Dorath's lips moving, but paid little attention to the words that came out of his mouth. Instead, his mind burned with wrath as the thoughts of all his hardships tumbled through his head: the chase from Nadir, Blynn's embarrassment of Jace in the North Wood, being forced to follow Blynn deep into the Clonesian Empire, left alone in Trailaden by their guide, losing Rae, betrayed and handed over to the dungeons, forced to watch the slaughter of other Keepers in the Kolosia, and return home hurt and demoralized. All these things flooded over the dam of his self-control. The final image that set the torrent free was Dorath standing before him. All his hurt, botched plans, and betrayal were focused on the kindly individual that strode toward him. All the malice and bitterness that Jace had pent up was finally released. A shadowy cloud seemed to cover his face as everyone looked on.

With inhuman strength, Jace jumped at the man. His teeth were clenched and his lips peeled back in rage. He drove his full force into Dorath. The unsuspecting man's face looked confused as Jace lunged at him. His hands dropped slightly and they both fell to the ground. Jace stood over him, his hands wrapped around Dorath's neck squeezing the life out of him with all his might. He was shaking the man's head and it pounded the floor several times. Jace was making uncontrollable high-pitched shrieks as he went about his work. Dorath struggled weakly, first dazed at the sudden attack from Jace and then his movement became more rapid as he fought to breathe. He grabbed Jace's hands and shook them, but the young man seemed to be filled with an enormous amount of power.

It all happened in the flash of an eye. Everyone watched, sucking in their breath, all stunned at Jace's reaction. Then they were on the crazed man, piling over him, ripping his hands from Dorath's neck and dragging him away by the arms. Jace kicked the air about Dorath as his Mentor leaned on his side, rubbing his neck and wheezing. A slew of curses spewed from Jace's mouth and the crowd's eyes grew wide with what they heard.

"What is the meaning of this?" roared Sturbin, his eye blazing menacingly. "To lay hands on another Keeper is forbidden, Jace! Speak, before we cast you from our presence!"

"Traitor!" he yelled. "This man left us for dead in the hands of a madman! I'll make him pay for it with his life!" he ended, lunging again.

The crowd grabbed him and he struggled furiously. The madness started to pass and his fighting became weaker. He turned limp, trying to catch his breath.

"Slow down, lad," Sturbin said, trying to make sense of Jace's ravings. The crowd was growing edgy from Jace's assault. They looked at him with burning eyes, threatening to drag him into the street. Sturbin settled them, commanding Jace to go on with his accusations.

"He vouched for Blynn!" Jace screamed. "The ugly man led us straight into the Clonesian Empire and then betrayed us! He turned his back on us and then handed us over to the Clonesians. We were sent to the Kolosia and left for dead because Dorath entrusted us into his care. He deserves to pay for what we went through!" Jace spat at him.

Dorath rose slowly to his feet. The words hit him like a slap in the face and he stared blankly at Jace not knowing what to say. The crowd was agitated now, focusing their attention on Dorath and waiting for his response. He hung his head wheezing and choking a moment and then straightened and looked about the room.

"Is this true?" asked Sturbin.

Dorath looked at the commander shaking his head. He wrinkled his brow in confusion.

"No," he said, but his voice was unsure. He stared into space while he recounted the facts. "I've known Blynn for many years. He's worked with me on many a mission. I've entrusted whole parties into his care before, and he has met each challenge with success."

"But is he a Keeper?" asked Sturbin slowly. "Does he cling to the teachings of the Song of the Ages and worship Yeshua as Lord of his life?"

Dorath scratched his head. "He told me," he babbled. "He told me he did. He said he was a Keeper and that he was from the Gap—"

"But did he confess that he believed in the Song of the Ages? Did he acknowledge that he followed Yeshua?" asked Sturbin again.

"He said he swore fealty," said Dorath, his eyes distant, "I believed him. He seemed so genuine at the time. We cannot judge a person by his unseemly figure. I took him at his word."

The crowd mumbled at Dorath's words. All could see he spoke honestly and did not doubt his story. They could see now that Dorath, as well as Jace, had both been duped by Blynn. The Mentor turned to Jace with meekness.

"Jace, I'm so sorry!" he exclaimed in sadness.

"No! You made me lose my brother!" Jace roared, struggling weakly. His anger fled and his voice trailed off into tears, "You made me lose Rae..."

He hung his head, his body shaking. Those around him were silent as he sobbed quietly. Alaric and Trel tried to pick him up, but he crumpled on the floor crying softly. They pulled him to his feet while he fought them off and led him from the hall followed by Lashara. Sturbin bid Hadran follow them, and the Mentor led them to Sturbin's quiet study. They laid Jace on the small bed in the corner of the tiny room. Jace had fallen asleep, his body drained in exhaustion from the days of riding and harboring his hatred. He slept, spent from the long journey that had brought him here.

He was never alone while he lay. At least one of his friends was with him while he slumbered. Lashara sat in the corner of the room for many long hours next to the crackling fire. It was hot and not suitable for summer, but the sound was welcoming.

She had visited Miss Pell briefly in the confusion of the camp. The infirmary was busy stocking supplies, fresh linen, plenty of water, and clean beds. It had grown in size, adding on two wings to the large white hall. The majority of the beds were empty, but Miss Pell had told Lashara that soon it would not be so. She had stayed and talked to her for a while, but the place was busy and she had to leave the kindly lady so she could supervise its organization. The two embraced and went their ways.

Others entered Sturbin's study. They checked on Jace and then huddled next to the fire to talk to Lashara. Trel was the first to arrive. He was wearing a heavy breastplate that rippled with muscles. His short sword bounced on his thigh and a short, conical helmet with a leather chinstrap that was a size too small was squished on his head. The man looked out of place in his uniform and Lashara stifled a laugh when he took off the helmet. His hair shot out at every angle. He grinned happily and the two talked of the preparations they had seen.

Trel had gone with Alaric to meet his friend Lumphar. They journeyed by foot down the road and through the forest to the staging area where Jace had first met the two architects. The short little man reminded Trel of Bartemus, but he was quite agitated and in no mood for games. Master Lumphar had taken over the production and design of the machines when Alaric had left. His stern face lit up when he saw his large friend walking through the camp. He ran up to Alaric, chattering away about the preparations and anxiously pulling him toward one of the machines.

The vehicle was mammoth. It was the length of three carts. Its sizable understructure was mostly raw wood that was held together with iron braces and thick leather lashings. Atop the carriage were two huge curve-shaped logs that shot out vertically on either side. A coarse rope, as thick as Alaric's arm was tied to each and strung to the log on the opposing side. A hoard of men and women climbed over the object, and when Master Lumphar ordered them to action, they set about their work with precision. They walked up next to the structure and Lumphar's eyes twinkled with glee.

"It was the fletchings, just as we thought," he said, smiling widely. "The added bow can make the bolt travel twice as far. I've given the commanders each a simple chart and guides which have improved the accuracy tremendously. Watch..."

The team dragged a log onto the carriage, fitting it through a hole in the rear. The long piece of wood had strange fins attached to the back of it and was covered with a thick black residue. As Trel and Alaric watched, the commander of the team ordered the large carriage turned slightly to the left. Four women turned a crank on one side of the machine and it moved slowly. Another team of women pulled a series of ropes on the far side and the carriage raised up at an angle. The leader sounded a trumpet and a mail-clad lady standing on top of thc housing touched a torch to the log. A flame engulfed the log with a puff, lighting up the night sky. The crew of women ran to the rear of the machine and handled a long rope waiting for the commander's signal. On his order, the women pulled hard on the rope, releasing the flaming log down range at a target. It shot up into the air, tracing a perfect arc in the night sky, and hit the center of the material, thrusting through it with a horrible sound and engulfing it in flames. Master Lumphar turned to Alaric with a look of satisfaction that showed through his weariness.

"...he said they had over one hundred of those!" Trel told Lashara excitedly. "They had other strange equipment also that I've never seen before: wooden towers that shot up into the air and giant creeping wagons that laid peculiar wooden walls! It was amazing! Alaric and Master Lumphar were very pleased. They said it may turn the tide of the battle!"

Lashara quieted Trel down while Jace turned over in his sleep. His stories seemed rather odd, but she let it pass. He had seen something extraordinary and though his descriptions were a bit sketchy, she was tired and let it be.

She slept for a few hours as the night wore on. A knock at the door jerked her from her sleep. She opened her eyes to see three people enter the room on tiptoe. The man who led them was middle-aged. His hair was swarthy black and neatly combed. He had on a simple woolen shirt and breeches over his medium build. His clothes were stained with dirt. His face was unshaven and littered with stubble. The man was tired, but his eyes took Jace's sleeping form in with yearning and happiness.

The lady that stood behind him was tall. She had a green shawl draped over her dress which hung to the floor. Her blue eyes were big and the look she gave Jace over her husband's shoulder betrayed her motherly relation to him. She went around her husband and knelt beside Jace, stroking his hair and laying her head on his chest.

In followed a little girl. She was not so young as Lashara assumed, and the second look she gave her revealed that she was on the verge of womanhood. She was dressed in a simple gray shirt and a black skirt that hung to her ankles. Her dark brown hair hung to her shoulders and her face bore many of the markings of her father's. She went up next to her mother peering over at Jace while touching her mother's shoulder.

Jace stirred on the bed and opened his eyes. He blinked twice and rubbed his eyes. Yawning, he stared at his father and sister. His eyes rested on his mother and the two embraced, the mother crying softly while Jace patted her back. He held her tenderly, kissing her hair while she laid in his arms. Finally, she looked at him, wiping the tears from her face.

"Is it true what Sturbin said, Jace? Is Rae not with you?" she asked with a trembling voice.

Jace nodded his head slowly, his face hard as stone.

"What happened?" she said, her voice on the edge of crying again.

Jace squirmed under the sheets, not wanting to speak. His hard face melted away and when the light from the fire cast on his head, his pain was clearly evident.

"I tried, Mum," he said, his voice breaking. His lips were shaking uncontrollably and he turned away, ashamed to show his tears. "He wouldn't listen to me. I begged him to come…"

His voice broke again and she cradled him in her arms.

"Shush, now," she said quietly and rocked him gently. His body shook and he held her tightly.

His father came and rested a hand on Jace's head. He knelt down by his wife and waited for Jace to look at him.

"It's alright, son," he said, a pained expression on his face as well. "You did what you could do. Don't ever be ashamed of that." Jace tried to wrench his face from his father's hands, but Sedd held him tenderly. "No one could ask for more than what you did."

The family huddled together while Lashara sat in the corner. They grieved for some time over the loss of Rae and then went to leave. As Mailyn and Amoriah walked out the door, Sedd turned to his son.

"You must let go of your pain, Jace," he said warmly. "We need you now. Yeshua has called us all here for a purpose. If you do not answer, He cannot use you and the Gap will lose another good Keeper."

Sedd shut the door behind him, and Lashara and Jace were left alone. He sat in the cot holding his head in his hands. When Lashara went to console him, he pushed her away.

"Leave me," he commanded, recoiling into the corner.

Lashara was taken aback while Jace sat crying. She looked at him for only a moment and then ran from the room in tears.

23

PIECES COME TOGETHER

Jace lay asleep late into the next morning. He could hear the sound of troops and carts moving by Sturbin's study on the streets below, but could not find the will to get up. Instead, he lay under the covers while the embers of the fire added to the heat of the day.

The sounds of the outside world were all around him. By late morning, the noise of the streets was tapering off. There were still sounds of horses, men, soldiers, and carts, but the volume did not carry as loud as before. The Gap seemed to be filled with a loathing expectation of what would happen. He could hear voices on the March Wall giving orders and speaking in quick commands to keep quiet and be on their guard, but there were no other signs or sounds of a coming war. Jace could also hear the groaning of heavy machines being hauled into their positions and the shouts of the teams of men and women who operated them. They struggled to unveil them from their canvas shrouds and ready them for the coming onslaught. By the sounds of it, troops were still trickling in to the area, and Jace could hear the quartermasters giving out commands to arm the soldiers with whatever they needed.

He viewed the noise with a kind of half-hearted concern, although he knew whatever was about to take place was of the utmost importance to the Gap, the world, and the future of mankind. He could feel it.

He had heard countless stories from the Constables and Mentors at East Haven. They told how he and every other member of the Gap had a responsibility to uphold and defend the earth from the clutches of Sa'vard. For the glory and honor of Yeshua and Elohim, they would stand in its defense under the guidance of the Counselor. Jace was told time and time again how they, as Keepers "wrestled not against flesh and blood, but against rulers, against authorities, against powers of this dark world and against spiritual forces of evil in the heavenly realms." He had seen the March Wall, looked on the living weeds, been chased by Watchers, heard their awful cries and urgings, and been in the depths of the Mines of Shorn. He had witnessed and been through all these things, but failed to make the connection that maybe those very things were what threatened the Gap now. None of his memories seemed to prick him to the point of getting up out of bed and taking his place upon the wall in defense of the Gap. He lay there while the world turned and time slowly passed.

It was Eckalus who first entered. He quietly shut the door, as if that would keep out all the noise that filtered through the windows and shook the floorboards. He poured some of the steaming water from over the fire into a cup and made himself some tea. After sipping some, he drew one of the chairs over to the bed and set himself down. He laid the large stack of papers he was carrying on the floor and took another taste of his drink. After adjusting his spectacles and looking Jace over, he cleared his throat and began.

"I figured it wouldn't hurt to drop by on my way back to the Pavilion. That's what they're calling the hall that Sturbin's been holed up in for over a week now. I suppose it's fitting. People always seem to find comfort in labeling things, though the musty place resembles a grand tent in no way at all."

He looked at Jace. The young man was playing with his blanket, pretending not to pay attention. He glanced at Eckalus who gave a brief smile back at him.

"They're worried, you know," the clerk said. "Not just your friends and family. Most of the Gap has heard your story by now, bits and pieces of it, or in one form or another. I heard one tale that said you bested Blynn by fighting him with both hands behind your back and blindfolded."

Jace snorted and continued to fondle the blanket.

"The truth of the matter is, Jace," said Eckalus, gently taking the blanket out of Jace's hands and waiting until he looked at him, "is that you are not to blame. If there were more time, you would have been taken before the Council and told to recount your journey from beginning to end. Even they would have told you that you bore no responsibility for Rae's actions. You were sent to warn him of his follies and ask him to come back. Everyone knows that part at least. You were not supposed to apprehend him or bring him back like some caged animal. That is not how Keepers operate, and it certainly is not what Yeshua commands or desires. What Rae did was his own choice. It was not your fault."

Jace tried to pick at the blanket, but Eckalus moved his hands away. He looked out the window and spoke while he observed the activity of the March Wall.

"It was not your fault, but neither was it Dorath's," he said, looking Jace straight in the eyes. "The poor Mentor was only doing his job. Everyone makes mistakes, Jace. Dorath could not see behind Blynn's deception, but neither could you. Don't fault the man for what you were fooled by also. No one can look into a man's heart except for our Master."

Jace grew agitated, but the practical clerk picked up on his feelings. "Yes, you did have to bear the brunt of Dorath's error, Jace, but so did everyone in your party. They suffered the same whippings, shared the same dungeon, and bear the same indelible memories of the Kolosia as you, though they bore no relation to Rae at all. We all are subject to things that are beyond our control, look at what Lashara endured for being a slave. Thank the Maker that you were under His care from the beginning, I say! He saw you through the obstacles that blocked your way, and you are alive to celebrate His victory in your life!

"We in the Gap had all felt that something was dreadfully wrong, but it was only Dorath who traveled about the countryside, asking others to intercede to Yeshua on your behalf. He was distraught and fasted until hearing of your return."

Jace looked at Eckalus in shocked surprise and the clerk nodded back at him. "Dorath admitted his faults, Jace. If anyone felt so strongly here about your safety, other than your family, it was Dorath. Give him a chance, Jace, we all make mistakes."

Jace shut his mouth and looked out the window. He looked back at Eckalus, nodding his agreement and closed his eyes. Eckalus nodded back, realizing that Jace had heard and understood what he said. He picked up his papers and drained his cup, setting it on the table by the fire.

"Don't think forever about what you must do, Jace. You've let the sun go down on your anger for too many nights. Release yourself from your burdens, casting them on Yeshua and take up your stand on the March Wall. Don't delay forever."

With that, he closed the door. His footsteps faded as he went down the stairs.

Jace turned over in the bed, playing with the blanket while he thought. Eckalus' observation that his friends paid for his mistakes was something that he had not thought of before. He was also surprised at Dorath's actions in his absence. He had not known how much his Mentor had cared for him and these two realizations left him feeling rather guilty. He mulled over these thoughts while picking at the blanket and vaguely listening to the world outside.

Before he knew it, he had drifted back to sleep. He awoke to the sound of someone coming up the stairs again. The sun had climbed halfway through the sky and he shielded his eyes from the light. Eckalus' words hung in his head and he immediately flung the blanket from the bed. He started putting on his clothes, hoping to look like he was busy for whoever was about to enter the room.

The door flew open and bounced back against the wall. Lashara blocked the doorway with her small form. She gave Jace a dark look and he started, throwing his clothes over his half-naked body. She wore a white smock over her riding dress that was stained scarlet in various places. Swiftly she strode across the room and planted her feet in front of Jace with her hands on her hips. Her golden brown hair cascaded down her shoulders and she gave him a long, hard look with her eyes ablaze.

"I will take no more of this, Jace!" She spat at him. Her face was pinched into a sad frown and her cheeks were stained with tears. "I have a right to let you know how I feel and I will tell you whether you want to hear it or not!"

Jace looked at her in shock, sputtering as he tried to cover up. Lashara paid him no mind and went on. "I am sick of waiting on you only to have you turn me away. You have no right to treat me as one of your servants that you can dismiss or beckon on a whim. I have watched over you since the Kolosia, and cleaned and bandaged your wounds despite your lack of thanks and your sullen attitude. You would certainly have died had I not done what was required of me. I did it not out of duty, but out of love. I thought we had something more than friendship, Jace, some stronger bond that was not treated with such disregard."

She whirled on him. "And this is how you repay me? Instead of offering any sort of thanks for my labor, you treat me like a dog and huddle in your corner, content to play the stricken fool."

She stabbed a finger in his face none too kindly, "I am a person, Jace! You've no right to be stuck in your self-pity while those around you are suffering the same problems. You've no right to push me away when a simple show of gratitude is all I need to feel rewarded.

"All you've done since we've journeyed from the Clonesian Empire is moan and wail about your hurts and expect to be cared for. Others have been hurting just as badly. Others went through exactly what you did. You may have lost something precious, but we all have at one time or another."

"Don't you dare talk about Rae!" Jace hollered.

"But I will," she seethed. "I will and you will listen. You've taken the fact that your brother went his separate way and made it into an ugly personal tragedy. Everyone has lost brothers or sisters—some fathers, mothers, or whole families. Whole towns, even, are lost and have never heard of Yeshua. You think your brother's choice is the worst that can become a man? There are heavier burdens to bear, Jace. Instead of letting go of your hurts and forcing yourself to carry on, you internalize them, letting them consume you, and drown under the pain they've caused you. Don't you see that everyone has been hurting from one problem or another? No, you'd rather wallow in slumber and let others deal with greater things."

She drew close to him, her small form towering over him. She loosened her smock and shoved it under his nose with a look of anger and pain. "See the blood of those who have already paid the price so you can sit up here and mope in solitude? You should be standing by their side instead of festering in your bitterness. As for me, I must go tend to those who fight for more noble a cause than selfishness!"

Jace had recovered and was ready to interject, but Lashara had spun or her heels and was headed toward the door. She turned and flung the smock at the foot of his bed, letting the bloodstained garment lie at his feet. With that she stomped out of the room leaving the door wide open.

Jace almost went after her, but then thought better of it. What would he say? He could not deny how he had behaved all this time. It was right for her to be so angry with him, but he still wanted to lay the blame elsewhere.

He sat and pondered what she and Eckalus had said to him. The more he digested their words, the more he realized that he had been sorely mistaken all along. They were right about everything. Rae had made the choice to turn away from Yeshua. Now that he thought about Eckalus' words, there was nothing he could have done to stop Rae that would not have produced more animosity.

Dorath was not to blame either. He could still recall how open his Mentor had been when he had met him in Nadir. He could even remember how he had stood up to Hadran when they had ridden all the way to East Haven on that long ago night and Jace had nearly tumbled from his saddle in exhaustion. Dorath had loved Jace all along: from his journey to East Haven, while standing in front of the Council, meeting him in Nadir, and even when he returned yesterday. That was the reason for the hurt Jace had seen in his eyes. He now saw his Mentor as he should: an individual who had watched over him as his son as he had grown up and loved him enough to help him when no love was given in return.

He had also come to the conclusion of his awful treatment to those around him. Never once had he thanked his companions for their loyalty and perseverance. He had never praised them for standing by his side as they crossed into the Clonesian Empire. They had always respected his role within the group, and though they doubted him several times, they chose to follow his lead even when it took them into the Kolosia. Even then, none of them had turned from his side. When he was sick, they had waited on him with all the steadfast love of a family. When he had pushed them away, they had remained close enough to offer their help when he asked for them. They had let him stumble and fall on his own only to swoop down and pick him up again. When he had never thanked them, still they remained by his side as faithful friends. They had been true companions and Yeshua's love had burned brightly through their actions.

It was Lashara whom he had dishonored the most. Of all the party, she had stayed closest to his side. When he was mortally wounded, she was the one who had nursed him back to health. The Maker had gifted her beyond measure with the ability to heal, and she had poured out her care on him with an unbridled passion. All those times that she had pushed her way through his sourness to check on his wounds, he had thought she was stubborn and manipulative. Now that he sat dumbfounded by her chastisement with his anger and sorrow melting away, it was clear how much she cared about him even when he refused her help. As much as Jace had tried to deny it, there was some special bond between them. A wave of guilt washed over him for his cruel treatment toward Lashara.

He had to find each of his party and let them know just how grateful he was for their friendship, especially Lashara. He had to right the wrongs he had made as best he could. He had to throw himself at Dorath's feet and ask forgiveness. Whatever it would take, he had to go and make amends. After he had done so, he would stand and take his rightful place with his fellow Keepers in defense of the Gap.

He limped across the floor and quietly shut the door. After smoothing the blanket, he knelt by the side of the bed and folded his hands.

"Father, how lost am I!" he cried out softly to Elohim. "All this time I have dwelt upon my misery allowing it to fester and ruin the relationships with those around me. Worse than that, Yeshua, I have dishonored You! My pride has built a wall that kept me from Your blessings. If it be Your will, I ask that You bless me as I go to make amends. I do not deserve either Your grace or mercy, but know that it is only from boundless wellsprings of both that I have found my way here. I confess, Lord, that I have done these things and go to make them right that I may stand pure with my brothers and sisters as You would have it while I go to the March Wall. In Yeshua's name I ask that You hear my cries and bless me, if only for Your glory. Ieysa!"

As he arose, he felt a sudden tingling run over his body. He slowly moved his hands over his bare chest down to his wound. The bandages were loose and soaked with fresh blood. He slowly unraveled the wet wrappings and exposed the poultice. Its hard mass was congealed to his skin like some large, gray leech. He touched the puckered wound and the poultice felt off into his hands. It was light and lay in his palms with a contour that outlined his side

He rubbed his fingers gently across his wound. The skin was tight and tender, but the cut had been replaced with sudden scarred tissue. The wet blood was still warm, but there was no sign of an open wound. He mopped the blood off and examined his abdomen closely. As best as he could tell, his opened side had been healed where he sat! His belly felt solid and the torn muscles underneath the skin, along with his cracked ribs seemed to be healed as well. He stood to his feet bending his back to the sides. The sun flared in the sky and he laughed out loud with a smile as wide as the heavens. Wonders never ceased! Clearly, Yeshua had blessed his life yet again.

In a matter of moments, Jace had dressed, washed, and eaten. After gathering his pack and his staff from the corner of the room, he tumbled down the stairs, still beaming with delight, and ran out the door into the sea of people. Minor cuts and scrapes still marked his body, but his spirit was rejuvenated and seemed to look past his pains now.

He had not gotten far when he realized he had no idea where he was headed. He walked about the area looking for someone he knew. Time found Jace standing next to the supplies. The depot stretched for miles in each direction. The crowd was not so full as it was yesterday, most of the people having been assigned to certain duties or areas around the March Wall. The parade ground was left open mostly to couriers and as a throughway for gigantic columns of troops and trains of goods. These passed along smoothly now, but the soldiers and drivers who sat at the heads of the carts and columns wore serious faces and moved urgently down the wide strip of land.

The quartermasters were a different story. Many of them looked considerably stressed since last he saw them. Their clothes were rumpled and their movements were lethargic. Many of them teetered on their feet trying to fight off the fatigue that pulled at their bodies. Some of them looked like they had been awake for days and by the looks of the goods, they would remain so for a long while more. In all actuality, most of the supplies that were before Jace would remain in place for the duration of the Calling. Most of the action had slumped off and quartermasters were being relieved as he watched. Porters and teamsters picked over the supplies, making sure they were in order and that the space was used efficiently.

Jace spied a familiar group down the line of goods. He went over to them and pardoned himself as he interrupted their work. The thick muscled teamsters rose up from around him to look at Jace. He excused himself again, mistaking them for people he knew. As he turned to leave, their foreman called him back.

"Don't I know you from somewhere, boy?" he said gingerly holding his pipe between his lips as he talked. His bald head glistened with sweat in the sun and his blue eyes suddenly went wide. "My, I almost didn't recognize you," he said, taking his pipe out of his mouth. "Hadran always did keep shady company, but you're a little old now to be under his wing, aren't you?"

Jace stared distrustfully at the squinty man, but then his memory clicked. He nodded politely to Dolmer and his wagonhands, giving them a short description of the past year. Dolmer and his team frowned as Jace bumbled through his story and then stopped him short.

"We've heard most of this already," said their diminutive leader pertly. "I bumped into Hadran and he spilled the news like a bag of hot air. He only does that when he's been worried, but don't tell him I told you," he ended with a smile and a wink.

Dolmer and Jace talked for a while, and the wagoneer told him where he could find his Mentor. The man was a virtual wellspring of information and chatted on about how smooth the preparations were going. He eyed Jace conspicuously as he chewed on his pipe. Before he let him go, he pulled him aside.

"Most of us have heard about your scuffle with Dorath," he said quietly. "I hope it's not true, but if it is, fix it as soon as possible. This could be an awfully long day and we don't need anything distracting us from our unity," he said raising his eyebrows and making sure Jace understood. Jace nodded to him and went away.

On the outskirts of the depot, he found his family. His mother and sister were helping with the seamstresses and his father was shoeing a horse. They all stopped their work while he came by. Jace smiled to them, but their brows were wrinkled in worry. They looked off at the March Wall with apprehensive stares while Jace talked to them. He went over his journeys in greater detail, but their thoughts seemed to be elsewhere. They jumped every now and then as if they heard voices or rumbles off in the distance. Jace looked about the sky, but when they saw him watching, they acted as if nothing was wrong. When he confronted their strange behavior, they played it off, saying they had been having a long day. He decided to leave, and kissed his mum and Amoriah. He walked off, a bit agitated.

Sedd put his hammer down and took Jace by the shoulders. His father walked with him for a spell. The two talked as if it were old times, and though Sedd seemed to be spooked by something, his words were firm.

"Whatever happens today, Jace, remember who you are. Don't try to be something you're not and listen to your superiors, doing what they say to the letter," said his father.

Sedd usually spoke deeply, but his advice always seemed to be mixed with riddles. Jace had an unusual feeling that there was some enormous thing about this place that he had missed all the while. He nodded politely and watched his da leave. While he walked away, his father would flinch every now and then.

Jace shook his head. The behavior was disturbing, but he didn't know what to make of it. We walked away, deciding he could put off his meeting with Dorath no longer. Reluctantly, he set out for the March Wall. Despite the crowds, the air was rather quiet. It almost seemed muffled in some way as if some thing or sound was missing from the world around him. The troops and couriers scurried and marched away with a purpose. Jace found their sullen stares and quiet demeanor unsettling.

By the time he had crossed the expanded parade ground, the crowd had thinned out considerably. Only a few dispatchers ran here and there and lone soldiers hurried to join up with their units. The entire scene had grown eerily quiet and the sky had darkened. A layer of unbroken clouds had moved in from the south and blocked the sun, sending the area into shadow and causing chills to creep up Jace's spine. The air was warm, hot even, but Jace still pulled his cloak about his shoulders.

He ran off into the houses and made his way closer to the March Wall. He passed by the Pavilion and stopped for a moment. The place looked almost empty. The guards still stood outside, but the two oak doors were flung open, revealing its vacant interior. Jace creased his brow and went on.

Instead of heading for the March Wall directly, he caught a glimpse of a large, white building some distance to the west. Less than an hour had passed and Jace figured he could spare another and go in to see his old friend.

He entered the infirmary and looked around. The place was busy. Men and women in bright white garments moved about the interior quietly. Most of the workspaces had been converted to make room for extra beds. The building was one gigantic room with the two added wings making it seem like some extravagant boarding house. The place was well-lit with bright torches that gave off a clean flame unlike the ones in the Pavilion.

There was no waiting space and Jace stood to the side of the doorway as people walked quickly by him. They spoke in low voices, but went about their business quickly and methodically.

As Jace stood against the wall, three soldiers carried in a man on a pallet. He was dressed in a leather riding vest and had a short sword tucked close to his body. He looked to be a courier of some kind and waited patiently while he was moved with a peaceful silence. His bearded face was fine, but he clutched his belly trying to hide a growing red spot on his clothes. He sat motionless on the pallet while his friends carried him into the hall and laid him on one of the empty beds. When they had positioned him, a swarm of white-clad figures gathered around him. They pushed his friends away and began muttering to each other as they bent over the man's body.

Jace could not tell what exactly was going on, but the glimpses he saw were not comforting. They had stripped the man to the waist and began applying some salve or ointment on the man's chest around his wound. Jace peered through the group of people as they passed sharp metal instruments to each other and touched the man's skin lightly. He could see one lady leaning over the outstretched courier. She seemed to be pressing down on the man's body with all of her weight. When Jace looked up at the man's face, he jumped and squeezed his eyes shut, looking away from the work that was being done on his chest with a pained grimace. He gave out a short cry and then others surrounded him as the action grew frantic.

Jace backed away from the scene. The infirmary was not a place where he was wholly comfortable. The foray around the courier was not the only thing going on in the large hall. Several groups of white-clad people stood around a number of beds. The majority of the spaces were empty, but the work on those that were here seemed to be busied, almost turbulent.

Off in one of the corners sat Miss Pell. The blind, old lady sat listening to the orders given around her, every now and then turning to someone near her and giving one herself in her kindly old voice. She stared into space, listening to the voices while in deep thought. Her lips were moving though no one was around her. Jace crept up to her and slipped up to her side.

"Hello, Jace," she said somberly. "Come to pay your respects at last?"

Jace's mouth fell open. He was never successful at sneaking up on the old lady and it always flustered him.

"I needed some coaxing," he said, trying not to show his consternation.

"So I've heard," she said with a whimsical smile.

Jace let it pass. She had probably heard all about Lashara's confrontation, or something of it. If Lashara had not told her directly, Miss Pell always had a way of finding out.

"Have you made up with her?" she asked, as if reading his mind.

Jace shook his head. "No. Can we please talk about something else, Miss Pell?"

"Of course," she said tapping her cane on the floor and then turning to face him in her chair. "Sit down," she said waving her hand.

Jace sat in the chair next to her. The lady placed one wrinkled hand on his face, running it over his brow, eyes, nose, and lips. She touched his side where the wound had been not five hours ago and he jumped. She gave him a warm smile and placed her hands in her lap.

"You've escaped rather unscathed, I should think, for all you've been through, my boy."

"Yes and no," he said with a sigh. "If only my outsides matched my spirit."

"But I've heard it said that you gave up your hurts for greater causes not too long ago."

"Where did you hear that?" he asked pointedly.

"Oh, it's whispered on the wind, you might say," she said with a mysterious smile. "Jace, why are you here?"

"I don't know, Miss Pell," he said shrugging his shoulders. "Something's happening in this place and I just thought I should see you. I guess I felt drawn."

"You're stalling, Jace," she said. "You want to talk to Dorath, but you don't know what to say, and you thought I might be of some assistance in the matter."

"Yes," he grinned, "but other things as well. It's been a long journey and I missed you. I felt the need to come by and sit with you for a while."

"So the truth comes out at last," she said leaning back in her chair.

The old lady was an enigma. For her to pluck thoughts out of the air and put them to words was an amazing quality that Jace had finally grown to accept. He could not hide much from her and despite how ornery it made him feel, he did not lie when he said he missed her. She was one of the few people he had grown up with, and her presence always eased his mind. She was like some ever-present watchful eye that pierced his being and reflected it back for him to see clearly—faults and all. She was much closer than a Mentor and though he did not talk to her much, now that he was too old to sit on her knee, he enjoyed her company and years of wisdom mixed with her subtle humor that had aged with her.

An hour passed while he sat and conversed. Miss Pell always found time enough for him while making sure that she did not neglect her duties to her post. Those of her staff that interrupted their conversation were given sound advice on their questions and sent back to their work with renewed knowledge and strength. She listened to all his journey, his trials, and losses. She frowned many times and laughed as well, for Jace's travels were not all filled with defeat and melancholy. Who could forget his mischievous antics with Lashara and the itching powder, or the beautiful landscapes of the open land? The pictures he painted of the escape from the Watcher in Nadir and the release from the Kolosia at the hands of their Lord were like a breath of fresh air. The lovely images of the Lord's host, his healed wounds, and Lashara's care brought a smile to Miss Pell's face that was lit with a warm glow of satisfaction.

"So, you've been though much, my friend." she said as he closed up his tale.

"Yes," he replied. "But as you know, I must make peace with those I have offended. It is only right that I ask for their forgiveness after all that I have done against them and all that they have done for me."

"Well spoken," she nodded. "It is time for you to be about your way. Hold to the promises that you have made to yourself, Jace, and when you are done, take your stand with Dorath and my dear friend Hadran."

He embraced her for a moment, holding her close. He kissed her cheek and turned to leave.

"Whatever happens, Jace, remember that Yeshua holds all things in His sway, and Sa'vard has no power beyond that which the Almighty has given him."

He gave her a quizzical glance, but she urged him on his way.

"I love you, Miss Pell. When this is over we will sit and talk for a long while, as it should be."

"And if that day never comes? Perhaps this is the last we shall see of each other until one far-off day in Par'lael," she said with one of her sly cackles.

"Don't say such things, Miss Pell," he rebuked tenderly and kissed her again. She pushed him away gently and bid him go.

More beds had been occupied since Jace walked in. The activity was speeding up and Jace stayed close to the walls away from the growing chaos. The place was filled with people in white robes and he made to leave as fast as he could. On his way out, he saw Lashara bending over a man with several other people standing around her. Her long hair was pulled back and that stern expression she always had when caring for another was plainly written on her face.

Against his better judgment, Jace walked her way. He happened to block her path just as she had finished her work on the man in the bed and turned to leave. Her eyes looked up at him quickly and then back down at her feet. She moved to go around him, but Jace cut her off again. She looked up at him and he grinned in embarrassment.

"Is something funny?" she said testily.

"No," he said and then tried his best to begin, "No, it's not, I've just come to apologize."

Lashara gave him a look of sarcasm and he moved back a step.

"What I mean is, I was wrong. I see that now, and I wanted to explain how sorry I was."

She sniffed at his words.

"Lashara, I'm trying to talk to you," he said quietly.

She flung her hands and looked around her. "Can't you see that I'm busy? You could have said something when you were alone in your room. Why wait until the worst possible time, or are you trying to change my response by confronting me in public?"

He was taken aback at her outburst. Apologizing to her had never been easy, but this time, something else seemed to be bothering her. She shifted on her feet, waiting for him to try again. He sighed and scratched his head.

"When you left, I had time to think. You were right. All this time I've been caught up in my own struggles and blinded to the pains of others. All my bitterness and anger spilled out on those around me. I took all of my friends for granted," he looked at her closely and lowered his voice, "I should not have been so coarse with you."

She sniffed at his remarks. "Is that all you've come to say? I suppose now you expect me to release you from all the pain you put me through and send you on your way with all my blessings."

People looked up as her words carried through the infirmary. Jace wanted to say yes to her question, but he knew that was not the answer she was looking for.

"I've seen the way you look at me now, Jace," she said coolly.

His eyes went wide with fear. He lowered his head in shame. It was not right for one to lust after another. How she had found out his concealed fantasies, he did not know. He had hidden them so deeply that he had fooled himself into believing all his feelings toward his former companion were inescapably pure. Subconsciously, that had been the reasons for pushing her away. Now she had discovered his secret and was going to expose him in front of everyone. He cringed and stood ready to accept his punishment.

"You see me as only a slave! I can't help you with that. As much as I'd like to change your view of me, I can't," she shuffled her feet, the words upsetting her to finally speak them. Her voice grew husky, but she went on despite the torture it caused her. "You only see what you want to see, but I am much more than that! I am saved and set apart as a Chosen of the Almighty. I have been washed and made clean, no matter what my former life was like. If you can only see some wretch who has a shaded past, then you've missed who I am. Shame on you!"

Jace sputtered at her eruptions. They were clearly not the accusations he had expected. Had she known his heart, she would have seen that his inward struggles had only hid his attraction toward her. He wished he could explain how he felt to her, seeing her standing there at that moment, but words failed him. Now that he was beyond his grief, he offered his consolation with a phrase that would mend her wounds. He sought to heal their relationship with as few words as possible, and hoped to quell her misery all at once. The effort was next to futile, but he gave one last push.

"Everyone has been a slave to one thing or another, Lashara," he mumbled.

"Don't patronize me," she said, her eyes boiling. "I think it's time you leave."

Jace stiffened. Rejected, he walked out of the infirmary. The bitter exchange had brought him to a new low after his hopes had soared. He did not look back as he left the place, but his heart was heavy.

Lashara watched him leave. She had steeled herself while in Jace's presence, but now that his back was turned it was all she could do not to fall apart. Her lower lip trembled as he walked away. Her rising feelings for Jace had scared her, but when she saw that they weren't returned with the same warmth she tried to give him, she knew what should happen. It broke her heart to push him away, but after thinking long and hard about her choices, she realized what she must do. She turned back to her work, wiping away a solitary tear and forcing herself to forget the young man. He would remain just another Keeper to her.

Jace walked out into the afternoon light. The sky was murky and gray, but it matched his feelings. A wind was building, coming up from Dredger's Lake, and he could almost smell the tiniest hint of rain. There was only one place left to go. After toying with the idea to skip the confrontation with Dorath altogether and head back to Sturbin's room, he forced himself to go to the March Wall.

He chanced a look over his shoulder. The parade ground had filled with a number of troops in his absence. They seemed to be jumbled together in a solid mass with no particular formation. Most of them were dressed in the simple black riding cloaks of the Keepers. They all were lightly armed with swords, bows, or staffs. None of them wore armor and they hunkered together like frightened cattle. Jace almost snorted, but he caught himself before slipping into another bout of depression. He thought he saw Trel in the group, but at this distance they all looked the same.

He weaved his way through the last of the houses and climbed the March Wall. The air was so muffled that it surprised Jace how many soldiers lined the Wall. They stood, their eyes pointed silently out into the wilderness of Sa'vard. A rumble seemed to rise from off over the low hills, but the troops stood motionless as if they had not heard. Jace leaned back on the inner parapet and watched them for a moment. None of them turned his way as if the weary landscape held some hidden entertainment that Jace had overlooked.

The land had been thoroughly pruned of all vines up to a quarter mile away. The tangled plants seemed to twist and turn with a life all their own, but from this distance Jace could not tell. If only the air were clearer, he would have heard their audible hissing. Besides the creeping plants and the quarter mile strand of turned earth at the base of the March Wall, it looked about as ordinary as could be.

He almost laughed at the soldier's serious expressions and how tense they were. Nearly all of them held their breath expectantly. Several of their lips were moving, like Miss Pell's had, but no sound came from them. It was as if giant wads of cotton had been shoved into his ears.

Whoever had organized the units had done an extremely thorough job. Highland archers were shielded in dense groups by shining knights. Swordsmen lined the wall and were intermixed with light infantry that carried everything from axes to cudgels. Bubbling kettles of pitch and oil were dotted across the wall. Regiments were drawn up around their flags. Where more than one mingled together, their banners were pitched beside each other in hollows of the March Wall. Their faces were grim and many of them thumbed their weapons patiently.

The breeze blew from the south, steadily picking up speed. It made the banners and pennons stand on end, pointing out into Sa'vard's Lair as if signaling the approach of some mighty force. Farther down the line to the east was staked a great flag. It was raised higher than the others and billowed freely in the wind. The flag of the Gap shown brightly even in the afternoon gloom. Its brilliant white danced in the wind and the red cross against the sea of blue was clearly evident a mile down the line. Jace stiffened to attention as he saw the flag: a symbol of their returning King, Yeshua, and all the promises He had bestowed on the land. His face beamed with pride and he moved through the crowd of entranced soldiers, making his way toward the banner.

Sturbin was under the flag as Jace had presumed. His former teacher was the picture of tranquility in the crowd of faces, his kindly face showing no sign of anxiety or fear. His retinue of staff was drawn up around him. Hadran stood at his side, the two bearing the same staunch countenances. They both looked worn as if they had aged another five or ten years since Jace had departed for his travels. They looked off to the north with the rest of Sturbin's staff and soldiers, their eyes peering into the gray land and focusing on some hidden vision. Jace shook his head and walked into the group.

All Sturbin's staff was silent and none of them seemed to notice Jace until he was a few paces from their leader. Even then did they only give him brief movements of acknowledgment. Jace saluted to Sturbin and nodded to his Mentor. He stole a glance around, but Dorath was nowhere in sight. Shereel stood on the other side of Hadran and her short nod to Jace was the only sign she gave to let him know that things between them were repaired. He nodded back at the lady, glad that she could understand his presence was a symbol of his apology. Sturbin beckoned him to come closer and he came to the Commander's side. Hadran moved to make room and he wedged himself between the two of them in their cramped quarters. The gray-headed Commander leaned close to Jace's ear.

"Soon that which we have waited for shall come the pass! We must remain strong, Jace, and stand together for the glory of the Almighty and Yeshua! Only then will we have victory!"

From the look of his face and the pitch of his voice, Sturbin was yelling the words. Even so, Jace could barely hear the man. He shook his head, hoping he wasn't getting ready to faint again. Sturbin pointed out across the March Wall.

"Here they come!" he roared in his strange whisper.

Jace looked, but saw nothing. The clouds that were slowly drifting north seemed to stop, like they had pressed against an invisible barrier, and then, quite suddenly, they changed direction. The sunlight poked through the broken clouds above them, but other than that, the circumstances seemed relatively normal. He looked at Sturbin and Hadran giving them each a confused frown. They turned to one another as if they had forgotten something and then turned back to Jace, each of them leaning toward him. All sound was almost muted now, and the two elders had to practically scream into his ears.

"Take our hands, Jace!" they yelled, "Close your eyes and call on Yeshua's name!"

As it was, the words they began to speak were only mumbles in the back of his head. Their eyes were closed and he knew they must be calling on Yeshua. He closed his eyes as well and began to do the same, calling on his Lord and Savior and asking for whatever strength he needed for that which he was about to face. If his ears were clear, he would have heard what the two elders were saying:

"Father in heaven, hear our cries! We ask that you free us from the sin that so easily entangles our lives. Let our eyes be opened to the Truth of Your Word, and let us see clearly the plans the enemy has laid against us. Stay our hearts on You and fill us with courage and the Counselor. Let our hearts be shielded in this time of trial as we are tested by forces that threaten all mankind! Let us shine like a city on a hill for Your glory and may what we do bring You praise. We ask all this not of our own power, but in Yeshua's name. Ieysa!"

As soon as Sturbin spoke the words, Jace's world gushed through all of his senses. The muffled scenery plunged Jace beneath a horrendous rush of sound that was mightier than ten thousand horses on the open plain. The avalanche of noise fell upon his ears with a deafening roar that stopped his heart. It was stronger than the waters of the Great River and threatened to knock him down where he stood. He sucked in his breath as the blast of overpowering thunder hit him, wavering on his feet as he fought to control his balance. His ears seemed to be ripped free from all that had once impeded his hearing and what he heard curdled his soul.

He was no stranger to the cry of the Watchers. Their calls had commanded him with an inhuman pull that was almost overwhelming. They had tempted him with subtle whispers and their violent song since Nadir. Their voices were nothing compared with what washed over him now. The sound of Sa'vard's host was thrust into his ears and entered his mind with a will that attempted to crush his soul. It almost pulled him under—its torrential song trying to whip him away into madness. He swayed between Hadran and Sturbin while he fought against its power.

Instead of reaching out to hold them, his arms moved to his chest, as if guided by an unseen hand. They rested on some rectangular object in his left breast pocket. His hand wrapped around it, slowly clutching it in a death-grip. Like a sudden beam of light that cut through the darkest storm, the Song of the Ages lit his world. A peace settled on his heart that chased away the cries of the Watchers and set his focus on the eternal Father and His Son.

It was not the book itself, but the act that it symbolized: the all-consuming need of crying out in hopeless abandon to his Master. His heart sang as he grabbed the book and he raised his other hand to the sky in a show of worship and dedication.

The moment passed and he opened his eyes. The world that met him was extremely different than the world where had stood before Sturbin's cry to the Maker. The March Wall was still there and the troops lined its width, clogging its battlements to overflowing. They looked the same but somehow their bland cloaks and polished armor seemed to be more pronounced and refined. Their swords and bows were sharper and sturdier than when he had last seen them. All the banners that hung in all the same places crackled loudly as they caught the wind. Only the faces of Sturbin and Hadran were no different.

The sky, however, sent him trembling. The gray, blustery afternoon of clouds were pulled back, revealing the deepest shade of azure blue Jace had seen anywhere in the world. Not a cloud shown in the sky and the sun burned down on the March Wall with a splendor like the Son of the Most High, Himself. The light showered the Gap with its goodness, glinting off the shiny breastplates and metal shields of the armed soldiers. The warm weather was perfect and if Jace had not known, he would have thought the day held no ill in it.

All the Keepers were looking out across the wilderness. They seemed focused on no other event. The only prevalent sound that weaved through the motionless troops was the Watchers' song that had all but fled from Jace's mind. By the looks of them, more than one soldier struggled with the song of Sa'vard's forces in their own private battle. Their faces were etched in contorted pain and some of their brows were beaded with sweat, but they faced northward, determined not to look away. By and large, the troops were grave and they waited somberly, like an army that knew what was to come.

Jace turned his head to the object of their attention and his heart jumped into his throat. Over the rolling hills stood a solid sheet of black. The majestic blue of the Gap sky ended at the foot of the darkness and as it came on, it consumed the sunlight leaving nothing but a bubbling shadow.

It was not dark as one could describe it, nor was it night where shadows stood in various strains of gray. It was the color of Sa'vard, like Jace had seen in the Mines of Shorn. It ate up all light as it advanced across the hills and tumbled down into the plain before the March Wall with a slow creeping that reached out to the Keepers with a sense of hatred and loathing.

Superimposed on the surface of the shadow were the Watchers. They filled the sky like Jace had seen through his dreams while deep inside the caves under the Great River. Their numberless forms swam in their shrouded bodies above the earth packed tight in the sky and took up every possible space in the air overhead. Their outcast images blotted out the light, and they flaunted themselves as they chanted their eerie song of temptation over the Keepers.

Below them marched a hideous sight. Jace had mistaken the sheet of black on the ground as a form of its own, but as it came forward, he saw that it was an endless sea of soldiers. The ranks were packed so tight that they left no room for light. They were dressed in the dread colors of Sa'vard's host and their numbers ran as far as the eye could see. They looked like a sea of midnight and roiled like a turgid river over the sloping terrain. The earth shook as they advanced towards the March Wall.

As they came closer, Jace could make out individual forms. Their shapes were macabre variations on things that walked the earth. Jace saw creatures that resembled wolves and goats that walked upright on their hind legs. They had long curved jowls and barred their razor-sharp teeth in terrible smiles of hunger. Their limbs were twisted and they carried spears and long-bladed axes. Others looked like insects, their black exoskeletons writhing with malice. Jace could hear the horrible sound of their mandibles clicking as they marched. He also saw the Bothian Horde spread out before him amidst the host. Their long arms and clawed hands looked ready to rake over the Keepers.

Their eyes were brimming with bloodlust. Other twisted shapes were fitted into the army. Some looked akin to the dreadful mass he had seen in the Mines of Shorn and others were indescribable. He saw some that were simply black, their thin forms shifting the light around them. They reminded him of what a soldier by the name of Grimly had once told him. He shivered at the thought of the army overrunning the Gap as he recounted Grimly's tale of horror.

Just when he thought they would charge, the army stopped as if ordered by some invisible voice. In the corner of his mind where the Watchers' song had dwindled came a hiss like the sound of rasping coils. Jace listened to it for only a moment before dismissing the voice of Sa'vard and turning his thoughts back to Yeshua.

The black mass halted before the March Wall. The two opposing armies stood facing one another: the brilliantly blue sky and golden sun over the Keepers shining brightly against the midnight black of the hosts of Sa'vard. His army stood just beyond bowshot and the two forces bristled openly at each other.

Hadran and Sturbin turned to Jace. From his look of awe, they saw that his eyes were opened to what was so blind to him in the beginning. Each of them adjusted their clothing. Sturbin tightened the leather straps of his breastplate and threw back his white cloak. Hadran unsheathed his oiled broadsword with a steely rasp and stood ready for the fight. Sturbin turned to Jace.

"Now it begins," he said in a hushed voice.

24

THE BATTLE OF THE MARCH

Jace stared at the sight before him. The armies of Sa'vard stood motionless while the black cloud of Watchers circled overhead. All along the wall, the Keepers stood silent. They watched the unearthly force with hard faces, waiting for a signal from their leaders. The air was as tight as a bowstring and rippled with expectancy.

Sturbin grabbed Jace by the shoulder and the young man wheeled around on him. The aged commander gave Jace a look of all seriousness. He spoke gruffly to him:

"Go to Alaric. Tell him to begin when he sees fit."

Jace stared at Sturbin, but the old man turned and pointed over the houses behind the Wall. A thin tower ran straight up into the sky. It swayed slightly in the breeze, the single flag atop its pinnacle fluttering furiously. The slender wooden structure had several lines of rope trailing out from along its height that were staked into the ground beneath. A lone figure stood in the small tower high in the sky. A gleam of light reflected off something that the man held and a small silhouette of an arm waved in Jace's direction. Jace raised his hand and gave a perfunctory wave in return.

"Go boy!" yelled Sturbin tightly, shaking him to his senses.

Jace darted into the crowd of soldiers. He unslung his staff from his pack and held it in his hands, using the long piece of wood to move the more dazed troops out of his way. Sturbin's voice and his sudden awakening had injected a need for urgency into Jace's bones, and he ran with all the speed he could muster toward the tower in the distance.

As he pushed through the crowds along the March Wall, several of the troops began stirring from their stationary positions. Knights and swordsmen were unsheathing their swords and picking up their lances. They tightened each other's armor and slid their visors over their faces, making their last preparations for the battle. Axemen and regulars began sharpening their weapons. They set about their work without a sound. Crews of men and women stoked fires in large braziers and others that were underneath the bubbling kettles of pitch and oil. The charred odor added to the mixture of battle smells that hit Jace's nose as he ran along the Wall. Archers began stringing their bows, flexing the strings and propping their quivers in an easy to reach place along the stone parapet. Some went so far as to knock a shaft, tense their weapon, point it out at the Enemy, and squint as if to judge exactly where the first volley would fall.

Jace dodged through the people and found the nearest set of stairs. He tumbled down the four flights, hitting the ground in full stride and ran between the houses. Few people hampered his mission now as most of the streets and alleys lay empty. Only crews of Keepers gathered around the oddcovered litters that housed the machines Trel had seen the day before. They were loosening the canvas as he passed by several of them, the men and women scurrying quietly as their leaders encouraged them in low voices.

A horse reared up in front of him. Jace sidestepped the animal as its rider brought the beast to a halt. He had been watching one crew uncover one of the strangely shaped weapons and not paid attention to where he was going. The rider gave him a harsh look while his beast pranced forward.

"Watch where you're going, boy!" the armored man yelled. It was not a threat of anger as much as it was a warning of safety. The man's voice was not hateful and he took Jace in with a worrisome manner, making sure he had not injured the young man. His helmet was low and covered his eyes, but Jace recognized the broadsword which hung from his side. Arthur raised a gauntleted fist and saluted Jace.

"May Yeshua protect you today, lad!" he said and wheeled his charger away into the houses. Jace stood alone in the empty street. He looked around cautiously to see if the roads were clear. He swallowed, trying to catch his breath and ran on.

The tower was higher than Jace had thought. The thin ropes that held it in place creaked and groaned as they fought against the wind. The wooden foundation had giant legs that jutted out along the ground. Iron spikes were driven into the earth and braced the tower somewhat from any major gusts. A hefty ladder ran up and over the gear house that Alaric had once shown Jace. It seemed pitifully small, vanishing into the wood as it stretched skyward. Jace gulped as he looked at the monstrosity lurching from side to side. He shook off his fear and began to climb up the rickety ladder.

Halfway up the tower, Jace chanced to look down. Objects seemed noticeably smaller at this height. He could see over the Gap Wall already, but still had plenty more rungs to climb. A gust of wind clutched at his cloak and he clawed at the steps of the ladder, almost losing his footing. He gripped it against his chest, closed his eyes and calmed himself. If he were to survive today, he would have to remind Alaric to install tethers to this beastly structure.

The climb ended below the lookout post. Jace struggled up to the bottom of the floor and tried to push the hatch open with his head. It didn't budge and he hung for a moment, prostrate on the ladder, fearing he would have to start back down. He banged as hard as he could on the underside of the wood, returning both hands to the ladder and gripped it hard. He squeezed his eyes shut, trying to shut out the feelings of the tower swaying in the wind and the noise of the groaning ropes and wood. He hung on for what seemed like an eternity while he listened to whoever was inside thump around the floor of the tower. Something was dragged across the cabin and several smaller objects seemed to fall on the wood and scatter across the floor. He heard a voice mutter in annoyance and then the hatch was raised with a squeak of its hinges.

Alaric stood peering down at him. His face was positively beaming and he looked as if he was having the time of his life. Something rolled out the hatch and plummeted to the ground. He watched it go with obvious dismay.

"I could have used that," he grumbled.

"Never mind that! Get me out of here!" Jace squealed, desperately clinging to the ladder.

Alaric grinned at him and pulled him up by the cloak with one large fist. For one horrible moment, Jace dangled in the air, suspended only by Alaric's burly arm and then the man set him on the floor. He turned and shut the hatch while Jace closed his eyes and caught his breath. Alaric gave him a smile and started picking up things that sprawled over the cabin.

"Sturbin sent me up here," he proclaimed to his friend.

"I know," he boomed, rummaging through several parchments and picking up a handful of tacks from the floor. "I requested for you to be dispatched to me after he had gotten done with you."

"What do you mean?" asked Jace curiously.

"I needed a helper," Alaric said shrugging his shoulders. He pointed off to his right and left at several smaller towers that stood in a row behind the buildings. Each held two crew members who scanned the formations of the Keepers as well as the layout of Sa'vard's army. "Sturbin thought these machines could prove useful and I've been assigned to oversee the whole operation. Actually, it's not that important. We have already discussed the order of events. All actions are prearranged, but he wanted me here, in case something went wrong. I would be able to communicate with him before anyone else did, and his hands would be freed for other matters without having to oversee the entire process."

Jace cocked his head to one side, but Alaric continued. He pulled Jace to his feet and picked up a round wooden cylinder.

"If we see something, we can place a message in here and send it down the wires to several places," he said pointing at the ropes that dangled from the cabin. Three ran off to the March Wall at diverging angles. Others trailed off to the sides to the other watchtowers behind the buildings and one ran out from behind the cabin to the parade ground. Alaric pointed along the March Wall, glowing excitedly. "We can communicate with them by rolling a parchment inside, fastening it to the wires and letting them slide down the lines. They would be picked up by couriers and sent to the commanders at their posts."

Jace had never heard of wires, but as Alaric showed him, they were smooth lines of rope. They were slick to the touch and extremely thin and delicate looking. The cylinder messages would have no trouble sliding down the finely woven strands. The man showed Jace around the tiny cabin, pointing out other odds and ends. He had sheets, maps, and several nick-knacks crammed into the small space that Jace had never seen before. He spread a map out on the floor which held a general sketch of the area.

"Sturbin and Hadran are stationed here," he said stabbing his finger at the center of the map. He lifted his head over the side of the cabin to point northward, showing Jace the correlation of places on the map to the real world. The large flag of the Gap did not need any introduction. Sturbin had made it known to all, including Sa'vard, where he would be. This settled the troops a little more and set the battle on a grand scale. Jace could almost see Sturbin and Hadran underneath the flag. The forces surrounding the two soldiers were fully armed and bore the markings of Sturbin's personal guard.

"Miss Pell is housed in the infirmary here, but she relieved Lashara and sent her to the rear to form another auxiliary station for an overflow of wounded troops. Lashara didn't like it, but she follows Miss Pell's instruction obediently.

"A strong willed women, that one," snorted Alaric. "I don't see how Hadran could butt heads with her all these years. She's raised Lashara up to be as bull-headed as she is herself. Still, if all goes well, she'll make a fine wife someday, provided she knows when and where to speak her mind." Alaric gave Jace a look as if he had said too much and went on, "Arthur and his mounted band have dispersed from protecting the archers with the rest of the knights. He did not let them go willingly. After a brief conversation with Hadran, the majority of his troops were positioned around the infirmary to our western flank."

"That must have been awkward," Jace interjected.

"At least they are speaking to each other," Alaric said in passing. "Do try to pay attention Jace, this is rather important. If there is a breakthrough, they can move in and plug a hole in the defenses, or be used to cover retreating troops from a rout." He set his hand sideways, making a wall on the map and then dragged his other hand across the map from north to south, giving Jace an example of what Arthur's position would be in a general retreat. "Constable Bilscen has lined his mounted troops on the eastern flank and will be covering the same responsibilities. Sturbin thought that Constable Wood should take the position, but he deferred it to Bilscen and took up stations along the Gap Wall farther to the east with the rest of the dismounted troops."

"Constable Wood is here?" Jace asked, taken by surprise.

Alaric knitted his eyebrows. "Didn't you know? East Haven has been emptied. Only a handful of people were left at the fortress to tend to custodial matters with a small compliment of guards in case anything should happen."

"But what about the students?" Jace asked.

"They came along with the troops," boomed Alaric, pointing to the wall of black-cloaked figures at the far side of the parade ground. "They certainly would have had a field day with all the Mentors gone, but Constable Wood thought we would need every man and woman we could use. This is, after all, a Calling, Jace. It is not as if we were going out for some grand picnic or dress formation. The forces of Sa'vard have assembled en masse directly on the other side of that wall. Every able bodied Keeper has been summoned in our defense."

"I know, I know, I guess I just wasn't thinking," he said prodding his big friend to continue. Instead, Alaric was looking south out of the cabin at the young mass of Keepers that had assembled. Behind their line was a formation of large, white tents marking the auxiliary infirmary. Jace squelched the memories of Lashara as soon as they began to rise. She was in the tents, no doubt, huddled over the casualties that were coming in from the west and had forgotten about him already. He wrenched his mind away from her image and examined the group of youthful Keepers. Their number was far larger than that which was on the March Wall. They were concentrated in one place with uniform colors and maybe that was why they seemed so formidable, but Jace frowned at their numbers.

"They are so young, " he mused. "Some are younger than I and have never been outside the Gap, let alone seen a war."

"They will shortly," said Alaric with seeming disregard. "We all have to grow up some time. Those children have tasted the freedom of the Gap that so many have paid for for so long. It is time they pitched in for its defenses. Sa'vard won't wait for them to finish their studies. Besides, they know all that it takes to stand in the Gap."

"They just seem so disordered," Jace said, eyeing the crowd in hopelessness.

"They better shape up, then," Alaric said gruffly. "If all else fails, they are our reserves. They will have to hold the line while the rest of our forces retreat and form up behind them."

Jace gave an audible groan. His growing confidence in the extravagant plans had been dashed when Alaric mentioned their fallback scheme.

"I hope we don't lose this," said Jace. He thought a moment and then asked a question. "Who's leading them?"

"Dorath chose to," Alaric said over his shoulder. He was rustling through the maps and pulling out a long folded parchment. "The man drew the short stick when the lots were cast. Some think he was quite happy to go to the rear after you two had it out. Others think he's turned coward."

Jace cast his eyes to the floor. He had hoped to find Dorath with Sturbin and reconcile their differences. Alaric's remarks stung him. If Dorath's confidence was shaken by what he had done, he would never forgive himself. The man was a reputed soldier, but if he was rattled, there was no telling what he would do. The impervious plan was starting to look like bad armor with chinks aplenty. Jace was growing agitated the more they talked. He looked over the lot of them, saying a silent word to Yeshua that their hearts would be calmed. Alaric stood by his side, looking down on the students with him.

"They're from all over the Gap, you know," he said waving his hand at them. "All the places of learning have emptied out. The commanders along the March could not send any troops, but they were able to send all the Keepers from those hidden places. What you see is almost the entire generation of youngsters that lives within the Gap."

Jace looked over them. They must have tallied in the thousands, though he was not a calculator of numbers. This high up, they all looked the same, but he knew they were vastly different. The students of East Haven took to the sword and staff. Those in the Western Highlands were brought up by the bow, taking after their fathers. Others had different weapons, but that was only the beginning of their disparities.

Some had peculiar teachings. East Haven instilled in its students the idea of "will-choice" and "immersion," and was quite conservative when it came to matters of the Counselor at work in the world today. However, he had been told that other secret places discussed such things as "forward-destiny," speaking in foreign and heavenly tongues, and were liberal with the laying on of hands. When you got right down to it, it was a wonder there was any unity among them, but their common bonds of all praise and worship to Yeshua and adherence to the fundamentals of their faith were stronger than all the differences that separated them. It would play havoc with the Gap if they ever saw differently.

Yet, looking over their numbers, Jace was still worried of their courage in battle. He could see Dorath riding up and down their lines with his silver sword drawn high and his black cape unfurled. He was encouraging them while making adjustments to their formations as his white stallion pranced along the parade ground. He did not look or act upset, but Jace still wondered if he had marred his Mentor in some deep way.

He ducked as he backed away from the side, his head nearly hitting on an iron contraption rigged to the top of the cabin. He gave Alaric a puzzled looked and reached out to examine the object.

"Do not touch it!" he said heatedly. He came between Jace and the twisted piece of metal, making sure it had not been tampered with.

"I'm sorry, Jace," he said, lowering his voice. "It's just, this was installed only yesterday and I don't want to have it meddled with just yet."

"What is it?" Jace asked, drawing close with curiosity.

"A means of evacuation," Alaric explained, scratching his head. He reached out of the cabin and jerked hard on the sides of the object. Two iron bars pulled down to rest horizontally. The piece was attached to the smooth wire that swooped down to the line of reserves where Dorath stood. Alaric grasped the handles. "You grab here and here. After swinging out of the cabin, your weight loosens the switch and you slide down the line away from the tower."

Jace pursed his lips trying to imagine the thing in action. The thin wires looked thick enough to hold only the tiny wooden canister Alaric had pointed out earlier. Surely, they would not bear the weight of a single individual—with or without armor. He shook his head, his face turning white.

"Have you ever made anything with tethers?"

Alaric shrugged, "I may decide to after today. I'll have to see how the ride is, I haven't tested it yet."

As if it weren't possible, Jace's face turned several shades whiter. He was now trapped in a tower, high in the air with the only means of escape besides the way they had come being two bars of metal attached to a wire that was not much thicker than one of his hairs. *Could the day get much worse*, he thought. He turned away from the machine feeling sick.

What Alaric showed him next boosted his spirits tremendously. They were the old sketches of his equipment that Jace had first seen in the forest a year ago. As he scanned the paper, he saw some minor adjustments. The drawings were of the three machines Alaric had showed him. He had no need to study the tower structure, having a thorough tour of that already. The "fence-laying" machines seemed vague and of little interest to Jace.

What really caught his eyes were the giant illustrations of the bow structures that rested on carriages. He had glimpsed them as he moved about the camp and had overheard some of their improvements. Alaric gave him a supreme smile as he went over the vehicles inner workings once more. Jace had seen the machine in action on its trial run and it looked rather devastating, if it was properly used.

"Will they work?"

Alaric gave Jace a hurt look. "Of course," he said with boyish arrogance. "I put the finishing touches on them myself. They were designed for massed formations and it looks like Sa'vard has obliged us with the perfect opportunity to test them in battle."

Jace sucked in his breath. "You mean they've never been battle-tested?"

Alaric shook his head. Somewhere a trumpet sounded. They both rose to their feet and stared out over the March Wall.

"No," said Alaric in a hushed voice, "but they will be now."

THE DAY DRAGGED ON. For some reason, the host of Sa'vard had not moved. The armies eyed each other, gauging the other's strengths, and matching their wills. The sheet of black stood plainly before the March Wall, spread out like some panoramic night sky on its side. The cry of the Watchers echoed through everyone's mind, searching for a foothold of fear and the army below them waited, unmoving. The Keepers seemed hesitant to open the engagements, and the sun moved across the sky ever so slowly. Alaric showed Jace a few of the other objects he had in the cabin. The things were interesting, but did little to quench the growing anxiety that churned inside him.

He handed Jace a set of flags. One was dyed bright orange like the setting of the sun. The other was an iridescent green that played with the sunlight as it twinkled on the fabric. By holding them in certain positions, Jace could communicate with the other towers in simple signals. He spent the day making use of the flags and practicing the signs that Alaric had shown him.

"You're getting quite good at that," his big friend grinned, looking over at him as he talked to the tower to their right. Alaric was holding a leather scroll that was rolled up and tied twice along its width. A heavy piece of glass protruded from each end and glowed in the sunlight. The glare caught Jace's eyes and he dropped the flags.

"What is that?" he asked, his jaw hanging open in astonishment.

"Don't know," mumbled Alaric, twirling it in his hands. "I found a merchant in the Clonesian Empire who was selling these on the streets. They had shiny rocks inside and made pretty images when you held them up to the sun. I found that by emptying out the rocks and trading out the glass, you could make images that were far away come closer."

"How does it work?"

"I don't know," Alaric said with a shrug. "You can try it, if you'd like."

Jace cradled the object in his hands. He brought it up to his eyes and squinted, mimicking Alaric. He pointed it at the March Wall and the people jumped out at him as if they were before his face. Jace nearly threw the object out of the cabin in excitement, but Alaric caught it. After calming down, he asked Alaric to try it again, but the hefty man shook his head.

"I only bought ten of them from the merchant. I gave one to each lookout and kept two for myself. I would let you have this one, but the other one fell out of the cabin when you arrived."

Jace remembered the object that almost hit his head when Alaric opened the hatch. He began to sulk at his loss, but things were moving too quickly now as the sun descended from its apex. One by one, torches sprang to life all along the March Wall. Alaric ordered him to look sharp, and they each grabbed their weapons, as if the light were a signal of some kind.

It was only mid-afternoon, but the shadows were long. They each stood in the cabin, watching the black army and March Wall for any preemptive attacks. The blackness before them added to the darkness, seeming to chase the sun from the sky. The blue heavens remained constant despite the leaning of the dark shadow in the north. Sa'vard's army stood in silence, seething coldly at the majestic sky.

The March Wall was quiet and the troops held their breath waiting for something to occur. Out across the hilly moors, a solitary drum began to play. Its rhythm was foreboding and with each beat another drum picked up the cadence. The black mass stood motionless as the instruments hammered out their rhythm. Both camps stood still as the sound filled the air, building until it overtook even the screams of the Watchers.

Alaric scribbled a short note on a parchment hastily and sealed it in one of his cylinders. He hinged it to the thin wire and with a hurl of his arm, sent it shooting down the line. All lightheartedness was removed from his face and he viewed the disappearing object with a frown and stood waiting. He picked up the leather scroll and pointed it down at the March Wall, holding it close to where archers stood on either side of Sturbin's staff.

He focused his view on a lone archer who dipped his arrow into a glowing brazier. The tip flamed to life and he pointed his weapon skyward. The shaft leapt from his hands and surged into the air. All sound stopped as both armies watched the lone arrow rise to its zenith and plunge to the ground. The flame stuck in the earth just a few paces shy of Sa'vard's host. The Watchers let out a shriek of fury.

Alaric pulled a curved horn from his belt and brought it to his lips. The note that blasted from its end pierced the cry of the Watchers and more horns bellowed from the line of watchtowers. As his ears cleared, Jace could make out the shouts of men and women that were hidden between the buildings. The short barks of their leaders rose above them as they rattled off commands. One by one, Jace saw intense glows erupt from behind the houses. Shrill horns sounded first from one place then another. Moments later, giant shafts of burning timbers were flung into the air as Alaric's ballistas revealed their positions. The fletched timbers rose high into the air, over a hundred strong, and dove down into Sa'vard's armies with devastating effect, their ignited lengths bursting into the massed troops with a shower of fire.

The host of the Gap let out a roar of victory as deep pockets were cleaved amidst the black soldiers. The horns were sounded again and the ballistas launched another volley that rained down on the motionless soldiers with unnatural results. Great holes lay in Sa'vard's army, but still they stood. The Keepers cheered again as the weapons thrust their horrible flaming bolts into Sa'vard's massed troops.

After three volleys, the Watchers let out a cry of their own. The sound drowned all others from the battle plain. As the terrible shriek faded, the hosts of Sa'vard began to form ranks. In spite of the damage that had been done, their troop was vast as the Unending Sea. They unsheathed their weapons and pushed in tight as they prepared to charge.

On Alaric's commanded, Jace waved his flags in a circular pattern. The signal showed its effect as all along the line, archers knocked their arrows. The black host advanced slowly and the archers waited until the army was well within range. Then, with a trumpet blast, the arrows rose into the sky, like thousands of blades of grass. The shafts poured down on the horde of advancing troops, causing whole lines of the Enemy to disappear as they came.

The cry of the Watchers became more urgent and the pace of the army quickened. Another time the archers loosed and the force crumbled before them, but they came on with a frightening resolve. The wave of night rolled up to the March Wall, crushing the few vines that were about their feet and attacking its stone base in fury. Archers fired into the shadows at will while the nightly host raised ladders in hopes of scaling the walls. One by one, the Keepers set about the army, pouring boiling pitch and oil on their heads as they dashed themselves against the March Wall. Torches were thrown down into the crowd, incinerating the army in a burst of flames. The work was thorough and the army withered under the attack. The host reformed and retreated as the Keepers let out a cheer, chasing the foul beings with arrows and spears. A number of them fell and the March Wall let out a roar of triumph at crushing the charge of Sa'vard's army.

Thrice more the throng of Sa'vard threatened to take the March Wall and thrice more it was beaten back. The Watchers trembled wickedly, shrieking their ghastly song and swooping about the battlefield in loathing. The terrible war drums of the enemy rolled on as the day ended, but the battle was in the hands of the Keepers. They gave glory to Yeshua with each victory and with each defeat of Sa'vard, their songs of praise grew louder.

Even so, the armies of Sa'vard did not waiver. They threw themselves at the foot of the Wall with a fervor and bloodlust that made the Keepers reel back in surprise. Each time they retreated, the field was littered with more of their number, but still they came on to no avail. Each time they withdrew, more troops of black slid over the moors to take their place. Their strength never faltered and they attacked always with the same zeal.

The sun tumbled from the sky and soon the earth was lost in shadows. The Keepers set about their stations, preparing for night while teamsters and porters drove a steady stream of supplies from the depot to replenish the front. Jace cheered each team that passed far below him as the night went on. His doubt had been replaced by awe as he watched the successful plan of Sturbin and his staff being carried out before his eyes. All troops set about their work with a determined effort to keep the March Wall alive and the Gap free from Sa'vard's minions. They knew if they fell, their numbers would be scattered, the world overtaken by Sa'vard's hand, and the earth would be plunged into unmitigated darkness.

25

THE FINAL BLOW

As night settled about the Gap, an eerie silence replaced the sounds of battle. Jace was at first euphoric with happiness, and he and Alaric stayed in the tower as they watched the troops go about their business. Most of the scene was doused with the thin glow of torchlight, but the space around the infirmaries was well lit. Jace could see a tiny stream of soldiers pouring into the buildings. Most of them were walking, but some had to be carried. Among them were some who did not move.

The sight suddenly made him feel hollow. He was removed from the chaos of the front, but the line of Keepers going into the infirmaries reminded him that this was a serious affair where some had paid the ultimate price in defense of the world. He was at a loss, feeling mournful and yet indifferent. He had not met most of the soldiers, and it seemed strange that people he had never known would die for him. He was aware that they had families and loved ones, and even though he did not know them, he felt a certain pain within his soul at the loss of his fellow Keepers. Their sacrifice had kept the rest of them safe. Though he was saddened at their loss, he was grateful for what they had accomplished. The torches in the rest of the place flickered about the camp, casting a multitude of shadows. The light was comforting, however, and everywhere else, people were busy working with little fear of Sa'vard's army breaking through.

The other side of the wall sat before them in silence. It was as if a huge barrier had been thrown up between the two forces. The black of Sa'vard's hosts loomed in the darkness since no fires were set in their camps. They seemed to remain in position as if they were asleep on their feet. Their actions were unnatural and Jace shivered and tried not to think about what the Enemy was doing.

Two hours after nightfall, Alaric called for Jace's assistance. He sent one cylinder to the towers on their right and left and then motioned for Jace to follow him. He opened the hatch and descended through the hole into the blackness beneath. Jace followed after him with a kind of reluctant obedience. The two of them climbed down the tower and set foot on the parade ground. The solid surface felt good under Jace's feet, but he had to get adjusted to the fact that the ground did not shift with the wind. They moved over the parade ground, through the buildings and found the Pavilion.

Bright light spilled out into the street from its doorway. Jace and Alaric walked past the two ceremonial guards and into the hall. People flooded the room, but talked in soft whispers and small groups. Most of them were officers and commanders of certain detachments from sections of the March Wall. Alaric pushed his way through the crowd, excusing himself several times, and made his way to the familiar table in the back of the room. Sturbin was leaning over it with Hadran at his side. Shereel stood next to them with Eckalus and Master Lumphar in the corner. Arthur was at the far end of the table with some white-smocked representatives from the infirmary. Jace did not see Lashara or

Dorath, but Trel was sidled up next to Arthur. Other leaders stood around Commander Sturbin: some of his general staff and a few quartermasters from the supply stations. He was hunched over the maps tilting on his arms and eyed the paperwork about him with a deep grimace.

"It was due in large part to the preparations," Eckalus was saying to him while everyone else listened. "The months that we have had in planning were not wasted today. All the time spent shipping supplies to the proper places, fortifying the March Wall, and assembling the troops was brought to fruition today. If I might say so, I was quite pleased with the results."

"As was I, Eckalus. We all did a splendid job and every one of us should feel a sense of accomplishment," said Sturbin. He stood up and rubbed his gray, stubbled chin pensively. "But, we all know that our plans mean nothing should they not be blest by our Lord. The work we do is in vain if Yeshua does not lead us."

He turned and looked at the people gathered around the table. Each one of them held his gaze as he went on. "Sa'vard does not have to defeat us by destroying our defenses. Should we take confidence in our own actions, we will surely falter." He paused and folded his arms in reflection. "We had great cause to cheer today, for the hosts of Sa'vard were dealt a mighty blow. Do not chastise your troops for their spirit, but warn them with all due speed that they and their actions mean nothing. The battle belongs to the Lord."

Many of them voiced their agreement with his words, but still he went on. "I must confess, I am wary. Sa'vard knows the hearts of men and his devious nature can draw out evilness and deceit like a river even in the driest land. Be on your guard and tell your soldiers to be also. The opening actions were merely a testing of our defenses. I fear Sa'vard has a deeper plan that we know nothing about."

Arthur stepped forward and looked at Sturbin. "What shall we do tonight? We do not know when the next attack shall be. How shall we set the watch?"

"Only half the troops shall remain on the March Wall with sentries posted every 20 paces," ordered Sturbin. "The rest should take shelter in the houses below, but let them keep their weapons within arms reach."

"What of the pickets?" asked Constable Bilscen. His face was spattered with mud, and he looked like he had been riding all day. "We have gotten spotty reports from them. I doubt they can see too clearly in the dead of night and several have had run-ins with the enemy. The last group that was sent out has not returned and they are well overdue."

Shereel stiffened at Constable Bilscen's comments. Her dress was spotted with mud about its fringes for she too had led troops of horsemen beyond the March Wall. She shifted uneasily waiting for Sturbin's answer.

The area around Sturbin's eyes wrinkled slightly at the news. They had all hoped to use the forward scouts as a buffer between them and Sa'vard, but the news of the latest group was not good.

"Stop the pickets," said Sturbin curtly. "We need every able bodied person in our defense. I would have enjoyed their reports, but we cannot afford to lose more men and women."

He turned to Master Lumphar. "The machines you and your apprentice have dreamed up have come in very useful today," he said casting a sidelong glance in Alaric's direction. "You and your crews are to be commended, Lumphar. They acted gallantly and caused the enemy to think twice before mounting another assault."

"Thank you, sir" said the little man quietly. He seemed oddly void of his usual anxieties and took in the brief moment with a hint of satisfaction.

Alaric stepped forward and gave his report. "From what we can see, everything went according to plan," he boomed quietly. "The ballistas opened fire at the proper range and the archers held their ground. The use of the oil and pitch kettles worked well, but I did see areas where Sa'vard's army did succeed in scaling the wall before being beaten back by swordsmen and regulars. This area, in my opinion, should be reinforced."

Sturbin turned toward Hadran. "Tell Grimly and Tover to spare some of their troops for those places."

Hadran nodded with a scowl.

Sturbin then bid Trel come forward. "How has Dorath made out?"

"The Keepers are nervous, sir," said Trel chattering away as he went. "Dorath has done an amazing amount of work in so short a time, but most of the students have never seen such a display of hostility. We have tried to encourage the younger ones to read the Song of the Ages in their spare time, but the sounds of battle do little to spark concentration."

Jace eyed his friend while he spoke. His bruises were fading from his face and, by the way he carried himself, most of the burns about his midsection caused him little trouble. It was good to see that Trel had regained some of his natural easiness. The thin man winked at Jace with a grin while Sturbin continued with his thoughts.

"Some things can't be helped," the commander simply said. "Tell Dorath to continue his labors. His work may be the hardest of all, but many of us feel that his actions and obedience to Yeshua may prove the outcome of the day."

Many of the leaders around the table knit their brows in confusion at Sturbin's words. On the whole, Alaric's assessment of Dorath was rampant throughout the camp. Several of the officers saw the man as a coward and thought the fight had been taken out of him at his meeting with Jace. Though they had heard the argument behind Dorath's decisions with Blynn, they still viewed him as a lesser Mentor, and some voiced their happiness that he had been relegated to reserve status.

Jace caught some of the haughty smiles of Sturbin's general staff. Their puffed-up views of self-importance stoked Jace's loyalty and he prepared to lash out at them in Dorath's defense. He would have, but he felt Alaric's hand slowly clutch his arm in warning. The two exchanged glances and Jace eased his temper.

They went their separate ways that night, all of them returning to their field positions. After eating their rations, Jace climbed his way up the tower at Alaric's feet and crawled into the cabin with exhaustion. Alaric let him sleep and he curled up in the corner.

Daylight found Alaric looking out across the field with his small scroll. The powerful lenses gave him superb vision of the entire battle and he used the flags and cylinders of parchment to communicate readily where he saw fit. Jace rose to his feet and surveyed the scene at Alaric's side. Besides some readjustments of troop placement, the place looked exactly like the day before. All traces of Sa'vard's dead had been removed from the field. The space between the two armies was clean once again and the vanishing of the midnight dead sent chills up and down Jace's spine.

"You cannot kill them, at least, not as we think it," said Alaric off-handedly. He glanced at Jace to see if he was listening and spread his hand over the arrayed armies of Sa'vard. "The images you see before you are shapes that Sa'vard's minions take. They live on a different plain of existence than we do and though we may see them, they are forever alive and will not die, much like the soul of man. The Watchers and Sa'vard's army are only seen by us, but no Keeper can kill them. They are only banished by Yeshua's power working through us and even then, they do not cease to exist. Their final doom awaits them in Scheil-duum, the lake of fire, when our Lord will set up His reign over the new earth as prophecies have foretold."

"Sa'vard's host was part of the Almighty's army at one time. He led them astray and caused a rebellion that threw him and his followers—a third of the Creator's host—out of Par'lael. They are powerful and immortal beings, much like you and I, but have turned to follow the Lord of the Night. What you see before you is not all of them, but remember, the army of the Almighty is greater and, even if it weren't, our Lord and Savior is."

Jace listened to Alaric silently as he brushed the sleep from his eyes. The day stretched out before them. Every so often a lone ballista would fire across the empty space between the armies. Its flaming timber would fall short more often than not. Once in a while, the shafts would sink into the unearthly host, scattering the army in a spray of fire. The Keepers would cheer, but the black army would simply ooze forward with more troops taking the space of their fallen comrades. The odd sight was disheartening and the Keepers began to grow uneasy at the persistency of Sa'vard's troops to stand under fire. The black sheet of soldiers eyed the March Wall like some juicy prize that would eventually succumb to its power.

At midday, the enemy mounted another assault. This time, the army broke off into several smaller units. Each of them moved over the ground with surprising speed. The archers and ballistas had trouble firing on the smaller bands, and only when they were right on top of the March Wall did they begin to take casualties. Some of the groups attacked the wall with ladders while others raked the parapet with a rain of black arrows.

The Keepers had not counted on the army to have missiles in their arsenal, and several of the troops were caught unaware. The first few volleys inflicted severe wounds on the Keepers until the unit leaders ordered their troops to take cover. A long line of wounded soldiers trailed from the March Wall to the infirmary, and the white-walled structure began to bulge with an excess of casualties. The more serious injuries were taken across the parade ground by cart and given into Lashara's care behind the line of Keeper-students. The hail of arrows made it hard for the soldiers to attack their counterparts, and a number of the black army succeeded in securing spots on the wall before being subdued by pikemen and swordsmen. The melee ensued late into the afternoon until the action subsided.

As the sun was setting, the black host tried again. This time, the Keepers had a different tactic. They waited until the smaller units had crossed close to the March Wall, keeping low and avoiding the rain of arrows. When they were nearly on top of the barrier, the Keepers brought oil and pitch kettle crews to the front and suppressed the enemy fire with their own spears and arrows. The solitary units moved to retreat, but a horn sounded and gates along the base of the March Wall opened. Constable Bilscen and Arthur's mounted knights rode forth, cutting off the individual units from retreat and trampling them under a flurry of hooves and lances. The dark soldiers tried to escape, but they were too far from the main army and the horsemen made quick work of their foes. The strategy worked flawlessly and as the sun set on the second day of battle, the Keepers were filled once again with high spirits. They let out a roar as the sun dipped its body behind the Withering Mountains and brought on the night.

Alaric and Jace descended from their perch, much as they had the previous night.

The camp was alive with activity. Soldiers were visiting fallen comrades, and carts were renewing supplies. There were even bands of small reinforcements that were still trickling in from the west.

It was almost midnight when they entered the Pavilion and gathered around the conference table. The same group that had been there before was present, but they looked a bit worn. The prolonged battle was beginning to take a toll on everyone, and several of them sported deep circles under their eyes. They paid attention to Sturbin and the reports, but they were far less animated than last night. Nevertheless, they listened to all that was said and gave special heed to the warnings that were given.

Dispatches from the west had come in that afternoon, and the news was read as it pertained to their situation. Apparently, the main force of Sa'vard was gathered here as Sturbin had suspected. Their faces were all grim as they listened to account after account of how the rest of the March had no more troops to offer. All resources had stopped coming in and supplies were slowly dwindling away. The troops and auxiliaries numbered over 10,000—including the reserves—and the toll that the population was taking on the food stores was incredible. If Sa'vard decided to sit his army out for the rest of the week, the soldiers would be forced to disperse. Many of them listened with growing agitation. The victories of the past two days seemed to amount to very little. Should they be forced to dismiss some of their troops, the situation would fall apart. Already they were hardly evenly matched with the black host and that was only if they maintained a defensive posture. A number of them stood in silence, mulling over every possible aspect in hopes of finding some means to take to their advantage.

After a while, Sturbin sighed. No further ideas existed and they were forced to play the strategy that they had devised all along. Since the last night had gone so smoothly, Sturbin decided to leave the March Wall only lightly armed. Most of the troops would take a long night's rest in the houses to be prepared for whatever tactic awaited them tomorrow. The horses were ordered to the stables and only those who needed use of the night, namely the teamsters and porters of the supply lines, were allowed to engage in their activity.

ALARIC AND JACE SLEPT IN THE BARRACKS that night along with the regulars. The entire camp was exhausted and went to sleep without much coaxing. Jace did not feel right sleeping less than a mile away from the spearhead of Sa'vard's forces, but he eventually succumbed to slumber as well.

They did not sleep long. Over the March Wall came far-off rumbling. The noise set the earth shaking and even the hardiest of soldiers tossed in his sleep. The sounds were like giant groans of unseen beasts. Mixed in with them were the rasping of chains and the grating of wood on wood. Many a person lay wide awake, staring at the ceiling as the sounds filled the night air. What awful beasts and machines laid claim to those noises, none could tell. Some soldiers questioned the sentries, but they could see nothing in the blackness. Archers that launched their flaming arrows into the darkness saw them extinguish as soon as they reached Sa'vard's army. The blanket of black-on-night spread out before the March Wall like the wings of a hideous dragon.

A shrill horn of the sentries cut through the night. At first, Jace thought he was dreaming, but another tore through the silence, sending the barracks into confusion. Before he knew what was going on, Jace was heaved from his bed by Alaric and caught up in the turmoil as soldiers darted about him in chaos. The alarms sounded as thousands of Keepers spilled out into the streets. The sky was dark and the smoky torches gave off only a fraction of the light he was used to. The images he saw were a tumble of troops and soldiers, regulars and the like, all running to their stations in the night air.

Alaric clutched at Jace's arm, pulling him through the turbulent crowd. They forced their way out onto the streets amidst a growing flood of screams and orders. A procession of knights was off to his right trying to make headway through the disordered mob, but they were pushed back as a torrent of young Keepers ran to their stations on the far side of the parade ground. They were all strapping on their cloaks and carried their weapons at their sides. Their eyes were big and they looked about them in fright as they ran, caught up in the chaos.

Alaric clutched at Jace's cloak again and pulled him into the mass as they headed for the tower. The torchlight was terribly dim, and he stumbled and almost lost his footing as he pushed across the parade ground. They climbed up the machine in a hurry, bursting through the hatch and setting about checking the flags and cylinders that were so key to their communication.

While Jace went over their supplies, Alaric checked the charts. They were engrossed in their work as the sea of Keepers ran about like chaotic ants far below them. A flash of light snapped their heads up and forward. They watched as a single shaft curved up into the sky and landed somewhere farther down the March Wall to the east.

Only then did they notice. Over the March Wall the landscape was filled with burning lights, torches, bonfires, and other strange flickering illuminations that lit up the wilderness and the moors. Even so, the blackness of the army sucked it in, not revealing a single solitary form. Within the darkness, Jace and Alaric could make out the faintest traces of shadows. It seemed that giant structures were hidden just beneath the blanket of darkness. The sight filled Jace with fear and he gripped the cabin as it shook in the night wind.

"It's always darkest before the dawn!" Alaric bellowed above the shouts of the Keepers. He lifted the strange leather tube up to his eyes and scanned the darkness, hoping to make out the shapes. They were hidden from view, but he could see the tide of soldiers as they climbed onto the battlements and ran to their positions. Alaric stifled a curse at the alarm. He was not given to harsh language, but being startled and surprised was never a good thing when it came to war. He watched as the soldiers climbed into their positions and formed their rag-tag line on the March Wall with more coming every moment.

Beyond the blackness, he could make out large shapes twisting and moving. He watched for a moment before raising the horn to his lips. As he did so, three other watch-towers sounded their alarms. He threw the horn down on the floor and set about scribbling notes on parchment before shoving them into cylinders. Jace was signaling to the towers and troops as Alaric finished writing. The broad flags billowed in the wind. Alaric yelled at him as he sent the cylinders down the wires.

"Put those away!" he ordered in a frantic voice. "Those won't work in this light! Come over here and help me!"

The two of them dove deep into a box sitting underneath the small counter while the horns still blared their warnings. Alaric pulled out his old steel and flint, and sprayed a loose liquid over the flags. Jace held the flags out of the tower while Alaric struck the steel against the flint. Flames jumped up the flags as the sparks took hold.

"Now!" yelled Alaric.

Jace turned away and began waving the giant torches to the towers at their side.

Alaric gave three short blasts of the trumpet and fumbled through his charts. The blackness was twisting and turning as the two moved about the platform. They could see large hidden objects turning toward the March Wall. Orbs of fire moved with them, glowing white hot. Alaric and Jace watched them as they moved, hoping their signals would not go unnoticed.

"Do you think anyone sees us?" Jace said over the hollering of the crowd.

"For Yeshua's sake, let's hope so!" roared Alaric.

Hadran was standing at the March Wall. He braced the parapet with his arms scowling down at the darkness as the troops fumbled their way about the wall in the dim light. He was one of the first to take his position and watched as the rest of the soldiers clamored up the stairs and about their equipment. Some of them had left their weapons on the wall, despite orders not to do so. They searched through the crowd, hopelessly lost in the growing disorder. Brazier fires had gone out during the middle of the night and soldiers worked furiously to set them ablaze. Behind him, ballista crews were readying their machines, making sure the lines were taut. They began loading the heavy timbers as soon as enough of them arrived.

Hadran sneered as the general staff congregated under the billowing flag. Despite their heavy armor and polished weapons, the do-gooders did little but follow Sturbin around while others did the work. They looked nervous, but ready for whatever had caused the alarm. Sturbin followed them, Shereel close in his wake. His face was as grave as hers.

"Where are we?" he asked Hadran, his voice out of breath from the long run to his station. He looked about him, taking in the order of things at a glance.

"Nearly half the troops have assembled in their respective positions," said Hadran flatly. "The eastern flank is ready, but the western flank has hardly a soul on the wall," he added, pointing at the empty parapet.

"Where are they?" shouted Sturbin with impatience.

"Grimly and Tover made the necessary adjustments like you ordered," Hadran replied. "I believe they moved much of their extra forces from the eastern flank. Either the troops forgot, or they are having a slow time forming in the confusion," Hadran said, pointing to the flood of soldiers who were still running through the houses to the March Wall.

"We need that place defended now!" cried Sturbin. He wheeled on Shereel, his eyes burning. "Find whoever you can and defend that position, you have my orders!"

Shereel nodded and disappeared in the crowd.

Behind them, a thin metal plate banged noisily. On its surface was a long round cylinder of wood. Sturbin took the object, stuffing his forefinger into the carved wood and pulled a parchment out. He unfolded it and scanned over the words hastily, turning to the massive tower behind him. He could see Alaric and Jace waving the torched flags wildly and turned to his general staff.

"How many ballistas are readied?"

The staff shifted on their feet, turning to look at each other, not knowing the exact count. Sturbin yelled at them and they fumbled for words. In rage he leaned over the rear parapet and hollered to the crew at its base.

"We need all crews to fire into the wilderness at will!" He screamed. He turned to order Hadran, but the black-cloaked figure already had a flaming arrow knocked in his bow. Sturbin nodded and Hadran sent the bolt into the night. The Commander of the Eastern March turned back to the ballista and nodded for their response.

"We're missing half our crew! We can't lifted the lumber into place and have no one to position the target."

Sturbin pointed at five of his staff and swung his arm down at the ballista.

"Get down their and help them!" He hollered. The men gave nervous glances, then jumped over the side of the wall, landing on the machine and slid to the ground. Under the leader's orders, they took up the ropes and began readying the machine.

Sturbin turned back to the wilderness, his eyes growing wide. The blackness twisted in contortions like a thin, impenetrable sheet. The shapes must have been less than 300 paces away, but they were still mostly imperceptible. Giant boulders of fire danced before his vision, their shapes moving in time with the shadows. He hollered back to the crew to hurry the ballista and turned to watch the shifting night.

Trumpets blared above the noise. All along the disorganized line of Keepers, a ragged volley of ballistas loosed their flaming timber. The long shafts tore the fabric of night apart, illuminating all that was hidden to the naked eye. The bolts soared over the thick mass of soldiers, plunging into their ranks and destroying whole units that were gathered in tight. The flaming trees sent the low brush ablaze and the soldiers could see beyond the tainted blackness as Sa'vard's army strode forward.

The bulked forces marched together, building momentum as they came. Their numbers filled the wilderness and continued on past the moors, disappearing over the darkened horizon. Another wooden cylinder fell on the metal plate, but Sturbin already knew what it read. He raised his voice over the chaos.

"Ready the archers!"

As more of the soldiers rolled up the stairs, they began stringing their bows and knocking arrows. They flexed the strings and angled them up, waiting for the command to loose.

"Fire!"

Arrows hissed from their arms even as they were met by a flurry from the enemy. The Keepers threw themselves to the ground as black shafts darted out of the night to land among the forming troops. Hadran peered into the darkness behind cover of the parapet. Their own arrows were falling into Sa'vard's soldiers, but the momentum of the black host now carried them over the slain as they made the final dash over the open land to the March Wall. He looked out into the night just in time to see the shrouded machines stop for one fateful moment and then release their boulders of molten fire. The hideous flickering light shot up into the night sky in a wide arch. Both armies seemed to hold their breath, watching where the flaming projectiles would land.

THE MARCH WALL WAS A BUBBLING MASS OF DISORDER as the soldiers ran through the houses. They pushed their way to the front only to stop at the crowded flights of stairs. They huddled about them, yelling and struggling to make headway as too many fought to climb the cluttered steps. Most of the students had assembled on the other side of the parade ground, but the turmoil amidst the houses up onto the March Wall was still in full swing.

All along the wall, units were beginning to form up. The trickling in of troops over the rising sound of battle was too slow and Alaric and Jace watched with growing dismay as the host of midnight closed the distance to the Gap. A lone arrow shot into the sky, its flaming tip visible to all. As it disappeared in the darkness, flaming timbers shot into the night, landing among the army with devastating results. The ground rose up and small fires of underbrush played about the roiling black mass. Despite the losses, the legions of Sa'vard rolled forward with one mind toward the March Wall. Arrows met them as they churned forward, their line staggering under the broken volleys, but still oozing ahead.

Behind the troops, shrouded in blackness, the great machines of the enemy were swallowed in the shadows. Their lumbering figures turned toward the March Wall, and Jace could see the emphatic glow of whatever strange ammunition they held in their chambers. The structures groaned as the black soldiers swung them into place; a moment of dread passed before the enormous machines released their cargo. The pulsing lights shot up high into the sky, almost disappearing from view as they hung in the air forever while those that watched held their breath. The flaming boulders hurled into the parade ground with a roar that shook the earth. Huge chunks of ground sprayed the air as they landed with explosions of light that ripped through the sky. The scene was cataclysmic, and the Keepers shied away from the carnage with terror.

Most of the artillery landed harmlessly in the field, and the Keepers breathed a sigh of relief. The ballistas returned the fire with their own, setting the night sky ablaze with their light. Their bolts could not miss, and the host took the punishment with resolve as they marched closer. The damage the machines did was enormous, but the sea of troops covered Sa'vard's Lair to the very horizon. Their fire was accented by a rain of arrows that rolled back the advancement of the black army. More and more shafts filled the sky as the walls gathered with soldiers. Brazier fires were finally started and soon flaming arrows leapt into the army as well. Crews were readying the pitch and oil, but the large kettles would take several moments before they could be used. Soldiers prepared to meet Sa'vard's host, unsheathing their swords and lowering their pikes and spears. Sa'vard's catapults launched their fiery boulders again and they fell harmlessly into the parade ground once more.

"They're overshooting the Wall!" Alaric boomed with growing excitement.

The volley of the army was growing less and less terrifying despite its awesome display in front of the reserves. Clusters of archers began singling out the large machines, raking the workers with arrows and sending flaming bolts into the wooden structures. The work around them wavered, but more soldiers picked up where their fallen comrades left off.

The sounds of battle were in full force now. As Sa'vard's army advanced over the last few yards to the base of the wall, the roar of the catapults was matched by the play of the ballistas. The arrows screamed from their bows, and men and women bellowed their orders to crews and units. Soldiers cheered on their fellow troops as they prepared to meet the onslaught of their enemy. Time seemed to be lost in the fray as the battle wore on.

The intermittent fire of the catapults was almost an afterthought in Alaric's mind. Jace and he were busy signaling reinforcements and noting enemy positions and the shuddering of the earth became second nature. They paid the chaos around them only brief regard as they went about their furious work. They only gave the fiery bombardment notice when it was too late.

Alaric was busy scrolling on a piece of parchment when it happened. As he stuffed the writing into the wooden cylinder and brought it up to the wire, a horrible sound filled his ears. He looked over in time to see a huge molten rock slam into one of his buildings, three towers down. The machine rent apart under a shower of splinters and burst into flames as the top two thirds started to topple over. With a resounding crash its length fell on the parade ground, disintegrating in a cloud of dust, fire and wood. The noise filled the battle scene, and Keepers turned from every direction to observe the destruction as three more towers burst into flames.

"They've targeted the towers!"

Alaric looked at Jace in bewilderment as he blurted out the obvious, his face going white. He stared at Jace, stunned, as the watchtowers crumbled around him. Jace looked at his big friend, waiting for him to give some order. He merely returned Jace's stare, his lips moving silently. Jace grabbed the horn and pushed out a shrill note. He waved his flags first to the towers on the right and then his left. All along the broken line, lookouts began to abandon the structures, climbing down them as fast as they could. One man slid down a thin wire. The line bounced and waved, but somehow held him until he reached the ground.

All around them the fragile towers fell as the catapults adjusted their fire. The line of molten flames receded, marching its way backward and began laying about the houses behind the March Wall. Most of the Gap's structures were stone exterior, but their thatched roofs and wooden innards burst to flames as the catapults found their targets. Several stores of ballista shafts were hit. The dry lumber exploded in flames as the pitch-laden wood caught fire. Huge holes punched through the housetops one moment and fire belched from them the next. The lines of houses were turned into a blazing inferno as excess troops, ballista crews, laymen, and clerks hopelessly doused the flames with pales of water.

Only the Pavilion and the infirmary survived the fiery bludgeoning. The hall was almost solid stone. The heavy boulders crashed into the building, most bouncing off it to land in the streets or on other houses. Those that succeeded in breaking through the top were immediately extinguished by the soldiers inside. The infirmary was the only structure that had been soaked in water. Miss Pell had ordered it done yesterday much to the frowning of the soldiers. The action now saved the building from the damage around it, though much of the bombardment was focused on the area to the center of the March Wall. Jace and Alaric watched helplessly as the buildings were pummeled into flaming wrecks. Through the fires, they could see the black army setting up ladders and rolling in huge siege machines as they finally approached the March Wall.

SHEREEL WATCHED THE ACTION to the center with horror. The blaze of the houses filled the air with smoke which was kicked up by the warm breeze. Soldiers were cutting makeshift troughs in the ground to protect the ballistas and their crews from the inferno as the teams went about their work. The weapons were still firing a steady stream of bolts into the dark army.

Sturbin's section was preparing to take the brunt of the assault. A number of the archers had put down their bows and replaced them with short swords and daggers. Shereel caught glimpses of the commander's white cape underneath the huge flag of the Gap. The black form of Hadran was close beside him, his broadsword drawn and waiting for Sa'vard's host. They came on, dashing themselves on the March Wall. Ladders were thrown up and siege machines thrust into place. The bridges of the machines slapped down on the parapet, and the enemy troops spilled across them, eyeing the Keepers. Black soldiers raced up the ladders only to be met by spears and pikes. The Keepers held the attack in place as the two sides exchanged volleys of arrows. Casualties mounted steadily on both sides as more and more Keepers flooded up the stairs and the black army met them from their ladders.

Shereel was pulled away from the view as the action grew furious along her section of the wall. She had gathered whatever spare troops would follow her as she rode to reinforce the flank position directly in front of the infirmary. Grimly and Tover were on their way bringing several other soldiers. She looked about her, wondering if the fires had delayed them.

A large machine loomed out of the darkness. In a matter of moments its siege ramp was flung down on the parapet in front of her. The soldiers attacked it, forming a solid row of pikes and showering arrows into the twisted forms that emerged from the thing's insides. Ladders sprang up along the wall and now her troops set about them, locking combat with the dread armies of Sa'vard. Her line thinned out as they spread to hold back the enemies. Black arrows of the army pushed her forces back even as they met the Bothians and the other twisted troops that threw themselves into the fight. She looked around her, realizing that the Keepers were severely outnumbered. They huddled into a semicircle, pointing their pikes and spears out in front of them. Short blades and broadswords met any who succeeded in breaking their barrier. Behind the wall of weapons, the archers fired into Sa'vard's minions as they poured over the walls.

The Watchers sang in the air. Their song shrieked out their triumph as they watched the army force the Keepers into the wall of flames behind them. Shereel spurred on her troops, but knew that they couldn't hold out much longer. The shifting images of maligned creatures pushed in on her band, suffocating their numbers and threatening to run them clean off the wall. Then, at the last possible moment, a squad of shining knights rushed into the fight, hacking back the black soldiers and regaining Shereel's position on the wall. Spears and swords thrust out causing the Enemy to retreat and abandon their assault.

All along the wall Arthur and Constable Bilscen's knights were plugging the holes in the Keepers' defenses, turning the tide of the battle and pushing back Sa'vard's attack. The black host trembled and broke as the spent troops watched with grim faces. Archers and ballistas chased the routed horde back across the littered field.

The members of the Gap stood and surveyed the damage as they reformed their lines. During the fight, the sun had risen over the mountains, revealing the full extent of the carnage wrought. All was met by the bright blue sky, save for the area over Sa'vard's army where the sheet of blackness stood unmoving. The houses stood in shambles while soldiers fought to quell the dying flames. Their empty carcasses smoldered in the thick haze as all around, the smoke billowed into the sky. Huge craters blackened the ground. Steam wafted from their depths and small fires laced the holes. Skeletons of the scorched watchtowers stood out against the sky, their bleak forms gaping at the Keepers. The troops had thinned severely, but the lines were strong enough to withstand several more assaults. They caught their breath during the brief lapse in combat.

Shereel looked at Arthur and his knights as the rest of her troops turned back the last of the black host. She leaned heavily on her staff and caught her breath.

"Where is Grimly?" she said starting to cough in the smoke. The fires had died, but the haze was getting thicker.

"I lost track of him in the fire. He and Tover were right behind me, but they dispatched some of their soldiers to quench the flames," he wiped the sweat from his brow as he spoke. His chainmail was gashed and bent in several places. He and his troops had no doubt been at work all along the wall throughout the three days of fighting. He looked off toward where the flag of the Gap stood fluttering in the breeze.

"They attacked the center hard, this time. We almost lost them if it weren't for Hadran and the ballista crews. The man is hard, but I dare say he enjoys the fight too much."

Shereel snorted. "One man does not win a battle, neither does our victory rest in the arms of mortals." She swept her hand over the battle plain, "If we are victorious today it will be by the blessings of Yeshua. No man can stop this," she ended looking out at the host of Sa'vard with dead eyes.

While the two sat in silence, Grimly and Tover climbed the battlements with their troops. Their faces were covered with soot and a number of them had cuts on their faces and clothing. Grimly clutched his side where a large red spot showed underneath his leather tunic.

"You came just in time," said Shereel acidly.

"Peace, Shereel," he said steadily, "We've all seen our fair share of battle today."

The old man eyed Arthur and the shepherdess.

"You and your troops are relieved from this position. Get some rest while my men watch this place for the remainder of the day."

Shereel twisted her face with rage, "Do men only stand guard in defense of the Gap? I shall stand where I was placed and only Yeshua shall move me."

"You shall go where you're ordered," Grimly said flatly without a hint of anger. "Sturbin and Hadran both agreed that you two will take up the flank behind the infirmary. We cannot leave that area exposed. If the action gets too heated, you are to retreat with as many as can follow you."

Shereel looked at Grimly for a long moment. Her face was a mixture of anger and fatigue. She left the man followed by Arthur and their troops.

JACE WATCHED THE EXCHANGE through the lenses of Alaric's scroll. Arthur and Shereel led their troops from the battlements to the area around the infirmary while other units reformed along the March Wall. The momentary break in battle gave him and his friend the chance to examine the area and they did so with heavy hearts.

Only from this height could the decimation be seen on so grand a scale. The houses next to the March Wall were covered in a low smoke that trailed into the sky. The acrid smell permeated the air and choked the lungs. The catapults had flattened nearly every structure, leaving everything but the Pavilion and the infirmary in shambles. Sporadic fires were still being fought throughout the buildings and narrow streets. Ballista teams had momentarily abandoned their stations and joined clerks and artisans to stave off the blazes. The soldiers atop the March Wall had stayed their ground, holding back the last charge, but many of the less disciplined units were in shambles and several of their officers were struggling to keep them from dissolving into complete chaos. The eastern flank had held strong, but the left wall around the infirmary was littered with fallen Keepers. Only Arthur's knights had succeeded in pushing back Sa'vard's foothold around Shereel's troops.

Even the Pavilion bore holes in its roof. One of its walls was slumped in ruin where several projectiles had glanced off its side and shaved chunks of stone into the street. The surrounding structures all about the large hall had been reduced to scorched heaps of rock. One craftsman's quarters had been filled to overflowing with dried parchments and roared to life after a fiery boulder had exploded on its roof. More than 20 porters and teamsters had moved up from the supply area and ringed the small building with pails as the flames licked out of control. Jace had never seen such devastation. He stood at Alaric's side, the two of them speechless.

The last of Sa'vard's army had gotten out of arrow range and turned to seethe at the soldiers on the March Wall. Ballistas hurled their missiles into the crowd, but the army took the losses with feigned indifference. They could tell that the last push had nearly broken through the defenses, and they reformed slowly for the final charge. The black mass bubbled with anticipation as they assembled behind the catapults. Figures climbed about the machines, and as the sounds of battle died off, Keepers could hear the clicking of iron against iron while the Enemy adjusted their war engines. The angle of the weapon's arms was dropped down and Jace and Alaric watched with a growing horror at what was evolving.

The army of shadow had grown silent. The Watchers overhead hovered in the air as the beastly machines were given their final settings. Slowly they lumbered forward and halted while the army oozed in behind them, still taking damage from the bolts of flaming timber. Archers joined the exchange, leveling Sa'vard's army as they stood in place. They attacked the host with unrelenting arrows, but many watched the army with uncertain fear. The air hushed as troops waited to see what would take place.

At the last moment, Jace realized what was unfolding. He pulled the horn from Alaric's side and blew the note of general retreat as loud as he could. The noise echoed down the March Wall, and Jace blew into the horn again. The Keepers lifted their ears to Jace's warning in disbelief. Several of them continued to fire as the line held, waiting for the actual order from their officers to abandon the March Wall. They first looked at the lone watchtower with annoyance and then out at the catapults.

Suddenly, the warning made sense, but it was too late. All along the wall, leaders began ordering the retreat, but the troops were caught. Still not understanding, Alaric fought the horn from Jace's grasp, ordering him to stop, but then he too looked out at the catapults with a dreadful realization.

As if waiting until all understood, the catapults released. The molten rocks of flame slammed into the March Wall at a flat angle. The impact shook the mighty battlements, jolting many Keepers off their feet. Shards of rock showered them as they regained their footing and pushed backward to forsake their positions. The catapults reloaded with lumbering slowness as all tried desperately to flee from their attack. The next wave of projectiles made the wall lurch and Jace could hear the Keepers scream out in sheer panic.

The final volley rushed into the high stone barrier while Jace and Alaric watched in terror. Whole sections of the wall seemed to disintegrate before their eyes. The areas disappeared in an avalanche of stone behind the smoldering ruins of the houses leaving giant holes. Jace could see the armies of Sa'vard directly ahead as they began their attack now in earnest. The Watchers pierced the air with their song, flooding the ears of the panicked army and quickening the steps of their troops.

Some sections of the wall still held strong and Jace stared woodenly as he watched Sturbin's troops hold the line. To the right of his position, a wide section had been ripped away, separating him from Commander Wood's remaining troops. The wall to his left was intact and ran all the way to the far flank of the army.

Jace watched helplessly as the catapults focused their attacks on Grimly's troops.

Several ballistas were still exchanging fire with the catapults even as the army advanced. Two flaming bolts ripped through the line of catapults, but the damage had been done already. The remaining awful machines launched their attack, sending Grimly's position up in flames. With a horrendous roar the wall in front of the infirmary buckled outwards in a plume of debris. Ballista crews now fired through the holes along the March Wall directly out into the charging army.

Alaric watched the chaos for one long horrible moment. The image burned into his mind and then he came to his senses. He clawed the horn away from Jace, lifting it to his lips. A long, low note wailed from the horn, stopping all in their tracks. Crews of porters and teamsters burst from the burning buildings, pulling long heavy carts with their teams of horses. The machines spread out across the gaping holes in the wall. At their rear, great wooden rams began thrusting giant fenced sections into the ground. In a matter of moments, the teams had hastily erected a secondary line of fire for the troops. The soldiers raced through the buildings and formed up behind the heavy wooden palisades even as Sa'vard's army rushed in. The action slowed the black army and they moved forward cautiously.

Archers fired over the walls as more troops formed up at their sides. The horsed machines had secured a makeshift barrier in every part of the collapsed wall. Mounted knights charged forward through the damaged buildings to await Sa'vard's host with their leveled lances. Some soldiers retreated through the charred remains to the parade ground while others turned to set up a hurried defense. Regulars and foot soldier units huddled behind the walls of broken houses preparing for one final stand before abandoning their positions and racing across the parade ground.

Alaric would always remember what happened next. The vast armies of Sa'vard seemed to swoon for a moment. The smoky haze over the houses swirled away and then the low drums of the dark host took up their rhythm. The sound rolled across the scene of ruin as here and there officers comforted their soldiers. The scattered remains of Grimly's troops squeezed in behind the fences, hoping beyond hope to stave off the assault from the infirmary. The Keepers bristled behind their defenses as the hideous army spread out before them. Sturbin's forces huddled around the flag of the Gap and eyed the black host with disdain. All were ready to confront their foe.

The drums suddenly stopped and for a brief moment, silence filled the battle scene. The arms of the catapults creaked loudly and released a spray of molten slivers. The rocks ripped through the wooden fences as if they were no more than parchment and the line of Keepers withered under its fire. While the unholy army advanced, the catapults fired again. Their boulders launched high into the sky, landing behind the houses and erupting into a solid sheet of fire.

Alaric looked over the scene, his heart sinking in despair. The forward line of Keepers was trapped between the wall of flames and Sa'vard's army. The black host rushed forward, sensing the hopelessness of the Keepers. The army came on like a flood now, its soldiers steeped in a rage of vengeance. They tumbled forward even as the Keepers set about them with arrows and ballistas. The host of Sa'vard crashed into the wall of Keepers. Lances, spears, pikes, and swords thrust out at the army behind a wall of shields and bucklers. The front line of the army went down under the weapons of the Keepers' all along their row defenses, but more spilled over them. The Keepers absorbed the first few waves. Their line seemed to buckle under the tide of the enemy and then Sa'vard's armies washed over the troops like a black wave. The row of Keepers disappeared before Jace's eyes as the legions of night pressed forward. The tide had turned and Jace and Alaric watched as the shadowy host bubbled over the March Wall in a sea of hatred.

"Do something!" cried Jace, grabbing Alaric by his shirt. The large man stared at Jace, his face as white as a sheet.

Off to the western flank, the twisted soldiers crashed through Grimly's ranks. The line wavered under the shock of the troops and was rolled back like a curtain. The dread host trampled over the Keepers and weaved through the houses. They surged through the hole in the March Wall and swarmed over the infirmary with indiscriminate regard for the healthy or wounded. Jace watched as the white building imploded before his eyes.

"Miss Pell!" he screamed at the top of his lungs.

All in front of him, Sa'vard's army pushed forward. It swept over the line of Keepers with indifference as if they were nothing. The dread host raced forward like a black, all-consuming wave and enveloped the Keepers even as they struggled to maintain a defense. The forms of the March Wall and Keepers alike were lost in the darkness as Sa'vard's army rolled them back. All along its length, the Gap's defense was dissipating.

Jace eyes came to rest on the March Wall to where a circle of Keepers stood around the flag of the Gap. He could see Hadran and Sturbin side by side as the sea of black pressed in around them. Their backs were to each other and their faces were set in stone. Sturbin's white cape and their two broadswords stood out against the dark host. Their blades flashed as they held the dread host at bay. Their soldiers defied Sa'vard's army even as it engulfed them. The troops were nearly overran and the flag wavered. Sturbin and Hadran's band was lost from view for one brief instant, and then the flag rose up high in the air as the army of night was beaten back. Only a small group of soldiers valiantly huddled around Hadran and Sturbin and then were lost as the black tide swept over them. The flag fell from view and was swallowed up as the hosts of Sa'vard advanced.

"Sturbin, Hadran! No!" he screamed, but his teacher and friend were gone. The swelling mass of blackness filled his view. The Watchers swam over the black army and the luminous shadow of night pulsed forward behind them. The army toppled through the shambles of houses and moved to the edge of the parade ground. Jace lurched forward out of the cabin, but Alaric pulled him back. He thrust Jace to the floor shaking him back to his senses.

"Jace, Jace, it's too late!" he hollered over the growing song of the Watchers.

Jace shook his head, sobbing uncontrollably.

"No! No!" he shouted over and over.

"You must leave this tower!" Alaric boomed.

"No, I won't do it!" he yelled, struggling against the large man.

"You must, Jace!" he roared, lifting Jace to his feet. With one hand he pulled the strange barred machine in the rear of the cabin into place. The shuddering mass of Sa'vard's minions were writhing slowly over the parade ground and Alaric could feel them climbing up the tower. The cabin shuddered again and he thrust Jace before the iron bars.

"Go!"

Jace struggled with his friend, screaming and kicking wildly, but Alaric pushed him over the edge of the platform. Jace gripped the bars, kicking his legs about the open air. The mechanism clicked into place and lurched forward. Jace watched below him as the line of Sa'vard's army clawed their way up the tower. They were lost from view as he sped over the parade ground along the thin wire, picking up speed. The remains of the routed army were fleeing across the field as fast as they could. Over the grass, the remaining reserves of the Gap army flew towards him. Jace could see Dorath atop his white stallion galloping up and down the line. Three soldiers broke out from their ranks and began running towards him. His screams were lost in the wind as the line of Keepers rapidly filled his vision.

He was some seven spans over the ground when the line slackened. It shook violently and then the line went limp. The ground flew up to meet him as he fell from the sky, still clutching the iron bars. He hit the ground and skidded over the grass a good 20 paces. Jumping to his feet, he turned around just in time to see Alaric's tower hurtling toward the ground, its form covered with the black shapes of Sa'vard's troops. The giant tower crashed into the earth, its fragments flying everywhere. Jace reached out his arms.

"Alaric!" he wailed.

He ran towards the tower, but something was holding him back. He crumpled to the ground as Trel, Clarissa, and Bartemus tumbled over him. They dragged him to his feet and pulled him the 50 paces to the reserve line.

Jace was crying uncontrollably and his friends huddled near him. As they dropped him to the ground, they hugged him, consoling him while he wept. His face was covered with mud and ashes mixed with tears. He came to his feet, his heart filled with anguish and rage.

Dorath stood before him, his gentle smile washing over Jace. He slid off his stallion and touched Jace on the shoulders, looking deep into his eyes with forgiveness and pity.

"It's alright, son," he cooed gently.

"I'm sorry, Dorath," he cried, hugging his Mentor fiercely.

Dorath cradled his head in his arms. "It's alright."

He let go of Jace and jumped on his horse. The white stallion stood before the Keepers, painted against the backdrop of flames and Sa'vard's menacing troops. Dorath rose up in his seat, waving his sword over his head till all looked his way. He pointed the silver blade at the host of night that was forming up on the other side of the parade ground.

"Friends, brothers and sisters, fellow Keepers!" He cried. His voice pierced the song of the Watchers and carried throughout the scared host of student-Keepers. He looked over the throng of young soldiers and pointed his blade low at the field toward the approaching shadow. "I stand before you today staring the very hosts of Sa'vard in the eyes. Our precious wall has crumbled, all our preparations have been quashed, and our friends, Mentors, yea, even our family lie crushed underneath the tide of our enemy."

The mass of Keepers was crying as he spoke, the actual events of what had occurred sinking into their hearts while he talked.

"But I say to you that all is not lost! The storm may blow and the wind may beat against our hearts, but the men and women of Yeshua will not forsake their Father! The battle is hopeless, but I say that is when our Master does His most awesome works! Our Savior has called us to stand in the Gap and we will. Join me as I offer my thanksgiving to our Lord and Master before we meet our foe. If the Almighty is for us, who can be against us?" he roared. "Join me!"

The 4000 students dropped to one knee as all along the parade ground, the armies of Sa'vard lined up. They twitched with hatred and the Watchers screamed malignantly as the Keepers closed their eyes.

"Our Father, hear our cries! We come not as victorious soldiers, but as humble servants. Our enemy has slain us today, but we know that You hold the victory! Let them see Your glory, Father! Let Sa'vard and all who witness this know that You are the One who alone has produced the victory which no other can claim! We bow our hearts before You and sing our praises! If we wake soon from now in Your everlasting presence, we will sing our praises still! Yet, if we leave here today with a victory that only comes from You, we will not forget Your faithfulness. Whatever happens, we give You glory for what is done here today!"

Dorath's words rose over the scream of the Watchers, touching both the ears of the Keepers and Sa'vard's army. The black host trembled and twitched as Dorath spoke, his crying out to Yeshua and the Almighty sending a chill through their souls. They shifted where they stood as more of their number washed over the March Wall and took their place opposite the Keepers. They sneered at the Chosen as Dorath spoke. The Watchers shrieked in fury while he continued.

Yet, even as the song of the Watchers rose in strength, it dwindled in volume, as if pushed from the senses by an overpowering calm. In its place came the faint whispering of another song. It sounded like the soft bubbling water in a mountain stream or that first ray of sunlight that tinges the morning sky. It was barely perceptible to the ears and some dismissed it as peculiar background noise. Even as they did, it grew steadily, tickling the ears as it progressed. The melodious song welled up around the Keepers as Dorath spoke. It had no words and when the Keepers were asked later to describe it, they would only say it was like the white of mountain snow and the smell of the freshest wild lilies. Its notes were pure and rang out to all in wonderment. The chorus washed over the hearts of the Keepers, turning their fear to peace, and chased away the terrifying song of the Watchers.

Something else happened as Jace knelt with his fellow Keepers. As the battle sounds around him died away and were replaced by the notes the joyful chorus like those that praised the Most High in Par'lael, the air began to stir. It was only the smallest of breezes, in fact, if you questioned someone else, they may have said it was nothing. The stillness shifted ever so slightly, running over and between the Keepers. Jace's eyes were closed, but he swore to himself that he could feel hundreds, perhaps thousands of other beings standing side by side with him and the Keepers. The air was electrifying and he could sense the hair on his neck prickle. A fabric of the softest texture seemed to brush across his cheek and he started, keeping his eyes closed while he spoke to Yeshua. At last Dorath was finished, and the throng of Keepers opened their eyes.

Directly before them stood a thick ribbon of blinding white that separated them from the bubbling mass of black soldiers. The swath was so close many of them could reach out and touch it. The Keepers threw their hands before their faces and Sa'vard's hordes reeled back in terror. As their eyes began to focus, they could see that the light was made up of thousands of figures. Their pure robes shined brightly about them. They stood side by side, their features the very essence of tranquility.

The beautiful song filled the ears of the Keepers as their eyes ran over the strange, silent men. Overhead the bright blue of morning shown in the heavens. The sun was in full view now and filled the scene with its glorious light. The brilliant colors ran to the very edge of Sa'vard's army and stopped. The sea of the black army stood in check while the Watchers circled high above them. The looming shadow that had flowed with their advance now lay billowing before the bright light of the sun and the shining white host.

Jace stared at the soldiers. Their ranks were massed together tightly. Every one of their robes was void of distinguishing characteristics. Their flowing garments ended at their wrists and ran down to their ankles. A golden belt was wrapped about each of their waists. From this hung a sheathed broadsword at each man's side. Their faces were timeless, having neither wrinkles nor beards, yet bearing no boyish resemblance to that of a youth's. They studied Sa'vard's forces without fear or malice. Only a look of finality filled their eyes. Jace picked out the familiar forms of Rendolph, Zax, Obban, and Torne from among the sea of faces. He could never forget the ones who had been the instruments of his salvation in the Mines of Shorn.

The image of the men in white was a sight that only a few of the Keepers had witnessed before. To those that had seen them, never were they amassed in so large a formation or assembled in a strength so great. Neither could anyone remember their forms being so stunning or majestic.

Only the glorious sound of the chorus filled the ears of the Keepers. Somewhere outside their heads, they heard the faint sound of the Watchers' song and the rasping, inaudible voice of Sa'vard himself. For a moment, the two melodies played in their heads: the one vibrant and lively, the other dark and foreboding.

A lone man stepped out in the field between the men in white and the black host. He stood up, calm and defiant against the sea of night and raised his hands. His robe was brighter than the sun, and his voice rang out like a bell for all to hear:

"In the name of the Almighty and His beloved Son, Yeshua, I command you to leave this place!"

His words were like steel and the midnight forms before him wavered under the reproach. From the shadows came the grating voice of their master and the horrible scream of the Watchers, urging them on to destroy the remaining Keepers where they stood. Their hideous shapes trembled with rage and they coiled up, prepared to meet the challenge of the heavenly warriors.

As one, the shining armies of Yeshua brought their swords to bear. Their blades blazed with white-hot light and they marched forward in a solid line halfway across the parade ground. The hosts of Sa'vard stretched through the smoldering forms of the houses, over the ruined March Wall, and out across the wilderness and moors all the way to the horizon. Their forms melded with the advancing shadow and the Watchers in the air, forming a churning mass of pure hatred to match the gleaming forms of the Creator's army.

Within the blackness, the war drums began to beat out their rhythm. The dark soldiers lining the parade ground stirred, formed ranks, and pushed across the field to meet the white host. As the sea of blackness advanced, they pushed forward with all their might, letting out great shrieks of rage and malice.

They crashed into the white army with a roar that shook the earth. Their spears and axes clashed against the blades of the men in white. The fury of the black host was met by the resolve of the gleaming soldiers. Their white forms lashed out at Sa'vard's army, their blades sweeping away the dread host as they advanced.

All about the front, the combat was heated while the two armies clashed and swayed, locked in a struggle of epic significance. The Creator's army shuddered under the ceaseless blows of Sa'vard's host. Their flaming swords reached out to their macabre counterparts. As their blades met bodies, the shrill forms would fizzle and fall. Beastly images of mandibled creatures and ghastly shadows threw themselves against the wall of white-clad figures with fearsome shrieks. Clawed arms of the Bothian Horde attempted to rake the men in white but they were cleaved asunder by the flaming swords. The faces of Yeshua's host set about the sea of black deliberately carving away the shadows as they came.

The Watchers dove upon the white-hot ribbon of men. From out of their tattered cloaks sprang great talons, and they whispered their icy promises to snatch away solitary forms and carry them to Scheil-duum. Their terrifying screams filled the air as they set about their prey. The unearthly shrouded harpies swooped down from the heavens, alighting on Yeshua's host, but their nails were turned away. Though they clutched about the men in white, their actions were to no avail. The gleaming army met each foul claw with resolve, hacking the limbs to pieces. The stormcloud reeled and churned, ceaselessly trying to capture their betters.

All along the host, the action persisted and the Keepers stood for a moment, shocked and awed at the presence of Yeshua's deliverance. With tears of sorrow still wet on their faces, they watched as their cries for mercy were answered through the hands of the white army.

Slowly, ever so slowly, the waves of the black sea began to recede. The white soldiers rolled them back with their swords, stabbing and striking as they tumbled forward only to be beaten back again. The black army roared out in extreme, unquenchable hatred as they realized they could not break through the gleaming line of soldiers. Still, they threw themselves relentlessly at the wall with dogged determination urged on by their master's orders. They howled and scratched, clawing at the men in white, but to no avail.

Great war horns sounded among the black army and the Watchers screeched relentlessly as they continued to swoop into the fray. Out of the sea of darkness rose the blazing orbs of molten rock, launched from the catapults. The hundreds of pulsing spheres shot high into the heavens and rose over the army of night toward the white host. As they passed over the white army, great slashes of light ripped from the sky. The bolts of lightening consumed the molten rock even as they descended upon the white host. The orbs vanished in a shower of sparks and flames as the jagged fingers reached out to them all along the front of men.

The Keepers watched breathlessly as their hour of doom was turned into triumph. All around them the armies of the enemy were beaten back, some breaking and running. The Keepers' brows of worry were replaced with smiles of joy. Their tears of defeat turned to cries of praise.

Dorath rode before the mass of soldiers. His stallion whinnied restlessly, standing on his hind parts before dashing to where Dorath rallied the Keepers. All who looked saw the hope and determination clearly written upon the Mentor's face as he watched the white host drive back Sa'vard's forces. His features glowed with excitement and renewed will as he urged the reserves to take up their arms. He raised his silver blade high in the air and pointed toward the sea of blackness. His voice was filled with triumph and elation as he roused his fellow Keepers to plunge into battle.

"For Yeshua and the Almighty!" he roared.

The Keepers joined him, cheering as one as they threw themselves into the fray. They rushed into the black hordes, fighting side by side with the men in white. Their staffs and swords lashed out at the enemy while the archers sprayed them with arrows. Sa'vard's army pushed into them, but their advance was stopped short.

The black host staggered under the shock. All along the lines, the hosts of Sa'vard fell or shrieked away as the wall of Keepers and shining soldiers pushed them ever back. The enemy's screams of triumph became desperate, and they hurled their mass into the troops to no avail. The catapults continued to launch their boulders, but a dreadful shower of explosions rocked the Gap as the fingers of lightening desecrated their attack.

Then, the jagged light pierced down into the roiling mass of blackness. Its bolts played about the catapults, setting them ablaze like a line of torches. The lightening struck out all along the plain of Sa'vard's soldiers, sending panic into their ranks with each horrible flash. The lights exploded about the ground, lifting up huge sections of earth and spraying the black hosts with dirt and rocks.

The armies of Sa'vard lurched forward in one desperate, final attack. As the line of Keepers and men in white beat them back, the churning mass of blackness reeled and broke. All along the plains, the armies of Sa'vard turned and fled as the jagged lightening danced through their ranks. The wall of Keepers and Yeshua's army moved forward, spurring on the rout until Sa'vard's soldiers ran about in sheer panic. All along the line cheers for Yeshua and the Almighty rang out as they turned back the shadow of night. The blue sky advanced, pushing back the bubbling tainted blackness as the forces of darkness fled.

All around Jace, the Keepers swarmed forward with the white host to pursue their foe. They ran over the parade ground and through the houses, following the black soldiers with vengeance in their hearts and praises to Yeshua on their lips.

Jace hung back from them a moment as they charged through the houses. The battle was a rout. His army would not miss one less pursuer. The heavy loss of all his friends began to weigh on his heart. Jace had been caught up in the awesome turn of events, but now his tear-stained face turned down the line to where the crumbled remains of the infirmary stood. So many friends had been lost today. It would take weeks before all the lost were found, counted, and all the bodies buried.

He had not seen Alaric's body when they had passed the splintered remains of the tower. Sturbin's section was far too wrecked and meaningful for him to approach just yet. He made his way to the western flank where Miss Pell and the destroyed infirmary were. Today was a day of miracles. Maybe his old friend was alive. He ran down the field, keeping close to the houses.

The place was ravaged. Sa'vard's soldiers had left no one alive and no stone unsettled. The devastation was only matched by the loss of life. Jace picked his way through the shambles looking for the diminutive woman. The sounds of the battle were growing distant and he suddenly felt very alone. Rubble was everywhere and he ended up in a dead end before a high stone section of wall. The piece was possibly the only section of the infirmary that was untouched. He secured his staff to his back and grabbed the craggy surface, scaling the wall and steeling himself for what lay on the other side.

The wall overlooked a scene of carnage. The roof of the infirmary had caved in, leaving nothing of the building but a buckled heap of stone. Solitary pillars stood amidst the chaos overlooking the horrible sight. A thin cloud of dust hung in the air over the destruction. Jace heard a pile of rocks fall to the ground behind him and he spun around on the wall.

At the base of the wall were stragglers of Sa'vard's army. Five hideous soldiers came forward. Three had huge hooked snouts, their jowls drooled profusely and curved into wicked smiles. They wore short, black vests of dyed wool and their furry legs ended in cloven hooves. Two held short spears in their gauntleted fists while the third grasped a long sword. The remaining solders were dressed in black cloaks. Their cowled faces were hidden, and they grasped two tall, black bows in their arms. A quiver of arrows hung on each of their backs. Their bows were strung and each had knocked an arrow. The five of them started as they caught sight of Jace and then slowly moved forward toward the solitary Keeper.

Jace scrambled on the wall, pulling his staff off his shoulders. He gave one look at the five and realized he was hopelessly outnumbered. He turned and jumped over the other side of the wall. The twisted forms shrieked with anger and began pounding on the stone barrier. Jace looked around for some place to hide, but the broken roof held little promise. The wall creaked behind him and he spun around just in time to see it collapse. He threw up his hands, letting go of his staff as he shielded his face. The boulders knocked him over and pinned him to the ground.

He tried to get up, but his leg was lodged beneath a large stone. It was bent at an odd angle and when he tried to move it, it only twitched. Jace struggled to his knees, but his shattered leg filled with pain and he cried out. The soldiers picked their way through the boulders and circled around him with growing hunger. They licked their snouts and lowered their weapons.

Jace clawed at his staff. The shrouded archers fired at his hand and he screamed out as the two shafts pierced his palm. He clutched his fist close to his chest, watching the soldiers as they pawed the ground, ready to move in for the kill.

As they lunged at him, Rendolph appeared out of nowhere. He stood over Jace's body, holding his flaming sword aloft. The black soldiers howled at the warrior and threw themselves at the lone white figure. Their weapons rang out as they crowded around Rendolph. They seethed openly and pushed in, hoping to overpower him. Rendolph deflected their blows, his fiery sword laying about the black soldiers with dreadful precision. The archers loosed their arrows at him, but he turned them away with one large swing of his blade. They pulled daggers from their belts and launched into the melee. Rendolph danced away from them, swiping and thrusting as they charged. His eyes were hard and he glowed with the power of his Maker. His attacks were swift as flashes of lightening, and before long, the five soldiers lay at his feet. Their black forms faded from view, vanishing to dust.

Rendolph came to Jace and heaved the boulder from off his shattered leg. Jace moaned as the gleaming figure kneeled down by his side. The leg was twisted and bent in several places. Blood soaked through his breeches. Jace lay motionless while Rendolph examined the damage. He came to Jace and lifted him to his feet. The young man groaned looking down at the appendage that flopped at his side.

"Come. I'll carry you," Rendolph said softly.

He picked Jace up in his arms and carried him through the piles of rubble.

The black host of the Enemy had long fled over the remains of the March Wall and the place was strangely quiet. The black shroud of Sa'vard had retreated and only unblemished sunlight shown down from the blue heavens. Rendolph carried him through the houses and over the parade ground to the auxiliary buildings. He walked through the secondary infirmary and laid Jace on a bed.

"Rest for a while, Jace. Much has happened today. Sa'vard has been defeated and Yeshua has been glorified. Think not on the losses of your friends. Rest."

As Rendolph finished speaking, Lashara stood over Jace. Her small form was dwarfed by the towering Rendolph. She was worn and exhausted and deep circles of stress were under her eyes. Her lips trembled as she examined Jace's wounds. Lashara looked into his eyes and burst into tears, embracing Jace's broken body. She buried her head in his chest, shaking with deep sobs.

"I thought I lost you!" she wailed, her voice thick with emotion as she clutched his cloak desperately. The two wept openly, embracing each other while Rendolph looked on.

EPILOGUE

"Jace, it's time."

Jace opened his eyes. Lashara was standing over him, dressed in her dark riding cloak. Her hair was pulled up and looped behind her head into several intricate braids. She wore a slender silver necklace with a heavy amber broach. It had been a gift from Miss Pell. The woman looked beautiful in spite of the somber mood that pervaded the Gap. He nodded to her with a thin smile.

"Okay," he said weakly.

He tore back the covers and propped up his body. Trel and Clarissa came forward. The two helped Lashara move Jace into position. They pulled him to his feet and steadied his body. Lashara nestled herself underneath his left shoulder while Trel held up his weak side and Clarissa walked behind. Inch by inch they moved him, resting halfway across the floor while he caught his breath. His face was twisted with pain, but he had stated several times that he would make the journey. Finally, Lashara had given in and his friends had pitched in to help.

Lashara had done her best with Jace's body. The man's leg was completely shattered. After she had done a closer inspection, she had not been pleased with her findings. The boulder had crushed Jace's leg. It was a wonder he was left with any appendage at all. His leg was broken in three places above the knee. They were mostly clean breaks and had not caused any major bleeding or swelling, but these were the least of her worries. Jace's lower leg and foot had broken through the skin in six places. When she had gone to set it, the skin and bones inside felt like a back of rocks in her hand. The skin was squishy and had a reddish-blue color and putrid smell. When she and Shereel had sterilized the cuts, Jace had howled and they had to sedate him.

His hand was another problem. The barbed arrows of Sa'vard had mangled his palm and when Jace had come to, he could not feel or work his fingers. Lashara had wrapped it and put it in a sling. She had set his hand and leg as best she could and cast them in a stern mixture of plaster and cloth after closing up the wounds with half a dozen poultices. All that could be done now was to wait. It would take another miracle for him to have any use of either of his limbs.

They walked out through the doorway to the long line of Keepers standing in the sun. Their horses pranced restlessly while the mounted Keepers waited for the small procession to get ready. They placed Jace in a sling and then carefully raised him up into a cart. Lashara made sure that he was properly cushioned, touching his cheek affectionately and smiling before taking her place in the front with Shereel. The two exchanged glances and Shereel nodded to Dorath.

He brought a horn to his lips. The low, mournful note ran down the line and the procession turned up into the Withering Mountains in silence. They departed through the gates of East Haven and followed the winding path which led to the Unending Sea.

Dorath rode in front with Arthur, Alaric, and Hadran at his sides. Hadran and Alaric were the worst of the four. Miraculously, the two had been found after Yeshua's army had purged the Gap clean of Sa'vard's forces. They had been taken to the infirmary and only Lashara and Shereel's skill had kept the two from losing more blood. Alaric's arm was in a sling and a bandage had just replaced the tourniquet that covered his leg. All were surprised that he had not suffered more when his watchtower had sheered apart and plummeted 60 cubits to the ground.

Hadran's jaw had been broken and his face was a puffy mess, but even that could not hide the scowl that always hung on his lips. He had been found buried under a large section of the March Wall that had collapsed outward. His body was next to Sturbin's, underneath the flag of the Gap and was discovered only when the soldiers had made a second pass of the area. He had said next to nothing since he had woken and only paced the broken remains of the March Wall in solitude while he grieved for his commander and friend.

Even Arthur had sustained a fair amount of contusions and lacerations. A deep gash ran the length of his right forearm and his large frame limped gingerly when he was out of the saddle.

Among them, only Dorath had minor cuts. His presence and words to the Almighty during the final stages of the Battle of the March had been whispered of amidst the Keepers and some of them eyed the man with a kind of reverent honor. The four acted as if nothing were wrong. They guided the long snaking column through the mountains for the next several days without a word.

Behind them rode Constable Bilscen and the knights of East Haven. The Council had hurriedly placed him in charge of East Haven's soldiers after the fall of Constable Wood. The troop was mixed in with what was left of Arthur's warriors—their shining armor now bearing many a gash and scar. The mounted knights were followed by scores of pikemen, swordsmen, and regulars—their numbers noticeably thinned. These gave way to the black-cloaked student-Keepers from all across the Gap. Teamsters, porters, artisans, clerks, and craftsman all brought up the rear of the column with several wagonloads of stores.

The procession traveled quietly around the bland peaks. For the early days of autumn, the sun shone very brightly, but the languished mood about the Keepers did not change. They stopped three times each day and ate their meals with nary a word. This journey was a ceremony of sorts, but even so, the Keepers' silence was much more than a ritual. After two weeks, the strong smell of sea-salt filled their nostrils, and the mountains gave way to the cliffs. The jagged rocks stared lonesomely out across the waters as the first blues of morning painted the horizon. The roar of the waves on the rocks far below and the cry of the gulls were the only sounds that hailed the coming sunrise. The Keepers spread out on the bluff, preparing for what they came here to do.

They dismounted in silence and formed all along the cliff. All of them waited quietly, going over the events of the past year in their heads. The joy of their victory through Yeshua had been dampened by the severe loss of life.

For Jace, the list was long. He would always remember his many friends that he had made along his journey and those that he had known before. He would never forget Dolmer's quirky phrases, his round belly, wispy hair, pipe, or his jovial narrations. Nor would Master Lumphar's angry tirade or high-strung temper pass soon from Jace's memory. Kindly Grimly and aged Tover were also gone. Their stalwart defense had allowed for many others to survive the retreat across the parade ground. He could still see Eckalus adjusting his tiny spectacles and clearing his throat for some extravagant explanation of the inner workings of the Gap. All the unsung work the man had done could never be replaced. Jace had never found the time to talk to quiet Master Klim. The steady man who was always at Miss Pell's side would be forever missed.

And how could he ever say good-bye to Sturbin and Miss Pell? The two individuals had always seemed so immovable and timeless like the very heights of the Withering

Mountains. Sturbin's gentle watch over his actions and instruction had played such a large role in shaping his life. His arrival from out of Jace's past had been too short-lived. Miss Pell's ever-listening ears, soft critique, and gentle persuasion were like an endless wellspring of knowledge that Jace had relied on for so many years. These and so many others had departed this world forever.

At least Jace's family was spared. It was not much consolation amidst the overwhelming loss, but Sedd, Mailyn, and Amoriah had all survived. They had been one of several families of craftsman who had escaped the bombardment of the food stores. Even Rae was still alive somewhere, but his memory was too hurtful for Jace to ponder atop his other losses.

Everyone in the Gap had lost either friends or family members. Whole villages had been sacked and destroyed from Noll all the way to Aider, but still the tide had turned through Yeshua's blessing. All sang in their hearts praises to their Lord even amidst their sorrow. Though they had sustained immeasurable losses, the Gap had not crumbled, and Sa'vard's forces were still held in check by Yeshua's faithful servants. These and other things went through the minds of the Keepers while they watched the horizon grow bright and listened to the cry of the birds and the crash of the waves.

The clouds in the distance caught the sun's approach in a rainbow of deep oranges and vibrant reds. Dorath moved from his place and stood before the throng of Keepers. His shoulders were bent for he bore the burden of speaking to those around him with the heaviest of hearts. He sighed deeply and began to speak, taking time to ponder his words before voicing each one.

"My brothers and sisters. Yeshua has taken us through the flames of our trials and created victory where there was defeat. For that I am thankful. I will forever sing praises to my Lord and King for what He has done for me, both in this life and in the next," he stopped for a moment and began again. "And yet, my heart is heavy. So many of my friends and teachers have left this earth to join the Almighty and Yeshua."

He pointed his finger out across the ocean. "They have crossed the Unending Sea to find their rest in the arms of the Creator on the sands of Par'lael. Pain can no longer touch their hearts. Fear, they will never know again. Let us weep for them a while, remembering what they have done, and then weep no more, for they are truly alive, at last!"

As his words ended, one by one Keepers came out of the crowd to stand on the cliffs. Each of them had in their hands small baskets made of reeds from the Lars Swamp. Inside them were wide-based candles. They stood before Dorath who lit the heavy wicks with one of his own. When he was finished, each of them said a silent word, thanking Elohim for their loved ones who had been lost and for Yeshua's faithfulness and protection in their time of need. As they finished, they tossed their baskets to the waves below.

The tiny boats were quite strong and survived the pounding surf. They were caught up into the waves and pulled out to sea. The Keepers watched as the line of candles trailed off into the horizon while the sun peeked over the waters. Each tiny candle represented the journey they would take one day when their life had passed from their body and they too crossed the Unending Sea to stand beside their friends and family and sing praises to Yeshua and the Creator.

The throng of Keepers stood out and watched as the tiny flames were consumed in the light of the sunrise. The burning orb shifted to a blazing white as it rose up from the water. The light expanded, growing brighter until a solid sheet of golden sun ran from the horizon to the cliffs where they stood. The Keepers watched, tears streaming down their faces as they said their final good-byes to their loved ones. As the sun climbed into the sky, the waters returned to a foamy sea of dark greens and blues. The lighted baskets had vanished, but this too was a mystery of the Almighty. As they finished, each one turned away from the turbulent water to ready themselves for the long trek back.

After all had left, only Hadran stood on the windy bluff. He had sunk to his knees and looked out at the bleak waves in sadness. The Keepers watched quietly as Jace's friends carried him out to where his Mentor stood. He knelt by Hadran, putting an arm over his shoulder in consolation. Jace could see that his friend had been weeping for some time. In one hand he clutched the giant broadsword of Sturbin. In the other was a piece of Miss Pell's tattered cloak. The ever-present scowl had been replaced momentarily with a look of severe anguish. His lips shook slightly and as he spoke, he struggled to steady his voice.

"So much loss..." he said letting his voice trail off as his tears began again. "So much pain to bear."

He looked at Jace and wiped his face. "He was like a father to me," he said, his voice breaking again. "No one will ever replace him."

He sat for a moment and looked out across the morning sky, shaking his head. His hands rubbed the tiny patch of cloth. "She was a sister in every sense of the word. Without her, I would still be a Clonesian slave, lost and alone."

Jace nodded at the Mentor's words, slightly shocked at the surreptitious connection between Hadran and Miss Pell that was now, at last revealed. The two sat in silence, listening to the waves crash below them. They grabbed each other's hands and began to quietly call on Yeshua. As they did, the sky seemed to brighten and they felt warm hands pressing gently down upon their shoulders. They lifted their heads and turned around.

Rendolph stood behind them, his white robe radiantly gleaming in the morning sun. Behind him were Zax, Obban, and Torne. Each of them stared out over the Unending Sea longingly for a while. Rendolph looked at Jace and Hadran, his lax features putting them at ease. He spread his hands as he began, his rich voice rising above the waves.

"Do not be afraid! Yeshua is pleased by your faithfulness, Jace and Hadran. Your deeds have not gone unnoticed by the Almighty," he let his words sink into the two heartbroken Keepers.

"Rarely are endings void of strife and grief. Though triumph and victory may come, it never is without loss. The March is secure and Keepers shall remain living in the land that Yeshua has set apart for them until His return. May you leave your agony here and take with you the blessings of peace that come only from Yeshua."

He looked deeply into the eyes of the two Keepers. "Take these words to heart. You shall see even greater things than that which you have seen before your lives pass. Yeshua and the Almighty have only begun a work in you!"

He stopped and for a moment, the world seemed to shine with light. Their hearts were quickened as the Counselor ministered to their souls. They smiled at Rendolph and his soldiers.

"Peace!" said Rendolph calmly.

All around, the Keepers watched as the white-robed figures glowed in a blaze of heavenly light. Tiny stars danced around their bodies and the sweet song of the host in Par'lael singing to El Shaddai filled their ears. Their forms shimmered and stretched. The men in white vanished from sight, returning the new day to its ordinary sheen. The Keepers stood alone in silence. A gentle breeze swirled about their faces, and up above them, the sound of great beating wings faded into the distance.

Glossary of Terms

Almaris – the star of true north. There is a tale behind this star.

Chosen - or the Chosen Ones. True followers of the Most High.

Council, The – the unanimous assembly of Keepers who make governing decisions of the Gap

The Counselor – The third part of the Holy Trinity. The Spirit of the Almighty that was sent to man after Yeshua left the earth to dwell in Par'lael until the Creator sends Him to take over the earth again. The Counselor provides wisdom to all Keepers, revealing the mysteries of the Song of Ages to them as they read it. He also intercedes to the Almighty on behalf of the Keepers.

Cubits – three feet

Enemy, the – Sa'vard and all his evil forces

Epistles – letters in the Song of the Ages written by the early Keepers

Fall of Man – the moment in time when Yahweh punished mankind with curses for their disobedience to Him.

Follower of Yeshua – see Keeper

Hands – approximately six inches

Ieysa – Amen

Keeper – those who recognize Yeshua as being the same nature as Elohim—holy, all knowing, all-powerful, and everywhere at once. These people believe that His death was the perfect sacrifice which would cover over anyone's wrongs if they claimed to follow Yeshua.

Kyrie Eleison – Lord be with us

Maranatha – Lord come quickly (lit.)

Na'tal – Sa'vard's minion in charge of persecution of the saints

Old Way – the laws of living found in the Song of the Ages prior to the time of Yeshua's walk on earth.

Oncan'lar – The Almighty's chosen people. Elohim sent Yeshua first to these men and women, but they turned Him away. After the destruction of their homeland, they were forced to wander the earth and make a living in other countries. Most of them became merchants and founded the Oncan'lar guild which is a far-reaching, powerful organization that hordes most of the wealth of Emblom.

The One (Yahweh) – The supreme being who made everything that is, was and will be. Also called the Keeper of Light, the Father, The Lord (Adonai), the Most High (El

Elyon), the Almighty (El Shaddai), Father of Goodness, Creator (Elohim), the Maker, the Master.

Par'lael – The dwelling place of the Almighty. It has been rumored to be across the Never Ending Sea, though none has ever returned to say it exists.

Sa'vard – Kra 'ken, Lord of the Night. Healer of Lies, Son of the Wicked. Cast out of the Par'lael by the Almighty and destined to wage war against Him and His Son till the Dawn of Time.

Scheil-duum – the lake of fire where all the Almighty's enemies and any mortal whose name is not written in the Book of Life will perish. This is the second death.

Sheol – the grave

Sealed – the point at which a person makes the choice to follow Yeshua whole-heartedly

Song of the Ages – the Bible, the Living Word of the Most High

Spirit – see the Counselor

Stalkers – other agents of Sa'vard. They, like the Bothian Horde are a legion that serves his will. These, he has entrusted to probe the Gap's defenses, keeping the Keepers constantly harassed and slowly weakening their resolve.

Strides – approximately three to four feet

The Way – the code of conduct which Yeshua taught His followers to live by

Truth – the knowledge that only comes from the Song of the Ages

Yeshua – Son of the Most High, the Maker of Heaven and Earth, and the rightful heir to the throne of all creation. Kyrie Christe, Adonai, The Lamb, Wonderful, Counselor, the Prince of Peace, the Master. According to the Song of the Ages, Yeshua and Yahweh are one and the same and yet they are two separate beings. These two, along with the Counselor, represent the Holy Trinity, a deity of three separate beings that are one in nature. This is called the Mystery of the Ages that only Keepers seem to fathom.

To contact the author:

E-mail: songoftheages@yahoo.com

Website: www.jonathanlewis.org

Printed in the United States
43285LVS00002B/88-408

9 781581 691900